BURNING ORCHARDS

Gurgen Mahari

translated by
Dickran and Haig Tahta
and Hasmik Ghazarian

First published in Great Britain by Black Apollo Press, 2007
Copyright © Gurgen Mahari
Translation © Haig Tahta and Dick Tahta
This translation is of the 1966 edition of *Ayrvogh Aygestanner* by Gurgen Mahari originally published in the USSR.

A CIP catalogue record of this book is available at the British Library.

All rights reserved; no part of this publication may be reproduced or transmitted by any means electronic, mechanical, photocopying or otherwise without the prior permission of the publisher.

ISBN: 9781900355575

Design: DCG DESIGN, Cambridge

The image on the cover is that used in the first edition of the novel *Ayrvogh Aygestanner* by Gurgen Mahari.

Contents

Map of Vaspourakan	5
Map of Van in context	6
Introduction	7
The Mouradkhanian family tree	12
Chapter 1	13
Chapter 2	32
Chapter 3	49
Chapter 4	73
Chapter 5	82
Chapter 6	98
Chapter 7	119
Chapter 8	126
Chapter 9	143
Chapter 10	167
Chapter 11	196
Chapter 12	212
Chapter 13	236
Chapter 14	253
Chapter 15	282
Chapter 16	312
Chapter 17	329
Interlude	339
Chapter 18	341
Chapter 19	363
Chapter 20	385
Chapter 21	397
Chapter 22	412
Chapter 23	435
Chapter 24	452
Chapter 25	468
Chapter 26	477
Chapter 27	491
Epilogue	517
Map of Aikesdan	521
Glossary	522

I began writing this book with unconscious enthusiasm in the thirties. I had in another book already portrayed Van through rosy spectacles. But this no longer satisfied me. I now wanted to smash the spectacles and turn the reader into an actual Vanetsi. My work was not completed until about thirty years later ...

May the political parties, past and present, forgive my not glorifying their leaders, but presenting them as they were. And may the people of Van living all over the world forgive my not portraying the characters in my novel as saints, but rather as the ordinary humans they were. I lovingly bear their sins myself so that my punishment balances my guilt.

I will only be able to live in peace with myself if I have succeeded in letting the smoke from the burning orchards rise to the heights achieved by other writers before me.

(from Mahari's brief preface, which was followed by a dedication to his friend, Shahan Shanour, 'with great love')

This book is dedicated to the memory of Dickran Tahta who died suddenly only days before the delivery of the first proof of this publication. He will be remembered for ever by us all.

Haig Tahta

Map of Vaspourakan

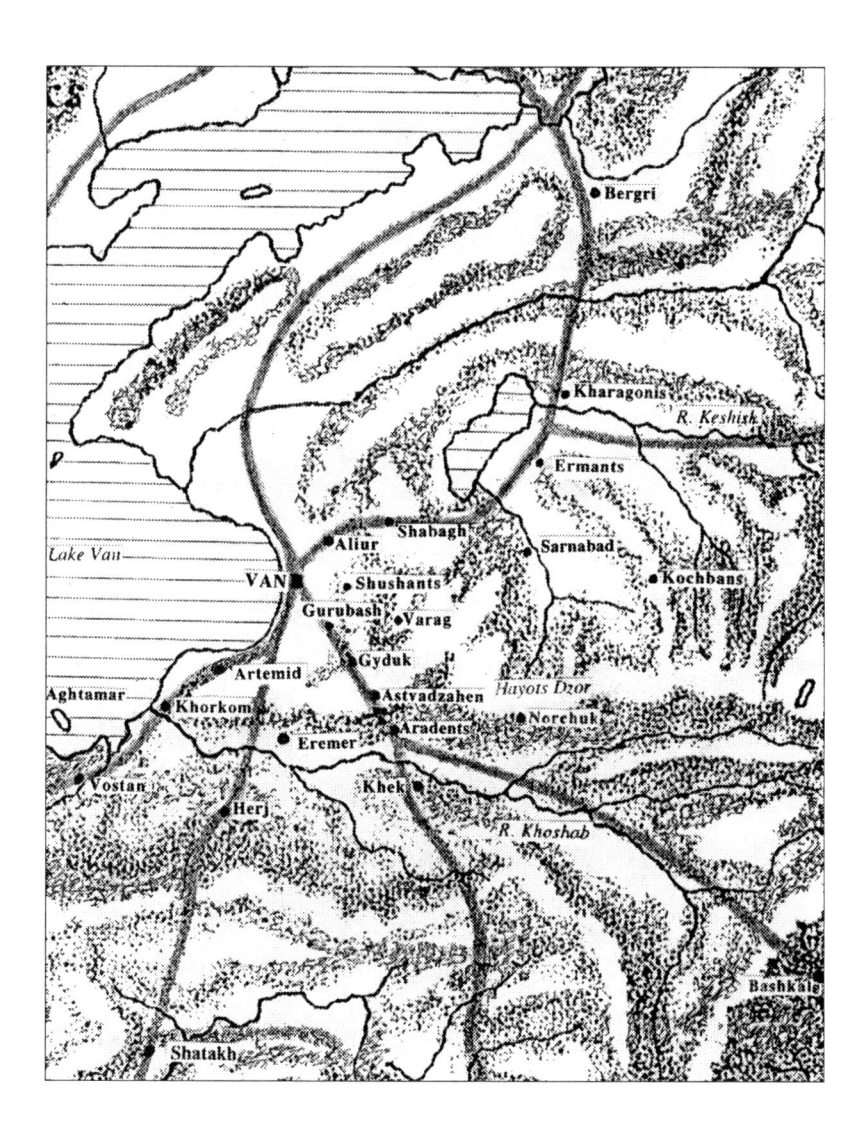

Map of Van in context

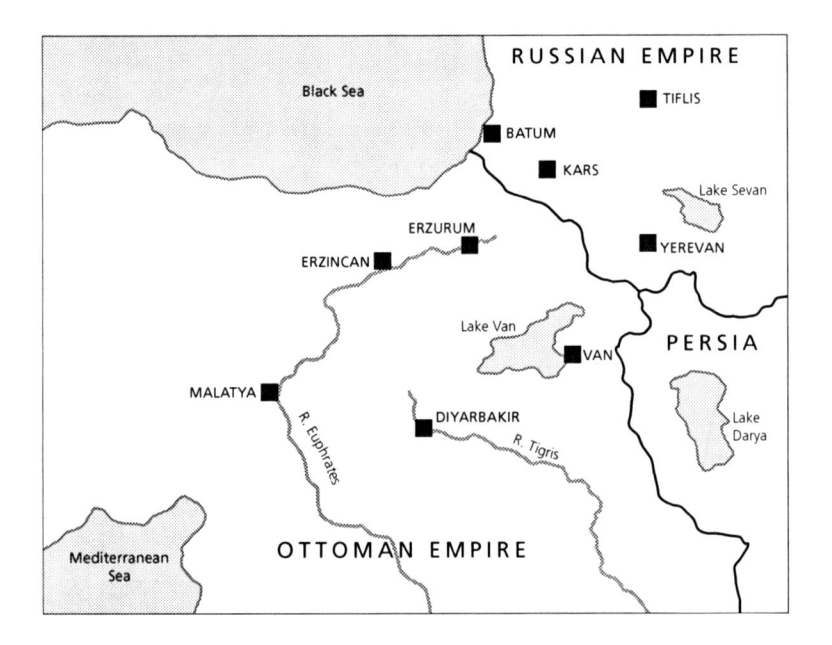

Introduction

Gurgen Mahari's novel, *Burning Orchards*, is set in Van, an ancient and beautiful town in Eastern Anatolia, during the five or so years before and leading up to April 1915. The orchards were those of the attractive suburb, known as Aikesdan, to the east of the small walled city. The burning was the result of Turkish bombardment.

An Armenian rebellion broke out in April 1915 and this resulted in a siege of the town by the Turkish regular army. The siege lasted about four weeks, and was a defining moment in Turkish-Armenian relations. One way or another it was the precursor of the Catastrophe that overcame the Armenian people during the rest of that year.

Van had a total population of about seventy thousand, over half of whom were Armenians, a third Turks, and the rest Kurds, with a few thousand Assyrians. It was the capital city of the district of the same name. Its governors, had always carefully maintained a traditional balance between the different races and religions in the area, albeit with the clear proviso that the state religion was Islam.

After the successful 1908 revolution, these traditional Ottoman governors throughout the Empire were slowly replaced by the tougher nationalists of the Young Turk movement. Relations between the Armenians and the Turks steadily deteriorated, and after the Turks fatally joined in the Great War in November 1914, these tensions increased daily.

The Armenians had been part of the Ottoman empire since the 15th century; the majority of them lived in eastern Anatolia, straddling the often disputed frontier region between Turkey and the Russian Caucasus. They were left in a particularly difficult position when the Turks joined the war as an ally of Germany, for they then had to face up to the fact that many of their fellow Armenians from the Caucasus were enthusiastically enrolling in the army of the Tsar. The Turks were aware of possible divided loyalties and were unsure how to deal with their Armenian subjects, particularly as relations between ordinary Turks and Armenians had been so drastically and deliberately ruined during the reign of the tyrannical Sultan Abdul Hamid.

In February 1915, the relatively gentle Ottoman governor of Van was replaced by Djevdet Bey, a cruel man who was notorious for having horse-shoes nailed to the soles of rebels. He established a vicious regime in Van, culminating at the beginning of April 1915 in the arrest and murder of the Armenian parliamentary deputies for the city. Not even the Turks have a good word to say for him. But did his actions justify rebellion? Much has been written about the rights and wrongs of the way this happened. The unquestionable fact is that there was a revolt, and that for four weeks about two thousand young men, with few arms but with much enthusiasm, held parts of Van against a force of about six thousand somewhat demoralised Turkish soldiers who had been sent to recapture the town.

Eventually the Russian army arrived and the Turkish army withdrew, and with them the Turkish civilian minority. But a few months later the Russians were in their turn forced back, and with them went most of the old-established Armenian population. Those who chose to remain were then lost in the wide-spread deportations which destroyed a population of well over a million.

Why is the Siege of Van particularly important in the whole sad story of the consequent catastrophe? The best analogy for a British reader would be the Easter Rising in Dublin in 1916, only a few months after the above events.

The Siege of Van remains a similar emotive issue, one that still divides people. Were the Armenians in Van justified in rising up in revolt just when the Ottomans were in such danger? Were the Turkish revolutionary leaders justified in then using that revolt as an excuse for the terrible elimination of the helpless Armenian peasantry during the rest of that year?

The Siege is not only an emotive issue between Armenian and Turk, it remains controversial between Armenian and Armenian, like the disagreements amongst the Irish. For instance, did any of the nationalist Armenian political party leaders consider for a moment the position of the rural population, bereft as they were of all their young men? The arguments rage on!

> *I carried my life like a flag*
> *up from the dark pits...*
> (Gurgen Mahari, trans, Diana der Hovanessian)

Gurgen Mahari was born in Van in 1903. He survived the siege, and was part of the mass exodus following the retreating Russian army; he ended up in an orphanage in Etchmiadzin, but eventually was able to meet up with his mother who had also survived. He became a writer, but was also politically involved and was eventually arrested in 1936 and sent to Siberia. He returned after the war only to be arrested and exiled again until 1954. Now 51 years old, with a second wife, a Lithuanian whom he had met in Siberia, he again took up his career as a writer with an account of his exile, pieces about his childhood and various works of poetry.

His novel, *Ayrvogh Aygestanner* (Burning Orchards), was published in Yerevan in 1966. The story offered a version of the events leading up to the siege of Van different from the received account of what was held to have been a heroic struggle, one that stood in marked contrast to the lack of resistance at the time by Armenians in general. Moreover the novel included a 'good' Turk and Mahari was even accused of being sympathetic to the Turkish version of events.

The novel reflected something of the loyalty that many Ottoman Armenians had felt towards the former Empire. Mahari's characters were portrayed as having different political views: in particular some of them were wary of the influence of the educated leaders who came from elsewhere and who were not primarily concerned with the safety or the future of the indigenous Armenian peasantry.

There was also a curious personal connection in that when Mahari was five years old, his father had been killed by his mother's brother in what was held by the latter's family to have been an accident. The men were of opposing political parties, the uncle being of the revolutionary nationalist party, whose version of the siege Mahari was to some extent disputing. The incident is echoed in the book with the same disputed ambiguity about what really happened.

The novel was officially denounced and an ugly campaign included copies being ceremoniously burned outside Mahari's house, and he himself was publicly criticised. During the next two years he was persuaded to remove some particularly offending passages – a revised edition was eventually published posthumously. He died, a somewhat broken man, in 1969 in Lithuania, his wife's country, where the couple used to take their summer holidays.

There has been a post-soviet re-appraisal of his work in which he is now seen as one of the few dissident Russian-Armenian writers of the soviet era. Mahari's point of view is, of course, no more valid than anyone else's, but his warmth, and his sympathy for all the ordinary citizens of Van, shines through and gives us an insight into events at the time which historians – Armenian and Turk – might have missed. According to Marc Nichanian, the critic who has written movingly about Mahari and his book, it is one of the great Armenian novels of the twentieth century.

Traductore traditore

All translation is treacherous and it is particularly difficult to express Mahari's distinctive style in English. In his novel, he shifts from present to past, from conversation to inner monologue, from memories to dreams, with corresponding sudden changes in tense. He uses a number of Turkish and Persian words, as well as words in a former local dialect of Van, some of which are virtually untranslatable.

Mahari wrote in Eastern Armenian, the version of the language spoken in Armenia. This pronounces some of the letters of the alphabet differently from Western Armenian, which was spoken in Turkey and now in the Diaspora. For example, the written name of the famous musicologist would be pronounced Gomidas in the Eastern version and Komitas in the Western version. We have used both versions for names of people or places.

The novel invokes a number of historical and cultural references, which would have been familiar to Armenian readers at the time. We have given a brief account of the historical background in our introduction and we also provide a couple of maps. We give some very brief notes on many of the references in a glossary at the end, for the benefit of readers who may be unfamiliar with them; these references include most of the characters in the novel who were actual people. The glossary also includes a few frequently used words like *tantun*, the main ground-floor room of a large house, and *tonir*, a stone hearth where the main cooking was done.

A person from Van would be called a *Vanetsi*, with similar expressions for natives of other towns. It would have been customary at the time to use formal titles regularly in conversations. Corresponding to *Mr, Mrs* would be Armenian *Baron, Digin*, or Turkish *Agha, Hanum* (the latter two being usually placed after the name). These are not italicised in the text. It should be noted that 'Baron' has a stress on the second syllable (as in 'upon').

Additional ways of politely addressing a man, roughly corresponding to *Sir*, would include *Bey* (a former turkish military title) and *Effendi* (originally the turkish title of a civil servant). Similarly, a polite addition to a woman's name would be *Hatun*. Within the family, people would usually address their parents as *hairig, mairig* (literally father, mother, but more like dad, mum).

The translation offered here is of the original 1966 edition. But it also includes a few paragraphs in chapter 5 which were in his original text, and had been censored before publication along with some passages that reflected his experience in Siberia. The State censors were not interested in Mahari's account of the siege of Van, which so upset his fellow Armenians. The censored text was restored in a 2004 edition which also contained an account of the various versions of the book.

The Mouradkhanian family

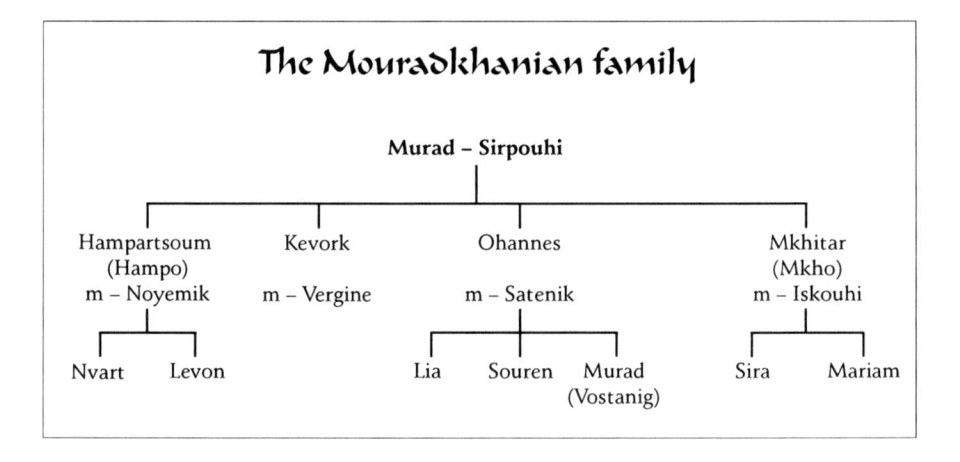

Murad – Sirpouhi

- Hampartsoum (Hampo)
  m – Noyemik
  - Nvart
  - Levon
- Kevork
  m – Vergine
- Ohannes
  m – Satenik
  - Lia
  - Souren
  - Murad (Vostanig)
- Mkhitar (Mkho)
  m – Iskouhi
  - Sira
  - Mariam

Chapter 1

The wind blew in from the sea in the evening, but swung to come down from the hill at sunrise. The leaves on the trees veered round; and not only the leaves on the trees: the waves of the peacefully flowing water, the washing that hung out on the flat roofs, the turn of the windmill looking over the town, the feathers of the birds spending the night in the tall ash and poplar trees, even the night itself, were all also turning round.

As was Ohannes himself.

He had gone to bed late, for the scream of the newly-born baby in the middle of the night had drowned out the screams of his persian carpet which had been trodden down all night by the midwife, by all his caring, close neighbours, and by his brother who had come over from some remote village. Yes, it was certainly that scream which jostled with his former memories.

When he first took that bawling and stinking mass wrapped in soft clothes from the midwife's hands, he seemed to be holding a parcel of merchandise trying to determine its value.

"How much is this worth, midwife Tarik?" he asked.

"A thousand sovereigns, a thousand, Baron Ohannes. Look between those legs."

Ohannes, who was numerate as well as literate, teased her. "Midwife Tarik, there aren't a thousand, there's only one between these legs."

The midwife was uneducated, but felt that she could not leave it there: "Does it need anything to become a thousand?" she asked.

"Well, yes, some round zeros."

"Baron Ohannes, if there's a one there'll be a couple of zeros as well. Happy birthday!"

Ohannes was delighted: "Midwife Tarik, it's a boy – I understand that much. But can you tell me what fruit he is?"

"He's a pear, a cherry. He's my baby, my baby with a royal birthmark."

The midwife answered Ohannes' somewhat scientific question with a fine humour, tinged with a certain flourish. Even Ohannes was pleased. He slipped some silver coins into her coat pocket, saying with suppressed joy, "Take him to his mother's breast, take him to his mother."

It was already morning. Ohannes woke up and turned over. The fresh June air blew into the room through the open window and he felt his moustache quiver. He took a deep breath and looked around the room with half-open eyes.

Everything was in its place. He smiled with pride at the new covers on the sofas. 'We're having some guests tomorrow,' he thought. The cushions on the stone bench along the wall seemed to be smiling with hospitality and soft warmth. The portrait of Reverend Father Khrimian sitting under an oak-tree was looking down from above the mirror on the wall. Ohannes could see neither the oak-tree, nor Khrimian, but he was looking at the mirror and knew that the portrait would be there above it.

His wife Satenik is lying alongside him a little apart. There is a carpet on the floorboards and under their bed. The baby is on Satenik's far side. Ohannes would like to hear his scream now, but instead of that, it is the baby's mother, Satenik, who is panting and restless. Ohannes stretches out his hand a little and lightly touches her brow.

"Are you awake, husband?"

"Yes. And you?"

"Going to the market today?"

"Do you think I should go?"

"It's up to you."

"Is the boy asleep?"

"He seems quiet, he isn't like the others. Husband, was he really necessary?"

"What should we have done then?"

"Medicine and doctors."

"Get up, get up and make coffee. I haven't married a woman to send her to that kind of doctor."

There was a silence.

"Make it yourself today, I can't," Satenik said in a shaky voice.

"Oh God, I'd forgotten," Ohannes groaned. He puffed and moved to get up, but then he remembered something.

"Daughter! Lia, Lia!"

"What's up?" came a reply from the room downstairs.

"Come upstairs and make coffee."

Silence. That meant that the order would be carried out. Ohannes lay back on the bed again. He stroked his wife's neck and whispered happily:

"Dear me, you've become too thin."

"Why shouldn't I? If you were in my shoes – ?"

"I would die," Ohannes interrupted, somewhat disappointed and then fell fast asleep, forgetting both Satenik and the baby, as well as Lia, who was to make coffee for him. Overcome by the fragrant and soporific morning air, he had a light nap again.

Now Khrimian appears clear and distinct. A few crows fly past croaking loudly and the sun lights up the tops of the tall poplars in the orchards, while the greyish-blue of the morning mist still lingers at their feet.

Ohannes was dreaming.

… The harvest had come in from the village. The full sacks of corn stood in the yard in a straight row, attached to each other in pairs. The peasants drove the oxen into the outer yard and asked for some grass for them. Ohannes took the key to the hayloft out of his pocket and gave it to the Assyrian servant, Hormuz.

"Go and bring some grass – dry grass. It's nutritious."

"Fresh grass?"

"No, no, dry grass." Ohannes shouted angrily in his sleep: "I tell you, dry!"

Hormuz left. A bit later, he came and stood in front of Ohannes with the strings of his hat loose.

"Baron Ohannes, come and see."

Ohannes opened the door of the hayloft. Instead of dry grass, he saw masses of green snakes wriggling and hissing. Ohannes was not frightened at first.

"Take it, let them have it."

"I will," said Hormuz.

There in the outer yard, not oxen but lions and tigers stood eating the green snakes. Ohannes now trembled with fear, but still he did not wake up. He was sitting on one of the sacks full of corn guarding them. The peasants began taking the sacks to the barn and emptying them. The sack he was sitting on stirred, moved, swayed under him and yet in his dream he was not surprised and simply sat there smoking. Then in came Satenik, tearing out her hair and crying.

"Ohannes, they've brought mice instead of corn."

Mice! And the mice rushed out of the granary, and chased one another, flowing like a flood towards the stairs and the rooms. They climbed up Satenik's legs, while the sack under him stirred and stirred, more and more. Mice! Mice! One of them – a more persistent and impertinent one – was looking for a way up to where Ohannes was sitting, and was digging and pecking at the sack, slipping and worming into it, and gnawing him. ...

Ohannes woke up, roaring with pain.

"Isn't the coffee ready yet?"

"No," Satenik answered. She had already placed the baby in the cradle and was rocking it to and fro. "What's up with you?"

"I had a bad dream, woman, I must have indigestion."

"What did you see?"

"A mouse," Ohannes said briefly.

"The mouse is here next to me."

"Also a snake," Ohannes insisted.

"You're the snake," Satenik concluded under her breath and occupied herself with the baby.

Ohannes got up, put on his black frock-coat over the long grey night-gown, took off his night-cap and covered his head with a fez. Then putting on his slippers, he walked slowly out onto the balcony. He was happy and in a peaceful frame of mind. In front of him, the sun-drenched Aikesdan was glistening in dew-covered green. The thick and luxuriant sorrel bush by the garden door seemed to be flowing into the yard, flooding it with green. The carefully tended terrace seemed cheerful and welcoming, and fruits were ripening in the garden.

Ohannes is feeling fine, very fine. He is murmuring under his breath and God knows whether he is praying or reflecting on something. Now he is stroking his moustache, rubbing his chin and thinking he should have shaved today. All of a sudden, he remembered his dream and murmured tolerantly, "Good Lord, I must have indigestion."

Being a practical person, he sometimes did not believe even in facts. He only believed in things he had discovered, touched and verified for himself. As an educated man, he did not attach any importance to dreams. He used to recount all his worst dreams in detail and even exaggerated them, but always concluded at the end, "I have indigestion" or "I probably didn't sleep well last night".

Meanwhile, the house was waking up. Lia came forward with all the washing utensils and stood ready with the pitcher in her hand to pour out water for him. Ohannes took off his fez and put it on Lia's head, making her look funny, but still pretty. Then he started washing noisily, splashing and spluttering, and sprinkling water over her. When he finished, Lia took the soft towel from her shoulder, placed it carefully into her father's hands and began to gather everything up.

"Haven't you made coffee?" Ohannes said, knowing full well that she had not, but as a confirmation of the fact, rather than a reproach.

"I've put on the coffee-pot." The girl blushed; she took the fez off her head, and held it out.

Ohannes threw the towel onto his daughter's shoulders, put the fez on his head and gently said: "Put on the samovar as well and tell your mother to roast some meat and prepare some bottles of wine and raki. Put your green dress on – you've a sister now, you know. The stork has brought her."

Lia corrected him: "It isn't a sister, it's a brother."

"Aha, you know this, too." He stroked the girl's nose tenderly with his finger.

A short, elderly woman shuffled slowly up the stairs onto the balcony. Lifting up her veil, she smiled affectionately at both of them. The old woman was Ohannes' mother; she would rather have been his elder sister – it was so unbelievable that Ohannes could still have a mother. Being called a mother no more suited this elderly woman than heavy, outdoor boots suit a seventy-year-old man. Ohannes was still very far from being seventy, yet still having a mother did not suit him at all – not at all

"Ohannes, are you going to the market today?"

"I don't know, mairig, whether I'm going or not," he replied. Then he thought a moment, smiled and said, "You've a grandson. He's the residue at the bottom of the pan – the tastiest parts of the dish are the cream on top and the residue at the bottom."

"Three is the number that God likes, my boy, but that's enough! Are we going to have visitors today?"

"We are. Go on, do something, make preparations. What's Mkho doing?"

"What can the poor boy do? He's sleeping," the old woman answered her eyes filling with tears.

"Wake him up, let's go to the market. I'll have a look at the shop, then we'll buy some things and come back."

"Aren't you going to shave?"

"I'll have coffee and leave."

"Let me go and make up the tonir. Praise be to God!" the old woman said thoughtfully before going out in a hurry.

"Aren't you going to see Satenik?"

"Oh, bless my soul, I'd forgotten." The old woman slapped her thighs and ran to the room of the recently confined mother.

Once there, she looked at her new-born grandson and remarked that the baby's eyes were like her father's and his forehead like that of her mother. Her daughter-in-law remembered with a forced smile that she had said exactly the same thing about both Souren and Lia, thus making sure Satenik or her husband would not ignore the genetic resemblance. The daughter-in-law, feeling it to be her duty, then said, "Hatun, I'd like to get up."

"No, no, darling, stay in bed today, and tomorrow as well."

However, she could not help adding that she herself had born her children on her feet, had done a mountain of washing the very next day, and yet had been as fit as a fiddle.

"We were quite different from you, we had something more," the old woman added as she left the room. "I'll go and make up the tonir. God be praised."

Puffs of smoke rising from the tonir have spread over the orchards. The morning looks bright, a morning as imposing and grand as God himself. God, who has no idea who really worships him or who only pretends to do so, who is afraid of him, or who looks at him with tender eyes. Even if there is no God, there is always a morning like this. It looks on the sky and mountains, on the windows and roofs, and it is wonderful. What does it matter that Mkho is sleeping in the corner of the tonir room, and that Ohannes is stroking his moustache and at last drinking his coffee.

By the time Ohannes finished his coffee and put on his clothes, Mkho had already got up and was saddling his grey donkey, and Ohannes' white one. The old lady came and opened the front gate to let the animals and her two sons out of the courtyard. They mounted the donkeys and the old woman watched them ride away until the sound of the bells hanging on the animals' necks could no longer be heard and they themselves had disappeared round the corner.

They trot along the broad avenue leading towards the town. Willows and poplars line the edge of the road. They are riding side-by-side, Ohannes on his white donkey with carpeted saddle and ringing bells, and Mkho on his more simply attired, grey donkey.

They are going to the market. Mkho has not eaten anything all morning. He wants to have something but he does not know how to ask for it. At last, he stops his donkey by a bakery and throwing down ten small coins takes a hot lavash from the stall and starts eating it with great gusto.

When his donkey catches up with the other one, Mkho says, "I don't like this town."

"Why so, isn't the bread tasty?"

"Well, I suppose it is quite tasty."

"Then why?"

"A man shouldn't have to pay for bread, should he?"

"You've got used to ... anyway what does it matter to you?" Ohannes said sharply, though good-naturedly.

"They say that in Stamboul one has to pay even for water. By the way, is there any news from Hampartsoum?"

"Yes, there is."

"How's he getting on?"

"He's expanded the shop and is doing good business. I've heard that Hampartsoum is well known in Bolis. Who can figure him out?"

They ride on side-by-side. The gay bells of Ohannes' white donkey have breathed new life into Mkho's grey animal as well. The latter is beginning to trot on with the same enthusiasm and with its ears pricked up, quite in pace with the other donkey.

"We've not yet spoken about our own affairs," Mkho said, when they had gone quite a long way down the road and he had already finished the last crumb of the fresh lavash.

"There's plenty of time. We'll talk later – I've a lot to do today."

"I understand. Today you're the father of a new boy. You can't think about business today, can you? Today's another day."

And Mkho started singing. He sang out loud, recalling his children, his wife Iskouhi, their village, the ploughing and sowing, the sheep and the cattle. In his mind's eye he sees the broad and winding way that stretches out of the town. It creeps along the mountain sides, rolls round the hills, and then goes up and up and over until, down below at the bottom of the valley full of water, there is the village, nestling in the mist. The road winds down and down into the valley, calms down and then goes on steadily and directly for ten kilometres – to the village!

Ermants! An Assyrian and Kurdish village where a few Armenian families have also settled. The Muradkhanians have owned land there for fifteen years – fields where Kurdish, Assyrian and Armenian shepherds and milkmaids look after about two hundred cattle, sheep and goats. They get on especially well with the Assyrians. The Muradkhanians were a family of four brothers: Hampartsoum, who now lives in Bolis and is engaged in business, Ohannes, Kevork the teacher, and finally, Mkho. Ten years ago,

Mkho went back to the village to look after the plowing and sowing for a time. However, once he got there he did not want to return to the town. He got married, had children and stayed. He took care of the family farm, drew his share each year and sent the rest to town.

Old Muradkhanian left a will before he died. According to that will he handed all his property on to Ohannes, considering him to be the most serious and deserving of his sons. He had, however, expressed a firm hope that his heir, Ohannes, would not give his three brothers the chance to curse their father's name and memory, but would give them their proper share. Only about a month after Murad's death, Hampartsoum took a tidy sum of money and left for Bolis. By now, he had already lived twelve years in Bolis and his business had expanded year by year. When Ohannes heard about Hambartsoum's success, he wrote a letter, making somewhat of a show of generosity and offering assistance from the main family property. A month later, he got a stiff reply to the effect that he was quite well and – thank God – he did not need any aid for the time being. And, in fact, he never did need any.

The other brother, the teacher who taught Religion and History in one of the local schools, eventually gave up the academic life. Having a soft spot for drinking, he could not reconcile the café with school, nor raki and wine with religion and history. His colleagues tried at first to shut their eyes to the problem, and even the headmaster managed to avoid noticing his red eyes whenever he entered the staffroom with shaky steps. But Kevork was gradually becoming unbearable. Bottles of raki appeared in his locker. It could no longer be ignored that drinking outside the school was not satisfying him, and he was obviously continuing this bad habit somewhere in the school. But where was he drinking? He dealt with his classes during lesson times like all the other teachers, while during the break time the staffroom was always full of teachers and the corridors were full of pupils.

The mystery was at last solved when one fine day (though really that day was not fine at all, the sky was cloudy and it had been drizzling since morning), the headmaster noticed an empty bottle of raki in a certain place and down a certain hole. Yes, there was no doubt that to slake his insatiable thirst, Kevork had chosen a place where everything was always performed behind locked doors.

The next day, the teacher on duty came up to him and said, "Baron Kevork, the headmaster wants to see you."

"Where is he?" Kevork asked, feeling instinctively that the headmaster would not really be asking to see him for something pleasant.

"Go to his office, please."

"All right, all right, I'll go."

"The head said, let him come right away," the duty master insisted.

"Is it so important?" Kevork asked, trying to smile and hoping to find out something.

"I don't know," the other replied curtly, and rang the bell.

Slowly and unwillingly, Kevork walked towards the headmaster's office.

While going quietly up the stairs, he heard his name spoken. He stopped: two of his colleagues were standing at the top of the stairs and talking softly together.

"It's inappropriate and really shameful," Mampren was saying.

"Has it been checked, though. What if it is simply not true." Yeghishé was expressing a doubt and fiddling meanwhile with his watch-chain.

"Come on, it can't be a delusion. The head himself has seen the empty bottle in the hole. Have you thrown it there, or did I?"

"I don't understand it. How can he be so desperate?"

"And not only that. If the boys find out, they'll play tricks on us. The head has already sent for him."

Kevork felt as though somebody had poured hot water over his head. He turned back silently and instead of going to the headmaster's office, he went to the staffroom. There, he opened his locker, took out a half-empty bottle of raki and hid it in one of his inner pockets. Then he put on his fez and left the school like a thief. And he never went back there again.

Meanwhile, the two brothers are continuing on the road in the shade under the willows, and each of them is musing to himself. Ohannes is smoking his long pipe set in yellow amber, with a bowl the size of a hen's egg. He is inhaling Trebizond tobacco deeply and puffing away. Mkho, who is a non-smoker, is thinking – counting up his income and trying to make ends meet. He is in fact very happy. He is looking at his brother. He has got so much to tell him, but this is a brother who is not available today. 'Today's another day,' he said to himself.

Mkho's mood suddenly changes. They have entered the market. He wants to buy three metres of wool for Iskouhi as he had promised, slippers for Sira, as also promised, and something else for Mariam, no matter whether she asked for it or not. But Mkho has not got any money. How could he have money? No: he thought he'd tell Ohannes, he'd tell him by all means, and surely his brother would get everything from his shop and give it to him to take home.

At last they came to Ohannes' shop. The usual procedure has always been that Ohannes enters the shop, while Mkho waits outside the door until his brother finishes his work. But this time, Mkho also gets down from his donkey and enters the shop immediately after Ohannes. Ohannes pretends not to notice this, but in fact does not like it at all: "Won't the animals wander away and get lost?"

"Oh no, don't worry, they won't go anywhere."

Now Mkho is looking around his brother's shop. What wealth! So much cloth, cotton, so many goods!

With an air of humble respect, a young man comes forward from the back of the shop. Meanwhile, the two shop-assistants stand anxiously looking into Ohannes' eyes. He gives his orders to the young man:

"Give those puppies," he pointed at the two assistants, "five kurush each as a gift. You yourself come to our place this evening, but don't bother to bring today's accounts." Ohannes smiled to make his manager understand that this was not to be a business visit.

Set – this was the name of the young man – twirled the ends of his moustache with his thumb and finger, and replied in a warm and respectful way:

"Already?"

"Yes, already, already."

"Is it a boy or ... A boy is very desirable, of course, but – er, er – a girl is of great importance in Bolis."

"It's a boy, a boy! Haven't we had any deliveries today?"

"Not yet."

"Send for the barber."

The barber came with all his equipment, got Ohannes to sit in the chair and stood before him, busily lathering him for a shave.

Mkho, for his part, was deep in thought. Where does all this fortune come from? Ohannes presents each of the young shop-assistants with five kurush apiece. If he had five kurush, he would be able to buy cloth and a shawl for Iskouhi.

At that moment, a Turkish official comes in with a porter following him. He buys three rolls of cloth, paying with gold pieces. Mkho can hardly breathe. So much wealth!

"Can I take some cloth for Iskouhi," Mkho cannot help saying. He is already twenty-six years old and as this is the first time he has asked for anything from his brother – he is depressed.

"Let's get going." Ohannes ignored his brother. He has already been shaved and is walking towards the door. Mkho follows him. He remembers his own surplus of corn and flour and his spirit lightens. He has already forgotten his brother's indirect refusal. He will go home to the village and open a shop himself. But who would buy flour in a village and pay for it? Mkho has never had more than one or two kurush in his whole life. He has only had that when a political group has come to his house, a gathering of perhaps eight or ten people who have lived, ate, and drank, under his roof for several days, and then given Sira and Mariam copper coins to make them happy. And this has been his only source of money.

Ohannes has already got on his musical donkey. Mkho is following him.

"Mkho!"

"Yes, here I am."

"Let's go to Araruts square"

"Why?"

"To buy a few things."

"Have you got any money on you?" asks Mkho, rather pointlessly.

They ride on in silence until they reached the square. This was a large square; there were shops on three sides and the Armenian church on the fourth.

"Good day, Baron Khatchadour," Ohannes called out, stopping in front of a shop.

"Good day, Baron Ohannes, good day," answered a man with a long, pointed moustache, and with a fez low on his forehead. He had been sitting cross-legged and was now making an effort to get up onto his feet.

"Be seated, be seated, Baron Khatchadour, please don't put yourself out."

"You don't come to my shop very often, so how can I not stand up?" At last Khatchadour managed to get up, bowing with a salaam.

"Baron Khatchadour, I've a special request."

"I'm your obedient servant."

Ohannes took a long purse out of his shirt front, jingled it in his palm, undid its knot, opened it up and poured out its contents. Several gold coins glittered before Mkho's eyes. Ohannes took one of them and handed it to Khatchadour. "Our Satenik has delivered ... Raki, wine, nuts, brandy – well you know better than I, what I need. And you –"

Suddenly, volleys of gunfire, one after another, exploded at the end of the square. The gold coin seemed to melt away between Ohannes' thumb and forefinger, while Khatchadour's stretched hand retreated into his own pocket, as he suddenly feared that someone was coming to rob them. In a moment, the windows of all the shops on the square were noisily shuttered up. Khatchadour closed his as well, without taking any notice of his respected customer.

"It was a drunken argument that blazed up, there's nothing serious," somebody called out from the square, and the shopkeepers breathed again. After opening up their shops, many of them even started boasting that they had not been frightened at all, that they had realized that nothing serious had happened, that if this had been an 'event', the guns would have sounded different ... and so on, and so forth.

Mkho thought about these events with a dull indifference. He was like a man swimming in the sea who does not feel the rain. Ohannes for his part was confused, but only for a moment; then he gained control over himself. Khatchadour murmured something about life and insecurity and wrote down Ohannes' order so as not to forget it. Then he closed up the shop.

"It's still early, Baron Khatchadour why did you close the shutters?"

"Baron Ohannes, I had a bad dream last night. I don't want any more business today."

"I think you must have indigestion."

"A dream has nothing to do with the stomach," said Khatchadour in an incontestable tone, thus throwing cold water on Ohannes' firm views on the issue, "Well, well, please excuse me."

"Don't forget, you know better the sort of things I need. Don't forget the olives, and you, yourself ... we'll have a good time."

"I'll manage, I'll manage, Baron Ohannes," he smiled and went off to do his own shopping. The two brothers set out for home exchanging no words the whole way. The sun shone over the yellow amber of Ohannes' pipe and on the tinkling bells of his white donkey.

Kevork had only just escaped from the school. However, he had an unpleasant pain constricting his chest. He had visited his brother several times recently and each time he had got a few gold coins out of him. Both parties now felt that there was not much to be given or taken any more. But what had just happened turned Kevork's mental accounting upside down – if indeed he ever had any such budgeting in mind at all. He had never particularly worried about his inheritance. He had considered his father's action to be perfectly natural, since he had never had any desire to do any of the kind of work involved in business and administration. And he had thought that the gold coins which he had got from his younger brother, were more a matter of fraternal support rather than his portion of the paternal inheritance. It goes without saying that after leaving the home where he had grown up, Kevork could not properly support his family. His salary of eighteen gold pieces a year would have been perfectly adequate if he had not been so fond of drinking wine and raki. A third of his salary was wasted in this unfortunate way. And, what a wrong path to take! All sorts of heroic thoughts, supernatural deeds, honest actions, many impressive words, vows and intentions, had been scattered in the fog of that wrong path.

When he had got up the morning after leaving the school, nothing seemed real other than his heavy head and light purse. Instead of the music in the café, it was the reproachful words of his wife Vergine, that had rung in his ears. Then the bells of the churches in the ancient town had rung, first to invite pious people to the church and then to call teachers and pupils to school.

He got up without looking at his wife, and threw the bath-towel over his shoulder. At one end of the light blue towel, the words 'good morning', were embroidered in white. In the first months of their marriage, when Vergine had first started humbly to express her displeasure, he would enter the bedroom and utter a formal 'good morning'. And when Vergine did not respond to his greeting and instead occupied herself by piling up the bedclothes spread on the floor he looked at the other end of the towel and teased her, saying, "Yes, you have a right not to respond to my 'good morning' - it isn't written here."

They had made up several times after rows thanks to this joke. But – oh dear! – where had those years gone? They had been married five years and during those five years Vergine had cried at least fifty times, cursed twenty-five times and had thrown his uselessness in his face twelve-and-a-half times, comparing him with Ohannes' cleverness, and her own situation with his wife's high status.

"Let me go and be a housemaid for Satenik Hanum, and you can go and be a servant for Baron Ohannes – otherwise what shall we do, how shall we live?"

Two years ago, he had commanded his wife sharply to have a little respect for him. She had then begun to 'respect' him. She stopped speaking either of his good or bad side. They had no children, and though they did not want to discuss who was to blame, it was a fact that bound them closely together. Vergine was a far-seeing woman. She went to her neighbours with her sewing and stayed there till late at night. When her husband came and found the door locked, he would go to the garden, or – in winter – to other neighbours. Then they asked around, found each other and came home. At home, Vergine continued to 'respect' her husband. She never asked where he had been and why he was late. She even tried not to notice that her husband could hardly stand upright when he got in.

In the mornings, after washing himself, he used to go out to the garden. The orchards behind the houses were separated by low, earthen walls. The neighbours, even those who were very short, could see and greet one another over the walls. That was why Baron Kevork – or Kevork Agha, or just plain Kevork – would go out into the garden and walk around quietly as though he had no cares in the world.

Yes, his only daily concern now was to check carefully that the pear tree was in its place, that the apple trees had not run away, and that the little stream had not been blocked. He also needed to check whether the birds flying over the narrow path had relieved themselves regularly or not. And if they had then why especially on the narrow path? Was that really proper?

"Good morning." Kevork heard the old, but welcoming, voice of Sarkis from the next-door garden.

"Good morning," he replied, "what's the news in the world?"

"Well, we're safe and sound," Sarkis said, and there is a smile, not only on his face but also in his voice. Kevork stays standing politely, musing on the fact that Sarkis is so eager to speak with his worthy neighbour, to inquire about his health, to relate any news about himself, and to shout it all out heartily and sincerely, so that the neighbour on the other side could hear as well. But then the church and school bells start ringing; they are ringing urgently –

and, it seems to Kevork, officially – and he hurries back into the house.

At home, Vergine continues to 'respect' him. She has wrapped some bread and cheese in a cloth and put it on the window sill. He takes this kind offering and implies that he is going proudly to school by leaving the house with a solemn air and weighty steps. He hears Vergine's customary exhortation, "Flour, butter, a few silver coins – don't drink raki – lentil, some potatoes. And I beg you, please don't drink."

And he set off as if going to the school.

Kevork had only just escaped from the school. However he had an unpleasant pain constricting his chest. For a moment, he was distracted by the most ordinary things: children playing knuckle-bones and citizens walking under the willows, especially one of them, the one who had a leather shoe on one foot and a rubber shoe on the other. And here is a watermelon, and there is a watch-maker; there is a baker and here – here, a café! Why had the headmaster sent for him? Who is he? What did the headmaster want of him? Where has he come from? What does he care about?

He entered the café, found a seat on the open balcony, took the bottle of raki out of his pocket, and called the waiter.

"Bring me some pasterma."

"One pas-ter-ma," called the waiter in a sing-song voice. A little later, he put the tasty, thin-cut, gritty and spicy meat on the table.

"Boy, what does a headmaster look like?"

"I've never seen one, Baron Kevork."

"Where on earth have you come from?"

"From a village – from Timar."

"Why did you come?"

"I'll go back if you want me to."

"Where? To Timar? No, no, bring me a glass for the raki."

"I'll bring it at once."

And thus he lost the school for ever. But school was not the most important thing. What was more important was that he lost those eighteen gold pieces he received annually; he had had a salary of one-and-a-half gold pieces a month and he had lost it. He remembered his last signature on the pay list. He had already received the whole month's one hundred and sixty-two kurush at his special request, and yet it was only the twelfth of May.

"Wonderful weather in the month of May, with the silver-waved lake ... Motherland ... Dearest ...," sang Kevork, and poured out his third glass. "What's a headmaster?"

He rolled a cigarette and looked around. A few Turkish officials were drinking round a table. Two Armenian gentlemen were sitting at another table and, stimulated by the strong, thick coffee, were whispering and talking together. They were stimulated, but then they got upset and began to spend the time cheering each other up. One of them made a long speech in a flat voice, and eventually they got up. They separated outside the café without saying good bye to each other; one went up the street, the other down the other way.

The one going up the street stopped a few steps and called out, "Simon Agha –"

"What is it?"

"We have to go and see Baron Ohannes Muradkhanian."

"Nothing can be done without him."

"So you ought to have known."

"I know, I know, don't worry."

Kevork overheard this conversation clearly and distinctly, but his mind became confused.

Gabriel Demirtchian, a habitual visitor to the café, a man of some education, a man interested in public life, was going up the stairs. He was rosy-cheeked, tall and slender, with a wavy moustache, and was neatly dressed. He settled his fez on his head and slowly went up. He looked at all the occupied tables with equal interest and friendly concern, and at last sat down on his own. Then he took the weekly newspaper out of his pocket and started reading. Kevork poured out the last but one glass and called the waiter.

"Invite that man to join me here," he said, pointing at Gabriel.

"I'll call him at once."

"Yes, right now." Kevork drank the raki.

Gabriel walked across the café balcony and took a seat in front of Kevork. "There's trouble," he said, still reading the weekly, "there's real trouble." He folded the paper, looked at the remainder of the raki and thin, sliced meat, and at Kevork's red eyes, then said with a somewhat twisted smile, "Did you sleep well last night?"

"Why shouldn't I?"

"I don't know. Let's go home, Baron Kevork."

"No, no, I won't go home."

"It's late, you've got to go to school tomorrow."

"No, I'm not going to school"

"Dear Baron Kevork –"

"Don't call me Baron Kevork. I'm a dog, a wolf, I'm just Kevork. I won't go home, I'll lie down here and die. Baron Kevork, Kevork Agha, dear ... Who am I to be dear to somebody? Go and call my brother 'dearest'. What am I compared with him?"

"So ... Baron Kevork, I'll be exhausted before I can get you home."

"I really don't remember," shouted Kevork, wanting to go home. But suddenly he remembered: "Look – what does a headmaster look like?"

"Eh, what does he look like?" Gabriel began at once. "What does he look like? He's like a pear tree. And what are you so upset about. You don't realize your own worth, you don't respect yourself. After all, your brother –"

"Is there anything more beautiful under the stars than –"

"Look, don't believe people. There are more desirable words than brother."

"For instance?"

"A friend."

"Are you my friend?"

"Yes, I am."

"Then I am grateful to you for being my friend; thank you for accepting my invitation. Waiter, come and take the money."

Gabriel Demirtchian looked once more at the empty bottle and the remains of the pasterma, pulled the weekly newspaper out of his pocket again and cast a sad glance at the café entrance as Kevork left.

Chapter 2

Puffs of the smoke from the tonir have spread over the orchards. The smoke goes up through the hole opened in the flat roof. Grandmother Sirpouhi, Ohannes' short, stout mother, is sitting under one of these smoke-holes. She is stoking up the tonir and thinking that the new boy's name should be Murad in memory of her late husband. But – oh, my God! – now the meat has to be prepared to make the kufteh.

Slap, slap, slap. Sirpouhi's hands pounded the meat as she thought back to fifty years ago.

She is crying under her veil and recalling the day some time before, when she was sweeping the front yard of their house under the balcony. Two young men had come and stood under the willows – both of them with waxed moustaches and carrying canes in the European manner.

Sirpouhi recalled that she had gone to the well with the broom in her hand. The broom had needed to be washed and cleaned. But had it really needed to be cleaned and washed? It was difficult to say. But now, when Sirpouhi is crying under her veil, and one of those Frenchified young men is coming to carry her away, she does not regret that she had gone to clean the broom. But which of the two had chosen her? The one who was tall and thin, or the other - full-cheeked and of middling height. What does it matter now to Sirpouhi? It is quite enough that she is a bride and that she is about to be taken to a rich man's house, to a finely furnished home, and that the young men standing under the willows and looking at her were brothers.

Slap, slap, slap. The brothers would not have fought each other for Sirpouhi. She was only the daughter of a small trader, the owner of one cow and a small garden. Sewing, Stove, Sorrow ... all that lay before her.

Click, click, click. This time it is the sound of amber worry beads. At last the two brothers came forward, inventing an excuse for approaching her. "We've heard you have a carpet for sale, show it to us." They inspected the rug, had it folded, then had it opened again, pulled a thread here and there, looked at it closely and then drew out their worry beads.

Slap, slap slap. Oh dear! What was she thinking about? She still had to make the kufteh, to roast the joint then make the pilaf, and prepare dry fruits and nuts. And the little grandmother pounds away with enthusiasm, kneads the mutton and remembers the day when they came to take her away.

Clap, clap clap. The wedding guests came on horseback with deafening thunder like an army. There were no carriages, and carts would not have been respectable in those days. And then the wedding guests came with deafening thunder like an army. They came and came and came in crowds. And the pipe and the drum seemed to be playing right behind her ears.

The little old woman finally finished pounding the meat and began choosing pans.

The sound of the pipe and drum merged with the rustling in the church and the clink of the censer. She was indeed carried away on horseback – pressing in her knee so as not to fall off. But from under her veil, she could see the two brothers riding their horses alongside with equal pride and panache. One was tall and thin, the other of middling height and full-cheeked. And she did not know which of them was to be her future husband, and with which of them she was to share her nuptial bed and her first maiden kiss.

They are leaving the church now and going to the bridegroom's house accompanied by deafening music and noise. Clap, clap, clap. This time it is the young people gathered at the church entrance, firing off their guns with glee, each of them aiming up at a star. "Let whoever is drunk, aim at the moon." Of course, no one brings a star down, nor is the moon dislodged but the words of the old wedding song resound: "God has appeared over Armenia, to join brave Armenians in marriage."

It turned out that the brave Armenian in this case was the full-cheeked young man of middling height sitting on the grey donkey-like mule – or mule-like donkey. His first words to Sirpouhi, when they had been left alone after the wedding party was over, were: "One of my trouser buttons has come off. Fix it, while I go and water the horses and come back." And he went away to water the horses.

Clop, clop, clop. The young bride Sirpouhi's heart is beating fast, beating like a door knocker, like the hooves of galloping horses, like the amber beads that click onto one another as if coming to an end (though they never do), and the bride's heart is beating as if it is fainting (but it isn't and it won't).

And after that, with light and shade, over days and years, in summer and winter, in the garden, in warm and mild rooms, beneath sun, moon, and stars, one after the other, Hampartsoum, Ohannes, Kevork, and Mkhitar were born. And no girls.

Clip, clap clop. The years passed like galloping horses, disappeared one after the other, some rushing, some limping. But life wore out, the heart wore out, the face became wrinkled and the sixty-year-old merchant Murad Khan died – the same full-cheeked young man of middling height, the one who had suffered from the unusual illness of eating earth and wetting his bed at the age of five.

There is a knock on the door. The old woman does not doubt that it is her son Ohannes. It is surely him. He knocks just three times. Now the servant will open the door. Her son will come in with Mkho. Her brave sons are coming in, one from the town and the other from the country. When Mkho, her youngest son, used to come to town from the country, the old woman's heart seemed to glow with sunshine. Hampartsoum has a sweet colour and fine appearance but is something like a rainbow for her – far away like an illusion. And then Ohannes – like earth and sky for Sirpouhi – and Mkho.

And what of Kevork? Sirpouhi hoped she would not hear his voice. She did not have anything left over for him. She knew he was also her son, but she could not relate to him. He, who was certainly born of her, had not given life to any child of his own. He treated his old home like a visitor, came in like a stranger to eat and drink, and then leave. He had got married to a woman without thinking whether she was good or bad. He had turned out to be a drunkard, and had been expelled from the school because of his drinking. He had not stirred a finger when Ohannes had sent him to the village to take care of the crops and lighten Mkho's burden. When Ohannes had offered to let him look after the shop in town, he had begun drinking in the neighbouring cafés and discrediting his brother's business with all the other merchants. Of course, the old woman wished him all the best, but really she did not want to see his face or hear his voice.

"Hello, mairig."

The old woman looked round, and there instead of Ohannes and Mkho, she saw Kevork's flushed countenance at the door.

"Ohannes has had a baby boy, I've come to congratulate him. Have I a right to?"

The old woman was impressed by the agitated tone of her son's voice. She noticed a touching change in both his looks and voice, as well as in his speech. She turned and stood up.

"Oh, my dearest, why shouldn't you have a right? This is your house, isn't it?"

"This isn't my house, mairig. I'm a dog, I'm a wolf." And he laughed and laughed like a child and pulled at his mother's shawl.

"Ohannes has gone to the market with Mkho to buy something," murmured the old woman.

"Isn't there anyone upstairs?'

"Satenik is."

"What about Lia?"

"What do you want of Lia?"

"I won't eat her, I won't eat her. Where is she?"

"She's picking rose-petals for tea."

Clenching his teeth, Kevork went out into the yard and called out: "Lia, Lia!"

Lia ran in through the garden door with a bunch of roses in her hand. She looked somewhat distraught.

"Lia, get me some raki and some bread, I'm hungry."

The old woman went to the pantry herself and prepared everything. She thought that Kevork was already drunk. Kevork sat cross-legged on the tattered old carpet spread out in the yard and Lia laid the small meal before him. He paid very little attention to the food but immediately started drinking. He saw his mother and heard her pleading voice. Then mists came down before his eyes, and in the middle of that he suddenly saw his two brothers' faces.

"Well I suppose I have to die," he said to Ohannes, taking the bottle of raki and pretending he wanted to throw it away. Ohannes feigned not to see the gesture, so Kevork put the bottle quietly back in its place. "I'm going to die."

"Oh for God's sake, go to sleep," said Ohannes. "Lia bring a pillow."

Lia ran out to fetch a pillow. Instead of sleeping, however, Kevork got up unsteadily and said drunkenly, "I won't go to sleep, I won't sleep. You have a sleep, you've the right to sleep peacefully. I must work. Ohannes, you have money, you go and sleep on your money. Mkho, Mkhitar, you're a peasant, you go and sleep on the earth. Hampartsoum is a great merchant, let him go and sleep on his gold. Lia take the pillows away, I don't deserve to sleep on a pillow."

There was a knock on the front door.

Ohannes gladly welcomed two unexpected, but honoured guests as a way of driving away the ugly atmosphere created by Kevork.

"Come in, come right in please. What welcome wind brought you here, to us? I can scarcely believe my eyes. You're both very welcome, the pleasure is mine."

He led them to the kiosk at the top of the house. This was a room level with the flat roof, built of polished boards and with wide windows that were always open from May to September every year, but which were shut in the winter months.

The kiosk was furnished half in Oriental style and half in European style. On one side of the room there were Viennese chairs with round little tables before them; a big table covered with a snow-white table-cloth; boxes of Turkish cigarettes; three faience dolls holding little baskets in which matches were carefully arranged – the matches lit when you struck them on the bottom of the basket; two green faience plates filled with gold-tipped cigarettes and with angry, open-mouthed lions on their lids, embraced by half-naked women; shining, clean ash-trays etched with Chinese women walking along the river bank holding fans and umbrellas, while not far from them, a young Chinese man was lying in a boat, looking at the women with suspicious calm. The standard painting of Mother Armenia was hanging on the front wall of the kiosk. and there were more paintings on the other walls: bear-hunting, the Russian Tsar and Tsarina surrounded by their nobles, Othello smothering Desdemona, the Resurrection of Jesus, a portrait of the great teacher, Stepan Nazarian. In the corner of the room – a sort of Asian corner – there were flat cushions on the carpet to sit on with an empty narghileh set in the middle of a heavy, steel tray. The narghileh was decorated, carved with camels and camel-drivers, Arabic characters and date-palm leaves.

"Would you like to sit in the French or Turkish style?" Ohannes asked his guests, stretching out one hand towards the chairs and sofas, and the other towards the Turkish cushions.

"I don't like the Turks, but I do respect their customs," said Baron Simon, a tall man with a withered body and slightly bent forward shoulders. He was in no way inferior to Ohannes in position or property.

The second man, Baron Panos, a short, gloomy person sporting a thick moustache, gesticulated and murmured: "They're one and the same thing, you see".

The guests sat down cross-legged on the cushions. Panos took a handkerchief out of his pocket and blew his nose with a snort while Simon began gently fingering his black worry-beads, looking down at the melodiously clicking beads with mock detachment. Each man's fez was perfectly groomed.

Ohannes left the room light-heartedly and went down to order coffee and inquire about the state of his brother. He met his mother coming up the stairs.

"How's Kevork?"

"He fell asleep," replied his worried mother, who was hoping to find out what was going on.

"Bring us coffee and something to eat."

"Why have they come?" his mother said with a gesture of her hand which meant, 'don't worry, son, everything is being prepared, but answer my question, please, and as soon as possible'.

"Why? They've come to congratulate me."

Sirpouhi calmed down and her anxious wrinkles dissolved. "Good, let me go down to deal with the food, and you go back upstairs."

And she went down in high spirits, while Ohannes suddenly became gloomy and was worried as he went upstairs.

– Why, indeed, have they come? What could they have come for? Who has died? Surely, they've come to congratulate me on the birth of the boy. What else? But how did they learn about the birth? –

He had got to the kiosk door. He paused for a moment, hoping to hear his guests' happy laughter or at least some conversation. But the kiosk was silent, only the melodious clicking of Simon's beads could just be heard, and, downstairs, Lia's warning voice forbidding Souren, her younger brother, to touch the roses. Ohannes was overcome by an unpleasant feeling. He tried getting annoyed in his mind with little Souren, who was touching the roses that had not yet blossomed; he praised Lia's vigilance in scolding her brother; he remembered his recently confined wife, then his new-born son. He smiled and finally went in.

"It's cool in your kiosk," said Panos not taking his eyes off his beads.

"Cool, yes," Ohannes felt a bit lighter. "Spring is coming soon. Then summer, when the wind blows down from Mt Varag on one side, and from the sea on the other, and the kiosk shakes."

He offered cigarettes to his guests who accepted them, and, with the same solemn, oriental courtesy, the match struck by Ohannes. They leant back against the cushions in a manner which clearly meant they should now pass onto the main issue. And Ohannes duly passed onto the 'main issue'.

"Well, I know I'm not young any more, but I'm not old either, I've got a few grey hairs, but never mind. But even if I am old, I would say, 'I can still break a few stones – let's see what the fruit will be like.' By the way, how did you come to find out ?"

"Do you mean to say that you also know," asked Simon, looking up from his beads for a moment, in an uncertain and doubting manner.

For a moment, Ohannes felt as if he were floating on air. He burst out laughing. "What do you mean? Ha, ha, ha! The boy was born in my house after all. Ha, ha, ha! Could I help knowing?"

Ohannes, almost weeping with laughter, met his guests' cold, glassy eyes. The laughter stuck in his throat and he remembered his mother asking him on the stairs why they had come and his own reply that it was to congratulate him He answered her once more in his mind and became anxious all over again.

"Really, Baron Ohannes, how did you learn of it?" asked Panos calmly this time and with serious interest.

"What, for God's sake?" exclaimed Ohannes, unable to conceal his suppressed unease any longer.

At that moment, the door opened and Sirpouhi and Lia entered, carrying the breakfast tray. The guests shifted slightly and returned the greeting of their hostess as her entry created a hospitable and warm atmosphere.

"Why are you sitting on the floor like peasants? Panos Effendi, I'm mortified. Baron Simon, do get up, get up and have a proper seat. Lia, set the table."

"We'll get up, Sirpouhi Hanum, don't worry," said Panos.

"I knew it would be a boy," asserted Sirpouhi, raising a finger. "When my son has a dream, he says it's due to indigestion. I don't believe in dreams very much myself, but there are dreams that are not mere dreams. When Lia was about to be born, I dreamed of a hundred, or should I say a thousand pegons that were flying over our roof. And two days ago, I saw a foal, a green foal, neighing over the door."

"Don't say pegons, say pigeons." Ohannes corrected her, just to say something.

"I don't use fancy words. Do get up, get up and be seated," Sirpouhi said, pretending to be irritated. "Let's get going, Lia. Get up, please be seated and help yourselves," she repeated, and left the kiosk with her granddaughter.

When the door closed behind her, she stopped; her face clouded with vague anxiety, her ear turned towards the door hoping to hear something, to catch some sound, but all in vain for there seemed to be no-one inside. She held Lia's hand and hurried down the steps.

The voice of the recently confined woman was heard from the next room. She was calling for Lia.

"Pluck a bunch of roses and take them to your mother," Sirpouhi said, and then called out, "Mkhitar!"

"What's up, mairig?"

"Come and have something to eat."

"I'm not hungry."

"What have you eaten?"

"Bread from the bakery."

"Come and have some fresh fish."

"Let me water the animals and then I'll come."

"All right, but be quick."

Kevork was snoring soundly, his arms stretched out like a cross. Sirpouhi anxiously lit a cigarette and went into the pantry.

'A pigeon? A foal?' she thought. She came out and looked at the long shadow of the sun in the yard. It was already midday.

A pigeon ... a foal.

Simon was sitting in his shop keeping one eye on the senior assistant and the cashier, his other staff, and the customers coming and going. The other eye was on the black beads in his hands. He was full of disappointment.

He was forty-five. He had seen the same number of summers and winters. In his youth he had been poor, bare-footed and frozen-toed. He had been a porter, an apprentice to a shoemaker, a travelling fishmonger, a shop-assistant, a peddler, a shopkeeper. Socks had appeared on his bare feet as he began climbing up the ladder of life. Then peasant's clogs covered his socks, followed by rough shoes, and then those common shoes had been replaced by delicate, expensive shoes and rubber boots in winter. And so these agile feet had climbed life's ladder up to his shop, up to his stylish seat, up to his ironic glance at the clicking black beads, and finally up to his position as Baron Simon.

It was morning. The itinerant tea-sellers were displaying

florally decorated glasses on their saucers, and holding up the hot, bright yellow teapots in their hands. The smell of boxes of goods being opened hung in the air. The thin, red line of all the fezes flowed continuously on both sides of the market. The tinkling sound of money would be heard, then a cough, another tea-seller, a yawn, yet another tea-seller, and the ripping of the boxes being opened, a tea-seller, glasses decorated with flowers, passing fezzes, coughs, yawns, trade – the market!

Simon was thinking that business was indeed not bad. But why, or how did he get where he was: an Armenian merchant with wealth; a three-storey house painted in blue with carpeted, light blue rooms; a large and safe hoard of capital; a wife and children; a private carriage; fame and respect. On the other hand, how happy he had been when he, a bare-footed Simon, was running after the cattle, to collect manure at his mother's command, then throwing the basketful of manure into a corner of the yard for his mother to make into bricks for the fire, then selling some of it to poor neighbours and keeping the rest as fuel for winter. He used to rush out of the house to play knucklebones, to snatch things out of other children's hands, to fight a few of them, or be attacked himself.

Now the beads were falling onto each other more and more rapidly. Simon could see his mother, clothed in rags and hardships, and the fishing-net – the only thing left by his father, fisherman Markar, after his death. He recalled the smell of choking smoke from the tonir and he found himself wishing that those sorrowful and fretful days would return. He was, of course, deceiving himself. He was cunningly scrambling his past, making it seem to have been happy and generously forgetting all his sorrows.

– You see, Simon, gold doesn't mean too much to you. What is gold? Gold is something dirty. What a pity! Where are those youthful and carefree days? Where the basket with the hole in it, the concern for winter manure? None of it can ever return. –

Eventually his mother had died. The neighbours, who had bought her manure, took care of her funeral. Simon thought that the cattle were of no use any more; her remaining manure bricks had to be sold and he had to think what he could do now.

It turned out that there had been no need to think long. Once, quite by chance, he patted a cushion, whether to soften it or simply by accident. His hand touched something hard. He unfastened the cushion without thinking and found ten gold coins wrapped in a dirty piece of cloth. And this set the young street-peddler walking along the road to where he had now arrived. He had endured the pitfalls with nimble feet and removed any obstacles in his way whenever he could with equally nimble fingers. He deceived people eloquently whenever he could, and charmed the influential people in the market. He came closer to them little by little; he flattered them and little by little drew closer; he smiled, he pretended to be poor and drew closer and closer.

At last he stood beside them, caught up with them, advanced with them, and when he felt that everything was just right, he took a step away and stabbed his companions in the back. He made many a man go bankrupt. Most men could not bear the onslaught of his violent will, hardened as it had become by earlier sorrows and poverty. The years slipped by and flowed away. Many men lost their position and influence in the market, dissolving like dust and mist, while he, Simon, smiled through that dust and mist with his inseparable worry-beads, his slight shoulders bent forward and with his all-seeing eyes fixed only on the beads.

Now he cunningly scrambles his past and his present, his world and his fate. What a pity! His carefree days are over! Carefree days? What carefree days? Hunger, sorrow, humiliation. Carefree days! His mother's curses and blows. What carefree days? Poverty, dirty knucklebones, a bleeding nose. Carefree days, indeed! Simon gathering manure, his mother selling bricks of it for fuel.

– No, no, Simon, enjoy the world, make your fortune. Save gold, Simon. Gold is a more secure fortune than knucklebones. Your brains turned out to be of more lasting value than the crumpled fishing net left by your father, which is kept in one of your trunks as a terribly galling relic. After all, these customers coming into your shop are more useful and nourishing than the fish that might have fallen into the net of your father, fisherman Markar. –

The shop-assistant put the usual glass of strong tea before Simon and left. Simon, with one eye on the steam rising from the tea, became anxious. He put the worry-beads on his right arm, took a black bone, tobacco case out of his pocket and rolled a cigarette. This time his eyes were fixed on his fingers. He seemed to be examining the way they were rolling the cigarette with languid dexterity.

The senior shop-assistant came up to him.

"A lot of military cloth has been bought today. It's a bad omen."

"Why should it be a bad omen?"

"The Armenian revolutionary committees are buying it."

"So what?"

"Isn't there something serious brewing?"

"What should there be?"

"I don't know, Sir."

"Mind your own business, if you don't know."

Simon lit his cigarette, smoked it, puffed the smoke straight above his moustache into the uncertainty now hanging in the air and asked: "Is there any military cloth left?"

"About two full lengths."

"Did they buy much of it?"

"Eleven bales."

"Did the Armenians buy it?"

"Yes, they did."

"Right! Put the price up. You may be right, there must be something brewing."

At that moment, one of the salesmen handed an envelope to Simon.

"Who gave you this?"

"A man in a carriage gave it and left."

Simon slowly and carefully slit the envelope open and took the sheet of paper out. He looked at the letter, at first in an unconcerned and absent-minded way. Gradually, however, his eyes strained, his face became more and more tense and his usually bright red face became as white as a sheet of paper.

He called the shop-assistant and impatiently demanded, "Who gave this letter to you?"

"A man gave it to me and left immediately in a carriage."

"Who was it?"

"Someone – I don't know."

"What did he say?"

"He told me to give it to Baron Simon."

"To Baron Simon?"

"No, sorry. He said, 'Give it to your master'."

"Why did you take it, why did you take it?" shouted Simon angrily at the lad for not having dealt with it properly. He realised that he himself had not heard his own voice raised in anger for a long time.

"What should I have done? He gave it and I took it."

"You, pumpkin head, do you think you should take anything you're given?"

He threw the beads onto the carpet and left the shop with his hands behind his back and his head thrust forward as if he were afraid of some terrible blow which was going to fall down on his wrinkled neck.

But that blow had in fact already fallen.

Simon walks on as if in a dream. He is breathing heavily and staggering as if he were drunk. The lines and the letters of the writing he has just read are burning in his brain like hot zigzags. An impenetrable and uncertain darkness overcomes him with the words of the letter flashing like bolts of lightning with flickering tails.

It was a cloudless, peaceful and joyful morning. He tried to look at everything about him in a normal manner as though nothing had happened, but he could not manage to do so. He hired a horsecab and directed the driver without even looking at him. The driver waved his whip respectfully and loosened the reins. The street swirled up, dipped down rose and began to flow along on either side of the carriage until it stopped in front of a two-storey house. The door was adorned with blue-painted iron. A hinged iron hand was hanging on the door with an iron ball clasped in its fingers. Simon got down, paid the driver and went up to the door. He lifted the iron hand twice and let it go. The door resounded sharply and deafeningly twice, followed by a muffled voice from deep inside the house.

"Who's that?"

"Open up," said Simon, stepping back from the door to be able to see better who opened it.

The door opened a little way and a servant's face appeared. He squinted through the narrow opening and when he saw Simon, he pushed the door wide open and stood with a welcoming smile.

"Is Panos Effendi in?"

"Yes, sure."

Simon entered and went across the cool, vaulted hall towards the stairs.

"He isn't in the sitting-room, Baron," said the servant politely

"Where is he then?"

"He's in the garden. He's having tea."

Simon's confused thoughts seemed to calm down: 'Thank God, the world has not after all yet come to an end. Here is Panos, sitting quietly and drinking tea, so it is still possible for life to go on.'

He came out into the bright yard from the dark hall. The yard was glistening with beautifully cultivated flowers. Ivy had climbed up the wall separating the yard from the garden. A low wood of sorrel delighted the eye with the intimate charm of all small thickets, while in the square niche set in the wall separating the yard there were three garden-pots with newly-flowered, velvet kadifa leaves. Panos' wife, with an early September bloom about her, welcomed Simon at the stony entrance leading to the garden. She had thrown a black shawl, decorated with roses, over her head. Peeping out of the shawl, a curl of black hair on her brow was divided by a single white hair. Just above the brow and the curl, one of the black roses on the white background of the shawl seemed to look back at Simon with dark yearning. She had a sieve under her arm full of green, still unripe, plums, with some thick, large roses scattered over the plums.

"Good morning," said Simon. "I see you've picked roses."

"Good morning. These are cherry-plums for the bitter pastille I'm making."

Simon wanted to insist they were roses, but she passed on, glancing back at him with just one of her black eyes.

"Panos Effendi is sitting in the rose-garden."

Simon walked ahead along the straight path edged by fruit trees, breathing in the fresh air of the garden. When he got to Panos' rose-garden, he was already smiling, though his eyes seemed full of tears.

Panos was sitting on a carpet spread out over a square area bordered by flowers. A boiling samovar was on the grass to his right, a glass of hot tea before him, and a long scroll for calculating dates beside him. In the mist of the steam rising from the samovar, Panos' face seemed to Simon so healthy, so smooth and clean. But as he came forward, Panos' face emerged from the steam, and he seemed much the same – with an unhealthy flush and a lot of wrinkles, folds and lines.

"Good morning," said Simon.

"Oh, good morning. Have a seat, you look sad."

"If I were only just sad."

"What's up, man?"

"Can there be anything worse?"

And he handed over the paper. Panos read it once and seemed to have understood a little of it. He then had a sip from his tea, looked at his knees, and read the letter a second time. This time he seemed to understood it more and picking up his glass he had two or three more sips. Finally he read it a third time – this time more slowly and word by word. He put the glass down, leant firmly on the ground with both hands and got up onto his feet.

"Let's go to the café."

"Let's go," agreed Simon fretfully, like a spoilt child. He had started playing with the ends of his red handkerchief instead of the worry-beads.

They walked off together.

"Well, well," observed Simon as they walked slowly back up the path, "suppose we do go to the café, what shall we do there?"

"We'll have a cup of coffee," came the answer.

"What do you think of all this?" said Simon, as he stopped and leant on the wall with his arm just as Panos was already going to enter the yard.

"Take it easy, take it easy. Let's go to the café first."

And so – the café again.

"Baron Simon –"

"Yes, what is it?"

"We should go and see Baron Ohannes Muradkhanian."

"Nothing can be done without him. We should see him by all means."

"So you ought to have known."

"I know, I know, take it easy."

Late that night, Panos approached his door thoughtfully, though with the sense of relief of a man who had got rid of a danger. He stopped and looked around. The dark street was already deserted. 'It would be nice, if they put up lamp-posts in the street,' he thought, and then he summarized to himself what had happened that day. 'Simon suffering, going to the cafe didn't help. It's always better to be on good terms with the Turks. We should go and see Ohannes; they haven't touched me yet, but who knows? I spent six kurush today.'

He lifted the iron hand on the door and let it drop. He did not hear the familiar ring. Lost in his thoughts, he looked at the dark and deserted length of the street, lifted the iron hand again and let it drop. There was again only a dull thud. He wondered. whether there was something wrong with the door. He lifted the iron hand again, and looking at it for the first time saw that under it there was a piece of paper, nailed in the very place where the ball of the iron hand fell. And the paper was not falling down because it was fixed.

Shivering with horror, he carefully took the piece of paper and knocked very loudly on the door three time, as if urgently seeking shelter from some terrible force following him.

"Baron Ohannes," began Panos playing with the glass of raki in his hand, "we indeed congratulate you on adding a branch to your house. May he have, as they say, an abundance of wine, and oil for the reins of his horse. May he enjoy this world, and may his parents be forever in glory. But this is not the reason we've knocked at your door, Baron Ohannes. I'm afraid we were born under a black star. Our happiness is not complete. We haven't brought good news to you."

There was a silence. Only the monotonous clicking of Simon's beads and the muted rustle of the Aikesdan trees could be heard.

"Take these and read them." Not finding anything more to say, Panos handed the two messages to Ohannes.

The latter took the unfortunate pieces of paper; their contents were the same but they were written in different handwriting. The messages demanded that three hundred gold coins be placed in a certain spot, at a certain hour, on a certain day. The demand was direct and unambiguous: if the recipients failed to fulfill it, they were threatened with death. Simon's message was signed 'Black Hat' and that of Panos, 'Red Hat'.

"Haven't you had one?" Panos broke the silence after Ohannes had already read the messages twice and was busy carefully straightening out the crumpled papers.

"They haven't taken me to be an important person," Ohannes said.

Silence again.

Ohannes continued: "I suppose they claim that this is for the nation's salvation."

"The nation doesn't only belong to them," Panos replied, getting annoyed. "We aren't worried any less about the nation than they are. Let them explain properly, fix a sum and give us a receipt so that we can control any money they spend. What manners are these! What is this 'black hat' or 'red hat'? What a disgraceful way to behave! Your health!"

He stretched out his glass for some more raki. They had a drink.

"I trust you enjoyed it?" said Ohannes.

"May your life be always in clover" replied the guests waiting to see who would speak again on the issue.

"We should inform the government," Ohannes proposed hesitantly

"They'll kill us for sure," said Simon at last.

"What should we do then?"

They had another drink, then a fourth, then a fifth. Little by little the nightmare seemed to vanish. They started talking about their business affairs and their plans. Each of them became inspired and did his best to inspire the others. Nobody wanted to get back to the original painful problem. They seemed to have agreed not to spoil the increasingly lively atmosphere. Sirpouhi came in and informed them that guests were gathering downstairs.

"Tell them to come up here," said Ohannes and then turned to his drinking companions.

"We won't betray our feelings to them. Look both of you, take it easy. You're my guests today. This is a day of happiness. Let's forget for today on which side the sun rises and on which it sets."

He raised his glass of raki, stared at its clear appearance and added in a spirit of innocent goodwill: "Today's another day."

Chapter 3

It is June. The ancient town lies not far from the lake, a miraculous green-haired enchantress from a fairy tale.

Gardens, gardens, gardens. Green – amazingly green – plush gardens with tall poplars and abundant orchards, where plump and fragrant malacha, malaghek and meghruk pears ripen, where the dalasli apples smell sweet, the bunches of grapes swell like the breasts of early motherhood, and the seductively ripe apricot charms and delights, where the quince hangs more heavily, the plums sing, the flowers smile and the paths wind round the gardens. And an enormous sun shines over all this, turning in its track, burning and pouring out its bright and fiery heat.

And the world is alive. And Van is alive.

And Van is alive with memories. And cradles: for the old recall their childhood as they sit under a tree, while their grandchildren play in the grass, screaming with shrill, childish happiness, so that their voices sound like those of a little bustard, a warbler, a swallow or a weaver-bird.

The houses, large and small, all in different European and Oriental styles, are hidden among the trees, gardens and orchards. From afar, the town looks like an extended forest and it is the same forest however close you approach it. When you enter through its green gates and see its houses and criss-crossing streets, you will come to think that they only exist in a fairy tale, that the streets and houses will soon completely vanish, and only the forest and streams will remain – and that you will remain. But the streets will be there, the houses will still be looking at them, the streams will flow, the orchards will still rustle.

And the world will be alive. And Van will be alive.

It is June. At noon, the grass will get warm, the trees will get warm, the fruit will get warmer, the flower petals will get warmer, while the marjoram growing in the shade will be moist and cool. At noon, the earth will be warm, the trees and gardens will be spellbound and still like a large landscape painting drawn on a magic canvas by an artistic genius. An intoxicating scent will permeate the air – the aroma of flowers, sap, seeds, and fruit, the aroma of incense, of the sun, of longing and sweat, of love and earth. Mt Varag will seem near and interlocked with the rocks bordering the town, the carved ones being decorated with mysterious enigmatic characters and incomprehensible signs.

The goldsmiths engrave churches and flowers on jewellery, the weavers at their looms weave cotton and chintz, the horsecab-driver Seno plies for hire, the typesetter Hmayak sets the *Ashkhadank* newspaper, and the only poet in the town, walks down the street alone – he had placed an announcement in the newspaper a few days before, asking his relatives and friends to be kind enough not to greet him.

The world must be alive. Van must be alive.

The market is noisy. The shopkeepers snatch peasants and teachers out of each other's hands. ("Baron Ohannes, how was trade today?" ... "It was a poor day; you see, neither teacher nor peasant came in.") The measuring stick flies along the flowery rolls of cloth, the street of the tailors roars with the noise of Singer sewing machines at work; the shoemaker sings a sad song and slowly bangs down a nail; the watchmaker always prefers the Zenith brand. The photographer, Arshak Dzetotian, has asked the painter, Mesrob Amsarian, to make him a sign for his workshop. And, incidentally, he has asked for the words 'STUDIO IDEAL: for accurate, vivid, and immediate photographs – from Arshak Dzituni', together with a drawing of him standing by the camera. But Mesrob has written IDIAL instead of IDEAL (a disgraceful mistake that would always be pointed out), and Dzetotian instead of Dzituni. The photographer thought this was done to make the whole town laugh at him.

"Take it easy, why should anyone tease you? Aren't you in fact Dzetotian?"

"No, professionally I'm Dzituni – yes, Dzituni."

"Why?"

"Mind you own business. And who's that standing by the camera? What's this? Am I so tall and thin?"

"The photo's still wet, that's why it looks like that, Baron Arshak, it will change when it dries."

The fishmonger walks along the street, following his exhausted donkey, laden with two baskets and waggling its ears. "Buy fish, buy fish!." Every fishmonger has his own way of calling out to his own particular customers, who appear with their pots and pans to buy from ten to a hundred fish – at one para each. This is the cheapest and most available food, enjoyed by both rich and poor. Then the travelling cloth merchant passes by. "Mustura, pasma, yasma yeo," sings the merchant, nobody knows why in so tearfully drawn out a way. There is also the chintz-seller and the street-musician, the fruiterer and the fortune-teller, the bear-trainer and the knife-grinder, and the fantastic stilt-walker standing five metres high on his wooden feet, decorated head to foot in a colourful silk costume, with neck and brow covered in beads and rattling coins, accompanied by a clown with his pipe and drum, and followed by an army of noisy children.

The man on stilts goes from street to street in huge steps, and dances in front of balconies and windows, while the clown made up with a goatee beard, painted face and colourful costume, makes funny faces, somersaults between the stilts and collects money from the audience with a copper bowl. When the solid army of children disturbs his act, he leaps out at them. The terrified children run away with piercing screams; the noise becomes ever more deafening and unpleasant. But the man on stilts strides on in huge steps, followed by the noise and the crowd. The beat of the drum can already be heard in the next street; and back where he has been, the gentle bubble of the stream and the rustle of the willows and poplars bordering it can be heard once again.

When a child becomes alarmed or sick with fright, its mother will hand it to the stilt man who, hugging the child, dances to get rid of its fear. The man somehow bends down and takes the child from the arms of the mother as she stands on a stone trough. He embraces the child and begins dancing with mysterious cries. The child screams in excitement, peering down from the unusual height to where the drum roars and the pipe howls, to where the crowd looks up as if from another world, while the stilt man jumps up and down uttering strange words. When the child has finally lost its fear, the man hands the weak and quivering child to its mother and moves on. The noise and the crowd follow him and the sound of the drum can be heard from another street.

As the stilt-walker entered the street where the Muradkhanians live, Ohannes was having dinner with his guests. These include Kevork Djidechian, as well as the manager of his shop, Set, and his beautiful wife, Khushush, dressed in Parisian style. Various relatives and close neighbours were in another room in the women's quarter, from where the sound of laughter and whispers could be heard. Ohannes' mother, a cigarette at her lips, was going round the dinner-table, persuading everyone to eat and drink more. The parish priest, Khoren, was also at the table: he was a merry person, a man of the world, who had assumed the cloth almost as a joke, just to amuse himself and others.

"It's not right, not right at all. Neither for God, nor for man."

"What do you mean, Reverend Father?"

"It's not right. I'm not interested myself, but I am anxious about you. Just think it over, aren't you sorry for your –"

"But what do you mean? What's the matter?" interposed Djidechian, impatiently toying with his wine glass.

Instead of replying, Khoren clears his throat and starts singing Armenian Girls with deep feeling:

"When the red wine is poured into my glass ..."

He raises the wine glass above his head, staring at it with bright, excited eyes,

"I see your beautiful face in it, my love."

Things are getting lively – blood is boiling – glasses are filled and a chorus is heard from the women's quarter.

> "A girl stood by the cool spring,
> Holding a jar, the darling.
> Mother, I'm smitten, I love her,
> But all she gave me was a brief glance."

Then midwife Tarik appears, boldly takes a seat beside Khoren and grasps his beard: "Aren't you ashamed of this beard?" She is drowned by a deafening roar of laughter from the women's quarter. She turns to him and tells him in a lively way that the stilt-walker has entered the street.

"What do you mean? Am I to go out and be a clown?" laughs the priest.

"Oh my, what a clergyman! He wasn't at all put out, but teased me instead."

"Midwife Tarik, how old are you?" asks Khoren, patting her shoulder amid everyone's laughter.

"Three times twenty-four."

"That'll be sixty-four."

"Don't say that, it's surely more. Say three-times-twenty-four, your tongue won't split, will it? I've made a vow at Varag's church of the Holy Sign to get married when I'm seventy."

Khoren sings A Modest Girl, addressing his words seductively to the midwife, and the joyful spirit at the table reaches its peak. Then the midwife sings a song about mothers in labour. The table calms down, bright lamps are lit, and candlesticks – each with ten candles – are placed before the two mirrors, but they cannot compete with the big oil lamps. Tarik sings in praise of the mother who gave birth to a boy, and in scorn of the one who gave birth to a girl.

"Take the boy's mother
to gather roses and smell them,
she's had a boy, had a boy.
Take the girl's mother
to pick onions and smell them,
she's had a girl, had a girl."

Ohannes is looking with misty eyes at the mirror hanging on the wall and at his grandfather's picture above it. That patriarch, that mythical person, looks down from the wall and artfully comments:

'Eh, Ohannes, Ohannes, you can't surprise me with your newborn babe, or your dinner table. I'd be surprised if you didn't have a baby, a home, a dinner table. Who knows further back than their grandfather? People often don't even know their grandfathers. They know only their mother and father. But if they knew everyone! ... The beginning for anyone is the very first day of mankind, isn't it? Get to know me, Ohannes, and make your children and grandchildren know us both. And you tell them to do the same to their children and grandchildren.'

The oriental music trio in the corner were playing a fine tune. Though it was far from being a dance tune, Ohannes got up and started dancing, with his eyes fixed on the portrait. He was dancing slowly, solemnly and unselfconsciously, as if lost and invisible. He was shaking his hips, moving his shoulders back and forth, throwing his handkerchief on the floor and lifting it with his teeth, and then straightening up to continue dancing with his eyes on the portrait. There was something moving and majestic about his spontaneous, improvised dance. That was why no-one spoke; everyone was looking at Ohannes with the awed attention of a circus audience watching a brave acrobat performing his dangerous and deadly turns.

To tell the truth, Ohannes's turns were neither dangerous nor deadly. It was true that he was dancing with impromptu boldness, though it was no different from what anyone else would have done. But all the spectators were stunned.

And the room? There was a haze in the room that was neither

from the smoke of cigarettes, nor the steam from the dishes, but which had got into everyone's eyes and souls. They were seeing ordinary things and events through the second, fifth and seventh layers of the haze. That was why Ohannes' dance had been so charming and unforeseen.

Then Simon stood up and announced he would like to say two words. But Ohannes was still dancing.

"Baron Ohannes, please, allow me to speak."

But Ohannes was still dancing.

"Baron Ohannes," Panos came to the aid of Simon. "Baron Simon speaks only once every ten years. Won't you let him do so now?"

But Ohannes was dancing before the portrait of his ancestor, to a tune that had nothing to do with any dance.

"Just two words," Simon insisted with tearful eyes.

Midwife Tarik brought out the swaddled baby from the next room and placed it solemnly in the outstretched arms of the dancing father. Joyful sounds arose, glasses were raised, and Ohannes lifted his load up to his ancestor's portrait.

"Just two words."

Ohannes handed the baby back to the midwife and his elated face took on its normal, straightforward look. He wiped the sweat off his forehead with a large, red handkerchief and at last sat down.

Simon stood up, holding his glass close to his chest: "We've seen many prosperous homes – let's drink to prosperous homes! We've seen people with generous hearts and souls – lets drink to them! A house should be built on firm foundations – lets drink to firm foundations!"

"Baron Simon," interrupted Khoren, "we can't drink to so many things with just one glass."

Simon paid no attention to the priest's interruption, but carried on: "My fellow diners, our ancestors used to say that where there's a thief living in the house, the ox can be removed even through the smoke-hole."

"Let's drink to the thief as well," Khoren interposed again.

"The thief mustn't be toasted," the orator replied, "a thief has to be consigned to the devil."

"Baron Simon, what are you saying? Let's drink to the devil, as well!"

"Reverend Father," murmured Panos, "there's no need to make a nuisance of yourself, let the man think."

"Let's drink to thought, as well."

"They've let down a rope from the hole in the roof, my fellow diners," continued Simon, suddenly inwardly troubled. "There's not much room left for them to get the ox out and slaughter it for the sake of the nation. What nation? It's a falsehood – who are the nation? That's me, you, him. If we aren't one heart and soul, in place of these homes and dinner tables, we'll see only the ruins of Ani." And here the speaker raised his voice: "We don't need any black, red, yellow or blue hats. Down with all hats!"

Simon drank and sat down. A shadow fell over the table. Many did not understand what Simon had been speaking about or what he had meant. But they felt that something dark and ominous had occurred. Only Khoren retained his merry mood.

"A black hat, a red hat, a long hat, a small hat. Good Lord! Who put forward this theory of hats? Fill your glasses, guard the smoke-hole so that no one could sneak out a hen, let alone an ox. As for the thief – well, lets catch him and rope him to the pillar, God willing."

Five minutes later, the musicians were again playing with zest, the wine was bubbling in the glasses, and the guests were singing and entertaining themselves at the richly laden table, having forgotten all about hats of any colour. Kevork, the teacher, came in. Ohannes, still holding his glass high over his head, froze intuitively. He had noticed a piece of folded paper in his brother's hand. The music stopped.

"What a surprising thing," Kevork's flat voice was heard in dead silence, "I'd just left, intending to go home. I'd no sooner walked a little way, than a man with his head and face covered with a hood came up to me and asked whether I was Ohannes Muradkhanian's brother. I said I was. The man told me to go back, rightaway, and hand this paper to him without delay. He then vanished. I called after him: 'Who are you? What are you?', but I didn't get any reply. Here it is!"

CHAPTER 3

The wind blew in from the sea in the evening, but swung to come down from the hill at sunrise. The leaves on the trees veered round; and not only the leaves on the trees: the waves of the peacefully flowing waters, the washing that hung out on the flat roofs, the turn of the windmill looking over the town, the feathers of the birds spending the night in the tall ash and poplar trees, even the night itself, were all also turning round.

As was Baron Ohannes himself. He had woken up early this morning. He had gone to bed late, as everyone had been treading down his Persian carpet till the early hours. But why had he woken up so early this morning?

– Souren, naughty Souren, had not left the roses to mature into thick blossoms. But Lia? Lia was mature. Hmm? But was that the important matter? Roses, rose ... 'A rose has flowered in the Aikesdan of Van' ... Reverend Khoren – what a strange priest he was. Was he a priest or a man? What an amazing clergyman the man was! So, that's how things are: Simon, Panos ... He recalled his dream. Mice! He remembered the portrait hanging on the wall and his dancing. He could dance; he had danced surprisingly well. Why dance? Who for? What for? For whose sake? 'In the name of the father and the son ...' Ah! Tarik, was it for you. I must dance for you on my knees. Midwife Tarik, midwife Tarik. –

His wife, Satenik, was lying a little apart. Their bed was on the carpet over the floorboards. The baby was on Satenik's other side. Would Ohannes now care to hear its scream? Not really! When you first take your own child in your hands, there is somethng amazing about it. A boy or a girl? Was it all the same? No, it wasn't the same. What was Lia? Nothing – destined to become a pillar of another house. Souren was something else, even though he spoilt the roses. He was a boy. He would go to school, become a teacher, get married, bring back a wife. Ohannes would have grandchildren. His grandchild would study, then become a teacher.

A teacher, a teacher! He remembered his brother Kevork, the teacher who used to drink. Well, let him drink. Did Kevork go hungry? No, he didn't. Ohannes would never leave him hungry. And now, only dancing and dancing. But – O, God! – now he remembers: there was Kevork with a piece of paper in his hand, asking him to take it.

> "Are you awake, husband?"
> "Yes. And you?"
> "Why did the guests run away."
> "Guests? What guests?"
> "Baron Simon, Baron Panos. The guests."
> "Run away ... ?"

Oh, he was very used to reading other people's handwriting. He wasn't superstitious, he didn't believe in dreams. But when he hurries to the market, riding his white donkey with the tinkling bells, he notices even the erratic zig-zags the hens' feet made in the fine dust of the summer avenue, stretching from Khatch Street to the centre of town. *Kher, Shar, Astvadz,* the zig-zags seem to say: Persian *Kher* was literally good, Armenian *Astvadz* was God and surely not bad, but Arabic *Sh – Sh – Sh – Shar* was competely evil. He was very used to reading even the most confused handwriting, let alone the one his brother Kevork gave him.

He had not put the glass down. He had held it with one hand high above his head, and he'd taken that terrible message in the other and read it:

At three o'clock tonight, place five hundred gold pieces in the stone trough in your garden. Don't stay there yourself. A refusal means certain death. Hat.

Impudent, shameless people! Simon and Panos had at least known the colour of their hats – a black hat, a red hat. But look at this villain – just Hat. What hat? What colour hat?

"Wife, what time is it? Oh, woman, I always forget your condition."

He groaned, got up, took matches out of his frock-coat pocket, felt for his waistcoat and pulled the flat watch and chain out of his pocket. He pressed the head of the watch handle with his thumbnail – the lid opened immediately. Then, he lit a match with his other hand. The mother, who had recently given birth, saw the anxious and worried face of her husband lit up by the flame of the match.

"It's two o'clock," he said "Go back to sleep. I'm going to nip out for a little walk. I've got indigestion. O God, O God!"

He put his frock-coat on over his night-gown, slipped the matches and the watch back into his pocket and swiftly left the room. He went downstairs and into the large room in the other wing of the house. It was called the large room because it really was the largest in the house. It was full of unnecessary things – carpets, rugs, a few beds for guests, numerous seats and armchairs, an old wall-clock that had been out of order for eight years and which had stopped at precisely twelve o'clock, whether midday or midnight nobody knew. He approached the door of this large room cautiously, being afraid to wake up his mother, or Lia and Souren, sleeping in the opposite room. Ohannes quietly pushed open the door and entered on tip-toes. He crossed the room and stood by one of the windows overlooking the garden; he opened it and cautiously put his head out, like a turtle popping its head out of its shell.

It was dead of night. The crescent moon peered through the two motionless poplars in front of the windows. But Ohannes was not looking at the moon: he was looking at the stone trough, near the well, in which wheat was pounded. The surprising thing was that there really did seem to be someone standing near the trough. It was difficult to distinguish anything in the dark; for example, the pail by the well was not visible, but the trough was and there was a shadow alongside it. Ohannes shivered and drew his head back. He went up to the large, built-in cupboard, took out a small bunch of keys from the pocket of his frock-coat, selected one of them without looking down, and opened the door of the cupboard. He then struck a match with trembling hand, lit a candle in one of the candlesticks on the table next to the cupboard. The candle lit up the silver, gold and gilded objects stacked up on the cupboard shelves – trays, saucers, glasses, glass-holders, piles of spoons and forks, expensive faience statuettes and boxes decorated with ornamental jewellery. Ohannes groaned out loud as though with toothache, and took out with both hands a plain, wooden box from the back of a lower shelf. He opened the box with a key and raised the lid. Every day – in fact several times a day – whenever he told someone that he had no ready cash and that his capital was tied up, he would bring this box and its contents to his mind.

He dipped his fingers into the box, groaned again, and started counting out five hundred gold coins, one by one, throwing them on top of each other onto the table beside him. When he had finished, he looked at the heap on the table, took the box, weighed it in his hands, replaced it, and murmured through clenched teeth, "I won't give them so much gold with my own hands. Let then kill me, the bandits. I won't give them any money."

He felt his brow getting damp with sweat. He looked at his watch – it was ten minutes to the fatal hour. A cricket squealed from a corner of the room and then went quiet with fright.

– Who invented night? Was God concerned about thieves or revolutionaries, who would not dare operate in the daytime? Why should he put this gold in the stone trough? What for? Who for? The result of a whole year's work! If it was for an honest cause, why didn't they come to the house or the shop in broad daylight? They could say, 'Baron Ohannes, give this much gold for the sake of the nation.' And he would count out and hand over the required sum. But what a way of proceeding! A vile, thievish business – for what? A Hat! –

"I won't give them any money," Ohannes exclaimed aloud.

He automatically glanced down at his watch, put the gold back into the box, closed the lid, locked the box, pushed it deep into the cupboard, and stood with his back to it, with hands stretched out on both sides as if to defend it from attack.

At that moment, two bursts of gunfire were heard from the garden. Suddenly it seemed the candlelight flared up and then went out. When he came to his senses, he realised that the reason why the light had vanished was that he was now facing the cupboard and pressing against it with his enormous belly. It meant that he must have turned round. It also meant that he was alive. He had not been shot.

Kevork read the stranger's unfortunate message and decided not to give it to his brother. Then he thought it would be wrong not to hand it over, that there could be serious consequences. Before going in, he had checked the mood of the guests gathered in the sitting-room, especially that of his brother. He had been irritated to see his brother dancing. He himself had been banished from school like a dog, deprived of his miserable salary, lost Vergine's 'respect' at home , and had been slighted by the waiters in the café. While Ohannes – his carefree brother – was dancing happily, dancing with untroubled confidence. He was light-hearted and oblivious of the impending calamity.

"Take it ...."

He had rushed out of the room after handing over the message, had ran downstairs and gone out into the street. He had not taken part in his brother's party, had not shared his happiness, and so did not want to share his alarm and confusion. He wanted neither his feast or his wake. No! But it was a hard blow – take five hundred clinking gold pieces and give it to God knows who. And why? Five hundred gold coins! How many years would he have to work to earn so much money? And now his brother has to give that huge sum to a Hat.

Mkho was approaching him, with a tool in his hand. He looked peaceful; only someone with a clear conscience could look so calm, someone who minded his own business, who had never spoiled the earth or cheated the cattle under his care, who had neither borrowed or lent money, someone who had seen his own needs as naturally subject to a divine tax, to be paid for with sweat and blood.

"Mkho, where are you going?"

"Home."

"To the party?"

"No, I'm going to bed early, and off to the village in the morning."

The thought occurred to Kevork that his brother may have had some money from Ohannes, and that they might therefore go to the café.

"Have you any money on you?" he asked, with the thought that the man was after all his brother.

"No," Mkho smiled, showing his healthy white teeth. "I had a few kurush and I bought a few things."

"Let's stay together, there's no need for you to go home just yet."

"But why?"

"I've something to tell you, of course. Let's go."

"Where?" persisted Mkho.

"Let's go. I won't take you anywhere bad."

Mkho turned round and they walked down to Khatch Street and carried on up it. Of an evening, the street was full of carriages and people passing through some of them returning from the market. There were few women; the older ones were swathed head to foot in snow-white gowns, while the young women were covered with delicate veils. The men, who were of varying age and status, all wore red fezzes, giving the street a cheerful look.

"Where are we going?" said Mkho.

His brother did not answer. They passed a number of houses and closed shops and reached a two-storey building. The people, crowded round the table on the ground floor, were having coffee, playing dominoes or cards.

Kevork went straight up to the first floor. Mkho followed him automatically, but reluctantly. They took their seats at a table on the open balcony. The waiter strolled up rather casually. He was a young man in black trousers, a blue waistcoat, and with a white napkin thrown carelessly over his shoulder. He looked at Kevork in a way that Mkho did not care for at all. Taking no notice of the waiter's manner, Kevork gave his order in a commanding, yet friendly, tone.

"Effendi, a bottle of raki, olives and pasturma."

"Why are you wasting money," asked a hesitant and uncertain Mkho, after the apparently unwilling waiter left. "We'd do better at home, there's raki there and wine."

"Home!" murmured Kevork. "Home! My poor crazy Mkho!"

Mkho did not ask why he was poor, why crazy. He just kept quiet, overcome with dark foreboding, and looked down at the street and the evening twilight.

The waiter appeared with a tray and put some fresh bread, several slices of pasturma, a few olives, a bottle of raki and two glasses on the table. Taking up the empty tray, he said, "Three kurush."

"We've got it," muttered Kevork, filling his glass.

"Three kurush!" echoed Mkho, looking aghast at the tiny meal on the table.

The waiter smiled softly: "Is anything wrong?"

"There's nothing wrong, go away," retorted Kevork as the glass of raki began to shake in his hand.

The waiter put the tray under his arm and went off.

"What a blockhead," Kevork said with anger and contempt. It was not clear whether the waiter heard or not.

"Let's drink. We can't look into this matter without a drink," Kevork added calmly, and swallowed the raki in one gulp. Mkho also drank and then began chewing some bread.

"Poor Mkho! Crazy Mkho!" Kevork exclaimed, this time with more firm conviction, when they had already emptied a fourth glass.

"Why, what's on the tip of your tongue? Come on, out with it properly, so I can know what's going on," said Mkho, apparently at ease, but still with the same unpleasant foreboding.

Kevork drank a fifth glass, sniffed some bread, put it back on the plate and at last related the whole affair. Mkho stood up.

"Where are you going?" said Kevork.

"Let's go and see what we can do."

"Sit down and drink. I'm no less worried than you are. But everything in good time. Let's think, consider, ponder. The affair is not about local thieves, it's national."

"Five hundred gold pieces!" muttered Mkho, trying to imagine that sum. Then he looked down at the dark street, and exclaimed, "One could buy a whole village with five hundred gold pieces!"

"Drink up," Kevork clinked glasses with a shaking hand. "Why one? Why not four, five, ten villages? Would you like me to buy and sell your village, Ermants, tomorrow?" Believing he had a fortune, he summoned the waiter.

"Aghavard, come here."

He recalled that he used to call his pupils to the blackboard in that tone. He wanted to smile, but remembering – he did not know why – the headmaster's face and the front of the school lavatory, he frowned.

"Three kurush," said the waiter, approaching the table.

"We have it. I'm not an arithmetic teacher, but I can add up, you know. A bottle of raki."

Mkho couldn't bear it anymore. "That's enough brother, you've already spent three kurush. With that sum I –"

"And what about five hundred gold coins?" Kevork rapped his hand on the table and turned to the waiter, "Aghavard, don't spoil my meal. Fetch a bottle of raki."

"Effendi, when are you going to pay up?" persisted the waiter in helpless despair. But it was clear that he was going to carry out his customer's order, whether the bill was settled at ten the next morning or in a year. Kevork was not a man to follow convention.

"Well, my lad," he exclaimed, stretching out both his hands towards the waiter, "a matter of five hundred gold coins is on the table. Just bring the raki."

It was not clear whether it was his irritable helplessness or the five hundred coins that impressed the waiter, but he went off in a hurry and in a moment brought another bottle.

The presence of the second bottle lowered Mkho's resolve. He was not used to drinking, and did not even like alcohol. He stared at the bottle of wine and the raki, as an ox working hard in a field might stare at a flock of cranes flying over. He was drinking now, and a certain calm, a strange peace, was spreading through his veins. He remembered his wife Iskouhi, his children Sirak and Mariam, and smiled. But suddenly the smile vanished as he recalled Ohannes' behaviour in the shop. He had asked if he could have some cotton for Iskouhi, and Ohannes had ignored him. And now some people were demanding five hundred gold pieces. Could Ohannes ignore that, too? Five hundred! Did Ohannes have so much money?

"Where from?" mused Mkho aloud, and then went quiet.

"Where from?" echoed Kevork. "We have five hundred gold

pieces, you and I, so what are you thinking of? Let's drink."

"How is Ohannes to pay?" Mhko clarified his question.

"How? Where from? From his purse of course. Who could wonder at that? There is one Van, and one Baron Ohannes. Now, Mkho, just think! Why should those others have the five hundred? We'll go at night, take the gold and share it out between us.

"They'd kill Ohannes," murmured Mkho.

"You're such a fount of wisdom," Kevork exclaimed, and then continued in a low voice. "We'll go from here to my house. You see it's not easy to find five hundred gold coins. We'll have to sweat blood, if necessary we'll have to shed blood."

"Blood? Why blood? I won't shed blood."

"Well, let the dogs have your brother's five hundred gold coins then. We can sing if you prefer."

When the doors of hope open ...

He began to sing, matching the rhythm with his feet, shaking his head and flashing his eyes. Kevork was singing and the thought of possessing the five hundred gold coins was searing his brain. He would dress Vergine from head to foot, and he himself would be dressed in the latest Stamboul style. He would also fill his house with furniture, with parties. That would show that headmaster.

I'd like to see my Cilicia ...

Mkho listened with a muzzy head to his brother's song, but he thought that something had to be done. But what? Something had to be done, lest Ohannes lose that sum and be ruined.

"Ohannes' home will be ruined," Mkho said, when Kevork had finished singing and had filled up the glasses.

Kevork laughed. "Ohannes' home will be ruined! Poor Mkho! Crazy Mkho! Just think about your own home. Holy cow! Think about my home. Ohannes' home indeed! Listen, just be reasonable. Let's go to my place now. I'll grab my pistol – it's old, but it can still kill a man – and also an axe. And we'll go to Ohannes' garden and hide behind the trees. When Ohannes brings out the money and puts it in the trough, we'll take it and sneak away. But if anyone interferes ... Do you understand my plan?"

The drink had worked on Mkho. In a remote part of his mind, only one thought was stirring – to save that fabulous sum and not let it fall into another's hands. Though drunk, he could clearly feel that this attempt to extort money was monstrous, unlawful and unjust. Well-bred people acting in a good cause would not be demanding that money be put into a trough for them to take away!

When there was no raki left and the waiter was busy serving other tables, Kevork seized the moment and stood up. "Let's get going."

Mkho followed him. On his way downstairs Kevork heard the waiter's loud comment: "His brother is so wealthy, while he …" He did not hear the rest, or did not want to.

It was past one in the morning when they entered Ohannes' garden through the vineyards. The weak light of the lamps could still be seen through the windows of some houses, whereas Ohannes' house and windows were plunged in darkness. It was a quiet, balmy night. Only a slight wind was blowing from garden to garden, from tree to tree, from leaf to leaf, and even the tender rustle of the trees seemed to be a silent whisper.

"The party's over," said Mkho in a hushed voice.

"They didn't have the usual lengthy party, did they?" said Kevork a little louder, perhaps to cheer up Mkho. "It's still early. We can have a little rest. Let me have one look and I'll come back."

He went out of the trees towards the shadowy trough. To do this, he had to cross over a paved area, since the well and the trough were not far from the garden door. He came back to Mkho; it was not clear at first why.

"Mkho?"

"Hmm?"

"I'm too tall," his voice was trembling. "Go carefully to the trough and feel it with your hand. If there's anything there, take it and come back. You're short and won't be seen."

At first, Mkho wanted to refuse; he thought it was like stealing, but then he remembered the complicated aspects of the matter and went off stealthily in the direction of the garden door. Kevork saw him approach the trough, bend down, straighten up and stay standing there for a moment. It occurred to him that Mkho had perhaps picked up the miraculous purse and was transferring a few dozen coins to his pocket.

"I won't take less than five hundred coins," he murmured to himself, but quite audibly.

Mkho came up quietly, empty-handed, and said, "There's a new moon tonight."

'What a blockhead.' thought Kevork. 'He's standing looking at the moon!'

They moved away to the low wall bordering the garden and sat, leaning against it, with their eyes glued to the trough. A moment later, Mkho heard Kevork's snoring.

"Kevork, Kevork."

"Yes, I won't be late. Well –," he murmured in his sleep.

"Kevork, give me the pistol."

Kevork woke up. "Have they come?"

"No, give me the pistol and go to sleep."

"Can you shoot?"

He could. With Shamash, the Assyrian, he had shot wild duck on the banks of the river Keshish, not far from his village, Ermants.

"Yes, I can."

Kevork put the heavy pistol into Mkho's hand and whispered, "I won't sleep, how can I? This isn't the time for sleep, is it?" And he fell fast asleep again.

'He'd meant to bring the axe as well!' thought Mkho, and he smiled in the dark. He shifted his gaze to the trough and leaned more comfortably against the wall. He rubbed his eyes. Two shadows came out of the trees and moved towards the trough. Mkho fired twice into the air.

At that moment, as Ohannes stood pressed against the cupboard, there was a knock on the garden door – soft at first, then more loud. In a part of his mind, he thought it could hardly be the 'Hats' who were knocking. Perhaps as they had not found anything, they had fired to show that they had been there, or as a threat, and had then gone away. Who, then, was knocking? He went with agitated steps to the west-facing window and looked out towards the garden door. Two shadows could be seen in the dark in front of it.

He opened the window quietly, leaned forward and called out in a low voice, "Who's there?"

"Ohannes, it's me, Mkho. Open the door."

Ohannes immediately shut the window, pulled on his slippers, grabbed the candlestick with the lit candle, quickly ran downstairs to the garden door and opened it to let in his two brothers. In other circumstances, Ohannes would scarcely have let them in with such pleasure, and at such a late hour of the night. He looked at their faces in the candlelight. Mkho was toying with something in his hand. Ohannes looked down – it was a pistol.

"Was it you who fired?" he asked Mkho.

Kevork answered instead: "I gave it to him."

They entered the tantun, sat down on a couch and leant back on the cushions. It was the first time since becoming adult that they had sat together like that, side by side.

Their mother, Sirpouhi, had been dreaming in a restless sleep. She had been running barefoot from one roof to another, laboriously catching up the washing blown away by the wind. Ohannes' shirt had got onto the top of the honey-sweet pear tree. A flock of crows was flying over the garden. They might sit in the pear tree and dirty Ohannes' shirt. 'Ksh, ksh,' the old woman waved the crows away.

Then she woke up, and anxiously went out to the balcony. The small, square window high up in the tantun opened onto the balcony. She noticed a faint light there, and went down. She could not help noticing the candlestick. How had it got there? The candle was low; that meant that it had been burning for a long time.

She came into the tantun. Her alarm subsided and she became radiant with joy. She had not seen her three sons sitting like that for ages. What had happened? The guests had left, one after another, almost without saying good-bye. And now, at this late hour, the three brothers were sitting up, not going to bed. Why were they sitting here?

"How are you all?" she asked as calmly as she could.

"Not bad, mairig. Have a seat. We're chatting."

"How did this candlestick get here?" She took it and lit the lamp on the wall. Then she asked, "Won't you have something to eat? Mkho hasn't eaten anything all day."

"No, mairig, I've fed."

But the old woman paid no attention. She knew Mkho's way. He would not eat for three days and then still refuse to eat. Whenever she asked if he would have something, he would say, "I'm not hungry, mairig." But when, without asking, she put a meal before him, he would eat it up with gusto. That was Mkho's way.

Kevork wanted to ask her to bring something, but seeing his mother go to the pantry he kept quiet. She returned, spread the red table-cloth before the three seated, cross-legged brothers, and set out lavash, roast meat, a whole fried chicken, some bacon, cheese, vegetables. Then she hesitated.

"Will you have wine?"

"Well, yes bring something," interposed Kevork, rather more confidently this time. A jug of red wine and three glasses appeared on the red table-cloth.

"Now, mairig, you go to bed. We'll eat and drink, talk about various things, and then go to sleep. You go and have a good night's sleep," said Ohannes in – unusually for him – a calm, quiet voice.

"There's something you don't want to tell me about," the old woman observed, pulling back the flowery head-scarf behind her ear as if to hear better.

"There's nothing, mairig. Go and sleep peacefully. We're sitting before you, safe and sound, drinking wine. What else could there be?" Ohannes calmed his mother down.

"Merciful Lord!" mumbled Sirpouhi, raising her eyes up to the smoke-blackened ceiling. Then she slipped away with quick, light steps.

Kevork filled the glasses.

"Now, come on, tell," said a rather subdued Ohannes, not in the calm voice with which he had just addressed his mother.

"Your health!" said Kevork, raising his glass.

The brothers automatically clinked glasses. Mkho wondered whether Kevork himself was going to drink. But Kevork did not leave his younger brother very long in any doubt. He emptied his glass in three gulps. Ohannes followed him without much thought, whereas Mkho put his glass down and took a piece of lavash – he was really quite hungry.

Kevork shouted out angrily: "There's nothing to say. I brought the paper, gave it to you and left with a burning fire in my soul. Such impudence! Just imagine, five hundred gold pieces. Why? Who for? Robbers, tell us, why? What are you going to spend it on? Maybe you've calculated incorrectly, maybe you don't need five hundred, but one hundred and one. And we'll give you ... Hat – what Hat? What a dishonourable way of proceeding this is. It's unbearable."

He re-filled his glass, raised it and toasting his brothers, drank quickly. Ohannes drank as well, hoping that this would lighten his spirits a little.

Kevork continued: "I must tell you, my brother, that I found Mkho and told him what had happened. We sat and thought how to help you, how to find a way to deal with your trouble and ease your pain. We decided, after some thought, that you shouldn't be left to be robbed. Whether it's a hat or a fez, it should be knocked off. We're brothers, aren't we?"

He replenished all their glasses, and continued. "We went to my place. Vergine has been insisting for a while that I should sell the pistol. We had no money to buy shoes, my clothes are worn-out. I should sell the pistol. I left Mkho at the door and went in. She was sitting darning some socks. 'Vergine,' I said, 'let me take the pistol, I've got a rich buyer – we need money and you need shoes, clothes.' My poor Vergine! She embraced me and cried and cried."

Kevork's voice trembled. "It's unbearable," he complained in the same voice and raising his glass, drank slowly and deeply. As he was drinking, he remembered how in fact he had gone in and asked Vergine for the pistol, how she had categorically refused, saying that he would only take it to the café and exchange it for some raki, how he had made a solemn promise and had gabbled away until Vergine had at last said, "Look here, you drunken fool, if you don't bring home the money you get for the revolver, I won't open the door to you again. Be off with you!"

"I took the pistol, kissed her brow and left. We got to your garden through vineyards and orchards. We looked into the stone trough, and found it was empty."

"What would you have done if it hadn't been?" asked Ohannes, casting an inviting glance at his brother, whose tongue had begun to betray him.

It was not clear whether Kevork was too engrossed in his invented narrative or whether he had not heard Ohannes' question; but he pretended he had not. As for Mkho, it did not even occur to him to object. He would not even mind if it was said that he had fallen asleep and that Kevork had fired the gun, or that Kevork had not fired in the air but had knocked two criminals down. No, he would not mind. Let Kevork tell it any way he thought appropriate, any way that pleased him.

"Who cares? I'd say, my good sir, that we sat down by the garden to wait. And that I told Mkho that Ohannes has decided not to give even one gold piece to those thieves, and that was the right decision, even though he has so much money. Why should he throw such a sum of money away? Why? Why? Doesn't he need that money? Don't his brothers need that money? Wouldn't it be better to offer a helping hand to his brothers instead of giving the money to strangers?"

Here, Kevork stopped talking, raised his glass and sang the next words: "What is there more beautiful and desirable than the name 'brother'?"

He slowly raised his glass, drank up, then wiped his moustache and lips with his left fingers, and continued. "I told Mkho we'd do such a good job that those rogues wouldn't even want to approach the trough. We were talking when suddenly two rascals came out of the trees and went up to the trough. I fired a shot. Then another shot."

"Did you or Mkho shoot?" Ohannes inquired softly.

Kevork did not lose his head this time either. His late imperfect experience as a teacher came to his aid.

"'To shoot' is the infinitive of a verb and can be conjugated in different ways: I shoot, he shoots, we've shot. But that's not important. The most important thing is that those terrified rascals ran away eastward towards Khanigian's garden, and who knows where else."

He sighed like a man who had fulfilled his duty and rolled a cigarette. There was a silence.

"If you had found money in the trough, what would you have done?" asked Ohannes, emphasising each word.

"That's an irrelevant question," Kevork got annoyed. "What could we have done? Isn't it clear what we would have had to do?"

Ohannes did not repeat his question, because his thoughts took another turn.

"And what if they kill me?"

"What right have they got to kill you? What an unjust thought?"

And Kevork replenished glasses excitedly. Ohannes groaned, stood up and quietly left the room. He returned five minute later, sat down, took his handkerchief out of his pocket, opened it and began to speak in a barely audible voice.

"Take one gold piece each, and spend it. Let's see what happens. I'm up to my ears in debt. I'm disgraced in the eyes of the Bolis trading companies. I'm on the edge of bankruptcy. If it goes on like this, I'll have to dance in the streets for a living."

The day was breaking. The church on Mt Varag opened its doors. The sun had risen and was shining over the Ourpad stream. Aikesdan dozed in delicious morning slumber. Mkho was asleep in the position he had been sitting in, leaning against a cushion. Ohannes was not asleep. In his mind, he could hear the sound of the recently confined mother's breathing. The baby was asleep. Ohannes' mother was not: she prayed, crossed herself, closed her eyes, but could not fall asleep. Kevork was not sleeping either. He was filling up the last glass of wine, looking at the dozing Mkho, raising his glass above his head and murmuring: "What is there more beautiful than the very name 'brother'?"

Then he remembered the headmaster's face, Vergine's bitter words, the waiter in the café, and the trough near the well. He felt in his pocket and smiled. He finished off the last glass, leaned his heavy and muzzy head on the cushion, and fell asleep with the empty glass in his hand.

Aikesdan was dozing in deep and peaceful morning slumber. A light breeze rippled from garden to garden, from tree to tree, from leaf to leaf, and even the light rustle of the leaves seemed to be a silent whisper.

And the world was alive. And Van was alive.

Chapter 4

Mkho reached the village late at night. Engrossed in his thoughts, he did not notice that his donkey had passed through two of the dark country lanes and had stopped in front of their door. He got down and knocked twice at the door with his stick. The door opened and a woman appeared. Mkho greeted her with rough affection and went in pulling the animal in after him.

"Is that you, husband? Where have you been?" Iskouhi scolded softly. She took the oil lamp and led her husband into the shed A dozen tethered cows stared at the lamp with puzzled eyes and carried on feeding. The one white horse whinnied softly. Mkho tied the donkey in its corner; then he brought in a big bundle of green grass from the yard and threw it into the manger.

"Satenik was delivered of a baby," Mkho said at last, spreading out the grass in the manger.

"Really?" Iskouhi asked with a woman's curiosity. "Is it a boy or a girl?"

"A boy." Mkho felt proud; he looked at his wife's face shining with rustic health, then he looked at her worn-out shirt and remembered the smart clothes piled up in his brother's shop.

"Are they happy?"

"Of course. They're eating and drinking – having a feast with music and lively conversation."

"And when can I go to town?" complained Iskouhi, drawing up

the wick of the oil lamp.

"Once in a blue moon," teased Mkho.

"Your donkey is better off than me. You take it to town but not me."

"Oh, aren't you ashamed?"

"Why should I be? What's my life like?"

They went into the yard and entered the large main room of the house, which at the same time doubled up as tonir chamber, dining-room, hall, pantry and a bedroom.

"Are you hungry?"

"No," Mkho said softly. He unwrapped the parcel he had brought with him.

"Is it cloth for a dress?"

"More than that. Here it all is. May Ohannes live long."

After the presents, Mkho took pears, apples, and a pie out of the parcel.

"Your mother-in-law gave it to me."

Iskouhi took a pie in her peasant's fingers, bit it and murmured, "What does she suppose I feed you on?"

"Do you need anything more?" Mkho again remembered the heavy rolls of flowery cloth in his brother's shop.

There was a silence. Only the rhythmic breathing of the sleeping children could be heard, together with the monotonous chirping of the cricket caught in the crack of the wall of the hall.

"It's not good," whispered Iskouhi.

"What's that?"

"The chirping cricket."

"Why?"

"It's an omen of disease."

"Nonsense."

"I don't know," Mkho's wife gave up and shook out her abundant hair onto her full shoulders, "I'm simply telling you what I've heard." And she yawned.

Mkho suddenly realised that he was dead tired; he began to take off his clothes, and Iskouhi put the light out. The hut was enveloped in darkness. The dark blue sky could be seen through the round smoke-hole, with one solitary star right in the centre. Mkho stared at that star and felt sleepy. A distant cock-crow was heard from the far end of the village. This was followed by another nearby, then yet another further away. All the cocks in the neighbourhood began to crow and the whole village seemed to turn over in bed and sleep more soundly.

There was a knock on the door, at first with a palm, then with a fist. The knocks became louder and louder.

...Iskouhi is dreaming that she has put on the new clothes and is standing on the threshing floor. The whole village is gossiping about her new clothes. A woman gestures rudely and calls out to her:

"Go to your stable, and your dress will become even newer."

"I'm not going to the stable any more, I'm going to town today."

"Mairig," Sira calls out from the house, "father wants his dinner."

"Let him look after himself. I'm not going into the pantry in these clothes."

Mariam comes and pulls at Iskouhi's hem, "Let's go home. Father wants you to come and milk the cow."

Mariam is tugging at her hem and one side of the dress rips off in her hand. Iskouhi notices that the Assyrian, Shamash is twirling his black moustache and staring at her exposed thighs from the other side of the threshing-floor. She grabs Mariam by the hand, runs into the house and shuts the door.

"Where's father?" she asks.

"He was moody and went to town," said Sira.

Meanwhile, someone is knocking at the door – knock, knock.

"Who's that?" screams Iskouhi.

"Open the door, Isko," Shamash whispers, "open the door. Mkho got upset and went to town."

Knock, knock, knock. Iskouhi woke up – someone really was knocking at the door. She raised her head from the pillow and strained her ears. Who could be knocking at their door at midnight as in her dream? With the new clothes, the threshing-floor,

Shamash...

Knock, knock, knock. "Mkho, Mkho, husband."

Mkho breathes deeply, and turns over murmuring, "Two metres, fifty metres. Oh..."

"Mkho, Mkho, somebody's knocking at the door. Wake up! Get up, man."

"What's that? Why are they knocking? Let me sleep."

Knock, knock, knock. Mkho woke up fully: "Iskouhi, what is it? Is that a knock on the door?"

"Yes, it is. They've been knocking for an hour."

"I wonder who that can be."

"I don't know. It's midnight."

Mkho got up sluggishly, went out barefoot into the yard and called out. "Who's there?"

"Open the door," a deep male voice called out. "Open, for God's sake."

A second voice was now heard. "Open, don't be afraid."

Mkho opened the door slowly and the first thing he saw was the dark glassses of one of the visitors. The other was a short man, holding the reins of two horses and talking to the carriage driver standing a little apart.

"Get them down one by one."

He then turned to Mkho and ordered him to light a lamp. Mkho went in mechanically and returned, barefoot and half-naked, with the oil lamp in his hand.

"Now take the horses and tether them in your stable. Have you any barley?"

Mkho, as if in a dream, held the reins of the horses and entered the stable with the lamp, tied up the horses and laid out barley for them. 'They're guests,' he was thinking sleepily, 'but what sort of guests are they, arriving at midnight with horses, a carriage and odd-looking pitchers?'

He came out. The driver was busy emptying the carriage; the man with the glasses showed Mkho a few large water-pitchers lying on the ground.

"Take these in."

Mkho rushed forward and tried to take two pitchers at the

same time. How amazing! He could not.

"Take them one by one," said the man with dark glasses.

"What's he saying?" babbled a confused Mkho.

"Take them one by one – they're heavy. Don't you understand? He's speaking Armenian, after all"

"What sort of Armenian is that?"

The man with the dark glasses smiled. Mkho lifted up the pitcher with all his strength and took it in. He had never lifted such a heavy pitcher in his life. In the same way, he took in a second, and a third. The driver, with the help of the short man, took down from the carriage three long boxes, which were also taken in and placed beside the pitchers in the yard. Then the man with dark glasses put something – probably money – into the driver's hand and said in a low voice, "If you tell anyone anything, you'll be in real trouble." And raising up one side of his short coat, he showed him what appeared to be the handle of a weapon.

"No, he's reliable," assured the short man.

"Come, sirs, do you think I'm out of my mind?" said the driver as the horses set off.

The short man turned to Mkho: "Could you put us up, brother? Are there any elderly people inside?"

"No, only small children."

"We're your guests for one night," interrupted the short man. "Are you keeping well?"

"So-so."

"What about Baron Ohannes' business? Your name's Mkhitar Muradkhanian, isn't it?"

Distrust vanished. Mkho hurried in to find Iskouhi standing half-naked behind the door. She had been listening to their conversation all the time.

"Make beds for them."

"Who are they?" whispered Iskouhi, with inquisitive eyes. "Are they from town?"

"Yes. It seems they know us. Lay out some good blankets."

Three minutes later, the short man's voice was heard from behind the door: "Mkhitar, my friend, is it ready?"

Mkho hustled Iskouhi into her bed and opened the door.

"You're welcome," he said, pointing to the newly made bed. They came in. The man with the dark glasses drew in his breath and murmured, "My God, it's not very elegant."

"Did you think this would be the Orient Hotel in Tiflis?" the short man replied.

The bed, laid on the ground, was a mattress with heavy blankets, a pillow, and no sheets. Mkho could not sleep, Iskouhi was not sleeping either. Mkho saw that one of the guests was lighting a match. Mkho raised his head, then the light went out and the red tip of the cigarette glittered in the dark. One of them was smoking.

"Aren't you sleeping?" the short man said.

"The bugs are biting me – outrageously," complained the one with the dark glasses. "Can't you feel them."

"You must bear it, my friend, for the sake of the Armenian nation. I've endured a lot worse, now it's your turn."

"May I be cursed!" The man with the glasses was annoyed and turned over.

"Let's make a plan, shall we?" said the other, hoping to cheer him.

"Let's keep quiet – something may come of that."

"So be it," agreed his friend and smiled in the darkness.

Mkho was listening, though he understood very little of their talk. But he certainly knew that one of his guests was complaining, while the other was calming him down, and that they were strange guests, sinister and scary people. He was thirsty, his throat was dry. He remembered where the pitchers full of water were – there, beneath the window. Mkho was overcome with sleep, but he had a burning thirst which carried on into his dream.

... Mkho is crossing broad fields, past Biar and up to Gyaduk. The clouds are resting on the grassy rocks of the mountain. Mkho is climbing to Gyaduk: he reaches the edge of the cloud covering the rocks, where the ground seems to level. The clear, cold water, dripping down the rock, appears to pour out of the cloud, which sparkles. Mkho presses his lips to the rock and drinks greedily, but with unquenched thirst. There is a wide-bellied jar near the rock.

Wanting to fill it, he tries in vain to lift it; he tries again but cannot shift it at all. Now he grabs the jar by its neck and tugs at it with all his strength. The jar splits in two, the smaller half remaining in his hand. Mkho peers into the other half: there are dark glasses at the bottom. . . .

Mkho woke up. The shining morning sun and a circle of light-blue sky could be seen through the smoke-hole. Mkho got up, dressed, and went to the corner for some water. He could smell cigarette smoke. He looked over towards the guests. The short one was asleep, while the other was smoking, lying on his back without his glasses. Then he threw the cigarette end behind the door, where the white tips of many other cigarette ends could be seen. He seemed to have spent a sleepless night smoking. His face looked gentler without the glasses and it would have probably looked even more so, were not for his thick, black moustache. Mkho drank some water from a small jar.

"Didn't you sleep well?" he said, feeling mystified.

"I was bitten abominably. How can you sleep here?"

Mkho understood him this time, but he was also wondering: 'What sort of Armenian was he speaking? He must have come from Russia. Who knows? Either from Stamboul or from Russia.'

"We're used to them," explained Mkho, "we're not bitten, and look how your friend is still fast asleep."

"It's clear that he's thick-skinned. Living among you, he's become a Turkish Armenian. That's the problem for Armenians in Turkey."

"Where've you come from?" asked Mkho, who had understood only the word 'thick-skinned'.

"From far away," answered the guest briefly, lying back and covering his face with a white handkerchief.

Mkho went out to the yard and entered the shed. The two labourers and their wives, who slept right there, had also woken up. They lived on the floor above the low rafter beams. The women were milking the cows, while the men were brushing down the animals.

"Good morning," greeted Mkho.

"Good morning," they answered, almost simultaneously.

A little later, Iskouhi came in and called Mkho aside: "Husband, it's time to prepare the tonir and they haven't woken up yet."

"You get it ready bit by bit, and they'll get up."

Mkho occupied himself with the animals. He loved the country – the heavy toil, the cattle and sheep, the field and the river bank. It had never occurred to him that he also could live in the town, wear clean clothes, sleep in a clean room, work less and enjoy himself more. He was frugal and tried to make sure his wife and children were frugal as well. He liked to take the produce to town, to fill the larders and barns in his mother's house. It had never mattered to him that in his mother's house his brother and his brother's wife were in charge, and not he himself and his wife Iskouhi. Never!

Mkho went to look at the guests' horses; he examined them as if he was a great expert, patted them, and gave them more barley. He recalled that one of the guests, the short one, seemed to know Ohannes and even Mkho himself; he wondered whether he should be glad about this or worried. Then he checked the pitchers and the boxes lying in one corner of the yard. He saw that they were in place, but did not dare approach them.

Iskouhi came out once again. "Husband, I've made up the tonir, but they haven't yet got up for me to be able to light it. I have to boil the milk, make yoghurt, bake bread, cook something. What shall I do?"

Mkho thought, and then said: "Start it up and let it burn a little, and they'll get up."

Nothing else could be done. Iskouhi went in, and within three minutes the house was filled with choking smoke. The guests rushed out coughing and sneezing, and fastening up their buttons. The short one was laughing and choking, trying to make light of their situation.

"This is how it is, brother. When you want to take honey from the hive, you first fill it with smoke. This draws the bees away, you can then finish the job. Our situation is the same."

"I don't understand," the other said angrily, putting on his glasses, "was this the time for that old woman to make up the fire.

I'd hardly closed my eyes."

"She isn't an old woman," whispered the short one, "she's a young woman – as explosive as cannon-shot!"

Mkho came up with a guilty smile. "Your sleep has been disturbed. What can we do? There's such a lot to get through."

"Never mind, brother, bring us some water to wash with."

After washing, they went out into the street, stood by the door and looked around. The village had woken up. Smoke was coming out of all the smoke-holes, the peasants had come out of their houses, hurrying to and fro, carrying out the day's tasks. They looked with surprised interest at the two strange visitors standing by Mkho's door.

"The village seems to be well-off," said the man with glasses.

"What makes you think so?"

"I don't know," he waved his hand lackadaisically, "my eyes ache due to lack of sleep."

The short man took a notebook out of his pocket, turned over a few pages, had a look, turned over another page and closed the book. "That's right, this is in fact a wealthy village."

"Didn't you know this village?"

"How could I have known it? We don't have an organization here. I came here once, five years ago."

"A wealthy village can't become poor in five years."

"A village in Turkish Armenia can become wealthy in ten years, brother, but it can become poor in a day," explained the short one.

"But that's not normal." asserted the one with glasses.

"There's neither a law about it, nor a decree."

They stopped talking. A few cows came bellowing out of their host's house and joined the herd passing through the street. The church bell rang over the village. A slight wind began to blow and the sounds of the bell seemed to turn into raindrops that spread over the houses, gardens and nearby fields.

Chapter 5

In the gloom of the ancient cathedral, the candle's flame flickered like a bird's tongue and finally died out in front of the faded painting of the crucifixion. The figure of the kneeling abbot was outlined in the half-light of the pale, blue dawn shining in through the narrow windows of the tall bell-tower. Flapping its wings, a pigeon flew in and out of the window. The monk raised his head, his face lit up by the faint morning light; his wistful, dark eyes peered out beneath black brows. He was praying.

A tall man came in through the open door of the church, quietly approached the abbot and stood at a respectful distance.

"What's up, Mihran?" the abbot inquired irritably, without turning round

"A sailing boat, Holy Father," the deacon reported. He was annoyed with himself for having to interrupt the abbot's prayers.

"A sailing boat?"

"Yes, Holy Father."

The abbot stood up, crossed himself in front of the image of the crucifixion and passed through the vestry. They went out together.

It was morning: the servants, who had just woken up, could be seen here and there in the large courtyard, milk-maids of all ages were hurrying to the cattle sheds with big cauldrons and small pails to milk the cows and sheep. One of them loudly threatened another. "Don't put on such airs, else I'll go to the Holy Father. He'll punish you and . . ." She added some profanities that were not part of the Holy Father's duties at all.

The two men had gone out through the church door. The large monastery garden with its ornamental and fruit-bearing trees lay before them. Beyond the garden was the calm, deep blue mirror of the sea. A boat was sailing towards the island.

"Go inside and prepare the room," the abbot ordered.

"Do you think?" said the other, holding one end of his moustache between his thumb and finger, as if holding a cigarette.

The abbot cut him short: "Yes, it's them."

Mihran went in purposefully, while the abbot wandered slowly towards the landing stage. Two people came out of the boat: one of them was tall, with dark glasses and a black moustache twisted like the horn of an ox, that emphasised his pale skin; the other was short with a thick beard – but we have met them both before in the village, under Mkho's hospitable roof. The abbot approached the guests, hesitating whether to receive them in a secular or ecclesiastic manner. The man with dark glasses set the tone by offering his hand to the abbot.

"Good day, sir, how are you?"

"Welcome," greeted the abbot, "you're welcome. Let's go in." He called over to Minas, the captain, to tie up the boat and follow them up to the church.

The abbot led his guests through the monastery gates and up stony stairs on the left of the courtyard to the room reserved for pilgrims. The room was just being prepared for them, and they were humbly greeted by Mihran himself, who took their small bags, which were heavy despite their size.

The windows overlooking the sea were open and the room was full of fresh morning air and early, golden sunshine. The blue mirror of the lake was motionless, but the faint noise of the small waves breaking on the stones of the shore could be heard. The monastery gardens were glowing in their vivid, beautiful greenery. A proud stork with a golden plume was standing domineeringly on one foot by its nest on top of the tall poplar; it seemed to be looking out from the broad canvas of a great artist.

The short man's eyes were smouldering. He opened his bag that had been placed on one of the window-sills, took out a revolver, rested its muzzle on the raised wrist of his left hand, and aimed at the stork. Mihran was the first to notice. He came up quickly and stood by the open window with both hands raised.

"Don't do it, Baron Ishkhan, I beg you."

"Don't stand in front of my gun, sir," Ishkhan softly, but threateningly, commanded.

"Put your gun away," the tall man interposed, "it's not hard to tell that the bird isn't a Turkish pasha or deputy. It's a proud Armenian stork, let it live!"

"Baron Aram is quite right, the stork is Armenian. If it weren't Armenian, would it stand for so long unarmed on top of the poplar?" the abbot said with a laugh.

Letting it live since it was Armenian, carried the day: Ishkhan sullenly obeyed and threw the gun onto a bed.

"And now let's have breakfast," the abbot said with evident relief that the issue was resolved in favour of the Armenian stork.

Mihran tip-toed out.

In the evening, the island and the church, as well as the crescent moon, shattered into thousands of pieces mirrored in the pale-blue sea. The deacon opened the door quietly and entered. He lit with a match the pair of candles in the two-branched candlestick on the table and made to leave.

"Mihran, you zealot, you."

"Yes, Baron Aram."

"In the name of the Father and the Son, have the samovar brought in."

"With pleasure." He made to leave again.

"Mihran, you old martyr."

"Yes, Baron Ishkhan."

"I'd like some fish."

"And some fish for this albatross, as well," added Aram. "And ask the Abbot to come in."

Mihran slipped out. He stopped for a moment on the balcony, caught by force of habit the end of his moustache between his thumb and finger, and glancing up at the rising clouds, he went downstairs.

"And if he doesn't agree?" Aram yawned heavily and lit a cigarette. "There'll be complications, problems, sermons."

"Well, what about the bullet we saved by not killing the stork? And all the difficulties and complications will be resolved."

"An axe?"

"But I didn't utter that word."

"It's all the same – an axe, a revolver, even a written threat, it's the same thing. You see, I'm in two minds. And I feel it more strongly the more I look into these matters."

Aram stopped talking. The murmur of the sea felt closer, and more threatening.

"The weather's changed," complained Ishkhan, clearly wanting to change the subject.

"The moon's come out. Don't get upset." Aram smiled at his thoughts and went on in a reflective tone. "To see this moon, or to believe in it, is the same as believing in the Turkish Constitution – or in European interference in Ottoman affairs. On the other hand, I think, why not believe, or pretend to believe, in it? At least, to gain some time. Do you suppose that our tsar is any better than your sultan? If you arm the Caucasus, take guns there and spread propaganda in a bid to overthrow the tsar and create a free Armenia, don't you think that the tsar would not drown the Caucasian Armenians in blood? I know, you'll say that the tsar is a Christian, while the sultan is a Moslem. But is there any difference, for those who perish, between being slaughtered for the sake of the Cross or for the Crescent?"

"Certainly," Ishkhan concurred, "but why in fact don't the Caucasian Armenians demand freedom? And why aren't they already armed?"

"And why do you think that is so? Why?"

"One more question," said Ishkhan, "do you think the Turks slaughter Armenians because they seek independence and freedom? That's not right, is it?"

"And what is right?"

"It's right that Armenians demand freedom because the Turks slau – slau – the Armenians"

"Say slaughter clearly, man," said Aram. "Why doesn't your tongue want to pronounce the word.? Slau- slau – !"

"There is slau – slaughter, and there is another slaughter as well. The tsar slaughters spiritually, while our rulers ..." And he flicked his finger across his throat.

"Yes," Ishkhan continued, narrowing his eyes at the burning candles. "What does an Armenian in Turkey want? All he wants is some simple respect, and not to be slaughtered like cattle. When he's tortured and screams with pain and then complains, Yildiz Kiosk cries out to the world that Armenians are demanding a free

Armenia. Just let them leave us alone, let them not close our churches and schools, not kill, not kidnap and not rape, and we'd live as peacefully here as in the Caucasus. When an Armenian demands freedom in Turkey, it only means he wants to be rid of massacres. When he demands independence, all it means is that he doesn't want to be hanged. And should we rise against the entire state for that? No, my friend. We're playing with fire. Yes, we're playing with fire and it's not difficult to guess how this game will end."

He stopped speaking, but then added, "Fire is not a toy." He continued with a smile, "I'm leaving the rest of my fish, and you, too, my brother, leave your tea. Let's go and tell Minas to get the ship ready. What do you say?"

"Just hear me out," Aram replied, rising from the bed and throwing his cigarette end out of the open window. "I, myself, agree with you as a common man, but I have another identity as well, that of a Party man. And that Party man thinks quite differently."

"What does that mean?"

"It means that the Party believes it to be necessary to apply violence, to arm the people, to raise the flag of rebellion, to have a new Ottoman Bank incident, a new Khanasor – to prove ourselves and show Europe that we have real guns and that, in the words of Khrimian, out ladles are made of iron not paper. And if we are defeated, it's better to die free than to live as a slave."

He was silent for a moment, then smiled and added, "Beautiful words, aren't they?"

Ishkhan felt inspired: "Those aren't words. What are words? Those are ideas, and sacred ideas."

"Ideas, sacred ideas. Why not?" Aram said ironically, "And who needs these ideas? The people? People live for better or worse, don't they? And we've grabbed them by the throat and are telling them it's 'death or freedom'. Why death? Who wants to die? A man wants to live even under the most difficult conditions. Life is dear and is only given once to a man. And yet we've seized him by the throat and are telling him that it is better to die as a hero than to live as a slave. I don't remember where, but I have read that it's better to be a live mouse than a dead lion."

The abbot came in at this point, and the conversation was interrupted. Aram turned to him, "Come in, abbot, take a seat and answer my question. Is it better to be a live mouse or a dead lion?"

The abbot sat down and smiled: "It's better to be a living lion."

The friends laughed. "Abbot, you've resolved the issue well," confirmed Aram in his deep voice. "It's good to explore thoughts with you. And now, let's pass on to the main issue."

He rose from the bed, stretched his hands right and left, then up and down, as if doing exercises and sat down at the table on a simple chair. Ishkhan did the same, contenting himself with just a protracted yawn, which was however not a token of fatigue but the yawn that comes after a long rest. Aram lit a cigarette, looked at the abbot very attentively and puffed away the smoke to left and right:

"Don't you want to know why we thought of your island, your monastery, and yourself? Do you think we've come to find protection under the wings of the abbey as believers, or that love for your milkmaids brought us here, or that we want to confess our bittersweet worldly sins to you? Well, you never asked."

The abbot smiled. "I didn't ask, because –"

"Because?"

"Because I know what wind has brought your boat here," replied the abbot.

"You're a sharp man," Aram said with a laugh. "Hey, Ishkhan, he knows the purpose of our visit. What do you say to that?"

Ishkhan tried to smile. The abbot took out of his pocket a piece of paper folded in four and handed it to Aram.

"We agreed, we confirmed the list, while they ..." exclaimed Aram, somewhat annoyed after reading the paper, "those Hats are overdoing things."

"What's the difference?" Ishkhan asked, after having read the paper in his turn.

"There's a huge difference," Aram raised his voice, almost snatching the paper out of the other's hand. "There's a huge difference, just understand that." He stopped speaking and looked at the abbot quizzically. "Would you leave us alone for a moment?"

"I'll go out," the abbot smiled sadly, "but I know what you're going to tell Baron Ishkhan. You're wondering whether the message sent by those Hats has been a warning for me, and that I might have hidden some of the possessions of the monastery. Aren't I right?"

Aram took off his dark glasses to see his interrogator more clearly.

"Let's suppose that's what it is," he said through clenched teeth, almost aggressively.

The abbot looked up at Aram, whose cold eyes looked sharply at him. It occurred to him that the man did not wear dark glasses in vain.

"There is no need to worry, Baron Aram. Both the reserved and unreserved property of the monastery are safe. I –"

"What do you mean by reserved property?" interrupted Aram with a scowl.

"Reserved property is that which is under the control of Etchmiadzin. You shouldn't forget that apart from being Abbot, I am also the bishop of the Aghtamar Patriarchate."

"You have a fine position, I didn't know that," mocked Aram, looking at Ishkhan.

The Abbot replied, "It's true what you said, that those Hats are overdoing things. Is there any need for threats or blackmail? Why do they think that they're the only ones in charge of this great business and that we can only be forced by terror into being accomplices in all of it? The property of the monastery belongs to the people. But if it's wanted for the national cause, doesn't the Abbot have the right to go against their will? The cause of the nation's freedom is not just the business of the Hats or of only one Party. It's a national cause, Baron Aram, a national cause."

"The Party should lead," Aram suggested in a barely audible voice.

"But with leadership, not with threatening letters and an axe."

There was silence – the increasing fury, protest and thunder of the sea was part of that silence. And this noisy silence would perhaps have lasted a long time if the steward had not come in with the boiling, gleaming, yellow samovar. The abbot left quietly.

"Well you can see who we're dealing with," Ishkhan turned to Aram, when they were left alone after supper.

"Yes, I can."

"And what about the deacon?"

"He's of the same metal."

"That was a thievish message, a clerical takeover."

"As a matter of fact, they're right, of course." Aram smiled, holding a cigarette to the thin flame of the candle.

"Are they?" Ishkhan was surprised.

"Why are you surprised? Of course they're right, only -" he blew out smoke, stopped speaking for a moment, thought for a while, and then said. "But that truth doesn't suit our Party's ideology."

"Does that mean that the ideology of the Party is wrong?"

"The Party also has its own truth, which doesn't go step by step with the truth of the Abbot and his deacon."

"Well?"

"Well, let the truths go their own way, but let us have the reserved and the unreserved and go our way."

A head stuck out of a square opening in the floor of the sailing boat's deck, followed by a neck and a waist. The figure took a deep breath, peered into the darkness, at the dark sky and the rough sea, at the darker outline of the monastery, and disappeared through the square hatch-door after closing it.

As he descended into the inner cabin, Dblosh Shavarsh announced, "It's the end of the world. Sky and earth have merged."

"Let them merge even more," scowled Kolocho, a young man with black brilliantined hair, who was sitting staring at the fire in the stove.

The third person, a tall man lying by the stove with his hands under his head, was singing.

> "Let Stamboul be drenched in blood,
> Let war arise from every side.
> Let Bashkale drown in death,
> and let us through . . ."

Dblosh interrupted the song: "Teacher, tell us again, what does Vaspourakan mean?"

"Sky and earth have merged," repeated Kevork, the teacher, "There's not a drop of raki in sight. One day the headmaster said my real home would be the River Nile, if it flowed with raki and I was a crocodile. I'll never forget his remark."

"No, tell us again what Vaspourakan means?" insisted Dblosh once more.

"It won't do," yelled Kevork, "the matter can't be settled without raki. I didn't come here on any other terms. Give me raki, and I'll tell you whatever I know. I won't accept any other conditions."

"Let him have some raki," Kolocho said, yawning idly.

"Here you are, you drunken pedant, drink it up, this is your day."

"Vas – pour – a – kan," Kevork began, pronouncing the syllables one by one and holding up a finger above his head to indicate he had finished his medium-sized glass of raki, "Vaspourakan is a compound word consisting of three parts: vas – meaning great, pour – meaning a son, and kan – meaning a country. So we have Vaspourakan which can be translated as 'a country of great sons'. Have I managed to explain? It's Persian, let's not forget that."

"Well, teacher," Kolocho declared, "looking at you, one can't help wondering whether you're one of those great sons."

"It's I, thou, he, we, you, they, me. Do you understand?"

"Well, if you know so much, why aren't you a boss like your brother?" needled Dblosh.

"There are three of us," Kevork got angry, "Ohannes' second name is Boghossian and Mkho's and mine is Aboghossian."

"We don't understand," said Kolocho.

"I've explained a thousand times," complained the teacher, "you can't understand the simplest things. The Boghossians are rich people – merchants, money-lenders, contractors – while the A-boghossians are simple, common folk. So Mkho and I are A-boghossians. But our elder brother is a merchant in Bolis, therefore a conservative, and therefore a Boghossian. Did I manage to make you understand? You take my science with ladles and give me raki with spoons!"

Dblosh thought it better to have another song.

> "Don't cry mother, don't cry sister,
> Don't cry for your brother,
> Don't cry for your husband.
> We fell here together,
> For the cause of our land."

He stopped singing, smiled, and then continued, changing the words.

> "We fell here together
> For two shots of raki."

Dblosh and Kolocho burst out laughing, while Kevork became serious.

"I won't accept rude comments. I'm a man of principle, I –"

He raised his voice but at that moment the trap-door in the ceiling of the inner cabin opened and Ishkhan quickly descended, bringing in the sea wind and the damp rain. He eyed the three of them.

"Follow me. But let me explain what you're to do. The business has got serious despite our original intentions."

"No explanation can be understood without raki, Baron Ishkhan," complained the teacher.

"The business is wet. Let him drink, and you have one as well," ordered Ishkhan.

"The business is wet? A wet business must have been made so with raki," Kevork became animated and only returned to the subject after pouring a full glass down his throat, "we don't understand what is wet and what is dry."

"You'll understand today what is wet and what is dry, you sozzled idiot," murmured Dblosh, filling the teacher's glass again.

The Aghtamar Abbot, Father Arsen, is asleep. He is dreaming through centuries of history, passing through Armenian land.

Haik laughs and strokes his mottled beard. Here is Mt Ararat and here is the native land. The giant Bel was crushed for Armenians to live, for Haik to live. And my people must live for centuries and all the Bels must be crushed and scattered in the wind. And the monk sees the Vaspourakan mountains move: Ardos cries with joy, Arnos turns green, Karkar laughs, Sipan shivers, Endzakh shudders, Kaputkogh is enveloped in blue mist and the mountains of the Mokats and Rshtouni, and those of the Zagros chain, begin to dance. And winged angels descend on the monasteries of Varag, Aghtamar, Khek, Eremer and so on – monasteries of a thousand saints and a thousand names. And the green-and-red flag waves its wings above Urartu and Armenia. Here, with millions of others, is Tigran, the king of Greater Armenia, and other Armenian kings – whether stupid or thoughtful, weak or creative. The monk knows them all one by one up to 1393, after which there were no more Armenian kings.

The Armenian mounted a horse and forgot God; he dismounted and forgot the horse. The monk turns away from 1393 and sees Armenia become a battlefield, a universal Avarayr. Then came the Mongols, the Tatars, Seljuks, Arabs, Persians and Greeks – Ctesiphon and Byzantium. Hundreds of years later the Ottoman Turks arrived and conquered all the Hayks – the master became a subject and captive slave, and the invader a commander.

King Gagik Artsrouni came to the shore of the Lake – named after Nairi, Biaina, Armenia, and then Van – a thousand years ago and founded this monastery. And Aghtamar has obeyed no power, no hand has ruled over it.

Who are these guests coming so timely and untimely to the shore? They are distinguished Caucasian Armenians. We also had leaders. They were all killed in the Bashkale hills, where St Bartholomew was martyred. Avetisian, Peto, Mardig perished. But these new nationalists tread over the tombstones of saints and want to rule over them. A pilgrim brings a threatening message to the church instead of an offering. He brings it, leaves it, and disappears. And these people claim they are saving the nation, sowing the seeds of freedom! Now they want to grab the property of the monastery. I won't give them a thing! It's the nation that owns church property and not these strange adventurers. I won't give them a thing!

The Aghtamar Abbot, Father Arsen is passing through

Armenian lands, he is going through centuries of history. He hears his own voice and wakes up for a moment. "I'll give them nothing."

There's a wedding ceremony in the Holy Cross church of Aghtamar – the wedding guests and the spectators shine in the light of the chandeliers and candles. And Abbot Arsen realises that he himself is the bridegroom in this big wedding, while the bride is – oh no! – none other than milkmaid Doghik, the plump and well-built Doghik, whose husband, Markar, the young labourer of the monastery, drowned at sea a year ago.

That was a nasty incident: Markar could have swum from Aghtamar to Artemid. How did it happen, how could he have drowned? No, there had to be a secret here. The answer lay with the beautiful maiden Doghik – someone in the monastery was her lover. Markar could have knocked the man down and thrown him so far into the sea that no splash would have been heard. Doghik's lover must therefore have been a man beyond Markar's control.

The abbot is standing beside Doghik and the priest marrying them – oh God! the priest marrying them is Markar, yes, labourer Markar but with the abbot's beard and moustache and dressed in his clothes. "Merciful Lord, I confess," murmurs the abbot, stroking his chin in terror – and he finds that his face is cleanly shaved.

"I confess, O Lord" And he hears the spectators loudly sing the words which they had sung at Markar's wedding, when he himself had married the couple.

> "Our bridegroom was dressed up
> Neatly from head to foot.
> The bride wore a fine sash
> Squeezed round her waist.
> An Armenian wedding.
> The bridegroom wore a cross on his chest.
> His crown was red, the ribbon was green.
> The buckle was red, the sun was green.
> His belt was red, the ribbon was green.
> The shoes were black, and the sun was green.

In Armenian or whatever mode,
May the lyre play and purify the mire."

The song thunders beneath the arches of the Aghtamar monastery, and the abbot accompanies the song at the top of his voice, "Purify the mire ..."

It seemed to the abbot that the door opened. He had not locked the door from the inside as he usually did, his ear caught the faint sound of rain. He sensed somebody breathing hard and caught a smell of raki, then felt a terrible burning round his neck. "Baron Aram!" he shouted, but he did not hear his own voice. In agony, he felt it was Doghik hanging from his neck throttling him with all her weight. The labourer Markar was raising a cross. And red blood was dripping from the arms of the cross, drop by drop by drop.

Deacon Mihran could not get to sleep. He got up and began to walk up and down the long chamber. He could feel instinctively that the two rascals had come with dire intentions. Well, even if they were rascals, the power was in their hands, and according to established and unspoken rules they could do whatever – and however – they wanted if it was expedient and suited their vicious purpose.

They had stopped at nothing, to get money, they had applied terror, blackmail, and murder. A bloody fist was dangling over Vaspourakan, and that fist had its own fist – a terrorist group, an executive committee, an assertive triumvirate, the Hats.

The deacon approached the windows and opened one quietly. It was raining, sea and sky, night and rain, had merged. The boat with its unfurled sail was in darkness; it seemed to the deacon that shadows moved on and around the boat. He closed the window and moved away from it. What nonsense! He was imagining things through fear. But was he afraid? Of what? Why should he be afraid? Clearly, some concessions would have to be made. Well, an hour of daylight is worth two at night.

The abbot had also been confused to the depth of his soul. He, too, had thought that something should have been offered them. It was easy to say that, but just try to decide on what that something is. Furthermore, two milkmaids, Antaram and Doghik, had quarreled that day and torn each other's hair. The abbot had ordered them to come to church to confess. He had received Antaram first and soon let her go, and then Doghik. The abbot had kept her a long time; perhaps beautiful Doghik had more sins.

The deacon was lying on his back, with his eyes glued to the dark. It was stifling, the rain had not yet stopped. Should he open the door to air the room? But, at that moment there seemed to be some people standing outside his door. And he was frightened again. He recalled the saying that fear is worse than death. He remembered the shadows on and around the boat. Nonsense! He rose and opened the door. It did not make much difference, it was dark and black outside. The only difference was that it was raining outside and not inside.

He recalled that the troubles had begun with blood, and anything that began with blood would also end with blood. There had been some renowned pioneers – Avetisian, Peto, and Mardig – but they had never raised a hand against fellow Armenians. Who could forget 1896? That Monday, June the sixteenth in Van? Who could forget the martyrdom of the seven brave Semerdjian brothers, born of one Armenian mother? Armenian mothers, Armenian mothers!

The year 1896 had passed away but another 1896 would come. The nation should not be forced to arm, but should decide to do so itself. There was no need to rush to a new 1896, time had to be gained. What could Van do alone against the rest of the entire Ottoman State?

And Mihran sang to himself in a barely audible voice, the song of a migrant:

> "The wind blew lightly from the sea.
> The curtain was green, though it seemed red –
> The face of my love showed up on it.
> Let me call up song and make the mountains
> cry out and turn the migrants back
> From the over-crowded Stamboul
> and the ruins of Üsküdar ...
> They sent my beloved away."

The revolutionary leaders and we two Aghtamar churchmen have been playing hide-and-seek with each other. But should this stupid game not be brought to an end? Should we persuade the workers to take up arms, go down to the quay and fire at the boat to force it to go away? Or should we perhaps extend a cordial welcome and offer hospitable entertainment, but then at night smother them or kill them with swords and, tying sacks full of stones round their necks, throw them into the sea? No, no – that won't do! An Armenian cannot raise a hand against an Armenian, an Armenian cannot kill an Armenian. What difference would there then be between Haik and Bel, what difference between Armenian and Turk.? Why not give that short stub of a man, the labourer Mokats Hairabed, two kurush to purchase his conscience? He would do anything. Should he not be woken up right now, and given five kurush instead of two? Let it be so, let the sea become a grave and a hell – a haven. Will that do? No, it will not!

The lightning flashed across the sky and its light seemed to last for a while. Mihran could see the tall outline of the monastery, the bell-tower and the gleaming cross, clearly and distinctly through the open door. Surprisingly, it seemed to him that short Hairabed passed swiftly by. It was now dark inside and out, and the billowing clouds spread over the sea. A sharp fear crept into his soul – now he wanted to get up and close the door. He wanted to call out for help to his strong workman, but then it seemed that Hairabed himself rushed in.

"Hai ..." the deacon cried out, and it seemed to him that the sea rose up to fill his room, and that the bitter and salty, boiling water poured down his throat. It occurred to him that he was dying. The deacon saw in a flash all the heads of his many friends bobbing up from the surface of the thick and black water. They were all staring at the deacon with wide open eyes. "I'm dying," he repeated.

And his friends were laughing and shouting in one voice, "Young man, are you sure?"

The sun rose on the world, on Vaspourakan, and on Aghtamar. The labourers and the milkmaids finished their work; the door of the guest-room was open and it was obvious that there was nobody there; the sailing boat had left the small quay. Some of the milkmaids and the labourers, half-asleep and half-awake, had heard hurried footsteps in the monastery yard. It had even seemed to them that the church door had opened and closed. Mokats Hairabed had not slept in his place that night; he was sitting now on one of the stones in the yard and was smoking one cigarette after another. He never lit a match, nor struck a flint, but lit each cigarette from the last.

The abbot and deacon had not yet come down, they had never slept so long before. A restrained but ominous whisper spread among the milkmaids and the labourers. Mokats Hairabed was aware of all the secrets of the monastery. He was sitting on a stone and smoking, and he himself was like a stone. Feeling everybody's strained eyes upon him, he rose casually and walked towards the stairs. He went up onto the wood-pillared balcony and glanced through the open door of the guest-room. He then walked to the end of the balcony and opened the door of the abbot's room. He went in, came out, then opened the deacon's door and went in and came out as before.

The milkmaids and labourers were gathered below the windows in the monastery yard. They were looking up at the balcony with bated breath, and following Hairabed. He came up and leant on the railing, and said in a strange voice:

"The abbot is slain, and the deacon's been strangled."

"And the guests?" someone asked.

"The guests have flown," answered Hairabed.

A general wailing rose up. The women mourned, slapping their own faces and tearing their hair. Doghik was crying at the top of her voice: "Holy Father, do you give me more pain? To whom shall I go to confess my sins, oh, my dear Holy Father!"

The men moved towards the church. The door was open and the church had been ransacked. The saints of both sexes were looking down from the walls and the vestry with impassive, holy eyes.

Chapter 6

A letter from Stamboul! Who should it be from if not from Hampartsoum, the eldest son of the Muradkhanians, the brother of Ohannes, Kevork and Mkhitar? A letter from Hampartsoum – what was up? They usually heard about him from people who came down from Bolis. These people had even brought his words: 'Baron Hampartsoum has asked me to tell you that he is well, and he's getting on quite well, and he doesn't need any help' or 'Tell them not to dishonour the name of the Muradkhanians, nor to look for help from any stranger, or even from a friend or relative.' Hagop Simsarian once arrived from Bolis. He entered Ohannes' room and without any words of greeting stretched out his two hands and sang out loud:

"Is there anything better
Than the desirable brother?"

"Baron Hagop, have you gone off your head?" asked Ohannes.

"No, you're mistaken, Baron Ohannes. I haven't gone off my head. It was Baron Hampartsoum who wanted me to greet you like that," answered Hagop.

Ohannes laughed heartily: "Satenik, bring some raki and soudjuk, and make some coffee. Our Hambartsoum has gone quite mad."

And now suddenly this letter. What was the matter? What had Hampartsoum written? Ohannes weighed up the envelope, turned it over and over and went down to the tantun. His mother was sitting on the carpet, knitting socks.

"Mairig, I've got a letter from Hampartsoum."

The old woman was surprised, "Oh, what's happened?"

"I had the same thought. What's happened? Does he need money?"

His mother was worried and scratched the back of her ear with the knitting needle. "Hampartsoum isn't one to ask for money."

Satenik came in holding the plump child in her arms.

"Your brother-in-law has sent a letter."

"Congratulations," said Satenik,

"Can you guess what he's written?"

She put the child on the bench and said, "How should I know? Maybe he needs something."

Ohannes turned to his mother in alarm "You see? I'm of the same opinion."

"Oh, good Lord," his mother got angry. "Open and read it, let's see what it's all about."

"We'll read it by all means," murmured Ohannes. "But can't you just guess what he's written?"

The letter, of course, could easily be opened and read. Ohannes was not uneducated. He had read the *Psalms, Nareg, Zen Hokevor*, even *Les Miserables*. He knew the four operations of arithmetic. But before reading a letter he wanted to guess its contents and that way he could take up a clear position and be able to read the letter without worrying.

He went up to the big window overlooking the garden. The frost had drawn delicate patterns on the glass. The garden, the winter garden with bare trees, could be seen covered with thick snow. A few crows were sitting in the tall poplars and peering into the distance with sad eyes. Who could believe that some day these trees would be dressed in green, roses would blossom in the orchards and the apricots would ripen. Ohannes looked for the sweet-stoned apricot tree and found it – it was Hampartsoum's favourite tree, Hampartsoum liked apricots a lot. Ohannes wondered what he had written. What did he want? Did he miss those apricots with the sweet stones?

Ohannes' ear caught his mother's voice asking if he had read the letter. "I'll do it now," he said with the obedient sigh of a man bowing to fate, and opened the envelope.

The letter did nor refer to his first concern and his worry about that had been unnecessary. The letter was signed by Hampartsoum's unknown wife with the words, 'Yours sincerely, the mourning Noyemik'. Digin Noyemik was informing Baron Ohannes with deep sorrow of the grievous death of her husband which had taken place on New Year's Eve because if he had woken up on January 1st he would have woken up bankrupt, leaving her, his twenty-year-old son Levonig and sixteen-year-old daughter Nvartig, deserted and homeless.

'So, for God's sake, I beg you to advise me whether I should take my children and come to live under your wing, or whether you could just assign a monthly allowance for me until Nvartig gets married and Levonig becomes a doctor.'

"Well, well," murmured Ohannes.

"Has anything happened?" his mother asked anxiously.

Ohannes did not answer. He felt his face was burning, but continued reading the letter:

'I'm finishing my tragic letter by sending my warmest regards to Sirpouhi Hanum and your whole family. Sorry to have troubled you. Yours sincerely, the mourning Noyemik.'

Ohannes sighed and felt his throat constrict. It was natural, his eldest brother had died. It was not shameful to cry, it was shameful not to cry. On the other hand had his brother behaved like a real man? To die and leave his family with nothing to eat.

– If you weren't able to support a family, why get married. Even suppose you got married, why did you have a child and not one but two. And now I'm supposed to send money to Stamboul until Nvart gets married and Levon becomes a doctor! What have things got to? Why should money reverse its usual flow? It should come to Van from Stamboul, not the other way round. No! Nothing can be done about that, there's no such rule. –

Ohannes shuddered. "Satenik, make up the fire, I've got gooseflesh."

"Oh," his mother was surprised, "I'm an old woman and yet I'm not cold. Are you? Tell me what he's written."

Ohannes wanted to put the letter back into the envelope, but he saw that there was another folded piece of paper there as well. He took it out, opened it and recognized his brother's handwriting. At the top of the letter, his brother's widow had written that her late husband Hampartsoum had written his first and last letter on December 31st, in a flippant mood, but had not been able to fin . . . And here, nobody knows why, Noyemik had not finished the sentence either.

"For God's sake tell me what he's written."

"Wait a little, mairig, I haven't finished reading."

Ohannes began reading his brother's last letter again, or should I say he tried to. It was hard work. Yes, Noyemik was right, the letter seemed to have been written in a very strange mood.

'My dear mother, my honourable brothers Ohannes, Kevork, Mkhitar, all my dear neighbours, friends and relatives, my dear flourishing and abundant Aikesdan: This letter has been written and signed by Hampartsoum of the Muradkhanians who was called Baron Hampartsum by some, before he became a man punished by God, a pitiful Hampo, who hid deep feelings though nobody realized it. Hampo, who burnt and shivered, but to whom nobody gave a drop of water; Hampo, whose home was ruined and nobody helped to re-build it. Living in Stamboul, Hampo sighed and chanted: Oh! Hampo misses Van and all its poplars and its flowers – violets, red, yellow and white roses, lilies and tulips, the primrose, the lilac and the walnut tree, and the perennial daffodils. Let me sigh and sing. Oh, how Hampo misses the sweet-stoned apricot, the juicy pear and apple, the succulent grapes, the Hadji-Nana plum. Hampo misses the herrings, the cheese, the spicy jajik, the soudjuk, the grilled beef, the fried pumpkin and the home-made harissa and pasta. May you be ruined Stamboul, with your Western way of life, with corruption from top to bottom – the Patriarch, the taverns, the brothels, a blood-sucking beast eating people's flesh and drinking their blood and turning Hampartsoum to dust. What shame! Farewell to you, Lake Van and Mt Varag. Farewell Mher's Door. Farewell Araruts Square and Aikesdan. You won't see me again, Van, and I won't see you or your roaring rivers and cold springs any more. With my sinful lips . . .'

The letter ended there. Ohannes wanted to lock himself up in his room, think, give way to tears and cry, read again and examine carefully every word in Hampartsoum's unfinished letter. A doubt crept into his heart like a snake.

"Haven't you finished? What's he written?"

"There's nothing serious, mairig," answered Ohannes trying to be casual. "He misses Van, the meals you make, Mt Varag. I don't know –"

"The boy misses the country. It's not easy being an emigrant, is it?" cried the old woman. "Write and tell him to come home."

"Yes, yes, I'll do that," Ohannes was choking with tears. He slipped out, went up to his room, sat down in front of the tall fireplace and held his frozen fingers over the fire, which seemed to be covered with snow. 'The ash of aspen logs is always white,' he thought, and was surprised by his banal words, as if nothing had happened.

He took his brother's letter out of his pocket and started reading it once more, this time more carefully. With the alert instinct of a merchant, he felt that this letter was not written by a bankrupt. And if there really was some sort of bankruptcy, it was far from being a financial one. Who could he show the letter to, and with whom could he get together in order to come to a conclusion? He thought of all his acquaintances. He recalled that two months ago a young lawyer, Hrant Kaligian had come to Van from Bolis. The man had to be found. He lived on the avenue stretching from Khatch Street to Arark, next to the French Consulate and just past the Freedom-and-Light library. He could usually be found at home on Sundays.

"Satenik," he called out, opening the door and then shutting it promptly, quite sure that his call would not end up as a cry in the wilderness. Indeed, within two minutes, the door opened and Satenik came in.

"Bring my clothes."

"Which clothes?"

"The Sunday best." Then he thought and changed his mind: "No, the ordinary ones."

Ohannes began to get dressed with Satenik's help.

"What's your brother written?"

At first it occurred to Ohannes to tell Satenik about the content of the two letters, but then he looked at her more closely and concluded that she would not be able to keep it all secret – his mother would be told. No, there was no need for his mother to learn about Hampartsoum's death for the moment.

"Bit by bit," thought Ohannes speaking out loud, looking at himself in the mirror hanging on the wall.

CHAPTER 6

"What's this 'bit by bit'?" asked Satenik, fastening the black buttons on her husband's waistcoat with skillful fingers.

"Everything. Everything should be bit by bit." Ohannes began to get annoyed.

"Don't get angry, do you want the watch?"

"No, there's no need."

"The beads?"

"Yes, give them to me. Now wish me good luck."

"Well, where are you going?"

Ohannes put the letter into his pocket. "I've told you a thousand times that a man shouldn't be asked where he's going."

"What about your galoshes?"

"I'd rather –"

But Ohannes put on the galoshes with Satenig's help, patted her on the nose as usual and tried to sidle out of the house without facing his mother. He did not manage to do so. When he went down the wooden stairs to open the street door, his mother came up from the yard.

"Why don't you get on the donkey, Ohannes?"

"What, use the donkey on Sunday, mairig? Let me go for a little walk."

"Where's Hampartsoum's letter?"

"It's on me."

"Why are you taking it with you? Leave it at home."

"Why should I leave the letter at home?"

"Because you've already read it. I thought, Kevork might come and read it to us."

"I don't want to hear that scoundrel's name." Ohannes became angry. "Don't let him ever set foot in my house again."

The old woman felt sad. "Ohannes, my son, he's your brother, isn't he?"

"I have no brother. My only brother is Mkho."

"What about Hampartsoum?"

Ohannes hesitated for a moment, but found a way out.

"Hampartsoum, what Hampartsoum? He's in Bolis and I'm in Van." He went out into the street, banging the door after him.

Ohannes' mother was reflecting.

– No, nobody else would stand for such treatment if they were in her shoes. If they were made of iron, they would melt, stone would wear out, dogs would perish. Four sons, four sons and each of them as stubborn as a ram. Oh husband, my soul, how did you know it was time to depart from this world? God rest your soul, Muradkhan. You never witnessed your sons' drifting apart. Hampartsoum took his share of the legacy and went to Bolis. Kevork drowned his in raki and wine, Ohannes started a business and became wealthy year by year. And Mkho – poor Mkho, innocent, harmless Mkho – went to the village, tied himself down to the farm and became only a memory in the town. What was going on in Ohannes' shop? How much gold had Ohannes amassed, how much did he gain and how much did he lose? –

Sirpouhi knew nothing of his affairs, but she was well aware of village matters. She knew what was sown in each field, how much milk the cows yielded, and how much wool the sheep. She even knew the names of the fields – Kerezako, Khmuk, Kamut. She had seen those fields with her own eyes.

She remembered the day when Mkho sent one of their best horses to town with his Assyrian labourer, Hormuz: She had expressed a wish to go to the village. In the morning, Hormuz had brought the horse out into the street, halted it by the stone trough and waited for her to come out. The cloth saddle-bag with provisions was thrown over the horse's saddle. Ohannes had come out with his mother. He patted her on her shoulder as tenderly as possible.

"So, mairig, you haven't walked across to my shop even once, yet now you're going all the way to Mkho on horseback."

"Well, I'll come to you, too, one day."

Ohannes was strong enough to be able to lift his mother and put her on the stone trough. The horse was brought closer. Sirpouhi raised one leg and slid onto the soft saddle. Hormuz then stepped out holding the reins, and the horse followed him.

"Hormuz," Ohannes called out, "keep an eye on her to make sure nothing goes wrong."

"Let broken my head but may nothing Hatun happen to,"

affirmed Hormuz in his poor Armenian, and they set off.

Ohannes watched the horse and the rider until they passed the neighbouring houses and turned towards the Little Kyanderchi spring. With Hormuz in front and the horse and rider following him, they passed through the inner districts and at last left Van behind.

"That's Aliur, a wealthy village," explained Hormuz as they went on their way, "The priest there is blind in one eye and lame, Hatun."

"Oh," Sirpouhi was surprised.

Six feet were carrying eight feet.

"If you were to go in that direction, you'd see the monastery of St Grigor. It has a spring called Sarnabad, with ice-cold sweet water. If you throw a water-melon into the water, it'll burst. Even if you were to eat two whole sheep, and then drink just a bowl of that water, you'd be hungry all over again".

"Oh," the rider was again surprised. Sirpouhi had been to the Varag and Karmravor monastery but had never seen St Grigor's monastery. She firmly decided that on her way back ... But, wait a moment, why on the way back?

"Hormuz."

"Yes, Hatun."

"Let's go to St Grigor's monastery now."

"Let's go – why not?" Hormuz turned round, smoothing his drooping, thick, grey moustache. He walked south along the path which climbed up a small hill and was lost in a small grove of enormous willows.

They entered the grove, which in fact consisted of only one tree. The great willow had grown a few huge branches, on which new willows had grown. Two branches had not grown upward but horizontally outward, and a few thick willow trunks had sprouted on them with new branches. The trunk of this tremendous tree had a wide cavity hollowed out inside it, in which twenty sheep could have rested. "Twenty sheep," insisted Hormuz.

The famous Sarnabad spring flowed silently, as it rose from the ground. The monastery was at the end of the grove. There had once been a congregation, with an abbot and servants. The monastery had had a flock of sheep, a herd of cows, and rich cellars, but in 1896, the year of that terrible event, the Turks had slaughtered the abbot and robbed the monastery of all its jewellery and silverware. So, it now sat – or rather knelt like a mourner – on the small hill, as if aware of its distressed state.

Sirpouhi got down from the horse with Hormuz' help and walked to the monastery door on stiff feet. She kissed the polished stone framing the door, remembered her late husband Muradkhan, wished him eternal peace. Then she remembered her four sons: Hampartsoum, Ohannes, Kevork and Mkhitar, made a wish for them to be healthy and successful, came back, sat down at the spring and washed in the fresh, cold water.

"Hormuz, bring the saddle bag."

"Yes, Hatun."

He got the bag down and put it at her feet. Sirpouhi took out cornflour cakes, boiled eggs, cheese, lavash, mint, tarragon. They both sat down to have a meal.

"Hormuz, will you have a glass of raki?" This was not just a polite gesture; Sirpouhi really had brought a large bottle of raki with her.

"No, Hatun, how can I have raki when there is such nice water?" Hormuz's refusal was not just a polite formality; he really was not fond of raki.

The rays of the midday sun were unable to penetrate the foliage of the enormous willow, but the grove was nevertheless flooded with sunlight, the crickets were chirping, beetles were buzzing. A cart passed along a road in the distance, and a flock of sheep appeared on the green slope of the nearest hill. They got ready to continue their interrupted way. Hormuz took the horse up to a big stone by the wall of the monastery. Sirpouhi got onto the stone with his help and sat on the soft saddle. Hormuz stepped out again with the reins in his hand and they began to descend to join the main road. It was level for a time and then it began to climb.

Hormuz began to sing. What was he singing? It sounded to Sirpouhi as if he was singing first in Armenian, then in Kurdish.

"Hormuz, what song is that?"

"Whatever comes to my mind. Armenian, Kurdish."

"Sing one of your own songs."

"We have no songs, Hatun. An Assyrian has no songs, we're left with none." He smoothed his grey moustaches with the leather of the rein in his hand. She thought he was crying. Here at last was the top of the road. Hormuz halted the horse and pointed downwards.

"There, Hatun, is your village – Ermants. Can you see it? Over there is the River Keshish. Can you see it? And there's Kharagonis."

The sun poured down gold over the treeless but green plain, the deep blue ribbon of the River Keshish stretched out in the distance, and the sown fields were scattered like colourful handkerchiefs on the small hills.

"What are in those fields?'

"Corn, barley, rye."

"What's that big one?"

"That's your corn – the Kerezako field. The lavash we just ate was made from the flour of that mealy corn"

They began the descent. Sirpouhi's heart was full of longing; this was where all the lavash, ring-shaped bread, thick loaves and pies came from. They approached the village. The flocks and herds, returning from the fields, could already be seen; the bleat of the sheep, the bellows of the cows and the cries of the people could be heard. The village stirred. Everybody knew the grand Hatun was coming that day. Hormuz was regally coming down the low hill near the village, pulling at the reins of his horse, with the grand old lady herself on horseback, wearing a green head-scarf and with a man's shiny, black boots.

Her youngest son, Mkho, was the first to approach the horse. He embraced his mother and helped her down. She kissed his forehead. Then Kasha, the Assyrian priest, came up with lavash on a griddle and some salt on a piece of broken pottery. Sirpouhi wondered what she was supposed to do with the bread and the salt, but she then remembered that the Assyrians were also Christians and she kissed the priest's hand. Then came the old people of the small village – they were all Assyrians – and kissed Sirpouhi's's hand. Younger people – women and children – stood at a proper distance watching the solemn scene. A few women were crying with excitement and wiping their tears with the ends of their head-scarves.

Sirpouhi stayed in the village for more than three weeks and during those three weeks she completely mastered both the simple and complex secrets of their big farm, made a few changes in the financial arrangements made by Mkho, and became fond of the village. Why shouldn't she? She looked at the cornfield and remembered the basin full of white lavash and the stone jar full of white flour in her house, she looked at the cows and sheep and remembered the larder in her house – the huge bowls of butter, cheese and roast beef. "The village is the source of life for the town," she murmured to herself every day. "Without Mkho, we would die."

Though now living in prosperity, Sirpouhi had suffered a lot, and now suddenly there was more trouble. Hampartsoum, it seemed, could not live in distant lands any longer. He missed Van, and the omelettes she used to make. A letter should be written to him. Let him come home! She lifted the lid of the tomir and took out the blackened earthenware pots, checking that the food was cooking properly. Everything was all right, only the quince needed a little salt. She put the pots back. The pots were boiling on the ashes at the bottom of the tonir and the room was full of the delicious smell of cooking.

Where was Mkho? When is he coming in to eat something?

Meanwhile, Ohannes quickly went down the street, entered Santi Street and then slowed down. Earlier in the morning, men using wooden slats had thrown the snow down from the flat roofs of the two-storey houses standing on either side of the street. A chain of snow hills now stretched along the middle of the street and the pedestrians on each side could not see each other. He came out into Khatch Street. Grigor, the tailor, was walking towards him.

"Good morning, Baron Ohannes."

"Good morning, Baron Grigor."

"Where are you going?"

"Nowhere special, I wanted to have a little walk around."

"Well, what sort of walk can there have in this cold? Let's go to my house, and play a game or two of tavlu."

"Baron Grigor, I have an urgent matter to deal with."

"What can there be to deal with on such a bitterly cold day? Let's go to my house, I'll treat you to some bitter melon."

"No, no, Baron Grigor, some other time, some other time."

They parted. Soon after, he met the merchant Simon Tutundjian, well-known for his deep voice and his jokes.

"It's rather cool, Baron Ohannes."

"Yes, you're quite right, Baron Simon."

"I must tell you something, something very important "

"Yes, Baron Simon."

"They say that the thinker has turned into a Turk."

"Well –"

"No, no, I'm not joking. I'm going to tell you something serious."

"Go on then, please."

But Simon Tutundjian, well-known for his deep voice and his jokes, suddenly took his leave and quickly dashed off.

"No brains, no thought," Ohannes murmured under his breath and continued on his way.

He stopped at the cross-roads and looked around – a few shops, a bakery, cabs standing one behind the other, bare willows. Misak, the butcher, usually simply called Miso, was dragging a goat by the horns to the slaughter-house. There was dark brutal terror in the eyes of the goat and it was bleating loudly.

"Couldn't you find something else to do on a Sunday?" Ohannes asked the butcher reproachfully.

"Baron Ohannes, look here, don't you have meat on Sundays?" Miso justified himself and continued dragging the condemned animal through the snow – the slaughter-house was not far away.

There was a moment when Ohannes forgot why he had found himself in the Khatch Street square this Sunday instead of sitting at home and smoking his nargileh. He looked around, stared at the passers-by. He saw Miso, who came out of the slaughter-house into the square and quickly walked up to him.

"Baron Ohannes. Alas, alas –"

"What's up?"

"Tell your brother to pay off his debt. He's had four piastres of meat from me."

"What brother?" Ohannes raised his voice, but nevertheless felt his brow sweat.

"Baron Kevork."

Ohannes came up to the butcher and softly demanded, "Have I ever bought any meat from you?"

"No, Baron Ohannes, never."

"As your answer is no, what then do you want of me?" said Ohannes and strode off and walked on towards the Citadel, towards the main market

"Meat ... four piastres ... brother," he murmured on his way. "He shouldn't have been born, he should have died."

And then he remembered Hampartsoum's death and the reason why he had left the house in this cold. He felt the letter in his pocket and turned back to the square. He then took the road down towards Arark to look for the house of the Kaligians.

'Give money, Baron Ohannes,' he said to himself. 'Give! Give to the Committee of Red Hats. Give clothes to Mkho. Pay off Kevork's debts. Send money now to Noyemik in Bolis so that Nvart can get married, and Levon can become a doctor. Give, Ohannes, give money, for the sake of the nation, for the sake of your brother. Give money!'

However, he did not pursue that thought. How could he wish the nation be left to its ruin? That would be treachery. How could he curse Hampartsoum, who had joined the great majority in a distant land, far from his motherland? And did he after all do much for Mkho? He only gave him a few metres of cheap cloth once a year. As for Kevork ... curses upon him.

Some dark rumours had lately been circulating in the city about Kevork Muradkhanian. Ohannes had heard terrible things. The news about the robbery in Aghtamar and of the murder of the bishop and deacon spread in Van at lightning speed and had stirred people's hearts. Whenever the criminals were referred to, the former teacher's name was also mentioned. Ohannes felt that some iron hand with iron fingers was pressing against his heart – a murderer in the family of the Muradkhanians, a robber of a monastery!

Furthermore, Ohannes heard that Kevork had become rich. Had the money been given to him by his brother? Anything was possible! And, even if his brother had given the money, he had made a big mistake. Kevork drank in the café, entertained people, got into a carriage and rode the streets of Aikesdan, giving away piastres. On the feast day of the Holy Cross of Varag he had slipped five gold pieces into the tray as a donation to the monastery, as if he was worried about its lack of prosperity.

"Baron Ohannes, where does Kevork's money come from? Have you given it him?"

What could he answer? If he said he had, people would consider him to be a fool. If he said he had not and that he'd have been a fool to give money to that drunkard, people would think it was obvious that the robbery and murder in Aghtamar … a hired thief, a hired assassin … akh, akh!

"You should have died rather than disgrace me before people," murmured Ohannes, and took the red handkerchief out of his pocket and wiped the sweat off his brow.

A young man had stopped in front of the door of a two-storey house. He lifted the doorknob and knocked twice; the usual doorknobs in the town clinked, whereas this one thundered. Ohannes could not help noticing that the young man's fine black coat was made of silk and that he sported a perfectly-shaped fez.

"Excuse me, young man," Ohannes came up to the man knocking at the door, "Which is the house of the Kaligians?"

The young man smiled. "When this door opens, we'll be entering the Kaligians' house together." The door opened and they went in.

"You're welcome," greeted the hostess who had opened the door, immediately recognizing the unexpected guest, "You're welcome, Baron Ohannes, how do you happen to be visiting us?"

"God knows all, sister," answered Ohannes gratified that she had recognized him.

"Do you know each other?" asked the young man.

"There is only one Van and only one Baron Ohannes. Is there anyone who doesn't know him? Come in, you're welcome. Have you come to see Hrant?"

"Yes, I have," said Ohannes.

They went upstairs to the first floor by stairs made of polished red boards. Ohannes was reminded that the stairs of his own house needed painting; he also realised that the young man was the jeweller's son, the lawyer, Hrant Kaligian. The lady of the house went ahead and opened the glazed door which opened, closed on its own springs. They entered the room and the door closed.

'Everything is westernised here,' thought Ohannes.

"Well, you just talk together, and let me go and see to the dinner. Hrant, shall I make djilbur?"

"Mairig, what is djilbur?"

"Oh, my son, you've even forgotten that – tarragon, butter, eggs. Baron Ohannes, you know what it is?"

Ohannes tried to smile. "Madam, are you making fun of me?"

The hostess left the room laughing. Ohannes looked around: a big mirror was hanging in the front part of the room and over the mirror there was a stuffed eagle with outstretched wings and angry looking eyes as though it were alive. On the other walls were portraits of Portugalian, Khrimian, Mardig, and a long landscape painting of the calm, blue sea with luxurious houses, palaces, and mosques along the sea-front.

'Is this Van?' thought Ohannes. 'Surely not. There aren't any such houses.'

Noticing the guest's puzzled glance, Hrant came to his aid: "This is Bolis."

"Oh, Stamboul!" he smiled with admiration, but the smile faded on his face as he remembered his brother Hampartsoum. He felt the letter in his pocket and wanted to get down to the problem, but his eye was caught by yet another picture in a brown frame, hanging on the wall. Who was that man? He looked neither a layman nor a clergyman.

Hrant came to his aid again: "This is Karl Marx".

"I haven't heard that name. Is he a hero?"

"Yes, he's a great hero." The host wanted to cut it short. "Do take your coat off, Baron Ohannes, you'll be cold later."

They sat at the round table covered with a white table-cloth.

"What can I do for you? But just a moment. Muradkhanian? Isn't there a merchant from Van in Bolis with that surname? I don't remember his first name."

"Hampartsoum."

"Yes, right, that's it – Hampartsoum."

"He was my brother – he is my brother. How's he getting on? Is he a success?"

"Yes, he's the most successful among those from Van. Once he invited me to dinner. He complained –"

"Did you go to his house?"

"No, I didn't, it was at the Tokatlian Hotel. A generous, clever man! He's highly trusted among the merchants of Bolis."

"What was he going to complain of?"

"I'd like to tell you about that. He isn't pleased with his wife, he says that she is avaricious, a despot. Hampartsoum has a weakness for the fair sex."

"What do you mean?"

"Look, Bolis isn't like Van, Baron Ohannes. When you walk along the streets, strange women and girls throw themselves at you."

"Why do they do that?"

"They earn money," said Hrant with a smile.

"Oh dear!" exclaimed Ohannes, realizing what he meant. "Did Hampartsoum have any dealings with them?"

"Yes, Baron Ohannes, yes, he did. He frequents brothels, looks for contacts, meetings on the bridge. Everyone from Van living in Bolis is aware of this."

Ohannes took the envelope out of his pocket and handed it to the lawyer with trembling hands.

"You're a lawyer. Please read this," he said quietly, "read it and decide what's true and what's false."

Hrant took the letters out of the envelope and began to read them one after the other.

"So, that's how things are," said the lawyer with a strained, preoccupied air after reading through the letters for a second time. "That's how things are," he repeated, putting the letters back into the envelope.

"Well?" asked Ohannes, who wanted to know what the lawyer thought.

"Write back to Digin Noyemik. Invite her to come to you with the children," said the lawyer, handing the envelope back to Ohannes.

"Are you joking?"

"I'm not, write to them, invite them to come."

"Why? What for?"

"Don't get excited, Baron Ohannes. Digin Noyemik, who grew up in Bolis and has taken the whole of Hampartsoum Muradkhanian's property into her hands, certainly won't come to Van."

"She's written that she's bankrupt."

"It's a lie."

"What does she want?"

"She has two aims. The late Baron Hampartsoum seems to have told the truth. Digin Noyemik really is avaricious, and her first aim is that she doesn't want you to demand anything from her. And her second aim is this. Would she lose anything if she was to get a sum of money from you each month? She'd lose nothing, she'd win something."

"Baron Ohannes," continued the lawyer, "at first sight, the affair is very simple: the man went bankrupt, died of a heart attack or committed suicide, leaving his wife and children to live from hand to mouth. Is that not so? But just look." He opened the envelope again and took the letters out. "His letter contains no word of any financial worries, there is indeed a sort of anxiety, but it's a moral rather than a financial one. Those sighs, those fits of home-sickness, have no material basis. He's written the letter on small pieces of paper, and where's the rest? There is no doubt that he would have gone on to give some instructions regarding his estate. I don't doubt either, that he hasn't bequeathed all his property only to his family. He was very wealthy, he can't have forgotten his kinsmen in Van. According to the French proverb –"

"I don't need his property, Baron Hrant," interrupted Ohannes, who was saddened and surprised by what the lawyer had been telling him. "I agree to whatever you said, your way of thinking is quite clear. That's fine. Now, could you work out what he died of?"

"Baron Ohannes –" He stopped talking for a moment and fixed his eyes on the big, blue lampshade hanging from the ceiling, then continued. "If I didn't know him and hadn't heard of him from the Van people in Bolis, I would hardly be able to answer your question, but –" He stopped again. "But as I know him and according to what I've seen or heard, I firmly believe that he was infected by some bad disease."

"What disease?" Ohannes almost whispered.

"A bad – a very bad – disease."

"Doesn't that disease have a name? Was it cholera? Or leprosy? Or pneumonia?" The unhappy man was getting upset.

"No, Baron Ohannes, no, something worse."

To clarify the matter Ohannes asked. "Baron Hrant, please express yourself clearly. What disease is it? Which part of a man's body aches? Is there such a disease in Van?"

The lawyer blinked his eyes rapidly. It was a sign that he was embarrassed. He lowered his voice: "Baron Ohannes, the disease is called the French pox. It probably originated in France and it can only be treated with difficulty. It's a shameful disease."

There was a silence.

"I don't understand." Ohannes seemed to be in another world.

The lawyer blinked his eyes again. "Baron Ohannes, your brother had wicked intercourse with a prostitute and got infected."

From the expression on Ohannes' face, the lawyer realized that at last Ohannes understood this time what his brother's disease was. He was hunched up in his chair, as if he had become smaller. Just to say something, he asked, "Well, are there no medicines or doctors in Stamboul?"

"Why not? People can be cured, sometimes successfully. But your brother didn't want to go to doctors or to hospital, in case anyone from Van saw him. This is a dishonourable, disgraceful disease, and your brother, in spite of the licentious life he led, was a proud and honourable man. He must have committed suicide."

Ohannes grasped the table with both hands, stood up and sat down again. "What shall I do?" he murmured. It was not clear whether the question was put to the lawyer or to himself.

"What should you do? You'll just have to put up with the grief."

The silence was broken by the lady of the house who came in and said, "Come on, let's go to the dining-room and have dinner now."

Ohannes stood up and collected his coat. "Excuse me, I have to go. Thank you very much, Baron Hrant."

"My work in the kitchen has become a waste of time," said the hostess, trying to take the coat out of Ohannes' hands. "You aren't going anywhere!"

"No, madam, I have to go. Many thanks – they're waiting for me at home."

"Good heavens, Baron Ohannes, I have fish, yoghurt, djilbur, bulghur, pilaf. I have Shabagh wine."

But Ohannes remained unshakable: "Thank you very much. Please do come and visit us sometime."

The hostess gave in. "This wasn't right, Baron Ohannes. I'll complain to my husband Hairo when he comes."

"Where has Hairabed gone?" asked Ohannes.

"A district committee meeting on a Sunday!" grumbled the hostess, though with obvious pride. She went downstairs quickly to open the front door for the guest.

"Baron Hrant," said Ohannes, "please don't say anything to your mother and father yet."

Hrant smiled: "A secret can be entrusted to a priest or a lawyer."

"Thank you very much."

The hostess opened the door wide. "Who lost out, you or me?" she said, "you didn't eat the djilbur I'd made. If a dead man ate my djilbur, he would revive."

"I'll come and eat it when I die. Please convey my regards to the member of the district committee. Please come to visit us soon."

The hostess waited until the guest walked away, and only then shut the door. A welcome guest should not hear the sound of the door closing behind him. Whereas, if the guest has been unpleasant, the door is slammed shut when he has hardly taken a few steps.

Ohannes went down into Khatch Street, cast an unfriendly glance at Miso's slaughter-house and took the road back to his house. He did not have any significant or important meetings with anyone the whole way, except for Vahan Chapudjian, working at the post-office, who recognized him from afar and coughed, in what seemed to be a feigned way, as Ohannes passed by. He came up and greeted him very respectfully. "Good afternoon, Baron Ohannes."

"Hello," said Ohannes pretendeding not to see Vahan's outstretched hand."

"What's the news, Baron?"

"We're all well."

"Health is the most important thing, the rest is hollow. Do you get letters from Baron Hampartsoum? Is he getting on well?"

"I had a letter from him today. He's well and so are his affairs."

Vahan was surprised: "Oh, a letter today? And he's said that he's very well?

Ohannes looked straight into the eyes of the impudent man. If he had a stick in his hand, he would certainly have struck him over the head. He wondered what was on the tip of the tongue of this son of a dog. The post-office clerk felt instinctively that he had better go away. He pressed his fez firmly down onto his head and disappeared behind one of the snow hills.

There was no doubt that the news of his brother's tragedy had reached Van, especially through the letters coming from Bolis. And there was equally no doubt that those letters were read at the post-office and that Vahan was one of those readers who never missed a chance to ask Ohannes questions, as he had done today. Sometimes these questions were too stupid; for instance, once when they were coming out of the church, he came up to greet Ohannes and, rubbing his hands, said:

"Baron Ohannes, let me ask you something? It's acceptable when guests knock at the front door and come in through it, but when they knock at the garden door and enter through that, there is nothing more unbearable. Baron, do your guests ever come to your house through the garden door?"

Surely a senseless question. You can walk round the whole of Van through the gardens. Many gardens are not separated by walls or are separated only by low walls, but why should an honoured guest come in through the gardens instead of the front door? A stupid question. Nobody knows what other abstract and everyday thoughts would have passed through his mind had not a woman with a delicate, white veil passed him with an elderly woman – perhaps her mother – beside her, She caused his thoughts to turn sharply away in some confusion. The woman glanced at Ohannes with burning, coal-black eyes; judging only by those eyes, he felt her smiling at him behind her veil. Ohannes' heart trembled and he remembered his unhappy brother Hampartsoum. He remembered the lawyer's words, 'Bolis isn't like Van. There you walk along the streets, strange women and girls throw themselves at you.'

"It's like that here as well. They aren't all that far behind Bolis in that business if you weaken," muttered Ohannes to himself.

Then he wondered how he would behave if that woman with the beautiful eyes threw her arms round his neck: would he free his neck and shout, 'Go away, you whore, go away'? Or would he give way and sin, like Hampartsoum. Ohannes hastened his steps, wishing to get rid of these unpleasant thoughts. He felt that he would hardly have the courage to shout at the woman with the delicate, white veil.

If it were not for a piece of frozen snow, the size of a five kurush coin, which fell right on Ohannes' neck from a branch of one of the willows and made him look around, he would not have realized that he was already in his own street, not far from his own house. He took a deep breath, went up to the door and knocked twice – klnk, klnk. Such was his knock, with a pause between the two klnks, that the those inside knew that it was nobody else but the head of the family, Baron Ohannes. His daughter, Lia, opened the door. She opened it wider than necessary and waited, smiling respectfully, for her father to enter. Ohannes came in and, as usual, took off his fez and put it on the girl's head. The red fez suited the white-faced, black-eyed and black-browed, pretty Lia very well.

Chapter 7

After dinner, Ohannes went to his oriental sitting-room, sat down on one of the mattresses placed on the carpet and rested his tired head on the soft cushion. Satenik placed a nargileh on a round, silver tray in front of him. Ohannes took the mouthpiece and fastened it to the long, snaking rubber tube. Stroking his moustache left to right, he put the mouthpiece between his lips and sucked. The clear water of the nargileh bubbled and gurgled, filling the room with the pleasant fragrance of the specially prepared tobacco.

Someone knocked at the front door, in just the way Ohannes would – klnk, klnk. But though it had the form it lacked the essence. It was not the self-confident knock of the master of the household. This hand was timid and unassured, which meant that it was that of Kevork, the teacher. Moreover, it meant he was drunk. It was only when he was drunk that he would knock at the door in the way his brother did. No-one knew whether he was mocking or whether he was referring to his share of power in the household.

Klnk, klnk. Ohannes heard the door open and then his brother's voice. "If I didn't come, would you care whether I was dead or alive?"

Ohannes thought that his mother had perhaps warned Kevork not to speak so loud, since his brother – that brute – was at home He was not mistaken, because later he heard Kevork's softly spoken protest: "It doesn't matter whether he's at home or not. I'm a man just as much as he is."

Then everything went quiet. Perhaps they had entered the other room, but had to speak quietly because the brute was at home. Ohannes had often heard people talking about him like that: "Ohannes of the Muradkhanians isn't a man, he's a brute. How could he have become so rich if he wasn't a brute?"

Does that mean that all rich men were brutes? Does it mean that Kapamadjian, the Houssians, and all the merchants of Van are brutes? Who knows, maybe they really are brutes. But is Ohannes himself also a brute? 'The dogs bark, but the caravans move on,' thought Ohannes, straightening his back. And the nargileh gurgled – glug, glug, glug.

Father was self-confidently looking down from the wall. With his fez tilted forward on his brow, and his moustache drooping on both sides, he seemed to be aware of everything going on.

– Do you see, hairig, what's happened to you? What a trick your sons have played on you? You were proud of having had four sons, four stout pillars to firmly suppport the Muradkhanians' large house. Look. Look at your Hampartsoum, dissolute and the prey of sinful women, such as the woman with the black eyes with a white veil I saw today. Look at your Kevork, a thief and a murderer. And Ohannes, a beast of the town; they who say so perhaps know something. And Mkhitar, a beast of the village. Is this a house? No, hairig, it's a den of beasts. –

Glug, glug, glug, agreed the narghileh.

– Someone is coming upstairs. Clearly it's my brother, they are a man's steps and there is no other man at home. Why's he coming? What does he want? How dare he come here? What impudence! He's coming to ask for the letter in order to read it downstairs. I'll show him! –

The door opened. Standing there – Ohannes could not believe his eyes – was Kevork in a new, dark suit. A black tie had worked loose from his starched collar, and the gold chain of a pocket watch hung out of his waistcoat. And the fez reminded Ohannes of the fez of the lawyer, Hrant Kaligian. But the most amazing thing was his brother's short beard.

"I left my coat downstairs, so as not to disturb you too much. Good evening –"

"You should have left your beard – defined as a hirsute growth – downstairs, as well," snapped Ohannes, trying to mimic his brother's pedantry, while examining his brother from head to foot.

"My beard's nothing to do with you. I don't refer to your merchant's moustache, so you leave my beard alone. Our mother wants you to let me read the letter from Bolis."

"I haven't got any letter to show you."

Kevork spoke softly: "Look, even if you give me the letter, I'll not read it to her."

"Why?" Ohannes was still anxious, but also curious. "Take and read it, if you want." He dipped a hand into his pocket as if to take the letter out.

"There's no need to play the fox with me. You aren't going to give that letter to me." Kevork lowered his voice even more, "I know the truth. Hampartsoum has been poisoned – he's dead. Hampartsoum isn't alive any more."

"What happened?"

"A shameful, incurable or hardly curable –"

Ohannes interrupted him: "Where did you hear about it?"

"People from Van, living in Bolis, have written to their relatives here. He's left a lot of property, but his wife's a bad one. He also has a son and daughter."

Ohannes handed the letter to his brother without a further word.

Sirpouhi was sitting in the room downstairs, tensely awaiting the outcome of the meeting of the two brothers. She was frightened and was expecting to hear loud shouts and mutual curses; but time passed and no sound came from the room upstairs. In the next room, Murad was being noisy; his mother calmed him down and became quiet herself. The children were shouting and throwing snowballs in the yard, but soon they were also not heard; they had probably moved on to continue playing in the neighbouring yard. There was a heavy silence and it wrung her heart. Let the brothers shout, swear and even hit each other, but not remain silent. If they but spoke in their usual tones, their mother would hear them. Why were they silent? Maybe they were whispering? Why should they whisper? What do they have to say to each other in a whisper? She remembered her dream.

She heard Ohannes' weak cough, and then silence reigned again. Now she had no doubt that they were speaking in whispers. Who about? What about? There was a lump in Sirpouhi's throat and tears began to pour down from her eyes, washing her face. Her dream!

There was a knock on the front door. Sirpouhi hurried to the outer yard, wiping her eyes and face with her apron.

"Who's there?"

"It's me, Sirpouhi Hatun, it's me."

It was midwife Tarik. Not a good time for a visit! Sirpouhi opens the door quickly.

"What's the matter, Sirpouhi Hatun, why are you crying?" Tarik asks even before entering. "Has anything happened to Baron Hampartsoum?"

"What could happen to Hampartsoum?" says the little, old woman bravely. "Have you heard anything?"

"I've heard that he's ill," Tarik stepped back, realising that the mother did not know what the whole of Van was talking about.

"We had a letter today. He misses Van, misses my djilbur. Ohannes wrote to him, telling him to come home and satisfy his longing for Van."

"May he come, by God's grace, may he come," said Tarik with feeling, as she entered the house.

Now it has become clear to Sirpouhi that something had happened to Hampartsoum. If it had been an ordinary letter from him, why would Ohannes waste time by walking here and there without opening it? And why then put it into his pocket without reading it, why go out and return so late? When Kevork entered the house, his first question had been to ask whether there was any news from Stamboul. She had answered that they had received a letter that day. Kevork had wanted to know what was written in it. She had told him that the letter was from Hampartsoum, who had written that he missed Van. Kevork had gone quiet, muttered to himself and had then asked where the letter was. "Where should it be?" she had said, "Ohannes has taken it." Kevork had then said he would go up and see.

And he has not yet returned. There is no sound coming from the upper room. It is clear that they are speaking about Hampartsoum in low voices; it is also clear that something is wrong with him. And here is Tarik: she had hardly stepped into the room before she asked whether anything had happened to Hampartsoum.

"Tarik –"

"Yes?"

"Please say something clearly. What have you heard?"

"I haven't heard anything, Hatun." She settled herself comfortably in the rocking-chair. "Listen, Hatun, it goes like this."

> "Hey my love, Ho my love:
> Lets line up the bright stars,
> Like a row of buttons,
> For the fearful shepherd
> To set his crook on fire.
> Let him have the ashes
> To make me a fine ring,
> Or a belt for my waist
> And sandals for my feet."

"Oh, Tarik, you are a happy woman – with no brains and no vices."

"Don't say that, I've both," Tarik rocked back and forth, "but let me finish my song."

> "The mill stones are turning,
> I want to stay awake.
> The mill doors are iron,
> You want to be like wood.
> The mill roofs are sloping,
> You want to come to me."

While Tarik was singing a well-known folk-song, Sirpouhi was drowning in the sea of her thoughts. 'This mad woman takes me for a fool or a child,' she mused. And in order to urge Tarik on and to set aside her own sad thoughts, she said: "All right now tell me about the bride taken to the bridegroom's house."

"I'll tell, I'll tell," Tarik became enthusiastic, believing that she could drive away the other's doubts. "It goes like this."

> "Hey welcome, Ho welcome,
> Here's a toast to the King:
> Long life, your Majesty,
> And long life to your Queen.

Come, mother of the king,
See what we have brought you:
We've brought you a housemaid,
A pretty one for you.
Come, mother of the king,
See what we have brought you:
We've brought you a nursemaid,
A gentle one for you.
Come, mother of the king
See what we have brought you:
We've brought you a milkmaid,
A rosy one for you.
Hey welcome, Ho welcome."

She stood up with her left hand on her waist and her right above her head. She glided back and forth, stamping with one foot and shouting at the top of her voice, "Shabash ... mahlabash." At that moment, a door opened and closed, and they could hear Kevork exclaim, "Well, well."

"Are there people at home?" whispered Tarik with exaggerated horror, holding her head between her hands, "I'm so ashamed."

Kevork entered, and without looking at Tarik turned to his mother. "I've read the letter, mairig. Hampartsoum is a bit unwell. Perhaps it's the sickness of nostalgia. If I were him, I'd have joined Abraham long ago. Thank God he was able to last this long."

"Where's the letter?" asked his mother in a hollow tone.

"Why do you need it?" Kevork felt weighed down.

"Don't lie to me, it's a sin," reproached his mother, "I've had a dream. My Hampo isn't alive."

Sirpouhi was not lying. Two weeks ago she really had seen it all in a dream.

Three huge poplars stood at the head of Ohannes' garden – three huge poplars with twisted branches. The fourth poplar stood on its own, a little apart from the first three. Sirpouhi comes out through the garden gate to pick up roses for tea and mint for yoghurt. She sees that the fourth poplar has fallen down across the orchard beneath the trunks of the others. "Oh, my God," murmurs Sirpouhi, and wakes up.

She gets up and looks through the window overlooking the garden. All the four poplars are in their places, three of them with twisted branches and the fourth one a little apart from the other three. She lay down again but could not sleep any more. She wondered whether everything was allright with Hampartsoum. She calmed herself down. What could happen to him? She recalled her mother. When someone recounted a strange dream, her mother would fall silent for a moment as if she was trying to find an explanation for the dream; then she would say, "Perhaps you haven't been properly tucked in".

"Don't lie to me, it's a sin. My Hampo's not alive."

The first one to give way was Tarik. She began to cry so loudly that one would think it was she who was the mother of the deceased. Kevork was struck dumb and looked at his mother. She was sitting on the carpet and rocking back and forth silently. Kevork rushed out and ran upstairs to tell Ohannes. Tarik was wailing in the customary style.

"O, my brave Baron Hampartsoum, why did you go to Stamboul? O, Sirpouhi Hatun, they say he died of a shameful disease. Couldn't someone else have got it, Baron Hampartsoum? Oh, what pain, what pain. Cry, mairig, cry. He's saying he'll not come back, his pain is sharp and there's no cure."

Taken up with her weeping, Tarik did not notice that Sirpouhi had stopped rocking. For a while it seemed she wanted to get up, but she could not and fell wide-eyed on the carpet.

"Water, water," screamed Tarik in great alarm. Satenik rushed into the room with tears in her eyes, and now probably aware of the tragedy. Tarik sprayed water over Sirpouhi's face. Sirpouhi closed her eyes – her eyelashes were quivering.

The brothers came down. Kevork took his mother's hand. It was warm. He lifted her up in his arms. "Get the bed ready – quickly!"

Satenik prepared it in a hurry and Kevork gently laid his mother on the bed. Ohannes, with his hands on his stomach, was looking at his mother, then at Tarik, then at a spot on Satenik's upper lip, then at his brother's ridiculous, short beard. He was thinking that one should not get so excited, it was not good for one's health.

The winter dusk was setting in. Four poplars were shivering – three of them side-by-side with twisted branches and the fourth standing well apart, alone, like an orphan.

Chapter 8

It was the dead of night. The full moon sailed out from the south edge of Mt Varag and quivered over the wintry town. Van is sad in winter, unhappy like the winter itself. The moon shone forth, seeking out all the secret highways and byways of the town. It found Ohannes Muradkhanian, standing by the window late at night, looking out at his orchard.

He could not fall asleep. When he had taken off his clothes and gone to bed, the day seemed to have been endless. He could not get the long and terrible events of the day out of his mind even as he caressed his wife's neck with his moustache.

Moonlight fell on the orchards of Van and it picked out a group of men moving forward from the Shaldjians' garden. They were walking along the frozen snow and, even though they wore heavy boots, they did not leave any footprints. They were marching in step and the frozen snow was crunching under their feet. They moved up to the Muradkhanians' garden. The sound of steps marching in unison reached Ohannes' ear; he got up quickly and went to the window. Some dark human shadows could be seen between the trees. They were coming up to the garden gate, they came right up to it and knocked at the door.

Tck, tck. The knock was quiet but determined. Ohannes immediately remembered postman Vahan and his words in the churchyard. Then, they had seemed senseless – all about guests entering through the garden gate. But now, here they were.

In came Sirpouhi Hatun, who had dressed hurriedly and had wrapped a black scarf round her head. "Ohannes my son, someone is knocking at the garden gate."

"Why did you get up?" said Ohannes angrily. "Go to bed. Have you forgotten what just happened to you? Go to bed, we'll be able to deal with anything without you."

"A creaking door hangs long on its hinges, my son. Only tell me whether they're Armenians or Turks?"

"It doesn't matter. The door has to be opened. Go to your room. I'll go and open up," Ohannes said, and put his coat on over his nightgown.

"You stay right here," said Sirpouhi, barring the way, "I'll open it myself."

And she went downstairs, though clearly with some difficulty. Ohannes went to the east window overlooking the yard. There was his mother. She went up to the garden gate and opened it. Ohannes counted six people coming in through the door, while the seventh said something to his mother at the threshold of the door and then also entered. Sirpouhi closed the door, walked ahead and led them all into the oriental room, the floor of which was covered with a large carpet with numerous mattresses and cushions on it. One of the visitors lit the lamp hung from the ceiling with his own match, and Sirpouhi could only then see that her guests were armed from head to foot. It was a political group, she thought. The guests put their firearms down with the pleasure of people who had come into the warmth from the cold. Sirpouhi went to her son.

"Ohannes, they're from some sort of committee, with Mausers, pistols, sheepskin hats, and cartridge belts. They're Armenians. They do speak Armenian, but some other dialect. I understood that they're proposing to stay here till tomorrow night, to eat and drink here, have a rest and then go on their way."

"And what's their business?" asked Ohannes with obvious distaste.

"Its a committee. It's bandits' business."

"Thieves' business," murmured Ohannes.

"It's not a good time to talk," she said anxiously, "we have to feed them. Let Satenik get up and help me to take some fried meat from the pan."

"I'll not let these dogs see Satenik," Ohannes said angrily.

"They won't see her. She'll prepare the food and I'll take it to them," Sirpouhi told her son in an effort to calm him down. "Don't shout, you can be heard."

"What a damned day and now a damned night," Ohanne groaned. He went across to his wife and woke her up gently, "Satenik, get up, my dearest."

Ohannes entered the room when he thought that the visitors would have finished eating. Some of those sitting round the big tray had already moved away from the table, one of them was cleaning his weapon assiduously, one was reading to the others from a newspaper, and another was pacing up and down the room.

Ohannes came in and raised a hand to his fez in silent greeting.

"Greetings, greetings!" exclaimed the guests.

"Are you the owner of the house?" one of them asked.

"He is indeed the host, Baron Aram," Ishkhan said helpfully. "Mkho's brother – Mkho from Ermants village – do you remember?"

"I remember, yes indeed, I remember," said Aram in his deep voice, twirling his sharp moustache. "You have a wonderful brother, Baron –"

"Ohannes," prompted Ishkhan, admiring Aram's ability to dissimulate.

"Baron Ohannes, you have a wonderful brother."

Ohannes was asking himself: 'Where do they know Mkho from? Why hasn't Mkho told me anything about them? Surely he couldn't have given any sheep to these wolves, could he?'

"Aren't there four of you?" asked Paramaz, a man who was long-haired and beardless, but with an elongated moustache. He smiled at Ohannes like someone who had known him for ages.

"There were four of us, but now we are three," answered Ohannes.

"Yes, really, in Bolis... er ..."

'These people know about our family as well as they know

their five fingers,' thought Ohannes. 'Well, let them know, there's nothing to be afraid of.' He took out a piece of paper from the pocket of his loose trousers and handed it to Paramaz.

"Who wrote this note?"

The paper then passed from hand to hand.

"And did you give the gold?" Paramaz said with a smile, taking back the note when all of them had read it.

"Why should I give any?" Ohannes said with spirit. "What a nerve. Only robbers act this way. If they need money for their business, let them come openly and ask for it, give a receipt and then take it. If you were in my shoes wouldn't you consider that to be proper?"

There was a deep silence.

"Yes, the method is not a good one," said a short man who had a thin moustache and a beard, and was wearing glasses. He turned to the others, "We should make an end of this story, my friends."

Ishkan tried to interfere: "Baron Vramian –"

"Listen. Firstly, as you all know, we don't get any significant results by this method, and secondly ... Baron Ohannes, go and have an unworried sleep, and if you ever get such a letter again, do as I do."

He took the letter from Paramaz, tore it up and threw the pieces into the corner of the room.

"Well done," cried Paramaz.

Ohannes was pacified. "Good night to you all. Excuse me, I have to go to work in the morning."

Not everybody in the room wished him a good night and a peaceful sleep.

Ohannes went to his mother's room. She was not yet asleep. Lying in bed, she was remembering Hampartsoum from the day of his birth to the day of his death, and recalling unimportant details of his life. For instance, some relatives once came to their house when he was seven, and among them was the newly-wed, rosy-cheeked Armenouhi Chantikian. Little Hampo could not bear to leave her side. The guests spent the night at their house and when they got up in the morning, they found Hampo sleeping under the blanket of the newly-wed woman. They all laughed a lot – what a child he was! He had got up at night and slipped under the blanket of the young woman and fallen asleep.

"Why don't you sleep, mairig?" said Ohannes, putting his hand on his mother's cold and moist brow.

"I can't sleep."

"What are you thinking about?"

"Nothing much," she groaned, "I'm thinking about those people. The one called Paramaz said to me at the gate, 'Mairig, all these men are your sons, this is Vramian, this is Ishkhan, this is Aram, this one is Armenak Yekarian, this is Grigor Bulgaretsi, and I'm Paramaz'."

"That's six of them," counted Ohannes.

"Six? Did I forget a name?"

"It's good you could remember that much. There's one thing I can't understand. I've heard about Paramaz, he's a Hunchak, while Armenak Yekarian's a Ramgavar. What have they got in common with those Dashnaks?"

Silence.

"And let me also say," Ohannes said, "if the Turks start a massacre, will they differentiate between a Hunchak or a Dashnak? It could be that they've united. But if they're united today, they'll separate tomorrow."

Silence again.

"Well, sleep, sleep. I've got to go – I must go to work in the morning. Perhaps the situation is really serious, if these... Well, sleep, sleep!"

And he went out on tiptoe.

But the guests are not sleeping. The lamp is burning and one voice can be heard. Only one of them is speaking, the others are silent. Ohannes moved cautiously up to the door of the guests' room and tried to hear what was being said.

"We've had some success from an organizational point of view," the speaker was saying. "The facts are clear. You know the names of the villages where we have supporters. This is the situation, my friends. Are there any questions?"

"What is the political situation in Aliur village?" one of them asked.

"We haven't yet succeeded in Aliur. They're all Ramgavars."

"Don't touch Aliur!" It was probably the Ramgavar supporter, Armenak Yekarian, who said that. All of them laughed.

Ohannes moved away from the door quietly like a thief. 'They've set the whole of Vaspourakan on fire, and we know nothing about it,' he thought.

He went to his room, took off his clothes, got under the blanket and curled up close to Satenik, who was sleeping peacefully after the earlier disturbance. The hair of her plait was touching Ohannes' nose and tickling it, so that he could hardly help sneezing. Then, who knows why, he remembered the woman in the fine, white veil, her eyes and her smile. Ohannes wanted to cross himself to prevent evil thoughts, but his eyes closed and he fell into a deep sleep.

The chapel could be seen from behind Mt Varag. In his dream, he was in Ermants. The fields were all ploughed. All the ploughmen were Assyrians, singing out gaily: "The ground fell, the master rose..."

Ohannes looks round and sees that there are no sheaves of wheat.

"Where's the wheat?" asks Ohannes, fearing the worst.

But Shamash, twirling his copper-coloured moustache, calms Ohannes down: "Master, the wheat went to Stamboul, in order to provide a dowry for Baron Hampartsoum's daughter and to help make his son into a doctor."

When Ohannes woke up the following day, the first thing that crossed his mind was that it was Monday. Then he remembered that Hampartsoum was dead. Finally he also remembered that the oriental room was full of terrible people, but that henceforth he need not be afraid of notes signed by Hats. And that was the most important thing.

While he was putting on his clothes with the help of his wife, the door opened and his brother Kevork came in. Ohannes immediately became gloomy: What was this unexpected visit? Why did his brother appear before him again in his new clothes, with a short beard. and with that awful smile? It is true that Ohannes had yesterday spoken with him at length and without argument about Stamboul and about their brother's illness. He had told him everything he had heard from the lawyer, Hrant Kaligian. But that did not mean that he had accepted him or forgiven his deadly – yes, deadly – faults.

"Are they sleeping?" Kevork asked, pointing back to the oriental room.

"Who?" asked Ohannes, not answering the question.

"The leaders."

Satenik went to get the breakfast ready. The brothers were left alone.

"Don't be angry," said Kevork in a conciliatory tone, "I haven't come to see you. I have some business with them." And again he pointed back over his shoulder.

"You've become a great b ———," Ohannes patted his moustache with a red handkerchief. "Did you have a hand in the Aghtamar robbery?"

"Don't be angry – and don't make me angry. I'm not accountable to you," Kevork arrogantly and vigorously replied.

Sirpouhi came in. She had stood trembling at the door listening to the brothers' quarrel, but entered the room quietly as if she had heard nothing.

"Ohannes, my dear, let's get going, you should eat something, it's late."

But Ohannes could not calm down: "How have you managed to get so much money which you spend so wastefully? You rob Aghtamar and then give the money to the Varag monastery?"

"Both of us are the sons of one father. Why should you be rich and me poor?" protested Kevork.

"I've gained my wealth by the sweat of my brow –"

"You have one brow, but I have one, too," interrupted Kevork and marched out of the room.

Sirpouhi breathed a sigh of relief.

After breakfast, Ohannes came in warm clothes into the outer yard where his white, dark-eyed donkey was standing. He got onto its large saddle with the help of his servant Usep and took the reins from his hand.

Usep wished him, as usual, a happy journey and a safe return, but did not receive the usual thanks from his master. With some effort, Ohannes took his purse out of his inner pocket, undid the knot and took out a silver forty-para coin, which he put it into Usep's hand. At the same time, he again remembered his dead brother and also recalled that he need not be afraid of papers from Hats any more.

Ohannes set off, leaving the surprised young man and his good wishes back at the house. Usep remained rooted to the spot, with the silver coin in his hand, until the jingle of the donkey's bells could be heard no longer and Ohannes had turned into Santi Street.

The guests – or 'the commitee' as they were called by Sirpouhi – woke up late. They came down one by one, washed at the well in the yard, took the towel from Lia's shoulder, dried themselves, threw the towel back onto Lia's shoulder, tapped her nose with their forefingers as if they had all agreed to do so beforehand, and went back up. Ishkhan also tapped her nose, but this made the girl blush deeply.

The breakfast was ready. Sirpouhi filled the tray with provisions from her larder: honey and butter, boiled eggs, cold meat, cheese, paklava and cakes. Sirpouhi wanted to feed Kevork, but he said he would sit down with the 'leaders'. And he sat down at the table with them.

He introduced himself with the confidence of a host, greeted them all, shook hands and made them welcome. He looked at the table and then went out quickly. On the stairs, he took the yellow boiling samovar off his mother's hands and said, "Bring some raki immediately, they want to drink."

The bottle of raki was placed in the middle of the table. It looked around like a prince, but only smiled at Kevork, who invited the guests to the table. They sat down cross-legged on the carpet round the well-polished tray. Kevork filled the glasses and breakfast began.

Kevork raised his glass: "Well, welcome. Here's to you all!"

Everyone took his glass and tapped Kevork's, but then put it down and continued eating in silence. Kevork did not let on that he had noticed this impolite behaviour of the guests, but he grasped the neck of the bottle, as if to strangle it, and filled his own glass again.

By the time they had eaten only half the breakfast, Kevork was already dead drunk. He was swinging the glass over his head and declaiming.

"There is no revolution without discipline and secrecy. And there is no revolution without blood, either. Away with revolution without blood!"

"Baron Kevork, calm down a bit," advised Ishkhan. He did not know why, but the presence of the former teacher and his speech were beginning to depress him and get on his nerves.

"This isn't a time to rest," Vramian said to Kevork, with a smile, his eyes shining behind his glasses.

"Now I would like to speak to Baron Kevork alone."

"I'm ready, Baron Vramian."

The two of them moved to a corner of the room, and sat close to each other, leaning on the cushions, and began a tough conversation. The others drew away from the table, lay down on the mattresses and one by one began drowsing off. Sirpouhi came in and began to clear away the table.

Vramian started by saying, "Don't keep secrets from me. I'm your friend. Tell me how you got to Aghtamar."

Kevork rubbed his face guiltily like a schoolboy who has not done his homework. Silence.

Vramian put his hand on Kevork's knee in a familiar manner and asked: "Who suggested that you should go to Aghtamar?"

"Baron Ishkhan."

"Where did you first meet him?"

"At the Askeran restaurant."

Oriental music was pounding out in the Askeran restaurant. The musicians were singing and playing Turkish music. The waiters were moving slowly between the tables to the rhythm of the music and seeing to the clients' orders. It is Saturday evening and there are many customer. Some of them are already well aroused;

they are singing with the music and clicking their fingers to the rhythm.

"Ach kapui, nazli hanum, ben geliyorum –"

Open the door, sulky lady. I'm coming in.

Kevork came in, peered at the three, large lamps, hanging down from the ceiling, as if to decide whether they were necessary or not. Then he looked round at all the other customers. Not seeing anyone known to him, he sat at the free table by the open window. The waiters all pretended not to notice his existence, guessing, probably correctly, that Kevork had no money and had come in hoping only that he would find some friend willing to pay for him, or that he might obtain more credit.

A short man with a thin moustache and a beard came in, and the waiters began taking notice. The newcomer looked round arrogantly at all the other customers and, to the waiters's astonishment, chose to approach Kevork's table.

"May I have this seat, Baron Kevork?"

Kevork looked with surprise at the stranger, sensing that he could probably rely on his having a generous pocket. He greeted him very politely.

"Yes, please, you're welcome."

"You don't know me, but I know you," said the new customer sitting himself comfortably on the opposite seat. "Well, how are you getting on? Have you already ordered anything?"

Kevork made a slight movement, only one small movement which meant all the following: yes and no, I was waiting for you to order, I have no money, what can I order? The newcomer realized only one thing from Kevork's expressive gesture: the former teacher had not ordered anything because he did not have a penny in his pocket.

It could be surmised that Kevork's poverty-stricken state had made the new arrival happy, as he immediately became the host at the table and turned to the waiter who was hovering in front of him, ready for his order.

"Aghavard –"

"Buyurun, Baron Ishkhan."

"What's this 'buyurun'? Can't you say 'at your service'?"

"A weakness for Turkish phrases!" Kevork declared loudly in a triumphant voice, feeling that he could not find a more convenient way to pay this Aghavard back for the many gross and petty insults he had suffered from him. Then to underline his supremacy, at least for this once and making use of the favourable occasion, he cast reproachful eyes on the waiter, and repeated, "A weakness for Turkish phrases."

The former teacher was no more than a zero in the waiter's eyes, but now there appeared a one near the zero and so the big 0 became 10. The waiter now listened to their orders respectfully and hurried to carry them out, although in truth it would be better to say 'his orders' and not 'their orders', because Kevork only took part by nodding his head.

A little later, the table was covered with fresh bread, salad, boiled eggs, fish, pasturma, and a high-necked bottle of raki dominating all of them. While the waiter was laying the table, Kevork felt that he was in seventh heaven. 'This is Baron Ishkhan, the famous Baron Ishkhan. Why did he take a seat at my table? What does he want?'

"I'm from Van too, my friend," said Ishkhan raising his glass of raki, "but I was born in the Caucasus, where I fell into a lot of whirlpools.

"Yes, getting into trouble is not good," said Kevork, emptying his glass in one gulp.

"Did I say trouble?" asked Ishkhan with a smile. "Never mind, they're the same. Where there's a whirlpool, there's usually trouble as well."

He stopped speaking and then asked, "Why did you give up teaching, Baron Kevork?"

"Ask the headmaster," murmured Kevork, re-filling the glasses.

"I have asked him." Ishkhan broke an egg and began to shell it.

Kevork looked at him, and wondered whether he was serious.

"I have asked him, " repeated Ishkhan.

"Damn him," said Kevork, avoiding the issue.

"He answered that you drank too much."

"Drink – don't drink," Kevork sneered, "Doesn't Sultan Abdul Hamid drink? Doesn't Khrimian Hairig drink? And Kapamadjian, and –¿"

"I said the same to him," exclaimed Ishkhan. "Everybody drinks. It isn't right to fire someone from their job for drinking, is it¿ He also said, however, that you had left without giving any explanation."

"Well, what would he have wanted me to do¿" said Kevork, getting heated. "Was that some sort of religious-political meeting where I would be required to explain myself, as if I was being questioned by the Bolis Patriarchate¿ I'm Kevork Muradkhanian and I can twist three such headmasters round my little finger."

"Yes, you're right," agreed Ishkhan, "but –"

"What 'but'¿" said Kevork impatiently, "we're four brothers, four guns, and we can roar all over the world."

"I know, I know," Ishkhan again tried gently to protest. "But in order to roar, it's not enough to have a throat. Any madman can do that. I know your three brothers. One of them roars in Bolis, the other in the village, and the third in the big market of Van. All of them are rich. And what about you¿ Where will your roaring take place¿"

"I'm Aboghossian," Kevork began trying to excuse himself, but Ishkhan interrupted him.

"Boghossian, A-Boghossian! These are stale stories. Now there's neither of those names. If you want to become a man, join us."

Oriental music was still pounding out in the Askeran restaurant. The musicians are singing and playing Turkish music. The customers sitting round the tables are already well aroused and are singing along with the musicians.

> "Aman doctor, djanum, gyozum doctor
> Derdime bir chare . . ."

So there it is. The weak rely on God and the saints, the ill go to the doctor, the poor beg. And Kevork¿ Kevork Muradkhanian – son of a rich man, accustomed to a wealthy life – what should he do¿ How, and with what income, should he support his house and raise his spirits to forty-per-cent proof or more¿ There was a time, when he could get home in fifteen minutes from Khatch Street. In just fifteen minutes! His pawned Zenith watch could have proved it.

But now, it often takes him no less than two hours to get home. How can he possibly get home early, when who should he see coming straight down towards him from the Kondachian sisters' school, but someone from whom he borrowed four gold pieces six months ago. He turns back and moves away in order not to meet the frightful creditor. He passes down the Shatvorians' street, reaches Atchem-Khacho's house, goes down to the Norashen church square. And there he notices, with horror, that leaving the church is yet another from whom he borrowed even more money eight months ago. So Kevork now has to hide his great height behind the willows and follow him, and so wander off in some wrong direction to get home another way. He reaches home tired and broken, swearing at all his creditors and often not sparing even the borrowers.

"Join us, get up onto the stage, make a man of yourself We're soon going to solve the Aghtamar problem, you could be quite useful there."

"What – do you want me to be consecrated as a learned priest?"

"Priest? What priest? You'll become so well-known that even the Bishop of the Aghtamar will quake before you."

"But that's impossible," exclaimed the former teacher taking the bottle and re-filling his glass. "I seem to be the only drinker here, Baron Ishkhan. You've put all the burden of drinking onto me."

Ishkhan pretended not to hear.

"Then your gun will fire like your brothers' guns. Long, long ago, I took some notice of you. You were walking in the street like a scared man, depressed and sad as if the weight of the world was on your shoulders. What's up, man? Even supposing you can't teach any more, you remain healthy and strong in body."

"Am I to become a porter carrying heavy loads?" Kevork was almost angry.

"Who said that? Are there only two jobs on earth – teaching and carrying loads?"

"Very well, just tell me what to do," exclaimed Kevork raising his hands towards the wooden ceiling of the restaurant, "I'll do anything you want to get out of this dreadful situation."

"Join us, and put your fate into my hands," said Ishkhan in a low, secretive voice.

"Very well, I trust you."

"Word of honour?"

"Word of honour!"

Ishkhan took a paper out of a wallet from his inner pocket. He called the waiter, "Aghavard!"

"Buyurun."

"Damn you and your 'buyurun'. Bring some ink and a pen."

Ishkhan took the pen, carefully dipped it into the ink, wrote down just 'Kevork Muradkhanian' after the word 'I' and put the paper in front of Kevork.

"Sign, please."

The former teacher's heart trembled. What signature? Why sign? He looked at the paper, on which there was some writing. At the top he read a preamble: 'Keep secrets and maintain discipline'. Then he read: 'There is no revolution without blood'. He did not like this 'blood' at all. Then: 'I, Kevork Muradkhanian, promise... must... otherwise...' They were all heavy commitments, not just light promises.

'A drowning man will clutch at a straw,' thought Kevork. Another minute passed and Kevork saw his own signature at the bottom of the paper. The ink was red and he did not like that, either. In a few more seconds, the ink dried and the paper disappeared into Ishkhan's wallet, and the wallet into his pocket.

There was an appropriate silence.

"So, this is how things look." said Ishkhan.

"And this is how this looks!" added Kevork, looking sadly at the empty bottle.

"Now you're a figure, a great revolutionary figure." Ishkhan pronounced the words distinctly, one by one, looking at the former teacher admiringly, as if seeing him for the first time. "Kharasho!"

"What does 'kharasho' mean?"

"It means 'good' in Russian."

"Kha-ra-sho," drawled Kevork, and they laughed. "Kha-ra-sho."

"I have to go now," said Ishkhan, looking serious. "You'll pay?"

One of Kevork's cheeks blushed and the other went white; the chair rocked under him and he would have probably fallen down if the skilled fisher of revolutionary figures had not picked out a few silver coins out of his pocket and put them in front of him.

"Three medjidie, you can spend it. We'll give you some other tasks when required. A good re-payment!"

He disappeared, and Kevork looked around. It was not a dream. 'Three medjidie, Kevork!' he thought, 'attractive goods find buyers easily.'

"Aghavard!" he called out.

The waiter approached and stood in front of him.

"Aghavard, keep secrets and maintain discipline."

"That's right, Baron Kevork."

"Aghavard."

"Buyurun."

"Damn you and your 'buyurun'. Listen, there's no revolution without blood."

"There isn't, indeed there isn't."

"Bring me half a bottle of raki."

"Certainly."

"Kharasho!"

The waiter rushed away. Kevork was astonished. The only thought still remaining in his befuddled brain was why the waiter had become so polite to him, and how had he known that he had got money to pay the bill. He had not noticed that the waiter had seen his two customers from where he was standing and had noticed that the well-known Baron Ishkhan had passed several medjidie to the customer who was nearly always short of money, and that Baron Kevork was suddenly not only able to pay this bill, but also perhaps able to settle his old debts.

When Kevork raised his heavy head, he saw not only a new bottle of raki before him on the table, but also Gabriel Demirtchian. He was neatly dressed, rosy-cheeked, with a pointed moustache, and with the local, weekly paper, *Van-Tosp*, in his hand.

"When did you come?" asked Kevork, almost happily, since a friend he could drink with had turned up.

"You mean come into the world?" Gabriel smiled, showing his white teeth. "That was in 1876 –"

"Oh no, not that."

"Come here? Well, I've been here for a long time. We were sitting in that corner. There was Ghevond Effendi Khanjian, Rouben Effendi Shatvorian –"

"In a word, you only deal with Effendis. Fill up the glasses and let's have a little drink."

"I'll do that," agreed Gabriel and filled up Kevork's glass.

"Fill your own glass, too."

"I shouldn't drink."

"Why," asked the former teacher in great surprise.

"I have indigestion and a bladder infection."

"What infection? What bladder? Come on, let's drink."

Gabriel inwardly laughed a lot at Kevork, who, although a teacher, knew nothing of anatomy. Gabriel did not fill his glass. He believed that one ought to have a strong will, and so he made an effort.

"Fill the glasses, man."

"No, Effendi, I'll get sick and die."

The truth was that Gabriel had been instructed by Rouben and Ghevond to take a seat at Kevork's table, not to drink a drop himself, but to find out in detail the subject of the conversation between the 'drunken idiot' and Ishkhan, who had appeared so unexpectedly in the restaurant. Of course, Gabriel could have ignored the Effendis' order and had a drink. However, after this talk with Kevork, he had to appear before them at Rouben Shatvorian's house and report.

'They'll probably smell my breath,' thought Gabriel. 'But I could say that I had one glass after finishing the conversation and leaving Kevork.' He did not recall quite how he took the bottle and filled his glass up as well. "Here's to you!"

"Oh, well done," shouted Kevork, "I don't like over-cautious people, you could hardly have avoided being included in my list of the over-cautious – but you recovered quickly. Let's drink up."

And the friends emptied their glasses in one gulp. Kevork banged his glass down on the table. Then, lifting one shoulder and shutting an eye, he began to sing in Turkish at the top of his voice and in tune with the band:

> "The clouds will soon pass by,
> They will have gone by noon."

"Your voice is too loud, Baron Kevork."
"You're right, let's make it quieter:

> "Hanum, don't be shy,
> Come to me sometime soon."

And this time he had lowered his voice to a murmur.

"Hey!", the voice of the former teacher and the present revolutionary figure got louder. "The owner of this dining hall is Armenian, the customers are all Armenian, and the musicians are Armenian as well. Why are they singing in Turkish?"

Gabriel turned pale, he wanted to stand up, but when he noticed a newly opened bottle, his feet did not obey him. He looked around. Four Turkish officials were sitting in the far corner. Of course, the voice of this drunken idiot could not reach them, but who knows whether there was not some un-Armenian Armenians among all these people, who might report Kevork's outburst, 'Why are they singing in Turkish?', to them. And then the Chief of Police, Agyah Effendi, would ask, 'Who was sitting at his table?' The answer would be, 'Gabriel Demirtchian'. And Agyah would surely then shout for them to be both taken to jail.

Gabriel could scarcely believe his eyes. The police chief Agyah, with his thin moustache and pale face, really did enter the café with his shining sabre flapping on his knee. He approached the Turkish officials who welcomed him cheerfully.

"Buyurun, Effendi, buyurun."

"Agyah, Agyah get into the Pagyah," Kevork shouted at the top of his voice through the noise of the band and the customers sitting at the dining tables.

The entrance of the police chief, and Kevork's insulting ditty – known to all the people of Van, young and old, who told it one another only in amused whispers – got Gabriel completely up onto his feet. He hurriedly put the weekly paper in his pocket, bade a regretful farewell to the half-empty bottle and rushed out of the restaurant without even completing the task he had been set.

Leaning upon the soft cushions and muddling up faces and events, teacher Kevork told Vramian how he had happened to become an agent and find himself on the island of Aghtamar.

"What did you do on the island?" asked Vramian.

Kevork's facial muscles creased with anxiety.

"I was drinking so-called raki in the ship's cabin. I didn't go onto the island," he answered like a criminal giving evidence in court.

"And then?"

"That naive idiot, Gabriel Demirtchian, sat next to me to draw information out of me and repeat it to his Effendis, but I made him leave the café in a hurry. Keep secrets! There's no revolution without blood!"

"So you had a drink in the ship's cabin. And then?" Vramian repeated his inquiry.

"Then – then I fell asleep."

"And then?"

"There isn't any 'then'. I fell asleep and had some bad dreams." He started weeping like a child.

"What did you dream?"

"I dreamt that I slaughtered an old man – a bearded old man," sighed the former teacher Kevork, weeping bitterly. Then he stopped speaking, groaned and fell asleep as if he had fainted – or he fainted as if he had fallen asleep.

Chapter 9

The bells were ringing. The winter sun was lightly warming the back of Ohannes' neck. The white snow shone with blinding intensity and Ohannes' tinkling donkey also sparkled on its way to market. It would have seemed to anyone looking on from afar that

Ohannes, clothed in black, was floating bizarrely through snowy-white clouds towards the town, towards the market.

In the morning, the wide street leading to the town was full of people on their way to work. People were hurrying to market: the rich merchants on their own sledges or on their thorough-bred donkeys, the shopkeepers walking sedately and slowly, and the craftsmen – simply dressed carpenters, furniture-makers and shoemakers – walking rapidly on their own, each of them absorbed in his own thoughts and plans, joys and sorrows. A stranger might think they did not know each other, but when one of them sneezed, good wishes could be heard from all sides.

"God bless you, Baron Sahag... Bless you, Baron Sahag."

"Thank you, thank you very much. God bless you, too," Sahag Djankoyan would reply to his left and right, front and back.

He tried at least to muffle a second sneeze, not to disturb his fellow-craftsmen again. He failed to do so and sneezed again, more heavily. This time, however, everyone around him – as if by common consent – assumed a second blessing would be too much and kept quiet. But Sahag, recovering after being overcome by the force of his sneezing, still said, "Thank you, I am grateful. God bless you."

Ohannes' donkey was behaving quite oddly that day. And one could not help being surprised, because the white thoroughbred sometimes rushed forward, if not like an arrow at least like a winged angel, and then sometimes slowed down and walked unwillingly, as if on its way to Miso's slaughter-house to be killed. But it would be unfair if the poor animal was blamed, since, in fact, it was not any less astonished at the behaviour of its master. Ohannes, either released the rein and struck senseless blows on the animal's sides, or drew the reins in tight enough to cause its lips to bleed, and make it go slower than necessary. At this point we should note that an alert reader would not be surprised at Ohannes' erratic behaviour: it was quite clear that when our epic hero remembered his brother, Hampartsoum, he became distressed and drew in the reins as he slouched in the saddle. BHhhhhhut when he remembered Vramian, he took the Hats' letter out and tore it up.

"Hats!" Ohannes murmured to himself, "I don't care a damn for your Hats." He released the reins and set off towards the market in the centre of the town, feeling free from the threats of the Hats.

The Citadel loomed ahead: an enormous, majestic monolith of heavy, reddish stone, stretching from west to east with winding battlements, mysterious holes, and magical, carved stone doors that were decorated with cuneiform inscriptions, which have never been deciphered.

The fortress protected the town; it was silent and dumb, not responding to any sound. The voices rising up from the town seemed to die out in the gloomy, ancient Urartian surroundings. Nor did it seem to have any organic connection with the living, laughing and crying, town. It was of some other world, an enigmatic, dreadful stone wonder, which would turn anyone climbing it into a stone sculpture. Even an eagle flying over it would fall on the teeth of the battlements and turn to stone. The Citadel, the fortress of Van!

Ever since Ohannes had lived in terror of the Hats, he had had strange thoughts every time he passed the Citadel. For instance, it seemed to him that the Hats lived within the stone doors of the fortress. At night, when everybody was in bed, the doors opened and they would come out secretly to conspire together, spread threatening letters and gather gold; then they would hide themselves again inside the fortress and the stone doors would silently close. But today, Ohannes completely ignored the Citadel, while laughing behind his moustache. His donkey, that swaggering angel without wings, entered the town. Ohannes looked back once more at the enchanted fortress, and it seemed to him that if he dismounted and gave it a hefty kick, it would collapse like a matchstick house.

The market of Van. Ohannes could be only five steps away from the market and yet be unable to see it. What a miracle! Perhaps it could be seen from above. Yet if somehow you climbed up to the top of the minaret of the Ulu mosque and looked down, there would still be no sign of a market. The most you could see would be an enormous expanse of flat roofs and glass skylights. Yet, under those roofs, the huge, covered market of Van was buzzing.

If we were lucky enough to enter the market together with Ohannes, we would find ourselves in some other world. It was really very prosperous, the Van market, amazingly rich and large. If you went to the tailors' quarter – a covered street with workshops on both sides – the noise of the Singer sewing machines followed you until you passed on to the shoemakers' quarter, where it was not so noisy. Here the toes and heels of shoes were being tapped – tak, tak, tak – and some of the shoemakers sang. They sang about love, about anxiety over the nation's troubles and sorrows, and they tapped the toes and heels appropriately, depending on how great was the sorrow. Often they hit neither toes nor heels but something else.

The noisiest quarter was certainly that of the tin-smiths. Here reigned a noise – chnk-cho, chnk-cho, chnk-cho – that could even drown a revolver shot. You passed from there into the world of locksmiths and carpenters, took a deep breath and felt the pleasant smell of damp and drying wood. Here was the only coffin-maker in Van, deaf Patur, whose deafness had given rise to funny stories. These tales spread round all parts of the market at telegraphic speed and in the evening they turned up in every house in all the districts of the town – on foot, or by carriages in the summer and sledges in winter.

Ohannes parked his donkey in the khan – for which he paid ten paras – and entered the market. When he passed the coffin-maker Patur, the man became flustered and wanted to offer his respects to his well-known countryman. He leaped up, ran to Ohannes, bowed needlessly low and asked with a mocking air, "Can I help you, Baron?" Ohannes looked at the coffin-maker and at his various sized coffins. He recalled the only way this Patur could serve him. He remembered Hampartsoum and chided Patur quietly: "You serve yourself, my lad, serve yourself."

Approaching his own shop, he saw Set and the two assistants. Ohannes did not like the way they were staring at him, as if they had agreed to determine his mood in order to greet him appropriately. There was no doubt that they had heard about the death of their master's brother. The expression on Ohannes' face which varied from joy to sorrow astonished them They were confused –

should they rejoice or be sad?

"Set."

"Yes, sir."

"How's trade?"

"So-so. In Bolis –"

"What's up in Bolis?"

"In Bolis ... Oh well, let's leave it," and Set squirmed.

"I don't want to hear the name of Bolis," said Ohannes, emphasising each word seperately, but without raising his voice, "Bolis is a city of prostitutes. I don't want to hear any more."

"I'm sorry –"

"Haven't the goods arrived yet?"

"Where from?"

Ohannes was caught out and nearly answered with the banned word, but soon recovered.

"Why do you want me to utter the name of that damned city?"

"Sorry, once more I beg your pardon. No, Baron Ohannes, the goods are on their way."

"Have you anything else to say?"

"No, sir."

"Give each of the boys three measures of cotton and take two gold pieces for yourself." He wondered why he had done that. Was it for Hampartsoum's soul, or was it for being saved from the Hats. He could not decide on the answer.

"Thank you in advance," Set touched his forehead with his hand.

"Everything's fine – in advance. I'm going."

And he walked off with slow steps, accepting one greeting, refusing two others and avoiding looking at people's faces.

Eventually he arrived at Simon's shop. Simon was sitting at a large table in a small room separated by windows from the main shop, looking with one eye on the senior shop assistant, the cashier, the other assistants and the customers coming in and out, and looking wryly with the other eye at his black worry-beads. What a coincidence! At that very moment, he was thinking about Ohannes, about his brother Hampartsoum's death, about his other brother, teacher Kevork, and about how the latter had had a hand in the terrible robbery at Aghtamar. How could Ohannes dare to show up among people? One brother dissolute, and the other a killer!

He rustled the beads between his two palms, then threw them onto the table as if wishing to get rid of bad thoughts. He wanted to change the drift of his thoughts, but at that moment he saw, through the windows, Ohannes himself walking towards his room. Were they carefree, or confused, steps? While Simon was trying to resolve this problem, Ohannes came in.

"Oh, I was just thinking about you. You're welcome, you're welcome. Have a seat, let's hear your news. Vostanig!" he called his senior assistant, "Vostanig!"

"Two coffees – in no time," short and broad-shouldered Vostanig shouted back, considering it needless to come in, since he always guessed his master's wishes correctly. This time, however, he was mistaken.

"Sit down, sit down, Baron Ohannes. It's cold. Armenians – in, Turks – out. Vostanig –"

Vostanig came in.

"Bring us some raki, nuts and raisins."

"And coffee afterwards?"

"Just listen to me," said Ohannes, "only two coffees, now and at the end. No need to bring any raki."

"Baron Ohannes, you're my guest. Don't meddle in your host's business."

"Oh, I didn't think it was necessary."

"It is, it is, Baron Ohannes. It's cold, let's warm ourselves."

Vostanig understood that his master was not ordering the raki for show, but that he really wanted to treat his countryman. He looked into the eyes of his master once more. He was experienced, he had been ordered before to bring raki, just like now. He had duly brought it, the master had drunk with his guest and after the guest had left in high spirits, he had called out:

"Why did you bring the raki?"

"Didn't you order it, sir?"

"Well, what of it? I ordered it out of courtesy. I offered, but he declined. You should have brought only coffee and that would have been the end of it."

However, this time, ordering raki was not a matter of courtesy. His master really wanted to treat Ohannes.

They sat down and were silent. Why were they silent? Was there nothing to talk about? Of course, there was a lot, but here they sat, competing in their silence. They did not find the silence inconvenient for they were waiting for the drink to be brought in by Vostanig, after which that would free the boneless one, called a tongue. Ohannes, while swallowing the first glass of raki, wondered whether Simon knew about Hampartsoum. Of course he knew – he answered his own question, rubbing a raisin between his thumb and forefinger, looking at Simon's face and trying to catch his eye, but in vain.

"From Stamboul," he began, but then coughed, "what's this – something's stuck in my throat?"

"Take it easy," said Simon and tapped twice on the back of his honoured compatriot, "Yes, you were speaking of Stamboul – of Stamboul."

"I had a letter from Stamboul."

"What about?" asked Simon with studied indifference.

"I don't know." He pulled out his handkerchief, put it back again, took a deep breath and almost shouted, "Our Hampartsum –"

He could not continue. Again he took out the handkerchief, but this time he raised it over his head and waved it back and forth like fine dancers brandishing scarves.

"What's happened to Hampartsoum, man?"

"He died."

"Who?"

"Hampar –"

"Have you gone crazy? You're not drunk. Why should Hampartsoum have died?"

"I don't know why he died?" whispered Ohannes like a petulant child.

After the next customer had left, Vostanig peered through the window with one eye into the room and saw the host and his guest. The guest seemed to be crying and the host was looking at him in surprise. Vostanig smiled. The expression on his master's face was known to him. He usually showed this kind of surprise when a customer informed him that the commodity he was selling for five gold pieces, was being sold for four by Djidechian. It was incredible!

"It's impossible. Why should Baron Hampartsoum...? Aman, Aman! There must be some mistake."

"No, no, there's no mistake. Hampartsoum is dead."

Simon stretched his hand towards the table, apparently looking for the bottle of raki.

"What can I say, Baron Ohannes?" The host picked up his glass. "I'll be brief, and you can fill in the details. I can say for sure that if he hadn't gone to Stamboul, he wouldn't have died. Both Stamboul and Van can be considered towns, but you see, Stamboul looks to its markets, Van to its monasteries. Van is a town where a young boy and girl can only kiss each other through a keyhole. While Stamboul, Baron Ohannes, is Sodom and Gomorrah – a veritable Tower of Babel. I lived in Bolis for two months."

He stopped speaking, looked vaguely into the distance, his face expressing his inner uncertainty. Simon quickly swallowed his raki and drew his fez down his forehead.

After the next customer had left, the senior assistant Vostanig peered through the window and did not believe his eyes. For the first time in his life, he saw something that could be called host and guest talking nose to nose. From a distance, it really seemed they were speaking with their noses literally touching. The speaker – it should be made clear – was Simon. He was telling Ohannes something with tactful care and Ohannes was listening with great interest. Then Simon laughed loudly; Ohannes also laughed – though his laugh was somewhat hollow – and shook his head. Simon tapped Ohannes' knee with his hand and spoke again.

"So, Baron Ohannes, Stamboul is a place to live in. And where you live, you may also die. I'll say in short and you'll understand more –"

Ohannes' brain suddenly brightened up as if by lightning and he remembered the woman with shining, black eyes whom he had seen the day before. "Aman, Aman!" he murmured, wiping his moist forehead with a dry handkerchief. "I met Vramian," he said casually, while slowly sipping raki.

"In your dream? It's good to see a great man in a dream."

"I showed them the Hats' letter."

"May your dream come true –"

"Have you any of those dogs' letters?"

"Sure, I've got one."

"Give it to me."

"What do you want with it?"

"Don't worry. Give it me, I won't eat it."

Simon groaned but pulled a bunch of silver keys out of his pocket, chose one of the small ones and, without looking away from Ohannes, skillfully opened the right drawer of his desk, pulled it out, found the required paper with nimble fingers and handed it to Ohannes.

"Here it is. So, satisfy your curiosity."

"Damn both your curiosity and mine," murmured Ohannes. He opened the paper, then folded it. He tore it into two parts, then into four, then into eight, then into sixteen.

"What are you doing, man?" Simon said, not believing his eyes.

"I'm carrying out Baron Vramian's instruction." Ohannes threw up the pieces of paper, which shook apart and fell on the floor.

After the next customer left, the senior assistant Vostanig again looked through the window. This time the scene had changed. Now, Ohannes was speaking and Simon was listening to him. Then Simon jumped up from his seat, embraced Ohannes and kissed him. Ohannes tried to get out of his arms, but Simon embraced him more tightly. Then he dropped his fez on the table and filled the glasses.

"I'm very grateful to you, Baron Ohannes. You've brought me very good news."

"I don't know whether to laugh or cry."

"Haven't you heard the words of Paramaz? No laughter, no tears – let's increase in number."

"Increase?"

"Don't you know Armenian history? There were millions of Armenians in the time of Tigran the Great. And now? If they massacre the people of Van, there will be less than half a million left."

"The situation is bad." Ohannes wanted to end the conversation.

"It's serious rather than bad. Let's drink one more glass and go – go to Baron Panos."

They drank and became rather flushed and cheerful. Absorbed in their thoughts they paced the length and width of the office several times and then went to the door in silence. Ohannes wanted to give way here to Simon, but the latter stood and pushed Ohannes forward.

"Vostanig, if anyone wants me, tell him that I'm with Baron Panos."

The two worthy citizens of Van were not walking, but hurrying down the streets.

"Aren't you sweating?" asked a concerned Ohannes, who was himself perspiring.

"No, I'm not yet so old. And you?"

"Just a little, because of the raki." He wiped his moist brow.

They were racing ahead, while that human ribbon – the river of red fezzes – streamed away beside them.

Panos was sitting at a desk in the corner of a large shop, with the still and inexpressive look of a Babylonian statue – a clean-shaven Baron Nebuchadnezzar in a fez. Though facing the entrance, he did not seem to notice his commercial and political friends enter the shop. They looked around them. Carpets! Carpets hanging like curtains on the walls, or piled on top of each other, hundreds of carpets of various sizes and periods, all very different. Panos was alone in his shop with his carpets. He had few customers, often one would not be seen for days, but when one did come he would leave without a significant part of the gold that had been in his purse. One of the lamps hanging from the ceiling shone on Panos' aged and wrinkled face.

"Good morning, Baron Panos." But Panos did not hear. "Good morning, Baron Panos," repeated Ohannes, this time more loudly.

"Don't shout, I'm not deaf," complained Panos, in a voice

seemingly rising up from the depth of centuries.

Simon stepped forward: "Good Lord! Baron Panos, what's happened?"

Panos moved at last, rubbed his eyes with both hands, and only then seemed to notice his guests.

"Good morning. Have a seat. Take no notice of me, I've gone off my head."

Simon tried to joke: "Oh, have you a head to go off?"

"You're right. What head? We don't even have a pistol. Only those villains have weapons."

"What villains?" Simon wanted to be precise.

"The Hats," shouted Panos, "the Hats." He repeated the words with special emphasis and drew out from his inner pocket a letter which he threw onto the table like a playing card. "This is not a personal or a national matter. This is daylight robbery."

Ohannes and Simon looked at each other and smiled. Simon winked slightly at Ohannes, who approached the table and picked up the terrible letter.

"God bless the soul of Baron Hampartsoum, who died and saved himself from the troubles of this world. What are you doing, man?" said Panos.

Ohannes, the man in question, threw up the torn pieces of paper. They opened, quivered and slowly floated down onto the carpet.

Simon replied this time: "He's carrying out Baron Vramian's order."

When Panos' understanding caught up with that of his commercial and political friends, he jumped up from his seat, put on his coat and declared, "Let's go to the Askeran. I'm paying for the meal."

They left the carpet shop in high spirits. Panos noisily closed the various shutters, fastened them with small, medium and large locks, checked them all, and they set off.

The passers-by could not help paying attention to this procession of the three worthy merchants through the labyrinth of the covered market. The market's alleyways had seen them separately many times, but now the three of them were walking together, side by side. They were moving as a unit, like a wall topped with three fezzes, and it seemed that if they split up they would disappear under some strange spell and only the three black-tasselled fezzes would continue to float along the labyrinth of the covered market.

The majestic procession of this worthy trio halted not far from the southern exit of the market, at the khan. As the reader may recall, this was the resting place for the few horses and many donkeys. The horses were harnessed to sledges in winter and to carriages in summer to bring the better-off merchants to the market – men like Hadji-Bey Bedros Kapamadjian, Kevork Djidechian, and the Shahbaghtian brothers. The admirable manager of this worthy establishment, Kurd Msto, who was gifted with the most awful ugliness, lived in the khan. One could not help noticing that he had an especially gentle attitude towards the white donkeys, but only respect towards the black and the grey ones, while horses did not interest him at all. Kurd Msto, of whom the most daring child would be frightened, saw his well-known customers from afar and rushed in to saddle the donkeys.

The three people in fezzes were going along the central avenue back into Aikesdan, sitting comfortably on their long-eared donkeys. They were silent, as if things were going to change completely and become more pleasant, anticipating that they were going to get warm in the atmosphere of a hot fire. They were silent, and that silence became more comfortable when it began to snow with large, cotton-like flakes. But that silence was probably unbearable and suffocating for the long-eared thoroughbreds.

In the Haykavan square, Ohannes' donkey slowed down a little, set its face towards Mt Varag, breathed in deeply and heaved up such a bray that Ohannes jogged up and down on its back several times. The other donkeys followed suit and reacted with almost the same persistence. A little later there was silence again, except for the tinkling bells which had always been part if it.

"Where are we going?" asked Ohannes, as if just to break the silence, although both he – and the reader – knew that they were invited to the Askeran restaurant. Panos had said he would be paying for the meal. But, no, Ohannes did not ask his question just to break the silence. He knew very well that one could not rely on Panos' promise. He could quite easily stop his donkey in Khatch Square and, rubbing his belly, say, "Oh, what's this, my stomach's hurting. Oh! Oh! Let's go to the Askeran some other time. Let's go home now – farewell."

Yes, Ohannes had meant to check whether or not Panos had repented of inviting them. Simon understood Ohannes' thought completely and, sharing his concern, he said: "Yes, it's very pleasant to sit in the café in such cold weather."

They did not need to be so sceptical. Panos had not today even thought of breaking his promise. What was more important was that he was free of fear of the Hats. Several gold coins might leave his pocket, but that would be no great loss. Then, however, it occurred to him to wonder why the others should not also pay for the meal? Was he the only one who had got rid of the Hats? Would it not be fairer if expenses were shared among the three of them? He wondered whether he should make a slight hint now. No, an awkward situation could arise, perhaps it would be easier at the table when the bill came.

As they came closer to Aikesdan, the street became noisier. Here were the Turkish baths where the soldiers crowded round, waiting for their turn. On the opposite side there was the shop of Arshak Dzetotian, the photographer, with a sign that read 'Arshak Dzituni' – yes, the mistake had been corrected. The bakery of Minas Palabeghian was still far away, but one could already smell the wonderful aroma of fresh bread. The group of three fez-wearers revived. Here was the bakery. Minas had a surprisingly long, blond moustache, as if to explain his surname. He had smiling and gentle, blue eyes.

Panos went up to him: "Baron Minas, give us two loaves of warm bread."

Minas tugged at the tips of his long, blond moustache with both hands.

"Oh, Baron Panos, are you having a wedding party?" He released the tips of his moustache that twisted like question-marks in double surprise. "A wedding?"

"What! A wedding? Do you think I'm Jesus of Nazareth to feed my wedding guests with only two loaves of bread?"

"Oh, Baron Panos!"

Panos took two warm and fragrant loaves, paid twenty paras, and joined his cavalry troop just when butcher Miso was grabbing a white goat, his next victim for slaughter. But this time, Miso's victim – possibly gifted with natural optimism – did not guess what its fate was going to be and came up meekly. Miso was amazed at such rare innocence. But his amazement did not last long. The condemned goat sneezed twice and it became clear that the goat was neither innocent, nor optimistic. It simply had a cold and could not sense the smell of animal blood on Miso.

There was no doubt that if butcher Miso were a politician or a journalist, he would write a leading article in the evening and send it to Bolis, Tiflis, Paris, Boston, or Geneva, to be published not to all, but only within one of these cities. Wait a moment: the reader, who does not have a cold but is really quite innocent, might well ask, "Why not to the local *Van-Tosp* or *Ashkhadank* weeklies?" It must therefore be explained that at that time Armenian nationalists lived in those particular cities and were brought in if needed. They published sensational patriotic newspapers there. Many of these politicians, and those trying to be like them, died for their motherland without ever seeing it. It was a miracle. Human history does not know of any case where a young man had been killed, or had committed a suicide, for a girl whom he had never seen.

We would like to say that if butcher Miso were indeed a politician or a journalist, he would certainly write an article – yes, a passionate article – comparing the Armenian people to a goat with a cold, which could not sense the terrible smell of blood closing in. And thanks to the fact that Miso was only a butcher and was illiterate, the Armenian people were spared, and that was why the patriotic foreign editors did not receive a fiery article containing the bitter truth.

Miso, together with his goat martyr, approached the three well-known travellers and turned to just one of them.

"Baron Ohannes, thank you very, very much."

"What for?" asked Ohannes in real astonishment.

"Baron Kevork paid his debt – with interest."

Ohannes understood. "Thank him, not me," he said and joined the fine duo to form a fine trio, that moved eastwards along Khatch Street. When they reached Vramian's house, they loosened their donkeys' bits and halted as if they had received a command from above or an instruction from below.

The whole town knew Vramian's two-storey house, with white walls, the wooden parts painted in blue. In front of the house was the second gas lamp in Van – no, the first gas lamp, because the second was at the door of Djevdet Bey, the governor of the province of Van. When it became known that Vramian had placed such a marvel in front of his door, the Armenians working at the governor's office assumed that the Turkish experts would not be able to solve the same technical problems and that the lamp placed at Djevdet's door would only get lit every so often. Djevdet, was said to have summoned his men and put them to shame. "The Armenians can manage to keep Vramoghlu's lamp lit even though they have no state, yet the great Ottoman Empire is not able to light even a lamp. You whoremongers!" Djevdet Bey had shouted – yes, he had sworn just like that, "Whoremongers!"

It was not difficult to guess why our worthy trio halted at Vramian's door. That house was for them today as a church is for a believer. Their faces were lit with joy and admiration.

"It's a fine house." The silence was broken this time by Ohannes, who really had the right – for a good reason, too – to express his opinion loudly.

"This is not a house, but a small palace," continued Simon in the second stage of the same right.

"The man sitting in that small palace is a minor king." Panos resolved the issue at a higher level and once more they directed their animals eastwards and hurried forward on twelve feet.

Here at last was the Askeran restaurant.

"Let's go!" grunted Ohannes, and he was the first to put his foot down on the ground. The others followed him, they tied the reins together and then all three donkeys to a willow tree. They went upstairs, shook off the snow and entered the restaurant without formality. They were tired.

The restaurant was almost empty. They went to the corner. The waiter approached, took their coats and went away. The two loaves bought by Panos were lying on the table.

"You were right to buy the bread – cheap and fresh," remarked Ohannes. Panos mumbled something like an agreement and they settled themselves comfortably on their chairs.

"I want to set a riddle," said Panos with a smile, taking up as much as he could of his part of the table, "What is it? I gave two and got back one."

Ohannes and Simon, both with tired eyes, began to think.

"I know," said Ohannes happily.

"Say it, please."

"I married off two daughters, then my son. That is –"

"That is –?"

"So, I married off my two daughters and acquired a daughter-in-law."

The three of them laughed heartily: Ohannes – ho, ho, ho, Simon – ha, ha, ha, and Panos – he, he, he.

"That's not bad," said Panos, "but it isn't my answer – he, he, he – no, that's not what I intended. Anyway, let's leave it. Aghavard! Aghavard!"

"Buyurun." The well-known Aghavard turned up, with his 'buyurun', which, as we already know, means 'at your service'.

"Take this bread, cut it up and bring it here while we're thinking."

"With pleasure," said Aghavard and rushed away with the bread.

"What shall we eat?" asked Panos.

It was amazing, but none of the three well-known merchants was thinking about eating, about the meal. Ohannes, was thinking that it was not so bad to come sometimes to the restaurant. He remembered the story told by Simon. The fact was that there were beautiful girls working in the cafés of Bolis. "It's not a girl, but really a rose," Simon had said, "one has to go to Bolis." He saw the rosy girls in his mind's eye, but then corrected himself. He thought they should have Hampartsoum's grave blessed – a mass... a rose.

As for Simon, he was alert. Panos had invited them to the restaurant for the first and the last time. Such a miracle would not happen again. He thought that they had to do their best to make the meal as expensive as possible. Meanwhile, Panos smoothed out his wrinkles, trying to think of a menu that would not be too expensive.

Aghavard brought the cut bread on a large, round plate, which he placed on the table and stood waiting for the order.

"Have you got jajik?" asked Panos.

"We have both jajik and cheese."

"I want the jajik."

Simon interfered casually as if his order was not considered so important: "Bring jajik, cheese with paprika, and some soudjuk, fish, olives. Oh, and bring pilaf with chicken, and some grilled kebab."

"Bring everything Baron Simon wants," confirmed Ohannes just to have said something as well. He was again absorbed in his own thoughts: 'a mass, a rose ... pilaf with chicken, Bolis ...'

It would not be correct to say that Simon's order did not make any impact on Panos. It would not be correct at all, but one would be unable to trace even the slightest muscular – or, to be more precise, cellular – twitch on his face, even were it under a microscope. However, something indeed quivered inside him, but externally he remained calm and indifferent.

"Now do you see what it meant when I said that I gave two and got back one?" asked Panos after Aghavard had rushed to the kitchen like Pegasus.

We consider it irrelevant to describe in detail this outstanding, unforgettable and wholesome dinner. We will only say that Panos' riddle (give two and get back one) concerned the two loaves, which were given to Aghavard to slice up and bring back. The suggestion was that he might steal one loaf and bring only one cut loaf back. We leave it to Panos' conscience, whether his accusation was true or whether it was a direct slander of the waiter. We will only say that the dinner proceeded in a warm atmosphere and with the highest level of conversation. Aghavard set out not only the required food, but also things that had not been ordered. He filled the empty bottles several times. It should be mentioned that the companions were eating with great appetite and drinking heavily. What were they talking about? About everything – about the economy and its ups and downs, about international problems and Khrimian, about the people who had arrived from the Caucasus and their mistaken policy, and, finally, about the villainous Hats. And here, in this place, their faces gleamed with joy; they took up their glasses and drank to Baron Vramian again and again. "Evallah!", they exclaimed.

The winter evening was weaving its grey apron like an invisible, huge weaver embracing the town of Van and its large and small suburbs. They suddenly noticed, almost simultaneously, that while engrossed in all this agreeable conversation they had not felt the hours pass and that it was now time to go home.

"I would say one thing," Ohannes said, "it's too early to go home. We aren't hens to perch so early, are we? Let's go –"

He stopped talking and looked at his table companions with an air of mystery.

"Where should we go?" asked Simon.

"To Baron-Bey-Effendi-Hadji Bedros Kapamadjian."

They saw the point. Simon and Panos immediately grasped the importance of Ohannes' suggestion. There really could not be any other reason for them to approach the Kapamadjian's smart house, a three-storey building buried behind poplars and willows. This stylish house had two entrances, the front door and a wide, iron gate through which the carriages and sledges in winter came in and out. Two similar, bronze lions, cat-sized but unnecessarily large and with almost human moustaches, sat on the iron gates. There were those, who, when passing by would stop and stare at one of the lions with befuddled eyes, until the lion took on the image of Bedros Bey-Hadji and shook its moustache at them.

The richest man in Van wielded power over the town. His name was spoken in every house. Bey-Effendi employed three housemaids, three servants, and a cook. His son, Set, used to go to school, to church, or to swim in the sea, in a carriage with a servant. Bey-Effendi had a brown moustache like the lions sitting on the iron gates; he was of medium height with an exaggerated and impressive stomach, a puckered neck, small, black eyes and large, white and soft, hands. His guest would respectfully approach his front gate, which had no knocker. What should he do? Knock at the gate with fist or foot to let them know about his arrival?

Oh, no, all Van knew that on the right of Kapamadjian's front gate there was a hole with an iron wire, which ended with a loop. This wire continued beyond the gate and changed into a rope of medium thickness that passed through a courtyard covered with trees and reached the actual door of the house, which had on its right a gleaming bell, looking just like a chamber pot. The end of this medium-thick rope was fastened to the tongue of the bell. Bey-Effendi's guest had to pull the iron wire two or three times, then the bell would ring and a servant would run to open up.

The fame of this wonderful bell had spread, not only in the town, but also in the surrounding villages. Here we should note one unusual fact. The impudence of the Van children was well-known to be considerable. They were not afraid of trashing the telegraph-poles with stones and so adding their own noise to the humming of telegraph wires. They knew this would reach Stamboul by those wires, right through to Sultan Abdul Hamid. Yes, any Van boy could put his lips against this pole and shout across the line between Van and Stamboul with a voice that could be heard by the Sultan – a telegraphed verbal curse addressed to him.

It did not matter which relative of the Sultan would then suffer: the most important thing was that the Van children were capable of performing such a heroic deed against the State. But despite this, the aforementioned bell, that was like a chamber pot, had not tempted the increasingly bold, younger generation. The teenagers hurrying to Norashen school looked with only one eye in the direction of the magic bell, the more courageous stopped for a moment, but nobody actually dared to take even a few steps towards the mysterious door of the mysterious house, which belonged to Baron-Bey-Effendi-Hadji Bedros Kapamadjian.

Simon put away his worry beads into his pocket: "Let's go. Let's go to the Bey, otherwise he may be offended if we ended up with five letters from the Hats."

"Bey-Effendi may well have received ten or twenty of them," Panos completed Simon's point.

"Yes, let's go. Let's go and make him as glad as we are. Aghavard!"

Ohannes was so inspired by, on the one hand, the thought of meeting Bey-Effendi-Hadji Kapamadjian, and on the other, with the taste of raki, that paying for the meal seemed to him as easy as floating up to the ceiling. That was why he addressed Aghavard with almost paternal warmth.

"Aghavard, my son, what's the bill?"

His two drinking companions, who were in the same emotional state, put their hands into their pockets simultaneously.

"Please, let me pay," begged Simon putting a gold coin on the table.

"Idle words," Panos raised his voice, "and an idle proposal. I invited you and I must pay."

"Eh, what invitation?" Ohannes was heated. "The restaurant isn't your house, is it?"

"Why are you insulting me, Baron Ohannes, why should my house be a restaurant?"

"He didn't say that to hurt you, man," interrupted Simon. "He simply wants to say that we're human too."

"Eh!" Panos lost patience, "who deprived you of the right to be human? I've brought you here, so I ought to pay. I'll pay the bill."

"Let the three of us pay." Ohannes wanted to negotiate, but at that moment Panos put a half gold piece in Aghavard's hand.

"Is that enough? Right, let's get going."

And now, our three heroes, travelling on twelve feet, were excited and pleasantly warm. The streets were dark and they faced into the cold wind. It seemed to Ohannes that it was his donkey's bells that were tinkling on the neck of Panos' donkey. "Halla, halla" he murmured and tried to find the stirrup. He could not find it, bent down and felt it. The stirrup had been shortened, it had risen up and was not in its usual place. Straining his brain a little, he realized that he was not sitting on his own donkey.

Panos was a prey to similar thoughts. As he was thin, his saddle was usually soft, and now he felt uncomfortable because his saddle was hard, more than hard. Before this it had seemed to him that the tinkling bells were on Ohannes' donkey, but now he pricked up his ears and realized they were on the donkey he was riding. Jingle, jingle, jingle: clearly, he was sitting on Ohannes' donkey.

'I hope he doesn't find out,' thought Ohannes, 'it's so hard to dismount and mount in such cold weather. When we leave Bey-Effendi's house we can get on our own donkeys.'

'What a stupid man he is,' thought Panos in turn, 'I hope he doesn't notice anything before we reach Bey-Effendi's house.'

Then, Simon made a discovery that made the others forget everything else. "My friends," Simon said in a panic, failing to keep up with the others, "my friends, this donkey's not mine."

What a fiasco! They tried to resolve the issue with their inebriated brains: Ohannes and Panos were also not on their own donkeys – so ...

Simon caught them up and just at that moment, as if by special request, a clipped moon showed up from behind the white clouds. Ohannes and Panos could not stifle their laughter. The issue clarified when Simon dismounted and saw the unfamiliar donkey illuminated in all its glory by the moon. It was a donkey with cropped tail, short, erect ears and an old saddle, a donkey with weatherbeaten face and eyes full of the aches of every donkey in the world.

"Baron Simon," exclaimed Ohannes, choking with laughter, "this donkey is the donkey of your donkey."

"Oh, no," added Panos, "Baron Simon made a mistake and mounted a rabbit."

"You've a right to laugh at me," muttered Simon under his breath. He looked round haphazardly as if seeking his lost donkey and suddenly noticed the one Ohannes was sitting on. Its long, white tail, decorated with black spots, was quite familiar and dear to him. He approached with trembling heart, held the lost donkey's head, looked into its eyes and smiled.

"Good Lord, you are sitting on my donkey, Baron Ohannes," he said in a low tone – the sort of tone in which one would speak in order not to wake a baby sleeping in its cradle.

Ohannes also whispered, "No. I'm on Baron Panos' donkey."

"Baron Ohannes," insisted Simon, "it isn't dark now, is it? The moon's bright. I recognise my donkey clearly."

"And Baron Panos' donkey?" inquired Ohannes, confused between the three donkeys.

"Isn't it obvious? They stole one of our donkeys at the restaurant and left us this poor one instead."

The problem was solved. Ohannes got down from the donkey and moved towards Panos, who was sitting asleep on the saddle with his head on his chest.

"Each take his own property," said Ohannes loudly.

There was a silence.

"Yes each to his own property," replied Simon, comfortably mounting his.

Panos was sleeping soundly. Ohannes shook Panos and embraced him in his arms. We have to say this was not done through love or desire. Without that precaution, Panos would have fallen into the snow, insensible of time and place, and in that case raising him would have required immense effort. That was why Ohannes embraced him as tightly as he could and kept him on the donkey, while trying to find a way of getting some simple thoughts across to Panos.

"Baron Panos, hey old man, get down, get down. Good Lord, get down old man."

Panos had vowed not to wake up.

Then Simon said loudly. "What are you doing? Do you imagine Bey-Effendi will sit up till midnight, waiting for us?"

A miracle occurred. Panos shook himself and raised his head. He looked around and by some inexplicable, inner strength grasped the importance of the point.

"Why have we stopped, why aren't we going on?" He got angry: "How shall we ever get there in such fits and starts?"

"Yes, Baron Panos, get down, get down. Let's each sit on our own property," Ohannes continued to exhort.

"Well," shouted Panos, "what's happened? Get down, get down? Here I am – I got down."

He really had got down, and half-sleep he approached the new donkey and mounted it effortlessly.

The three riders set off, There was a moment when, as if by command from above, their thoughts converged. How would Bedros Bey Kapamadjian take their visit? What would he say, how would he look? Here it should be mentioned unequivocally that none of our heroes had ever set foot in the house of that famous and great Bedros Bey. Not for the first time, they were flying on the wings of imagination into the house, to find themselves in the wealthy man's fine, large room, with its ceiling and floors covered with carpets. And Hadji-Bey was smiling: he was the roll of huge and thick oriental carpet, his moustache was the golden fringe of a Persian rug, and he was saying in a soft, carpet-like voice: 'Thanks be to God. May Vramian live long. Have a glass of brandy.'

With such thoughts they passed the Little Kyanderchi spring, passed by the Shatvorians' house and also the house of the Kondakchian sisters. Here was Norashen Street, with the faintly lit, narrow windows of the Norashen café, Atchem-Khacho's house, the Norashen and Sandghtian schools, and then Kapamadjian's renowned house.

They paid no attention to two dark shadows that came out of a café, passed through the snow-laden, leafless willows, and went up to the left side of the front door of Kapamadjian's brightly-lit house. But they did see, as if in daylight, a two-horse sledge glide through the gate and stop at the front door. Then everything happened very suddenly. The famous and almighty Bedros Bey, muffled in black fur coat and accompanied by two servants, came out of the front door and settled himself into the sledge, while the servants draped his legs with a soft rug, even though they were already clothed in fur.

What was he thinking at that moment? It was difficult to say. He was going to the house of Kevork Djidechian, one of the wealthy men of Van, where there was to be a grand party that night, at which not only eminent Armenians would be present, but also influential Turkish figures as a token of Armenian and Turkish friendship. Kusho's band would be there and the chef, Simon, had been especially invited to prepare grilled kebab. The so-called 'extreme' activists had already been intimidating people with their written threats, their bringing in arms from abroad and their appeals for armed rebellion. This party was, therefore, important because the American, Dr Ussher, the German representative, Herr Spörri, and the Italian Vice-Consul, Signor Spordoni, would all be there, and the Armenian and Turkish élites would be able to show them their solidarity and disavow the disloyal 'foreigners' who were sowing seeds of discord between the Ottoman state and the Armenian nation, between the free, equal and fraternal, families of the Armenian and Turkish people.

Perhaps Kapamadjian was engrossed in these very thoughts while settling himself comfortably in the sledge. The driver took his seat and, pursing his lips, prepared to whistle and shake the reins. The two servants stepped back to make way for the sledge, but at that moment, from behind the willows to the left of the front door, two revolver shots were fired and Bedros Bey-Effendi-Hadji Kapamadjian, wounded in his head with two bullets from ear to ear, stopped thinking at all. The two horses reared up with their usual whinny and sledge-driver could only exclaim one syllable to express his surprise and horror: "Ya!" This did not remain without response. No, there was a triple response from the three riders who had become involuntary witnesses of this tragedy. "Ya! Ya! Ya!"

The still warm body of the moderate and conservative Bedros Bey was taken up hastily to the second floor by the three servants. His mother began to lament and recount with mournful wails the whole biography of Bedros, her 'crown', up to the time when the villains had appeared, and then about the evil letters that had unexpectedly arrived. She even described all the physical and spiritual attributes of the master of the house.

We would rather not describe what happened to our three riders after that. We would only say that they lost each other at midnight in the deserted streets. How could such a marvel happen? We consider it right not to speak about that either, assuming that readers can solve this simple question, which would be as clear as two and two making four, if they take into account what had happened and the terrible psychological shock our three heroes had experienced. After that, they were not able to look at each other or exchange even half a word. We can only add, as a detail, that one of the riders, – either in surprise or in horror, but probably both – gently fell down from his height and sat unhurt on the soft snow. We think it needless to name the person who experienced this. It goes without saying that only the one who did not feel secure at his new height, and had not got used to his new position, could afford such extravagance.

Let us not speak either about how they got home. We can only confirm that when Ohannes put his head on the soft pillow, he conducted a brief review of the events that had taken place and could not help wondering at the raised hopes and dashed disappointments known to the reader. 'Mashallah! Well done, Vramian. It's not true that all of them are tarred with the same brush.'

Chapter 10

Spring spread its wings over the world and over Van.

Ohannes was floating on the sea of his thoughts. He was sitting in the open balcony on the divan, which was covered with carpets. He was leaning against the soft cushions with his elbows and brushing his moustache to each side with the mouthpiece of the narghile. He was so absorbed in his thoughts that he noted neither the deep, velvet sound of the narghile, nor its blue smoke. It was Sunday: on that day, Ohannes used to go to the balcony in a blue nightgown, shuffling along in his slippers. He would then go down to the yard, and on into the garden, singing his favourite song under his breath:

"Father, father, your Motherland
Is our country Vaspourakan."

When he reached the pear tree called Hadji-Nana, he used to stop for a moment, let out deep breath like a sigh, and remember, as if in a dream, his grandmother, Hadji Nana, who had planted this very same unkempt tree after returning from a pilgrimage to Jerusalem. None of the other pear-trees could ever compete with the fruit of this one.

"Father said his country's thorn
Was sweeter than the rose."

He would raise his voice and then be embarrassed at how loud it was. Then he would look around at the paths of the neighbouring gardens, and seeing nobody, would be pleased that no-one could therefore have heard his voice, which he assumed was not a very pleasant one.

The usual course of a spring Sunday was indeed disturbed today. He no longer wanted either to be in the garden or to sing. He no longer felt as secure as usual. Although it was long after the Hats and their nasty letters had disappeared, although people spoke more and more about Armenian-Turkish friendship, although time had passed since Kapamadjian's murder, and although the bloody and treacherous fratricide seemed to have ended, nevertheless the atmosphere was daily becoming more suffocating and the silence more threatening.

The most tragic thing was his mother's death. It does not matter how old you are, while you still have a mother, you feel well protected and able to enjoy the pleasures due to you as a son. Ohannes, that tall man with a thick moustache, cried like a twelve-year-boy and felt what it meant to be an orphan.

That day, the little old woman had made up the tonir as usual and asked Ohannes not to go to the shop.

"Why shouldn't I go?" said Ohannes, stubbornly.

"Perhaps, as your mother says so, she knows something," said the old woman briefly.

"But I want to know as well," insisted her son.

The old woman became helpless. "Don't go today. Oh God, please don't go."

The son was left disarmed. He looked carefully at his mother's face, tried to smile, and wanted his mother to smile as well.

She did not smile. "Mkho will come today," she said.

"Maybe."

She raised her voice: "No, he will come."

"Don't get angry. Very well, he'll come."

"Kevork will come as well."

"Yes, yes."

"And only Hampartsoum won't come."

"No, he won't."

The subject was changed.

"What would you like me to cook for you today?"

"You know better than I," he replied.

"You used to like fried pumpkin very much when you were a child – let me go and fry some." The old woman's spirits revived.

"Fine," Ohannes said happily like a little child, "Yes, fry some pumpkin."

"Mkho likes fried herring," recalled the old woman, "and Kevork ... Hey, Satenik!"

"I'm all ears." The voice of her daughter-in-law was heard from the room upstairs.

"Prepare some ghavurma. Give some to that child of yours."

The meal was glorious. The old woman's premonition had not deceived her. Mkho indeed came from the village, and he had no sooner sat down than he said:

"I don't know why I came. The devil persuaded me, and I came. I left everything – and just came."

"My prayers brought you here, my son," murmured the old woman.

But Ohannes became gloomy and wondered what was going on. His mother had not let him go to the shop, Mkho had left all his affairs and had come in to town. What was going on? Then Kevork appeared in the doorway.

The meal was grand, especially for the latter, for the old woman did not let the bottles remain empty. Along with the fried pumpkin, herring and mutton ghavurma, she had also prepared a meal with quince.

"This was Hampartsoum's favourite meal," murmured the old woman. Ohannes heard this but pretended he had not.

"The situation is serious, we Armenians are face to face with great events." declared Kevork filling his glass again.

Their mother put a small plate with two Turkish gold pieces on it in front of Ohannes.

"Ohannes – for heaven's sake – go to Stamboul. Don't forget. Place a stone on Hampartsoum's grave. These two gold pieces are from me."

The last piece of fried pumpkin felt bitter in Ohannes' mouth.

He was annoyed: "It's unnecessary, quite unnecessary. Do you think I need your money to go to Stamboul, or to erect a gravestone?"

"Listen to me. Just you listen to me today. I'm your mother, aren't I?" She lit a cigarette and walked slowly and thoughtfully out of the room. She returned with a roll of embroidered cotton in her hand.

"Mkho, my son, give this cloth to my daughter-in-law. Let her make a new dress and wear it."

"Thank you, mairig." said Mkho, who was both pleased and moved.

"What's the matter with you today, mairig?" Ohannes was openly irritated but kept calm. "There's plenty of cloth in my shop, so why are you giving some to Mkho from your own trunk? The shop is Mkho's as well and he can take anything he likes from it, whenever he likes."

"And this purse is for you, Kevork, my son. They say you now have a lot of money." She handed the silver-threaded purse to Kevork.

"A dress, a purse," murmured Ohannes, "what's the matter with mother?"

His mother had heard the sound of approaching death. That evening, she closed her eyes, slept deeply and never opened her eyes again. She slept the sleep that knows no waking, and joined the great majority.

There was a funeral and a great funeral feast. Ohannes spared no expense. For a long time he could not reconcile himself to his mother's death and he never lost the feeling of being left an orphan.

Yes, the heaviest blow for him, was indeed his mother's death, but then it was followed by other scarcely less heavy ones. More and more often, there would be a knock at midnight at his garden door, and his stable was no longer a stable but had become an arms depot. With a noise like thunder, Burnaz's cart would stop in front of his door full of long, wooden boxes and earthenware jugs. Kotcho would be in the driver's seat and in the back of the large cart sat Kuzh-Kuzh – careless and drunk, clever but crazy. "Buy jugs, jugs, buy jugs," he used to cry in a sing-song voice, and when some naive, old woman approached the cart, Kuzh-Kuzh would become sober for a moment and say in a voice audible only to the woman: "They're not for sale, mother, not for sale!"

The cart would come and stop at Ohannes' door. Then Kotcho and Kuzh-Kuzh would get down and knock at the door. The door would open and they, together with the man who had opened it, would silently carry the boxes and earthenware jugs into the stable and place them one on top of the other with a lot of effort. Finishing their hard work, they would go into the large yard, wipe the sweat from their foreheads, drink a glass of cold water and would get on the cart and rumble away, God knows where.

Of course, Ohannes did not lack nationalistic feelings and he was even often proud at the bottom of his heart to be trusted by 'those dogs', but what if by any chance those other dog, the government officials, smelled it and what if the affair came to light? When his thoughts reached this point, he would, if walking, slow down; if sitting and playing with his beads, he would throw them onto the carpet; if eating he would stop chewing for a moment look around with anxious eyes and then continue his meal, but always with less enthusiasm and appetite.

One night, some people came asking for pincers, hatchets, and other similar things. And the breaking began! They broke the jugs with the hatchets; bullets and gunpowder poured out. They broke the boxes, and out of them poured Mausers, Colt and Smith-Wilson revolvers, Brownings, all deadly weapons, terrible, death-dealing arms. Ohannes had never handled anything like them in his life.

'They're playing with a hornets' nest,' Ohannes thought, 'one shouldn't play with hornets' nests.' And Ohannes remembered...

He was small, he could hardly have been twelve or thirteen years old. Bees had made their nest in the earthen wall of the outer yard and they were buzzing in and out of it. They were joyful and lively, golden, black striped bees and their wings shone in the sunlight. The devil tempted him to take a stick, stand by the nest and hit the bees flying in and out. For a whole two hours he only managed to kill two bees and trample them down with his feet. The stick was thin and he failed to hit most of them. He considered for a long time what he ought to do to kill more bees. He began to strike at them with a thicker stick. It was no use. The stick was heavy and it was impossible to strike quickly enough. Then he found a way out. He took the large school ruler and now he began to have great success. The ruler seldom missed, and the wounded bee fell to the ground moving their wings and legs, until he trampled them down and continued – slap, and the next – slap, slap.

He was ambitious: he was trying to kill all the bees, but somehow they did not come to an end, and indeed they did not even seem to decrease. The next morning, he took a glass of hot water from the samovar and threw it over the hole in the nest. One bee was burnt, but in a few minutes their usual routine was restored. They flew out buzzing, disappeared in some direction, then returned and flew back into the entrance, as long as the blows from the ruler did not kill them. In the evening, he took some mud from the garden stream and closed up the entrance of the nest. He was delighted with his idea, and was confident that the bees would now be destroyed, being deprived of freedom. He was amazed the next morning when he saw that the bees had pierced the mud and were flying in and out, buzzing joyfully.

Seeing what he was doing, his grandmother warned him several times: "For heaven's sake, don't play with the hornets' nest."

He heard her, but pretended not to and continued his labours. Seeing that the mud had not worked, he began to use the ruler again, while trying to think of more effective actions. Ohannes was standing quietly with the ruler in his hand. The bees stopped flying in and out. He wondered why they had stopped. Had they come to an end? Surely not! Many bees had flown in but he had killed only three of them. Slap, slap, slap. What had happened to the bees? Why were they not flying out? And then, suddenly, the bees flew out of the hole straight towards Ohannes, alighting on his neck, forehead, face, lips, and nose. Ohannes was fiercely and painfully stung; he screamed out loud. His grandmother, for whom such a climax to his activity had not been unexpected, hurried to help. The bees retreated and Ohannes' swollen head and face were rubbed with vinegar used as first aid.

"I told you not to play with the hornets' nest, didn't I?"

And now, each time when those quiet foot-steps were heard from the garden and there was a cautious but resolute knock at the garden door, he would remember his grandmother's warning from the remote past: "Don't play with the hornets' nest!"

'We're playing with a hornets' nest. Some hornets' nest,' he thought, and drew on the narghileh. There were a few red seeds bobbing up and down in the bubbling water of the narghileh bottle; they were only there to entertain the eye and for nothing else, but today Ohannes did not even see the red seeds.

Spring was surprising this year. The fruit trees had blossomed so abundantly that the branches seemed about to break under the weight of the flowers. It was as if a deep snowfall had settled on the apple-trees, the pear, apricot, peach, and plum trees, as well as on the quince trees edging the orchard on three sides. It was as if the green leaves were covered with snow and the garden lit with thousands of lamps. But the flowers fell down, some of them earlier, some later, and when the trees began to bear fruit, it became obvious that the year was going to be fruitless and that the abundance of blossom had been a delusion.

"How will all this end?" Ohannes said to himself out loud.

"The end of what?" he heard his wife Satenik say. She was busy cleaning the dust from the balustrade of the balcony with a damp cloth. It was clear to anyone that the balustrade was not dusty at all. Satenik was simply worried about the despondent mood of her husband and she wanted to get him out of the dark and gloomy depth of his thoughts.

"Did they get rid of those dirty things in the stable?" he asked suddenly. The question referred to the pitchers and boxes which had arrived the previous evening.

"How could they in the daytime? Why are you annoyed? Oh! let them take them away whenever they want."

Ohannes saw this as a woman's way of thinking, and not replying to his wife's question, carried on with his own reflections.

People were playing the game of the new Liberal Constitution; the priest and the mullah were kissing each other; the Armenian and the Turk were declaring eternal friendship; Armenian children were singing Turkish songs: 'Vatan bizim djanemez, Feda olsun kanemez ...' Damn all your Vatans, your motherlands, your willing sacrifices! It's all a lie, a lie. Arms are being collected again, there are still secret depots, and massacres once more in Cilicia. The lamb remained a lamb and the wolf remained a wolf. What troubles they all brought to Van, the Turks on the one hand, and the Armenians on the other. The Armenians carried on what the Turks began. Davo of Dher, traitor Davo! Was he right to have done as he did? Is a girl worth betraying a whole nation? What is a girl? –

He remembered his Lia. 'It's time Lia got married,' he thought, 'What is a girl? A flame to light up another home, a pillar for an alien house.'

The pungent smell of fish roasting on the fire diverted Ohannes' thoughts and he realised that he was hungry.

Lia appeared. "Mairig is calling you to dinner."

Ohannes raised his head. Lia was standing before him with the glowing face and eyes of a newly-matured girl. Her hair was plaited in two branches; she had a good figure, and was bright and lovable. Ohannes could not help saying: "I'm going to marry you off."

Lia blushed, but did not lose her head. "I won't go away from this house."

"Oh, yes!" her father pretended to be surprised. "Does that mean you want to bring a son-in-law into our house?"

"I don't," she asserted.

"Then what do you want?"

"I want ... " the girl thought a moment. "Oh, let's go and have dinner."

"Oh, you holo-molo," he laughed, and holding onto the outstretched hand of his daughter stood up from his cross-legged position. He raised his two hands towards the ceiling, went up and down on his toes several times as an exercise. He again remembered the Constitution and his terrible stable; he yawned and again rose up and down on his toes. "Well, well," he concluded and went downstairs to have dinner.

"Sourig, come to dinner," called Lia with the half-commanding and half-inviting voice of an elder sister. Souren rushed in, grabbed the match-box and ran back into the garden. He was engaged in some dark business on the main path dividing the garden into two parts. He came back with an uneasy, but triumphant, look on his face. A moment later, a loud explosion was heard from the garden – boo-mm!

"Was that the sound of a revolver?" Ohannes said.

Sourig wanted to shout with inner satisfaction, but had to avoid doing so. Only Lia knew about her brother's business but she was not the sort of sister to betray him. The fact was that Sourig would regularly take a little gun-powder from the stable and collect it in a tin box. Once he had seen Sahag, who was two years older, show him his arms-manufacturing skill in his garden. He had taken the empty bullet of a gun, made a hole in one end of it, filled it with gunpowder and fastened it down with rubble and pieces of cloth; then he had taken a piece of wire and covered it with wax.

Sourig remembered it as if it were yesterday. Sahag had put the bullet he had prepared onto the garden path. He had inserted one end of the wire into the bullet hole, lit the other end with a match and shouted, "Run back, it'll explode now." The flame of the waxed wire drew near to the bullet hole. Everybody ran back. The flame reached the hole and ... there was a miracle. Boo-mm! The powder exploded, emitting blue smoke. The bullet flew up and fell on the other side of the rose garden. They found it still smoking.

From that day on, Sourig had lost his peace of mind. Using Sahag's experience, he carried out several trials of exploding bullets with more or less success, but still he was not satisfied. He was engrossed with the idea of increasing the effect. He who seeks finds! And indeed he found a stick-thick, span-long tube with one open end. He needed only to make a hole in it. After school, he came home, hurriedly ate something, then appeared at the forge with the piece of iron in his hand and watched the work of blacksmith Arabo.

Arabo's workshop was small and everything in it was also small – Sourig liked it a lot. Arabo used to work alone: he worked the bellows with one hand and put a piece of iron on the fire with the other. Then he kept the red-hot iron on the anvil with one hand and hit it with a hammer in his other hand, uttering 'huh, huh' with each blow. Sourig especially liked the moment when Arabo threw the hot iron into the tin tub, half-filled with water which then spluttered, releasing a lot of steam.

On the third or fourth day, the blacksmith paid some attention to the boy. "Whose son are you?" he asked Sourig, stroking his scorched moustache.

"The Muradkhanians'."

"Oh, which of the Muradkhanians?"

"Baron Ohannes."

"Oh, oh!" The blacksmith was surprised. "Are you Baron Ohannes' son? You don't say! Hm, hm, what are you going to be when you grow up?" He patted the boy's cheek with his sooty finger.

"A blacksmith," Sourig replied with a smile.

"Oh, oh, oh!" This time Arabo was really surprised. "Your father a rich merchant and you a blacksmith? No, it can't be true, it can't be." He rolled a cigarette and recited in a soft voice: "A man with no education can't be a perfect man ... Studying a few things can't make a man wise enough. Large and expensive clothes can't make any man an educated one."

"Who said these words?"

"You did," the boy smiled again.

"Teacher Dikran said it was Columbus," laughed the blacksmith, choking with the smoke.

"Who's Columbus?" The boy also laughed, but was interested.

"Columbus was the man who found America,"

"What's America?"

"It's a country," answered Arabo and throwing his cigarette end into the fire, added, "There's a country in the world larger than our Vaspourakan, and that's America. Do you see?"

Sourig was standing in front of the forge with his hands behind his back, holding the valuable piece of iron and considering whether it was, or was not, now the time to open his heart to Arabo.

"Why do you want to become a blacksmith?" asked Arabo.

"To make a hole in this iron," answered the boy and revealed his treasure at last. The blacksmith took the short pipe with one flat side from the boy's hand and turned it over and over several times.

"Where do you want to make the hole?"

"Just here," the boy showed the place.

Arabo hesitated: "What for?"

"To make a weapon," the boy answered honestly.

"A weapon?" There was a silence, then Arabo said, "What weapon?"

"A bomb," explained the boy.

The blacksmith smiled. Then he added some coal to the furnace, threw the piece of iron onto the coals and began to work the bellows – puh, puh, puh. Little by little the iron got red. The smith placed it on the anvil, and then put a pointed rod like a nail on the spot the boy had indicated.

"Here?"

The boy nodded. Two light blows of the hammer and the iron had a hole. The smith effortlessly took the pierced rod and threw it into the water. The water spluttered giving off steam and was soon still.

"Is that all?" asked Arabo.

Sourig could not find anything further to say.

"Boy," said the blacksmith, "let's have a heart-to-heart talk until your bomb cools down."

He was going to say something, but at that moment a boy of Sourig's age, in clean but patched-up clothes, boldly entered the forge.

"Mairig told me to get twenty paras from you to buy bread from the bakery," said the boy. He looked at Sourig with curiousity.

The blacksmith groaned, looked at his son, took an empty cloth purse out of his pocket and turned it upside down in the air.

"Tell your mother that I haven't earned anything since morning. You go home. I'll bring some bread myself later." And he smiled sadly.

Sourig had got just twenty paras in his pocket. He had saved that amount from the money given to him for school extras. He had decided to buy marbles or a top. The blacksmith's son had no sooner gone some paces from the forge than Sourig, running after him, caught up and taking the twenty-para coin out of his pocket, handed it to the boy. "Take this."

The blacksmith's son took the money, looked towards the forge, turned and ran on. He looked back only once as if to check whether the strange and well-dressed boy had not regretted his action and was not calling him back to return the money. No, the well-dressed boy had not regretted, he never thought of calling the other back to return the money. Sourig returned slowly and happily to the forge.

"Did you give money to my rascally splpoch?"

"Who's a splpoch?" said Sourig, avoiding an answer.

"My son – his name is Mukuch, but I call him splpoch. I saw you give him money. How much?"

"Twenty paras."

"Good for you, thank you. We'll have bread today. You gave the money with your small hand. Despite being so small, you played the father on my behalf. Yes, despite being so small."

He bent down, took the warm piece of iron out of the water, wiped it with his apron – it was impossible to tell it's original colour – and handed it to the boy.

"Is this what you wanted?"

The boy nodded his head positively, "Yes, it is."

"If you need anything else, come to me, don't be shy."

Sourig said goodbye to the master magician and returned home happily. A few days later, he appeared in the forge again. He asked for some small pieces of iron to enable him to seal the hole of the pipe after he filled it with gunpowder. Arabo would not take the ten paras offered by Sourig.

"The small iron pieces are not worth any money, my boy. I haven't done any work, why should I take money for it? Go, my son, go and make your bomb." He tapped the boy's nose with his finger.

And this was the improved weapon that was now being tested by the little gunner. His father was not of course aware of the matter.
"Was that the sound of a revolver?"
After dinner, Sourig stood up and took a few steps towards the door, then, remembering something, returned, took the box of matches out of his pocket, put it back on the windowsill and went out.
Ohannes wondered why Sourig needed matches. Did he smoke secretly? He stood up and followed the boy without realising that even if he did smoke secretly, he could not be caught red-handed, because he had not taken the matchbox, but on the contrary had put it back in its place. He came up unnoticed, at the very moment when Sourig was lifting the sealed pipe off the grass.
"What's this?" asked his father, taking the iron pipe away from the boy.
"A piece of iron," said Sourig, looking innocent.
The piece of iron was still warm. Ohannes remembered the explosion and understood everything. The boy was playing with gunpowder. That day, for the second time, he remembered his own childhood and the bees. He also thought that gunpowder was not a bee, and that it's revenge would be a good deal more serious and disastrous than that of the bees.
"Don't play with gunpowder."
He put the piece of iron into his pocket and said nothing else. On his way back to the house, he thought to himself, 'What sort of generation is this that's growing up? They're playing with gunpowder, making arms.'
Sourig, left alone, began to examine the site of the explosion. The earth was burnt over quite a large area and had acquired the colour of reddish coal. The thin vegetation on both sides of the path was burnt. And the little pieces of iron? The boy looked up instinctively. The leaves of the lower part of the apple tree

spreading its branches over the path were torn as if they had been hit by large hailstones. Parts of the green leaves had fallen here and there on the road, not far from spot where the explosion had been. That was the power of the terrible weapon made by the little gunsmith. As for the pipe, Sourig was not at all sorry about its confiscation. He would find a new one, a larger one, and when it exploded, people would ask one another: "Was that the sound of a bomb?"

Meanwhile, Ohannes entered the yard deeply confused and uncertain. Where should he go? What should he do? Should he go to the café and play one or two rounds of tavlu? Who with? Let it be just Hagop Kandoyan, a regular player. He was always at the café, no matter who was there or who was not. He was considered to be one of the best tavlu players. But Ohannes had beaten him last time and the overall score was level.

Passing by the woodshed, he stopped for a moment, then entered and threw the iron with all his might on top of the carefully arranged wood. Look at the little shndo and his games – Ohannes smiled to himself. He used to call Sourig by this name when he was still a baby and still held in his father's arms. Now, he gave the name to his younger son Vostanig, who was currently playing quietly with small stones in one corner of the yard.

He walked to the stable. Dark-eyed Usep was sitting on the stone near the stable door and was cleaning his raffia shoes. Seeing his master approaching, he stood up.

"How are you, Usep?"

"Quite well, Master."

Ohannes entered the stable. In the front there was a raised level on which there were tall piles of hay. Ohannes knew very well what there was under that innocent and fragrant hay. Under the hayloft, there was a great heap of large and small pieces of the broken jugs and pitchers. If they had been remainders of old crockery, one could perhaps understand, but these ... Anyone seeing all that might well ask why all this new crockery had been broken and piled up there, would they not?

"Usep."

"Yes, Master."

"Bring a stone to the stable, take a hammer and break up all these pieces."

"Very well, Master."

"Turn it into sand, red sand."

"I'll make it red sand, Master."

"And spread it on the wide garden path. Let the road through the green grass be red."

"Let it be red. It'll be beautiful, Master."

"Yes, it will be very beautiful."

Ohannes smiled, pleased that he had found a way out of the situation. Then he went out of the stable.

And again, the same questions: Where should he go? What should he do? He went upstairs onto the balcony again. He settled down on his sofa and picked up the daily *Van-Tosp*. There were two newspapers in town – *Van-Tosp* and *Ashkhadank*. Being conservative, Ohannes, took the former. On the last page he read a report about how some Turks had raped a peasant woman in one of the villages of the province.

"Oh, what barbarians, oh," he murmured and his thoughts flew away again.

What do they want of us poor Armenians? Aren't Armenians created by God? Don't they have a right to live? If you're an Armenian, you have to suffer. But in Uncle's country, in Russia, Armenians lived in freedom, didn't they? Christian countries are something else. Where are you Uncle? Why don't you turn your weapons and your wrath against these vandals? We didn't want a kingdom, we didn't want a king, but we did want freedom. Haven't the Armenians got a right to live free? There's no other way! Blood against blood? So be it – blood against blood. As the New Testament says, a tooth for a tooth. It's too much to bear. –

He remembered the well-known song and began to sing under his breath.

> "Mother, it's enough to caress me.
> I want to drink blood instead of water,
> I want to fight, I want to die …"

He returned to his thoughts: – What stupid words. Nonsense.

'I want to fight' is fine; after all you don't want to die like an ass. But the other bit, 'I want to die', what kind of a wish is that? Which stupid oaf would want to die? –

He corrected the song in his mind and sang an edited version:

"I want to fight,
I don't want to die..."

Ohannes smiled, pleased with himself and stroked his moustache. He narrowed his eyes and took in with one glance the garden and the view of Aikesdan spread out beyond him. The bright green orchards flowed with fruit trees like waves. In some places the poplars bunched up, dominating the fruit trees and embellishing the gardens with particular beauty. There were no houses visible in all this green expanse; but in some places there could be seen part of a balcony, a wooden stair stretching across from roof to roof, or a gleaming window. And a solemn Sunday silence lay over the gardens. Then came a loud cock-a-doodle-doo from the depths of the green garden and the barking of a dog from the Dankovians' garden.

What do they want of us poor Armenians? Do they want to ruin and destroy Van, to throw the people into the lake, to kill them, to slaughter the women and the children? – He became angry, and who knows in what direction his thoughts would have gone if there had not been a knock at the street door. – Who can that be? Nobody has ever knocked at our door like this. –

The door was opened. Ohannes heard his name uttered in an unknown voice. The newcomer began to come slowly but resolutely upstairs. The Chief of Police, Agyah, entered the kiosk.

The police chief Agyah, known as Agyah Effendi, had appeared early in the morning that day in the Armenian district. Walking slowly, he went up the crowded, wide street leading from Arark to Khatch Square. He was dressed as a civilian, not wearing his usual uniform and probably unarmed. Those who recognised him were shrugging their shoulders in confusion. They wondered what he was looking for on a Sunday, and did not know whether to greet him or not. As if to release the passers-by from such indecision, the police chief was walking with his eyes fixed firmly ahead, without looking left or right.

At the same time, a young man was knocking at the door of a two-storey house situated in one of the remoter streets of the town. The door opened, this young man entered and just as the door was about to close, a second young man dashed in. They both simultaneously asked for Baron Aram.

"Baron Aram is in his room," answered the landlady, more formally than necessary but with a smile that meant that she was very proud of her prominent lodger.

It was not the first time that Digin Makrouhi had received these young men. Their ages hardly added up to forty years. They were both dark and tanned, lively and shrewd, and both of them were called Peto. To differentiate them, one was called Monarchic Peto and the other Republican Peto. Monarchic Peto was an only child, whereas the Republican one had four brothers and four sisters.

Aram's room was furnished in European style, except for the oriental sofa. Aram was sitting at his desk and setting down his impressions of the day in a notebook.

I went to church today, the church was full of a dense crowd. My appearance in the church caused a considerable stir –

He was interrupted by the knock on the door and called out, "Come in."

"Oh," he exclaimed, looking back and seeing the two Petos at the door, "come in, and have a seat. What's the news?"

Monarchic Peto: "The Chief of Police Agyah, Baron Aram..."

Republican Peto: "He entered Khatch Street and from there, Baron Aram..."

Monarchic Peto: "Baron Aram, he turned towards Arark from Khatch Street..."

Republican Peto: "And he went, and he went..."

"And you ran to me like bull-calves," said Aram, "let me see your heels. Who did he greet? Who did he speak to? And, if you know, what did he speak about? That's what I need. And all you can say is 'he walked, he walked'."

The two Petos were confused and looked at each other. They

then almost simultaneously dashed out, ran down the stairs, and came out into the street where, like the ends of a spring one of them went to the right and the other to the left.

Alone again, Aram continued the interrupted sentence:

– yes, my entrance did not remain unnoticed. The people seemed to be asking themselves what was this heretic doing in church. That heretic is now seated, writing these lines. Our struggle is a pointless labour and a waste of time compared with the beard of an eternal God. However, if there is no God, how could we be wasting time? And if even there is one, we should enroll him in order to lead our struggle. The so-called 'new generation' movement should be extinguished. We are on the eve of great events. The lessons of Aghtamar...

For a moment, Ohannes did not believe his eye. It was the police chief himself, lean, stooping a little, and with a drooping moustache. "You're welcome." Ohannes rose from his seat, greeting his unexpected guest. He raised the fingers of his right hand from chin to brow several times as a mark of deepest respect. He went up to his guest and instinctively bent down a little in order not to appear higher than his influential and cunning visitor.

"Buyurun, Agyah Effendi. Please take a seat – here, it's softer here."

Perhaps the police chief was not used to sitting in a soft place, for he sat down on the small, three-legged, round chair at the table, inwardly pleased at his host's confusion.

"Well, how are you?"

"Well, Allah be praised," answered Ohannes, "Allah be praised. And how are you?"

"Eh, how would a government official be? One day's good, another's bad. Could I have some coffee?"

Ohannes smiled: "Coffee! You come to my house so rarely – and you ask only for coffee? No, Bey-Effendi, it can't be so. What would you like – brandy, raki, wine?"

"Coffee, Ohannes Effendi, coffee, the time for brandy and raki has passed."

The police chief began to sing, while drumming on his chair

with a self-satisfied expression.

> "Getdi gyul, getdi byulbyul,
> uster aghla, ister gyul ...
> The rose and the nightingale went away
> you may cry, you may laugh ... "

Ohannes left his guest alone, but soon returned with the coffee and a glass of rose-syrup on a clean plate. There was a silence, during which the police chief drank the coffee in small sips without paying any attention to the syrup. He then stood up.

"I beg your pardon. I was passing by and just wanted to know how you are. I see you're well. Pass on my greetings to your family. Goodbye."

Ohannes accompanied his guest to the street door. When he closed the door behind Agyah, he stood for a moment and wondered why the dog had come and then just gone. His face was tense. Chakhk, chukhk, chakhk, chukhk – that was Usep crushing the bits of pottery. Has he heard about the arms being kept in the house? If so, surely he would have come with his dogs and made a proper search. Or he would have asked some vague question or made a faint allusion. 'Getdi gyul, getdi byulbyul ... '

Now Ohannes happened to be standing on the same balcony and looking again at the view of Aikesdan spread out before him. The cone-shaped, far end of the Sudjians' kiosk showed up for a moment through the branches swaying in the slight breeze, then disappeared again. But the end of that kiosk pierced Ohannes' memory like a bolt of lightening. 'Oh, you scoundrel! You brigand!'

"Satenik, Satenik," he shouted as if stung by a snake – even he was frightened by his own voice.

Satenik came upstairs: "What's happened?"

"Plague on him. Give me my clothes quickly."

He began to put on his clothes with his wife's help. His mind was working rapidly and accurately. That was it – there was no doubt now – it was clear to him that Markar Sudjian was innocent. Poor Markar, that tall, able-bodied man with his thick moustache and ever-smiling, black eyes, that amicable and well-liked resident of Van, of whom it was said that when he laughed heartily – and he always used to laugh heartily – the sound would reach the Varag monastery. Some people had noted that on the day before vengeance had fallen on him, the police chief had knocked at Markar's door, entered the house and came out half-an-hour later.

Ohannes now had no doubts that there had also been a cache of arms in Markar's stable or in his barn. And so? Well, the next day, three young, Armenian peasants – or rather some citizens dressed as peasants – had entered the house, locked the family members in one room, then draggd Markar into the garden and slaughtered him like a sheep. Ohannes understood that he might expect the same fate. That child of Tartarus, Agyah, had found an easy way to kill some 'dogs' by using other 'dogs'. Why should the government appear in the wrong by searching or arresting people? Whenever the police chief heard that there were weapons in this or that house, he simply knocked at that door, entered, asked for a cup of coffee and left again. There was no doubt that the Committee would be informed that he had visited that house, and it was clear that no-one would then be spared. They had not had mercy on Markar – and not only Markar. Ohannes recollected one by one all the citizens that had disappeared or had been killed under puzzling circumstances. 'It's impossible to remember them all. What luck, Ohannes Muradkhanian, you've also got onto that black list.'

"—— your list! —— your drooping moustache!" He swore coarsely and energetically rubbed his neck with a red handkerchief, as if to check whether his head was in its place or not. Already dressed, he went quickly downstairs. Satenik followed him to open the street door – the uncertainty had left her more anxious.

"Husband, say something so that I'll also understand what's happened?"

"Things have taken a very dangerous turn, woman."

Saying no more, he ran out into the street.

He stopped walking for a moment and took a deep breath. Which of the three dogs should he go to? Baron Vramian, Baron Aram or that rascal Ishkhan? It was not worth going to Vramian – he remembered Kapamadjian's murder. Nor to Ishkhan – he remembered the Aghtamar events. Only Aram Pasha remained. But then he remembered the story of Davo's betrayal and the fact, according to rumours, that Davo had been driven by jealously to commit that extremely evil act, and because of that very Aram, who had seduced the girl whom Davo of Dher loved. He also remembered that there was nasty gossip going round from house to house that Aram cohabited with his landlady, Digin Makrouhi, the wife of Setrak Yapundjiants.

– Well, it's none of my business. Let him do whatever he likes, it's not of any political significance. Let Setrak himself worry about that – that fool doesn't think about such things. No, no, it's not my business, let him pretend not to be aware. I've decided: it's a matter of life and death, I'll go to Aram Pasha. –

And he went up to the Miravi Chadr and into the deserted street where Aram Pasha lived. Makrouhi opened the door; she was portly and very attractive, in a flowery dress and with a shawl thrown over her shoulders. Perhaps she would not have been so surprised if it had been her husband who knocked, because that fool Setrak was never at home in the daytime. On weekdays, he used to go to the shop early in the morning, and on Sundays, he would be in the Shirak café all day playing tavlu. When he won he would boast: "My name is Setrak Yapundjiants. Go and learn how to play and only then come and play with me." When he was defeated, however, he got angry and depressed: "And you'll stick your nose up at me and say you've won!"

Makrouhi had a right to be surprised, because she was more interested in the affairs of her lodger then in matters concerning her husband or the house. When someone entered her eminent lodger's room, she had a habit of coming up to the door noiselessly and eavesdropping on the conversation inside. Makrouhi knew many things, she was aware of many very important, dark matters. She led a lonely and secretive life; she did not receive anyone nor visit her neighbours, as she was afraid of revealing secrets which would mean losing her well-known lodger. Makrouhi loved Aram very much. She could divide the whole world into two parts – Aram and the rest. How could she help being surprised at Ohannes Muradkhanian's visit, as she already knew about the police chief's visit to him as a result of the conversation of the Monarchic and Republican Petos, overheard behind the closed doors. Makrouhi knew how such matters were likely to end. And suddenly ...

"I'd like to see Baron Aram," Ohannes said without any preamble.

"Is the matter so important?" asked the woman as if to check whether the man was still alive or whether it was his ghost.

"No, no, it couldn't be an important matter, could it? Do you suppose I've come just to hop up and down with him?"

Makrouhi realised the impertinence of her question and invited her unexpected guest to go up. Before going up the steep, broad, wooden stairs, Ohannes looked at the hostess once more out of the corner of his eye. He saw her white neck with two black beauty-spots on it, and then the scarred lobes of her ears. Perhaps as a young girl, she had heavy earrings, which had cut her lobes; together with the beauty spots on her neck these gave her an inexplicable charm.

'She really is beautiful,' Ohannes thought, 'that Aram knows which side his bread is buttered.'

"Knock gently at the door Baron Ohannes," she directed

"How can I? There isn't a door-knocker," Ohannes was confused, he had never heard of an inner door having one.

Instead of answering, Makrouhi tapped at the door three times with her finger – tek, tek, tek – and Ohannes heard an invitation from within to enter.

"May I go in?" whispered Ohannes, confused by this mysterious ceremony. Makrouhi opened the door and the visitor slipped in.

Aram stared at the newcomer, narrowing his eyes as if he did not believe them. He stood up, rubbing his clean-shaven chin and asked, "Is that you, Muradkhanian?"

"Yes, Baron Aram, did you recognize me?"

"Of course. I've been to your house. How are you? Please, take a seat."

The famous political leader pondered: 'Perhaps Agyah has sent him to me. It's very interesting. Now we'll see what interests the

Chief Constable. But this man must be killed tonight.' He smiled at the worthy citizen of Van sitting on the edge of his chair.

"I'm sorry, Baron Aram. I'm so sorry." Ohannes wiped the sweat from his brow and neck with a red handkerchief, then raised his fez to wipe his head as well.

Aram smiled again. "What's up? Don't be confused. Just ask. What do you want to know?"

"I don't want to know anything, Baron Aram, I haven't come to learn about anything," said Ohannes, as if to justify himself, and instinctively guessing the unfortunate drift of the famous leader's thoughts. "I'd like you to know that Agyah Effendi came to our house today."

"Agyah? To your house?" Aram pretended to be surprised. "Tell me more."

"I came to do that, but there's nothing to tell. He came, sat down, asked how we were, had a cup of coffee and went away."

Aram was sombre, and just to say something asked, "Where did he go?"

"To the devil. How should I know?"

Aram was thinking: – This cunning Vanetsi, this citizen of Van, is lying. Perhaps, he's learnt that I'm aware of the events and has come to pull the wool over my eyes. Or, maybe Agyah himself has sent him, telling him to come and tell me about his visit and to report back what I might say. –

"Baron Muradkhanian," he turned to the visitor and said softly, "you're a clever man. Is it possible that a Turkish official knocks at the door of a man like you, inquires about your health, drinks a cup of coffee, says goodbye and then goes away? If I believed your words, wouldn't you think me naive?"

"So," Ohannes choked, "does that mean you don't believe what I am telling you?"

"No, I don't believe you," said the eminent man rudely and raised his voice, "I don't believe." He took a revolver out of his pocket and put it on the table; he sat down with his hands on his knees, looked long and hard at Ohannes and asked, "Why did you come to me?"

Ohannes was terrified by the sight of the revolver. He

wondered why he had really come to this man, who seemed ready to attack and kill him. Only beasts about to attack their victims could have such a look. 'This is not a man, this is a beast,' he thought and instinctively looked towards the door.

"You came to me to tell me that Agyah visited you, drank coffee and went away? If that's true, is it something to tell me about? Do I need to know who visits whom to drink coffee? You'd better tell me how you showed him the arms, what he said, and how he then ordered you to come to me. Do you think I don't know what's going on at your house?"

Ohannes felt as if someone had grabbed him by the throat. He stood up, then sat down and shouted at the top of his voice: "You have no conscience, you're an unscrupulous revolutionary. You're not even a revolutionary – you're a Turk, and even worse than a Turk. And what you're up to is a messy affair, like that of a Turk. With the Turks on the one hand and you lot on the other, you've ruined the people."

He stood up and sat down again. "You want to know why I've come to you? I've come so as not to be slaughtered tomorrow like poor Markar Sudjian. I've come to tell you about that dog, that child of Tartarus, who enters the houses of people he suspects and leaves the rest to you. It's very easy for you. You've already killed many people. You're very good at performing evil deeds but idiotic at fine ones. Tear us to pieces – the Turks on the one hand and you on the other. Devour Van and then, to digest it better, drink the water of the lake."

There was a silence, broken only by Ohannes' gasps. But a careful ear would have also heard another's, no less excited, breathing from behind the door.

Aram began to think more rationally. He remembered that Vramian had always been against these 'cleansings' and had often expressed the opinion that everything should first be checked and that they should not be prematurely provoked. But he and Ishkhan had preferred their extreme methods. Had they made a mistake? 'Nothing ventured, nothing gained' – he remembered a headline in one of their official newspapers published in Geneva. He now had almost no doubt about the sincerity of this honest citizen of Van.

And if he hadn't come? It's clear that he would have ordered avengers to … No! Nothing ventured …

Aram was not offended by Ohannes' grave words.

One should not be offended by the words of a man condemned to death. On the other hand, see what an interesting thing this fellow said: 'You're very good at performing evil deeds but idiotic at fine ones … devour Van and drink the water of the lake.' Yes, the nation is wise. And what should be done with this Vanetsi, this flawed martyr? –

And the influential and prominent political figure, known as Aram, remembered the names of a few past martyrs. They had been sent to the other world on his and Ishkhan's orders. Well, if there is no God, there is no life beyond the grave either. Otherwise, he and Ishkhan would be in Hell. And Vramian? Perhaps he would be sent to Paradise, accompanied by the guardian angels, the Seraphim and Cherubim. He smiled to himself and wondered whether Vramian would walk in the gardens of Paradise with or without his glasses on.

He went to the door, thought for a moment, then half opened it and called, "Digin Makrouhi!"

Makrouhi came in promptly.

"Digin Makrouhi, would you mind bringing us two cups of coffee?"

"Why not?" She went out in a flirtatious way.

"Baron Muradkhanian, please sit down at this table. We'll have a cup of coffee together and talk."

Ohannes changed seats automatically. He took a deep breath. Now it was clear that his righteous anger had found its target, that beast. He stood up and said, "Say something, so that I can go away. I've told you even more than what I wanted to say. I regret my uncalled-for words. Now, it's up to your conscience and your God to decide – do whatever you want."

"Take a seat, Baron Muradkhanian, take a seat," said Aram putting his two hands on Ohannes' shoulders and making him sit down. "Now we're going to have coffee together. You were right to come and tell me about it. The things you said are I suppose reasonable. It's possible that black soul does go to houses whose owners he suspects in order to dishonour them in our eyes. Who would imagine it? What infernal people these Agyahs are."

Ohannes felt reassured. "Infernal is not a good enough word for them. Their place is at the bottom of a hell-pit – and that isn't enough either."

Makrouhi brought in the coffee. On her way out with the empty tray, she turned back and taking advantage of the fact that Ohannes was looking at the coffee placed in front of him, she smiled at her famous lodger. Ohannes saw that smile without looking. His boast was not groundless, when he often used to say to his shop assistants, 'I've got eyes in the back of my head. I can see everything.'

They were drinking silently, sip by sip, each staring at his cup, preoccupied with his thoughts. The great man was thinking: 'He must be sent to Ishkhan and Vramian. Vramian may gloat of course, but for the sake of the cause and our collective leadership, it's necessary. Yes, indeed, for the sake of our great cause and collective leadership.'

He heard his visitor saying, "Baron Aram, will I able to sleep quietly at night?"

Aram looked at his questioner as if seeing him for the first time. "Baron Muradkhanian, are you Armenian?" he asked.

"And what do you think I am?" said Ohannes, rather surprised.

"Then answer this question: does any Armenian ever sleep quietly at night, for you to have a quiet sleep?"

There was silence. The voice of the fishmonger could be heard from the street, "Buy fish, buy fish. Ten paras."

"There's always trouble, but there are also different kinds of trouble," said Ohannes, as if speaking to himself, "There's the trouble coming from the Turks, we know that. But shouldn't we at least trust other Armenians today?"

"It's allright," said the leader, smiling. "You can feel safe. You can trust us."

Ohannes remembered Vramian, remembered Bedros Bey Kapamadjian. What was this so-called safety? Could he be sure that Ishkhan would not send his people to kill him?

"Should I go to Baron Ishkhan and Baron Vramian?" he

inquired.

"Yes, you should." confirmed Aram. "Go and tell them what you told me. Perhaps, we ought to look into some circumstances – review them. Nothing ventured, nothing gained! Am I not right?"

This time the voice of the pedlar rose up from outside: "Buy small trinkets, buy some trinkets."

Ohannes stood up and as he got to the door, the great man tapped him on a shoulder and said, "Goodbye, you clever Armenian you, goodbye."

As she opened the street door for him, Makrouhi smiled and said, "You're very welcome'. The door closed. Ohannes took a deep breath, looked right and left, remembered where Ishkhan's hous was and walked towards the north-east.

Ishkhan lived just opposite the Sandkhtian girls' school. It was a two-storey house which had become well-known thanks to its famous owner. The street door was opened by a young man in knee-high boots. He let Ohannes in and asked why he had come.

"I want to see Baron Ishkhan."

The young man went quickly up the stairs two steps at a time and returned at the same speed.

"Go up, Baron Ohannes, knock at the second door on the left."

"I know, I know," murmured Ohannes, pleased that the young man had recognized him.

While going upstairs, he looked back and saw the young man's eyes fixed on him. He got exasperated, it occured to him that the man must also be one of Ishkhan's people. He again remembered the slaughter of Markar Sudjian and he came out in a sweat.

There was no need to knock at the door. Standing there was a tall, slender woman, with white skin and sad, black eyes, who let him in and then went away. She would be Ishkhan's wife, thought Ohannes.

In the discreetly furnished room with its two big mirrors, Ishkhan seemed shorter than when he had been at Ohannes' house. He had a pale face, a small moustache and a smaller thin beard, he was slim and muscular. He was standing with his back towards the street window. Ohannes entered and stood in the doorway. Ishkhan stroked the thin growth on his chin with his fingers.

"Come in, take a seat, Baron Ohannes."

"Thank you. I'm sorry to trouble you, Baron Ishkhan. You'll ask why I've come."

Ishkhan thought to himself: 'Agyah's been to his house today. Why has he really come to me? Perhaps Agyah's sent him.'

"Sit down. And now explain."

"Baron Ishkhan, Agyah came to my house today."

Ishkhan had not expected such a confession. He was surprised, not so much at the fact of the visit which was already well-known to him, but rather at Ohannes having mentioned it. The interesting thought occured to him that perhaps the man had gone mad.

"What's surprising about that?" he said with a smile, "I think he's always visited you. And you've visited him as well, haven't you? He's a very good man – a good man deserves to be one's friend, doesn't he?"

Ohannes had not expected such a blow. He stood up and sat down again, as he had done in Aram's house; he held his head between his hands as if to protect himself. He remembered the cautious glance of the young man in knee-high boots, who had let him in. The thought crossed his mind that he would not leave this house alive.

"I've come from Baron Aram," he said, not in his normal voice. "I explained everything to him. It's up to you whether to believe me or not."

"What did you explain to him," Ishkhan asked sardonically. "Tell me, I'd like to know as well."

And almost in the same words and with the same hysterical passion as there had been in Aram's room, Ohannes condemned the party's behaviour and emphasized the innocence of victims like Markar Sudjian and himself. But in his great rage, he could not pronounce his final sentence correctly. "That's enough," he said, "you've devoured the Sea of Van and drunk Van over it."

Ishkhan began to walk up and down the room, slowly at first and then more quickly. He recalled those residents of Van, who had been proved on undisputable evidence to have had relations with the Ottoman Government and who had been killed on the party's orders. But Markar Sudjian? He and a few others had only been killed because that conspirator Agyah had entered their houses or shops and this had been considered enough to blacklist them as traitors. If this man was telling the truth, it meant they had made mistakes in their terroristic activities several times. Ishkhan recalled that Vramian had often repeated: 'Be careful, lads , you may punish the innocent as well as the guilty.'

And now one of those innocents was sitting in his room. Another day, and he would have joined the dead of a thousand years. Was the man acting? No, he felt he was dealing with someone honest. Only a man feeling he had fallen into a trap would be so anxiously concerned to find how to reveal the truth. Ishkhan once more remembered Chief Constable Agyah's victims. Why did they not come to tell the truth? Clearly, they were afraid – they had not seen that far. But this innocent?

"You said you've come from Aram?" said Ishkhan.

"Yes."

"And what did he say?"

"What he said was: 'Go and trust us, you will be safe from us'. That is what he said. 'Go and tell Ishkhan and Vramian,' he added."

Ishkhan stood by the window and looked into the street. There was a silence.

"Well," he turned to the worthy Vanetsi placing a finger on his thin beard, "go and don't worry. As for Vramian –" He thought for a moment and waved his hand in the air: "Go to Vramian, go to him as well. Go and tell him. It's all the same – better late than never, as the proverb goes."

"Later but better, you mean!" said Ohannes and stood up. "I'm sorry if I used harsh words."

Ishkhan tried to smile. "You didn't leave anything unsaid, but don't repeat elsewhere what you've said here."

"Indeed not," assured Ohannes and went towards the door.

Ishkhan followed him. "Do you know the way to Vramian's house?"

"Who doesn't know the way to Vramian's house?" replied

Ohannes, going down the stairs. "Open the door, boy," he said to the young man in knee-high boots whom he no longer feared.

Ohannes came out into the street, looked right, then left, and walked northwards.

Chapter 11

Ohannes passed by the Norashen school, the mill and the café and turned westwards. The Sunday market was in full swing in the Norashen church square. He briefly greeted some acquaintances and, trying to avoid them, he entered a street of one-storey houses with, at its end, the attractive two-storey house of the Tutundjians. The spacious park stretched alongside the whole street; the foundations for a new building had been laid at the far end. Ohannes had heard that there was going to be a new Dashnak Centre, with a theatre and a library. 'Why not?' he thought. 'Nothing's too difficult for them, they'll take money from people and build a palace with it. Let's wait and see! What a long Sunday, full of trouble, this has been.'

Ohannes sighed and continued bravely on his way. He turned towards the new Khamurkyasan well and on to the street of the main secondary school, where he met Simon.

"Good afternoon, Baron Ohannes."
"Good afternoon, Baron Simon."
"Where've you come from?"
"From Aram Pasha and Ishkhan."
"Oh!"
"Don't you want to know where I'm going now?"
"Where?"
"To Baron Vramian."
"Oh!"

"Well, so what!"

"Have you had anything to drink?"

"Yes, I have. Only ask me what? Coffee! And ask me who with?"

"Who with?"

"With Agyah Effendi."

Simon thought Ohannes had gone mad.

Ohannes guessed what he was thinking. "No, I'm not off my head. Moreover, I've become wiser. It's a long story. Come over in the evening and I'll tell you all about it."

"I'll come, but aren't you joking?"

"What joke, for heaven's sake, what joke? Just come."

"Very well, very well."

"See you soon."

"Goodbye."

Ohannes carried on westwards. He saw a large sign with the word 'Books'. There was a huge, three-metre long pen hanging beside the entire length of the sign. 'It's a lie,' he thought, 'Books and pens are only a cover. They circulate clandestine newspapers there and collect money for that business of theirs.'

He entered the bookshop, where a young man sat smoking. He was Hagop Simsarian's son, handsome Ara, who had recently returned from Bolis with a higher-education diploma.

"Ten kurush from me."

"Whose name shall I write?" asked the young man.

"Write Hnazant."

The young man wrote out the receipt, put the money into his pocket and slipped a few copies of a newspaper into Ohannes' inner pocket.

"Only be careful," the young man said crisply.

"Certainly!"

Ohannes came out into the street feeling better. He felt protected and invulnerable now that the receipt for his donation to the 'sacred cause', as well as the secret newspapers, were in his pocket. He even began to sing to himself under his breath:

"Islamic armies, fierce and furious,

Besieged our great mountains."

He did not like his performance. 'Good singing is a fine skill,' he thought, and comforted himself: 'It's not easy and not everyone can do it well. But the song's not a good one either.'

He was in a musical mood and involuntarily began another song, but with the same lack of success.

"And you got up at sunrise,
Tied a belt round your proud back,
Turned your eye towards the stars
To get in front of the light."

Here was Vramian's house. The main door was open and through it could be seen the small sun-drenched yard. There was a small pond, round which narcissus and marigold climbed up the lilies and hollyhocks. Ohannes immediately noted that there was a horsecab waiting in front of Vramian's door. Vramian himself was coming down the stairs with a rolled-up piece of paper in his hand. He recognized the Vanetsi and acknowledged his greeting.

"Have you come to see me," he asked, cautiously peering over the rim of his spectacles at Ohannes.

"Yes, I have."

Vramian cast an anxious glance at the cab, at the paper in his hand, and then at Ohannes.

"Let's go upstairs."

They went up to the first floor. In a corner of the open balcony, there was a round table, covered by a white table-cloth and with a bowl of fresh flowers in the middle of it. Ohannes reckoned his host liked flowers a lot. They sat down opposite each other.

"Agyah came to my house today," reported Ohannes without further ado.

"Accompanied by policemen?"

"No, alone."

"And what did he say?"

"Nothing. He drank a cup of coffee and went away."

"Well, you have had a nice guest."

"Oh, yes, indeed."

"Then?" Vramian was getting anxious.

"So I came to ask you, why he came and why he went?" Vramian smiled. "Baron Ishkhan understands such things well and also –"

"Baron Aram," interrupted Ohannes.

"Yes, yes, and also Baron Aram."

A briar leaf fell on the white table-cloth. Vramian picked up the leaf, smelled it and placed it carefully on the edge of the porcelain plate under the bowl of flowers.

"I saw both of them. But I came to you. You're the most important leader." Vramian smiled and screwed up his eyes.

"Tell me about your visits."

Ohannes related every detail of his two meetings with Agyah. Vramian's face clouded during this account. There was a moment when it seemed to Ohannes that Vramian was not listening to him. But as if guessing those thoughts, Vramian encouraged him to continue.

"Do go on! I'm listening, I'm listening."

"I must tell you, my brother …"

Ohannes prolonged his personal Odyssey. He had forgotten to whom he was speaking, and was so much engrossed in his story, that if Vramian had been sitting beside he would have patted him on the shoulder to make his thoughts more convincing, in the way he usually did when speaking to Simon. "I would also like to tell my brother that …"

Before getting into the cab, Vramian shook Ohannes' hand and said, "In any case, go to work in peace. I'll pass on instructions."

'What instructions?' wondered Ohannes, looking at the receding cab. In his account he had also reminded Vramian of the events that had taken place in his house a few years ago, when Vramian had torn the Hats' threatening letter to pieces and Kapamadjian had been murdered immediately afterwards. 'Will he instruct Kapamadjian to resurrect himself?' he asked himself bitterly. Vramian had inquired whether the Hats continued to pester him, and Ohannes had stretched his arms out wide and exclaimed: "Nothing's been heard from them, but what's the use of that? There's no safety, no security." And now the worthy Vanetsi wondered whether these 'instructions' would be for his safety.

It was difficult to say what turn his thoughts might have taken but for the noise of military music heard from ahead. Ohannes moved aside and stopped. It was a military band followed by lines of Turkish soldiers. They were marching with their guns on their shoulders, stamping on the main avenue in step with the military music. It seemed to him that the soldiers looked very alike, not only in their uniforms, but also in their faces. But when he looked at them more carefully, he noticed that like all people they were quite different. One soldier's face, in particular, stayed in his memory: he had a pointed nose and a thin moustache, he had looked at the windows of the houses and smiled. The soldiers passed and the resulting silence calmed Ohannes down and he slowly carried on. 'They're terrible people,' he thought contemptuously.

Passing by the café, his nose caught the spicy smell of a grill and he felt hungry. He recalled various meetings and remembered that it was Sunday. He heard the sound of tavlu coming from the open balcony of the café as he went in without thinking. He took a seat at a free table on the balcony. He rubbed his hands together, grating his knuckles in the way he would do before or after a successful business deal. This had been a successful deal! He moved his fez back and rubbed his brow with a handkerchief, though he was not sweating. A successful deal! He briefly reviewed what had happened: he recalled Agyah's drooping moustache, then Marouhi's split lobes, Ishkhan's finger on his thin beard, and Vramian's disappearing cab. Had he actually carried out any successful business deal? No, he had not. He felt in his pocket, he remembered the huge pen on the front of the bookshop, then found the newspapers in his pocket – clandestine newspapers!

"Aghavard!"

"Yes, Baron Ohannes."

Ohannes pondered: 'To drink or not to drink?' He stared fixedly at the waiter's almond-shaped eyes and gentle features. "A skewer of kebab. Some kidneys."

"Wine or raki?"

The decision became easier. The question had been put with such emphasis that one had to be ordered, if not both. "Raki. I'd like just raki."

"Anything else?"

"Bring other things as well," Ohannes conceded, and Aghavard dashed off.

The raki arrived together with the other things that included thin-cut slices of soudjuk, olives, cheese, fresh cucumber, and so on. Ohannes took a small pocket-knife out of his waistcoat pocket and began to peel the cucumber carefully; the skin hung down from his hand like a green ribbon. He put the peeled cucumber on the edge of the plate and enjoyed its pleasant, sharp smell. Then he folded the knife, returned it to his pocket, raised his hand and threw the skin onto the table. To the thoughtful Vanetsi, the twisted green heap seemed like a snake – a bad omen. Such peelings sometimes look like a horseshoe and this is taken to signal good fortune; sometimes they lie in a circle and that means no profit; and sometimes in a green tangle which might not mean anything, though it was usually taken to indicate confused affairs. But this time he thought it was a snake, and he filled his glass.

The grilled meat arrived. Ohannes set to: he ate and drank, hoping every now and then that he would remember something important, but he could not. The raki did not fail to have an effect, but at the very moment he was going to recall that very important thing, a man came up onto the café balcony. It was Gabriel Demirtchian with the Van-Tosp in his hand. He immediately saw Ohannes, smiled and approached him without losing his smile amidst the tables and chairs.

"Bon appétit!"

"Good afternoon. Take a seat."

Gabriel was carefully and neatly dressed as usual. He sat down, checking his tie and sizing up the table and its contents with one eye.

"It's not bad, not bad," Gabriel said, appreciating not only Ohannes' outdoor, Sunday meal on the table, but also the arrangement of his own tie. Ohannes caught Aghavard's eye across the room and raised his empty glass. Aghavard came up with a clean plate, knife, fork, and another glass.

What would you like to order, Baron Gabriel?" Ohannes asked his guest.

"Please don't order anything, Baron Ohannes, what's here is quite enough. If there was chicken pilaf like at the Tokatlian restaurant in Bolis –"

"We do have chicken pilaf," asserted Aghavard.

"Yes, you may have. But it won't be the same as the chicken pilaf at Tokatlian's! Well, bring some. Let's try it once – bring some."

"Bring it," confirmed Ohannes. "Bring pilaf with chicken. And raki – yes, add some raki as well. So – what's the news?"

The balcony where they were sitting was separated from the inner part of the café by a door and four windows, which were closed. One of the customers sitting inside opened a window and the noise from inside wafted into the balcony – a Bolis melody played on a zither and a voice that was shouting: "Call me, oh, my little sea! Call me, oh, my little sea!"

Ohannes did not want to believe his ears, but he could not deny that it was his brother Kevork's voice. Gabriel confirmed the matter by pointing his thumb over his shoulder towards the window. "That's Baron Kevork! He seems to be in a cheerful mood."

"I think so. So – what's the news?" Ohannes returned to his question while filling up the glasses. Then he picked up the green snake from the table and looked in vain for somewhere suitable to hide it. Willow branches were swinging lazily almost at the level of the balcony. The green cucumber-skin flew onto one of them and hung there just like a snake. He pretended not to see it.

"Vramian went into town in a cab. Something's up!"

"What can it be?"

"Who knows? Perhaps Djevdet has sent for him."

"What kind of a man is Vramian?" asked Ohannes casually.

Gabriel took a slice of cucumber. "If there is one of them who's more or less reasonable, that's Vramian. The rest –"

"The rest are nothing?"

"The rest –"

The chicken pilaf arrived and the atmosphere round the table significantly warmed up.

"And Ishkhan?" hinted Ohannes.

Gabriel shook his collar: "What happened at Aghtamar…" He did not continue, they understood each other.

"And what about Aram Pasha?" asked Ohannes with a furtive smile.

Although they understood each other, Gabriel felt that it was perfectly reasonable to add a further comment: "What a figure a libertine can be."

"I don't know," Ohannes feigned ignorance, "I've never heard or seen one."

"Why don't you know?" complained Gabriel, whose teeth were as white as the rice he was eating. "All Van knows – and you don't?"

Ohannes wanted to change the subject. "Baron Gabriel, tell me, what is a revolution?"

"Let's drink and I'll tell you. A revolution is change – I mean a change in the state of affairs."

Ohannes considered this. "A change? Right! But for better, or for worse?"

"For the better, of course, Baron Ohannes, for the better, of course."

"Well, let's say for the better. Everyone wants his business to go well, but it's a business after all and it could end in failure. What then?"

"And then," smiled Gabriel, "it won't be a revolution but a constitution!"

"Ha, ha, ha!" laughed the Vanetsi at the top of his voice, "you spoke very well. A constitution! Con-sti-tu… Ha, ha, ha!"

Gabriel, who had not thought he had said anything very clever, began to laugh as well. "So, what can I say?" he concluded, and cleaned his moustache with a green silk handkerchief.

Ohannes picked up his glass and offered it forward. Gabriel's glass did the same: the full glasses tapped each other; they were raised and emptied, and then set down on the table facing each other each other, as if asking, 'What now?'

Ohannes sighed and said, "Well, Baron Gabriel, what did the constitution do for us, and what will the revolution do?"

"Well – let's accept that the Armenian issue is quite a serious problem. Let's admit that." Gabriel lost the thread of his thoughts, but he found the other end of the thread and tugged at it: "There are thousands of people, all of whom live in and enjoy God's world. What do these Turks want of us? Perhaps you can tell me, Baron Ohannes, what do these Turks want of us?"

"The Turk doesn't want anything of us, Baron Gabriel," said Ohannes lowering his voice, "we want something from him."

"Nonsense!" The other got excited and pulled the silk handkerchief out of his pocket again. "What do we want from the Turks?"

"Freedom."

"Oh, is it something shameful to wish to be free?" Gabriel continued.

"It's not shameful. But it doesn't suit them."

"Damn their schemes. Do we have to abide by their rules?"

"And what do you imagine? They constitute the state, and we're only subjects."

"Well, we're certainly subject! But on what grounds do they enslave their subjects and slaughter them?"

"If you behave properly, they won't kill you," said Ohannes.

"I haven't done anything wrong."

"You've said you want freedom."

"Baron Ohannes, answer my question" insisted Gabriel. "Should they seize a man and slit his throat simply because he wants freedom?"

"Not only slit his throat, but hang him and gouge out his eyes as well."

"Is that a Government?"

"And, what would you like, Effendi?" Ohannes felt he was floating on a cloud of raki and raised his voice: "Under the very nose of the Government, you bring in guns and convert churches and houses into armament dumps; you print clandestine newspapers and books criticising the government; you send terrorists to train in the hills; you kill officials and district governors; you sing songs day and night; and you shout, 'call me, oh my little sea'. And after all this, you want them to pat you on the head and applaud you! Finish with it, for God's sake, and don't make me have to speak again."

Gabriel was surprised, for Ohannes was echoing his own thoughts. He himself had always given similar answers to those who accused the government and defended the nationalists. Perhaps it was the raki that had led him to other points of view. At any rate, he would not think of giving way or changing his position, though he would defend himself, if not his views.

"What can we do? There's robbery everywhere, ideas as well as people are murdered, human rights as well as women are raped," complained Gabriel like a hurt child. "Should we go and be slaughtered like sheep? What about Vartan Mamigonian, Antranik...?"

"I say A and you reply B! We can't communicate," said Ohannes bitterly. "In order to understand, to clarify things, you have to say A and B and carry on to Y and Z."

"Look, there's Vramian returning in his cab." Gabriel spoke very quietly. "He had a piece of paper in his hand when he left, but now his hand is empty. What's going on? We're told nothing."

Aghavard placed a bottle of raki on the table, said something under his breath, and left. The two men looked at each other: 'I didn't notice him order that,' thought Gabriel. While Ohannes thought: 'Has this peacock Gabriel got enough money to order another raki?'

"Aghavard!" Ohannes called the waiter, needing to do something to clear the confusion: "Bring the bill."

"It's already paid."

"Who paid?" Ohannes was surprised.

"Teacher Kevork".

Afterwards, as Ohannes thought back, he was not entirely sure whether these were his thoughts or Gabriel's. He worked it out like this:

– Think of the government as the father of a family; his sons are his citizens, they want freedom. 'You're nothing,' they say, 'we're the owners of the house and garden, the owners of the shop. If you don't agree, go to hell! Long live freedom! Long live revolution!' What father would agree to that? What government? –

But there is an alternative argument, and once again was it his idea or Gabriel's? He thought of it like this:

– These lands are ours, our people own them. We once had a kingdom. You've come and snatched our land, made us slaves and captives, and now you want to wipe us off the face of the earth. What right have you? By what law? –

Did he bang on the table with a fist or did Gabriel?

– Well, we understand the situation is serious, we carry on living a dog's life. But what can we do? What can we do against the State, against the Army? If you batter your head against a brick wall, that won't make it fall down. What about European intervention? Don't be childish! Would any Europeans lose their life for you? Hunchak, Dashnak, Armenak – three Armenians – three parties! As if those are not enough a fourth has come from abroad to trouble us. Damn their revolutions! People want to live. Let them live, whether well or badly. Let them live in hardship, but let them live. –

His brother appeared with an empty glass. He sat down at their table and filled all the glasses. Raising his, he proclaimed:

"… to capture the girls and women
And make them suffer terribly.
The men are looking from afar
At their lovely wives and daughters,
Who are thrown into the vast sea."

Then he raised the cane in his left hand up to his glass and began to sing as if shouting.

> "The hills of our nation cry out
> Cry out for *Van-Tosp* and for Van."

And what happened after that? Ohannes said, "Go and settle your debts, you worthless being. You've no place at my table. Take your raki and get out of here!"

"Baron Ohannes, for shame, people are looking at us," interposed Gabriel.

"Don't poke your nose between two brothers," said Kevork, "Tell me, brother, tell me –"

"Go to hell!"

"I will! I will!"

"You've lost all your sense of shame. Of respect."

"Why are you insulting Baron Gabriel?" said Kevork, "He's not a bad man, and he has a sense of shame as well."

Gabriel leapt up as if stung by a snake: "He's speaking about you and not me."

"Of course, it's about you, Kevork," said Ohannes. "Do you imagine we don't understand that?"

He remembered the cucumber skin, swinging from the willow branch and already yellow and wrinkled; he remembered Gabriel's bent fez and the shouting, but not what was shouted, and his brother's polished cane brandished in the air. He then sensed that he was sitting in a cab, turning from Khatch Street into the wide road leading to Arark, and passing the green windows of the British Consulate. Gee-up! The driver's call woke him up. Gabriel was sitting beside him, clasping his shoulders and imploring him not to shout.

"Don't shout, Baron Ohannes, I'll agree with anything you say, I'll believe all of it. Only, please speak lower, for God's sake."

"You believe that Agyah came and had coffee with me today?"

"Yes, I do. I believe you."

"And that I went to Aram Pasha?"

"Yes, indeed."

"That I had coffee?"

"Clearly."

"That Aram Pasha's landlady made the coffee?"

"Don't shout."

"And that I then went to Ishkhan?"

"You were right to do that. Speak in a lower voice."

"Do you think I'm shouting now? You should have seen how I shouted at Aram and Ishkhan."

"Oh!" Gabriel pretended to be surprised, but was struck by Ohannes' vivid imagination.

"I left out nothing. I told them everything."

"Well done."

"I scolded those political leaders passionately."

"Good for you, but please don't shout."

Driver Seno slowed down the cab several times to check out what he was hearing. Then he winked at Gabriel in a way that meant 'let him tell his stories.'

"I left Ishkhan's ..." Gabriel did not think this was to go to Vramian, but Ohannes added, "And drove straight to Baron Vramian."

Ohannes continued his heroic tale. 'How lucky that we're nearly there,' thought Gabriel, 'otherwise he might carry on to Djevdet, as well.'

But Ohannes thought that dreaming was better than going to Djevdet. "Gee-up!" He heard the cry as if it came from the depths of a well.

And now, having woken up with a terrible thirst and blinking his eyes in the dark, he tried to remember how he had got home and who had successfully helped him lay his head on the pillow. The last thing he could recall was the green windows of the British Consulate and driver Seno's call, "Gee-up!"

Ohannes was now sitting in the back of his shop, with a glass of strong tea in front of him, and fingering his worry-beads – chuk, chuk, chuk. Set paced up and down giving instructions, the shop-assistants ran from corner to corner carrying packages, and one of them stood on the short ladder to receive the packages and arrange them on the shelves.

Ohannes' head felt as heavy as lead, but the pleasant fragrance of the strong tea was soothing him. He took a deep breath and changed position. Something rustled in his pocket. He pulled out the two small newspapers printed on fine paper.

"I've got it," he murmured under his breath, "Set!"

"Yes, Baron Ohannes."

"Are you very busy? Sit down beside me."

"This instant – I'll serve this customer and come."

"Yes, serve him and come." Ohannes managed to smile.

At last, the senior assistant – or manager as he used to call himself – took a seat beside Ohannes at a respectful distance.

"Sit closer. Look through these papers."

"Baron Ohannes," said Set taking the papers, "they're buying a lot of common grey cloth. It's much in demand." He lowered his voice: "Turkish officials are taking it."

"Why do you think they're after?" asked the merchant.

"Isn't it clear?" He lowered his voice again. "They're making up uniforms for soldiers.

"Of course. Why shouldn't soldiers have uniforms?"

"Yes, but they're taking a lot. In my opinion, they're preparing for some great event."

"Look through these papers."

"Hm, Droshak." Set examined one of the papers, "this isn't an Armenian newspaper."

"No, it isn't."

"And not Russian."

"No, it isn't."

"And not from Bolis either."

"Oh, no, no."

"It's from Europe."

"Yes, from Europe," Ohannes felt proud, though no-one would know why.

"Baron Ohannes," whispered the capable young man, having read a few headlines, "these papers are dangerous and harmful."

"Dangerous indeeed – but why harmful?"

"They're writing against the Turks, Baron Ohannes."

"That means they're telling the truth," insisted Ohannes.

"It depends ... on the standpoint."

"There's no standpoint, it's just the truth."

"That may be. But just look at what they're writing."

"People mustn't slumber."

"Why should people lose sleep?"

"Sleeping's a bad thing."

"On the contrary, from a medical point of view –"

"They'll come and cut your throat if you sleep."

"If such newspapers –" He wanted to say 'are read by you' but then changed his words, "– if such newspapers are published, they'll cut not only the throat, but also ... "

Ohannes stirred his tea thoughtfully, took a sip and became

impatient while Set read through the pages of the small newspaper to himself, shaking his head. The silence was broken by Ohannes.

"I agree. Weighing up all the pros and cons, I think like you as well. But I can't see how it will all end."

"Geneva!" Set read out. "If I'm not mistaken, Geneva is a European city. They're sitting in Geneva waving a big stick at Turkey and stirring up a hornets' nest. Oh, what rascals!"

"Why?" Ohannes complained. "Many of them have been here themselves and have perished, haven't they?"

"Who asked them to come? Who asked them to perish? Did the people of Van invite them to come? What do they want from poor people? You just look at the names of their groups, all names for lightning – *Shant, Paylak, Kaytsak*. The government will certainly see this newspaper."

"This one?" Ohannes was frightened.

Set smiled. "This newspaper has been published in thousands of copies, Baron Ohannes, do you think the Government won't manage to get hold of one?"

"Yes, it might."

"And what would you do if you were in their place?"

"I'd kill them."

"Who?"

"Those who publish, send, receive and read them." The merchant was getting angry.

"Do you see any real names? Look at this list of donors – these are all false names."

"Read them out."

"Look: they're divided into two sections: devils and poor, peaceful people." He began reading out the false names. Halfway through he asked whether he should continue.

"No, don't. My head's spinning!"

"The second lot," Set went on with his analysis, "are honest neutrals."

"Which group am I in?" asked Ohannes, finishing his tea.

"How should I know? In Arark? In Varag? You're in twenty places."

"I'm in the second group, my boy," declared Ohannes firmly to Set, and implicitly to the world. Then he stopped talking, became sad, and began musing aloud: "If I spit upwards – there's God. If I spit down – there's my beard. Well, well."

The day was long, it seemed to be crawling along. No one he knew turned up, and in any case, he did not want to see anyone. Simon had come to his house the previous the evening, as arranged, and had been told by a clearly worried Satenik that her husband had left in the morning and had not yet returned.

"Where did he go," Simon had asked, hoping to learn something by concealing his previous meeting with Ohannes.

"He didn't say, Baron Simon, he didn't say," Satenik had replied.

Simon had then remembered Agyah. "Did anyone come to see him this morning?"

"No, nobody," Satenik had considered it wiser to say.

Simon had left thoughtfully.

Satenik had also whispered something very important in his ear that day. Now Ohannes wanted to remember that thing but he failed to do so. Set approached with a roll of newly arrived silk in his hand.

"A fine piece of cloth. A dress for Lia?"

Ohannes imagined Lia in that dress, and then at last remembered the 'important thing' that Satenik had whispered in his ear, namely that an informal delegation of three people had come from the Manasserians to see the girl. 'Mihran Manasserian?' he mused, 'So! His mother's only child, a monastery, land, wealth … But –'

His thoughts were interrupted. Simon came in.

Chapter 12

A man on horseback emerged from one of the gates on the south side of Van in the afternoon. A short street with poor one-storey earthen houses on both sides, led up to this gate. The horse passed down the road by the Arark cemetery and went on without stopping towards the south. Not far from the town lay the village of Gurubash. The rider rode on fast down the main street and did not notice, or pretended not to notice, the respectful greetings of some of the peasants. Mt Varag seemed to be following him as he rode, sometimes near and sometimes far. Eventually it became far away and disappeared from sight. He rode on towards the south, always the south. The road was wide enough for two carriages and stretched straight ahead. It then wound round, reaching a spot where the road seemed to touch the clouds. When he reached this spot, he stopped and got down.

The rider was Mihran Manasserian, the principal – and only – member of the 'committee' of Hayots Dzor, the owner of the Khek monastery and other adjoining land.

He loosened the reins from the horse's mouth, took down the cloth saddle-bag, and put it on the grass not far from the road-side. He also took the black blanket down from the horse's saddle and spread it on the grass. Finally he patted the horse on its flank. He was not much taller than the horse, and was wearing black boots over civilian trousers together with a white, broad-rimmed hat of African style which emphasised his thin, brown face and short moustache. The horse took a few steps off the road, snorted and started grazing quietly.

Mihran – or Baron Mihran as he was called in the town, and Mihran Effendi in the village – took some lavash, cheese, boiled eggs, pokhind, fresh tarragon, and raki out of the saddle-bag and before sitting down looked out at the panorama stretching out below him.

There lay Hayots Dzor spreading from east to west. In front, hills covered the horizon. To the east, there was a higher, unnamed hill with the ruined St Abraham monastery sitting like a medal on its chest, and to the west the view ended with Lake Van. These were the horizons which framed Hayots Dzor. At a glance, Mihran could take in Khek village, the domeless Khek Monastery, the Astvadzashen and Aradents villages, and, to the west, the Eremer village, which had an abbey of the same name with its chapel hidden by willows. The river Khoshab flowed like a blue ribbon. Down the hills and in the valleys, there were patches of green, yellow, yellowish-green and yellowish-red, fields spread out like different sized handkerchiefs or cut-up pieces of cloth. Remote sounds, which were more like silence than sound, came up from the valley below. To the west, the rays of the sun filled the valley, and Hayots Dzor was smiling with all its colours and with the familiar and heart-felt charm of the fields, roads and paths. Mihran's fleeting look ended back at the Khek Monastery sitting on the shoulder of the small hill like a grey box. He took a deep breath of fresh air, sat down on the blanket and started having both his breakfast and his lunch.

As he was eating, he was thoughtful and in low spirits. A Turk from Bolis had been appointed to be the district governor of Hayots Dzor. The previous governor had been great, he would do nothing but drink and sleep, day and night. Perhaps he was dismissed for that very reason. He would come to a village with the tax collectors, stop at the headman's house, drink and then sleep. His subordinates did the same. The news about the tax collectors would reach the monastery and the farmhands Andro and Avdo would then take some sheep and two or three cows to the monastery to show them to the collectors. They would register that number, then have some more to drink and go away.

Things remained like this for many years. They were not interested in the affairs of any of the 'committees' or 'groups'. Hayots Dzor could have been armed to the teeth but its governor would simply drink and sleep. Hayots Dzor could declare itself an independent Armenia, but it would still be the same – the governor would just drink and sleep. You could remove Hayots Dzor to Erzurum, or to the Caucasus, but the governor would not pay the slightest attention – he would drink and sleep.

But the new governor? Mihran had not seen him yet, but he had heard that he came from Bolis, spoke French, and according to Aram's information, he was a free-thinking Turk. What did 'free-thinking' mean? His wife was also 'free-thinking'; it was said that she rode a horse dressed like a man, walked arm-in-arm with her husband and with her face unveiled.

Being engrossed in his thoughts, it was only after he had eaten his fill that he realized he had not yet had any raki. That was not unusual. Though he always had drinks with him at home and when travelling, he was not particularly fond of them. After finishing his meal, he stretched himself on the blanket and fell asleep.

He even dreamed – a muddled senseless and incoherent dream. Every time he awoke from an unusual dream, he would recount it to his mother. His mother believed in dreams and could explain them. But when Mihran told her one which had no beginning and no end, his mother would call it a meaningless nightmare and would shake her head, cutting him short: "You've been sleeping with your eyes open!" He also saw dreams that could not be told to anyone. Personal dreams about dark secrets, dreams about women, about girls he had seen or had never seen, and these dreams he guiltily kept to himself, becoming ever more gloomy.

Aram Pasha is sitting at his desk with his feet on the chair. One lens of his spectacles is black and the other is plain, one hand is ordinary and the other is a bear's paw. He is not speaking but wheezing, in fact not wheezing but screeching like an old gramophone record.

"What? That is the question! At this moment the most imperative task is the li-qui-da-tion of all Armenaks. You Vanetsi, do you know what liquidation is? No? Yes? Here is the list, three people. Your revolutionary duty is to do away with them. Freedom or death? Freedom or being killed, being slaughtered like donkeys."

Aram Pasha was speaking like that, and Mihran was in front of him with that revolver in his hand.

"Why are you showing me your revolver? You killed your brother-in-law with it, didn't you? What? Just like that. But as a result you acquired an entire monastery, lands and herds from me.

The whole of Hayots Dzor, political fame and influence. The Committee of Hayots Dzor ... What? Just like that."

And now he sees that his revolver is not in his hand but in Aram Pasha's. Aram throws the revolver up and catches it in his fist.

"Mihran, Mihran," he is wheezing, "you're a weak character, you have no spirit, no backbone. You aren't a man. How could you make your sister a widow and make her children orphans just for your own material gain? Was it for the sake of the cause and discipline? But wasn't your brother-in-law a perfectly honest Armenian, no matter that he was a rival?"

"I didn't kill my brother-in-law," moaned Mihran. "It happened accidentally when I was cleaning my revolver."

"Ho, ho, ho," Aram burst out laughing. "Well now, take this revolver and this list. Let that same accident happen again to these three people. We don't need the party of the Armenaks, we don't need local diplomats. Clean them out. Clear them away and that'll be that. Or else, I'll take back the monastery, the lands and the herds, and in addition I'll banish you from the paradise of Hayots Dzor. You Cain! You horned, miserable devil, with the mark of Cain."

And now he was dreaming of a big, luxurious funeral, an overcrowded funeral. School-children are carrying wreaths and bunches of flowers. Representatives of all the political parties are present. The huge procession is moving forward and the open coffin, with the victim of either a deliberate, fratricidal bullet or an accident, is also moving ahead, swaying on people's shoulders. His face is visible. He has a wide forehead, a white face and black moustache. Mihran is also walking in the procession and is crying with real tears. He cannot bear the looks people are directing towards him, confused, inquiring and even angry, looks. He leaves the funeral, noticed or not, and gets home through the gardens and deserted streets. Once at home, he becomes aware of all the wailing and crying. His mother, his widowed sister with four orphans, the eldest of whom is ten and the youngest a new-born baby, the women-neighbours, and the female relatives, none of whom took part in the funeral, are all weeping. It was like the shrieks of a wedding party heard from afar. He slipped in through the garden door, went up like a thief and locked himself in his room. He looked at himself in the mirror and stepped back in fear. Grigor, his sister's husband, was looking straight back at him from the mirror.

Then, as if bewitched and hypnotized, he went up closer and looked at the mirror again. He moved his head, but the figure in the mirror did not move. Mihran was scared and blinked rapidly, but Grigor's implacable and penetrating look stared back at him from the mirror. The 'committee' of Hayots Dzor bit his lips so as not to shout out and at that moment the man in the mirror opened his mouth.

"You're a shameless creature. You killed me under your own roof, on a peaceful spring evening. It doesn't make any difference whether it was a premeditated murder or an unlucky accident. Let those who are still alive solve that problem. The fact is that I am not alive and that's the most important thing. I left four orphans, three boys and my eight-year-old eldest daughter Adrineh. My four children are the most wonderful and clever children in the world. My daughter will become an Armenian Jeanne d'Arc, my elder son an Armenian Lamartine, the middle one a Victor Hugo, and the youngest one a Cicero. Take all this into account. You're responsible for getting them to the position I had planned for them, or else I'll not leave you and your conscience, if you have one, in peace. As for the parties, it's clear that your party is one of madmen and epileptics and can't win. You'll have to take pride in your defeats and you'll deserve to be the grave-diggers of your own dead. Your favourite music will always be the funeral song, your favourite color black, and your favourite perfume the smell of incense. One cannot conquer the world by hatred; nobody can grow flowers with oil and salt water. Flowers don't blossom just to decorate the coffins and graves of the dead."

Mihran sees that the mirror is shining with a strange brightness. He is standing right in front of it but cannot see himself. A moment passes and now Aram Pasha is looking out at him from the mirror. He is shaking his head reproachfully, with regret and clicking with his tongue – chrt, chrt, chrt. Then, as if stung by an inner pain, he pushes his black hat back, and appears to want to come out of the mirror frame, groaning loudly.

And Mihran woke up. The horse was neighing, probably now well fed, and shaking its tail with boredom. Sleep had not done him any good; on the contrary, as usual after these awful dreams, he still felt tired and shattered. He pulled the horse close, put on the reins, adjusted the saddle, put back the saddle-bag, shook the left-overs out of the blanket and placed it on the horse. Judging by the position of the sun, not much time had passed. He had read somewhere that even the longest dreams only last a very short time.

He went ahead holding the reins and began to go down the steep slope with small, weary steps, the horse following behind him. Before reaching Astvadzashen, he got back on the horse, which began to play its usual role. It stepped forward nimbly. A slight, cool wind blew onto Mihran's face and he felt a bit fresher himself.

He entered the village. When passing by the one-storey school, he could not help smiling. An old peasant woman standing below one of the six windows of the school was crying out with a pleading voice. "Teacher, dear teacher, let our Ared come and have his meal before it gets cold." He stopped the horse near a hut and called out, "Armaghan!" A woman appeared with her forehead and chin covered with a worn-out scarf. He asked for water. The herd was coming back into the village. The village revived, becoming noisy and dusty. The day sharpened up. He drank the water, quickly acknowledged several greetings, returned them, and left the village.

The sun set. Hayots Dzor was getting filled with evening shadows. The horseman arrived at Aradents village, which stretched along the Khoshab river. He wanted to pass straight through, but noticed that the headman of the village, Naho, an old man with a very full beard, stopped at the edge of the street and raised his long and thin pipe at him.

The rider pulled up the reins and stopped. "Good evening, headman Naho."

"Good evening, Mihran Effendi."

"What's the news?"

"Nothing special," said the old man loudly, then added in a low voice, "two horsemen have just gone into the monastery."

"From the town?"

"They came from Eremer, but they're townspeople." He blew down his pipe to clean it and added, "yes indeed, from town – peasants can't ride a horse properly." He screwed up his eyes and looked down the pipe, to see if it was clean.

The horse shifted about like Mihran's thoughts. Children wearing dirty linen shirts came out of the low earthen huts and a few shy women with covered or half-covered faces appeared in the doorways.

"Let's get going," said Mihran and the horse set off.

"God be with you," said the old man.

When the horse was crossing the Khoshab river after leaving Aradents, Mihran looked up at the monastery sitting on the hill not far away. The round-shaped wall of his own room stuck out where the walls, stretching from east to west on one side and from north to south on the other, crossed. Though it was just getting dark, the two windows were lit up. That meant there were guests in the house. His mother usually sat on the stone at the right of the monastery door when waiting for her son. Each time her son returned home late at night, nobody knew where from, the same conversation would take place:

"Why are you sitting in the dark like a blind owl, why don't you light the lamp?"

"Who should I do that for, my son?" the mother would defend herself. "You're not at home, I'm alone, and everyone's asleep. Who for?"

Now there was light in the windows. Mother had lit the lamps, and furthermore had done so earlier than required, so there must be guests. Mihran spurred on his horse, passed the grove spread out below the hill, carried on up and dismounted at the monastery door. "Andro!" he shouted, "Andro!"

A short young man with a tanned face ran out of the stable and took hold of the horse's reins. Mihran's mother came forward with quick, light steps and her usual anxious expression, that of a woman of fifty, or one of sixty, depending on her mood.

"The new district governor is inside," she said to her son.

"Alone?"

"No, he's not alone, but with a shameless woman. In a man's trousers. I think she's his wife." She smiled and gestured towards the room. "May she die. May such a woman die!"

"What have you cooked?"

"I've made pilaf and chicken."

Mihran slowed down. "What kind of man is this governor?" asked Mihran, relying on his mother's astute instincts.

"He isn't like a usual Turk," she answered in a whisper, "go in, go in."

He entered. He felt the presence of the strange and unexpected guests. The air in the room was full of the fine fragrance of a woman's perfume. Then his ear caught the silver sounds of the woman's laughter and only then did he see the cleanly shaved, pale face of the newly appointed district governor, who had a well-groomed, triangular moustache and serene eyes looking from under a new, bright-red fez. A youthful looking woman with luxurious hair, in beautiful knee-high boots and a man's grey clothes, was sitting on the knees of the man and cutting the hair in his ears and nose with small scissors. She was pulling her husband's ears right and left to ease her work. The governor obeyed the girl's whims with an expression on his face that seemed to mean 'I've fallen into the hands of a mad woman, and I can do nothing but bear it.'

When Mihran came in, the girl jumped off her husband's knees, threw the scissors onto the wide sadr along the entire wall of the room, clapped her hands and exclaimed with gay and childish delight: "Here's the host and the owner of the monastery. But why hasn't he got a beard?"

The girl approached Mihran, put her small hand into Mihran's palm and pulled him towards her husband. The governor stood up politely and smiled modestly. The girl joined their hands.

"Kamal," the governor gave his name.

"Mihran."

"Mihran?" The girl turned to her husband, "Bey, do you remember, we knew a Mihran Effendi in Bolis – a doctor, yes? A doctor?"

"He wasn't a doctor," corrected the man, "he ran a drugstore."

"It's the same, he smelled of medicine like a doctor. It's the same."

They were speaking in Turkish: Mihran in the language he had learnt in the local school, and the guests in a pure Bolsetsi accent.

"And my name is Nana. Do you like it?"

The host and the guest looked at the girl with similar smiles. Such are the smiles cast on beloved, spoilt children. Kamal felt no need to explain to Mihran what kind of a bird Nana was.

Mihran invited the guests to have seats on the sadr. They sat down cross-legged, leaning on the soft cushions. The talk was first about the weather, then the advantages and disadvantages of Hayots Dzor and of the town.

"Has Effendi arrived from Bolis?" asked Mihran.

"Yes, I'm from Bolis," answered the guest, "I've studied in Paris. Now perhaps you will want to know what's brought me to Van. I was simply interested. Nana likes to travel."

"And to dress up. Mihran Effendi, my dear, tell your mother to come and dress me."

"Mairig," called Mihran, "mairig!"

His mother entered. "Mairig, help this girl to change her clothes."

"Come, let's go, you shameless girl," said the old woman, pretending to be kind-hearted.

Nana took some clothes out of a soft leather bag, put her arms round the old woman, and they went out. Nana was vigorously explaining that she was not a man, but a girl, and that she would soon prove it. The woman could only understand intuitively what Nana was saying and she agreed: "Yes, you shameless girl, yes."

In a few minutes, while the guest and the host were smoking silently as if waiting for Nana's transformation, a young woman, or should I say a girl, entered the room – a gentle, feminine figure, in a short dress and with naked arms and neck. She knelt on the sadr, fell on her husband and said: "Bey, do you love me?"

Her husband caressed her hair and replied, "I can't say for sure."

"Don't repeat my own words." Turning to Mihran, she said, "Mihran Effendi, when he was seeking my hand three years ago, he asked me whether I loved him. My answer then was 'I can't say for sure', but now I can say for sure that I do love him. I like Mihran Effendi as well – and his mother. Bey, she doesn't know Turkish, but she understood everything I said. What a clever mother she is."

The clever mother came in, smiling, "Are you going to have some dinner?"

"Bring it, they may be hungry."

She deftly spread a white table-cloth before them and placed some nice-smelling lavash, cheese, and olives on it, followed by knives and forks in honour of the guests, and finally a boat-like dish with rice pilaf and sliced chicken.

"Fetch some brandy, mairig." Mihran smiled at the girl, waiting for her response. It came without delay, she clapped her hands.with pleasure. "Bey, Bey, we're going to have brandy."

Nana was determined not to eat in western style. She held the lavash with her thumb, forefinger and middle finger in the local way, scooped up pilaf and put it into her mouth without dropping a single grain of rice. Nana's mouth could not be considered small, her large mouth well matched her big, black eyes.

The brandy made the conversation more animated. The young governor was describing Paris, and Bolis, while Nana kept reminding her husband with her comments. Mihran was listening with real interest. The last memories of his nightmarish dreams were cleared away. He was greatly taken by Nana and her feminine extravagance. 'So this is a free-thinking Turkish woman,' he thought.

Armenians appeared in all the stories Kamal recounted. He remembered their names with warmth and sympathy, remembered their professions, details of their biographies and their way of life – usually adding: "He was a very, very good man."

Mairig kept filling up the flask. "Mother dear, I'm already drunk," said Nana, and she embraced and kissed the old woman.

"God forgive us," exclaimed the old woman, smiling slightly and with a thoughtful air. "What does this shameless girl want of me?"

Nana kissed her husband. She didn't even spare Mihran.

"Mother dear, take me wherever you want, take me for a walk, take me anywhere. Let these men sit at home, while we women go for a walk."

"Let's go then, you blaze of light, let's go. I understand what you're saying."

They went out and Kamal addressed Mihran. "All people should live in peace and solidarity. Armenians are great builders, but the rulers of the state are the Turks. The Armenians must realize this simple – and at the same time complex – fact. As for the rest ..."

He lit a cigarette and blew the smoke out though the triangle of his moustache. "Nothing further is needed than to carry out a fair division of obligations and rights and mutual respect. Without these there can be no life, Mihran Effendi, without these it could yet get critical."

Kamal was speaking in Bolsetsi Turkish and it seemed to Mihran that he was not speaking but reciting. Nana's distant, ringing laugh was heard outside the open window. Mairig's troubled voice was also heard: "You'll catch cold – the devil take you, my girl." Nana appeared to be bathing in the river that flowed by the edge of the grove at the foot of the monastery hill.

"As for the local governors, judge for yourself, Kamal Bey. All those who are more or less humane are recalled or disgraced, and are then replaced with ones who have even had Armenians horse-shoed – yes, yes, just like that, shod just like horses!"

Mihran went quiet. Ought he to speak to a Turkish district governor like that? Should he, moreover, speak about the present governor of Van, even though not actually naming him.

"Of course," Mihran went on, wanting to take a half-step back, but the Bey interrupted.

"It depends – it depends on the political situation. And the political situation depends on the Armenian revolutionaries. When it was relatively calm, the government sent someone like Tahir Pasha. And what's your opinion of him?"

"Tahir was a good man."

The Turk smiled. "So, you see, the situation is not so desperate."

They laughed and drank together.

"As for Tahir Pasha's son, Djevdet. Yes, certainly, he's not like his father, just as the present political situation is not like the one at Tahir's time. The sea takes its colour from the sky. But this is only one side of the issue, Mihran Effendi." The governor lowered his voice. "There are two people living inside me: as a Turk I think in one way, and as a man – as a man, I think in another." He paused and then added: "Well, I think about many things."

There was a silence. Kamal resumed as if in another voice.

"The whole matter is spoilt by a third outside force. There's the Turkish national state and there are Armenians living within the boundaries of that national state. If this is indeed the case, the interference of any third party is not only unnecessary but even harmful. If prophets of freedom are needed, let people here produce them together with their own heroes. There are things which are both expensive and potentially dangerous to import."

The hint was clear. Even if unconsciously, the governor had touched on concerns of the Hayots Dzor Committee, and on Mihran's more personal issues. Kamal's hint had been about the newcomers from abroad. Even if there were no outsiders involved – as for instance in the Khanasor attack, or the seizure of the Ottoman Bank – it would still be the same, the situation would not be changed, the despot would remain a despot. Mihran remembered again the last version of that dream which he had seen several times, the nightmarish dream that would probably follow him all his life. Ownership of the monastery had really cost him too much.

He recognised the quick steps in the corridor. "Mairig?" He saw the smiling face of his mother in the doorway with a snow-white towel in her hands. "The girl went into the water. I'm afraid she'll catch cold. What a girl she is, just a blaze of light. Son, is she the governor's wife or his daughter?" And she hurried away without waiting for the answer.

Mihran translated his mother's question with inward amusement. The governor smiled sadly and stroked his temples where several white hairs were hidden. 'He's a handsome man,' thought Mihran, looking at the governor, 'but surely he's much older than Nana. I wonder if they have any children?'

"Have you any children?" he asked.

"No," replied the governor, "God didn't will it."

"Perhaps it's early to blame God."

"Do you believe in God," asked the governor looking straight into Mihran's eyes.

He was taken unawares. Did he believe in God or not? Mihran had neither thought about it, nor even considered thinking about it. At school he had studied the subject known as Religion: the Old Testament, the New Testament, Jacob born of Isaac, and whoever was born of Jacob – he could not remember, and in any case how could Isaac or Jacob give birth, what were their beloved wives doing at the time? Then there was Mount Sinai, the prophet Moses, Jesus born of a virgin, who entered Nazareth – or was it Jerusalem? – on his donkey, just like Mughsagha entering the Van market. And some Mary or other, a Magdalene, a crowd throwing stones at her, Pilate-Milate …

"I can see you don't believe," said Kamal, smiling gently and indulgently, and looking at Mihran's sardonically screwed-up eyes and tight lips. "I believe in God, but I believe neither in our Mohammed nor in your Jesus. No, even if they existed, they weren't good peacekeepers. There is a supreme being, a great, inexplicable and superior power. I do believe in that."

"And does that power play any role in politics," asked Mihran half-seriously.

Kamal smiled. "Politics is a mundane, human affair."

"And is there a heavenly politics? And a more serious question: does that inexplicable supreme being concern itself with human affairs?"

"No doubt," replied the governor.

They heard steps in the corridor. Nana threw herself into the room full of gaiety and short of breath. "Bey, I had a swim. And how I enjoyed it, what a pleasure!"

The oil lamp hanging from the ceiling lit up her golden face, her dark-blue eyes were peering through her long eyelashes with drowsy pleasure. Mihran's mother came in as well. She took the wet towel out of Nana's hand and gave her a new dry one.

"Take this, you little devil and dry your hair. Oh dear, she is a master at making everybody like her," she said and wished that such a girl would come to her house.

"Bey, I asked her whether she would take me as a daughter-in-law if I were unmarried, and she answered yes. She understands everything. I said, 'But I am a Turk, a Turkish girl,' and what do you think she said? 'Gyozal arvad Turk, Hay yok – Turkish women beautiful, Armenians not.' You couldn't find such clever people even in Bolis. Then she said – oh, I forget, what did you say, mother?"

"Splpoch," laughed the mother.

"And what does that mean?" she asked Mihran.

"Quick-witted," explained Mihran.

Nana embraced the old woman and lifted her off the ground.

"This time you are wrong, mother dear. I'm more like a child, and indeed even more foolish than a child. Ask the Bey."

"Oh, girl, you've broken my back, the devil take you," exclaimed the mother, evidently delighted at this extraordinary demonstration of affection. "And now, gentlemen, go out, you've drunk quite enough without me."

They got down from the sadr. "We never finished our chat," said Kamal, "but perhaps this discussion has no end."

"You're my guests for a few days," said Mihran smiling, "and we'll have enough time for more such discussions."

"A few days? No, Effendi, tomorrow we're going to Khorkom."

"Let's stay, Bey, let's stay. Your Khorkom won't run away." Nana hung from her husband's neck. "Mihran Effendi will treat us to brandy every day."

"Every day," confirmed Mihran.

"And now, do go out."

It was a beautiful, starry night with no moon. They passed through the wide yard, came out through the monastery gate and walked round the monastery walls.

"In Bergri," said Mihran, "a Turk killed a few Armenians, gathered their blood in a basin and had a bath, a bath in that blood. What delight! And you speak of some supreme being. Well, what can I say, Bey? I know many songs, but lack a voice to sing them."

"Blood calls for blood, Mihran Effendi, he who sheds blood can't live in peace or remain unpunished," said Kamal out of the dark.

Mihran's heart pounded so audibly that he thought Kamal was bound to hear it. Nonsense! A pigeon shivered and shifted its position in one of the holes in the monastery wall, and all was quiet again. Mihran was upset. "Bey, let's go in, you must be tired and need to rest."

When they re-entered the room, they found that the light had been dimmed. Mother and Nana were lying almost side by side in separate beds, and there were two more beds prepared on the sadr.

"Why did you separate the couple," asked Mihran.

"It's what she wanted," his mother cut him short without opening her eyes.

Mihran climbed onto the sadr and puffed three times at the lamp. The room seemed smaller in the dark.

"Mihran Effendi, don't try to see me in your dreams, I'm not interested in dreams." Nana's sleepy voice came out of the darkness.

Mihran smiled. When they began to undress, it seemed to Mihran that the governor was singing. Yes, yes, he was singing.

"Bey, are you singing?"

"Yes, it's a foolish song: 'Niazi, Enver, became leaders …' I believe you have many songs too."

"The world can't be built with songs." Mihran tried to philosophise.

"I don't know about the world, but there are songs which can destroy homes, especially when those songs come from far away, from Geneva or Tiflis for instance. I knew an Armenian barber in Bolis called Arshak and he used to say that it was well known that the drum sounds sweeter when heard from afar."

The governor took his small revolver out of his pocket and put it on the window sill. Mihran mechanically did the same. This act of disarmament was performed completely naturally. Then, each of them stretched out on his bed.

Silence reigned. A slight wind blew in through the open window as if spraying their eyelashes with sleeping powder. Hayots Dzor fell asleep.

It seemed to Mihran that somebody had woken him up. No one. It was early in the morning. He felt his heart beating strangely. Was he sweating? As usual, his mother was not there. She always got up before daybreak, dressed quickly, made her bed, took a towel, went out through the monastery gate and down carefully to the river bank. She washed herself, came back up to the monastery and went into the church, where she knelt on the damp ground and prayed. If the saint of the monastery, St Kevork, heard her prayers, everything would be in order, everything would be fine, with no murders, no Djevdet Bey, no oppression, no revolution, and no Aram-Ishkhan.

But all these did exist and, in addition, her joints ached, she could not sleep at night sometimes and she saw nightmares. That surely meant that her prayers had not reached their destination. But she was not disappointed, she had got hold of an icon of St Kevork, and of the Varag Holy Cross when she had gone into town, and so could repeat the same prayers in the morning and in the evening, and briefly, on occasions such as when making up the tonir, or doing something like darning socks. Nothing proved that the Saints existed in any form, but that did not change her faith. She prayed and was afraid of them, was afraid of them and prayed – prayed and believed in life after death. "Let me continue to live before I have to go to the dark, murky, sombre and eternal underworld where there is no light and no human life."

Nana was lying with the blanket thrown aside, her naked, white body tucked up, as if in an embryonic position with her knees close up to her chin. For the first time in his thirty years, he saw a woman's real, and almost touchable, nude body. That is why he had woken up. Perhaps a man wakes up in this way when he is in danger, when a snake is crawling towards him, or when there is a naked woman lying nearby on a white bed. She had not approached him like a snake, but had not moved away either, as she was fast asleep. That was why Mihran's heart was beating in quite a new way. Both pleasant and agonising. Was he sweating? The governor was sleeping quietly and peacefully and did not even think of waking up. Nana, shameless Nana! Mihran closed his eyes and decided he had to change the direction of his thoughts.

There are songs that destroy homes, especially when those

songs come from far away – from Geneva or Tiflis. Wasn't the allusion clear? Wasn't it completely clear? Allusion? A compound word meaning 'to cast a glance', that is to make a sign with your eyes. Yesterday evening, when they were sitting and talking together in the way two Armenians or two Turks would, Nana was swimming in the river, shrieking with pleasure – here Nana moved, but Mihran shut his eyes tighter – and, yes, he wanted to imagine Nana swimming naked but felt unable to do so as it was wrong and in any case unnecessary. And now Nana was not moving. Could he just look at her with one eye, with just a half-open eye? She might even have covered herself with the blanket as she turned.

And he looked, first with one half-open eye, and then he could not help looking at her with both his eyes wide open. Nana was now lying on her stomach just like people swimming in the sea, embracing the pillow with two hands and motionless as if held back by the waves. 'Oh, the Devil!' his mother would have exclaimed such an unexpected immoral situation. Yes, the Devil, not God. Because only a Devil could have planned such a thing. It seemed to Mihran, who could see only one of Nana's eyes, that her eyelashes were moving just like those of a man only pretending to be asleep.

A devil! But is there such a thing as a good devil? If yes, it could only be Nana, a kind, white devil. A white, white devil. And what if he touched her body? Very carefully, very devoutly? Nonsense! He should simply get up and cover her, as would a respectable and hospitable host who liked everything to be in order. She might even catch a cold and fall ill. Since she was under his roof, he was responsible for her health and welfare.

He carefully got down from the sadr. He was trembling. What if she woke up? Surely nothing terrible, even if Kamal woke up. After all, Nana might fall ill, she should not sleep like this. He had to cover her up with the blanket. And he quickly did so with gentle care.

But then something unexpected happened. Without opening her eye and without changing her position, Nana spoke in such a friendly and warm tone that Mihran remained leaning over her:

"Thank you for your thoughtfulness, but the blanket's too warm. It's more pleasant without it."

Mihran cast an anxious glance towards the sleeping governor.

"Don't worry. You could put your whole monastery on horseback and ride to Bitlis and he still wouldn't wake up." Nana smiled and then added, "He is forty-five, but sleeps like a child. While I'm twenty-three, but can't fall asleep at all. You're still young, Mihran Effendi, you shouldn't be told such things."

"I'm older than you, Nana," whispered Mihran.

"It's all the same. By how many years? Five or six? It's all the same. You're not married, so you're younger than me!"

The governor stirred. Mihran threw himself back on the sadr. Nana laughed. She laughed quietly and provocatively. Mihran put his clothes on quickly and went out. Away from temptation.

From behind Mt Abraham, above the Khek Monastery, the sun was just beginning to catch Hayots Dzor in its rays and the monastery was waking up to its daily routines. Just as he did every day, Andro had taken the already milked cows to the meadows. His wife was boiling milk in the large cauldrons on the gridiron of the stove in order to make cheese, while her mother-in-law was kneading the daily dough to bake bread. Andro's father, who was called 'crazy Avdo' – but only out of earshot, was cleaning the stables, shouting and swearing. The work of the monastery had eased, as a few days ago the sheep had been taken up to the summer pastures. In spite of that, Avdo had become angrier and was swearing even more loudly and forcefully than usual.

"I'll ——— the owner of this monastery, that Mihran."

But the monastery owner was standing right beside him. "Good morning Avdo, it's not clear what you are saying. What's the matter?"

"Good morning." Avdo quietened down. "Good morning, Baron Mihran."

"I said that you couldn't be heard properly," insisted Mihran.

Avdo was defensive: "Well, why should it be heard?" He was dividing the manure piled in the corner into two parts with a wooden paddle, but then he could not help shouting: "This part of the dung is for the Father – the creator of it – and this part is for you." He turned to Mihran, brushing his moustache to left and right with the handle of the paddle, and fixed his big eyes on him.

"Where are the governor's horses?" said Mihran.

"I've washed them down, together with your own horse, and tied them both to the tree. About that governor, who's the handsome boy, his son?"

Mihran smiled. "What boy, Avdo, what do you mean? It's his wife."

"Wife?" gasped Avdo.

"So what?"

"Oh," exclaimed Avdo, "and I was thinking..." He went quiet and shook his head. "Crazy Avdo! I'd better go and throw myself into the river, Baron Mihran."

"Why Avdo, what have you done?" Mihran was really interested.

Avdo said almost in a whisper, "I embraced the governor's wife, Baron Mihran. Yes, yes, don't laugh! When she was getting off the horse, I thought it was a young boy and decided to help him. I lifted her and put her on the ground."

Mihran went out of the stable laughing and left Avdo motionless and bewildered. Mihran went up the short, stone staircase to the monastery yard.

His mother pushed the church door open with her knee and went in with a deep bowl and a wooden spoon in her hand. She had suffered a lot of spiritual anguish before reconciling herself to a practical insight. In one corner of the church there were various pots of all sizes, together with a large cauldron. Here she kept all the food that was likely to spoil quickly. Here she kept the large cauldron filled with all the previous day's milk, so she could skim off the raw cream the next morning. She knelt beside this cauldron, put its lid aside and began to skim off the cream with a skilful hand and fill the bowl with it. She met Mihran at the door.

"Cook some eggs," ordered Mihran, "and get cream, butter and honey."

"Have they got up?" asked the mother.

"I'll go and see."

CHAPTER 12   231

Kamal and Nana were already dressed. Mihran took a clean towel and turned to them. "Shall we go and wash?"

"Let's go to the river." Nana clapped her hands and smoothed out the crumpled folds of her light-blue dress with its red-spotted hem.

"Mihran Effendi, have you got an iron in your monastery?"

"We've got everything in our monastery," answered Mihran.

"Surely not! I bet that there's no Koran in your monastery," said Kamal.

"I was thinking of Nana's needs," replied Mihran defensively.

On the river bank, everyone washed themselves as best they could. Nana even expressed a wish to have a swim, but Kamal protested.

"The water is too cold, my girl. In the evening – it's always warmer."

'My girl!' Mihran repeated to himself, 'they really are more like father and daughter rather than –'

"Very well, I'll have a swim in the evening," said Nana decisively.

"Yes, but today we –"

Nana interrupted him. "No way, Bey, no way. We won't go anywhere away from here until Mihran Effendi turns us out of the house."

"But Mihran Effendi will never turn us out," laughed Kamal.

"Why won't he?" said Nana with spirit, throwing the towel to Kamal, "because you're a governor? Don't forget, Bey, that he's a revolutionary committee member. I'm seeing a real such committee member for the first time. A committee member – it's even frightening to utter the words."

Then she came up to Mihran, took hold of his hand, looked straight into his eyes and asked: "Mihran Effendi, are all committee members like you? No, no, another question. Could you kill anyone?"

At that moment Kamal handed the towel to Mihran who quickly covered his face with it, leaving Nana without an answer.

"You never answered my question, Mihran Effendi," said Nana as they were going back up the hill. "Don't take any notice of

Kamal's revolver; he couldn't even kill a chicken."

"Yes," protested Kamal, "but Mihran Effendi hasn't yet answered your question as to whether he could kill a man or not."

Instead of answering, Mihran looked at Nana hoping for some help from her.

"And there's no need for him to answer. His eyes alone show that he couldn't even kill a fly," Nana decreed and took Mihran's arm.

The breakfast took place in a warm and happy atmosphere. The bottle of brandy was emptied. Nana was unable to find enough words to praise the smell and taste of the country food.

"Bey, to think that sitting in our city we believe that we live well. I've never before had such a breakfast in my life, and with such a good appetite. Bey, let's live in the monastery and let Mihran Effendi become the governor."

"In that case both of us will have to change our faith," said Kamal.

"I don't think it is a great sin to change one's faith for the sake of such cream and eggs, Bey."

The governor stroked his grey temples with two fingers. "Well, Nana, let's suppose that we change our faith for the sake of such eggs and cream. But what would Mihran Effendi change his faith for?"

Nana blurted out without thinking, "He wouldn't get killed during massacres. Is that not worth … ?"

There was an unpleasant silence. If they laughed, Nana's unfortunate statement might have been considered a joke, but none of them could laugh, instead they went quiet – even Nana.

Mairig, coming in, saved the situation. "Are they well fed?" she asked Mihran, who translated his mother's question. In response, Nana leaped up from her place, embraced the old woman and sang in Turkish.

> "Mother, mother, sweet and gentle,
> There's no-one like you in the world."

"Leave me alone, girl. What a devil! You've broken my bones again."

CHAPTER 12   233

Taking advantage of the change in the atmosphere, Kamal stood up and said, "We'll meet again, Mihran Effendi, thank you so much for your hospitality."

This time, Nana left the mother's side and rushed up to her husband. "Bey, Khorkom will not go away. I beg you, Bey, let's stay here."

The governor became serious. "Nana, my girl, whatever happens I have to be in Khorkom today. A man from Van is coming to see me. I'm an official, after all."

"I'll not go away from here," pleaded Nana and snuggled comfortably on the window sill.

The mother who was following the conversation, could only understood it intuitively, but she turned to Mihran and said, "Why does he break the girl's heart? Let her stay in the monastery."

Mihran translated what his mother had said and added, as Nana's eyes grew larger, "Of course, it's up to you, Bey. Nana and you are welcome to stay here as long as you want."

The Bey took up his revolver. "I see," he said, "but today I have to be in Khorkom whatever the circumstances. Won't you be unhappy without me, Nana, my girl?"

"I'll wait for you, Bey." She slipped out.

"Mairig, tell Avdo to prepare both my and Kamal Bey's horses."

"And where are you going?" asked Kamal, seeing Mihran pick up his revolver as well.

"I'll accompany you, Bey, as far as the Eremer monastery."

"There's really no need, Mihran Effendi."

"It would be a great pleasure for me, Bey."

The governor looked older, and at the same time more influential, when he put on his red fez. Avdo was standing at the monastery door holding the reins of both horses. Kamal was followed by Mihran and the two women. When Avdo saw Nana, he turned his head away; Mihran could not help noticing.

"Avdo," he exclaimed, "This is the governor's son. Isn't he beautiful?"

"Don't say another word, Baron Mihran, I'm mortified," murmured Avdo.

The governor put a silver coin into Avdo's hand. The horses

moved off.

"Bey, I'll be expecting you in the evening," Nana called after him.

"I'll do my best," he promised.

The riders went down the hill and came out into the open field by the road dividing the grove. The road was almost straight and it stretched on to the west, along the edge of the stream. The road that went to Aratents and Astvatsashen turned off to the right. The morning was full of sunshine, the smell of grass and the chirping of the crickets. The morning was filled with light, smell and sound, heard and unheard. it spread out over the hills, the sown fields, the pasture and paths of Hayots Dzor. The horsemen were silent, each of them engrossed in his own thoughts, or maybe they were simply listening to the clatter of their horses' hooves and were trying not to think at all.

But they could not help thinking. Kamal broke the silence.

"Hayots Dzor, and all Vaspourakan is beautiful."

"Beautiful, but accursed," replied Mihran.

"Everything depends on people, Mihran Effendi."

"People? Isn't that too many, Bey? It seems to me that it depends not on people but on one man. One district or one provincial governor – a Tahsin or a Djevdet Pasha. It will always be so, wherever the law of power reigns rather than the power of law."

"I can't object to that," said the governor, "it's necessary to know each other well. When I decided to come to your home instead of requiring you to come to me, there were people who advised me to give up that idea. I didn't listen to them and in order not to treat my visit as a cold and official one, I brought my wife with me. As a result I have come to know what motivates and moves Hayots Dzor Committee Member Mihran. Yes, yes, don't laugh. I know they won't congratulate me and there may well be some complaints regarding this step. However, I don't worry about my own position. I can leave Hayots Dzor and Van whenever they want me to, or anytime I want to."

"It has always been so," said Mihran, "the good ones leave and the bad ones come in their place. A man like you, Bey, can't remain in this position for long they wouldn't allow it."

The road ended in the grove of green willows. The fresh, damp air caressed the riders' faces pleasantly. The horses too seemed to be feeling well. They slowed their gallop and neighed with pleasure. There was a light wind with an oleaster fragrance; a stream covered in light and shade flowed on the right; a rooster solemnly crowed out at length and the hens clucked and strutted by the stone walls. The Eremer Monastery, built of black stone, stood before them.

"Manvel!" Mihran called out and then turned to the governor, "Bey, let's get down and have a little rest."

A young man, with a short neck and a tanned face, dressed partly in country, and partly in city, clothes, came out through the monastery door.

"Manvel," Mihran addressed him in Turkish, "I and the governor are to be your guests for half an hour."

"Welcome," answered the young man in good Turkish. He took the reins of both horses and went towards the grove. One did not need to have a sharp eye to see that Manvel was limping.

There were trimmed stones under the willow to sit on. They sat down side by side.

"He studies at the college in Van and has come here for his holidays. He speaks French and Turkish well. You can even find a Koran in this monastery."

"Really?" laughed the governor. He turned to the approaching young man who had a somewhat serious face, but smiling eyes, and said in French "Manvel Effendi, you live in a beautiful place. I bet you write poems."

"Lamartine's muse can't reach this sort of place, Bey," replied Manvel also in French, "the roads are too unsafe."

The governor laughed and laughed heartily.

"What would my guests like to drink?" asked the young man in Turkish.

"Give us cold yoghurt, Manvel."

Kamal drank it sip by sip with a good appetite. "Nana was right to admire. Everything is really delicious in your village."

The governor stood up returned the deep earthenware jug to the host and thanked him. He wiped his lips with a green handkerchief and smiled.

"Yesterday, when I passed by this monastery, and then saw the Khek monastery in the distance, it seemed to me that many armed fedayeen with fiery eyes were waiting in ambush in these two monasteries. I had to face that very prejudice. I decided that I would go to the main den, and then if I managed to leave it alive, I would then come to this monastery as well and check and see with my own eyes those 'beasts', of whom I had been told such terrible things. Now that I know what the Khek and Eremer monasteries are really like, I've left my wife in Khek and I'm going to move my own government house to this very place. So, you see, it's simply necessary to get to know people."

A slight breeze stirred as if bringing some very important news, the willows swayed whispering to each other, the monastery dog ran off causing the hens to cackle and then once again peace reigned.

"It's time to start," said the governor, "I to the west – and you to the east."

Manvel came up holding the horses' reins and smiled, showing his white teeth.

Chapter 13

Ever eastward, ever eastward!

Mihran was not in any hurry; the horse seemed to understand that and carried slowly on, nodding away as if counting its paces. Mihran had become more nervous and uneasy lately. What could that be ascribed to? His distressing dreams were becoming more tangible, more real than reality itself. Very often he took reality to be a dream and a dream to be reality. He would remember, but how could anyone know whether it was fiction or fact? What about a naked, white devil called Nana?

CHAPTER 13   237

He had also had such such a dream that spring. What day was it today? It was Friday, yes Friday. What a coincidence! That was the name of the Ourpad creek. Surrounded by a lawn with very few trees, it lay to the east of Van and to the west of the monastery where people from Van would go for a stroll. They would take food with them – boiled eggs, paprika-spiced cheese, grilled beef, fried chicken, raki, wine, even a samovar with things to make tea with – and there they would enjoy the gifts of nature. There would be singing and dancing to the music of pipe and drum, and even the school bugle. There would be someone down from Bolis who would organize a football match. The Ourpad creek was often like that.

Was it a dream or had it really happened? One thing was clear: what he had seen was a girl in a pink dress, with two plaits of brown hair, black eyes and white skin. She had been staring at the distant Mt Varag. Her father had called out, 'Lia, sit down'. And she had sat down on a rug. Mihran had recognised her father, Baron Ohannes Muradkhanian, his wife, his two sons, and Lia.

But it was not Lia, it was ...

And when a few weeks later, his aunt Aghavni wanted to discover what he thought about getting married, and whether any girl in town had attracted his attention, he could not help but remember Ohannes Muradkhanian's daughter. "Then, why have you given your mother such anxious moments, my boy?" his aunt had said, half-joking. "I'll go with Aregnazan and see the girl for you."

Aregnazan was his other aunt. Mihran never knew whether they went or not, saw her or not, such negotiations generally occurred more often in the autumn. Mihran would have left Van and gone elsewhere rather than get married. It would not matter where – Tiflis, Bolis, Varna, anywhere, just to get away. But here there were many pressing matters: the monastery, his mother, the Ourpad stream ...

He came to, sensing the keen scent of the oleasters in the monastery meadows – they smelled stronger in the midday sun. He got down from his horse, tied it to a tree, gathered up the saddle and slowly went up the hill. Avdo came up, took the saddle from him and strode ahead. Then he slowed down and said, "Baron Mihran, the governor's wife is crazy." Mihran smiled. "Don't laugh," Avdo said, "you'll say it's me that's mad. But I'm very sane compared with her." And the very sane man went ahead with the saddle in his hands.

Nana rapturously welcomed Mihran. Earlier that day, she had looked through the window of her room and followed the two men, one with a red fez, the other with a white hat, going along the wide road. They had got gradually smaller until they were red and white points. Nana would have preferred to wait and see Mihran return, but she had not just there sat with folded arms. She was helping his mother with important household chores. Nana liked the monastery a lot and was ready to spend all her life there.

"And now, Mihran Effendi, you must entertain me so that I shan't be sad."

Nana was tinting her already made-up nose with her finger. "What? Shall I go and see what my face is like?" She ran off and came back screaming hysterically. "I've seen a monkey in the mirror. Don't look at me! I'll be back." And she ran towards the river.

Nana would not eat; she had fed and did not want any more. Nana wanted to go for a walk or a ride, it did not matter which. Was there nowhere nearby worth seeing? Hardly! St Abraham? What was that? A ruined monastery?

"I like ancient things. It's not too far? That means we can go there on foot, I like walking ... We're off! Don't be afraid, I'll not eat your son. What fine weather! What are those mounds? Oh, it's the village graveyard. Why are there so few graves?"

"Because the villagers often don't die a natural death," Mihran replied. "They die in obscure, far-away places, and remain unburied."

"And why do they leave their village?"

"They go to seek justice and freedom. And they die on the road to that justice and freedom."

Nana did not want to hear or think about sad things. "How bitter and deadly this bush smells. It only grows in graveyards. And this flower? It's called 'gedja safasi' in Turkish – a night's joy, or something like that. Yet isn't there any daytime joy? The day is for work, for dreary and joyless, everyday matters. But the night! Oh, how terrible life would be if there was no night, if it was always day. Just think – beautiful flowers blossom at night."

Nana stopped and shook a finger at him: "What are you thinking about? What did you just remember? Don't bother – it was only a dream! What am I feeling? The shadow that the big rock casts on the road. The smell of the herds that passed by – I wouldn't change that smell for anything sweeter. Take my arm! Or better, let me take yours."

The road coiled up the hill. Below its three sharp peaks lay the ruined monastery of St Abraham which was covered with the leaves of old willows. Like all other sanctuaries, this also had its own water from a spring coming out from under a rock. The spring water flowed down the hills, leaving in its wake a touch of green growth which gradually got narrower and then vanished.

"Don't worry, you mischieveous boy."

Nana had been to great cities. "Do you know about the Eiffel Tower or Notre Dame? Or the midnight cabarets? But I prefer ancient churches like this – at least today, at this moment. And what magnificent mosques there are in Stamboul!"

"Armenians built them."

"So, it turns out that what an Armenian builds for someone else survives, and what he builds for himself ends up in ruins. Who arranged matters that way?

"Who arranged it that way? History, Geography, Religion, and such elementary disciplines, which are not school subjects but national disasters."

The road wound up the broad base of the hill, which seemed to be supporting the three peaks, left, right and centre, below which was the ancient ruined monastery of St Abraham, grieving beneath the willow leaves.

"Nana wouldn't exchange the cities she has seen for these hills, for that rock, this road, this grass, this insect, and these incredible smells. No, Nana would live here with pleasure. Alone? Oh, no, I'm afraid of loneliness! With Kamal? Wouldn't that be sad? Now,

I'll... Did that hurt? Kiss me and it'll go away. Did it? You don't even know how to kiss. Despite that, I wouldn't mind if we were together, the three of us. Far from towns, in a deserted place like this. And we also need a mother, otherwise who'll feed us? What a good mother! I'm thirsty."

"I'll get you some cold milk."

"In this deserted monastery?"

"Yes, in this deserted monastery."

"Let's hope you're right."

A left turn wound up the hill towards the south and disappeared into the distance, where there appeared to be a huge insect moving, which stopped and then crept forward again. A driver's call dissolved in the yellow rays of the sun and everything went quiet again. It was a cart loaded with grass – 'Gee-up!' What a large and amazing world it is.

One more bend, and the sad, lonely St Abraham stood before them, looming proudly out of the willows. It had walls in which there were some missing stones, an entrance without a door, and a roof covered with grass and wild flowers. And further on where the water-course turned, the fresh water could be seen to be quietly flowing. At one end of a wide basin there was a round, clay bowl, half-immersed in the water.

"Milk, Mihran Effendi! What magic!"

No magic – the monastery shepherd had finished milking and had put it there to cool. His herd was somewhere nearby. He would run back here several times a day to quench his thirst.

"This is not milk. It's a miracle!"

Now, when it was past noon, the eastern side of the monastery was in the shade. There was dry moss by the wall, then warm earth, grass getting thicker and thicker, flowers and insects.

"Sit down here by my feet, with your head like this. I want to sleep. You're trembling! You're a child, just a child."

An invisible hand brushed up the fields, meadows and mountains with a broom, the bristles of which were sunbeams. Then the broom shrivelled and the hand turned into an invisible, fine dust which spread all over the world.

Nana was scared. "Mihran Effendi, can you see anything? The

sun's darkened over the hills. The sky seems clear, but there's no shadow any more. The world's under an endless, grey veil. It's too dark, Mihran Effendi, to see anything other than our open eyes? I can't shut mine. Stars! I see stars and stars and stars. Didn't I tell you that beautiful flowers bloom at night? The sun's faded, Mihran, the moon has gone across the sun!"

Was the scent that of the earth or of Nana's warm lips? Was it the earth or Nana herself that trembled? A disturbed flock of wild birds swarmed onto the pinnacles of the monastery, the cattle stampeded down the opposite hill with terrified bellows. Was it the monastery or Nana herself that sighed? Mihran freed himself from Nana's strong arms. Her hands fell back, closed and helpless, on the grass. A glistening, small worm slid across the girl's bare thigh. One side of the grey disk of the moon covering the sun seemed to disintegrate, and the rays of the sun stabbed the earth like fiery spears.

There had been a girl standing near the Ourpad creek, watching Mt Varag in the distance. Then that wonderful girl turned into white smoke which faded away. Mihran's heart ached. The weak and delicate Nana had fallen, but the strong and earthy Nana had become the dream of his life, the only thing he would fight for, one he would strive for and not achieve, though the longer he tried, the fuller his life would be, the richer and happier his soul. Where did this Turkish woman come from to steal his soul, impoverish him, and leave him bankrupt and homeless?

"Tidy yourself up," Mihran said, "it's already light."

"What a short night that was," Nana yawned. "What was it – a solar eclipse?"

"An eclipse of everything," he replied.

An eclipse of everything! Mihran found the way back long, even tedious, despite the gentle descent. Nana, light and slim, was walking in front. Sometimes she went off the road to pick a flower and smell it; sometimes she lagged behind Mihran and then dashed forward singing some sad, oriental song, occasionally with, and occasionally without, words.

"And I'll leave in your memory

A bitter kiss and a sweet wound."

Mihran listened to the song and reflected that the Turks had some fine, moving songs. Clearly, Sultan Hamid had not created the songs of the Turkish people, any more than Djevdet Bey. It was unknown, simple and law-abiding, people who expressed their hopes in song. They sighed with grieving hearts and their sighs turned into entrancing melodies.

> "Let me water your roses
> With the moist rain of my eyes,
> You'd like to kill me, I know,
> Let me sharpen your knife."

As she sang, Nana sighed 'Aman' at the end of each line. And Mihran also instinctively sighed – Aman, Aman! – in his mind while looking around him in the boundless and all-inclusive, golden, midday sun. The displaced and fading moon faced the cheerful sun and seemed to be seeking a way to approach it again. But that was impossible for there was no longer any way it could cover the golden-haired sun. Such an amazing miracle only occurs once in a hundred years Once in one hundred years – Aman, Aman!

It seemed to Mihran that he was the tired and fading moon, while Nana, singing sprightly near and about him, was the sun. Like the sun and moon, they were now as far away from each after having been so close. No, the comparison was not right. Mihran – if he only wanted it enough – could go up to Nana, catch her, kiss her and kiss her, and wrap her up in his soul. The earth would not then go dark for the sun would certainly continue to light up the world, but a large, black shadow would spread over the Ourpad creek, and in that dark shadow the youthful, slim figure of Ohannes Muradkhanian's daughter gazing at Mt Varag in the distance would vanish ... 'Lia, sit down!'

As if frightened by some unknown danger, Nana was now walking slightly apart from him in silence.

"What are you thinking of? Why have you gone quiet?" he asked.

"I went quiet when the song came to an end."

He grabbed the girl's arm: "Can a song come to an end?"

"The one I was singing did. There are many songs in the world. Must I sing all of them? As for what I'm thinking about – it was about my man, my Bey."

He felt a dagger pierce his heart. Nana tried to free her arm but could not.

"Nana, let's leave the road, go up this hill and then down to the monastery."

Nana looked at Mihran. On leaving the monastery that morning, Nana had been ready to go along any road he wanted. She would have gone down every dark abyss and up the most dangerous peak. She would not have been apprehensive, would not have been frightened, even if the sun had melted away. But now – what was happening to her, why was she anxious and afraid? Of whom? Of what?

"Nana, let's go up this hill, you'll see everything from the top, and nobody will see us. There'll be beautiful flowers flourishing in the sun. And if you hurl an apple down from there, it'll fall on St Abraham's nose. Shall we go, Nana?"

"Let's take the road we came by. It's hot and I'm too tired to able to climb up the hill."

"I'll help you," replied Mihran and put his arms round her waist, hoping to help her off the road. But she did not want to go.

"Nana is tired. Let go of me – it's too hot. Let's take the road we came by, the Bey will have already returned."

Mihran felt her withdrawing from him. She was reviving. And, yes, she was the wife of the governor of Hayots Dzor. Now she had become cold, even formal. She shook off his arms, looked into his eyes with the look of a surprised stranger: "Excuse me, who are you?"

Mihran shuddered and thought to himself:

– Who am I really, my humble lady? First of all, I'm Armenian; secondly, remember that though your husband is the governor of Hayots Dzor, I'm its council. What is a governor? A tax-collector, a nobody! Whereas I'm the heart and soul of Hayots Dzor. I'm all its seven senses. I'm the most powerful lord of Hayots Dzor, and if I wanted – .

Mihran was only now aware of what Nana had been feeling.

What had been in his mind? Why had he wanted to leave the road and take the girl up into the hills? Desire? No, not now with her cold look. He felt that he had been badly humiliated, deprived and left impoverished. The image of Lia left him restless. Who was he? What was he? He knew how he was looked upon in Van. He was greeted there with pleasure, even with some respect, because he was rich and influential. But he felt deeply that he was neither liked, not fully respected – they were simply afraid of him. Why? Because he was considered to be a murderer, a fratricide, a villain. But he had been open and pure as far as Lia was concerned, and he had never previously kissed any girl, any woman, he had not known what a woman was.

No girl? Another image came before his eyes: a girl with big eyes and rosy cheeks like Artemis' apple. She was their lodgers's daughter, Karmileh, with whom he had innocently flirted. But was that any more than the possible flirtation of a brother and sister? Brother and sister?

Mihran now had only one thought in his mind: to take possession of Nana again, not with love but with hate, to hurt the woman in her, to pollute her, to humiliate her, to suffocate her and then cover her breathless and still warm corpse with stones, or throw her into the ravine. On his return to the monastery, his mother would ask, 'Where's Nana?' He would reply, 'Hasn't she arrived yet? She went ahead of me to return to the monastery.' The governor would return to collect her in the evening. 'Nana left the monastery,' he would have said, 'then the sun went down and she didn't return. Perhaps she was kidnapped by Turks.'

Nana seemed to have read all this in his eyes. She ran down the hill, like a deer running away from a furious hunter, and disappeared round the first bend of the path leading to the monastery. The idea of catching up with her was even amusing. Mihran thought of several possibilities, such as taking a short cut and blocking her path, but he felt that they were all impractical. He could at best, meet the girl at the doors of the monastery, if he went up the steep hill and came straight down to the monastery on the other side. Which is what he did.

When he got to the top of the hill and looked around, he

seemed to wake up from a deep nightmare, as he had done the day before. He took a breath and seemed to be seeing the deep beauty of nature for the first time. The valley of Hayots Dzor stretched out to the east and far way beyond its western border was the Van lake. The peaceful sight of the large and small villages on and below the hills, some near and some far from the river Khoshab, filled Mihran's heart with a sweet yet bitter longing. How splendid nature was and how mighty man was! From this barren earth, he reaped a golden harvest and fed not only himself and his family, but also thousands of people who had never seen a village, a cornfield or a sickle. The river Khoshab was shimmering like a silver snake, flowing from east to west. As if the beauties of Hayots Dzor were not enough, God had given it this river as well. Take it and live! And Hayots Dzor was alive.

The monastery was below him. From where he stood, it looked like a small dwarf stuck to the ground. A sound came up from somewhere below, and this made the space around him seem wider, deeper and endless. The hills were looking around. Each had its own nature: there were sad and thoughtful hills; there were happy and light, even light-headed, hills; there were naive hills and sly hills; there were crooked and tired hills; there were hills which had just pushed up out of the earth and looking around defiantly were surprised and would return underground; there were even sleeping hills, and fainting hills, or hills pretending to be dead. The more Mihran looked around, the wilder and more absurd seemed the thing which had happened, and even more absurd the thing that might have happened.

And now he wanted to find Nana and apologize to this incomparable and unusual woman in the surroundings of this wide and benevolent land. 'Forgive me, Nana, forgive me for the crime I didn't commit. Forgive me for the hurt I've done you, voluntarily or involuntarily, consciously or unconsciously.'

Mihran began to descend. He remembered Moses's descent from Sinai. But he was hardly an honest Moses – he could not be so compared. Dust was rising up from the road that went from the village of Nor to Khek. Mihran stopped for a moment and stared at the dust-cloud creeping towards him. 'It's a gang,' thought

Mihran, 'only gangs gallop on horseback like that.' He hurried down. Nana would probably be in the monastery by now. And what if she complained to her husband, to his mother, even to the gang. 'You see he claimed he was the council of Hayots Dzor. He wanted to take me to the mountains and then throw me into the ravine – me, the wife of the governor of Hayots Dzor.'

Mihran was some metres from the monastery, when he noticed Nana come out from the western corner of the monastery wall and go up to the door. Seeing him, she raised her right hand, waved her slender fingers and said in a ringing voice, "You've lost your bet. I got here before you."

At that moment a group of riders on horseback arrived at the monastery grounds. Mihran did not enter the monastery but continued down light-heartedly to meet the group. A gunshot was heard, then a second and a third. Those who had dismounted cheered in unison – bravo! The man thus hailed was Ishkhan who had just shot down two birds while galloping rapidly. "May you always succeed," exclaimed Kotcho, a short, broad-shouldered man with a thin face, He was the only peasant fedayeen in trousers of Shatakh wool and with a hat.

Avdo, bare-footed, long-haired and open-shirted, came down the hill and without paying attention to anyone, took the horses one by one off to the meadows. Irritated by the group's lack of care for their horses and murmuring something under his breath, he left the horses to rest and graze in the meadow.

"Bravo to you too, priest," said Aram in his pleasant, deep voice, shaking the supposed priest's hand, "Has a lost angel appeared in the monastery as a result of the solar eclipse? Or have you brought a lady to the monastery without having had a wedding party?"

Mihran smiled complaisantly, shook hands with everybody and said: "She's the new governor's wife. They spent the night in the monastery. The governor went to Khorkom."

"So, the wolf has to guard the lamb, does he, Mihran?" Ishkhan ruffled his beard with his finger.

"So his great Mohammedan majesty has deigned to spend the night with his wife in a Christian-Armenian monastery. How courageous!"

"He is a very liberal man, Baron Aram," said Mihran.

"I'm not sure about that." Aram shook his head. "That's what I've been told, but –"

"Is his wife also liberal?" asked Ishkhan, squinting with one eye into the barrel of his gun, as if he hoped to see the answer to his question there.

"Yes, she is as well." Mihran was a little bewildered.

"Well, we'll talk about that later," interrupted Aram wiping his dark glasses with a white handkerchief. "Now, the men are hungry."

It was not the first time that the monastery had turned out to feed the group. It was not the first time that Avdo, swearing under his breath, had slaughtered hens and lambs for the sake of the revolution, or that Mihran's mother had come down with piles of lavash, with some cheese and butter. The guests spread their cloaks on the grass, took raki and wine out of their bags. Kotcho sang some Kurdish songs and the smoke of the fire under the cauldron of the cooking meat spread over the green foliage of the park like blue lace. It was not the first time.

The solar eclipse had had a terrifying effect on the mother. She saw the phenomenon as an ominous evil, the start of black misfortunes. She did not say anything aloud to anyone and even when Avdo, standing in the middle of the monastery yard, raised his long arms to the sky and promised with a voice of doom that the world would be destroyed, she warned him: "Don't talk nonsense, the moon and the sun suddenly met up with each other. It's nothing more than that." The monastery gongs rang out with an unbearable, corrosive sound. Ordinary people have always behaved this way in times of natural disasters like hail or flood. Deeply shocked in her soul, but with outward composure, the mother was calming everybody down and trying even to laugh. "It's nothing serious, nothing serious, they suddenly ..."

The suddenness really lasted only a few moments. The sun came out from under the silver lid of the moon and reasserted its rights. The horrified hens and roosters slipped out of their holes in the earthen wall, looked around in confusion, and having made sure that the danger had passed, began to cackle lightly. The sound of a long crow was heard from Khek. The most powerful of the young roosters – Avdo called it 'tossoun' – jumped on the wall like a trained athlete and sounded such a loud cock-a-doodle-do that it could be heard throughout the universe. It was not the tall tossoun, but most probably the newly-freed sun which now rang its unrestrained and resounding cock-crow all over the world.

"May we be the next to be free?" said the mother.

When Nana had appeared in the monastery yard, Mihran's mother was distressed. Why was the girl alone and looking sad? Nana felt the mother's anxiety, put on a happy face and made it clear to her that Mihran had arrived, but that he had gone to the riders. No, Nana had not been frightened by the solar eclipse. Nana was afraid of the people who had just arrived – were they bandits with guns, knives, hats? Mother made the sign of a curse in the direction of the meadow and said, "They can't be compared to a governor. A governor's wife mustn't be afraid of them. That would be a mistake, a shame."

They laughed.

The sun was setting in the west. The group had eaten and drank, had rested and were on their feet again. Some of them were washing themselves, some were smoking and one was assiduously cleaning his weapons. Only Ishkhan and Aram were lying with their bags under their heads, with closed eyes though they were awake.

"It wouldn't be bad," murmured Aram.

"What wouldn't be bad?" asked Ishkhan without opening his eyes.

"Aren't you asleep? It wouldn't be bad if we made use of the meeting to solve the problem with that Mushegh. Hard times lie ahead."

"Do you recall any easy times?" Ishkhan said.

"At any rate," Aram suggested, "there have been some hard times, which have been light compared to the really hard ones."

"That's philosophy," Ishkhan yawned. "As for Mushegh, why must his problem be discussed at any meeting? The question is more than clear, the crime has been proved and confirmed. Can't you and I ...?" He looked at Aram with a searching glance. Was Ishkhan speaking seriously?

"No," said Aram abruptly, "neither you nor I. I don't want you to hear Vramian shout at me or myself to hear him shouting at you. He's become quite unbearable lately – malevolent, nervous, quarrelsome. Let it not be a formal arrangement, let it be the way he wanted it."

"Very well!" Ishkhan gave way. "And now?"

"And now – come here, everyone," called Aram, sitting up.

Ishkhan also sat up. "Have you noticed that the Mohammedan angel hasn't left the window?"

"Stop, man, this isn't the right time for that."

Aram turned to the bearded men sitting on the blankets and the trunks of the felled trees. "Dear colleagues," he began – he thought they should all be sent to the barber's – and then continued in his deep voice, "you all know Mushegh Baldoshian. You also know that he's been put on the black list because of his way of life and his suspicious contacts. Yes, recent evidence proves that Mushegh Baldoshian is a traitor."

"May God be with him," someone called out.

"We believe in neither God nor Devil." Aram wanted to smile, but his face took on a stricter expression. "Boghos, was that you? But this time, may Hell be with him."

Boghos rubbed his forehead. Then Kotcho spoke up: "Give that withered cockerel to me. I'll twist its neck." Everybody burst into laughter.

"Be serious," Aram could not help smiling now. "That man's regular meetings with the Police Chief Agyah have been confirmed. Please don't think that we're so naïve that any Vanetsi speaking to Agyah would be accused of betrayal. We shouldn't forget that Agyah himself sets up some subtle provocations. He enters the house of this or that completely innocent man as if he's an intimate friend, in order to confuse us. If you remember, he did once in this way try to involve ... er, er ... Muradkhanian."

"Ohannes," prompted Ishkhan.

"Yes – he involved Ohannes. But we saw through Agyah's

provocation in time and avoided shedding … er … innocent blood."

'He's blustering, but from the right side,' thought Ishkhan, now stroking his beard with his palm to conceal his smile. While Aram continued talking and proving poor Mushegh Baldoshian's betrayal with irrefutable evidence, Ishkhan remembered the day when Ohannes Muradkhanian, wild with rage, had boldy told him things which had disturbed his sleep or given him nightmares for a few nights. One thought tortured his mind about these men who had left their homes and parents, crossed the border risking their lives, and come to this peaceful town to sow the seeds of revolution: did they help or harm people?

– Was their cause good or evil? Could they be a Moses for this tribe and take it to a Canaan of happiness? Could one Ottoman Bank incident, one Khanasor, one pasha killed, and all such single events, lead to liberation from the Turkish yoke? Was that not a dream? What about European intervention? But how many times had the alarm bells rung over the blood of thousands of victims and over the flames of the burning villages and towns of Ottoman Armenia, while those civilized European countries remained content simply to print articles and photographs. Then people came from outside the Empire, started a movement, excited the people, created songs of freedom in glory of the victims, in praise of the struggle. And what songs! These songs showed that the business they had started was doomed from the start, that those who spoke of sacrificing themselves for the sake of victory, would die – but never win. Songs, what songs!

> "Love for freedom
> Thundered strongly in my heart,
> The sacred name of my home
> Calls me to go to war."

And all of a sudden, in this glorious national song – tra-la-la-la. What wretch had invented that la-la-la? Was that not a sardonic attitude to this revolution? Was it not a mockery when people sang:

> "The leaders are strong in spirit,

So that though we lack
A sword, a sabre or a spear,
We'll kill all our enemies
With our spades, with our spades."

So, look at these people who are so strong in spirit. The Turk does not sing. What song could there be while he is working? He does his work – he slaughters. An Armenian gets slaughtered and dies singing.

One more question. Did people really like them, especially the outsiders? No, you did not have to be wise to realise that people did not like the newcomers. People were simply afraid of them. Could men who relied on frightening people ever succeed, could any undertaking based on fear ever be a success? Fear, fear, fear! Ohannes Muradkhanian had not been afraid, even for a moment, and what had he said? And if people were not afraid, would they not rise up one day and say with one voice: 'Take the seeds of your freedom, your clandestine leaflets, your newspapers and secret weapons, go! And may God go with you. There are no loyal subjects and no fair masters. A whip is a whip even if its handle is made of gold. We were under one whip, but have fallen under two when you appeared. We were under one yoke and the yoke has now doubled. Go – go away by the road you came on, and may your heels be blessed.' –

"All Baldoshians must be killed – anyone who interferes with the sacred national cause." Aram's warlike speech seemed to Ishkhan to be from another world. "That's why it was decided that Baldoshian has to be killed. The organisation sets you the task of resolving this situation. Does anyone want to speak?"

Yes, there is one. Boghos from Van, Ishkhan's bodyguard, wants to say something.

"We can certainly clean things up. Purity is not a bad thing. Baron Aram spoke in detail. But we heard very little about what Mushegh Baldoshian's treachery was. There are no facts. So he and Agyah, met, spoke, heard – these are no facts. When we mention the traitor Davo, we can immediately recall the armoury unearthed and the secret cases opened up with his help."

"We can't allow it to get as far as that," said Aram.

"Well, let's consider whether Baldoshian could become a Davo or not. No, he couldn't. It's not enough to have a finger to be a traitor. It has to be pointing at something critical. Baldoshian doesn't know anything of that sort. Davo's case was quite different."

"What's your conclusion?" Aram said seriously.

Broad-shouldered, low-necked, short Boghos stood up firmly and stepped up to Aram. "Baron Aram, you know the cases of both Davo and Mushegh Baldoshian better than I do. Baldoshian isn't a Davo."

"He curses our Party, he soils everything we hold sacred," objected Aram.

"Baron Aram, I haven't heard him curse the Party, nor has anybody else. As to the other thing you said, well, I can't agree to that either. Who says that criticizing this or that member means you're cursing the Party or soiling what we hold sacred? It's shameful even to speak about it – it's shameful."

Ishkhan wrapped his hands round his knees, and rocked backwards and forwards as if wanting to concentrate. Now he realised that the question of murdering Baldoshian was not nearly as clear and straightforward as he had earlier suggested to Aram. Perhaps he had been wrong in trying to persuade Aram that there was no need to discuss it at any meeting, or that he and Aram could deal with the matter with the help of one of their men as they had done so often before.

Yes, Van was excited, the people's hearts had been stirring like the orchards in the wind. Now they had calmed down and the orchards were quiet – but only until there was a new so-called treachery, to be followed by a new terror.

Chapter 14

The most important incident was of course the Davo affair. What was the so-called Davo affair? Davo was from Dher, a peasant boy and a hot-headed patriot. The 'sacred national cause' was dear to his heart. At the same time he had fallen deeply in love with a girl named Marineh. She had limpid cheeks like dalasli apples and eyes as black as the cave of Zum Zum Maghara. It had always seemed to Ishkhan that if Father Mesrob in Araruts or Father Khoren in the church at Norashen had only put their heads together, the hot-headed youth would have sung the wedding hymn,'Come on native bridegroom', and carriages full of wedding guests would have driven away, following the bride and bridegroom's carriage along the broad avenue stretching from Arark to Khatch Street. In that event there would have been no Davo affair.

"David, am I greater or is Mesrob?" Aram asked the young lover.

"You are greater, Baron Aram, you're greater, what sort of question is that?" Davo answered.

"In that case I must marry you off," Aram replied, "in the Aghtamar monastery where the gods of the Dashnak party reign with St Ishkhan at their head."

"Well that will be a great honour, Baron Aram, thank you."

"What nice socks you're wearing, David. They could almost be a carpet."

"A carpet can't be compared with this. The girl I'm engaged to knitted it."

"What a gifted girl she must be, David, what's her name?"

"Her name is Marineh, Baron Aram. I'll tell her to knit another pair for you."

"Let her do so, David, let her do that. And I'll deal with the wedding expenses."

Ill-starred socks! What need was there for measurements in order to knit socks. However, Davo wanted Marineh to measure Aram's feet, so that the socks should be neither too big nor too small, neither tight nor loose, neither long nor short, and so that the socks knit by Marineh would fit Aram's feet perfectly. So Marineh went round to measure Aram Pasha's feet.

With one ear still turned towards the hot quarrel still going on outside the monastery, Ishkhan's thoughts went back into the past and he smiled to himself. No future historian would imagine for a moment that the terrible Davo affair had begun at the moment when Marineh, who had limpid cheeks like dalasli apple and black eyes like Zum-Zum Maghara, had put the first loop of the thread, as red as blood, on one of the four parts of the sock.

And Ishkhan remembered again that Aram's weakness for women was even then well-known. Aram, himself, once told him that while crossing the border he was staying in the village of Davalu. Attracted by the affectionate looks of his host's young wife, he had taken explosives and grenades out of his pack, ostensibly to clean them, but in fact to drive the lovely village lass out of her mind. Was Aram the sort of man to keep a cool head in the presence of a pretty woman? Due clearly to carelessness – what eyes she had! – one of the grenades had exploded and both he and his hosts were covered with blood. And this was on the border where he was just about to cross to look for fortune and glory. And here, he was now called Aram Pasha by the people and even if people did not like him, they were afraid of him, they respected him because of that fear. Could Marineh resist the rakish Aram, sitting in the armchair, smiling and speaking Caucasian Armenian? Could Aram resist a rose-like girl kneeling before him and measuring his feet?

And the knitting began. It began with necessary, and then unnecessary, measurements, and the longer the socks got, the shorter became Marineh's and Davo's meetings. Davo was slow to realize which way the wind was blowing. Love itself had not faded, the flame of love was still strong in Marineh's heart, but it was no longer there for Davo, but for another. Ishkhan remembered well the evening when he went up the wooden stairs to Aram's chamber. He was half-way up when the door of Aram's room opened and closed and Ishkhan had seen that a woman or a girl, covered with a white scarf, had slipped quickly down the stairs and had run towards the garden door. It was clearly Marineh. Had she been knitting a second pair of socks?

In the dim light of the lamp hanging from the ceiling, Ishkhan saw Aram stretched out on the sofa, staring up dreamily.

"Man, you're busy on an important matter tonight," said Ishkhan just for something to say.

"Are you laughing at me?" Aram sat up. "You're married and can distance yourself from such things."

"Well, you too get married and stop dallying," Ishkhan interrupted. "I don't like these relationships of yours. She's engaged to David, isn't she?"

"She was," yawned Aram, "she was, but now she isn't. She says she doesn't love him anymore. Look, have you read – er – that novel. What's it called? I'm a Man? Yes, that's it – *Homo Sum* by George Ebbers. Have you read it?"

"No, I haven't."

"Do read it if you can." Aram smiled and added, "Good Lord, you don't read anything else but your own poems. I think that this poem of yours – 'You got up at sunrise and tied the belt round your waist with pride' – will last. I'm not joking. You've done it well."

"You always tend to suggest that all my literary efforts will last."

"Why?" asked Aram.

"You aren't behaving well, you aren't behaving at all decently." Ishkhan was striding up and down the room.

"I admit it," Aram raised his hand to the switch and the room was pleasantly illuminated. "I have become totally besotted with the girl, you see. As for decency is there any decency in what we're doing politically? David has told the girl that he'll kill himself, then the girl, then me."

"That's impossible."

"Why?"

"Because it's impossible to shoot anyone after committing suicide."

"Let's stop joking. He's said he'll kill us, then himself."

"Very well, that is possible. And what do you think?"

"David's a hot-tempered man. You can expect anything from him."

"Yes, that's true."

"So, I'm declaring that tonight is going to be a sleepless night, when we'll talk the whole things through."

"Sleepless nights are obligatory for those who are in love."

"In this matter love is the fifth foot of a dog! I've never been afraid of death and we're all condemned to die, but is it normal to survive fire and water only to be drowned in a bath full of soapy water? Well, let's leave it at that. Come take a seat, let's get down to work."

And they got down to work.

But Davo got down to work too. Blind with jealousy, once he was sure that he had lost Marineh, he planned a great revenge. Davo was an active and senior member in the great cause, and no conspiracy, no business, no affair had been carried out without his participation. He had been a fanatically active organizer of all the dark and secret matters, the stores of arms, the important hiding places. He had been a flame burning for the great cause, with whom Aram had so foolishly and irresponsibly amused himself. The fire which had been scorching the Turks veered the other way. David went to the local Turkish authorities and offered his services, "Effendi..."

And the Davo affair exploded! All the arms and ammunition acquired at heavy cost were lost, hidden stores were unearthed, lists were drawn up, and arrests were made. The Turkish newspapers buzzed:

> 'A few terrorists have crossed the border and initiated a conspiracy in Van against the Ottoman state. It has been prevented, although similar groups of conspirators have been established in all the Armenian vilayets. Our Motherland is in danger! Turks, keep your powder dry.'

And what happened? All the leaders of the movement went underground to avoid being arrested. They went underground literally. A hide-out was soon excavated by experts to enable those leaders to live at the bottom of it like snakes and scorpions. They all went underground one after the other down a long rope. A heroic old woman would send them baskets of bread, cheese, cold meat and jars of yogurt. Early in the morning, she would lower a boiling samovar down the hole, and wish everyone below a good morning.

Meanwhile life in Van was becoming a nightmare. When all the depots were discovered and emptied, searches began in the private houses. Fear spread everywhere. The town was given over to beatings, violence, and barbarity. And terrible Davo from Dher was everywhere, committing all his perfidious, black deeds in the company of a group of Turkish guards. Often, especially in the middle of the night, Davo would awake to a memory of how he had been before – the David who had been trusted by everybody.

At such moments he was horrified with himself and his eyes, already black as coal, would become even darker. Where was he, what was he doing? From the day that he had crossed over, that is to say had asked the Turks for political asylum, he had lived in the house of the police chief, in a room which had been put at his disposal. He remained under the protection, or rather under the control, of a strengthened group of Turkish guards.

At those moments of self-awareness, when his conscience awoke, he fell into a fit of rage and was ready to run away back to his native district, and stand before … stand before whom? Aram? Ishkhan? Sarkis? Those outsiders, who came and polluted the pure air of Van like cuckoos that lay their eggs in other birds' nests?

Van was for people born in Van. Down with all those foreigners, especially that scoundrel Aram with his dark glasses, who had taken the pure and modest Marineh away from him, and turned her into a free-thinking, licentious whore. Davo walked to and fro in his chamber, like a beast locked in its cage, and when he remembered Marineh slipping through the door of Aram's room at night, his steps became faster and he became furious. No turning back, no regrets. He would go to the end, to the bitter end.

The police chief entered in a nightgown and cap.

"Why don't you go to bed? Are you worried? Are you ill?"

"I am neither worried, nor ill, Effendi. I don't know why but I can't get to sleep."

"I can't either. Do you think that the Padishah can fall asleep in the Yildiz Palace? No, he can't sleep, either. The great Abdul Hamid who thinks about his people, about destroying evil and bringing calm, can't sleep easily either. That's why you can't sleep. However, take off your clothes, get into bed and try to rest. You've a lot to do tomorrow."

Davo came to a halt at the mouth of the secret hole, which was covered with a heavy slab. He was surrounded by policemen and guards, all of them armed and with the Police Chief at their head.

"The leaders are all here," declared Davo, indicating the slab with his foot.

The slab was pulled aside. The Police Chief himself bent down; he could see nothing but darkness.

"The dogs are in there," insisted Davo.

"Is there anyone here in this hole? Dead or alive?" the police chief shouted down into the depths of the hole.

The inhabitants of the pit were in a state of shock. "That's the police chief's voice," said someone. "We're betrayed," Aram moaned. "David is implacable."

"Speak up, otherwise we'll fill the pit with water," threatened the voice from above.

There was no way out, they were forced to surrender. They had to face death either by drowning, or now that a guard could be put at the entrance, by starvation.

They had to surrender. And Ishkhan began to sing one of his favourite songs:

> "I'm walking at midnight
> Beneath the full new moon.
> Due to your love, darling,
> I've lost my peace of mind."

Ishkhan sang in a loud and resonant voice, remembering the many times he had sung this song while hiding in different houses. He always sung in a loud voice from the bottom of his heart, and the host or hostess who were hiding him would run to his hiding place and beg him not to sing so loudly as Turkish soldiers were wandering the streets and gardens looking for outlawed fugitives. And now? Now he was singing the same song just as loud to make the people above understand that they were there at the bottom of the sunless well, and that they had no other option but to surrender. 'We're here, alive – and we surrender.'

The negotiations lasted only a short time. The men above shouted and those below agreed. The men at the bottom shouted and those at the top agreed. Those in the pit promised to leave their arms at the bottom and clamber up the rope totally unarmed, and those at the top promised that their person and honour would not be violated.

And so these Illuminators of the early twentieth century came out of their pit like the founding father of the Armenian Church did out of his, sixteen hundred years before. This great event became a lively entertainment for the Turks. Cannibals might have rejoiced like this when taking out the corpses of half-drowned European sailors, wrecked not far from the coast of a deserted island. No, the promise of keeping the honour of the hole-dwellers intact was not kept and each time the next Illuminator appeared up the rope, a great clamour of laughter, swearing and humiliation arose. Aram was greeted with particular exultation; the Police Chief even pulled his hair, obviously meaning to tear some off, and spat in his face.

"You have no right to insult our honour – you promised not to," Aram complained.

Instead of replying the police chief turned to Davo.

"Look who's talking of honour, David Effendi."

It could not be said that Davo showed any great interest or enthusiasm during all this activity. No, he sat smoking on the stone slab or walked to and fro and behaved like a man who was not concerned with whatever was going on and was quite bored waiting for the matter to be done with. But when Aram Pasha, who did not look like a pasha at all, but was thin, bearded and dishevelled, was taken out of the pit, David became tense. To conceal his trembling, he struck a match and lit a cigarette. Perhaps he was distraught at the fact that Aram was wearing slippers, and over his civilian trousers were the long colourful socks. The colours had faded a little in the pit, but they were neither long nor short, neither big nor small, neither tight nor loose – in a word, they fitted Aram's feet perfectly.

Eventually, however, something happened that was bound to occur sooner or later. On an early spring morning, when Davo was walking along Khatch Street accompanied by guards, a teenager, with a worn-out sack over his shoulder, was casually strolling in the direction of the town, taking no notice of the lively bustle and activity in the street. No-one knew exactly what happened, but everyone heard the three shots of a gun. The news flew like it always does from street to street, from district to district, from house to house.

"Davo's been shot ... Where? ... In Khatch Street ... Who shot him? ... It's not known ... Oh, may the assassin's hand be ever blessed.! ... But Davo wasn't guilty ... Good Lord, so many betrayals, so much misfortune, and yet he wasn't guilty? ... Well, you have to take into account his emotional state and all the circumstances ... No emotional state, no circumstances, can excuse a man who betrays his motherland to the enemy for a girl – he doesn't deserve to be alive ... And the other one, that Aram – isn't he at all guilty? ... His fault was only the natural weakness of a human ... Yes, but that's no excuse ... Well, man, history has many similar examples."

Davo's murder and the whole story was examined and analyzed differently by the women.

"May Marineh be accursed! See what harm she's brought to Van ... Well, was Aram's part in it right? ... Mothers and sisters, a man is a man, you can't expect any better ... But he could have behaved more properly ... If a woman is virtuous, she'll withstand any amount of male misbehaviour. Neither Aram nor Davo are to be blamed in this affair; Marineh is to blame, may she be accursed!"

And so a convenient moment had at last presented itself to an alert supporter of the Great Cause to cut out ferociously the malignant tumour named Davo. But by an evil irony of history, that deed was carried out by a still beardless teenager, who had nothing to do with the Great Cause. Grabbing his opportunity following the great excitement and panic in Khatch Street, the young terrorist, Tachat Terlemezian, managed to rush off and disappear into the gardens, while the bleeding victim, Davo of Dher, was taken to the Police Chief's house in a carriage.

Davo was still alive. The dying man opened his dimming eyes. While his eyes had been closed, he had imagined, with a touch of that conscience that had returned to him, that he was dying because he had been shot by a Turk. He was dying for the sake of a sacred cause, for the great cause, dying as the heroic leaders, Peto Giumretsi and Serop Aghbiur, had died. But now, when he opened his weary and sweating eyelids, he saw that instead of Marineh, his kinsmen or his fighter friends, he was surrounded by Turkish soldiers and the Police Chief himself. He groaned deeply.

"David, my son, what do you need?"

Davo shook his head.

"Be a little patient, the military doctor is coming."

"Send for a priest, Effendi," Davo could only just whisper.

The police chief respected Davo's last request – a priest was sent for.

Father Housik, the old priest of one of the smaller churches in Van, arrived. Without looking at anyone, he quickly went up to the dying man, took a small prayer-book out of his pocket with the confidence of an expert drawing a revolver, and only then turned and looked at the people in the room.

The police chief signalled that everyone should leave the room. Left alone, the priest moved his lips quickly, sometimes looking at the pages of the open book and sometimes casting a glance up at the blue-painted boards of the ceiling. Then he took a small round tin box out of his other pocket, opened it skillfully without putting the prayer-book down, dabbed the contents of the box with his thumb and finger and then touched the dying man's lips. This was the sacrament and the remission of sins in normal conditions. In normal conditions?

"Holy Father, let me die as an Armenian," said Davo, gathering all his strength into his hands.

Instead of answering, the priest moved the prayer book up and down, but not in the shape of a cross, that is without also moving it left and right. The dying man made an effort to raise his head and was able to utter: "Long live ..." He could not continue. He made some convulsive movements, breathed deeply and died. Death had not allowed him to finish his last words, his last credo: "Long live ..." Long live what? Long live who? Maybe Tachat Terlemezian?

All this, together with the news, suppositions and his own personal imaginings, had occurred to Ishkhan several times like magic visions, and the whole memory of the Davo affair was with him again, now that an open-air meeting was going on under Aram's chairmanship, in which the issue of another presumed traitor, Mushegh Baldoshian, was being examined.

They were unable to arrive at any agreement. At this point Aram looked in Ishkhan's direction in an attempt to catch his eye and make him understand that he should interfere and give the meeting his opinion. A vain effort! Aram realised that Ishkhan's thoughts were far away and that it was impossible to involve him in this matter. Aram began feeling uneasy.

Where had they got to? As if it was not enough that the killing of that minor character Baldoshian had become an issue for the meeting, it was if any particular decision always invoked certain general principles. This seemed to be a perennial Armenian problem.

Aram felt power slipping out of his hands – no, not just his but out of all their hands. He felt that the group had lost the benefit of leadership and would no longer be able to act decisively and at the right moment as they had done before. What a fiasco! Had they already reached the sad day when the revolutionaries would be without a revolution and the Tashnaks would be without allies? 'Tashnak' – Aram liked to pronounce this word like that, and in that T, rather than a D, he felt a sense of power. Where was that power? Where was the former trust? Aram felt that his influence was disappearing and that a nameless great ideal was getting lost. Perhaps David had felt the same way when he sensed Marineh drifting away from him. And perhaps Mihran had also felt the same that day in the hills behind the monastery of St Abraham, when Nana, trembling under his influence, had changed and become someone else, and looking at Mihran's eyes like a stranger had said, "Excuse me, who are you?"

And, indeed, who are they? Mothers had given birth to them and sung lullabies over their cradles. Mothers, poor mothers, who thought that their sons would become the future pillars of their fathers' homes, and the smoke of the family hearth. And when that future came, these sons left their homes and houses, went out into the dark world to give it some light, leaving their mothers with tears in their eyes. Mothers, poor mothers!

And what was the end result? They built their hearths in this world of conspirators, in the mountains of Sassoun, the fields of Moush and Bitlis, and the mountains and valleys of Vaspourakan. They came separately and in groups, and many died on the way, and that way was called the way to freedom. They brought sparks of fire from the chapels and forges of Tiflis, Geneva, and other well-known cities, to rouse the fire of the glorious cause, which would be seen by the whole of the civilized world. Leaving all their normal life, they would hasten to help create a free and independent Armenian kingdom. And the day and the time would come when a flag would be seen on the top of Masis with the naked eye, when all Armenians would return to their beautiful motherland – a motherland as beautiful as Marineh.

But the result, the actual end result? The end of the glorious cause could have been seen from the start, when their original great leader made a bomb, a fearful machine which was intended to send the blood-thirsty Sultan Abdul Hamid to Hell. The bomb exploded, but instead of taking the Sultan to Hell, it took that leader, according to most people, to Paradise. The blood-soaked sultan remained unhurt on his throne, and instead of him, the leader and expert in hellish affairs was torn to pieces. Was not this to be the end of the cause as well?

And the result? They left their homes, but they did not do much for their motherland. They came to the Ottoman Empire for the sake of their great cause, but as a result of their crazy policy they became hard, fratricidal Cains. They brought in forbidden books, forbidden arms, forbidden songs and, now at the moment that calamity was threatening to spread all over the world threatening to sink whole nations, they were sitting here and discussing the question of killing one Mushegh Baldoshian. Why? Because he had dared to criticize the outsiders – especially Aram.

Absorbed in similat thoughts, Ishkhan guessed from the pleased look now on Aram's face that a black mark had at last been placed against the name of Baldoshian. Encouraged by his success, Aram, with the consistency of a man striking while the iron was hot, suggested to all present that they should choose someone to carry out the decision. One of them suggested Mihran.

"I couldn't do it," said Mihran, "it's beyond my capability."

A shadow passed over the faces of those who were present; a slight smile was hidden in Aram's thick moustaches.

"The matter is beyond Mihran's power," he said softly. "We need a strong fighting hand and not a talker-balker." Someone laughed, perhaps a talker-balker. They decided on Kotcho neither a talker nor a balker, he was a natural fighter with a strong arm. Aram asked him what he felt about this. Kotcho looked around, rubbing his neck, and swearing at the chairman and all the other participants of the meeting, at the way they had come and the way they would go.

"What can I say, Pasha? Kotcho's job is to sing Kurdish songs, but now if you tell me to do this as well, I must do it, even if I die."

"The meeting is over," announced Aram.

Just then horse-hooves were heard. 'That's the district governor,' thought Mihran and was upset. The horseman came out from the road on the right that cut through the meadow. He had an oval face, wheat-coloured skin and unkempt hair, and was dressed in light clothes, without a cap and with the collar of his shirt open. He had a stick in his hand and was swaying to the right and to the left on his horse as if he was beating out the rhythm of a song. It was Mushegh Baldoshian.

Only Ishkhan was not surprised. He was in such an emotional state that if even Davo from Dher had appeared on horseback he would not have been surprised. 'The quarry itself has come into the hunter's trap,' he thought. Aram took a white handkerchief out of his pocket and began to wipe his glasses energetically.

Mihran, who had wanted to go back up to the monastery, changed his mind and remained rooted to the spot. Confusion and hesitation could be read on every face, a circumstance which the condemned would not have failed to notice, had not Kotcho saved the situation.

"Now, would you all like me to sing the song of the Zilana gorge? Mushegh, you just sit and listen. What wind brought you here? Listen everyone! Two Kurdish clans have been warring for many years. The head of one of these families, Msto, shot the brother of Djndo, the head of the other family, last autumn. Spring came and Djndo went down into the Zilana gorge with a weapon in his hand seeking to kill Msto. I'll sing the song and you just chant tra-la-la'."

Everyone, even Aram, sighed with relief. Mushegh stretched out on the grass.

"Why," he complained, "didn't you let me know that you were all going away into the countryside? I was at home and I got bored. I had some raki, but my heart was still heavy. So I came out and decided to look for one of you. But, whichever door I knocked at, I was told that he had ridden away. My instinct told me you would be in this part of the world. I don't know why my heart is so heavy."

What a surprising thing! Why was Mushegh's heart so heavy?

Kotcho closed his right ear with his right hand, shook his head as if to get rid of some thoughts, and began to sing. The song flowed, sometimes slow and heart-breaking, sometimes the Kurdish words were pouring out as fast as hail. Kotcho was singing with an infectious, impersonal warmth, sometimes begging and repentant, sometimes cruel and sharp like a stick.

"Spring has put on its neat, green clothes,
The Zilana gorge smells of blood.
Djndo, the head of his tribe,
Lies in ambush to take revenge.
His brother was fatally shot
By Msto, the head of his tribe.
He lies waiting to take revenge,

to blend Msto's soul with the earth.
The others joined in – tra, la, la.
The mother of Msto tells him:
Lao, don't go to the chasm,
Don't go through the Zilana gorge,
Go away to Van for a while.
I've had such a terrible dream:
Black smoke rose from your silver knife,
Black smoke rose from Zilana gorge,
Black smoke spread over our village.
Mother, mother, I'll soon come home,
I'll bring my wife green fruit and rhubarb,
And I'll shoot a partridge for you.
She hung onto his horse's neck:
Lao, don't leave the village now.
It's a bad day to go, lao,
Just obey your mother, lao."

The others joined in – tra, la, la.

Which son has ever obeyed his mother for Msto now to obey his. And every son that has not listened to his mother has been hurt. Msto rode his horse along the road of the Zilana gorge. Msto, turn the head of your horse. Msto, may your home be ruined. Msto – tra, la, la.

Djndo has been lying in wait – hungry and thirsty – behind the big rock for four days and nights, guarding the Zilana gorge. Spring has arrived and the mountains and the valleys are dressed in green. Msto is impatient. He comes to gather green fruit and rhubarb. The killer is lying in ambush like a black snake, like a wicked wolf.

Tra, la, la ...

Djndo, it is not honourable to stab a man in the back, put your gun away. If you are brave, come down onto the road, stop Msto and fight face to face. Whoever dies, may his soul go to heaven. Whoever survives, may he live long.

Tra, la, la ...

May you be lucky. Msto is coming on horseback and the wind is blowing black dust over his hat. Djndo's heart is thumping, he is lying on his stomach and shutting one eye to take aim. O, Zilana gorge! O, gorge of disaster! O, fate – fate – fate!

There was a silence. As if with one accord, everyone looked at Mushegh Baldoshian lying on the grass. No, no one knew why he was so sad that day.

Without any preliminary arrangement, but as if it had been agreed, Aram and Ishkhan went to one side. "What's the matter with you today, man?" asked Aram warily, leaning on the broad trunk of the ash tree.

Ishkhan linked his fingers and twiddled his thumbs rapidly. "I'm si-ick and ti-red," he stammered.

"What of?"

"Of all these things."

Aram smiled. 'This is going to be his next bit of madness,' he thought, and then addressed Ishkhan in the way spoilt children are spoken to: "What must we do to allay your boredom Your Majesty."

"I don't know, I don't know myself," said Ishkhan thoughtfully. "I do know one thing, however, that all this is not right. The path we've chosen isn't right. Maybe we're going in the wrong direction. I don't know."

Aram again smiled. "I know – I don't know. I know one thing for certain, I can see that today you're unrecognizable."

"Why only I? It seems to me that little by little we're all becoming unrecognizable."

"In what respect?"

"In every respect."

Ishkhan moved off; he went a little way up the hill and sat on the stone where Mihran had sat and gazed at the panorama before him. The others were sitting or standing in the glade of the meadow. They were all wearing red fezzes, they were like huge tulips against the background of the greenery. Some of them were walking under the rich green trees that edged the glade. Crowded into the small space, they were like walking red tulips.

There was Maghak – Baron Maghak to the children at school – with his sad, dark eyes and small moustache. He kept quiet most of the time watching the face of each speaker with strained attention, but now he was walking up and down, looking at the grass under his feet, and stroking his small moustache. There was Barunak, fair-haired, broad-shouldered, with a solemn childish face and almost completely blue eyes. He had a gift for writing and the voice of an orator, and was now sitting silently on the trunk of a felled tree, with elbow on knee and fist under chin, as if posing for a photograph. And there was Onnik, the most outstanding feature on his face was his round chin, and to appear more dignified he was wearing glasses on his crooked nose. He was now walking up and down reciting Siamanto out loud and pushing his glasses up into their right position all the time. He looked so inspired today that it seemed that he was about to stop, fold his hands across his breast and declaim with Siamanto: "Yes yerkelov gouzem mernil – I want to die singing."

There was Maksapetian – thin, with long arms and legs – sitting under a tree leaning back against it vacillating between unhappy thoughts. Ishkhan wondered what the man was thinking about. There was Hmayak, and here were Vagharshak, Set, Arshak, Khatchig, and Arsen, all young men full of enthusiasm and conviction, with long hair and the obligatory moustache, though not all of them had beards. They were honourable soldiers individually, but could vote for any black deed when they acted as a group.

What a pure parade of death and dying. These people seemed to have entered into the cause not to live but to die, to die whatever happened – their attitude being what possible revolution could there be without death.

No, the temperature of the revolutionary spirit must be kept at a high level so as to equal that of the shed blood. This yearning for death, by whatever means, was so great that these people were unable to give up the habit of dying. If they ever achieved their aim, if the time came when there was no need any more to sigh for an independent Armenia, but to live for it, they would still prefer to die. And the revolution? The revolution would come to an end just like that, would it not?

And songs like this were sung by all these young men:

> I wish I could achieve my aim
> But even if I'm to be hanged

> From the very gallows I'll shout
> a strangled cry, 'O Armenia'.

What a terrible habit this readiness to die. Even after gaining freedom, people were prepared to be hanged in order to have a chance to shout 'O, Armenia' from the gallows. How ironic it would be, how history would burst into laughter, if these standard-bearers of death were still shouting aggressively from the gallows 'O, Armenia', when there might be a time when there was an Armenia with a flag and state insignia, and when emigrated Armenians from all over the world could visit their motherland.

Aram went up to Kotcho and took him aside. It was clear what he was speaking about, and Kotcho was listening anxiously. Aram was not the sort of man to leave till tomorrow work that had to be done today. The quarry had walked into the hunter's trap so why should he not take advantage of this opportune fact. Kotcho took off his sharp, turned-up shoes, hit the tree with them, put them on again and said something to Aram, who had been bending down a little. Aram straightened up and his face now had a quiet, confident expression again. Ishkhan felt that Kotcho must have agreed to the plan: this famous singer of Kurdish songs, that primitive man of the mountains understood that a revolution demands victims.

Poor Mushegh went up to Mihran like an estranged son of the family and whispered, "Did you just have a meeting?"

Mihran could not think fast enough and answered the question with a question, "What meeting?"

"A meeting. Wherever Aram is, there will always be a meeting. When so many people gather together, could Aram do without a meeting?"

"No, no, what meeting?" stammered Mihran and added, "We did have some discussions on different topics."

Mushegh wandered over and found Boghos. He was lying on the grass on his back, probably feeling ill. He wanted to go up to him, to say a joyful, heart-felt word to him and to hear a warm word in reply, but when he approached, he saw that Boghos's eyes were tightly closed – perhaps he had closed them just now when he saw him approaching.

"Boghos."

There was no reply. Mushegh sat beside him on the grass.

"Boghos, I'm speaking to you."

"What's up?" asked Boghos without opening his eyes.

"Are you feeling sick?" asked Mushegh as he noted Aram's careful glance from afar.

"Oh," groaned Boghos, "I do have a terrible headache." He turned over onto his stomach and buried his head in the grass.

The sun was setting unsociably in the west. It was gathering up its skirt from the hills of Hayots Dzor, and the shadows of the night were lengthening. The Khoshab river had acquired the colour of lead and seemed to be motionless. Nana appeared at a window of the monastery, but only Aram noticed. Then her face was also shrouded in the veils of night.

"We're leaving, men," Aram called out. "Our thanks go to the monastery and its priest."

The horses were gathered in from the meadow. Avdo came and saddled Ishkhan's and Aram's horses and then helped those who were having difficulty. Avdo asked Mihran why everybody was in such a bad mood that day.

"What makes you think so?" said Mihran.

"They didn't sing the goat song."

Indeed, nobody had sung the goat song that day and Avdo liked that song very much.

Go and see who's eaten the goat.

They went and saw

that the wolf had eaten the goat.

Aram went up to Mushegh: "Baldoshian, you and Kotcho will leave us at Gyduk and go to Varag."

"What for?" asked Mushegh, taken aback by this unexpected command.

Aram cut him short, "Kotcho will tell you."

The group set off. Usually they would sing 'There was no moon' or some other march, but this time no-one was in the mood for singing anything. They passed through the sleeping villages of

Aradents, and Astvadzashen. The village dogs were still not asleep, but they did not seem very lively, an inevitable bark was occasionally heard but everything soon became silent again.

Mushegh was riding next to Kotcho. He wanted to find out what they were going to do in Varag, whether Kotcho had been aware of that decision or whether he too had been taken unawares. When had it been decided that he would go to Varag with Kotcho? And how had they guessed that he would be coming at all? Mushegh felt that there was something dark and obscure here, something unpleasant. 'Taken all in all, today's been evil and unintelligible,' he thought, 'why did I come out from Van?'

The moon could be seen in the sky and it could not be said that it was a dark night. The group was not riding by at any speed. It was clearly not a group of brave brigands, though some were indeed armed with rifles, others with revolvers, and Ishkhan just with a shotgun.

When this group had left Gyduk behind, Kotcho rode away from the group. He called out, "Mushegh come, we're leaving them." Mushegh joined him. All the other horses had halted in their tracks. The other riders only appeared to realize this fact when the horses suddenly ceased stamping as if controlled by a supernatural power. There was a massive dead silence, during which Mushegh strained to see Boghos – why particularly him? – but he could not make out anyone as the dark shadow of the hill had fallen across them all. The fact that the group had halted also seemed suspicious and ominous to him. Why had they stopped?

Mushegh and Kotcho turned to the left and took a narrow road which later wound round and crept up Mt Varag. The thudding of the horses started up again. 'They've been standing and watching us – why?' thought Mushegh. Why, indeed? Kotcho's song echoed round the shadows of the mountains, and the horses slowed down as if aware of the tragedy of Zilana.

> "Msto stood up and got on his horse.
> Mother, mother, I'll soon come home,
> I'll bring my wife green fruit and rhubarb,
> And I'll shoot a partridge for you.

She hung onto the horse's neck
Lao, don't leave the village now,
It's a bad day to go, lao,
Just obey your mother, lao."

"Mushegh, lao" Kotcho called out, "sing tra-la-la."

Meanwhile Mushegh seemed to have solved the puzzle: they were probably being sent to kill Artak Darbinian, the supervisor of the Varag monastery school. Artak was a follower of Portugalian and Avetisian, Armenak opponents of Aram's party. Another victim! Mushegh had never interfered in such matters. This was his first time – that was why they had stood staring after them! But why was Kotcho not talking about it, not saying what they were to do? At this point Mushegh decided that he would never shed blood at any price. He would not harm Artak under any circumstances. Kotcho had been given the task, let Kotcho solve the problem. "Kotcho knows," Aram had said. Very well, let Kotcho not forget what he knows; he himself did not want to know anything.

Djndo, it is not honourable to stab a man in the back, put your gun away. If you are brave, come down onto the road, stop Msto and fight face-to-face. Whoever dies, may his soul go to heaven. Whoever survives, may he live long.

"Mushegh, lao, sing tra-la-la."

"Tra, la, la," Mushegh kept singing, relieved at last of his gloomy thoughts. And he thought to himself: 'You're going to stab Aram in the back. Shame on you, Kotcho!'

And the end of the song rang out.

Djndo's heart is thumping, he is lying on his stomach and shutting one eye to take aim. O, Zilana gorge! O, gorge of disaster! O, fate – fate – fate!

Kotcho halted by a big rock and looked around. Varag monastery lay before him with its verdant grassland. The outline of the domes could be against the background of the mountain, and the soft sound of the monastery's water-mills could be heard. Down below, Van was a mass of dark gardens, and the lake merged with the sky and nobody could tell where the water ended and the sky began.

Kotcho got down from his horse. Mushegh dismounted as well; he went up to the rock, three metres away, and stood staring fixedly at it. Kotcho reflected, 'So, this is the so-called traitor'. He took his gun down from his shoulder and aimed it at Mushegh. Then he coughed, and sat down on a stone with the gun at his feet and rolled a cigarette. Mushegh came up and sat down beside him.

"Well, what are we supposed to do?" He took a box of matches out of his pocket and handed it to Kotcho.

"My flint's good enough for me, lao," murmured Kotcho and took it out of his pocket. He held a burnt match on the flint firmly with one finger, hit the flint with a piece of iron – one, two, three ... the match began to smoulder. He lit his cigarette and inhaled deeply. Mushegh was now thinking about how he could persuade Kotcho to give up the idea of killing Artak. Then he laughed at his own naiveté. Could anyone get these savage mountain men to understand anything? They were only cut out for such barbarities.

"What are we supposed to do?" echoed Kotcho, making himself more comfortable on the stone. "We won't do anything. You were standing near the rock just now doing nothing, and I shot and killed you. My task then came to an end, as did yours. I would now get on my horse, ride home and sleep peacefully, while your corpse would be eaten by the wolves. I would get up in the morning, calmly have a meal, then go and find Aram Pasha and tell him I carried out his orders – I killed Mushegh. Do you understand?"

Mushegh appeared to be waking up from a sleep. At the same time, however, it seemed to him that he was still having a terrible, stupid dream. "Oh!" he exclaimed and his cry was full of surprise, hesitation, fury and disgust.

"Oh, for God's sake I tell you, lao, ride away. Save yourself until we see what becomes of the world. Brains or courage aren't enough in this world, lao. Clever people go to prison, brave people to the graveyard. Go away, lao, get out of the country."

"What about you?" asked Mushegh with a lump in his throat.

"Me? I'll go and tell him you ran away and I wasn't able to kill you, or I'll say I have killed you, and if they ask where the corpse is, I'll tell them I've eaten it. A murderer of a fellow Armenian, and a cannibal – aren't they the same thing? Lao, have you got any money on you?"

"I've a little," replied Mushegh feeling his pocket.

"I also have a little. Two littles will make one much – take this, you'll need it. There are many Armenians out there, you won't die. If I didn't kill you, you won't die any more."

The silvery cock-crow was heard from Varag monastery, a light breeze passed over the world and the night seemed to lighten.

"Get on your horse, lao. Good luck to you, and may I also get out of this mess successfully."

Mushegh stood up, fastened his belt, came up to Kotcho, embraced and kissed him. He wanted to say something more but could not.

"Go away, lao. Leave this country, may God be with you."

"Please, see my mother and tell her everything."

"I'll whisper in her ear. Get on your horse, lao, and good luck to you."

Mushegh took the road leading to the Aparandgan spring as if in a dream. Kotcho stared after him, looking relieved, threw himself onto his horse and rode down the wide road to Van.

Someone seemed to be waking Mihran up, as on the previous day. Nana was covered with a blanket and the bed looked empty, with nobody in it. Where was last night's Nana? No, the bed was not empty, there was a fringe of her short hair sticking out from under the blanket. The district governor had not returned. And yesterday...

Mihran shut his eyes to try to fall asleep again, but felt that he could not. Nonsense, he must sleep, sleep, sleep and forget everything.

His mother turned over in her bed and gabbled something in her sleep. 'She's certainly speaking to me,' thought Mihran, 'she speaks only to me in her dreams'. There was, by God's grace, another speaker: a rooster called from Khek village, got an answer from the chief rooster of the monastery, and then silence fell again.

A bird screeched from the meadow.

'I must sleep, I must sleep.' Mihran closed his eyes tight. Something green spun like a wheel and stopped in front of his closed eyes. It was Nana's head. Did he smile? No, he became angry, or rather both at the same time. He was simply frightened.

What a dreadful experience it had been. Everything, everything in one day. Had he been right to reject the Baldoshian business? Of, course, he'd been right. He didn't want to specialise in murder. And if Nana agreed today to go off the road and up the hill with him … Well, it had turned out that twice in a day he had avoided murdering – no, murder had avoided him. What an unusual person this Nana was. A surprising Nana! And where did this free-thinking district governor with his free-thinking Nana come from? What a dreadful experience!

What makes you so narrow-minded and wretched, Mihran, and what after all has actually happened for you to get so upset? Look at Arshak Mandaburian, who lived in Stamboul for a few years. He has just returned to Van. He goes on and on – he has done such a lot.

"Is it true that there are bad houses in Stamboul?" Mihran once asked Arshak who had not understood.

"Good as well as bad houses can be found in any town," Arshak had said in a pure Bolsetsi accent.

"All the houses in Van except a few are bad houses." Mihran had clarified his question: "Is it true that there are houses – you know – of ill repute?"

Arshak had laughed. "Oh, now I get the point of your question. But the houses you mean are the best in Bolis. You're a man, Effendi, a young man, and you're not married. You've got money, you can go to Aphrodite's temple, as they say in Bolis. You go in and take a seat at a round table. You're given an album with pictures of girls of any nationality, flavour or age. You can choose anyone you like. Perhaps you find a great difference between the picture and the girl. You'll be able to say it won't do, and look for another until you find the one you like."

Mihran had objected, "But there are bad diseases."

"There aren't good or bad diseases. All diseases are bad. There are no Aphrodite's temples in Van, but there are nevertheless lots of diseases."

"And what happened to Hampartsoum Muradkhanian then?" Mihran had reminded this fanatic priest of Aphrodite's temple.

"That was bad luck, Effendi, just bad luck. It can happen to anyone."

The conversation had not ended there. Arshak had leant forward and whispered in Mihran's ear: "I'll you something. If there had been bad houses, as you call them, in Van, the Davo affair wouldn't have occurred. Well now, I didn't say anything, and you didn't hear anything from me. Goodbye, Baron Mihran. Please come and visit us."

This is the truth. Be reasonable, Mihran, nothing particularly terrible has happened. Both the Ourpad creek and Ohannes Muradkhanian's daughter are still there – 'Lia, sit down!'

After leading such a dissolute life in Bolis, did not that same Arshak Mandaburian come to Van like an innocent lamb and get married. He drew a red veil over his wife's head and took her to Arshak Dzetotian where they had their photographs taken side by side. Who had ever seen a husband and a wife have their photographs taken together before. He brought liberalism to Van. Bravo to liberalism!

This was the truth.

Mihran was reflecting that Kotcho would have finished his job by now. What a job. The man existed, lived, ate, drank, got happy, unhappy and suddenly he stopped being. Had Aram and Kotcho given birth to Mushegh to have the right to kill him now? What a terrible affair! Aram called Mihran a talker-balker and yet what was he himself, what did it matter that he was called Pasha, was he not also a talker-balker. He even kept a notebook. He even sent articles to Azadamart and Droshk under pseudonyms. But has he ever shot a man himself? He's a specialist in bragging – a talker-balker!

And Mihran began to dream.

... Mihran is picking quince flowers in the garden. They smell strongly and Mihran is sorry that it is impossible to make up a bunch of them. Ohannes Muradkhanian's daughter, the very modest Lia, is looking over the low wall of the Terdzakians. If some day Mihran gets round to writing a letter to her he will address her like that: 'To very modest Lia'. With a big bunch of quince flowers in his hand, Mihran comes up to the wall. Lia is smiling. She is not running away. Mihran hands the bunch of flowers to her.

"I've picked them for you," he says.

"You haven't picked them for me, take them to the one you've picked them for."

"I have picked them for you," repeats Mihran and insists on the girl taking the bunch.

Lia teases him. "Don't bother! I won't take that bunch, go and give it to your Nana. You love a Turkish woman! Couldn't you have found anyone better?" Lia is laughing.

The district governor is looking sad, riding along the road by the meadow. When he catches up with Mihran, he halts and silently looks at Mihran straight in the eye. And then he mournfully and slowly rides off.

Now Mihran sees that it is not Lia before him on the other side of the wall. It's clearly Nana.

"Shall I tell the Bey to kill you? What would you say?"

"What can you say? It's not clear yet whom the district governor would kill, you or me?"

"Why should he kill me? I'm his wife and I love him faithfully."

"Faithfully?" Mihran bursts out laughing. "The district governor is going away with shaking shoulders! You see, he's laughing, too."

Nana looks after the governor and catches hold of Mihran's hand, like a scared little girl. "Can't you see, he's crying bitterly, Mihran Effendi. The Bey is crying … Come, give me your flowers, let me take them to the governor and let him give them to me. We love each other, but we have no flowers."

"These flowers are for Lia. She loves me with a maiden's love."

"Maiden love? Marineh, too, loved Davo of Dher with a maiden love." …

Mihran woke up. It was morning. His mother was not there. She had got up early as usual. The fringe of Nana's hair had disappeared and instead, her slender fingers could be seen on the white pillow. What a stupid dream. Yes, he had had many foolish nightmares over the last few years. Should he go to the American hospital to see the American, Doctor Ussher? But what should he say, and how should he say it? It was said that the doctor had strange instruments and that he examined patients with these instruments to diagnose their disease.

Odd things were said about this Dr Ussher. For example, when Aram contracted arthritis, he was sent to this American hospital. Ussher came in to examine his patient. Aram's name was of course known to the doctor like every one else. He decided to test his patient's nerves. After a thorough examination, he said in his fair but rather shaky Armenian:

"Baron Aram you am to die."

Aram was terrified. "Am I to die, or you?"

"You are – you," the doctor corrected himself. "I'm healthy."

Aram fainted.

Ussher was thinking: 'You aren't very brave and you' re certainly not going to liberate Van from the Turks.' And he helped Aram to regain consciousness with the aid of some medicine. The doctor spoke to the recovered patient:

"I said you were going to die, but I didn't say you were going to die right now. All I wanted to say was that some day you're going to die."

"We're all going to die some day, doctor," groaned Aram.

"That's right, that's just what I meant to say."

Yes, Mihran had often thought of going to that famous doctor to tell him about his troubles. Once he even went to see him in a dream. He dreamt that he entered the waiting room of Doctrusher, as the people of Van called him.

… There was a long queue. Turkish soldiers were standing in the queue, as well as Aram Pasha, Avdo of the monastery, Ishkhan and others. He wanted to go back, to escape, but at that moment Doctrusher came out and said: "Come in, I'll see you out of turn." And Mihran went in.

"What seems to be the trouble?"

"My mother, my house, my land."

The doctor was irritated. "What's your illness?"

"I see very bad dreams and because of that I feel like a patient.

Please, cure me."

Doctrusher opened the iron door of a cupboard set in the wall, pressed a switch whereupon strong lights lit up on each side and at the top of the cupboard.

"Go in, I'll shut the door and look through this round hole to see what's wrong in your head, then I'll look through the other to find out what's wrong in your heart, your stomach."

Mihran was horrified at the thought that this man could see inside him with his accursed lights.

Mihran woke up. 'Of course,' he thought, 'it was ridiculous to think that there were really such things as magic lights and cupboards'. Nevertheless, he felt that he should go to that American doctor, he had to get rid of these terrible nightmares.

What had happened at yesterday's meeting in the meadow? What was the world busy with and what were the leaders coming in from outside busy with? Who knows? The sound of a drum always seems sweeter at a distance. Maybe, when these leaders died, they would be made saints the following day to rule over us.

Nana stirred – no, the blanket stirred and Nana's fingers disappeared. There was no Nana left now. He remembered his dream and all yesterday's events. He seemed to have forgotten Nana. An irresistible urge rose in him, to get down from the sadr and raise the blanket to check whether Nana was there or not and to see what she was doing. It was clear she was asleep, and that it did not suit her.

It was also clear that the district governor would come that day. They might leave in the evening or they might stay for another night as well. How could Mihran talk with him after all this? He felt that it would be difficult, even unpleasant to meet him again, to talk with him, and to sense Nana looking at him with penetrating, childish eyes. He would listen to himself talking and laugh in his mind, knowing the falsehood of what he was saying. Furthermore Nana was so direct that she might be unable to suppress the desire to interrupt him, 'Hey, Mihran Effendi, you're lying, you'd better tell about yesterday'.

So, did that mean he was guilty, and should be ashamed for

what had happened. What about Nana? Everything had happened as a result of her initiative, had it not? How surprising and bizarre the events had been. Nana was hovering over his head like an innocent angel, with only her soul under the blanket, while he himself could not even fall asleep. Mihran remembered Arshak Mandaburian again. It was true, if there were temples of Aphrodite in Van, the Nana affair might not have occurred.

In order for such matters not to recur, it was necessary to get married. And the sooner, the better. Of course, Ohannes Muradkhanian's daughter was young for him, but what did that matter? The most important thing was that they should love each other. The district governor was much older than Nana, but what did that matter? Mihran turned over – he did not much care for that comparison.

He recalled his dream about the park of the Ourpad stream, where the people of Van made a lot of noise and enjoyed themselves every Sunday, and where a girl was standing and looking at the distant view of Mt Varag. That girl's name was Lia and when people asked who had married Mihran Manasserian, the answer would be 'Lia Muradkhanian'. That was how things stood.

Mihran recalled one of Ishkhan's favourite love songs. He stared at the ceiling and sang in his mind:

> 'O, mountain girl, oh, lovely girl,
> Come out and let me see your face.
> O, Armenian boy, you brave boy,
> Haven't you been onto the roof,
> and haven't you there seen the moon?
> O, a deer girl, a golden girl
> Come out and let me see your brows.
> O, Armenian boy, you faithless boy
> Haven't you gone into a church,
> and haven't you there seen an arch?'

The song would have gone on in the silence if Nana had not moved. She moved, but was then still – there was no change!

The district governor! The hardest thing for Mihran now was to meet him. Whatever had happened would pass, but he saw many difficulties ahead. What if he got up and rode off to the town? Who could blame him? No one, of course, but it was surely not proper. Mihran stretched, yawned, got longer and then shorter – and then at last fell asleep.

Everything in fact passed more easily and smoothly than he had expected. The district governor did not come. Instead of him, Dikran from Khorkom appeared with two short letters. One of the letters, written of course from right to left, was for Mihran.

> 'Mihran Effendi, I am unable to keep my promise to return and enjoy your hospitality and friendliness once more and to pick up Nana. Please arrange for Nana to come with this messenger. I think she has probably already managed to bore you. I wish we could meet more frequently.
> Kamal'

Nana read the letter addressed to her and ran into the room, then she changed her mind and came out again. She called out to Mihran's mother, who was at the door of the church.

"Mother, the governor has sent for me. I'm leaving right now."

"Oh, God bless my soul, what shall I do without you?" The mother slapped her knees with both hands with comic intent.

The rest was dealt with very quickly. Nana came out of the room, quite ready, dressed as before in boy's clothes. Mihran brought the carpet bag out of the room, Avdo saddled the horse and brought it to the stone mortar. Everything was quickly and easily tied onto the horse. Dikran of Khorkom, clean-shaved and with a thick moustache as black as resin, looking very impressive – and interesting – in his peasant clothes, forgot everything when he saw Nana dressed in boy's clothes.

"Good Lord! Is it a dream?" he whispered to Avdo.

"She's not a dream, she's the district governor's wife, and you're her escort, so get her to her husband, safe and sound," Avdo said with authority.

Nana embraced the mother and kissed her without a word. She lightly jumped onto the edge of the well, and then onto the saddle. There was a moment when Mihran felt Nana coldly staring at him.

He pretended not to notice. A new mental torment – what was she going to tell the governor about him? The fact that Nana was not the slightest bit afraid of what Mihran might say was the most amazing and painful part of it all – he was shuddering at the very thought. The horses set off and slowly began to climb down the hill from the monastery.

"So, that went well," said the mother, looking at her son with an inquistive eye. Avdo wanted to say something, but shook his hand instead and went in. Mihran looked after the departing riders and at last realized the truth: 'Nana will keep silent,' he reflected, 'whether she wants to or not.'

Chapter 15

The city being described had many centres. For instance, there was the Arark square, known as the Araruts market, because it was surrounded by stalls and shops. The main commercial and artisan shops were in the town centre. But Aikesdan still had its own such centres, such as the Araruts church and its parish school, as well as a vegetable-oil processing plant. These were all part of the Araruts market, where there were many grocery stalls, small shops selling cloth and those selling ironware such as scythes or rakes, a workshop making candles and soap, a barber's shop, and a bakery. Here also was the small forge of blacksmith Arabo, and an attractive shop selling school supplies – the children were very excited by the small rubber balls on sale there. On Sundays, Araruts square would become the town centre, especially in summer and autumn when peasants came in from the neighbouring villages with their carts drawn by mules and oxen and laden with food. There would be piles of water-melons, tall baskets full of herrings, and lots of peaches, grapes, apples, and pears. The melons dominated all other smells, the square was always full of their sharp aroma.

There was also in the square a two-storey police station, as well as a small café, though no restaurants, and a low, square, wooden building, the only one of its kind in the town, where for ten paras one could see a shadow-graph, that early form of cinema with fantastic moving shadows of people and animals projected onto the white wall of a darkened room.

Despite all these advantages, the people of Arark were always described by those who lived in the Norashen district as going without food, and they in turn called the latter poor and proud. The square in Norashen was much smaller, in fact scarcely a square at all, just the Norashen church and its grave-yard with a few stalls opposite it But the wealthier people of Van lived in Norashen. The Kapamadjian and Terzibashian houses, and Simon Tutundjian's house with its large orchard, were nearby. The local schools – the Norashen for boys and the Sandkhtian for girls – were here, as was the American quarter with its mixed schools and protestant church, hospital and pharmacy. There was also the massive windmill which could be seen from all parts of the town; it was more of a proud symbol than of any very practical use. Moreover, as if to underline the superiority of the Norashen district, Iskhan lived just opposite the girls' school.

Next to the boys' school, there was a water-mill and then a café, which was well-known for being just a café and nothing else. Opposite it was Atchem-Khatchoyan's two-storey house, with its long, open verandahs overlooking a large yard. Houses of this sort traditionally had plain walls facing the street with just one door with a square hole above it, from which whoever was knocking could be seen. The verandahs opened up the front of the house; they were literally yeress-pats – face-open; in the local dialect they were called orospats.

Garabed Atchem-Khachoyan was one of the conscientious teachers at the school in Arark. But this was not the only significant thing about this short man with his dark face, big, black eyes, and thick, black moustache. He had won great fame for his acting in the roles of headman Mno in *The valley of tears*, the Abbot in *Ancient Gods* and Iago in *Othello*. His Iago had especially stirred

Van. Some excitable people had tried to throw chairs at this deceitful Iago, others had decided to accost the scoundrel in the street and beat him black and blue, and there were some self-styled intellectuals who had wanted to influence the performance by shouting out: "You stupid idiot, don't believe that villain ... He's got the handkerchief, you black fool ... Desdemona's innocent, you beast ... May your handkerchief be accursed!"

Garabed-Iago's father, Sarkis, was sitting in the front row. He could not bear his son's disgrace and left before the end, feeling quite ashamed. He came home and told his wife what shameful things their respectable son was doing in front of people. She was very upset and blamed her husband for having left early and come home instead of trying to bring their son to his senses. When the father saw his son the following day, he said just four words: "Were you not ashamed?"

Of course, Garabed spared no effort explaining in detail that it was just a play, *Othello*, written by Shakespeare, that everyone had been just acting a part, that Desdemona – Digin Trchunian – had gone home safe and sound, and that ...

"Don't treat me like a simpleton," his father said. "Whoever wrote it – that Shakespeare or whoever – had his own reasons. But an actor should try to play the role of a good man so that he himself gets better, and so that people appreciate him. Let somebody else act that shameless man's role. Let Garabed Dantoyan do it. Why should it be you?"

It is not clear how sound and correct Sarkis' aesthetic views were, and whether they could have stood up against other views, but it is certain that the son could cope with his father's criticism – the young are fairly resolute.

Meanwhile, an uninformed reader needs to know some further details. There were three political parties in the town and each of them had its own company of actors. It should also be said that the party which had the most influential role on the stage of everyday life, did not excel in the great dramatic roles of the theatre. In contrast, the other two parties whose political roles were not nearly so influential, provided such great actors as Artashes

Solakian, Abraham Broutian, Garabed Atchem-Khatchoyan and countless others.

There were three libraries in the town: the biggest was, of course, the Freedom-and-Light library, the Mardig library was also well-known, as was the Avetisian library which was next to the Little Kyanderchi spring. The leafy willows rustling by the spring created a fine, cool spot that gave the Avetisian a special atmosphere. The library was on the first floor of the building, while the celebrated Shirak café was on the ground floor. The difference between this café and the library above it was that the library was generally empty, whereas the café was always full. Yes, this was the place where the former Armenaks – now Ramgavars – held their formal and informal meetings. Formal, in that they left their homes and came to the club to keep alight the flame lit by Khrimian, Portugalian, and Avetisian; informal in that they gathered in their ideological home under its patronage, and what did it matter that they did so sitting at tables, drinking cups of Turkish coffee and playing tavlu, card games and dominoes.

By a surprising and inexplicable coincidence, the three immortal spirits – Khrimian, Portugalian, Avetisian – who watched over this Armenak-Ramgavar centre, were all called Mgirditch. What a historic, almost incredible, coincidence! Several people had been baptised in these three Mgirditch's shadows. Many of them had fallen in the blind alleys of the roads to freedom. Many writers have tried to prove that in any case there is no true path to freedom of any sort.

It was also surprising that the orbit of these three impressive stars passed through this well-known centre. Just a few steps away was the house of Hovaness Kouloghlian, a prominent orator and historian, an outstanding figure among the Ramgavar intelligentsia, who had experienced great hardship throughout his life. He worked at the Varag school and was highly respected. But there were Iagos in the world of education, who went out of their way to disgrace him and get him expelled from the monastery. They could do nothing, the muddy waves of their intrigues broke nowhere near him. His rivals then took more extreme steps, and one fine day – not fine, of course, for Mair-aness Kouloghlian, as he was called by his students – some Bolis newspapers carried a report from their correspondent in Van according to which Hovaness Kouloghlian ... The libel was mean and cruel, and his rivals achieved their immediate aim, the schoolteacher left Varag.

He went to see the bishop, His Grace Saradjian.

"Well, Hovaness, my son, what's up? Why are you drooping like an autumn leaf?" the bishop said scornfully.

"Holy Father, those lawless –"

"I know, I know," the bishop interrupted him, "I've read it all."

"So, what do you advise, Holy Father, what should I do?"

The bishop stroked his beard. "What can I say, my son? You'll have to be on your guard from now on."

"Holy Father, I've never been in such a situation." The poor victim was getting worked up.

"You should keep an eye on your rivals, my son. It pays to be vigilant. Go and teach at the girls' school."

To get to the Kondakchian sisters' private school for girls, Hovaness had to pass by the Ramgavar centre, and he always left his house in good time in order to have coffee under the patronage of Khrimian, Portugalian, and Avetisian, or to sit beside tavlu players and give them the benefit of his experience.

"Make that six door! ... Now throw a double! ... Go on, hit him!"

"Baron Hovaness, don't interfere," complained the one who was losing, Mgirditch Atchemian a teacher at the Hankoysner school. He kept records of all the games and always carried a few old ones with him.

"Whether I interfere or not it would still be the same – your goose is cooked," said Hovaness.

"Baron Mgirditch looks well today," said Michael Baronikian, who was always well himself. "You're welcome, have some coffee."

"No, thank you, I'll be late," Mgirditch would answer, shaking his head in a way that meant both 'hello' and 'goodbye' at the same time.

The clicking sound of dominoes would let you know at once that Ghevond Effendi Khandjian was also there: a tall person with bright eyes, a smiling face, and wearing military uniform, he was the brains of the party. But no dominoes could be heard today, only laughter and shouting on a Homeric scale. Some party members were looking through the satirical newspaper Ner, published by some of the younger members, which contained a brilliant cartoon of Ghevond Effendi.

Another no less influential man would often ride past the café: Rouben Shatvorian was a tall and handsome official, who had some influence in government circles. As he passed by, he would raise his whip and shake it with a friendly smile, as if to say, 'Good day, all you lazy-bones, good day'.

The rank-and-file Ramgavars used to waste any free time they had in this place. The warm and affable atmosphere was sometimes disturbed when a young man, Hrant Bagratouni, passed by and shouted an enthusiastic greeting to 'you class of dunces'. Nobody answered, and the loud-mouthed representative of a new generation group departed, chuckling at his own wit. It was clear that he was going to Karkar, a rocky hill beyond the Hankoysner river, where the new generation group held their meetings. Van had suffered a lot at the hands of those cynical and irreligious, local extremists, those spiritual brigands.

And it is still going to suffer. Van is going to suffer.

The Ramgavars also had had a leader who came from outside the city, and the Dashnaks had spitefully commented on this several times. But in fact, the Ramgavars had not brought him in from the Caucasus – from abroad – but only from Arabkir. Yes, the young man, Sebouh, who was only just twenty years old, came from Arabkir. He had been killed by a Turkish soldier while escaping over the wall of the Houssians' garden. All Van mourned his death: someone wrote the Lament of Sebouh's Mother and this was sung at gatherings of all sorts. Even the Dashnak leaders attended the funeral. His grave at Arark Church was the beginning of a Van Pantheon. Van was not to be the inferior of Paris, it too came to have a Pantheon. And now, Sebouh, with his thick, black beard, bow-tie and black coat, looked down from a wall of the Avetisian library. The photo had been taken beneath a lilac tree in the Mughsaghian's rose-garden, and no one believed that such a serious, even stern-looking, man was only twenty years old.

The word 'pantheon' had just appeared in the vocabulary of people in Van. They already knew about 'propaganda' ('Dashnak propaganda urged people to vote for Vramian and not for Paramaz') and they had long mastered the word 'terror' ('the Dashnaks terrorized Kapamadjian'), which they often deliberately mispronounced. And now the new pantheon was enthusiastically adopted in Van as well as among the small circle of Ramgavars.

"Well, when they say that Sebouh was buried in Pantheon, what sort of word is that," asked Armenak Sossoyan, throwing a four-three with his tavlu dice.

"A Pantheon," explained Kouloghlian in an authoritative tone, "is a place where famous people should be buried. Hit that piece of his, you fool, don't hold back."

"If so, why wasn't Kapamadjian buried there?" said Grigor Manasserian – no relation of Mihran Manasserian – as he threw a double-two.

"There was no Pantheon then," explained Kouloghlian patiently. "Don't throw any more, you idiot. Pocket your dice, go home and learn how to improve your game."

"So, if by God's grace Aram dies, will he be buried in the Pantheon as well?" asked Aram Mardigian as he finished his coffee, wanting perhaps to set some limits on who might be considered famous.

A regular customer, Hagop Kandoyan, now took over from Kouloghlian and said with some heat, "Well, Sebouh was a man, and what's Aram?"

The meaning of Pantheon was completely clarified.

The Mardig centre of the Hunchaks, one of the three political parties in Van, was a more formal, more unattractive, place. It was in the centre of the town, in Khatch Street, on the first floor of the Terlemezians' house. The only man who was always there at certain hours of the morning and evening, was Hamazasp Hundstantsian, a young man with long, fair hair and a wide pointed moustache. He did not have many customers, mainly a few students. There was no catalogue at the library; the students were offered magazines – **Hasker** and **Aghbiur**, but not **Taraz** which only the adults could read – with anything else they could lay their hands on. One of the customers, returned the colourful *Taraz* and asked what its name signified. The librarian looked up at the ceiling, then smiled amiably at the man who had asked the question.

"It's the name of a river. You must know: 'Hey, my Taraz, your water is high'. Surely, you've heard that song?"

The customer also looked up at the ceiling. "As far as I know," he cautiously said, "the song says Araz."

"Araz – Taraz," the librarian hesitated for a moment, "it's all the same, a difference of one letter doesn't matter."

The Hunchak Party was small, four members and all of them leaders. There were good generals among them but very few soldiers. Here was Abraham Broutian, a fine figure always neatly dressed and shaven, a born leader and the first member of this party. He rarely smiled and when alone he liked to walk up and down the room, looking at Mardig's portrait on his right, admiring Zhirair Boyadjian's beard on his left, and getting inspired to go on working at his half-finished article. Yes, Abraham Broutian was the editor of the new periodical *Kaits* with the motto that stood out on its masthead: 'Break the brutal chain, let a new sun arise!'.

And there was Artashes Solakian, a brilliant person inside and out, a talented man from head to foot, a teacher, an authority on theatre, an actor – and a leader, above all a leader. There was Garabed Dantoyan, broad-shouldered, calm and composed but decisive, a teacher, a figure – a leader, unreservedly a leader. Then there was Hrant Kaligian, the lawyer – and a leader. And Zhirair Mirzakhanian, the orator – and a leader. There was only one person, Haykak Yeremishian, who might be considered to have been an ordinary member of the Hunchak Party before, alas, he also became a leader by marrying Abraham Broutian's sister, Noyemik.

Moreover, the party even brought in a leader from abroad, from Karabagh. They might at least have chosen someone from Arabkir, but, no, it had to be a leader from Karabagh, a fellow countryman of Ishkhan. The local Hunchaks were slow to realize that on the day Paramaz, the leader they had brought in, arrived in Van, they all became ordinary members.

The brightest page in the history of the Hunchak party was, in fact, Abraham Broutian's wedding party. If the novelist, Berdj Broshian, had been born by mistake in Van instead of Ashtarak, the wedding parties of Van, and especially Abraham Broutian's, would have been immortalised in our literature. The people of Van were deeply sad people. They were deprived of everything – including Berdj Broshian.

The solemn ceremony of the shaving of the bridegroom lasted two-and-a-half hours. The wedding guests, especially the women, counted twenty-five sorts of dry and wet, hot and cold, food prepared by skilful cooks for a special price. For dessert there was a pastry made of quince, a complete novelty in Van. The most daring guest, Mariam Sudjian, the bridegroom's aunt, asked her sister, Veronik, what it was called. Veronik did not know either. She ran into the kitchen, learned its name from the cooks but forgot it on the way back.

"I've forgotten it," she said, laughing in Mariam's ear, "it was a strange name."

Everybody immediately became even more curious.

"You clumsy girl," Mariam said reproachfully, "go back again with pencil and paper and write it down."

Veronik went down into the kitchen, this time armed with a pencil and a piece of paper, and read it out syllabically, "kom – pos – to."

The strange word 'komposto' was passed from mouth to mouth. There were competent and inquisitive women, who managed to penetrate the kitchen and find out the recipe for this so-called komposto for themselves. After that the dessert became the hallmark of luxury for any wedding party or feast: "Was there komposto? ... Can anything be settled without it? ... Of course there was komposto."

Yes, Abraham Broutian's wedding party was not of huge, everyday importance but it turned out to be an outstanding political event. Not only were the Hunchaks there, but also the Ramgavars. This wedding showed what these two parties could do, how successful they might be, if they could only join together against the mother party, the Dashnaks. They could do much harm to that party if only they had a delegate in the Turkish Parliament. It is true that the mother party's candidate, Vramian, had won the election, but that misfortune only occurred because Paramaz was not a Turkish subject, but a Russian one, and because the uncommitted had not cast their votes. Paramaz had shouted in vain from all his platforms: "Uncommitted people are unnecessary people."

Hagop Kandoyan maintained that there were more than forty-five carriages at the wedding. The ceremony was stage-managed by Paramaz himself and his every toast had a forceful message for a political programme of moral legislation. It was not a wedding party but a general ceremony.

There were so many people inside and outside the church that the ground could not be seen. According to the same Hagop Kandoyan, five hundred – or was it five thousand? – candles were burning. He maintained that as the newly-married couple were leaving the church the young people had been singing 'Stuck in a foreign land, you pilgrim' instead of the hymn 'Crowned in your own land', and that so many celebratory gun-shots had then been fired off that the Turks thought that there was a revolt in the town. The same Hagop Kandoyan also related how the Vali had been worried, and had sent for Agyah, the police chief, and told him there had been a revolt in Aikesdan and that no-one was doing anything about it.

"Go and find out how serious the revolt is," he had ordered, "and tell me how many soldiers I should send."

Agyah had taken a cab to Aikesdan, had searched around, and had then reported back to the Vali: "Pasha, there's no revolt in Aikesdan."

"Then, what's all that noise been about?"

Agyah had bent down and whispered in the Vali's ear, "It was the wedding party of the Hunchak leader, Abraham Broutoghlu."

"Oh, let him get married. Marriage is not forbidden in the free Ottoman Empire."

Not everything that happened at that famous wedding left everyone expressing amazement and appreciation. Alas – as has been related – many Ramgavar leaders and their families were among the guests, a circumstance that could not help having consequences. The coaliton was a coalition, but what sort of merging of beliefs could there be? No concessions were made. Moreover, there was criticism, especially from the women who disapproved of the young people, headed by the bridegroom's friend, Arshak, who had sung the Hunchak anthem instead of the usual 'Come native bridegroom'. They also criticised Paramaz who had kissed the bride on her cheeks and had given a speech at the dinner-table on the role of Armenian women, in which he had said that there would come a day when women would be in parliament as well as men.

The wives of those with conservative views grumbled: "What an evil parliament that would be. What have women to do with parliaments?" The fact that the bride, beautiful Ripsimé, the well-known daughter of Atchem-Khatchoyan, sat at the head of the table between her husband Abraham and Paramaz without a veil and often laid her head on her husband's shoulder, and furthermore spoke lovingly to Paramaz, was particularly strongly criticized. It was disgraceful, was it not?

The other cultural centre in Van was the Freedom and Light library, which was in fact not a library but a headquarters – a civilian headquarters if not a military one. People came in from various districts to be trained how to fight for freedom. There were now some very skilful specialists in this subject, yet you could not detect any sign of this freedom, whether with the sharpest of eyes, with binoculars, or even with Ishkhan's telescope. This well-known building was on three floors; it had many rooms and there was not one that was ever closed and not used. The library was on the first floor. Passers-by could see typesetter Hmayak standing at the open window, a young, bespectacled lad who was setting the local *Ashkhadank* newspaper.

From a modest point of view, one of pure principle and consistency, a Vanetsi remains unsurpassed. Two weekly newspapers were published in the town, *Van-Tosp* and *Ashkhadank*. It was impossible to find a fan of one newspaper who would read the other. In particular, no Hunchak or Ramgavar had ever been in the building, this stronghold of pure principle. This strict demarcation could be seen even in everyday matters. Hunchak and Ramgavar men would not marry off their daughters to Dashnaks, nor would they themselves marry Dashnak daughters. This division became especially acute on the day girls had begun to attend the Freedom and Light library, when Yevkineh Manougian, had sung *Like an Eagle* in a darkened room of the centre. Why had they darkened the room? Just to show pictures of various people projected onto a white screen by a magic lantern. Of course, these were not like the moving shadows shown on Sundays in the familiar wooden building in Arark square. No, it was not like that at all, indeed the difference was even greater; the audience there used to laugh at the Karagyoz shadow play, while here, even though people were not actually weeping, there was a sad atmosphere in the hall, almost as if a liturgy was being sung.

And when a figure on horseback appeared on the screen as the first lines of *Like an Eagle* were sung, there had been a sudden hush, followed by confused whispers between a man and the girl Yevkineh.

"It doesn't go like that."

"I made a mistake." And then she said, "You mustn't –"

"I'm very sorry, I was wrong."

To tell the truth, nothing special had happened and if Yevkineh had not been foolhardy and told everyone, an exaggerated version would not have spread round Van. Instead of 'Let Armenian maidens weave a laurel wreath', Yevkineh had sung 'Let Armenian maidens weave a laurel purse'. The conductor, Onnig Mkhitarian, had reproached the girl – "It doesn't go like that" – and the girl had been confused. To punish the girl, hot-tempered Onnig had pinched her arm. The girl had been angry and had protested – "You mustn't" – and Onnig had then apologized. Such was the truth. But it became a chronicle passed from mouth-to-mouth. It was this innocent event that made the rift between the 'free-thinkers' and the 'conservatives' even deeper.

There were rumours that there were lots of weapons and military provisions in the cellars of the Freedom and Light centre, and that young men came in from the villages under the pretext of taking out a book, but each took instead a ten-bullet gun which he tied to his body beneath his clothes, and departed with an innocent air. It is said that mysterious meetings and gatherings were held behind closed doors in this house. Many other things were said, but though the people who came and went had seen much, no one – yes, no one – ever said that there really ever was a flame of freedom or light. For no sign of freedom's light, however far away, could be detected, whether with the sharpest of eyes, with binoculars, or even with Ishkhan's telescope.

The Hunchak anthem was *The Remote Country*; but the Ramgavars had no anthem, or perhaps it should be said that what they had was a dirge, *The Song of Sebouh's Mother*, rather than an anthem.

> Oh, my wounded heart,
> when are you going to be joyful?
> Who'll bring me news from my beloved son?

"What sort of a party is it," Aram had said, "that would sing a dirge instead of an anthem? It would be a tragic party."

As for the Dashnak hymn? Oh, the Dashnak hymn! When the young men sang that, the foundations of the Freedom and Light centre shook.

> Labourer, worker, peasant – brothers
> Come, let's join up and march on,
> Lawyers defending labour
> Salute Dashnaks as well.

This warlike appeal reached neither labourer, nor worker, nor peasant. No lawyer busied himself defending labour, and no one thought of saluting Dashnaks, unless they did it out of fear. However, Aram saluted Ishkhan and Ishkhan saluted Vardan, the hero of Khanasor.

There also existed a so-called 'neutral' party, whose members, Ohannes, Simon, and Hagop, distrusted the three other parties, but often had some sympathy, which they kept secret from each other, for the actions of one or other of them. For instance, a few years ago, Ohannes Muradkhanian had gone to the Gir bookshop for some unknown reason and donated – under the pseudonym,

Hnazand – a 'small sum of money' for the success of a great cause. Later he looked forward to seeing this contribution published in a list of donors, but he could not find which was his among those of the many Hnazands.

When thinking of the memorable and remarkable party centres, and in particular that of the neutrals, it is impossible to ignore the latter's leader, Hampartsoum Yeramian and the secondary school he had established, naming it the Yeramian School and appointing himself as its headmaster. He only had four senses, instead of five. Yes, he had been blind since early childhood. The black spectacles he wore were not to improve his sight, but were simply plain glass, which could have been made of any opaque material. It was all the same for Baron Hampartsoum, there was no visible world for him.

But, oh, what a miracle of natural goodwill! As a result of one blind law of nature, though his eyes had lost their ability to see, the headmaster himself had not. Light went through his eyes to his brain. Memory was the sight and strength of this man who had been both punished and rewarded by nature. And he went forth, armed with light. He was the best student at school and a model boy in the streets. And the ears of wheat ripened and the cornfield grew heavier. He became an expert in Armenian, Turkish and French, in Geography and History, even in Economics and Politics; he started his own school and carefully gathered together a teaching staff.

He achieved much. He would repeat his slogan: 'You should either come first in the marathon of public education or not be in it at all.' and would threaten to dig out the eyes of other influential educational figures. Horrible Hampartsoum Yeramian! On the tall side, this usually sad-looking man was always dressed neatly and buttoned up from top to bottom; he knew all his pupils either by their voices or simply by touching their faces. Being a head, he taught various classes. He would enter the classroom like a bold gladiator of ancient Rome rushing into the Coliseum, and he approached the subject he taught in the way a modern football player would a ball. The only difference was that his unfaltering kick always sent the ball into the net – in this case, into the pupil's brain – no matter how much narrower the net was than it needed to be and no matter how stupid the pupil was. It was not in vain that he was spoken of with admiration in the town. People said that he melted down any subject he taught and poured the molten metal into the pupil's ear.

When he was not teaching, he used to go into some classroom and observe the lesson. During the year he came to know all the students, especially those who had stood out in some way, whether good or bad. He knew where everyone sat, who their parents were and whether they had paid the school fees or not. In the presence of the students, he treated the teachers with tact and great respect, but in the staff-room or in his office he was strict, even cruel. In short, Hampartsoum Yeramian was a fine teacher.

He had a model family; his eldest son would read the local and Bolis newspapers to him whenever he asked. Whatever caugh his ear, whatever he gathered from the books of authors, whether famous or not, turned into erudite comments etched safely on pages in his brain. Those pages piled up and became books in his mind, on economics, history, geography, politics as well as fiction, all of them in their appropriate place. When he was taking a class, making a speech or dictating an article for some Bolis newspaper, he imagined the appropriate book in his mind, turned over its pages, found unerringly what he required, melted the matter down and poured it out wherever necessary. Yes indeed, Hampartsoum Yeramian was an educated man.

His garden lay between his house and the school. As the students arrived early in the morning, they would see their methodical and punctilious headmaster walking briskly up and down the garden path, absorbed in reciting one of Victor Hugo's poems and deciding what he was going to say when he made a courtesy visit to the new assistant director of education.

"Baron Hampartsoum," one of the students called out, "what are you doing?"

"I'm taking in the fresh air," he replied and cheerfully carried on walking.

"_____ _____." The student muttered some obscene words.

When school had begun, the strict headmaster entered one of the classrooms and passed between the desks where the petrified students were sitting in silence, and unerringly picked out the impudent and foul-speaking student. He grabbed the boy's ears, dragged him onto his feet, then slapped him on the face – one, two, three, four times. Then he quietly went off to his own class, as impassive as ever.

"Last time, we saw that Alexander the Great ..."

At break, the whole school – and in the evening, every house of this ancient town – heard about what had happened. So, the headmaster smacked children! Well done, Baron Hampartsoum!

He was neutral – in the strictest sense of the word. And because he really was neutral, he felt free and uncommitted in all matters. He was the best-known of the neutral people in town; he could be called their leader and might have gathered them all around him. But, mercifully, nothing of the sort happened, for if it had, this Urartian town would have had four, not three, parties. No, this blind man had no such intention and never had. But when a new asssistant-director in charge of recent education policy arrived in Van, and the three parties held closed meetings to determine what attitude to adopt, the headmaster, accompanied by one of his teachers called on the assistant-director one Sunday to welcome him cordially, to show respect, and to emphasize the need for peaceful harmony between Armenians and Turks. He also invited the new arrival to visit his school to see what went on there and to have a cup of coffee.

"I have nothing to do with any party," he would say. "My party is that of true and devoted obedience to the supreme Ottoman Throne and my only desire is to be a reliable citizen and to defend the great reputation of His Majesty with my hand on my heart – *dente et unguibus.*"

Well, well – with tooth and nail! Hampartsoum Yeramian was a great politician!

This sort of meeting with a Turkish official usually passed in an atmosphere of mutual understanding and friendship. There were some who naively tried to sniff out his ideas by cross-questioning him, but they soon gave up when they sensed the iron veil protecting Hampartsoum's inner world. They could really find no fault in him on these occasions, for this famous Vanetsi could create the illusion that he had bared his soul to his Turkish interrogators, that they could treat him in any way they wanted. But any slight hint or question that seemed a bit problematic, or could not even be seen through a microscope, was enough for the gentle, even naïve, Yeramian Effendi Bey sitting in front of them to disappear. Whereupon all they could then see was an invincible force, armed against them with those dark and inaccessible, resolute and obstinate, spectacles, which were impossible to ignore. In such cases, this amazing man, who normally hid inside his shell like a tortoise, would show some signs of life and come out of his shell with a smile, in so far as a tortoise could smile, only soon to withdraw again.

And then he would become once more the ever-accessible, and easy to communicate with, Hampartsoum Effendi, with his witticisms, his perfect Turkish and elegant French phrases, and his historical anecdotes, parables and proverbs. Whenever he managed to create – or re-create – a favourable atmosphere, he would stand up and take his leave in a warm but dignified way. He would express gratitude for an exceptionally warm, almost brotherly, reception, and would promise never to forget this auspicious day; he would offer his best wishes for the success of his host's hard work for the glory of the great Ottoman Motherland, and would invite him to return the visit. Well, Hampartsoum was pretty good at what he did.

The return visit would not be delayed. He would receive the honoured guests in his study. After enjoying cups of coffee, he would take them to sit in on classes, especially drawing attention to the high level of Turkish language teaching and then to the chemistry laboratory.

"Effendi, your school compares favourably with Stamboul schools – in fact, it's ahead of them," they used to say.

"We work as much as we can for the glory of the Ottoman –"

"Good, Effendi, very good."

"This blind man is really clever," the important Turkish officials said about him after his departure, or after they left him, "he's very good."

"But he's a snake," someone would object.

Hampartsoum was outwardly polite, but inwardly could not stand others in the education field, especially headteachers. He particularly mocked the Kondakchian sisters and their school. He energetically carried out a campaign against Krikor, the head of the Norashen and Sandkhtian schools, by spreading the unverified rumours that he and Marina Kondakchian wrote love-letters to each other. In all fairness to Krikor, it should be said that he had answered only one of the three letters written by this woman, and that he kept all her letters in a large box which he had marked in pencil with the words 'a disgusting box'. Krikor was reputed to be a decent man and he had never directly quoted any ridiculous or improper words from the letters.

But it was obvious that she had circulated them and had tried to influence public opinion about their relationship. Surely it mattered that she had written, 'You are my Saint Gregory the Illuminator, you just light up the body of your wearied Marina with your illuminating light.' Was that not a disgrace? She might at least have had a better body, one not so tall and skinny. In another letter, this unrestrained woman had written in violet ink on a sheet of white paper, 'I'm your garden – entirely and unconditionally. Save me and take care of me.' Was that not shameless? She might at least have been worth saving, but she was dismal, loud-mouthed, and really very ugly.

There was a knock at Hampartsoum's door; he recognised Hagop Kandoyan's way of knocking and in any case heard his voice in the yard.

"I missed you, so I thought I'd come and see."

The far-sighted, blind man knew very well what had brought Hagop to his house. It was plain as two times two that he had come to learn how the meeting with the Turkish official had gone, and what had been spoken about. But how could Hampartsoum find out who had sent the man – was it Aram, Paramaz, or someone else? Hagop Kandoyan was in fact a so-called go-between, he served all the three leaders with the same faithful devotion and without expecting any reward.

It would not be completely true to say that Hagop had neither family nor friends, nor a house. In fact, he was one of the few people in the town who rented one. His situation was however completely different from that of say Armenak Sossoyan who lived with his mother, younger brother and sister in Mihran Manasserian's house as tenants: they rented a large room with five windows – two overlooking the garden and three overlooking the yard – and had the use of the kitchen and cellar. No, Hagop's case was different. His shelter was a shack with an earth floor and and a hole in one wall overlooking the yard – a fairly inconvenient place to spend the night. The landlord did not charge any rent saying, "He's a poor man. Well, let him live here, and his neighbour, widow Antaram, can wash his clothes once a fortnight." But there was still the question of food: Hagop would sometimes go to the Shirak café, sometimes to this or that bakery. He would occasionally appear in the restaurants, or go to the houses of people he knew to talk pleasantly, and to houses of strangers just to get acquainted. He was fed and, it should be said, fed well, sometimes with pleasure, at others as a duty, but he was always fed however grudgingly.

Hagop came to Hampartsoum's house precisely at dinner time. For many years he had investigated the meal-times at a number of prominent people's homes and had been very seldom mistaken. Amusing tales about this spread from house to house. Markos Shahbaghtsian asked his mother whether dinner was ready. "Yes, everything's ready. Only Kando is missing," his mother answered in jest, and just at that moment, Hagop appeared smiling, and with his worry-beads in his hand: "I was passing by and I thought I'd come and see how you all are." As another example, if the table was set for a meal and nobody had appeared, the head of the family used to say, "Why don't you come and sit down. Are you waiting for Hagop Kandoyan?"

Hambartsoum received his guest cautiously, but amicably: "Welcome, Baron Hagop, welcome."

"Blessings upon you, your house and your work. The whole town is speaking of you today." He fired away without losing time: "Well, you were lucky to come back alive! Come now, tell me, Baron Hampartsoum, there's trouble everywhere these days."

This frontal attack met strong resistance, it retreated – after which, the initiative passed into Hampartsoum's hands. "Take a seat, and let's have dinner," he said with cold condescension.

"Oh, I've already eaten."

"Well, I didn't suggest you only came to have dinner. Take a seat, we've got some quince to go with the food."

"I do like a meal with quince."

"In that case, take a seat."

"Well, I'll have a couple of bites – my tail is drooping."

"Don't use that idiom elsewhere." Hampartsoum was serious.

"What idiom?"

"The last one. People from Van are laughed at in Bolis and other towns for their use of that ambiguous expression."

They started eating. No one could blame Hagop for lacking a sense of propriety. He was eating moderately and only spoke to extol the great culinary skill of the hostess, and also to achieve his main purpose which was to glean some information about the important visit, now that his direct attack had failed.

"There wouldn't have been such an excellent meal at the Vali's table, would there?"

"We had coffee."

"Only that?"

"I hadn't gone to a feast, my friend," Hampartsoum raised an edge of the veil a little. "It was a welcome visit."

"Well, that's clear," said Hagop swallowing the last bit of food, "a short coffee and a long talk."

"It didn't last very long." Hampartsoum smiled, put down his napkin, and added, "How long should I say? Probably no more than a school break."

"So, you talked together. Don't you want to tell me about it?"

"Well, there was nothing special."

Hagop closed his one eye and opened his mouth: "Was nothing important said? I know that talking involves asking questions and getting answers. It isn't straightforward, not everyone can manage it – an Aram or a Paramaz could do it. Thank God, there's also a far-sighted and competent man like yourself."

Hampartsoum laughed quietly, his face creased with laughter, but not his eyes. "Did you say far-sighted?"

"Yes, I said far-sighted," said Hagop gravely, "and I'll insist on what I said. If only those with good eye-sight saw half of what you can see!"

This warm wave of sugary flattery also bounced off the rock of Yeramian's soul. Anyone else in Hagop's shoes, would have sounded a retreat and turned back to where he had come from. But our intrepid explorer of mind and soul, merely moved to a seat closer to Hampartsoum and prepared to try again. But at the same moment, his host acted in a way that left Hagop overwhelmed and feeling almost buried. Hampartsoum leant back, yawned casually and asked, equally casually, "Well, come on, tell me. What's the news?"

Moreover, Hagop felt that this fearsome man, buttoned up with forty padlocks, was not even waiting for his question to be answered. No, he was sitting back comfortably on the cushions, and Hagop very soon heard Hampartsoum's snores. There was no point in staying; he felt like getting up and leaving the field of his defeat, but it seemed to him that something like a smile passed over the sleeping man's face. 'The old man's pretending to be asleep, hoping I'll go away,' he thought. He further reflected that he had adopted the wrong approach. He was strong enough but had not been able to get a foothold. What he should have done was to have opened his own door, slowly let the man in and then grab hold of him. How improvident he had been. But now how could he check whether Hampartsoum was really sleeping or just being impolite.

"Avetis Effendi went to the bishop today." Hagop pronounced the words distinctly while carefully looking at the other's face.

"Avetis Effendi? To the bishop? Why?" said Hampartsoum, as if continuing an uninterrupted conversation.

"Weren't you asleep?"

"No, I wasn't."

"Then why were you snoring?"

"I had a slight nap," replied Hampartsoum, looking up as if he was not blind and enjoying it. "Why did Avetis Effendi go there?"

"Who? Where?"

"Didn't you say that –?"

"I said that only to find out whether you were asleep or awake."

"I am going to sleep now. You never told me what the news was."

Hagop was disappointed with the world and with Hampartsoum Yeramian. He risked offering a riddle: "There isn't now what existed before, Baron Hampartsoum, whereas there is now what didn't exist before."

"So? What was there before, that doesn't exist now?"

"There were Hunchak leaders who don't exist now."

"Have they ascended to heaven?"

"Further than that."

"For instance?"

"It's said they've gone to Constanza."

"What for?"

"How should I know?"

There was a silence. 'It's no use speaking to this blind man,' thought Hagop. 'I'd better go to the Shirak café for a cup of coffee, and then to the Muradkhanians.'

"And what is there now, that didn't exist before?" Hampartsoum's voice seemed to come from far away.

Hagop thought, smiled under his fine moustache, and found the answer: "There was no disagreement about anything between Ishkhan and Aram before, whereas now there is."

"Disagreement? Between Ishkhan and Aram?" Hampartsoum became anxious and really surprised.

"Yes indeed, Effendi. Don't you believe me?"

"Well, what's the cause of this dispute?"

Hagop was uneasy with the word 'dispute'. "I don't know. It's said to be a matter of words." He relaxed a little.

"Well, there are a lot of those," said Hampartsoum, leaning back comfortably on the cushions again. He reflected that this silly scrounger did not deserve to have any time wasted on him and that he would be better off going to sleep. But he did ask whether his guest had anything else to say.

Hagop realised once more that he had not learned anything

about the question he was interested in. In fact, he had not been assigned the task of finding out the details of Hampartsoum's recent meeting, the initiative had been entirely his. He often behaved like that; with important and interesting news as a passport, he bravely went wherever he wanted and spent the day, or even days, there. Hagop knew his business no less than Hampartsoum did his. He had very wide interests and did not confine himself just to social and political affairs. No, he would get involved in all sorts of ordinary family matters, and depending on their nature he would advise people how to solve their problems or how to dispose of them. He carried out these operations as impartially and delicately as possible though always with skill. His motto was to win everyone's heart and have as few enemies as possible, for then every house was his for at least a few hours.

It goes without saying that Hagop Kandoyan was a man, and nothing human was alien to him. He had his outbursts and made unavoidable mistakes. But he had the gift of skilfully meeting crises, whether avoidable or not, by letting the situation grow, like a snowball rolling down a hill, and then after puncturing it he would, without losing time, immediately dab the wound with cotton-wool. For instance, it was known that, in the Shirak café, he once caught the attention of the Ramgavars with one of his impatient, extreme announcements, yet on the other hand set all the Dashnaks against him. This event happened on the day when the meaning of the word 'pantheon' and the question of who had the right to be buried there was being considered. This was when one of those who were present had asked whether Aram had the right, authority or merit, to be buried in the pantheon in eternal sleep. And it was also when Hagop had closed his eyes, opened his mouth and sung the Ramgavar anthem, Sebouh was a man, which had led to him being favoured by the Ramgavars and no longer by the Dashnaks.

What was said could not be unsaid, but Hagop, the sworn knight or priest of even-handed, objective impartiality, was not the sort of man to neglect his business and deprive hundreds of houses of his friendship. No, after he had analysed the situation he was taken up that very day, and the three following it, with dabbing cotton-wool on the wound. To staunch the wound further, he made up a list in his mind of several of Aram's most important followers and went to see them to mend the broken relationships and retrieve favour with the Dashnaks. He carried out this hard task with perfect ease and skill. He informed the Armenak leader with heartfelt joy that the question, whether when Aram died – God preserve him – he should or should not be buried in the pantheon, had been discussed in the Shirak café and that he, Hagop Kandoyan, had insisted that Aram indeed deserved to lie in the pantheon in eternal sleep. And what was even more joyful, was that the Ramgavars had agreed.

Is that all clear?

The reason for this particular visit to the headteacher had been something else. But not only did that man not want to speak about the subject, which Hagop needed to know, but he also kept on asking, "What's the news in the world?"

Hagop offered something from his mental file of varied and colourful items of news: "There are rumours that Mihran Manasserian wants to marry Baron Ohannes Muradkhanian's daughter."

"Is the girl pretty?" asked Hampartsoum.

"She's like a rose," answered Hagop. "But I don't understand. Mihran Manasserian flirts with Karmileh, the daughter of his tenants, the Sossoyans. How's he going to deal with that?"

There was no answer to this crucial question, so Hagop continued his probing. "People can be separated into two."

"People? Which two?" Hampartsoum appeared to be slightly interested.

"Yes, one lot think that nothing special took place during your visit to the Turkish official, only welcomes and farewells."

"That's right,"

"While the other lot," added Hagop, "insist that many important problems –"

"That's true, too. Go and tell everyone that what Khrimian Hairig couldn't sort out at the Congress of Berlin with his open eyes, Hampartsoum Yeramian managed with his blind eyes. From now on, there's no Armenian problem. The Armenian problem is resolved! Is that all?"

No, that was not all. Hagop, that bright and blue-eyed anthropologist and expert on human affairs, realised that Hampartsoum was angry. He fiddled with his moustache. 'God save me from a blind man's fury. I'll flatter him a little and take my leave,' he thought and he called upon his reliable and irresistible charm. He began to sing Hairig's song. Hagop had a thin, melodious voice and a rich repertoire of both Armenian and Turkish songs. Oh, yes, he owed much to the art of singing, without which he could not have mastered various challenges, or be the camel who could indeed pass through the eye of a needle. Hagop was not someone God created casually and hastily. No, he was a carefully and comprehensively created work of art, a well-considered, perfect and complete, composition.

He began singing, as if for himself, whether or not for pleasure, and as quietly as possible so as not to frighten the flies, or confuse the nightingale singing in the rose garden.

Hairig, hairig, your motherland ...

The first line could be sung in a cautious, quiet style, but it would have demanded enormous effort and superhuman self-control to sing the beginning of the second line in that way. No, it had to be:

Vas-pour-ak-a-a-a-n!

How could the name of the province be pronounced in a restrained way when a whole country, a whole world, a whole universe, throbs in that word. It is surely not too outrageous to claim that? Just try and reflect to the world the charms of Vaspourakan – real or imagined, permanent or temporary, explicable or mysterious – even in the brightest of mirrors.

Vas-pour-ak-a-a-a-n! This country of great men, which has so many undamaged ancient monuments with their still undecipherable inscriptions and mysterious decorations, and which has the famous Citadel of Van with its battlements, where the great Artsrouni kings, the Senekerims and the Gagiks, had reigned. It also has the Varag monastery, that eternal memorial of Artsrouni wealth, where Senekerim was buried and where perhaps he still lies in eternal slumber. But where precisely that might be would have to be found out from Baron Kevork Muradkhanian, the former teacher, who was now unemployed and a well-known political figure. Or even, for that matter, from the Varag monastery itself.

How could you not help shouting 'Vas-pour-ak-a-a-a-n' if the shrines of Astghik and Vahagn were placed on Mt Varag and you were able to see Mt Ararat from the top of Astghik with your naked eye? Shoemaker Sahag Bournazian – well-known to be a liar, nobody knew why – insisted that his father had told him that he had seen the standard raised by Khatchadour Abovian on top of Masis from the Astghik castle. "Who's this Khatchadour?" sceptical listeners had asked and Sahag had angrily hurled a shoe onto the floor and shouted, "If you still don't know who Khatchadour Abovian is, why are you still alive?"

The general attitude to Sahag was on the whole unjust. He was called a vrdji – a liar. He would no sooner open his mouth when he was called upon from all sides to close it – don't vri! Raphael, the teacher of Russian at the Yeramian school, where Hampartsoum had managed with great difficulty to get Russian included in the curriculum, would pay special attention to the words 'vri, don't vri' used in Van. According to Raphael, this word had the same meaning, the same root, in Russian and as the Armenians were a more ancient people than the Russians, there could be no doubt that the latter must have acquired the word from the people of Van and made it one of their own.

You just try to sing about Van in all its glory and pride in a quiet voice. Vas-pour-ak-a-a-a-n! Van has been proud of its crafts ever since ancient times. Was it not for this very reason that many families and dynasties were named after craftsmen? For example, Terdzakian (tailor), Houssian (carpenter), and Broutian (potter). These craftsmen included not only ordinary people but also some outstanding leaders whose qualities were reflected in the 'bashian' ending of many surnames, such as Terzibashian.

The noise of the weaving mills could be heard all over the town, the young workers, a few of them women, sat at the looms and flung the shuttles from right to left and back. The cloth was woven thread by thread, and was later dyed in various colours and spread out on the flat roofs to dry; this is why the Terdzakians' house looked so festive and gay. The lively, grey-haired cotton-combers went round from house to house with their combs that looked like single-stringed musical instruments on their shoulders. They sat before the pile of cotton, struck their strings, which trembled, quivered, and sang, as the cotton was slowly worked over and freed from the useless waste. By the time they finished, had been paid and were leaving, their faces were covered with white cotton fluff and with their tools on their shoulders, they looked very much like minstrels from Goghtan, or at least medieval troubadours.

These craftsmen were the heartbeat of the town, they worked with pride and pleasure, contributing to its welfare and charm. Outwardly calm but inwardly anxious and cautious, these obedient people could hear the ominous whisper of the great Catastrophe amidst the noise and tension of their work. They were as sensitive as their instruments, and when they felt that the danger was real, that the enemy was planning intrigue, and that – as they put it – Mt Varag was covered in mist, then these industrious knights of peaceful work threw their tools aside, took up arms and prepared to defend themselves heroically in fierce battles.

It had always been like this and it would always be like this.

How could you sing Vas-pour-ak-a-a-a-n! quietly when teacher Kevork authoritatively insisted that 'Vaspourakan' was grammatically a compound word, which includes the syllables 'vas, pour, kan' meaning 'country of great sons'. Would you take that to be a joke? The whole world – yes, would you imagine, the whole world – came to believe the saying, 'Van in this world: Paradise in the next.'

May Almighty God bear witness! Name some other city as beautiful as Van, as honest as wealthy, as heavenly, as natural, as reasonable, as Van. It is certainly not a question of only natural wealth. That is very important, but you should not forget that the famous Grigor Naregatsi lived and wrote here, and is now lying in his private pantheon. Writers like Grigor Vanetsi or at any rate Mesrob Khizanetsi, or for instance a painter like Ignatios, lived and worked here and left us their immortal creations. And what about Khrimian or Avetisian, the famous heroines Mariam Pasha and Zarouhi Teroyan, and our Sebouh who was not a Vanetsi, but died for the sake of Van, and became immortal because of Van?

When the sun lights up the tops of the poplars in Aikesdan early in the morning, and the sea surges in golden waves, get up people of Van, rise Armenian youth, and look around you. What other town in the world has got a Zum-Zum drum, or a centuries-old underground canal, which according to Sahag Bournazian reaches the Citadel? Queen Semiramis lived here, but because she was a woman, she did not create anything. That does not mean that she did not get some things done. She designed the hanging gardens round the Citadel, and, of course it is a fact that she ordered the digging of the Semiramid canal from the lake so that she could bathe in its waters every day to keep clean and healthy.

And what about the majestic and mysterious Mher's Door, the terrifying stone statues of the bride and the bridegroom standing among the Ak-Küpri rocks, and the stone on the shore of Aghtamar, on which Raffi sat with paper and pen, and sang with chin on hand, "Call out to me, little sea, why are you silent?"

How could you, dear reader, sing 'Vas-pour-ak-a-a-a-n!' quietly when Van is the heart of Vaspourakan. You would need a thousand and one nights to enumerate the charms of this city one by one. You would need a thousand and one nights, and after that, another one thousand and one nights.

The town was particularly welcoming at holidays – the most important being, of course, New Year.

It was cold. It had snowed so much that the narrow streets had become almost impassable. If there had been radios there would certainly have been weather forecasts of heavy snow and and sudden falls in temperature in these months. The face of any poor Vanetsi returning home from work on December 31st would provide a weather forecast that was unerringly accurate – not something that could be said of modern forecasts.

People are returning home loaded with baskets, parcels and sacks.

"Good evening, Baron Oksen."

"Good evening, Baron Melkon, is your nose where it should be?"

"Yes. Where else? How cold it is!"

"Yes, you can say that again. Oh, I forgot, Happy New Year!"

"One can't think in this cold. The same to you! Goodbye."

"Goodbye. My regards to your family."

And they separated – one went to the right, the other to the left. The windows of the houses lit up one by one. Everyone was happy – rich and poor, each according to their means. There were no completely poor people in Van; even in the years of peace, the poorest family had one or two goats, and a small stretch of land in front of their door – was this poverty? It is true that there were houses made of earth, houses with no beds where the family would sleep on thick felt rugs with their clothes on, and where half-naked and barefoot children would run after the cows to collect manure for the tonir. There were also some very poor peasants, who had come to town with their families; the men worked as porters or in similar poorly-paid jobs, the women washed the clothes of the rich or were simply engaged in begging. These people lived as tenants in the rich men's stables with their animals and so were free of the difficult matter of getting some manure. The only fruit their children ate was wild berry which was brought to town on Sundays by peasants from the villages. But there was no absolute poverty in Van, everyone lived according to their means.

So the fact that Father Christmas could not completely fulfill his duties and visit every house should not be a surprise. Father Christmas also knew his place; he knew which house he should enter and which he should not, which door he should pass by without letting people living there know, and which door he should dutifully knock at and leave quickly.

The New Year table was laid out on the small square tonir. There were plates and saucers full of dry fruit on the large tray. And what could not be found on the table? There were Baghdad dates, Persian raisins, Shatakh nuts, hazelnuts, local dry fruit, roasted wheat grains – the list could be endless!

The most exciting moment of New Year's Eve, one that made a great impression on children, was, of course, the arrival of the Alleluia. Could Van's Alleluia be found anywhere else? No, nowhere. Footsteps would be heard on the stairs, it meant that the

Alleluia was on its way. Candles were lit round the table, and the festive atmosphere got denser and warmer. At last the door opened, and fifteen- and sixteen-year-old teenagers, shivering with cold, rushed one after the other into the room. The leader of the group stood in the front row, swingng a lamp at the end of a rope forward and backward like a censer, and they all sang:

"Today is the birthday, Alleluia ..."

They sang in such a sweet voice. Nowhere are there Alleluia singers like those from Van.

> "Mary went to the Father's door, Alleluia,
> Lay on the khatchkar, Alleluia,
> And Jesus was born, Alleluia."

At last, the keenly expected moment came. The song was interrupted, the lamp hung motionless and the leader solemnly and sternly inquired, "What's your son's name?" The head of the family said it was Arshavir.

> "Arshavir's ——- got longer, Alleluia,
> Mother ate it and got happy, Alleluia,
> Father ate it and got immortal, Alleluia,
> Brother ate it and got immortal, Alleluia,
> Sister ate it, and fell into the tonir
> And burnt her head, Alleluia."

Everyone rejoiced. The singers were paid in silver coins and dry fruit, and went out and knocked at the door of the neighbouring house.

The light in the houses went out one by one and the town was immersed in total darkness. The wind was blowing from roof to roof, from street to street, and now it was singing Alleluia down the chimneys. The town was asleep, though people lying on their beds could not sleep. One more New Year's Eve over. What will tomorrow bring? Lord, if it's beyond your power to give peace to the whole world, at least give Van some quiet and security. At least to small, beautiful Van.

Vas-pour-ak-a-a-a-n!

Contrasting with the pleasures of the New Year, the later festival of Easter was celebrated solemnly, with a deep sense of responsibility and serious theological meaning. It lasted three days. For three days the women received calls and the men paid calls. The wives made a list of who had called and showed the list to their husbands in the evening, and the husbands then made up lists of the calls they should return. Dinner was almost never served. The guests were treated to raki, wine, light dessert, and especially to Turkish coffee. And, like everything in this town, the hospitality was always tasteful – though not every hostess had the skill.

Chapter 16

A woman like Kalipseh Atchemian, an atadan-babadan woman, could be found not only in Van but also even in Stamboul. Kalipseh was from head to foot a distinguished person; she inherited this from both her parents. Her way of life, the manner in which she received guests, talked with them, and saw them off was unique. She knew exactly what to talk about with everybody, how she should treat each one, and where to get people to sit. Where to actually receive guests was a question of the utmost delicacy, requiring a great deal of tact. Some visitors were to be just welcomed, some were to be met on a red carpet, and others on the sadr with cushions. Some, on the other hand, were to be received on the sadr without cushions, some on the sofas and finally some others just on the hard chairs.

"You're very welcome, Baron Paramaz. How are you? I'm so glad to see you. Come in, come in. Help yourself to raki, or to the wine. Have some soudjuk. Why don't you get married, Baron Paramaz? ... Nobody loves you? That's not true, Baron Paramaz, that's not true. There's only one Van and there's only one Paramaz.

Who could not help loving you?"

"You're welcome, Baron Armenak, you're welcome. How are you, Baron Armenak. How's Digin Antaram and how are the children? ... And how are you getting on? ... Yes of course, you're always busy. There's only one Ramgavar party and there's only one Armenak Yekarian ... What's that? Why should you allow Van to be ruined? Did they build Van? Why should they be allowed to ruin it? Just show them your strength. How sad our Van has become. Would you like something to drink, Baron Armenak – wine, coffee?"

"Oh, you've come at last, Roupen Effendi – better late than never! Have a seat on the sadr, lean on the cushion. Yesterday, Mgirditch wondered why Baron Shatvorian didn't come. How's your family? Did Aghasi get to the Central? ... Well, that's good, very good. If it's Central School, why do they call it Haikazyan as well? I wonder when summer will finally arrive so that we can come to your garden and have some grapes. What was the name of those small, black tomatoes like grapes?... Lolik? ... Shall I make coffee?"

"You're welcome, terrible Iago. Have a seat. How are you? ... Well, if we don't come to visit you, you forget us. Get up, get up and make some coffee. Let's drink it together ... Yes, it's a brotherly duty. Look, don't talk too much, I'm not in the mood. When is *Ancient Gods* coming on? Get me some tickets, or never set foot in this house again, you disgusting Iago. Best wishes!"

And if the guest was not respected and admired, Kalipseh knew perfectly well how to speak to him: "I congratulate ... No, he's been paying visits since the morning. Yes ... No ... Of course ... Winter also has its beauty ... Why not? ... Maybe ... Why are you hurrying? ... Yes, that's Sebouh. That's Baron Hovsep Kouyumdjian. And Simon Hovivian is next to him. It's not a bad photo – Arshak Dzetotian enlarged it ... Go in peace."

The young men of Van, in black overcoats and with red fezzes, passed along the snow-covered streets. Most of them were already drunk, the others were on the way to getting drunk. Kalipseh looked out into the street through the icy decoration on the windows.

Kalipseh knew very well how to treat whoever called – but not Syusli Der Aristakesian. His name was Sahag but the whole of Van called him Syusli which meant 'dressed up', or perhaps 'dandy'. He had been in Tiflis and spoke Russian Armenian. He was handsome and gallant, smooth-tongued and a breaker of hearts. Kalipseh did not know what to speak to him about.

Standing by the window, Kalipseh was thinking that there were less and less young men in Van. There were so many red fezzes that they covered the whiteness of the snow. But there were no young people left, everyone had been taken to be trained as soldiers. A few young Armenians in Turkish military uniform passed by. These were perhaps being trained in the outskirts of the town, and had obtained a three-day Easter Pass.

Kalipseh's thoughts were interrupted; Syusli Der-Aristakesian himself was standing in the doorway with his big smiling eyes and cleanly-shaven, pink face, and with the ends of his moustache as sharp as bayonets.

"My best wishes to you Digin Kalipseh Let me shake your little hand. Merry Christmas! Thanks be to Jesus' birth, as otherwise I wouldn't have had this chance of seeing you today. Thanks, I'm all right like this. Take a seat, don't worry ... I don't want anything. We'd better chat. Baron Mgirditch is a brave man ... Why? Well, if he weren't brave, would he leave a beautiful woman like you alone and flit about here and there? Wouldn't he be afraid of scoundrels like me? ... Siran is very well, she's safe and sound ... Why, she's certainly a nice woman, but roosters tend to prefer their neighbours' hens. So, though I'm not a rooster, nevertheless I feel ... "

Kalipseh got up and rushed out of the room as if she had just remembered something. Syusli was left alone. He rose to his feet and looked at himself in the mirror, which was in the front part of the room. He realized that he had put himself in a very foolish position. He looked at the photographs hanging on the walls. He stood in front of Sebouh's photo for a long time. Pretending that nothing had happened, he tried to sing the song of Sebouh's mother under his breath, but nothing came of it. 'You, fool,' he said angrily to himself, 'when are you going to understand that Van is neither Yerevan nor Tiflis?' He remembered the English park in

Yerevan, and Mushtaid in the beautiful capital of Georgia, and his heart became bitter. 'The women in Van,' he thought, 'are dismal and old-fashioned, they don't know what a graceful compliment is.' He was going to put his coat on and go away when suddenly Kalipseh re-appeared.

"It was lucky I remembered, the fish could have burnt. Do you have good fish in Russia?"

Syusli thought that she was making fun of him, but he answered her with great dignity: "Yes, there are. The best known is the ishkhan trout of Lake Sevan – not, however, the equal of the Van herring."

"Is the fish called Ishkhan?"

"Well, yes."

"So the local people eat Ishkhan?"

"Well yes, they kill ishkhan, clean its stomach, wash it, fry it and eat it."

"Oh, how interesting!" said Kalipseh. She wanted to ask whether that was why Ishkhan had come to Van, but she said nothing.

Somewhat encouraged, Syusli wanted to return to what he knew best. "Digin Kalipseh, there are many interesting things there. And if you went into the Mushtaid garden in Tiflis, you'd see men and women walking arm in arm, and embracing each other."

Kalipseh pretended not to have heard. "And which is bigger, ishkhan or herring?" she asked.

"Ishkhan is bigger," answered Syusli in an exasperated tone. "But what does it matter, the Van herring is tastier."

'We must really finish all this fish stuff,' he thought, noticing at the same time that Kalipseh seemed to have remembered something once again.

"Let me just go and check that the fish isn't burnt."

"And I too must leave." Syusli leaped up and put on his coat. "My best regards to Baron Mgirtditch. Goodbye."

And not daring to shake Kalipseh's 'little hand' once more, Syusli rushed into the street like a burnt fish himself.

Vaspouraka-a-a-a-n ...

At last, Kalipseh took a slight breath. She realised that he had arrived just as she had thought of him. She looked out of the window again – the youth of Van streamed along the street with their black coats and red fezzes. An Armenian soldier, whose face seemed familiar to her, passed by. Yes, he was Hmayak Sossoyan, the brother of Armenak and of Karmileh – the one who flirted with Mihran Manasserian.

Armenian soldiers in the Turkish army were not employed as such. It was as plain as 'two times two is four' that the Turkish commanders did not trust them with proper weapons. They were employed instead on road construction. If there were any doubts about this situation, it was enough to look at Hmayak Sossoyan's unmilitary bearing as he walked along the street Armenian young men got out of the army in various ways; the sons of the rich, for instance, paid huge sums to be excused such service. And they were right to do so. No, the Turkish sepherberlik – military call-up – was not popular, neither were the route-marches. The men of Van did not want to fight. A Vanetsi wanted to work as a jeweller, to learn a craft, to trade, to produce a play, to work like a busy bee, to generate life. No, a Vanetsi did not want to fight. In any case against whom? There were Armenian soldiers in the Russian army and they not only did not get out of the army, but in fact joined it as volunteers. Should a Vanetsi fight against Armenians? No, he should not; it would be quite senseless. Not because he is a coward – for he has no fear – but simply because this was an aimless, pointless, crazy war. And the men of Van were not crazy.

Another Armenian soldier walked past. He was drunk, and proud that he was wearing high military boots and not common ones. He was happy, but his face was nevertheless sad. It was undeniable that he had drunk a lot of wine and that he was ploughing through the snow with his boots instead of walking like everyone else along the path already trodden down by others. It was a holiday, but many people were on their flat roofs, pushing and throwing the snow down into the street with spades. The Armenian soldier was kicking the snow and singing, in the joyful voice of a drunkard, the recently popular, sad and heart-breaking song:

"In the year of the outbreak of the war
They gathered at the door of the barracks,
They took down and read the call-up order:
I'm going, I'm going –"

His song was rudely interrupted. Snow fell down on him from one of the roofs. He looked up surprised, then moved over to the path and walked on with relief, but also with some difficulty, almost as if he was choking.

"I'm going, I'm going, I'm a soldier,
I'm going ..."

"... a-a-a -n!"

Hagop Kandoyan was also singing, but at that moment, Hampartsoum Yeramian shifted about on the cushions and said in a flat voice, as if in a dream, "Sing a bit louder, don't swallow the words."

At last, Hagop felt that the impenetrable fortress was about to crumble. He let his voice swell,

"Our land ... instead of a rose –"

"No, that won't do," interrupted Yeramian, "go back to the start."

The victory was complete. Hagop pushed his fez back, stared at the lamp hanging from the ceiling, sighed heavily and gave his silvery voice full rein.

"O Father, father, your homeland,
Vaspourakan, this land of ours
Brought you thorns instead of a rose,
Increased your cares a thousand time."

"Go on, go on," whispered Hampartsoum excitedly. Hagop, with the spirit of a true artist, was delighted by his success and carried on.

"And my father then said – the thorns
We have are sweeter than a rose.
Even among those prickly thorns
I will find a beautiful rose."

Like everything in this world, the song eventually came to an end, and there was a stony silence for a while. Hagop shifted back and forth where he sat as the sound of the completed song faded away.

Hampartsoum was inspired by the words; he sat up and firmly said, "Such people mustn't be lost." Then he looked for his handkerchief, dried his tearful eyes and added, "I can see our future as clearly as sunlight. Van must live."

"It will live, indeed it will live." Hagop, fingering his black beads, poured oil on the flames. "Woe to the future that you're seeing. Why should we lose Van? Don't talk nonsense! Is Van a needle to be lost in the hay? Is Van the missing ring of Abbot Arsen of Aghtamar? After all even that ring did not vanish. They say it was taken by teacher Kevork. Why then should Van disappear? Everything depends on people like you whose motto has always been, look before you leap."

"If I had supreme power," he continued, "I would appoint you as both the Minister of Foreign Affairs and Home Affairs in the future republic of the Van to come. I would not of course have that right, but just for you I would make a new law. Now, let's get on, you are here to learn at any price about my visit and what I talked about with the Turkish officials. I had made up my mind not to tell you anything but you've won."

Hagop wanted to protest: "But, Baron Hampartsoum –"

"Don't say a word," said Hampartsoum, "I must tell you with my hand on my heart, that I remained true today, as always, to my political and social beliefs. I always try, when dealing with people, to look for a language in common, which I sometimes find and sometimes not. I believe in diplomatic and peaceful methods, and quite often – it's bitter for me to have to say this – I have often found it easier to speak with a Turkish official than with an Armenian leader. I won't mention any names. It was in this spirit that I paid my courtesy visit to the Turks today. Are you happy now?"

Hagop winked: if Hampartsoum's eyesight had been better, he would never have made such a gesture.

"You trouble your self needlessly, Baron Hampartsoum. Who

am I to interfere in your affairs? I'm just an ordinary Vanetsi, a dervish. I spend my days wandering about and chatting to people. I missed you a lot and thought I'd come and visit you. Well, I'll be on my way to the Manasserians. They say that Mihran Manasserian wants to marry Ohannes Muradkhanian's daughter."

"Very well, let him marry," said Hampartsoum with an off-hand, mocking air.

"But they say that Mihran Manasserian flirts with the daughter of his tenants, the Sossoyans. I don't know what will come of that."

"Either a boy or a girl – what else?"

"Oh, no," said Hagop, "there's nothing very special – they're only playing ailoz-pailoz."

Hampartsoum was amused: "What's this ailoz-pailoz?"

"You see, at last I've found something which you don't know."

"No, really, I've never heard it before."

"It's a puzzle: ailoz is sitting in front of pailoz, when is it going to ailoz for me to pailoz?"

"Which means what?"

"The cat is sitting in front of the mouse-hole, waiting for the mouse to come out for it to be caught and eaten."

"What a splendid puzzle!" Hampartsoum was sincerely impressed. "No, Van must live on."

"Certainly," confirmed Hagop, modestly proud or perhaps proudly modest. "But look, our Mihran's and Karmileh's affair is 'ailoz-pailoz' – that is, they're playing cat and mouse with each other."

They could hear some conversation going on in the yard.

"Is he at home? Is he alone?"

"He is at home, but he isn't alone."

"Who's there?"

The answer could not be heard.

"Oh, so the yoghurt fly and the djilbur busy bee has come, has he?"

This was the phrase used for people who were unexpected, unpleasant but unavoidable, guests. The man who had asked the question was Hampartsoum's deputy, Mardiros Nalbandian, and the one who had answered was his wife. Both guest and host pretended not to have heard anything. But Hampartsoum thought that Hagop's ear really had not caught this insulting and inappropriate comment, and Hagop thought the same about his host, who had said that he wanted him in the government of the future republic of Van.

Hagop rose to his feet. "Well, I'm leaving now."

"Do come more often."

"Thank you."

Mardiros Nalbandian appeared in the doorway. He, too, was wearing dark glasses. Hagop passed by him, leaving his greeting unanswered, said goodbye to his hostess and went out into the street. He stopped for a moment at the front door. He wanted to remember the precise, offensive word which would suit this Mardiros Nalbandian. What was it? Infantile? That Lenten doll, Aklatiz? It was on the tip of his tongue! His face shone with delight. He had just remembered it. He raised his stick, turned towards the door. Addressing the deputy head of the Yeramian School, he cried out only one word: "Lackey!"

It was hot. The sun shone down on the vineyards, houses, and streets. It was hot: on such a day, one should only go to the beach, have a swim, get cool and then saunter home only in the evening. It was really hot: there was no shelter from the heat under the leafy willows, nor by the streams flowing along the streets. On such a day, one should only go to the garden, lie on the grass, breathe in the mixed scent of parsley and apricot and have a nap. On such a day, one should sit in the Muradkhanians' kiosk – no matter how hot it was, there was always a light breeze there. The kiosk was high, it looked over the orchards and it seemed from there that one could actually count the numerous fruits, and even leaves, in the gardens. On such a day, one should wrap up some bread, boiled eggs, fried bulghur, and wander slowly up to the Varag or St Grigor monasteries to get some spiritual and physical satisfaction.

So thought Hagop Kandoyan from the bottom of his heart – though not a poet, he had many poetic experiences and emotions in his whole being. Hagop was braving the heat and heroically marching on with the aid of his stick. 'The sun is intense,' he thought, 'on such a day, the café Shirak is the place to be in.'

On the opposite side of the street, Simon Tutundjian was leaving the Maksapetians' house. He went straight ahead towards his own carriage waiting almost in the middle of the street. He got in loudly ordered the driver to go to the house of Kevork Djidechian. He did not notice Hagop, or pretended not to notice him. This upset Hagop's self-confidence. Blind Hampartsoum had promised him the post of the Minister of Foreign and Home Affairs; but now this corrupt merchant did not even offer him a formal greeting. Hagop could not suppress his anger: "Well, damn your carriage!" But then he also thought that if some day – who knows? – Van gained its independence and the government was taken over by these wealthy merchants – Kapamadjian and Terzibashian, the Shahbaghtsian brothers, Tutundjian and Djitechian – they would never allow blind Hampartsoum to be at the head of the government, for him be able to appoint Hagop a minister. Well, it could never happen anyway. A minister? What about the leaders?

The Khatch Street square was sleepily dozing today. There were no customers; the shopkeepers' snores were frightening away the flies. Even the dominating aroma of the apricots made people sleepy today. Clearly one ought to sleep on such a day. The coachmen had all disappeared. They had stretched out in their cabs across the customer's seats and were all fast asleep. There were very few people walking by. The windows of all the houses were wide open. 'This too will pass,' Hagop said to himself, 'autumn will come, then spring... they will all come and go.'

At Arark square, he turned left into a narrow street and walked eastwards. Another merchant, Ohannes Khanikian, lived here – he had a thick moustache and sympathetic eyes. In this narrow street, called Khanikents, or just Khanike, there was also another influential, impressive house, that of the five Houssian brothers. This was why the street was also sometimes called the Houssians' Street. Father Mesrob the priest of the Arark church also lived here; he was famous for his skilful and inspired sermons and for his capable delivery of the liturgy. This was why the parishioners of the church also called it Father Mesrob's Street. Moreover, Hamazasp Hundstantsian, the librarian of the Mardig library of the Hunchaks, also lived in this street, but his existence had failed to influence its name, and very few people in the street knew that this well-known librarian also lived there.

Hagop Kandoyan, the so on and so forth of the coming future republic of Van, stopped at a closed door set neatly in a high wall. This was the entrance of the Manasserians' house, sporting an ordinary doorknob. Before knocking on the door, he took off his fez, wiped his sweaty face and neck with a grey handkerchief. He was thinking that it was still not clear, after all, whether this worthless fellow Mihran had shot his brother-in-law or if it had been an accident. He knocked three times but while doing so he suddenly remembered that the Manasserians were never at home at this time of the year, and that both mother and son would be at the monastery.

But what was done could not be undone. A woman's head appeared at the square hole above the door. Perhaps not recognising him, she called out: "Who's that?"

Hagop looked up. "It's me, Karmileh, it's me. Don't you recognize me?"

"Is that you, Baron Hagop? I'll come and open the door for you." She shuffled down the wooden stairs in her slippers and unlocked the door.

"Aren't the Manasserians at home?" he asked.

"They haven't come back from the monastery yet," answered Karmileh carrying on with her needlework. "Come in, come in. Takouhi is ill in bed."

"Oh, really? Let's go in and see her."

Takouhi was Karmileh's mother: she was lying on the bed laid in the hall, an elderly woman with a the colour of an unripe quince and big deep-set eyes that looked scared.

"Hello, Hatun, what's the matter with you?" asked Hagop, bending bending over the sick woman.

"I'm dying, Baron Hagop. It's serious – I'm dying," she replied in the tone of one who had accepted the idea of death.

"You won't die, Hatun. People couldn't die in this heat even if they wanted to."

"They will die, Baron Hagop, when their time is up. It won't matter whether it's hot or cold, I'll die and join the great majority."

That was basically the end of their conversation, there was nothing more to be said. Karmileh showed Hagop into their only large room, where two windows looked onto the garden and the other three onto the yard. Karmileh was just as keen to speak to this yoghurt fly and djilbur bee as Hagop was to speak to her. She wanted to find out what he knew about the marriage of their landlady's son Mihran to Ohannes Muradkhanian's daughter, the modest Lia.

They sat down on the colourful divan, though at a proper distance from each other and without leaning back on the cushions, partly not to get too hot, but also for the sake of propriety. Karmileh bent over her needle-work. She had mastered that handicraft – almost a pure art – in special courses laid on by the American missionaries. She had completed the course successfully while managing to avoid becoming a Protestant. There was only one way in which Karmileh, who had apple-red cheeks and who was twenty-six years old, was a Protestant: she protested against her fate which had left her childless, whereas many of her numerous friends had two or three children already.

"Good for you Karmileh. What a fine piece you've knitted." Hagop traced the embroidered flowers of the white lace with his fingers.

"Well, Baron Hagop, who'll be around to appreciate it?" complained Karmileh cutting the thread with her white, healthy teeth. "A girl is always born with a sigh – akh!"

Hagop put his fez on his kneee, took out his handkerchief, and developed the issue: "A girl is saltless meat. You need to sprinkle some salt on her so that she won't spoil. She'll say the one word, the great yes, in good time – that is, get married."

Karmileh looked brightly at her interrogator who seemed more than a confessor. "I wouldn't mind. But someone has to ask for her to be able to answer with your great 'yes'. Or even a little 'no'."

They had almost reached the main question exercising them both. Hagop pointed to Mihran Manasserian's quarters opposite the windows overlooking the yard. "Isn't there someone living there, making any promise, or proposal?"

This led Karmileh to advance no further, but rather to retreat. She threaded another needle and said, "Baron Hagop, why don't you get married?"

"Are you mad, girl? Are high boots suitable for an old bird?"

"Why? Isn't there some widow out there with a house, whom you could go and live with.?"

"A son-in-law who lives with his in-laws?" asked the old bird, for whom high boots were unsuitable – as if they had ever been at all suitable for a young one. "A man living with his wife's family? Don't you know the story."

"What story? The history of Assyria?"

"What are you talking about – Assyria? I mean the story of the fox. The fox was grilled on the flames of the tonir, and was asked, 'Monsieur Fox, how are you?' The animal answered: 'I'm like a son-in-law living with his in-laws.' Ah well, none of that is to the point. Tell me, how is it going between you and Mihran?"

At last the direct attack was crowned with success. What was said between them after this was difficult to hear and impossible to write down properly. Why was that? Well, both their voices became lower and more mysterious; their talk was seasoned with metaphors, ambiguous expressions, monosyllablic words, short questions and answers, denials, confirmations, confessions. And the conversation went on and on. Finally at the hour when the sun went down into the lake to relax from its tiring, hot day's journey, when the tops of the trees in Aikesdan were bathed in a rosy radiance when the scent of the oleaster in front of the door became – it was not clear why – sharper and soporific at that last hour of the day, Hagop Kandoyan got onto his feet to take his leave.

"Cheer up, don't be upset." The instructor was very experienced in such affairs and did not spare her an explanation: "A broken heart ruins your health."

Out in the hall, they passed silently by the old lady, who appeared to have fallen asleep, and went down the stairs. Karmileh went ahead, opened the front door and said in a whisper, "Whatever I said, let it be between you and me, Baron Hagop."

"Are you mad, girl?" the visitor was almost angry as he went out into the street. "Goodbye."

"Go in peace."

He had already gone some way when he heard, or rather felt, the door being closed behind him. 'Two parties in one house,' thought Hagop, hitting the stones on the road with his stick as he went along the street called Miravi Chadr towards the district of Norashen. "Two parties in one house," he repeated aloud, as if giving both the political and social explanations of the situation. Karmileh's two brothers, Armenak and Hmayak were ordinary Ramgavars. Mihran Manasserian, on the other hand, was a sour Dashnak. "If there are two parties in one house, can there be unity – and especially love – in that house? Certainly not!"

As a rule, Mihran went to bed late at night and woke up late in the morning. He used to get up when his mother was engaged in cooking and washing. Why should Mihran get up early? He had nothing to do, he had no shop. His business was the monastery in Hayots Dzor, with which he occupied himself from the end of spring to the beginning of autumn. For the rest of the time he was as free as a bird. And his house was always filled with wheat, flour, butter, cheese and other stores – and in good time. He was not greedy like Ohannes Muradkhanian who had relations in a village and was at the same time involved in trade in the town. Mihran was an idealist, who generously kept open house for his political friends, who came to his house several times a month. They ate and drank, and sang *The Goat* or *My scarf is lost*. Why not? Ohannes Muradkhanian's lands were his ancestors' lands while this upstart Mihran … Why would Aram have handed over the monastery and its lands to be maintained by him? For what advantage?

While speaking to Karmileh, Hagop had asked, as if casually, about the circumstances of the murder of Mihran's brother-in-law, Grigor.

"Well, it happened at a distance of only two feet," she had replied. "How could you not draw the inevitable conclusion that the revolver was in Mihran's hand."

Hagop had been angry, but had not raised his voice. "In Mihran's hand? But they say that the man shot himself."

Karmileh had smiled. "People say many things, but consider – why ever should Baron Grigor play with Mihran's revolver, or clean it? Didn't he have anything better to do?"

Hagop had continued his interrogation. "Well, was it an accident or not?"

Until then, Karmileh had always answered this question positively. "Of course it was an accident," she used to say, "You should have seen Mihran crying bitterly." But this time, the girl – excited perhaps by the rumours about Mihran's marriage – had not only made her usual crucial comment that the revolver had been fired by Mihran rather than the deceased, but had added a new unexpected reply: "Don't make me talk? Do you want me to tell the whole truth? I don't meddle in the affairs of the political parties. Do you understand?"

It can be firmly said that there was nothing special about the relationship between Mihran and Karmileh. They played 'ailoz-pailoz' but to be completely impartial it should be observed that what was considered to be play for the cat, was tragically serious for the mouse. The Grand Mother would say, "Karmileh, the boy's got up – go and make his bed."

Karmileh would obey without a word. Every day, when Mihran got up and went down to wash with a towel over his shoulder, she went to his room to tidy it up, trying to finish and go to her own unattractive room before Mihran came back. Once, when she had finished her work and was about to leave the room, Mihran came in and greeted her casually, patting her cheeks lightly, as if she was a child. And as time went on the greeting became less and less casual.

This should not cause too much concern. Who could be blamed that the soul of this girl, who had grown up in a sheltered way, responded even to the smallest sound as if it was thunder from the Zum Zum Maghara. How could Mihran have known that these innocent jokes had seeded in Karmileh's soul, like ivy in fertile ground. The seeds had sprouted and grown into branches which were to climb up and embrace Mihran's neck, in the way that ivy does whenever it can. Mihran did not see – or pretended not to see – the light in the girl's large eyes shining out at him sadly like a thoughtful, inquiring searchlight. He could not know that the happiest moments in the girl's life were the times when she came to clear up his room, which had become untidy during the previous twenty-four hours whether there had been any guests there or not. The room was furnished in the fashion of Western Europe – very different from her own dull room – and when she was there, she felt as if she was in paradise. The oil-cloth blinds, decorated with green flowers, pulled down effortlessly; if you wanted to raise them, it was enough just to tug the them down a little, and they would fly up with a cheerful noise.

There were many other miracles in this room: for instance, the walls were decorated with photographs of prominent men and armed groups, which were covered with fine, transparent, blue tulle to protect them from the flies. No one knew why the flies liked to sit right on the nose or the mouth of these men or on the horses of the armed groups. But the most surprising thing was the large album next to the heavy, leather-bound Bible. Colourful postcards with amazing pictures were stuck on its many pages: there were Easter postcards with pretty girls and handsome boys coming out of red eggs, and family postcards showing a young couple standing by the cradle of a sleeping baby – the mother had a finger to her lip, perhaps asking for quiet lest the baby woke up.

For Karmileh, the most tempting cards were the so-called love postcards. Girls with naked arms, half-open breasts, red lips, long and short hair, and boys neatly dressed with starched, snow-white collars and colourful ties, clean-shaven with small moustaches, and all with bold looks. Karmileh stared and could not believe her eyes: the couples were kissing each other on the lips, and here the girl was sitting on the boy's knee. What surprising, incredible scenes! She blushed, her heart beat anxiously, and she closed the album. She was more excited than she need have been, perhaps because she imagined herself sitting on Mihran's knee!

Mihran was not, of course, involved in all this. Even to think that way would have been wrong if for no other reason than the fact that Karmileh's two brothers were Ramgavars, while he himself would die as a Dashnak. As for the kiss – well, something like that did happen once. How did it happen? Karmileh could now no longer quite remember. Mihran had been brushing his clothes. Karmileh wanted to take the brush from Mihran's hand to brush him herself. Mihran would not give it up, whereupon the girl had insisted on taking it. And then, it seemed to Karmileh that Mihran's lips had touched her ear or neck. She had been stirred and had joyfully rushed out of the room; Mihran had carried on singing his favourite song:

Don't ask me, I won't sing...

One day Karmileh said with a smile, "You say, 'I won't sing'. But you do."

"Those are just the words of a song," explained Mihran.

Hagop Kandoyan was a man who always looked for a hair in an egg and found it. If there were something serious going on, he would certainly ferret it out. He entered the street of the Bournazians, having concluded that the relationship between Mihran and Karmileh had gone no further than 'ailoz-pailoz'.

Near the house of the Shaldjians, a scene he had witnessed several times before caught his attention. The children of the district were chasing an elderly man with worn-out clothes and thick moustache. They were shouting, "Let it flow, I've paid for it." It was the well-known, crazy Levon of Van. The evidence for his craziness and for the harm he caused lay in the fact that he was drunk all the time, and also that he used to urinate in the street or against a wall, in broad daylight.

But the matter did not end there. While behaving so improperly, he would shout loudly as if inspired: "Let it flow. Let it flow, I've paid for it. I've drunk Shabagh wine." This was the most disgraceful part. And now, mad Levon was running away from the noisy boys. He stopped to pick up a stone and throw it at the urchins, cursing them in great detail, and then ran away again.

As usual, Hagop raised his stick and shouted: "Aren't you ashamed to chase an elderly man like that. Go home – it's bedtime!" As usual, and this time as well, Hagop's interference did have an effect. The children unwillingly retreated and Levon stopped running away, but hurried on looking back all the time. Meanwhile Hagop stopped in front of the Muradkhanians' door, took off his fez dusted and then replaced it, lowering the tassel towards his right ear, and raised the doorknob.

Knock, knock, knock.

Chapter 17

Ohannes was thinking:

– And we should take into consideration the fact that Mihran Manasserian's position in society, his wealth, and his lands, are really all of no value. As against that I have both land and wealth. Furthermore, has anyone confirmed that he really had a hand in that business? Was there any trial, was he sentenced, was he taken to jail? Nothing happened at all, the case was dropped. But there's another question: as far as I know, Mihran Manasserian was only the head of the Freedom and Light library – how did he happen to come into wealth and land all of a sudden? It's said he's Aram's favourite. Why? For what particular act of bravery? Above all, there's a more important question: what's actually happened for you to get so worried – has there been any formal proposal? No, there's nothing. Mihran's aunt Aghavni approached Satenik and Lia in the Norashen churchyard after the service. She praised Lia's beauty and said she wouldn't be at all worried if she could only find such a beautiful girl as Lia for Mihran. That's all that's happened, and it could be said that nothing's happened, rather than that something has. –

Absorbed in these thoughts, Ohannes was waiting for supper. He was sitting on a rug laden with cushions, a little beyond the rose garden and away from the big apple-tree. In this season, he found it particularly healthy and pleasant to be outdoors as much as possible. 'The world is alarmed and you're just sitting and mulling things over,' Ohannes said to himself as he reviewed the day.

That intrepid trio, Ohannes, Panos and Simon, had met that day quite by chance. After that famous night, it seemed that they had become angry with each other. This surprising and inexplicable coolness between them had lasted two or three years. Why? What had happened? Were they to blame that Bedros-Bey Kapamadjian had fallen down splattered in blood before their very eyes? Were the three worthies to blame because they had been late and were unable to shake hands with him for at least once in their lives? There was no real discord; it was something else, a nameless and incomprehensible – well, yes, discord. It was more a matter of a feeling of shame. They were ashamed of one another and were ashamed to be ashamed in this way. It was a devilish business, almost as if they had shot the well-known merchant themselves and were now ashamed of what they had done. They had needed a few years to stop pretending not to have noticed when they happened to meet, to stop avoiding each other and to start remembering to look out for each other. "Well, time is powerfully restorative," Hrant Bagratouni would say.

And so, today they had met one another on the upper balcony of the first floor of the restaurant. It cannot be said that they had given up drinking – drinking had simply given up them. Indeed, their meetings had recently warmed up only on black coffee or rose juice. The time had passed when after the raki came wine and after the wine the raki and after the raki...

Ohannes called out for Satenik and she called back from the yard, where she was roasting salted herring on an open stove. The sharp smell of the herring had pervaded the yard and street, and even the garden. Every housewife thought that it was the smell of her own herring that wafted over the whole of Aikesdan, for at that hour of the day herring was being cooked everywhere. Yes, the Vanetsi menu was really rich with flavour.

Satenik came out through the garden door with a lamp in her

hand. She hung the lamp on the hawthorn tree and bent over her husband who was leaning on the cushions. Ohannes had closed his eyes and was resting with his face supported by a hand.

"It's been seven days and seven nights since Hagop Kando last came to sing, " she said affectionately not wishing to wake her husband up.

"I'll give you Hagop Kando if I get up." Ohannes smiled without opening his eyes and played with the ends of his wife's dress in a suggestive way. "Come, bring me some raki, fish, and boiled egg."

At that moment there was a knock on the door.

"Don't be a saucy rascal, husband," Satenik said, slipping away from his wandering hand. "What's this about some raki? Have you been dreaming? Who's that knocking at the door? Lia, open the door!"

"Who should it be but your favourite Kando," Ohannes murmured under his breath. It was at this moment that the man in question could be seen, despite the dark, framed from head to foot by the garden doorway.

"Oh, bless my soul, is this a dream?" Satenik was astonished and made the sign of the cross. Ohannes was also surprised but recovered more quickly.

"Come in, Baron Hagop, come in," he exclaimed, though still scarcely believing his eyes. Then he turned to his wife, "Didn't I tell you to bring raki, fish, and boiled egg?"

"Good evening." Kando was not impressed by Ohannes' enthusiastic welcome and noticed the confusion of the hostess. He decided to make the situation clear right from the start: "I was at Mihran Manasserian's and I thought I should come and see you straight away."

It was this statement that made a magical impression on the host and the hostess. Hagop would never knock at any door if he had nothing up his sleeve to impart.

"Take a seat, Baron Hagop. You haven't been here for ages. We've been thinking of you and wondering where you've been."

"Well, here I am. How are you and your children?"

"The children are fine," Ohannes replied and took the worry-beads from Hagop's hands. "Look – one, two, three, Kher, Shar, Astvadz – this one is Lia, this is Sourig, and this is little Vostanig. Lia's affairs are fine, she's a beautiful girl. I don't want to praise her too much, but all roads are open for her. As for Sourig, his position is not so good. He does something mysterious all day and night with that blacksmith Arabo, they're very close. Well, that's him. And as for Vostanig, well, he reads and writes very fluently."

"Blood is thicker than water, Baron Ohannes. Come on, tell me, if there's anything to tell."

Satenik set the table by their feet. She spread the white tablecloth on a rug and put some lavash, cheese, fish, boiled eggs, and fresh cucumber on it.

"Baron Hagop, would you like to drink anything?" She prepared for the guest's refusal by adding, "Why should we always drink?"

"Yes why should we drink? Are we like that mad Levon?"

Ohannes interrupted: "That mad Levon is crazy, he gets drunk day and night. A guest shouldn't be asked whether he would like to have a drink or not. One glass won't do us any harm."

"Of course," said Hagop, "let it be one or two glasses. What Levon does is something unnatural and excessive."

Satenig reproached her husband amiably: "You're a bit muddled today."

"Yes indeed, my beautiful wife," Ohannes said cheerfully. "Of course you know I'm a bit muddled today."

"Saucy rascal!" Satenik was pleased with herself and her husband and walked to the house swaying her hips. She returned with a tray, containing a bottle of raki and clean glasses, which she set beside the food. The glasses sparkled joyfully in the light of the lamp. Ohannes became merry: "Let there be light! I haven't had a drink for ages."

"Nor I, "said Hagop. "We live in hard times, Baron Ohannes. I don't know what will come of all this?"

"Take your glass, let's drink." Ohannes was getting bothered. "Has Van ever lived in easy times? Your health!"

"And yours!"

"Well, what's the news?" asked Ohannes after their first glass, as if they had just met. He wanted to get quickly to the main issue: whether there had been any talk of Mihran's marriage at the Manasserians.

"What's the news?" said Hagop while breaking an egg. "Something that existed before no longer exists, while something now exists which was not there before."

"For instance?"

"Do you know Mushegh Baldoshian?"

"Sure."

"Well, the Mushegh Baldoshian you used to know doesn't exist now," said Hagop, wondering at the same time whether blind Hampartsoum had been aware of this and if so why he had not spoken about it.

Ohannes froze. "What? Why doesn't he exist?"

"He doesn't," Hagop asserted casually. "Mushegh Baldoshian has joined the great majority."

"Has he died?"

Hagop stuttered as he took a fish bone off his tongue. "No, there's no news of his death, nor of his being alive. In a word, the man has vanished."

There was a silence. Ohannes filled up the glasses thoughtfully, and then immediately drained his. Hagop followed his example, possibly out of politeness.

"You seem greatly affected, Baron Ohannes. Were you close to him?"

It was true, Hagop's eyes were a sort of liquid blue, but nothing, whether important or not, escaped them. It seemed clear that Mushegh Baldoshian had been considered as a possible fiancé for Lia and that he had been more likely to succeed than even Mihran Manasserian. Why not? An only son, a splendid watchmaker, with a house, garden, and an orchard of fruit-trees. This question – the issue of Mushegh's likely, and certainly welcome, proposal – had been examined at the highest level during Ohannes' and Satenik's night-time consultations and negotiations, and had been confirmed and agreed between them unanimously.

Ohannes called out for his wife. Satenik appeared in the garden doorway bathed in moonlight. She was now dressed from head to foot in green. She slowly approached and stood under the lamp hanging from a tree.

"What do you want, my master?"

"Oh!" Ohannes was taken by surprise, "Are you remembering your youth?" He smiled and then added, "My dear, Mushegh Baldoshian has died."

"What dreadful news!" Satenik sat down beside her husband. "Who says so?"

Ohannes indicated Hagop with a jerk of his chin.

"Look here, don't exaggerate," said Hagop. "It's not certain that he's dead. A few days ago, he went on horseback to Hayots Dzor and he hasn't yet returned."

'This is Aram's doing,' Ohannes thought, 'Mushegh didn't like Aram.'

"I went to their house," Hagop continued.

"Did you see his mother?" Ohannes was getting impatient.

"Certainly, why else should I have gone?"

Satenik was touched. "Was his mother crying?"

"Not at all. She looked a little worried, that's all."

"What a mother!" Satenik was surprised.

There was a silence. A light breeze blew up from somewhere and spread over Aikesdan. The trees rustled, the ripe fruit fell onto the flower-beds. Water-distributor Harutioun could be heard asking for the water to be turned off from the garden of the Dankovians. Then there was silence again. Ohannes stretched for the bottle of raki.

"That's enough, man," protested Satenik. "What other news is there today?"

"What other news could there be. A healthy, sane man has disappeared in broad daylight!" said Ohannes bitterly as he filled up the glasses.

"Well, let's turn to Hampartsoum Yeramian," Hagop suggested. "He said he'd paid a courtesy visit today to the newly appointed education director."

"You see?" Satenik was delighted.

'He's found a new ear to tell his tales to,' Ohannes thought, and said aloud, "If he's such a diplomat why doesn't he go and see the blacksmith of Bashkale?"

The blacksmith was none other than Tahir Bey's son, Djevdet. He had been given that name when he had been the district governor in Bashkale. He had not done anything special: he had simply had horse-shoes nailed onto the feet of Armenians. 'Worthless son of a virtuous father' or 'The Horseshoer of Bashkale' were the titles which the people bestowed on Djevdet, the last governor of Van.

Hagop lowered his voice. "Would Yeramian be interested in doing that? He'd go if it was necessary. He's a mischievous rogue and now he's sitting around making up lists for the free government of Van."

"Is he going to be the head of the government?" Satenik inquired.

"Who else?"

"Everything's possible in this blind world, why not a blind king for a blind country?" Ohannes drained his glass.

Satemik was annoyed: "That's enough drink, husband!"

"Let's turn to the Manasserians." Ohannes was impatient.

"Let's," agreed Hagop. "There's no special news. The mother and the son haven't yet come down from the monastery. Takouhi Sossoyan is seriously ill. I spoke to Karmileh about one or two things. That's all."

"They say that Mihran Manasserian flirts with that girl Karmileh," said Satenik carefully.

"I've looked into that situation," replied Hagop in a quiet and confident way, "and I came to the conclusion that there's nothing between them – well, nothing serious. As they say in Van, 'girls and boys kiss each other through key-holes'."

"Why?" said Satenik, "Free-thinking is coming little by little to us all."

"It will seem so if you look at it from above, but if you examine it, and think about it from below, you'll see that there's nothing there. One Arshak Mandaburian, one Ourpad Creek picnic, one piece of theatre – is that free-thinking?" argued Hagop, stroking his fair moustache.

Night was approaching and its footsteps could not fail to be overheard by Hagop's large, though quite delicate, ears – he had a good sense of time. He put his beads back into his pocket, pushed himself off the ground with both hands and stood up.

"Well, good night to you and good luck to me," he said. "How is Lia? Has she many suitors?"

"You can't build a house on the sand, can you?" said Satenik. "Is this the time to marry a girl off?"

"That's true as well," agreed Hagop. "Good night."

"That's that," sighed Ohannes after the guest had gone. It was not clear whether he was relieved or, on the contrary, disturbed. "Go and make the beds. Let's go to sleep. No, wait a moment – tell me, why the pretty dress?"

"Why not? Can't I dress up once in a year? Who knows what'll happen to us?"

"You're right, woman, your judgement's very shrewd. These are complicated times. What about Baldoshian? The man disappeared in broad daylight!"

"What about him? One day the whole of Van will disappear."

Ohannes became angry. "Why do you start up such nonsense? Why should Van disappear?"

"Well, don't be angry." Satenik had brought in the bedspread and wanted to soothe him. "One can expect anything in a time of war."

Ohannes took down the lamp from the tree, blew it out and hung it back in its place. Then he undressed and got into bed.

"Are the children asleep?" he asked, in order to say something.

"Long ago."

A huge full moon watched over the vineyards. One of its beams had found its way through the foliage and was now quivering on Ohannes' brow. 'There's nothing like sleeping in the open air,' he was thinking, as the pleasant fragrance of the garden caressed his nose.

"You've come up in the world! You've washed with lavender soap."

"Go to sleep, man, don't talk so much."

The silence was broken by a rippling sound, it seemed of sand, rather than water. There were hedgehogs and even a turtle in the garden. Perhaps they slept in the daytime and grazed at night. The flapping of wings was heard. A stork lived on the top of the huge poplar. Perhaps it had been dreaming and it had flapped its wings when it woke up. What sort of dream could it have been?

Today had been the day the great trio had met on the café balcony. Each swore that he had not had a drink for a long time, but perhaps the others had also, like Ohannes himself, had a drink in the privacy of their home. They deliberated, weighed the pros and cons and always came to the same conclusion – the situation in the town was serious. Panos said: "Take it easy, one day we're born and one day we're going to die." That is what he said, but there was both fear and sadness in his eyes. Simon said: "What would happen if we battered our heads against a wall? All that would happen is that our head would suffer." That's what he said, but it could be seen in his eyes that he was in fact ready to batter his head against the wall, no matter what happened. He kept quiet and said no more – or perhaps it was he who had said, "Blood is thicker than water." To which Simon had replied, "Yes, blood is thicker than water, but water can become blood." What did Simon mean? Clearly, Ohannes understood Simon's hint very well: he was inferring that there might be a massacre. And that this was harmful, disgusting, and unhealthy – even the word 'massacre' was something terrible.

'Anything is possible,' Ohannes said to himself hoping that there would be no massacre, and stroked Satenik's neck with his moustache as usual. And now, it seemed again that somewhere water – no, sand – was rippling. Had Satenik fallen asleep? She had never slept so soundly.

"It's the hedgehog grazing," he whispered in Satenik's ear.

"What hedgehog?" she asked, also in a whisper.

"A hedgehog. Don't you know? The one with quills."

"It's you who's got quills," Satenik said in a sleepy voice, "you're the one with bristles."

The night crept on silently in velvet slippers and cautiously pricked up its ears. Then Satenik could be heard complaining in the faint voice of someone who had only just fallen asleep or had only just woken up: "I could tell your brain was muddled today. Did you have much to drink?"

A distant cock-crow was heard in Aikesdan. It lingered, drew out like the fiery ribbon of a flame, and then petered out. And the next sound was like that of a tiny saw cutting a thin piece of wood, or the meal sizzling in a pot on the hot tonir, or the rustling and wheezing of the gleaming yellow samovar on the boil. No, it was the snores of Ohannes, who was fast asleep, and at last in harmony with the night.

Ohannes had guessed correctly. A hedgehog came out from under the earth wall of the quince garden. It seemed to be curious about everything – in, it might be said, a simple-minded way – as it passed across the clover-bed and carried on towards the snoring Ohannes. Then it felt, presumably with its quills, the pleasant presence of something unusual. The hedgehog crept forward rubbing itself against Ohannes' soft pillow.

And perhaps it was at this very moment that Ohannes, a virtuoso of extraordinary dreams, had one of his recurrent nightmares: he was drinking wine in the sitting-room with Simon and Panos; Hagop Kandoyan was singing the ballad of Mushkil Gusha; Satenik entered in a skimpy, silk dress, shamelessly grabbed Ohannes by the arm and said with a laugh, "Get up, man, get up. Let's dance. The massacre's begun. A bloodthirsty massacre. Let the Armenians weep!"

Interlude

Sitting here by the shores of the Baltic sea, it has fallen on me to sing a lullaby to Vaspourakan, that country of great sons with its Lake and its enchanting city of Van. You are sleeping, as the great poet has said, like a queen. You have been buried ignobly and, in the poet's words, without murmur or complaint. But I say we need not protest. We can say Amen to all that, because we should listen to the voice of the future as well as that of the past or the present. Why can we not fore-hear if we can fore-see?

How am I going to answer God who created the world? I suppose I could deceive him, but how would I answer future generations if I did not tell them about what is happening and about the fate of the various known and unknown heroes? It would ease my burden if there was a single epic hero. But every living person in my story is a hero and has gained the right to live and die, and to become immortal.

All these characters have knocked at my door for almost fifty years. They have asked me, commanded and forced me, to write about them and to include their names and deeds in the glorious story. Wherever I have been, whether rich or poor, well or ill, they have discovered my address, and have come knocking at the door. I tried for many years to get rid of them by moving house and sitting behind securely locked doors.

One night, when I was resting after some enjoyable work and had made sure I was to be left undisturbed, the door suddenly creaked open. Who should come in but some of my characters! Hagop Kandoyan first, then Ohannes and Panos, followed by my other heroes – whether political, domestic, clerical, educational, military, royalist, republican, men or women – who all felt that I was betraying them.

The meeting was, however, warm – indeeed more emotional than was necessary. As their unworthy, but nevertheless diplomatic, countryman, I pretended I was glad to see them and that I was very sad without them. They settled in and did not cause any disruption in my household since I was the only one who could see them. They did not work and did not ask for bread and water, but they talked a lot about the food of Van, especially the herring and the djilbur. They followed me around, often disturbing me, yet they sometimes helped me when I grew tired: one of them would speak to me about the past and I would be inspired to continue writing. They were not rewarded for their good deeds, nor punished for their faults, for they were but memories, shadows, illusions, reflections. They followed me around in this way for years, for decades. They observed me intently, even now when I was fully determined to let go of them.

But I am also accountable to all those future generations. You can sin against the past and the present, but if you are deaf to the future, or hearing it pretend you did not, you deprive yourself of the right to speak. You become voiceless, and as Paramaz would say, the voiceless are worthless.

The fact is that there was once a city, and now that city no longer exists. Could you rebuild Pompeii or Ani in fifty years? What an astounding Pompeii or Ani it would be if its worthy citizens sat playing tavlu in Yerevan and complaining of the heat.

Just as blind Hampartsoum Yeramian saw our heroic future, I hear its voice asking what happened to Van. Why did Van stop being Van? Did it get lost like Abbot Arsen's ring? Did it disappear like Mushegh Baldoshian? But wait! The ring was never actually lost, teacher Kevork had it and people have seen it. And as for Mushegh Baldoshian, he opened a watchmaker's shop in Persia and now regulates the unsettled times.

Chapter 18

It is late at night, but Aram cannot sleep. He sat at his desk wishing there were telephones in this awful city. But he then decided that he would not know whom he would be able to ring, even if there were telephones. He remembered Ishkhan and Vramian. No, Aram had nothing to say to them. And even if they had a telephone, they would be just the same as him; he had no doubt that they would not ring him up either.

What had happened? Why had the feelings of the three leaders diverged into such separate streams? Why did they now see each other only at specially arranged meetings? The three leaders could not have given the same answer to these questions.

It was late at night. Were the situation to be viewed impartially and with no ulterior motive, it would be clear that nothing special had actually taken place to affect the relationships within this great trinity. No, it was simply that times had changed. What had been close, now seemed far away and out of sight, while that which had been far away now seemed close. Nothing appeared to be as miraculous and attractively bright as before.

Aram was as usual beseeching Lake Van to speak to him but he could feel that his appeal had lost its power. The lake might answer right away and call out to him, but it would not have anything special to say. In any case, everything was quite clear. Vanity of vanities and deceit of deceits! It had turned out that there had never been a civilized Europe, let alone any justice.

'We were deceived, but who deceived us?' Aram reflected, 'but who deceived us? We deceived ourselves.' He opened his notebook and with his blue pen wrote in his usual small script:

> Let us not persuade the people or ourselves that we have been deceived. We ourselves deceived ourselves.

Aram read what he had written and could not believe his eyes. What he had written was so terrible and so true.

> Before we came here, the people were shedding tears of

frustration. We came to tell them they should shed blood and not tears. Were we wrong to intervene like that? Were we to sit in Baku, Gandzak, Tiflis, Alexandropol, Kars or Yerevan and calmly look on at the torture and anguish of our brothers in Turkey?

And so those outsiders came and interfered. They said they had travelled on 'the road to freedom'. They shed the blood of their unselfish compatriots on that road and never encountered anything like freedom. No, the road they had opened up was not the road to freedom, it was simply a road of blood. 'There is no freedom without blood,' they wrote on their flag. When they were asked whether there might be blood without freedom, they had no answer, but it was clearly 'as much blood as you want'.

And so there was blood but there was no freedom. The great cause should not be underestimated. There was freedom of a sort – freedom to dream, to be obstinate and vain. There was freedom to imagine as much as possible. Consider what had already happened – the dramatic Ottoman Bank incident or the earth-shattering attack on the Kurds at Khanasor. Imagine that you are one of the new leaders. Imagine that you spurn the bridge and ride your donkey into the turbulent river. And when the donkey and its luggage has been carried away, you raise your hat in a moment's silent tribute. You see the death as a historical necessity and you yourself cross safely over the bridge. To be a hero you have to be vainglorious. For it has been found that it was not for heroism that people were crowned with laurel wreath; it was rather that they sought glory and having found it only then thought about performing heroic deeds. Yes, that is all it was.

Aram could not sleep. He recalled his life, and how he had felt when still a teenager, how the sacred motherland was calling for a war. A war? Well, no one wanted that, a conflict sounded better; a conflict was indeed a war but it was a more harmless version. After all there could be conflict between husband and wife, between mother and daughter-in-law or son-in-law, just as much as between Armenian and Turk. Even children fight with each other. Yes, there was no doubt that for various reasons it would be better to call this a conflict rather than a war.

And this of course came down to a matter of personality. Ishkhan was belligerent rather than a fighter, while Vramian was neither. There was a time when Ishkhan and Aram did not refer to Vramian by name, but simply called him 'teacher' – of course only in his absence. He had always stood against their political actions, their radical measures. Yes, he was just a teacher but all agreed that he had a great reputation. The exiles in Geneva and Tiflis believed that Vramian was the head of the great movement in Van, while Ishkhan and Aram were merely his right and left hand.

Could anyone believe that? Was Ishkhan only a right hand? No, Ishkhan was not the sort of man to suffer this. He did his best, went to any extreme to prove that he was not less 'left' than the others. In a revolution, being on the right was like being a man living with his in-laws. The events in Aghtamar showed that Ishkhan was really a true man of the left. Certainly, Aram was also present at those events but his position was more restrained, more to the right. That affair had taken such a turn that Vramian, in one of his secret messages to Tiflis or Geneva, asked – suggested, demanded and even ordered – the party to free him from these two hands, even by the most serious act, because both of his hands were now left-hands and it was impossible to work with them, whether with pen, knife or fork. It was beyond doubt that if Vramian had complained that both his hands were right-hands, he would have been immediately assisted, even by abrupt surgery and his request, suggestion, demand and order, would have been fulfilled.

It was impossible to sleep. Aram had always been susceptible to women; this has already been referred to as a simple matter of personality and, at the same time, as an accusation. He had always acknowledged it as a fact, but had always protested if the fact was formulated as an accusation. When alone with his conscience and analysing himself, he concluded that his brief but overwhelming fits of passion for this or that Eve or Titania, were nature's punishment. Either his heart was in the wrong place, or perhaps a wrong heart was in the right place. Yes, that was it, nature had given him just the one heart which was more suitable for a poet than for a politician. The painful events involving Marineh proved that nature had played a trick on him, that he, the famous leader could turn into an ordinary rooster in front of a beautiful woman or indeed any woman at all. Cock-a-doodle-do!

Something moved behind the door. Aram knew what that meant: it was Makrouhi, his landlady, who had got out of bed and come barefooted to check whether he was asleep or not. Of course, she would first peep through the key-hole; if the light was on, she would not come in, but if there was no light, she would enter cautiously, check whether her famous tenant was sleeping naked, in which case she would carefully cover him and leave. Sometimes Aram would happen to catch hold of her hand. "Why aren't you sleeping?" young Makrouhi would whisper, almost trembling with excitement.

Yes, something certainly moved behind the door. He wanted a cup of coffee and nothing else; he wanted to feel that at this midnight hour someone else was also awake in this sleeping city. He wanted ... Aram got up and quickly walked to the door. He had been right, but with a small difference. It was the mewing Van cat rubbing itself against the door. Shuffling with his slippers – or paboush, as they were called – across the floor, he returned and sat at his desk to write again.

> Whoever thinks that there are only three political parties in Van is naïve. In fact, there are five parties in this astonishing town. There is our party, with Vramian [he crossed him out], Ishkhan [he crossed him out], myself [he crossed himself out as well] ...

He thought for a moment and then continued:

> ... us at the head. Then there are the Ramgavars, perhaps with Terzibashian or Yekarian at their head. And the Hunchaks with Abraham Broutian. Besides these, there is a party of neutrals led by Hampartsoum Yeramian, and finally I should mention the party of the women of Van – from Mariam Pasha and Zarouhi Teroyan up to Grand Mother Manasserian, and others.

There was a knock on the front door, which he heard being opened. What a time to visit! He remembered Ohannes

Muradkhanian's visit long ago. Someone came – no, flew – nimbly up the stairs. Republican Peto's head appeared in the doorway.

"What's up, what's the matter?" Aram asked.

The messenger took off his fez, took another fez of the same size out of it, and handed Aram the folded letter which had been between the two fezzes. He said it had come from Vramian.

> Dear Aram,
>
> The three of us have been called to attend on Djevdet early tomorrow morning. Ishkhan is going to Herj with several men to try to calm down the Armenian-Turkish disturbances there. I don't know what Djevdet wants from us, but I'll go and find out. But meanwhile you stay put.
>
> Farewell, Vramian.

Aram sent the messenger away. He went up to the lamp and peered more closely at the letter It was written in purple ink, on an ordinary piece of paper in calm, careful handwriting. Under Vramian's signature there was a winding tail which looked more like a question mark. The whole letter was essentially a question, a seriously alarming question. Why was Ishkhan going to Herj to 'calm down the disturbances'? What a surprising thing to do, to go and put out the fire which had been stirred up for years, perhaps centuries, to go and extinguish the blaze. And why had the governor sent for them? He was not missing their company, was he? Was it not clear that there was some dark conspiracy here?

Aram opened the window. The smells of the early spring night filled his heart with a strange desire. Life, life! A hand seemed to be throttling him. What was life, a public figure's life? He brought to mind dozens of faces and names with whom he had acted, played tavlu, drunk coffee. They were not alive now. As the saying goes, they had fallen victims on the road to freedom and with their blood ... and so on and so forth. The road to freedom was not closed, it was open and it required new victims. And now their turn had come. How astonishing, how terrible – to die and not to know how the cause to which you gave all your life would end. To die and to become a headline in a newspaper, or become a picture hung on a wall. A fine prospect, is it not?

Makrouhi came in, delayed by a conversation with her husband which had gone something like this:

"Just tell me whether there is anything between you and him or not, just let me know."

"Don't talk nonsense. There is nothing to tell."

"But the whole town is talking about it."

"There is one Van and there is only one Aram. Why shouldn't he be talked about?"

"Just tell me whether there's anything."

"Yes, there is one thing – there's even two. Is that all?"

"Tell me, I'd like to understand."

Aram asked her to get his black suit ready.

"At midnight?"

Aram was not in the habit of telling his landlady about his affairs or showing her any papers, whether important or not, but this time he pointed at the message on the table like an actor playing Hamlet. Makrouhi, who had left Sandkhtian school when she had only reached the third grade, clumsily picked up the letter, went up to the lamp and read it. She then turned it over and seeing that it was blank, read the first side again, and finally put the letter back on the table.

"You don't need to go, Aram Pasha. It's quite unnecessary."

Aram was surprised. "What do you mean? Would you want me to betray my friends? Never!"

He crossed his two hands on his breast, again like a Hamlet, and his eyes appeared to Makrouhi to flash behind the dark glasses.

"Don't get excited," said Delilah of Van to her Samson from Karabagh. "It's night ... time to dream."

"Get my black suit ready," repeated Aram, but with less resolve.

'I knew this man was a hero but I didn't realise he was quite so heroic,' thought Makrouhi, and her heart filled with tenderness, and at the same time a deep and boundless pride.

"What would my Aram Pasha like to have?" she asked, coming a step forward towards the object of her pride and affection, her pasha.

"Poison," the candidate for bravery almost roared.

Delilah, who was very moved, stroked the already short hair of our modern Samson.

"Let Djevdet have poison, let Agyah have poison. I'll bring coffee for my pasha, I'll bring wine and raki. What else shall I bring?"

"I can't, Makrouhi. Do you understand what my not going would be? It would be treason. It's true Vramian wrote that I should stay put, but what of that? He couldn't very well write 'I am going to die, come and go ahead of me, you cur.' He couldn't have written that, could he?"

"Let's think first –"

"In such cases, logic is the fifth leg of the dog."

"Let's suppose –"

"Without any suppositions, just go and get my black –"

"Coffee – right now!"

And she rushed out like a girl of sixteen. Aram looked after her and reflected –

– If Vramian is going to die, it would really be neither heroic nor clever to follow him saying: 'Let's go and die together'. There's no need to worry and break discipline. As he's written telling me to stay put and that he would come and tell me everything, I should indeed stay here. Let him come and tell me everything. I mustn't disobey Vramian's order. The men in Geneva and Tiflis knew something when they considered him to be the head of the movement in Van. –

The black suit demanded by Aram turned into black coffee. The difference was not very great. As Makrouhi looked at Aram, drinking his coffee in angry, large sips, clearly worried about his friends and all the other Armenians in Van, she felt great admiration and compassion. Surely, she thought, if he was not stopped, he would get up immediately and go straight to the Vali, Djevdet Bey, with his friend and ask him what he wanted. He would do that – you could expect anything of such a hero.

Meanwhile, like everything in this world, Aram's coffee also came to an end, and he again turned to his faithful landlady with a request:

"I don't know how all this is going to turn out for me, but I beg you, for the sake of all the victims who have fallen or are going to fall, wake me up early in the morning as the first rays of the dawn hit Lake Van from Mt Varag so I can have a bath. Wake me up, even if the Semiramid canal overflows and washes away the whole of Turkish Armenia."

While the Samson of Van was persuading his landlady with the force of impossible and terrible images to wake him up in the morning by any means, Delilah of Van was listening to all this with her eyes fixed on his lips and on his small, pale ears. She was wondering how she had managed not to go mad with happiness having such an eminent person under her roof, one whom destiny had entrusted to her and whose every step she ought to guard, especially at this fateful moment. Seeing that Aram had no intention of finishing his spontaneous poetic oration and feeling that time was slipping by, she quickly made up the bed of the man who was going to wake up early. Not daring to interrupt his speech, she pointed at the bed with her finger.

"To sleep, yes, to sleep," said Aram, understanding her silent command, "but how can I fall asleep if the great scoundrel –"

Just at those words, which surely referred to Djevdet, the landlord's voice was heard calling for her from downstairs. She was surprised: "What does the man want of me at midnight," she murmured audibly as she left the room.

"Vanitas vanitatum."

She heard these words as she left, but not knowing the meaning of this desperate exclamation thought to herself: 'What did he say? Vani-tas – tas means cup, so that is cup of Van. Then Vani-tutun, and that must be tobacco of Van. Can the poor man be going mad?'

Meanwhile another surprise was awaiting her in her room.

As ill luck would have it, Setrak had also been unable to get to sleep. If sleep had been a person, Setrak could have told his wife about it, his wife would then tell their powerful tenant, who would then stir up all the several political families and they would find the absent fellow and return him to his lawful owner. Aram would spare no effort in trying to provide for his landlord's immediate, and even eternal, sleep. There is no need to go into deep explanations and make the complicated situation even more complicated. This whole affair was known only to Setrak himself and to God, but also of course to his wife and Aram – and them only, so long as we disregard the whole town of Van. But let those fools not think of him as a fool. There had been times that he had pretended to be asleep and had seen how his wife, to check whether he was asleep or awake, had whispered several times, "Oh, husband, somebody's knocking at the door. Oh, man, haven't you slept enough?" And when he had kept quiet and even deliberately snored, she had got up very cautiously, opened the dowry trunk, taken some things out and put them on, but nevertheless had gone half-naked to her seventh heaven.

Only Setrak knew what he had suffered and it was not in vain that when speaking to different people he often repeated, without rhyme or reason, the saying: 'If I spit up, there's God, if I spit down, there's my beard'.

Setrak had always clenched his teeth and stayed silent. He had thought that if the fool was not ashamed, the master would have to be. However up to that day he had not been able to find out whether the so-called fool was his wife or their honourable tenant. And if it was the latter how could he, Setrak, be the master.

No, Setrak was not completely naïve, he knew perfectly well that the great secret had ceased being shared only with God, and that in fact his secret had evidently gone round the town from house to house, from café to café. Sometimes, when he had felt miserable at home and had gone to a café, he had felt how the sounds of the chatter, which could have been heard even outside in the street, had stopped and there had been an awkward silence. He had taken such blows with the detachment of a philosopher or a hero. He had taken an empty chair, ordered coffee and turned to those who were present:

"Why, aren't you talking? Why are you silent? Has Nasreddin Hodja become an Armenian?" And after the first pleasurable and noisy sip of his strong coffee, he completed his thought, 'Well, If I spit up, there's God, if I spit down, there's my beard.'

To tell the truth, it should be noted that the history that had had developed in Setrak's house, the geography of it (the space between Aram's and the landlord's rooms, open to the landlady but a forbidden zone for the landlord), the arithmetic and the trigonometry (the Setrak-Makrouhi-Aram triangle), had only given pain to Setrak. There had been times when the town had been seriously alarmed.

"Baron Setrak, please come in … Welcome, welcome, Baron Setrak. Come and sit with us … Bring him some coffee. Baron Setrak knows where to sit … Do take a seat. Well, come on, tell us – what's the news?"

Setrak knew very well what these careful welcomes meant. Knowing his tenant's reputation, people wanted to know what the tenant thought about the complicated situation that had developed, what measures he intended to take and what measures he had already taken. They all, without exception, wondered whether the news that was being spread about – to the effect that 'Uncle' had set out and was coming – was true. Anyone who unaware of what was going on in the world asked in surprise who the uncle was, would be laughed at by everyone in the café. "Stupid idiot, don't you know who the uncle is? The uncle is Russia."

Today more than ever, Setrak had no peace. He had heard nothing. He had been to the café on his way home and had been surprised that the customers were sitting separately with no games or chatter. He had seen some anxious-looking acquaintances in the street, who had been so engrossed in their own thoughts that they passed him without any greeting. That was not so unusual, but the fact was that some of his own thoughts were tormenting him today and he could not fall asleep. These thoughts were emotional rather than rational. He felt that there was some shapeless, immaterial and nameless danger in the air. Sometimes that danger seemed to be in the street, wanting to come in; sometimes he thought it was right behind the door, looking for him and about to take him by the throat. He sat up in bed and wanted to catch at least a sound, a whisper, but there was only a silence around him, and that silence was more suspicious than if he really had heard some sounds.

People say that mice on ships are the first to feel the danger of a forthcoming storm and that they escape at the first port. The whole town said the same when Hampartsoum Yeramian left for the Caucasus to go to Egypt through Batum. The whispers passed round: "The blind man knows what's what, something's going to happen to Van." But in his favour they did say that in the forest the lion was the first to sense an approaching hurricane and defend itself in its den. But Setrak had nowhere to go. It was so astonishing to poor Setrak. While there was such an influential person living in his house, it seemed nonsense to be afraid. Just that man's presence in his house was enough for Setrak to feel as safe as an eaglet under the wings of its parent. So had he thought, so had he felt up to that day. But now he had just the opposite feeling: because of that great, but dangerous, man, both he and his house could be ruined.

His wife was sleeping as usual on the sadr. Perhaps she was not asleep but simply waiting for her husband to begin snoring, when she would say, "I'll just go and have a look." Let her go and have a look and do something more; only let there be peace and quiet and may the lustre of that man always reflect on Setrak and his house. But today it seemed to him the lustre was darker and more ominous than necessary.

Was that a knock at the door or did it only seem so to him? His wife stirred and sat up: "Husband, was that a knock on the door?"

He did not want to pretend to be sleeping; on the contrary, he wanted to emphasize that he was not asleep and was not going to sleep that day.

"Yes, it was the door," he confirmed, "see who it is and then come back. I want to tell you something."

'Even a mouse eats roasted wheat,' thought Makrouhi, 'he's going to say something.'

She dressed quickly and left the room. Setrak heard the front door open and someone coming quickly up the stairs. His wife came in with her finger on her lips, though Setrak could not see that in the dark.

"Who was that?" he asked, pretending to be unconcerned.

"Sh-sh," reproached his wife.

Setrak's heart missed a beat. It meant that all his worrying, his heavy premonitions and his sleeplessness had been justified that day.

The same footsteps were heard going downstairs. His wife went out again, locked the front door and came back in.

"Who was that?" asked her husband, now fully alert.

"A messenger. Didn't you want to say something to me?"

Setrak knew nothing of *Othello* and it was not the furious jealousy of the Moor that had awoken in his soul at this eleventh hour. No, he simply wanted to show that he was not interested in the messenger and that he did not feel bad at all. Life flowed on as usual – he was the owner of this house and this woman's husband, and he could even demand an explanation, he could even judge. This led to the conversation that has already been recalled.

"Yes, there is one thing – there's even two. Is that all?"

"Tell me – I'd like to understand."

"Have you anything else to say?"

"Yes, I have."

"Well, say it quickly, and let me go and see what's going on upstairs."

"I think the ghavurma should be made earlier than usual this year," he said carefully and waited for an answer.

Makrouhi thought the man had gone mad. "Well, go to sleep and I'll go to Golgotha and see what the news is."

"Crucifixion! Crucifixion! Go, don't be late. I have something else to tell you."

Makrouhi went up to her seventh heaven.

We have already seen how all this transpired. But now, Setrak was alone again. He, himself had referred to the tenant's room as the seventh heaven, while Makrouhi had called it Golgotha. Often, when he felt that his wife was anxious and irritated without rhyme or reason, he, like a considerate husband or rather with the tenderness of a loving father, would say almost kindly, "Go, go up to your seventh heaven, relax, and see what the news is." The young landlady would fix her large, brown eyes on her husband and would usually complain, "Do you think that it's pleasant for me? That it's not difficult to go up to Golgotha?" Nevertheless, she would go up heavily and angrily and then come down a little later – light, kind, gentle, soft, just like turkish delight.

Setrak wondered what was going on:

– Why did a messenger come at midnight? Why did he immediately go away ? If he came, it's obvious he had to go away but why did he come? The world's in a real state, there's war everywhere. –

He had heard a rumour that Armenians in Anatolia had been massacred and deported.

– Anatolia? Where's Anatolia? Where's the revolution we're supposed to be having? What became of the refrain, 'Let's attack, brothers, let's kill Turks and save Armenia'? But just the opposite seems to be going on: 'Let's kill Armenians and save Turkey'. –

"Oh my God!" Setrak groaned out loud and tried to think of other things.

– The wall of the pantry looking out at the snow-well has become damp. It ought to be repaired. If I don't do the work around the house myself who else would do it? Would Aram Pasha? God has punished me – who knows for what sin? – by depriving me of any children. Blessed be the will of God. Makrouhi is thirteen years younger than me; she could almost have been my daughter. Would she re-marry when I die? Why not? As a widow with property couldn't she find some Hagop Kandoyan? But I have no intention of dying. I'll live as long as Van lives. Why shouldn't I? The most important thing now is that the wall of the pantry looking out at the snow-well has become very damp and needs urgent repair. –

He sat up in his bed, then got up quickly, opened the door of the room in his bare feet to shout out in the dark for Makrouhi and ran back into his bed. It was at this moment that Makrouhi, while still fascinated by Aram's eloquence, realised she was not in heaven but on earth, and that the man who had called her was her husband. She went out leaving the great man's vanitas-vanitatum behind.

"What do you want, husband?" she called out in the direction of her husband's bed in surprise and hesitation. Why are you shouting like that at the top of your voice?"

"Sit down, I must tell you something."

She heard his voice in the dark, but it was not that of the well-known poet who had pleaded for Van:

> I hear your voice in the dark;
> Have mercy, show us your holy truth.

"The wall of our pantry overlooking the snow-well has become very damp, something must be done," said Setrak pronouncing the words carefully one by one and then became silent, which meant: 'I, your lawful husband Setrak, am looking forward to your answer.'

The answer was slow in coming. Setrak's lawful wife felt not only that she had come down to earth from the clouds, but that she had also fallen right under that damp wall.

"Husband, have you gone mad, or are you perhaps running a temperature?" she asked angrily.

"Why?" Setrak replied calmly, "Does speaking about such maintenance problems mean I'm going mad?"

"The house is on fire and you're looking for a hammer."

"What's up? Has Hamid become a Turk?"

"Djevdet has sent for Aram and Vramian."

"If they've been sent for, obviously they must go. The man who has sent for them is the Vali after all. I, too, called you – didn't you come at once? What's so special about all this?"

"Vramian has written to Aram telling him not to go anywhere but to stay put. He himself will go and find out what's going on."

"Very well then let him stay here. Vramian knows something if that's what he is saying."

"Aram's revolutionary conscience is restless."

"That's also natural. What's natural can't be unnatural."

"He wants to go with Vramian."

"That would not be revolutionary, but childish. Don't let him go."

"Husband, he's suffering a lot." Makrouhi's eyes filled with tears.

There was a silence. Setrak continued his masterful summary. "Well, the life of a revolutionary is something terrible."

"I'm afraid, he may go mad," the great man's student said with tears in her eyes. "He's sighing and murmuring 'Vani-tas, Vani-tutun'."

Setrak became deeply worried. "There can be only two possibilities. Either you've misunderstood him or our leader has gone off his head. What does 'cup of Van' mean? A cup is a cup, and what does Van tobacco mean? Van has no tobacco. Our tobacco comes from Trebizond or from Samsoun." He stopped talking and remembered the rumours. "Just go and ask him where Anatolia is."

"What's all this about Anatol?" Makrouhi now became frightened herself for her husband's state of mind.

I'm going to go on a trip," Setrak replied casually. "They say there are such big water-melons in Anatolia that if you sit on them, your feet won't reach the ground." He was pleased he was remaining calm, he began to sing:

"The Sultan's executioner
Gave orders from Yildiz Kiosk."

'What misfortune!' thought Makrouhi, 'both of them have gone mad.'

"I don't know what to do," she said. "What shall I do? Suppose he suddenly gets up and leaves while I'm sleeping. I can't relax while he is talking away to himself."

"Is he running a temperature? Who can tell whether a revolutionary is hot or cold? Go and do something," said Setrak.

"It's important he doesn't leave the house."

"Try to get him to undress. Once he's in bed, take his clothes and shoes away, put them under your pillow and sleep soundly. There's no other way."

"What if he doesn't take off his clothes?"

"If he doesn't undress willingly, undress him by force." Setrak corrected himself feeling that he should not have said such a thing: "Make him undress himself."

"Husband", complained Makrouhi, "you sound as if we're dealing with a child."

"Well he is a child. All leading politicians are children."

"Oh, don't speak nonsense, man." Makrouhi had got bored and she left the room.

By now, Aram was not suffering from any nameless fear and terror. No, now it was clear to him that a dangerous ambush was being prepared. Djevdet had sent for both Vramian and Aram, Armenians were being massacred in Anatolia. In 1895 there had been one Sultan Abdul Hamid, and all Armenians – old and young – had cursed him. But then he had been supplanted and whom could one curse now? There were so many separate Abdul Hamids now. What should he do? Go to Varag and light a candle?

Setrak was thinking:

– I wonder if our national hero has relaxed or not? The people of Van did not call Makrouhi Aram's guardian angel in vain. I wonder in what state the guardian angel is now. That bloodthirsty executioner Abdul Hamid is said to have had six or seven hundred wives. We have only one wife and even then we find ourselves always in trouble. How could that odious beast get his seven hundred wives to understand anything? –

Setrak got annoyed with himself, not because he could not make seven hundred women understand what he was saying, but with his one wife who was late. It occurred to him to get up, go upstairs quietly to the door of the room and eavesdrop, to learn what was going on. But Setrak said to himself out loud, while stroking his moustache with pleasure, "I'll do nothing of the sort, a man must have respect for his moustache."

But then another thought stirred like a caterpillar in one corner of his brain.

– One has to be all eyes when playing tavlu with Avetis Boshian, he always cheats ... We never managed to find out anything about Anatolia, about the Armenians in Anatolia being massacred ... Let me light a candle. –

And he feel asleep.

... It is the Varag festival. People from the villages and the town come in carts and carriages, on horses and donkeys, and on foot. They are coming and filling up the meadows, the large yard and the rooms of the pilgrims. They are singing and dancing on their way. They are coming with a few days' supply of food and with samovars and beds.

CHAPTER 18

Dng, dng, dng. The huge drum thunders so loudly it could burst one's heart and the flute is screeching so loudly it could deafen one's ear. The pilgrims are lying on carpets and rugs spread over the grass. Sheep and lambs, hens and cocks are being slaughtered at the entrance of the monastery and smoke rises from the improvised fires and spreads over the green meadow, over the monastery fields. It is the festival of the Holy Sign at Varag.

The silence of Mt Varag fell upon the monastery and its surroundings. The people fell silent; their belongings and their music, the lambs and sheep being slaughtered at the walls of the monastery and the seven mill-stones all fell silent.

Dust hovers like a cloud over the wide road. Three horsemen are approaching – Ishkhan, Aram, and Vramian. And now only the twelve thuds of the three horses can be heard.

The people seemed petrified like stone statues. Those who had been dancing stood motionless with one foot in the air; those who had been speaking stood with open mouths; those who had been bending over a samovar remained bent over it; anyone who had been pouring out tea stood motionless with the teapot in one hand and a glass in the other; one of the drummer's sticks stayed in the air with the other on the drum; those who had been drinking raki still had an empty glass at their lips and their eyes remained fixed on the monastery's dome; and the tavlu players were like statues with the dice still in their hands.

Everyone was frozen in whatever position they had been in. The water had stopped flowing and the smoke of the fires – for cooking or for sacrifice – had stopped wafting over the fields. Only Setrak remained unaffected. Sitting on a stone by the door of the monastery he was watching this drastic miracle with horror. The horsemen approach and halt. Ishkhan's horse rises twice on its hind legs and neighs. Aram speaks in a voice like thunder.

"Why were you frightened of us? Does it matter that we are new-comers? All Anatolia is afire. Aikesdan is burning bit by bit. Djevdet has called Aram and Vramian to drink raki with him – and Ishkhan to sing a song. This will be the last festival at Varag. So sing and rejoice – for there won't be any Varag in future."

Ishkhan and Vramian were listening sadly, still sitting on their horses. Aram jumped down, stretched his hands and moved them up and down.

"Bang the drum, blow the flute. I must dance."

As he spoke, Setrak saw the drummer's stick rise and fall down on the drum, and the flute player's cheek puffed and the instrument screeched. People began to move – they danced, poured out tea, and drank raki; the animals being sacrificed began to bleat and the seven huge millstones started turning. And people were clapping as Aram danced. But Setrak sees that Ishkhan and Vramian are motionless, frozen like statues on their horses. Aram got people to form a circle dancing round the petrified horsemen. Then the ground shook! A large, polished, square slab of stone came up from under the ground and took Ishkhan and Vramian up into the air. The horsemen made such an amazing picture that Arshak Dzetotian took out his camera. Aram led the dancers round the statues, the drum roared and the flute screamed.

And just at that moment, a tall, half-naked man with unkempt hair and beard, looking almost like a corpse and smelling like one, came out of the monastery. Setrak saw very clearly that his rags were of expensive, fine silk. On one side of his head there was a dirty crown looking like a monk's skullcap. He had green shoes, but he had hardly walked two steps when they broke into pieces and he continued on bare feet.

"Woe is me, woe is me, woe is me," said the crazy man.

Everyone shouted out, "It's King Senekerim. The king's been resurrected."

"Woe is me," repeated the pitiful Senekerim, "you'll leave me and go to foreign lands, leaving my tomb to outlaws. How can I reign over outlaws?"

Aram noticed the king, ran up to him and embraced him. "Brother Senekerim, cheer up. I'll continue the work you began."

The king laughed like a madman and patted Aram on the shoulder. "Woe is me. What I began died. You begin something new, if you can. Baron Setrak's pantry wall is damp, repair it if you can. Digin Makrouhi has a fever, give her brandy, cure her if you can."

"Oh," Setrak shouted in horror, "my domestic affairs have also come to the attention of King Senekerim. Alas! Alas!" ...

It was already morning when Setrak woke up, confused by his strange dream. His wife was sleeping on the sadr in fine clothes and he wondered when she had found the time to put them on. He called out to her. She shifted a little in her sleep and settled herself more comfortably.

"Woman, I'm speaking to you."

"What do you want, man, let me sleep."

"Woman, get up. I've had a bad dream. Has the great man left?"

"It was really hard to persuade him, but he finally fell asleep. Go and find out from typesetter Hmayak. Find out what's happened to the others."

"Damn all of them. Let typesetter Hmayak come and find out from me."

"Not again. Let me sleep."

"Sleep. Sleep peacefully, your affairs have reached the ears of King Senekerim."

"Have you had a dream?"

"Certainly – and what a dream! Something terrible."

"Well?"

"In my dream I saw thousands of people at Varag monastery."

And Setrak reported his dream – including every detail without exaggeration, and with his eyes fixed on the ceiling. When he got to the part about her fever and the brandy, he looked over to see what impression his account had made, only then to realise that she was fast asleep, and that the account of his preposterous dream had only been heard by him. He felt a wave of unrestrained anger. He defiantly, but not too loudly, described his wife with an ugly and un-Armenian adjective, not a generally acceptable one but in this case, who knows, perhaps quite suitable.

Nevertheless.

Leaving the house, Setrak set out for the Shirak café. The fresh spring air gave him a surprising feeling of pride. He remembered his dream and the feeling of pride turned into one of bitterness. What a senseless, absurd dream! Yes, it was only a dream, but the truth was that they had to keep Aram at home and not let him out of the house. When he himself had left, the great revolutionary and his guardian angel were both fast asleep.

At the cross-roads he met Hagop Kandoyan. When he first saw him in the distance, he had decided not to say anything to this walking newspaper. Yes, nothing. But the terrible thing about Hagop Kandoyan was that he knew how to make you pour out your news. Setrak had reproached himself, 'Well, are you a child, just hold your tongue,' and had walked bravely on.

"Good morning," he said to Hagop, hoping not to stop.

But Hagop intercepted him. "Is this a time when you can tell anyone the morning's good?" he said angrily.

"What's up, has the mullah become Turkish?"

"I wish he had. It's the priest who's become Turkish."

"So what's up?"

"You don't know a thing, you poor man, why should you?" said Hagop and walked on.

Setrak was dumbfounded, he felt as if he had been stabbed in the back. What a disgrace! He went after the wandering newspaper

"Stop, stop, let's exchange a few words at least."

"Did anyone come to your house last night?"

"Yes, someone did."

"Was he Djevdet's man?"

"What are you talking about? He was a messenger."

Hagop pretended to be surprised. "So, a mess-en-ger ... There are so many rumours flying about. I thought I should go to typesetter Hmayak but then I thought why should I go to him, why should I go to a child instead of to a reliable man. And so I decided to come to you. It's a good thing we met."

Setrak melted like butter and he poured out everything he himself – rather than his wife – had seen or heard with his own eyes.and ears. He told Hagop about Vramian's letter and how Aram had got so excited and had decided to go and kill Djevdet; and how he, Setrak, had shouted at that big child and commanded – yes, commanded – him to undress and go to bed, after which he had locked the door, depriving Aram for a while of the right to move about freely.

"And is he locked in now?" asked Hagop anxiously.

"Yes, he is at the moment."

"You've made a bad mistake – a very, very bad mistake,"

"Why?"

"What if," Hagop lowered his voice, "he wants to go to the lavatory?"

"Oh, Baron Hagop," Setrak laughed heartily, "what a curious man you are. If he wants –"

"If he wants? How can he help wanting in such a serious situation?"

"Well, Makrouhi's at home – she'll see that he has a serious need to come out and she'll let him out."

"So, the key is with Digin Makrouhi?"

"Certainly."

Setrak was pleased with his quick thinking. Hagop's thoughts now took another turn.

– What a stupid idiot, your wife and Aram Pasha have locked the door and are playing at revolutions together, and you are wandering the streets like mad Levon boasting or, as they say, selling pickles. –

"Yes," Hagop said, "but he could come out to go to the lavatory and then escape to Djevdet Bey."

"He can't."

"Why can't he? He could easily run away."

"He can't, if I say he can't. It means that I know something."

"Well, tell me, so that I know it as well?"

Setrak whispered in Hagop's ear: "We've hidden his shoes in a safe place. He won't run off to Djevdet in slippers."

"That's a point," Hagop conceded, but did not want to give in completely. "But if I were you, I'd let him do whatever he wants. Let him go if he wants to, and let him stay if he feels like it."

"He mustn't, Baron Hagop, for heaven's sake. Vramian knows something if he's written telling him to stay where he is."

"Well, let him stay where he is." Hagop finally agreed, hoping however that Aram would not only stay where he was, but would never get up.

"Let's go to the café, shall we?" Setrak suggested, regretting from the bottom of his heart that he had been so open with this walking newspaper.

"No, thank you, I must go to the restaurant." Hagop said and walked on.

"Baron Hagop," Setrak ran after him anxiously, "please let whatever I told you be between you and me."

"What! Am I a gossip¿" said Hagop angrily as he walked firmly on. And he continued on his way, thinking he would in fact go to the Manasserians rather than the restaurant.

Setrak stared after him. He no longer wanted to go the café.

– Is this the time to go to the café. I'd better go home and make sure that Makrouhi understands not to get involved in revolutionary affairs. Let Aram go or let him stay – whatever he wants. It's none of our business. Kando was quite right. –

He turned and went back the way he had come. He had only just got back to the house when he noticed that yet another messenger was knocking at the door and was then let in. Setrak stood listening at the door There was no sound coming from inside.

– What have I to do at home¿ Let them do whatever they want. I'd better go to the Araruts café after all. I'm living like a stranger in my own house. Ah well, if I spit up, there's God, if I spit down, there's my beard. –

It is not yet clear whether Setrak got to the Araruts café or changed his mind again half-way. But it is said that some people did see him in the Araruts café, that he had sat at a separate table, ordered a cup of coffee and when some acquaintance had approached him and asked him an innocent question, he had answered very briefly, "I don't know."

Chapter 19

The wind blew in from the sea in the evening, but swung to come down from the hill at sunrise ...

We could begin warmly this way, and be happy to return to the balcony of the home of Ohannes Muradkhanian and look at the leaves and the new buds, the apricot trees bathed in white light, the flowering bardisapakhs and the barely flowering crocuses, but alas ...

In fact it had rained, and the overflowing gutters had wept or sung all night. The news of the arrest of the Hunchaks had invaded every house and heart like a cold wind, everyone was paralysed with fear. Djevdet had sent for Vramian, who had gone but had not yet returned. Ishkhan, accompanied by a few young men, had gone on Djevdet's orders to Shatakh to look into the disturbances there between Armenians and Turks. That was surprising, since Ishkhan had himself been sowing discord in the villages day and night. Now there he was, destroying the seeds he had sown. Was there any reason for that? Indeed, there was not.

News of the Hunchak meeting in Constanza had spread. A decision had been taken there to eliminate the Turkish leaders, Enver, Talaat, and others. Some Hunchaks from Van had also taken part. Could they get something going and see it completely and successfully through to the end? A copy of the agenda, which included a list of the participants from Van, had been seized in Bolis. That was the most terrible thing.

And now Ohannes wanted to find out where Constanza was, just as Setrak had wanted to know where Anatolia was.

– Hmm, Constanza. I must look it up. But suppose I do learn where it is, what use would that be? It's by that deep, Black Sea. So what? The fact is that the Hunchaks are all young men, and they've all been arrested. –

Images of them flashed before his eyes: Garabed Dantoyan, as strong as an ox, thick-set and heavy like his name; Artashes Solakian, with his fair beard and clear blue, intelligent eyes;

Abraham Broutian, with his high forehead, gloomy features and tightly-held, soft lips; Haykak Yeremishian, who was thin and stiff, and had never seen Constanza but had been arrested because ... well, is there any need to carry on?

Ohannes did not go to town today. The meeting of the trio had so decided. Both Panos and Simon had agreed with his comment that profit in these days was cursed. The situation had become really serious. Aram stayed at home; there was a rumour that Vramian had ordered him not to leave the house until he returned. Had Aram ever taken any notice of Vramian's commands? Well, yes, but only when it suited him!

Satenik called out downstairs. "Lia, get some water from the well."

Ohannes' thoughts took another turn. Lia was still a mere child, how could there be a marriage? He was a liberally minded man. When last autumn, a formal delegation had come to see the girl on Mihran Manasserian's behalf, Lia had been prepared for this the day before. She was told that a certain Mihran wanted to marry her. Lia was surprised and asked who this Mihran was and what he wanted of her? They told her that she should get married and go to live with Mihran. She cried and said she would not go away, that she would not live with any man other than her father. They were not able to dress her up in the new clothes for the delegation of three women, which included Mihran's mother. Lia grumbled, "It's not a play like *Ancient Gods*, it's not a holiday – why should I wear new clothes?" And she ran away from the house and took refuge with her friend Arpenik next door. When Satenik told the guests candidly about the behaviour of the bride-to-be, adding that the girl was still very young and ignorant, and not mature enough to get married, Mihran's mother had deeply resented what she imagined had been a rejection that had already been decided. She loved Mihran with a mother's devotion and the fact that he had a bad reputation touched her heart.

But the most surprising thing was what happened in the evening after the delegation had left. When the 'refugee' came back home, Ohannes, called her to him.

"Why didn't you have anything to say to the guests?" he

complained, nevertheless admiring her innocent eyes full of fear, "you disgraced your parents in front of others."

Lia embraced her father: "Don't be angry, I won't do it again."

Ohannes could hardly suppress his laughter. "The girl's mad", he shouted out, "she's too mad to be betrothed."

"I don't love that Mihran," Lia said and wrapped her arms round her father's neck.

"Look at the girl! Come on, my lady, tell us whom you love? Tell us, let us know who it is."

"I love Ishkhan," the girl confessed openly.

Ohannes could not believe his ears. "What? What did you say? Say it again."

The girl was scared. "Is it a crime to love Ishkhan?"

"You blockhead!" exclained her father. "Ishkhan has a wife and a son."

The girl was surprised. "Is it not possible to love a man who has a wife and a son?"

'She's no more than a child,' thought Ohannes. And he took hold of Lia's ear and enacted a sort of children's game with her.

Ohannes, (pulling Lia's ear): "have you given the donkey water?"

Lia: "Yes, I have."

Ohannes: "Is the water hot or cold?"

Lia: "It's cold."

Ohannes: "Heat it up."

Lia (already suffering from earache): "I have heated it."

Ohannes: "It's too hot. Cool it down."

Lia: "I have cooled it."

Ohannes: "It's too cold. Heat it up."

This was repeated endlessly until the girl pulled away from him.

"What's all this?" she complained grimly, "Am I a child for you to play that game with? I'll go and tell Ishkhan."

How could he explain things to her. And in any case, looking at the issue calmly, was this really a good moment to be thinking of marriage. Here was Van, critically wounded, terminally ill! Was this a suitable moment for marriage celebrations when there was so much death in the air.

Boom! A distant explosion was heard from the far end of the garden. Clearly that was Souren. Where did he get the pistol? He must have got it from blacksmith Arabo, with whom he was on quite good terms. Ohannes would have liked to get angry with both of them, but he could not. 'The times call out for it,' he thought, 'Perhaps, the day has come for everyone, old and young, to take up arms. How many such dangerously fatal periods have there been in the course of history?'

Tack, tack – tack,tack. Someone was banging the front door. Only beggars or children, who could not reach the knocker, banged on the door like that. A drunk might knock at the door like that. 'It's Kevork, that prickly bush,' thought Ohannes. 'No, wait, the more he's drunk, the more recognisable would be his knocking.'

He felt agitated and shouted down to Satenik that there was someone at the door. He heard it being opened and then the sound of someone tramping upstairs. He came in from the balcony with heavy foreboding and peered out of the open window to see who had come. He wondered whether it could be Agyah? Ohannes held his breath. Panos appeared on the balcony and Ohannes, hiding away, did not like his expression or the way he walked in. He wondered whether Panos was drunk, and shouted out with unsuccessfully assumed gaiety, "Come in, I'm inside."

Panos came in with a pale face and tired eyes. He offered no greeting, but threw himself onto the sofa, pulled a handkerchief out of his pocket with trembling hands and wiped his forehead.

"Good Lord, what's up?" Ohannes said in a hoarse voice.

"Haven't you heard?"

"No, what's up?"

"I wish I were you. Tell them to bring a jug of water. I really wish I were you."

"Lia," Ohannes called out through the open window, "bring a jug of water."

Lia soon came in with a jug of cold water and gave it to her father. Ohannes took it and passed it on to Panos. The water gurgled out from the narrow mouth of the jug into Panos' throat, which seemed almost as large as the jug.

"You're lucky," repeated the bearer of bad news for the third time, returning the almost empty jug to a blissfully unaware Ohannes and wiping his mouth with a handkerchief. Assuming that he had suffered some personal tragedy, Ohannes adopted the manner of a comforter.

"Alas, Baron Panos, misfortunes happen to men and men happen to misfortunes. A man can endure anything in cold blood. Calm down, my friend, calm down. Tell me what the matter is and perhaps we can sort it out."

"The Turks caught some Armenians returning to Aikesdan from the city centre, and butchered them – our friend Simon among them."

"No, not that!" exclaimed Ohannes striking Panos' thigh with such force that the latter momentarily forgot in his own pain, that of the loss of Simon. "Not our friend, Simon?"

"Yes, our Simon," said an exasperated Panos, rubbing his aching thigh. "And not only Simon. That villainous cur, Djevdet, has had Vramian thrown alive into the sea to drown. Moreover ..."

"Anything else?"

"Yes, there is. Ishkhan and his bodyguards were all shot one by one in Herj on their way to Shatakh."

Something stirred behind the closed door. Was that someone moving or breathing? Ohannes, taken aback and broken-hearted, heard nothing. If he had opened the door at that moment he would have seen Lia with the jug in her hand, kneeling and sobbing quietly. She had overheard the bad news – each item worse than the next. Could it be assumed that what had affected her was the heavy news about Simon's – or perhaps Vramian's – death?

"It could be a lie. So many murders! And if it is true, then it's the end of the world and we'd better go and throw ourselves into the sea," Ohannes called out in alarm – nobody knew whether addressing God, the world, Panos, or himself.

Panos got really frightened that Ohannes might go and drown himself in the sea leaving him alone, absolutely alone. With whom would he then be able to sit and drink raki in the café? Or to sit and drink rose-tea in the garden and speak of the good and the evil in the world, the old and the new, the here and the now? With whom? He passed on to Ohannes' previous comment.

"Baron Ohannes, alas misfortunes happen to men and men happen to misfortunes. Men –"

"I don't understand. We met the other day, and decided –"

"When we left you, Simon complained that he'd left his documents in the shop. I suggested to him that no guarantee, no insurance was reliable any more in this country. I begged him not to go. He didn't take my advice. Well, if you don't take an old man's advice, you'll get –"

"So, he became an unnecessary victim?"

"Yes, more than unnecessary."

There was a silence.

Ohannes counted the arrested Hunchaks on his fingers, "Ishkhan and his bodyguards are killed – one, two! Vramian is drowned in the Lake – three! Simon and other Armenians are killed – four!"

He raised his hand with four closed fingers and an open thumb, moved the other hand up and down and exclaimed, "This is the end of the world."

"It's not the end of the world, but of Van," objected Panos.

"The end of Van is the end of the world, Baron Panos. Aren't I right?"

Ohannes had counted with the accuracy and speed of a an adding machine. There was again a silence.

Panos felt exhausted: "The world is large. I don't understand what is going on in the world. But I'm sure that our Van is going to turn into ruins like Ani." He changed the subject abruptly, "Have you any raki in the house?"

"Why not?" Ohannes cheered up as if remembering the old days and went off to order something, almost as he would have done so before.

"Satenik, let's have some raki, meat and fish."

Satenik laid the table. When Ohannes asked what Lia was doing, Satenik said she was not in the mood. She asked nothing, and the men told her nothing; but they did not realise that Satenik already knew everything. A little while before, a deathly-pale Lia had gone downstairs with the jug in her hand and had related with barely restrained excitement what she had overheard. While Satenik was setting the table, each worthy Vanetsi was thinking about the third, whom they would never see again, and whose voice they would never hear any more.

"Simon is late." Ohannes blustered in his distress: "Oh God save us from the worst –"

"He won't be coming any more," Panos' eyes filled with tears and he reached for the raki bottle. "God bless your soul, Baron Simon."

They drank and Panos pursued his thought about Ani. "The city of Ani was lucky. Mother Armenia mourns for Ani."

He pointed to the picture hanging on the wall as grounds for thinking that the day would come when there would be nobody to mourn for Van, nobody to tell it not to cry.

> "The city of Ani is crying.
> No one is saying,
> don't cry, don't cry."

Panos sang, or rather recited, the words dramatically.

There was silence again – a different sort of silence. And then Ohannes said:

"Did I say it was the end of the world? I'm sorry, I was wrong. Neither the world, nor Van will come to an end. One Vanetsi like Baron Simon can be lost. What you call the the world is Van, and Van is the world. Do you think that the seas and oceans are bigger than our Lake Van? That Masis is higher than our Varag? That those cities, Bolis-molis and Paris-maris, are more beautiful than our Aikesdan? Let's admit that there's a bit more water in an ocean than in our lake. But the most important thing is not being long or short, big or small, great or average. The most important thing is the meaning. Like it or not, Van is of very great importance. Glory be to our Van! Long live our Van – and the world with it!"

Boom! A distant explosion was heard from the far end of the garden.

"It's the sound of a gun." Panos froze with his glass in his hand.

"No, my friend," Ohanne calmed him down, "that's our Sourig playing with his weapon."

Wiping his mouth with his handkerchief, Panos said: "Baron Ohannes, for heaven's sake, don't I also want our town to live? May the whole world live too. However, you will see that they won't let our sons follow us. Where is the great, traditional Van of our grandfathers? Van has lived and survived for thousands of years – from King Senekerim to Baron Simon. What winds have blown over Van and what waters have flown through it? Van has lived and suffered idolatry, Christianity, Islamic invasion, Turkish rule, rape, robbery, and murder. If Van has said 'how terrible' once, it has said 'how wonderful' ten times. Van has lived and survived until outsiders stirred up our Van leaving no fellowship, no respect, no honour, no sanctity, no humanity. You've said what Van is for you. But can there be a Van with only herring, dalasli apples and Hagop Kandoyan, with only a library, an Ourpad creek, with only the songs *A girl with a red bicycle* and *Come down dreams, come down*. Is this all that Van is? If so, let it fall into ruins – we don't want it."

An excited and agitated Ohannes now replied, "I'm very surprised, Baron Panos. I'm surpriserd and quite frankly, angry. What's the matter – why worry? Is a library a bad thing? When did you become an enemy of reading and writing? You're an odd man, what harm has the Ourpad creek done to you? Let people go there and breathe fresh air – is there anything but good in that? *A girl with a red bicycle*? That's a song: let it be sung. Why should they only sing *The city of Ani*? As for *Come down dreams, come down*, is that such a bad story? Levon Shant knew a thing or two when he wrote it. When the monk exclaims, "Open your arms, Seda," and jumps into the lake, it's worth a thousand sponges. A man should be a little progressive, Panos my friend."

"Well, I don't know." Panos was angry and stood up. "You acted the way you did and got where you are. When were you ever progressive? Answer me that. They say better an open enemy than a false friend, and that's true. I'm going. I'm sorry to have troubled you. " And he moved towards the door.

"Baron Panos, are you off your head? Where are –"

"To Baron Simon. Are you satisfied?"

It is hard to imagine how this agitated scene might have ended.

Ohannes was holding Panos back with both hands to prevent his going, while Panos, judging by the expression on his face, was making an enormous effort to rush out. But just at that moment there was a short, loud knock on the front door – tack, tack, tack. Yes, the sound of the front door had a magical, disrupting effect on the two old friends and seemed to bring them back to the reality of their serious situation. Who was knocking at the door? They stood back and looked at each other like guilty children, then remained standing like tired, gaunt wrestlers waiting for some third party.

Who's coming up the stairs? Thmp, thmp, thmp. It's Simon, he's late! But he won't be coming any more. There is no Simon any more.

The door of the room opened quietly, and the former teacher, Kevork Muradkhanian, once a public figure and now a man of no definite occupation, appeared in the doorway: "And our Lord said that drink was a friend not only to happiness but also to grief and bitterness. You've behaved very correctly, you're very wise, you're very beautiful."

Kevork's appearance would hardly have been considered a welcome intrusion in other circumstances, but now his entrance was a sort of blessing. Indeed even if it had been the Devil rather than Kevork, he would have been seen in that alarming atmosphere as a desirable third party, a welcome guest, a much appreciated resolution of the awkward situation. Had a satanic whirlwind in fact taken over Panos – a man who was to all appearances self-controlled and who always looked before he leapt – and led him to jeopardise his devoted and long-standing, intimate friendship with Ohannes, especially at a time when both of them had lost their dear and irreplaceable, third part?

How had it happened, at a time when they should have been standing side by side, hand in hand, heart to heart, in memory of the tragically deceased Simon, that their friendship had been about to drown in a sea of discord? There must surely have been some volcanic eruption for there to have been such a disturbance. The unconscious life of a human being is an unfathomable and enigmatic mystery, a deep and impenetrable abyss.

There had been an occasion when the amazing news had spread

round Van that Ishkhan had a pocket lamp. What sort of lamp was that? What Ishkhan always kept in his pocket was a torch, an amazing, wonderful thing with a strong lens and an unusual shape. Whenever he was somewhere dark, he took that magic thing out of his pocket, pressed on a sort of button to light up the place with rays that were too bright, like those of the sun, to look at directly. Ishkhan could see whatever was revealed by his torch, and while remaining invisible himself, he could see everyone but nobody could see him.

The point of this digression is that if we had such a torch with which to explore the human soul and if its light was cast on Panos' inner world, it would become clear why he had been driven to such extremes. The issue was that Panos could just as well have claimed for himself the role of a free-thinking progressive, and assigned Ohannes to the marshes of ignorance. Had not Ohannes himself directly criticised the Freedom and Light library as well as the shameless songs, *A girl with a red bicycle* and *Come down, come down dreams*? It had never occurred to Panos to interpret those critical comments politically. And now in this unstable political situation, when all the Hunchaks had been imprisoned, when Vramian and Ishkhan had been stealthily killed and one of their trio had been slaughtered in the middle of the town, when all Van was in a state of alarm and at the edge of more terrible, historic events, he, Panos, had been accused of being ignorant while Ohannes had been intelligent. 'Well, I'm ignorant, but when did you become progressive?'

No, Kevork had appeared just in time. Panos, the ignoramus, and Ohannes, the intellectual, now came to agree with each other, having forgot their ideological disagreements. They greeted the former teacher: "Why are you standing? You must be tired. Oh, I get it – you want to pay respect to Baron Simon. You've surely heard? Alas, alas, our dear Simon."

Kevork went up to the table, picked up a full glass, and leaned back, supported by his cane.

"This is in memory of the patriarch, the – the –" He looked up at the ceiling and found the word he sought with surprising adroitness, "– the victim. In memory of the experienced member of a prosperous business – Van's loss in these barbarous times. All praise to his two orphaned friends who are to continue his cause, if circumstances allow them to do so. Let's drink up and sit down."

He did so himself and suggested with a slight gesture that they did so as well. It was not at all surprising at this stage that the two orphaned friends followed his example. But they did not care for the expression 'if circumstances allow them to do so'.

"Well, what's up? What's worrying you now? What's been left at home and what bone's been given to the dog to chew over?" Kevork demanded in an aggressive tone.

"What do you mean?" Ohannes did not really catch what his brother in his euphoric mood meant. "What home? What dog?"

"The dog is all that's left of the market, of your shops," explained Kevork with great enthusiasm, "Give a farewell blessing on their souls. All that's left is whatever you've got here."

The orphaned friends looked at each other. What nonsense was he spouting?

"But why bless their souls?" asked Ohannes, assuming that brothers would understand each other.

"My brother, why can't you understand," Kevork was almost angry, though inwardly rejoicing that the two merchants had lost their property. "The link between the town and Aikesdan is broken. The central market has been taken over by the Turks. Let's bid a fond farewell to the great market of Van!"

Ohannes and Panos wanted to look at each other again, but that felt awkward, indeed impossible.

"You're talking nonsense," Ohannes said, facing up to the real situation, but taking advantage of being the more affluent brother. "The world hasn't come to an end. Trade will resume in a few days."

"Van has been beheaded." Kevork paid no attention to what his brother had said and carried on with his account. "Vramian is drowned, Ishkhan is dead in Herj, the Hunchak leaders are in jail. And – an incredible thing – Van is leaderless. Aram is considered to be an outlaw because he never went to Djevdet Bey when summoned. Djevdet has sent a message to the bishop demanding that all the young men of Van should surrender their arms and promising in that case not to harm anyone. It's clear that he is acting like a fox. He simply wants to make it easier to slaughter the people. In a word, it's time for the go-ahead. War is inevitable. You must say farewell to your great market. For better or worse, you're no longer merchants, you're common soldiers. Did you leave much to the Turks?"

The curtain was up. The two unfortunate merchants were exposed to the horrible truth. Each of them imagined his own shop for a moment and saw it as organised as they had last seen it. Then Panos left his shop and imagined the other, and Ohannes did similarly. They peeped in on each other's shop, but came to no conclusion as to whose loss had been the greater.

Kevork raised his finger above his head while the two former merchants, now common soldiers, followed his gesture with their eyes. "But," he said in a different, more hopeful and steady, voice, "but, as the song goes, 'You shouldn't get desperate, my friend'. It's true we're in the foaming waves, but we shouldn't lose hope. Van must endure until Uncle arrives."

Panos, with a great sigh, wiped his sweating brow and recited: "Before the water flows in the stream –"

"– the frog will die." continued Ohannes, also sighing and wiping his brow.

"Well, whatever you say," commented Kevork.

He then addressed his brother. "I don't know what to do about our Mkho. If fighting breaks out in Van, Djevdet won't spare the villages. Let's write to tell him to bring his wife and children here."

Ohannes raised his big eyes and looked at the cruel messenger. "What do you want of Mkho? How can he leave all that property and come here?"

Kevork became absolutely desperate. "Baron Panos, my brother and I can't communicate. Make him understand that it is not a question of property any more. Now everyone has to save his neck."

It now appeared clear to Panos that Ohannes had suffered the greater loss. He felt quite relieved, as if nothing had happened to him, as if he had lost nothing, and that it was Ohannes who had lost everything.

"What's done can't be undone, Baron Ohannes. What

property? There's no property left. Now everyone has –" he paused, gave a sigh and delivered a final sting, "– to be a little intellectual."

Ohannes had in fact already flown in his imagination to Ermants and seen the newly-sown cornfields, the herds of cows with full udders and the flocks of sheep raising dust. Then he had seen Mkho, with sad eyes, confused, standing lonely and helpless at the door. He was now reflecting.

– Panos has lost a shop with all its merchandise. It'll be the death of him, but now he'll be happy when he sees what I've lost. The fact is that both of us have lost. My ten's become nothing – ten minus ten equals zero. He had two and lost two – two minus two equals zero. Both of us have ended with nothing, so there's nothing to be happy about. As for this djaghdi-lalo Kevork, he's always been a zero – and zero minus zero equals zero again. Each of us should swallow our zeros and choke on them. That's all."

Boom! An explosion was heard from the far end of the garden.

"What was that?" Kevork quickly went to the window. "Martin, Browning, or Colt? Is it Armenians, or –?"

"Don't be afraid, it's nothing special." Ohannes calmed down the excited Kevork. "That's our hero Souren. He's playing with a gun."

"Good for Souren," exclaimed Kevork. "Perhaps Souren's gun is a cannon. Oh, what a mischievous boy. I was about to shoot as well."

He patted his back pocket for no particular reason. This gesture made no impression on the two former merchants, now ordinary unarmed soldiers; it would have been laughed at in any other circumstances. Needless to say, there was nothing like a revolver in Kevork's pocket.

It was late at night and everyone was asleep. Satenik's gentle breathing could be heard. If she was asleep then there could be no doubt that so was everyone else in the house, and not just in the house but in the street, in the whole of Van, in the whole world.

But Ohannes had lost his sleep. He had had many sleepless nights, kept awake by joy or sadness, by great business profits or losses. 'I have lost my sleep ...' He appreciated those words of the song that Satenik, and now Lia, used to sing. The second line of the song – 'The garden door's just opening' – had led to quarrels between father and daughter. For Lia, the meaning of the garden door that was opening was that of the dawn. What is the door of the dawn? For Ohannes, it was the actual garden door: he could imagine the moment it was opening when he would be catching the pleasant aroma of marjoram, tarragon and mint. But today, it was one of the last lines of the song that was churning over in his mind: 'And I am swallowing my bitter tears'. Today, it was this line that was closer to his heart, mind, and soul. Ohannes was not crying – no, not in the least – he was merely swallowing his tears.

He was reflecting again on the day's events and remembering every conversation in detail. He was weighing up the evidence and reaching the same conclusion: the shop and the village – everything he owned – had gone, and on top of that there might be a massacre. What advantage would Armenians in Van have compared with Armenians in other regions? Why should Armenians in Van be an exception?

At a crucial moment in the earlier conversation, when Kevork was eagerly proving that in a state of siege a gold piece would not be worth as much as a para and that the most important things would be arms and food, the door opened and in came Set, the senior shop assistant and self-styled manager. Ohannes wondered how he had got in without knocking at the front door? It turned out that the streets were almost deserted and that Set had entered through the garden. Then Khatchadour, Ohannes' regular grocery supplier, also came in from the garden.

"So, have you closed up your shutters as well ?"asked Kevork.

"No," replied Khatchadour with his usual friendly smile, "the two locks with their keys are still in my pocket". He actually took them out of his pocket.

Ohannes was quite surprised. "And what about the contents?".

"What contents? I packed most of them onto Burnaz' cart and brought it home, leaving the rest for the Turks."

Well done, Khatchadour! And Set? He had probably come to

ask for his monthly payment. He usually took various goods, some at a discount, instead of cash. But, perhaps sensing Ohannes' mood or the atmosphere in general, he gave up the idea of asking for anything. It was clear what Ohannes would say, something like. 'Baron Set, have I ever failed to fulfill my obligations? When by God's grace the road to town is open again and trade resumes, I will do my duty.' Set was not wrong. Ohannes had prepared exactly that answer in his mind to ward off any request. But with his innate discretion, Set did not refer to the matter. He was content to make polite Bolsetsi inquiries into the other's health and mood.

"It's not for me to advise you," Set added, "but I hope you won't take everything to heart. There's a second door, and a third. One of them will open, won't it?"

Ohannes was reflecting on what Kevork had said about gold having no value: 'Oh, you blockhead, so gold is of no value? Oh, you donkey of Christ, if gold is of no value, then what is of value? Your wooden head! Gold is of no value! Oh, for shame!'

He had not for a long time looked at the boxes, hidden away in a dark corner of a cupboard, where he kept what he called 'a little sum of money for a rainy day'. Month after month, week after week, he would shake out two or three gold coins just to hear them tinkling. He did not dare to count the lot. Why should he? There could not be any more than there was before. He would feel proud of his strong will.

'For a rainy day?' he was now thinking. 'Is there worse to come? There can't be. This is the rainy day. It's as rainy as it's ever going to be.'

He turned over in the bed, listened to Satenik's gentle breathing and became more absorbed in his thoughts. If this was the so-called rainy day, then from tomorrow onwards he should start spending that little sum of money. He had been adding and multiplying, but now he had to put all that aside and begin subtracting and dividing. That's Arithmetic!

Ohannes' thoughts were interrupted by a half-awake, half-asleep, exclamation. "Herj! What's Herj? Where is it?" Then he immediately remembered that Lia was sleeping on the divan beside Satenik and himself. Satenik had arranged this, saying, "The girl's in low spirits She's not well, let her sleep in our room." And now she might be running a temperature and was speaking in her sleep. "Herj! What's Herj? Where is it?" Ohannes wondered about that too, but could not recall anything.

He returned to his arithmetic:

– The store's half-full of flour. Thanks be to God, there's butter, ghavurma, bulghur, cracked wheat, cheese, jajig, lentils, beans, herring and pickled fish. There's a few months' food, praise the Lord. Before all this comes to an end either the donkey or its owner will die – and at the worst, both of them. Yes, that's how matters stood. But another thing had to be considered – prudence is a fine thing. What if the Turks attacked the Armenians tomorrow or the following day, and began to rob and slaughter them? Clearly the gold would be first to go. His 'small sum' was in such a place that even an Armenian infant would find it let alone a Turk. How stupid! How could he have failed to think about that? Who knows? The Turks might even attack tonight or in the morning. –

Ohannes sat up in bed, blinking his eyes in the dark, and felt that his forehead was sweating. What should he do? Wake Satenik up and share his worries with her? No, that would be pointless. Satenik would try to smooth away his concern and get him to go back to sleep. 'The man's mad. Go to sleep, we'll think it over in the morning.' That is what she would say.

He found his clothes in the darkness and began to dress slowly and silently. This lasted rather a long time, a circumstance which gave him a chance to think and decide what he was going to do. So that by the time he put on his strong shoes rather than his slippers, tied up the laces and stood up, it was clear to him in every detail what he should do. He took the candlestick and matches off the table and crept out quietly.

First, he took a brand new, medium-sized jug from the pantry; it rang clearly when he tapped it with his finger. With the lighted candlestick in his left hand and the jug in his right, he went upstairs, entered the large sitting-room and went up to the cupboard. He leaned the jug against the wall and opened the door of the cupboard. It creaked with a familiar sound – tchr-r-r. He put the candlestick on one of the shelves of the cupboard and pulled out the box.

Things were moving fast. Ohannes counted out one hundred gold pieces, wrapped them in a handkerchief, and put them at the back of a shelf. He started slipping the rest in twos, threes and fours down the throat of the jug. At first Ohannes was counting, but then he lost count. Why should he bother to count? There was this much, no more. And if he was going to lose everything what did it matter whether he lost one-and-a-half thousand or three thousand gold pieces. When the horse died, did it matter how many teeth it had?

"O Lord, save us from the worst," he murmured audibly, pouring the last of the gold coins into the jug. The task was done. He lifted the jug from the floor; it was half-full, but he thought it was heavy enough.

The first part of the plan had been successfully accomplished. Ohannes now firmly picked up the candlestick and the heavy jug – a common enough jug, but now with uncommon contents – and went steadily downstairs to the woodshed where he chose the most suitable of the three spades. He blew out the candle, left the candlestick in the woodshed and went bravely and decisively to the garden with the spade and the jug in his hands.

The garden ... Ohannes stopped on the path dividing the garden in two and looked around. The early spring night was soundless, though it seemed as if it wanted to capture some sound. Ohannes went ahead and stopped at the malacha pear tree with its thick branches, spreading out on each side. This was where Ohannes' grandmother had planted a pear tree on her return from her pilgrimage to Jerusalem, which is why it was now referred to as the pear tree of Hadji-Nana. Over the years after her death it came to be thought of as a sort of saintly tree; for instance, though stones could be thrown at other fruit trees they would never be thrown at the pear tree, or hawthorn, planted by Hadji-Nana – never.

Ohannes left the spade there and went to put the jug in the stream near the quince trees. He returned to the pear tree and began to dig. He went on digging until he got tired, but he took a deep breath and started digging again. The soil was soft, soaked as it was by the melted snow. For a moment, it seemed to him that there was some movement in the next-door garden of the tailor, and the same in the garden of the Houssians. He decided it must have been an illusion, and went on digging and digging.

Crmp, crmp, crmp. Digging was not as hard as clearing out the bottom of the hole. He dropped into the hole, it came up to his waist. He went on digging deeper. The work was gradually becoming harder. Now, he was digging and throwing out the soil, bent down on his knees.

Ohannes heard a slight rustle from the side of the wide-leafed mulberry tree. It sounded as if someone was sharpening a knife against a whetstone – sst, st, sst. He stopped working for a minute, and smiled. 'The mulberry's not yet ripe, and the sparrow thinks it's eating it in its sleep,' he thought.

He also thought that it would be better if there were harmony and peace in the world, then no one would kill anyone and no one would have to hide his gold at night for it not to be stolen. 'Vramian was very fond of flowers.' he recalled. 'How could they take a man who loved flowers to the sea and drown him?' Ohannes also remembered the sight of Ishkhan at the window looking down at the street. He remembered Kevork's words: 'Ishkhan was killed in Herj.' He stopped digging for a moment and racked his brain. "Herj," he repeated and seemed to hear Lia's fevered words: 'Herj! What's Herj? Where is it.' Ohannes remembered this and he also remembered Lia saying that day, whether seriously or jokingly, that she loved Ishkhan. What a wicked devil she was, he thought, refusing to see the obvious connection in all this.

Ohannes' actions apparently acceptable to God were coming to the end. He flung the last spadeful of wet sods out of the hole, bent down to inspect the bottom of the hole – now a pit. He saw nothing but darkness. He stood up, leant the spade on the pear tree, shook the soil off his knees and went towards the stream with numb feet. It was here that thousands of ants suddenly stirred and ran up and down his skin. The jug was missing!

Ohannes went into shock. He heard himself saying, "What the devil! Did the sparrow take it away?"

He bent down and waved his hands about for something to do. No, the jug was there, after all. "You blockhead," he murmured, "Why didn't you look for it where you put it. What if you had had a heart attack.?" No, Ohannes did not have a heart attack. What else might it have been – an apoplectic fit? There is no need to speculate further, but if his fingers had not found the jug at that moment … But that is all better left alone.

He took the jug, climbed up the slope and brought it back to the hole. The valuable load seemed to be heavier this time. He placed it carefully in the hole, then stood up and picked up the spade again. "O Saint Mary of Varag, keep it safe," he said quietly, and began to fill up the hole.

When it was full and level with the ground, he scattered the rest of the soil in all directions. The full moon could not conceal its curiosity – it came out from the top of Mt Varag and peered down through the trees at Ohannes' work. There was a round, open patch in the grass beneath Hadji-Nana's short, thick pear tree. He had not thought about this but it did not need a great, wise man to sort this out. He picked up the spade again and went down to the end of the garden, where some grass had grown beside the low wall separating his garden from that of the Dankovians. Ohannes cut a few different-sized strips of turf, carried them back and laid them over the hole. You would have to have very keen eyesight to notice this green patch.

When he had just been about to leave the wall, it seemed to him that something had moved on the other side. He had gone up to the wall, risen on his toes and looked over. How surprised he had been to see Sirak Dankovian bathed in moonlight. Sirak might also have heard his footsteps and he had poked his head over the wall to see what was up. So they met in this way, very close to each other.

"Oh!" Ohannes was surprised. "Are you a vision, Sirak?"

"It's me, Sirak, Baron Ohannes. I'm Sirak at the moment, but, who knows, I may turn into a vision one day."

"You speak wisely." Ohannes appreciated Sirak's untimely early morning wit. "What are you busy with?"

"Busy? Nothing special. I've been digging here and there, tidying up the rose garden so that Djevdet can come and sit here with his ladies and have tea with the roses and enjoy himself."

"Well, is that possible?

"Why not? It's most possible."

Ohannes felt bitter. "Well, what can we do to make it unlikely?" he asked.

"We must fight, Baron Ohannes, we must fight to the last breath," replied Sirak, wanting to get away.

"Where there's fighting, there has to be victory," said Ohannes to scatter a few rays of hope over the gloomy conversation.

"I can't judge that." Sirak became gloomier: "What can a Vanetsi do faced with the weapons of the State?"

"What can a Vanetsi do?" Ohannes raised his voice and passed on to the decisive point: "A Vanetsi must endure until Uncle comes."

"I wish, I could believe that, Baron Ohannes," acknowledged Sirak, without, however, giving in. "But we may not be able to endure till then and the whole of Van may be ruined."

"The houses may be ruined but why should the gardens be?" Ohannes was getting worried.

"The gardens will dry out and die."

"And the earth?"

"The abandoned earth – left without water, without fruit – what would it become? It will be a pile of stones."

"Yes, it will become rock-hard, and if anyone tries to dig it, his spade would end up broken." This time Ohannes announced the conclusion and the two men understood each other without looking into each other's eyes.

"Good night, Baron Ohannes, it'll soon be dawn."

"And good night to you. Don't worry too much. God's in his Heaven –"

"Yes," agreed Sirak, as he set off back to his house, "but Djevdet's down here."

"Damn Djevdet!" Ohannes almost shouted. Completing the swearing in his mind, he began walking along the path home that divided the garden into two. A drop of spring rain fell onto his brow, then a second and a third. Clouds passed over the moon and Ohannes started singing one of his favourite songs, at first in his mind and then aloud.

> "Silence fell. The clouds came
> To cover up the sky.
> And the moon …"

He washed his hands and his moist brow at the well, and dried himself with a big, coloured handkerchief.

> "And the moon was taken
> Then away from my eyes.
> I was left …"

He took off his slightly muddy shoes on the terrace and quietly entered the room.

> "I was left alone with
> A stirred and sad soul.
> And my hands …"

He began to undress, continuing the song in his mind. He reproached himself: Was this the right time to be singing? But the song continued without taking his will into account.

> 'And my hands at my chest
> With my head bent over.
> Rise sad moon …'

Lia and Satenik were both sleeping peacefully on the divan. Ohannes thought of Herj. It was not clear why – his thoughts were confused.

> 'Rise sad moon every night
> Shine peacefully on us.
> And the throne …'

He covered himself with a blanket, he felt dead tired and wanted to sleep, but the song that kept on turning round in his mind, would not let him do so. A few raindrops tapped at the windows.

> 'And the throne of our kings.

How great was Vartan's love
For his fine Motherland.'

The song came to an end. He could sleep now.

– Mother … land … Did it matter that it was the motherland? What would become of it without water and fruit, without care? It would get stony, and when it did, would the jug not crack? Oh, let it crack! The jug would break, its owner might die, but that which was in the jug would never die. So it was immortal. A source of immortality! –

He wanted to pray but his thoughts flew back to the song. Vartan loved Armenia … but why was there no mention of Van? Something, for instance, like this: 'How great was Ohannes' love for his town, for his Van'. Yes, Ohannes was not to be underestimated. He had changed the song many times into something better. But this line of the song had been missing.

'Well, let it be sung again with a missing line. What did it matter? One line more or less! No ma – tt – er.'

And Ohannes fell asleep. He had a dream the moment he fell asleep: Ohannes is digging a hole on a clear, moonlit night and goes to take the jug out of the stream. What does he see? The jug has broken into two, the gold pieces have spilled out and hundreds, or you might say thousands, of mice are running away all over the garden with the gold between their teeth. Ohannes shouts in terror: "Mice, mice, catch the mice."

He heard his own voice and woke up. Satenik woke up as well.

"Let's sleep, man. What do you want with mice?"

"You're unfeeling," he complained. "It's always me who sees the bad dreams."

"You just have normal dreams. Are they worth shouting about?"

Let us leave Ohannes in his confused house and garden, quarrelling with his wife. Let the day break over Van and Ohannes' house and let Satenik be surprised by the muddy shoes, the muddy spade, and the candlestick in the woodshed. Let her consider, weigh up and judge, without coming to any conclusion. Let her not ask her husband to find out where he had gone that night. Why? Well, why should she ask, when she knows full well what her loving, though secretive, husband would say: 'I've told you a thousand times not to interfere in a man's business.'

There is no need to conceal from the reader the fact that after eating his breakfast without appetite, Ohannes threw his coat over his shoulder and casually went into the garden. It could not be said to be cold, but after the night rain, there was freshness in the air. Ohannes remembered his former neighbour, who had died several years before. This time it seemed to him as if he was still hearing his early morning greeting: 'Good day, Baron Ohannes, it's cool' In the past his reply would have been 'It's cool but pleasant' and their conversation would then be exhausted. In spite of his cold and soulless occupation, Ohannes had undoubtedly a poetic soul and he had been greatly affected by his neighbour's death. He was now sadly hearing the screams and whistles of the sparrows and other spring birds. He also recalled one of little Sourig's favourite poems:

> The March days passed away,
> Beautiful April came ...

After the night rain, the green patch was invisible even to Ohannes. 'Glory be to God,' he thought, 'and as for beautiful April, who knows what April will bring. O my blessed soul, O mother!'

Any more of this and Ohannes will never be got rid of. Let him be left where he is. It is time to think of the Manasserians.

Chapter 20

In the autumn of 1914, Mihran Manasserian's house was filled with the abundant harvest of Hayots Dzor and the Khek monastery for the last time. After the stores had been filled with wheat, flour, butter and cheese, and after the oxen and donkeys had been unloaded and had left, Mihran's mother, known as the

Grand Mother, closed the front door and stood thoughtfully for a moment wondering what she had just been about to do.

She tentatively entered the tantun, the large space with a high ceiling, a round smoke-hole and blackened walls and beams, where they used to bake and cook in different-sized tonirs and even sometimes have dinner in winter. She looked around, took out of an alcove a grey, half-knitted sock, came out into the yard, sat down on the step of the garden door and began knitting.

It is autumn. The gardens, the trees and the glades, the grass and the bushes, were all dressed in gold, the rose garden and the sun were also golden. The sunflower, the corn grown in front of the garden door and the sorrel were all equally golden. And now, the sun reflected from the Darbinians' roof has lit up the Grand Mother's knitting needles turning each of them into sunbeams. But she herself was deeply depressed. She had never experienced such an abundant and generous, though hard, autumn.

The moaning of the sick woman in the hall was heard from the terrace. Patients usually need water and in this respect Takouhi was normal, which was why she too wanted water. It had to be cold water taken out of the well, so Karmileh got her some.

After going back to the town, Kamal, the district governor, had re-appeared once more. He had sat in the upper room with Mihran, drinking raki and speaking quietly. The gatherings in the monastery, the eclipse of the sun, the sight of Mihran's face becoming gloomier day by day, and more importantly, her own instinct, told his mother that something really serious, unusual and dangerous, was about to happen. And she longed for time to pass quickly so that whatever had to happen would do so as soon as possible.

And God heard her cry and fulfilled her wish. The north winds blew, the gardens were left naked, and when she lit the tonir the smoke went through the smoke-hole, into the clouds and up to God's beard. She sent her heart-felt prayer for God's blessing up with the smoke.

There were fewer and fewer visits from Mihran's friends. There had been a time, when they would have got together somewhere and feeling like having a good dinner after one or two glasses, they would unanimously cry out, "Let's go to the Manasserians!" And they really would go there, whether it was morning or evening, day or night. They ate and drank, sang the goat song and danced, kissed Mihran's mother's hand, and eventually returned to their homes. Now they seldom came, but when they did Mihran tried to make the table even richer and their meal longer – as if he had committed a crime and now wanted to atone for it.

At last, one winter night, their tenant, Takouhi, died. Her two adult sons – Armenak and Hmayak, the soldier, grieved over her cruel death. Karmileh spread her hair over her mother, sang and lamented like a professional mourner. The special corpse-washers arrived in the cold light of morning, and washed Takouhi's emaciated body in the middle of the yard. She looked as if she were wanting them to finish it all quickly. Takouhi was then carefully sewn up in a shroud and placed in an unpainted, wooden coffin, with its lid loosely nailed so that she could arise easily at the Last Judgement and not be late when Archangel Gabriel blew the last trump.

Neighbours and relatives gathered and took the coffin out of the front door on their shoulders, but there were no speeches and no elegy. But, after the coffin and the mourners had left, the Grand Mother closed the door and dramatically addressed those left in the yard: "You were lucky, Takouhi Hatun, you died in your house and were buried in peace. Who knows, under what rock or mountain our own bodies will lie, and what wolves or dogs will devour them."

In fact, it turned out exactly like that.

As for what had happened in the monastery previously, the Grand Mother now remembered it all with a heavy heart. What had taken place between Mihran and Nana? She did not know anything, but felt instinctively that something unpleasant had occurred. After Nana's departure, Mihran had become more curt and thoughtful. She had deliberately spoken about Nana several times, but Mihran either had not heard her or had avoided the subject. The situation grew more complicated when the Muradkhanians refused to marry off their daughter, claiming that she was too young.

No, it was quite clear, that people did not like her Mihran. It was true that from the day when her son-in-law had been murdered in their house, Mihran had gained the favour of the Dashnaks; but had instead lost peoples' respect, and his mother bitterly cursed that day.

And now, something inexplicable was taking place. Mihran's friends had turned their backs on him. Inexplicable? Well no, she understood very well what was going on and reasoned that they had first made him do what they wanted and then turned against him. Certainly that was it. She had hoped that he would find his feet by getting married. That had not happened either. They had refused to marry Lia off. Well, were there not other girls in the world, was the world relying only on Lia? Mihran wanted her and had no eye for any other girl.

Was Karmileh any worse? She was good at housework, washing and cooking, but what was the use if he did not want her? He was not a mere boy to have him married by force, he was already over thirty. Poor Karmileh, she went crazy seeing him every day, but what was the use of it all? One of the main reasons for Karmileh's failure was, of course, the fact that both of her carpenter brother were Ramgavars. The Grand Mother remembered very well the day when Mihran and Karmileh had exchanged a few words, quite unaware that they were being overheard.

"You're undoubtedly a rose, but you've blossomed among thorns."

"Well, take the rose and throw the thorns away."

"I can't – the rose and the thorns are inseparable."

The mention of thorns clearly referred to the Ramgavars. Mihran had meant by this that though she was a fine girl, her brothers were Ramgavars.

'Hunchaks, Dashnaks, Armenak,' thought the Grand Mother, 'who invented these parties? They brought only disorder and dissension into Van. Three brains, three different directions! May they be buried and leave us alone.'

Her son-in-law had become a victim of their differences. Her daughter had been widowed and the four small children had been orphaned. It was true that an Egyptian charity assigned her an allowance of twelve gold pieces a year. God knew that Mihran did take care of all his sister's needs and did not allow the children to be in any way deprived. She was well aware that her grandchildren would grow up and take their father's place – blood being thicker than water.

Mihran would order her every autumn to take some butter, cheese, and meat to Aram. Aram would joyfully say, "Mother, you're the mother of all Dashnaks." But last autumn, when she had reminded Mihran about the presents for Aram, he had become gloomy and had told her that there was no need to send anything and she had then ceased to be the 'mother of all Dashnaks' and now wanted them all dead.

The first bad news was brought by Hagop Kandoyan. He came at dinner time, sat down, asked how Mihran was, and then told them that Djevdet had summoned Vramian and Aram, while Ishkhan had been sent to Herj with his bodyguard. Vramian had gone, but Aram had not. There was no news from Vramian, and Aram was in deadly danger.

"Why is he in deadly danger?" the Grand Mother said, "Let him go to Djevdet."

"Vramian told Aram the day before to stay put," Hagop replied, tucking into his potatoes with great appetite. "We told him not to leave the house, and took some steps to keep him there."

"Who are the 'we'?" the Grand Mother asked, suppressing a smile.

"We… the party."

After a brief silence she said: "Vramian and Ishkhan have joined the great majority."

"Oh! Who said that?"

"I did – I had to say something. Aram saved his own skin."

Hagop started taking his leave. He praised Mihran, and he praised the dinner: "If a dead man ate it, he would come back to life." He spoke of the arrest of the Hunchaks as a national shame, and of Hampartsoum Yeramian as a cunning and experienced diplomat. "He left Van in flames and is now sitting on the banks of the Nile shedding crocodile tears".

"Good bye, Mother Hatun, may your home be always safe."

"Good bye, Baron Hagop. Where are you going to now? To the Party?"

"Yes, yes, let me go and see what is to be done. The situation is very serious."

Hagop hurried off to the restaurant to inform everyone that Vramian and Ishkhan had joined the great majority, and that Aram had saved his own skin. Meanwhile the Grand Mother, shutting the front door, was thinking. 'That Hagop Kando has become a party all on his own. Van will be saved and liberated! To hell with your parties!'

Entering the main courtyard, she tried to recall something important but failed to do so. Acting on impulse, she went up the stairs and entered Mihran's room. The photos of all those dead heroes – soldiers on horseback and those without horses – were looking down at her like modest sons-in-law, though she had never had any special respect for them. She then remembered the important thing she had been trying to recall. It was a white, sealed envelope on which nothing had been written.

Someone had knocked timidly at the street door the previous evening. While Karmileh had looked out of the square hole overlooking the street to see who it was, the Grand Mother had opened the door. A woman covered in a white cloth had come in quickly.

"Mihran Effendi var?" she had asked in Turkish.

"Yok – no."

"Mother var?" the woman with a yellow face and black eyes had asked.

"Var. I am the mother."

The strange woman had then handed over an envelope saying something, from which the Grand Mother had understood that the envelope was important, and that it should be handed to Mihran Effendi and to no one else.

She now took the envelope, turned it over in her hands and began to worry. She had no doubt that the letter was from Kamal. Was there any relation between this letter and the fact that Djevdet had summoned Vramian, Ishkhan, and Aram? And

Mihran had not been home for the last three days. He had gone to Vostan two days ago, to buy a black horse from some Kurd or other. That is what he had said, but who could know what he was up to? Was this a good time to go out of town? 'To hell with black horse,' she thought, 'or even blue ones!'

Mihran finally appeared that evening, and having stabled and fed the horse, asked whether there was anything to eat. His mother gave him the white envelope. Mihran opened it, read it and his face became even darker.

"Is it from Kamal?" she asked.

Mihran nodded his head.

"What has he written about?"

"Nothing special. There isn't anything important in it."

"The person, who brought it, said it was important."

"I said there's nothing important." Mihran was angry and sat down to have his dinner.

The letter was, of course, extremely important. It was so important that it could be said that no Turk had ever written such a letter to any Armenian since the Armenian nation and its people had lost their sovereignty to the Ottoman Empire. The letter was written in a manner that only Mihran could understand what the writer intended to say and what he had wanted Mihran to understand. They had worked out that provisional coding when Kamal had visited Mihran once or twice without Nana. On each occasion, he had conveyed Nana's greetings and had said that Nana was missing 'mother' a great deal. The letter said that the situation had become very serious and a storm was most probable; that meant that the Turks might attack Armenians. The sheep should be locked up in the sheepcotes to protect them from the storm. If the black shepherd summoned the rams, they should not go. It would be bad. The black shepherd was of course Djevdet and the rams were the leaders. It meant that if Djevdet called for Ishkhan, Aram, or Vramian, they should not go to him. 'We're too late,' thought Mihran, 'we've already lost two rams.'

Mihran thought for a moment that he should go to Aram and show him the letter. What then? What was the point of that?

Aram would get furious: he would ask why the letter was brought to him so late. And if Mihran explained he had been in Vostan, he would be asked what he was doing there.

No, he had better keep quiet and destroy the evidence. And what if the matter was eventually revealed? No, it could not be revealed – like his relationship with Nana, like his ...

Mihran went up to his room. Karmileh had made up his bed and had left one window open. He went across to close the window and saw her sitting with some embroidery by the open window opposite. The girl looked up at Mihran with a sad smile. Mihran pretended not to notice, closed the window and lowered the blinds of the four windows overlooking the yard.

He took a box of matches from the round table, lit a match and held the letter, which was decorated with violet patterns over the flame. The matter was done with. A corner of the scorched paper crumbled and fell into the ash-tray, where it struggled and shivered before coming to rest.

Mihran lit a cigarette and looked around. He began to put together his books. He put the books by Raffi, Siamanto and Varujan to one side in a large pile. He went quickly out of the room down to the woodshed, and returned with a big, empty box. Then he carefully arranged the selected books of various sizes in the box until it was half-full. He began to take the pictures down from the wall, and put them in the box. He wiped the sweat off his brow. His mother came in, saw what her son was doing and disapproved.

"God save us! If they come for you, they won't care whether you're Dashnak or Hunchak" she said, and then added, " My boy, have you got a weapon?"

"Why do you ask?"

"You've been singing day and night 'We have to fight and not weep.' Well, the moment for that has come."

She went out without waiting for an answer. Mihran opened the drawer and took out a Colt revolver with lots of bullets, put them into the box and covered everything up with paper. He called for Karmileh from the door. She came and was taken aback on seeing the bare walls, but she said nothing. They carried the heavy box together to one corner of the woodshed, and covered it with pieces of wood.

"Is there anything else to do?" Karmileh said.

"No, thank you. Don't say anything to your brothers."

"Why? Are you afraid?"

"Yes – of needless rumours."

Karmileh went back to her room reflecting on the fact that being a Dashnak, Mihran was afraid of rumours.

Mihran went down and washed, then came back to his room and went to bed. He had heard recently that Ramgavar Ghevond Khanjian had called him a man with no character and no backbone. At a dinner given by Simon Tutundjian, when Hagop Simsarian was delivering brilliant speeches and toasts, that well-kown clown, Dikran, had shouted: "Baron Hagop, don't talk so wisely, or they will think you're too clever and will send you to Jerusalem." There had been laughter and applause. Simsarian had wittily replied. "Luckily, my brother-in-law is a Ramgavar," and had continued his speech.

Mihran continued reflecting:

– What do they want of me, why can't they leave me alone? Yes, Ghevond Khanjian is a Ramgavar, his son is the brightest pupil in in all Van. But what right has he or those former Armenaks, now Ramgavars, who have been gnawing my flesh day and night for several years, to insult me? How have I sinned? Whatever I did was for the sake of the great cause. –

It had all started on a fresh spring day just like this one. Aram called for him, spoke about various things and then began to complain of their adversaries including Mihran's respected brother-in-law. Aram opened a bottle of brandy and said:

"It's impossible to continue working under these conditions. All our rivals should be eliminated. We can't now do it by terrorism. That method of cleansing has now gone out of fashion. Do you know how many cases there have been in world history, where brother killed brother, a father his son, and the son his father – all for a great cause? Millions of people have come and gone, but these people have remained and are remembered in history. Let's drink to those immortals ... How old are you.? Twenty-four? It's an age when every young man wants to make his name. And what is yours – a librarian?"

The conversation lasted a long time. They were drinking brandy as they chatted, but it was mainly Aram who was doing all the speaking. Mihran only spoke when he had to answer a question.

"A few people must be eliminated, and the first of these has to be your brother-in-law who has gone beyond all bounds. It's true he has children, but the Dashnaks will take care of them. Mihran, find a suitable man, an honest, brave, and idealistic one, able to do the job successfully. We have monasteries and lands, we'll make him a rich proprietor, and he will be able to provide for himself and take care of the children and your sister as well. Think of it, Mihran, an immortal name in history together with wealth. What else could anyone want? While some skilful, future historian can be found to describe your brother-in-law as a traitor and not a victim, and the one who killed him as a hero. Think about this, Mihran."

Mihran had lost all his composure since that day. Glory and wealth – these were things he had been offered. And what a fool any young man would be to turn his back on both the wreath of glory and the purse of gold?

His brother-in-law often used to visit him. They used to argue endlessly and with passion, drink coffee together and then continue to argue.

Then that fatal evening came. All the family were sitting round the table; they had finished supper and were now all drinking coffee, he and his brother-in-law were also drinking raki. The lamp was lit and was on the middle of the table. He had been more nervous that day than usual, for a Turkish officer had been murdered earlier, and several Armenian families had been slaughtered in retaliation.

"This is not revolution, but simply devastation," his brother-in-law said.

What happened next was in no way premeditated. This was really true. Mihran suffered ever after from that thought, but on that day he was not thinking of Aram's sly proposal at all. He just took the revolver out of his pocket and began to clean it.

"Is this a good time to be doing that?"

"It's empty," Mihran replied with a smile, pointing the revolver at the other's chest and pulling the trigger ... Bang!

What happened after that was not all that important. Mihran could not remember now whether the light had gone off before, during or after the explosion of the gun. Nor did he remember who had switched the light on again. He did remember his mother's and sister's screams and his own open but dimmed eyes.

He got up, lit a cigarette and began to smoke in a state of tension.

Yes, it was true that after all that he did become wealthy. However, he did not see even the shadow of the glory that had been suggested. Aram had otherwise kept his promise, and now he was rich and could support his sister and her children. But he was not able to look at them. He tried to be kind and gentle to them, but at the same time, each of those orphaned children seemed to be a walking accusation. He reflected that in a few years, the eldest could be sent to Sanasarian College in Erzerum or to Central College in Bolis. This sometimes salved his conscience.

But why, did it all seem to be too late? Well, it had soon become clear that there was none of the so-called glory either for him or for them. Mihran now knew why. Because their so-called great cause was not honest, because the edifice they had been building had no foundation, because the builders of the cause of 'national-liberation' had been inefficient; willfulness and tyranny had been the two-wheeled chariot, which Aram called the Dashnak party.

Mihran brought to mind the story of the Hermit and the Bear. They had become friends, and shared their troubles and joys with each other. One day, the tired hermit wanted to have a rest and to sleep, so he asked his friend to guard him. He duly fell asleep and the bear began to carry out its duty. An impudent and bloodthirsty fly kept alighting all the time on the hermit's nose disturbing his sleep. At first, the bear carried out the simple Ramgavar policy and strategy. He patiently drove the fly away. But the fly was persistent and spiteful, and continued its defiance. At last, the spirit of the Dashnaks awoke in the bear and he decided to kill the insidious fly and thus save the hermit. He took a big stone, and ... And he sent his beloved friend to the other world, where there was neither joy nor eternal love, nor spring bringing pearls and diamonds.

Before coming home, Mihran had gone to Hmayak, the typesetter of the Ashkhadank weekly, to learn the latest news. Hmayak told him about all that was going on. Ishkhan had gone to Herj with some of his men to restore order, that is, he had gone to drive the fly away. But that mission would have been much more suitable for his Ramgavar brother-in-law, rather than Ishkhan, would it not? Then why so many victims and sacrifices? There would have to be a retreat in all directions – not because they had to but because they had been defeated so severely.

So, why did he not just leave Van and go away to the Caucasus or to Bolis? He could open a shop in either place and live in peace. He might even be able to find peace of mind for his troubled soul. What, after all, could the people of Van look forward to? Only to defend themselves until the Russian army arrived? And what would they be defending – simply their own skins, because that is all they would be left with. Only those mortally afraid for their lives could succeed in such a fight.

But now there was for him no Lia dreaming at the Ourpad stream, no future!

Black, thick, smoke spread from beneath the ancient citadel towards the east, towards the orchards, which seemed to be burning without flames.

Chapter 21

Ohannes woke up late that morning. The sun, the size of three Martin guns, had moved down from Mt Varag to Aikesdan The traders and craftsmen did not go to work that day and the schools remained closed. The shepherds did not take the cattle out to the fields. But the church bell-ringers vigorously struck the gongs and pulled on the strong ropes of the wooden bells, which rang out, some of them sounding sad and imploring, others sounding threatened and alarmed. Only the bells of the high tower of the American Protestant compound pealed in their usual formal way – ding, dang, dong – ding, dang, dong.

Ohannes was not hungry, and after a small breakfast he sat smoking his nargileh. Just as he was exhaling, the dramatic moment came – or to be more exact, as the old song has it, a sound was heard. It came not from the mountains to the east but from the Ourpad stream and the Solakians' garden. Armenian hearts beat faster with those first shots of this last, decisive battle.

Bang, bang. Tchk, tchk. Ohannes caught the far-off sound of gunfire, followed by more shots which then spread in all directions – the shooting encircled the town. Encircled! Ohannes' heart also beat fast. He stood up and hurried to the window overlooking the garden and looked for Hadji-Nana's pear tree. It is not clear why he did this, or what he was thinking about, or what he would have thought next, for just when his eyes settled on the leafy branches of the magic tree with a heart-felt wave of relief, three cannons started firing from the Turkish position on the rocky Toprak-Kale hill looking over the town from the north. The thunder of the bombardment was deafening. The whine of cannon-balls was heard in the distance and it seemed to Ohannes that one of them, and perhaps all three, was coming straight towards his house and his windows. He was horror-stricken, but had the time to reflect that he should have dug two pits under the pear tree, one for the jug, and the other for himself, for his own safety.

Satenik rushed in, alarmed. "Why are you standing at the

window, husband? Are you that brave?"

Her last question prompted Ohannes to recover himself. He could certainly be brave! Why not? Was he a woman to be so frightened? He turned round and even wanted to tease his wife to show that nothing had happened, but could only ask, "Was that Souren's bomb that exploded?"

"The man's gone mad," exclaimed Satenik, "that wasn't Souren's bomb. The war's begun. Get downstairs, take your nargileh and get below. It's dangerous up here."

"Woman, has the war really begun, or are you joking?"

"Aman!" Satenik was annoyed, "Aman! You aren't being sensible." She took the tray with the burning nargileh and went out.

Ohannes followed. "So, you say the war's begun. And I'm wondering why my fingers have been itching since yesterday evening."

They went downstairs.

And now, Ohannes was sitting in the tantun, leaning on the old cushions of the oriental corner, smoking his nargileh and listening with more than two ears to the various gunshots coming from all directions. He wanted to call to mind the history of Van, beginning with Queen Semiramis, then on to King Senekerim, and finally to Avetissian, Khrimian Hairig and the recent dead. His outline could be illustrated or not, though he realised pages of his mental review would be blank, since he did not have the knowledge or ability to do the hard research required to get to this fatal April of 1915. He wanted to reach some conclusion, even perhaps to predict the course of the future events. He would even be pleased if his worthless brother Kevork came in, so that he could ask him some questions. For instance, whether there was any country in the world that had only one party, and solved all its national problems with one heart, one soul, and one decision? And whether it was possible for Van also to have just one party instead of three? And whether such a single party could lead the people to a happy future? Logical questions, surely.

And now that the war had finally begun, who was to be in charge of the defense? It was clear that people would fight, but who was going to be in command? The Hunchaks, the Dashnaks, or the Ramgavars? Or perhaps some poor neutral?

"There won't be any neutrals," Ohannes said aloud to himself, just as Satenik came through the room to go to the pantry.

"What did you say, husband?"

Ohannes repeated his brilliant throught: "I said, there won't be any neutrals."

"Stick to your narghileh, politics is not your business."

"The Hunchaks will have to be taken off the list. Four or five of the six or seven of them are in jail, so only Dashnaks and Ramgavars are left."

"What are you thinking about?"

"I'm wondering who is to lead the fighting."

"Does it make any difference? Let it be whoever wants to."

"Oh my God!" Ohannes was surprised. "What reckless indifference! Leadership is a matter of life and death."

There was a cannon-burst and a bomb roared through the air. It seemed to them that it could immediately fly in and Ohannes would never know who the leader of the fighting might be. But no, the bomb passed over their roof, the noise faded and died out. And now gunshots could be heard nearby as well as from afar.

"Where are the children?" Ohannes asked.

"They went away, all three of them went away."

"Why did you allow them to go?"

"They went through the gardens to my mother's house."

"Is it advisable to wander off anywhere during the fighting?" The father of the family was annoyed.

"Husband, they went off before the war started."

"Before the war?" Ohannes suddenly seemed to become aware of the reality of the situation. "Before the war? So now there is a war!"

It was indeed a war, a real, actual war. During his long and full, yet brief and uneventful, life, he had seen such a day many times in his dreams, and he had often woken his wife before dawn to tell her happily with relief that he had only dreamed of war. Here was that war, here was what he had always feared, what he had seen in his dreams and had woken up from in terror. And now, perhaps this also was a dream, too. Perhaps he would also wake up this time and whisper that he had dreamed of war.

"Satenik!" he called out, "Satenik!"

She came up from the pantry. "Yes?"

"Do me a favour – pull on my ear."

Satenik was surprised. "What for?"

"Pull my ear and pinch it. Perhaps I'm dreaming."

"I wish I had your brains, husband. The whole world's alarmed, and you're dreaming!"

"I'm not dreaming, woman," he exclaimed, throwing the tip of of the narghileh pipe onto a plate. "I wish I were, but ..."

Satenik looked into her husband's eyes and saw that they were full of horror and realised that he was feeling the terrible situation more deeply than she was with her groans. She realised that now, as always, Ohannes was trying to hide the tragedy behind the smoke of the nargileh and was joking in order not to betray his anxiety. When he spoke of who was to lead the fighting, his only concern had been to cope with the harsh reality more easily. It also now seemed to her that it was really no longer so important for him whether the first gunshots in the morning had destroyed his shop full of merchandise or his possessions and property in Ermants. No, the central issue for him had been the question of who was going to lead the fighting, or who was already doing so, whether Dashnak, Hunchak, Ramgavar or some neutral. If only this important issue was clearer.

Satenik wanted to keep Ohannes hanging onto the thread which she was only just holding onto herself, but where she felt more comfortable than if she were standing on firm, but scorched, ground.

"Aram Pasha will be in charge. Is there anybody else available? Not Ishkhan. Not Vramian. Only Aram," she said, in the tone of someone speaking to a child to stop it crying.

"Aram Pasha?" said Ohannes, laughing bitterly. "Aram Pasha! That's impossible, there's no Aram Pasha any more."

"Has something happened to him as well?"

"What else could happen? Is Aram worth anything without Ishkhan and Vramian?"

In asking the question, Ohannes made it clear that there was no need for her to answer since it was completely obvious that Aram was not worth a para without them. But an answer was forthcoming. Satenik put forward the bold idea that, on the contrary, as long as Aram was with Ishkhan and Vramian, he had not been worth half a para, whereas now he was worth millions. Aram would act now, and Makrouhi, his guardian-angel would shine and sing.

Ohannes was inwardly astonished by his wife's wisdom, but he did not give in. "There's no Aram Pasha any more. Aram Pasha has lost the game."

Perhaps it was at that very moment that Aram in a suit and tie was approaching the Command Centre. He was accompanied by guards, who went ahead to make a way through the crowd gathered in front of the building – needlessly, because the crowd immediately parted on seeing them. Aram looked tired and depressed, his head leaned forward as if under the weight of his red fez, which had also tilted forward. The revolver hanging from a shoulder-strap made a strange impression. Just as he wanted to go in, three soldiers came out of the building. This was the so-called Defense Command, a single body that consisted of three men – Armenak Yekarian, Grigor Bulgaretsi, and Gaidsag Arakel.

Armenak Yekarian, with piercing eyes and a neat moustache, casually dressed and armed, looked nervously and impatiently at the gathered crowd, and muttered something to Aram. Grigor Bulgaretsi, a gentle, modest man with sharp eyes, seemed ill at ease in a military uniform. Gaidsag Arakel, with nothing reckless about him but his upturned moustache ends and beaming eyes, approached Aram, shook hands with him and stood stock-still in a solemn pose.

Though what was now the Command Centre was in the middle of the town, not far from Norashen square, the place resounded with the noise of gunshots, from nearby as well as from afar. The residents were terrified, especially of the cannons thundering from the Toprak-Kale hill dominating the town, since as well as aiming at certain specific targets they were also firing randomly into the district – at the churches and at civilian houses

– to cause fear, horror and panic. The people were pouring in towards the Command Centre from all directions. The forest of red fezzes became agitated as the crowd opened up for two stretchers bearing the first two victims of the fighting from the Ourpad stream position. The stretchers were laid down in front of the centre. The men seemed calm and impassive, one of them was clean-shaven, the other not; one of them had his eyes open, the other not; one of them was Yeghia Nakhshounian, the other Hagop Dyurzian. But both of them were dead. Something like a sigh passed from person to person.

A short, hunched old man came out of the crowd and without any help climbed onto a stone block, leaning on his cane. "People of Van!" he bellowed, to everyone's surprise. It was Hovaness Kouloghlian, the mentor-teacher-historian-orator-poet and skilful tavlu consultant. He was a devoted follower of Portugalian and a true Armenak, famous for his nickname – Crazy-Bahloul.

"People of Van, we are standing today –"

"On the stone block," Dikran, the wit, whispered to teacher Kevork standing beside him. The latter was taken unawares and wanted to laugh, but sensing the solemnity of the occasion he murmured under his breath, "Be serious."

"People of Van," continued the orator, "our glorious ancestor Haik Nahabed once stood where we are now standing. It was here that he fought against the perfidious Bel and defeated him."

"Was Haik Nahabed from Van?" Dikran quietly asked Kevork.

"Most probably," the teacher replied.

"Was he from the Arark or Norashen district?"

"Quiet!" someone yelled from the back.

"People of Van, you are the citizens of one of the most ancient towns on earth. Van is as old as Nineveh, as Rome. The Chaldeans and Urartians lived in and around our Citadel. Queen Semiramis lived here. She made sacrifice in Astghik's shrine, and when tired of pagan feasting, bathed in our lake to ease her sinful soul and body."

"I wish I could see her," murmured the clown, Dikran.

"People of Van, our brave ancestors are watching us: King Senekerim from Varag, Grigor Naregatsi from Nareg, Nahabed Koutchag from Kharagonis. The immortal martyrs of 1896 –

Avetisian, Peto, and Mardig – are watching us. The recently perished Ishkhan and his bodyguard are watching us, as are the still-warm corpses of the heroes of today right here before your eyes – the bodies of our own first martyrs, Yeghia Nakhshounian and Hagop Dyurzian. People of Van ..."

The crowd listening to the inspired orator was tense and excited and could only just hear his loud, inspired voice above the gunshots. Even that incorrigible jester, Dikran, was excited; he took a deep breath and rubbed his inflamed eyes.

"Are you crying, my boy?" Kevork asked softly.

"My heart is throbbing."

"You see, you're becoming a man little by little."

The orator was also getting excited. His words were already being heard less clearly, and there was a moment, when the cannon fire and gunshots drowned them out completely.

"People of Van! (boom, boom) Let's make a vow. (thump, thump) The voluntary death of our martyrs (bang. crash) for the sake of freedom – to die for freedom – than live as slaves (tchayt, tchayt) – as one person – people of Van! – Avarayr – Vartan (bam, bam) – ahead to our posts – for the sake of the mothers who have lost their sons (crk, crk, crk) – to your posts – widowed and orphaned – the holy fire of revenge – to our positions – (drrr, drrr) – death or freedom."

The orator staggered, his face was pale and his eyes, shining with inner fire, grew misty. Strong arms lifted him off the stone block onto the firm ground; Kevork and Dikran held him on both sides. The teacher was formally dressed – but this is scarcely the right moment to mention that.

"Don't get so excited, Baron Hovaness," the teacher said quietly.

"It'll affect your heart," Dikran added.

By chance or demand, a carriage drew up, cutting its way through the crowd. The two self-appointed guardians put the orator into the carriage to take him home. Dikran took a seat on his right. Kevork began to go round to take a seat on the orator's left, reflecting that Hovaness's wife would undoubtedly set out some soudjuk, pasterma and raki. It was spring, but she still had pears, apples and grapes from their own large garden hanging from the larder ceiling. Hovaness' daughter, pretty Papoush, would come running out and sit on his knee. Dikran would start talking, and Kevork would scold him, saying "Cease your idle chatter. The situation is serious, fill up the glasses."

These charming images passed through Kevork's mind at lightening speed as he was walking to the other side of the carriage – the strong smell of the pasterma and raki seemed so real, so near. He finally reached the other side of the carriage, to find his place miraculously already occupied by Hagop Kandoyan. Let history itself decide whether Kevork remained unconcerned or was taken aback as if struck by lightning. We would have left a calmer person alone and followed the carriage, but just then something happened which petrified everyone and rooted them to the spot.

Drim, drum – crish, crash. The college military band, with its gleaming brass instruments, arrived at the Command Centre and almost drowned out the sound of gunfire and exploding bombs, by playing the well-known formidable anthem, *Our Motherland*. Yes, there have been many military bands in the world, but none of them have performed a piece like this.

It can now be claimed, repeatedly and without any exaggeration, that it was this very band, this neutral college band, that managed to do what all the Ramgavats, the Hunchaks and even the Dashnaks – however much they insist – were unable to do.

The crowd forgot everything for a moment. The people did not notice that the gunfire was becoming louder and louder. They stopped noticing the shining, peaceful faces of the first victims. They had been stirred and were ready for any heroics or sacrifice.

"Our military positions are firm," Armenak Yekarian was saying, "but they need to be strengthened even more. Our reserves are organised, but need more training. Sex and age don't matter. Political membership doesn't matter. Sign up for whatever you can do."

Aram was looking with sad, tired eyes at the crowd moving into the yard of the Command Centre. Was this what he had longed for since his youth? Was it for this day that brave and devoted fighters had been killed on what they called the road to freedom. Was this what he and his friends dead or alive had wanted. Here it was, the great war, the war of all wars, the battle of all battles. And Yekarian said that there were less than a thousand guns and only about twenty thousand bullets. Against a whole state! A few hundred fighters against an entire state! The eastern headquarters of the party were in Tiflis and the western in Geneva. The Ottomans were everywhere, east to west, north to south. And Djevdet was right here.

Fight, men, fight bravely! Those, who have already fallen were now free of any responsibility. And those who remain alive have to answer both for themselves and for the dead. Would it not be better to die and be saved than to live and ...

"Aram, recent events have shaken your nerves," said Armenak Yekarian. "Go home and rest for a few days."

"And what will be the result of all this?" Aram asked in a tired voice.

Perhaps Gaidsag Arakel realised the meaning of the question. "The end will be either death or victory," he said.

"Suppose we win. What then?" Aram insisted.

Grigor Bulgaretsi joined in, with a cold, but not malevolent, smile. "At the end, we'll crown you King of Van."

"That's just what the fighting is for," Armenak concluded with comic seriousness. "Go, go and have a rest."

Dr Ussher entered his room feeling rather tired. He lived in the American compound in the eastern part of the town. A few American men and women comprised the soul and spirit of the place. Ussher was the soul of these souls and the spirit of these spirits. It had already been some time since he threw in his lot with this ancient town and its citizens. He was not only a physician and a surgeon, but also a public, even political, figure. He spared no effort to learn Armenian, he even studied Armenian history. His profession meant that he went into many houses, whether wealthy or not, for he always said that a Vanetsi, rich or poor, was a citizen of Van before anything else.

The shooting became more intense at night.

Dr Ussher saw to wounded soldiers, bandaged their wounds

and ordered that he should be told if there were other casualties, whether he was asleep or awake. Though he had never used a weapon in his life, he had a light-green military uniform and knee-high boots under his snow-white gown. He was a blond man with a short beard and blue eyes, more than thirty years old but certainly younger than thirty-five.

He mixed a little soda in a glass of water with a tea-spoon, added some citric acid, drank up and said 'good' a few times. "That was good, good," he repeated and sat down at the desk. Then he tried to find words to describe the war, he thought it was a – – – – – – , a very impolite word!

He took his notebook out of the drawer. It was a carefully crafted book about the size of a small Bible. It was already half-full of his daily thoughts and impressions, written in purple ink, from the day he had settled in Van. Several years before he had received a letter from a university friend in Chicago: 'So, my dear friend, you've decided to settle down in Van.' Ussher had written in his note-book: 'Settling down is a pure and simple American notion. It's as impossible to settle down in Van as it would be to settle down on Vesuvius'.

He began to turn over the pages of the note-book. He stopped and began to read:

> This town is as ancient as the Egyptian pyramids, and its history is as long and tangled as the beard of the pharoah Rameses. To the east, is Mt Varag; the monastery, named after it, clusters comfortably below it, or, to be more precise, below its right edge. Under the trimmed stones of its altar, one of their kings lies in eternal sleep.

He turned over the pages, stopping now and again to read some of the entries.

> ... the existence of a gold mine is quite probable. The hill on which our compound is situated is said to date from the Bronze Age. The ground at the bottom is covered in white sand, as fine as flour, with bright, golden specks. The local people pour this on anything they write to act as a blotter.

To the north, on the Ak-Küpri rock, there are the naturally formed shapes, known as the bride and bridegroom, and the subject of many moving legends. Then there are the cliffs with the huge, hewn slab called Mher's Door. This Mher is one of the mythological heroes of the Armenian people. He shut himself up in these rocks and vowed not to come out until there was an end to violence and injustice in the world. As far as I can see, this gentleman named Mher will have to wait in his stone prison for a long – yes, quite a long – time. Then to the east…

The architecture of this ancient town is oriental – a few western-type buildings cannot change the general appearance of the town at all. The houses are built with unbaked bricks and have flat roofs, where people dry fruit during the day and where they sleep at night in the summer and autumn. It must be assumed that this habit, besides being healthy, is also undoubtedly romantic.

… Lake Van, which is called a sea by the locals, is one of the most beautiful lakes I have ever seen in the world. The lake has small islands and both the shore and the islands are wonderfully suitable places in which to take a holiday. My compatriots would love to have the opportunity to come here for at least a month, even living in tents without any of that fastidious American comfort. As for the so-called sea herring!

… If the statement, 'Van in this world: paradise in the next', is true, then it also has to be said that public affairs in this worldly paradise are not conducted by angels, as in the heavenly Van, but by senior officials and ordinary devils. These include the various ranks of governors – vali, kaimakam, myudur – as well as the police, the soldiers and so on. The ordinary citizens are creating and building with steady, hard labour, while the rulers are pulling down and ruining.

Today, I went with Dr. Grace Kimball to collect …

December 26: This town has a special fragrance, and that fragrance can be sensed whether it is spring or summer, autumn or winter, day or night. No one knows if this fragrance comes from the sea or the orchards, the water flowing along the streets, or the peaceful bells of the numerous churches. The women spray water in front of their houses and sweep vigorously. Perhaps the damp ground smells so good because – I don't know – maybe the rising …

I went to that Armenian revolutionary today on some unpleasant occasion. And had the following conversation:

"Are you arming the people to attack, or just to defend themselves?"

"It depends – it depends on what the strategy for freedom will dictate."

"Couldn't you employ a more diplomatic approach in order to gain a few peaceful years while you gather your forces?"

"In that case the revolution might die and the revolutionaries would have nothing to do."

"And what if the Turkish Government was to lay down its arms and ignore your movement? What then?"

"Then we would attack."

"Why? Isn't your goal to ensure a peaceful life for your people?"

"Only if that peace is achieved by fighting."

I got very angry. For these people, revolution is a goal in itself and not a means.

… It's true that Djevdet is spiteful and hates Armenians. It's also true that he wasn't appointed at this particular time by chance. It's well-known that this gentleman is so inventive that he nailed horseshoes onto Armenians to punish them. He had them shod and then ordered them to run about on all fours. I'm not aware how well the victims managed to carry out that order, but it's well-known that further villainous atrocities are now being prepared for these fine people, who are caught between two fires. The appointment of Djevdet and his presence in Van are not accidental. Today ...

... I met that spiteful Djevdet again. If we are to believe him, the Armenians are malicious beasts and the Turks are desperate hunters. The Governor has studied carefully those earlier years when Armenians ignored the fact that they were Armenians and lived peacefully and calmly under the powerful government of the Ottoman Sultanate. So, are Armenians now guilty for remembering they are Armenians? Are they guilty for bringing to mind their religion and nationality? If they became Turks, would they live in peace and happiness?

"Don't you think that this sort of reward is not merited for such an ancient nation?" I asked.

"There's no ancient or modern nation," he said, "there's only a subject minority. This is what the Armenians must not forget. Among domestic birds, geese have the same rights as hens, ducks, or turkeys. They're also caught, killed and fried without taking into account that their ancestors saved Rome."

This was cynicism and nothing else. "So, in your opinion, Armenians are geese?"

"Like all the minorities. Put yourself in our place for a moment. Turkey is now at war against Russia. God bless us in this war of Turks against Russians! This is neither the first nor will it be the last time. But that's not what's most important. The most important thing is that Armenians have formed Armenian battalions in Russia, so-called groups of 'volunteers', who are coming to Turkey to liberate the Armenians living here. That's a fine thing, isn't it? And if you were in our place, tell me please, what you would do? Perhaps you would sit the Armenian down on a soft divan, offer him some raisin and nuts, stroke his head and say, 'Calm down, don't be offended, your brother will come soon and liberate you. Eat up the raisins and nuts, take this gun and bullets, and when he comes, join him in killing us.' Is that not so? We're not Christians, we'll do our best not to leave a single Armenian on Turkish soil before his Russian brother gets here."

… The most terrible thing is that Aram and his friends approve of the policy carried out by their central committee in Tiflis, especially that of developing Armenian battalions.

… Spring has gently opened its heavy gates. It's Sunday today. I went to church and prayed.

Events have taken a tragic turn. Ishkhan's murder. I'll pray today for his salvation. I can't forget how he once laughed at me. I was riding to Varag. On my way, two ugly Kurds appeared, dragged me off my horse, and went away with it, as well as with my coat and watch. I hadn't an American flag with me to warn them off. They took the small prayer-book out of the pocket of my coat and gave it back to me politely. I told them I didn't need it and that they should read it and end their thieving. Ishkhan laughed long at me when he heard this story. Poor man, perhaps he remembered me at the last moment. If the Turks who killed him and his friends had only read the Gospel, they would have been scared of the Almighty and wouldn't have committed that shameful deed …

… Djevdet proposed today that he be allowed to place a Turkish brigade inside the American compound, for our safety! I consulted the newly elected Armenian military leader, Yekarian, about this. As I had imagined, he was definitely against the idea, saying that Djevdet was not worried about the safety of Americans. The American compound overlooks Aikesdan, and if war broke out any

Turkish soldiers here would clearly not be concerned about our security but would fire at the Armenians. One must not forget that Djevdet hasn't read the Gospels, either. I recall the unfortunate Ishkhan again.

The distant sounds of gunfire and the incessant cannon shots could be heard. Ussher took up his pen and wrote.

April 7, 1915

This morning saw the start of what has been awaited for a long time. As expected, the fighting was begun by the Turks. If this was the dream of the Armenians, it's come to pass. But, no, it wasn't the dream of Armenians. Even the most hot-headed figures had recently been following a cautious policy. It's child's play to fight in songs, articles and books, especially when such fighting always ends with the triumph of the good. But now, the people of Van have to fight against the whole army and the state. A bad dream, a terrible dream. Armenians have always dreamt of heroic battles, but in the event they've always ended up having to defend themselves. A horrible reality – a sad reality.

… It's late at night. It seems the world has come to an end. The town shakes with the thunder of guns. Will the Armenians be able to stand up to it? In such cases … I think the people of Van will win if they fear the Turks enough. The fear will make them defend themselves – fight on to victory.

It's a paradox! You need to be afraid in order to win.

Chapter 22

Meanwhile, Ohannes was sitting in his corner of the tantun, listening to all the gunfire going off all around him and considering the events of this first day of the war while clicking his worry-beads. Just when he had decided to get properly dressed to go out, as it was already nearly midday, someone knocked vigorously at the garden door. He called out to his wife and she went to open the door. Satenik soon re-appeared with his younger son Murad, or, as he was called, Vostanig.

"Who brought him back?" Ohannes asked, and as if answering his question, Noyemik appeared. She was a tall, strong and well-built, young woman, who was more Noyem than Noyemik. She was the daughter of Ohannes' sister and at the same time the sister of Hunchak Abraham Broutian and the wife of another Hunchak, Haykak Yeremishian. After the arrest of her brother and husband she had been living in her father's house.

"Where are Lia and Souren?" Ohannes said.

"At the Command Centre." Noyemik replied. Her large black eyes shone sadly as she sat down cross-legged beside her uncle, took the worry-beads and began to count out the amber pieces: "Kher, Shar, Astvadz, Kher, Shar ... "

"Command Centre? What Command Centre?"

"... Astvadz. The beads have stopped on God three times today." Noyem felt encouraged and she carefully put the beads on her uncle's knee. "It's the Defense Command Centre."

Satenik was angry. "Tell us why they've gone there."

"Why shouldn't they?" Noyemik replied. "Lia enlisted as a Sister of Mercy. Souren was sent to the Chantigian post and this little rascal wanted to go too, but I didn't let him."

"Yes, yes," Ohannes approved, "Murad will make a good ball-player. The name suits him well – Murad the striker."

Nobody was in the mood to laugh. Only Murad chuckled.

"Who's in command?" Ohannes asked.

"Armenak Yekarian."

"Really? On his own?" Ohannes was surprised and pleased.

"Gaidsag Arakel, Grigor Bulgaretsi –"

"Great! And Aram?"

"Aram appeared with his bodyguards, stood frowning among the people, exchanged a word or two with Yekarian and then –"

"Then?"

"Then he went away haughtily, followed by his guards."

"Where did he go?"

"Where? To the battlefield, of course," interrupted Satenik.

Ohannes turned to his wife angrily. "Think what you're saying. First of all, what battlefield? Do you think Van is the battlefield of Avarayr? Or maybe you think Aram and Djevdet will fight together in single combat – like the epic heroes David of Sassoun and Melik of Misra – on the banks of the Ourpad stream."

"Oh yes! Yeghia Nakhshounian and Hagop Dyurzian were killed in the Ourpad stream," Noyemik said.

This fact shocked Ohannes, but as usual he was able to hide his feelings. It was contradicting his comment that since the Ourpad stream was not an Avarayr – no battle could take place there. In order to maintain his dignity, he considered it suitable not to take Noyemik's remark too seriously and he said, "Was this the proper time to have a swim?"

Noyemik began to give a lot of detailed information, mentioning in particular the solemn military demonstration in front of the Command Centre. Ohannes was deeply shocked by her story but did not want to expose his feelings. He pulled a red handkerchief out of his pocket and pretending not only to clean his nose but also to smooth his moustache, managed to wipe the tears from his eyes. He decided to criticise Noyemik to relieve his own anxiety.

"And what were you doing in front of the Command Centre?"

It turned out that Noyemik had registered as a volunteer tailor to sew linen for wounded soldiers. At this point Ohannes had almost ceased to be a 'Baron Ohannes'. Only Satenik realized. And in order to conceal her husband's complete confusion, as well as to change the subject of the conversation, she asked, "Is there any news from the prison?"

"What news can there be from the prison. Any news only means death. Kalipseh Solakian and our own Hrep have already been executed."

'Our Hrep' was the beautiful Ripsimé, the wife of Noyemik's brother, Abraham Broutian, and the daughter of Atchem-Khatcho. The marriages of these Hunchaks lasted such a short time, that they had not even managed to have children to continue their unfortunate fathers' line. What an unhappy fate! The Hunchaks had placed a slogan at the top of their bland newspaper – 'Break our brutal chains and let a new sun arise' – yet they themselves ended up in this dark and sunless jail. It was clear that they would not see the sun ever again no matter how the battle ended.

All three of them were thinking about this and no one would have known how long the silence would have lasted if a deserter from the Turkish army had not appeared on the threshold of the tantun. Yes, a real soldier in knee-high boots, a dishevelled fez, and unarmed.

"Oh, my God, is this an illusion?" Satenik was the first to be able to utter a word, as she recognized teacher Kevork in the uniform of a Turkish soldier. Kevork came in gradually getting accustomed to the half-dark of the tantun.

"What get-up is this?" Ohannes at last found his voice.

"Is there anything to be surprised at? I'm a preacher."

"Catholic or Protestant?" Ohannes asked.

"Neither. My task is to pass from one post to the other to encourage the fighters."

"A profitable business," murmured Ohannes.

"There isn't any profit in it, it's simply a job. Satenik, give me something to eat after which I can back go to the posts."

Satenik looked at her husband trying to catch his eye.

"Feed him and let him go back to the defense posts, for if he's late they'll all be overrun one after another," said Ohannes, taking up his worry-beads.

Noyemik took her leave and went out, casting an unfriendly glance at the preacher.

"Come more often, my dear," Ohannes called out after her. "Don't worry too much: ba du gechar – this will all pass away."

Kevork rubbed his hands. "It will indeed pass away. Van has seen many storms, and this one will also pass."

He sat cross-legged on the woollen cushion beside his brother. In peaceful times he would hardly have dared, but in wartime ... During peace, you must weigh up all the pros and cons of any action, you must look before you leap. Whereas now in this whirlpool of battle, everything is exactly the opposite: leap before you look, and since even looking is pointless, just leap!

Satenik put the small, low table, with lavash, cheese and cold meat on it, at the feet of the preacher, and asked him to help himself. Kevork did not move.

"Come on, set to work," Ohannes said.

"Brother Ohannes," murmured Kevork, "Food can't go down without a drink during a war."

"I've seen you in peacetime as well, brother. Do you want wine or raki?"

Kevork cheered up. "Only raki, wine should only be drunk on peaceful days."

"Woman, bring some raki," Ohannes groaned, and suddenly feeling a desire to drink himself, automatically added, "also bring a couple of fish, pasterma, soudjuk, ghavurma."

"May your home prosper, brother, and may it always be safe," exclaimed the former teacher, his heart filled with joy and his eyes with tears. As far as we now know, Ohannes would not in former days have permitted such luxury, particularly in honour of Kevork. But the deep sounds of various weapons exploding outside, continually confirmed that life had totally changed and was heading rapidly into some terrible uncertainty.

Boum, boum. Trak, trak, traaa-a-a-k. Vsh-sh-sh.

Satenik put a bottle of raki and two gleaming glasses on the table, looked at her husband with thoughtful eyes and was about to say something, when her husband's brother said, while filling the glasses, "There is no news from Mkho. I had a dream two days ago –"

He could not continue, because something surprising happened. Ohannes took his glass and emptied it silently. Kevork was taken aback. Nothing like this had ever occurred before. He had always been the first to raise his glass, at all times and at all tables. However, he recovered from the shock, emptied his own glass and continued reporting his dream.

"Mkho came in and said goodbye. I asked him where he was going, leaving everything. He said he was going to Stamboul. I asked him what he had to do there. He said that Hampartsoum had called him, so he had to go."

He re-filled the glasses. "It wasn't a good dream," he concluded.

"Why did you have it then?" Ohannes' heart was stirred. "Or even if you did, why did you tell it to me?"

"I know you don't attach any importance to dreams."

"And what about you?"

"Well, yes," Kevork confessed.

"You see? Maybe you're right. I didn't believe in dreams when there was no war. But now when the fighting is going on, I believe in everything, and at the same time I believe in nothing."

"Include my dream in that 'nothing' and let's leave it at that."

"Just answer this question: how many days will Van be able to hold out?"

Ohannes stared at Kevork, who was again taken aback. He had never been honoured like this by his brother, who was sitting beside him, eating and drinking, and, moreover, had asked him a question, which should have been put to the military committee members, or at least someone close to them.

Satenik put grilled herrings on the table. In order for these fish to fit neatly over the fire and be grilled well, the hostess had twisted their tails into their mouths. This was an unwritten rule: to be properly grilled the mouth of the famous Van herring should be closed over its own tail. It was just like this that Djevdet Bey wanted to grill the people of Van. In order not to be accused of plagiarism, however, we should hasten to add that this parallel between grilled herring and the people of Van did not originate with us.

"Yes, my brother, it's just like this fish," said the experienced military commentator, teacher Kevork, holding his glass of raki above his head. "That villain Djevdet wants to grill the people of Van and swallow them. Now let's turn to your clever and direct question as to how many days, weeks, months, or hours, that Van will be able to resist."

"Hours?" Ohannes was worried.

"Why are you surprised. Here we are sitting and eating in a brotherly manner, and we're talking about vital issues, aren't we? But is there any certainty that the Turkish rabble hasn't already overrun Chantigian's post and broken into Aikesdan. What certainty can there be? None at all."

He fell silent and slowly lifted his glass to Ohannes. But the latter was only thinking of being in the Chantigian post himself. Three cannons thundered one after the other, perhaps at the post. Ohannes imagined Turkish soldiers and a Turkish mob, armed with sabres and knives, breaking into Aikesdan. Destruction and slaughter begin! Salavat!

"Bu-u-u-ut," thundered the new-born preacher, and this 'but' took Ohannes out of his nightmarish illusions in a flash. He clinked his brother's outstretched glass with his own and drank up quickly.

"You'd better say more about that 'but'."

"But Van must endure. It will endure. Why?"

He filled the glass yet again. "Why?" he repeated, looking at Ohannes as if he were a teacher looking at his pupil.

"Why?" repeated Ohannes, like a pupil.

"Because, first, second, third, fourth, tenth, twentieth, hundredth – there are many reasons. But all these reasons will bow before one reason – the reason of reasons, the main reason. And what is that main reason?" Kevork, raised his glass, this time looking at Ohannes like a teacher looking at a stupid pupil.

"Well, what is it?" Ohannes repeated the question, and at last began to realise that this drunken idiot was taking him to be a fool and that perhaps he should grab him by the neck and throw him into the garden. The great military commentator seemed to read his thoughts and spoke more gently.

"Van will hold out, my brother, because Van has remained leaderless. Wherever there are leaders, there is defeat. Van will hold out so long as there are no leaders: leaderless people can work wonders."

Ohannes actually approved of this conclusion, though not how it had been arrived at, yet he decided to object. As for Kevork, he had not had a clue what he was going to say when he began. He looked like a man, who about to jump from a great height into an abyss, was now very pleased to find that he had landed successfully on firm ground.

"Van will hold out so long as there are no leaders: leaderless people can work wonders," he repeated. He emptied his glass with self-satisfaction, took a fish, carefully beheaded it, removed the bones, and put it on a piece of lavash.

"There can be neither peace nor war without leaders," said Ohannes firmly, pronouncing the words distinctly. "There can be no flock without a shepherd."

"People are not a flock, and men are not sheep."

"Men are worse than sheep. Ishkhan and Vramian disappeared, and Yekarian, Bulgaretsi, and Arakel took their place. Is there any difference? A leader is a leader."

"Not all leaders are the same," said Kevork.

"I accept that shepherds are different. You only say that because now one of the shepherds is from Van. It would appear that Aram has failed and the leader is now Yekarian. What is more important is that the outsiders aren't concerned, they've neither home nor family here and they can get on their horses, turn towards Mt Varag, ride to Aghbak and cross the border into Persia any time they want. Yekarian, however, has a family and is a good citizen of Van. He won't give Van to Turks. No, a Vanetsi would die before giving up Van!"

The level of the raki in the bottle was now quite low and the mood of the Muradkhanian brothers had significantly changed; to say 'for the better' would be to sin against truth and to misunderstand their psychological state. During peacetime, after having drunk that much, they would have sung 'Father, father, your motherland' or quarrelled, but in this new, war-time situation, their perception and understanding had changed, some new feelings had arisen and some old ones had ceased.

Kevork continued with an evermore rising voice:

"We started from different points, but got to the same place.

Van is for the people of Van. Let the guns thunder and let thousands and thousands of bullets fly towards the Armenian lines. Van must live! Van must see each Spring, when the last scraps of snow disappear; when the green blades of bardisapakhs appear from under the ground; when the spring birds fill the gardens and orchards with their sweet song; when the diligent Vanetsi takes a spade into his hands and digs and digs the ground; when the soil gives off the fragrance of the fruits which will ripen later; when the smell of the carrot, of apricot and marjoram ...

Van must see each Summer, when the sea and the sky are blue and Aikesdan is green; when the sun transfers its taste and colour to the fragrant fruits and berries, vegetables and flowers; when the thirsty orchards want to be watered in the evening and the water distributor with a strong blow of his spade changes the direction of the water to flow into your orchards. Purling and bubbling, the water will flow into the gardens and flower beds bringing along some twigs and grass. The moon will rise from behind Mt Varag, and now the gardens previously longing for water will be quiet and content. You'll hear the ripe apricot, and the early apples and pears falling into the already watered beds.

Van must see each Autumn, when the wheat, the flour, and all the harvest pours into the town from the villages and monasteries; when the bells of the churches ring sweetly; when the pupils hurry noisily to school; when ..."

Kevork fell silent. He filled his brother's glass with the remaining raki and hung his head. Perhaps he remembered his school and that fatal day when he came out of the building, ashamed and never to return there again. Then he raised his head and called out for Lia.

"Lia's not at home. What's up?" Ohannes said gently, having been fully absorbed in his 'bad' brother's eloquence.

Kevork was not put off and called for Souren.

"Souren isn't in, either."

"Where are they?"

"At the Command Centre. They're volunteers," Ohannes said, no one knew whether with pride or sarcasm.

"Don't joke," said Kevork.

"What joke? One shouldn't joke in war time. Lia sews linen for the soldiers, and Souren runs from one post to another."

"As a messenger?"

"It seems so?"

"Mashallah, Lia! Mashallah, Souren! So, tell Satenik to bring more raki for us to drink to Van, to Lia, and to Souren."

Ohannes did not mind, but he wondered what all this was for. 'It's because,' he thought, 'the world is anxious and this man is entertaining me with his eloquence and knowledge. Only it's necessary to have some raki to get any information of a higher quality out of him.' So he said: "It's easy enough to solve the raki problem, but in my opinion your speech is off the point."

"How is that? I've made this speech in almost every house, and at every table for years and I have heard only words of admiration, and now you say –"

"Don't you see? According to the Gospel, you're caught up by your own words."

"It's not like that."

"What I mean is this. In peacetime, you've taken that speech of yours from house to house, from table to table. And now, when there's a fatal war, you want to sell your worn-out goods to me!"

"Listen to me –" Kevork began.

"No, you listen to me. You say that when spring comes the snow will melt and the birds will sing; when summer comes, the fruit will ripen and the gardens will be watered and the apples and pears will fall down from the trees. Flan-fstan! Doesn't the snow melt in Russia, in England and in Germany? Don't the flowers blossom there and the birds sing in spring? And when summer comes in other countries, doesn't the fruit ripen and aren't the gardens watered and don't the apples and pears fall down from the trees into the water? You talk about the smell of the carrot. What is a carrot to smell sweet? Do you think only Van cantalaloupes and water-melons smell like cantaloupes and water-melons? We say Van, Van – but is this your Van? When autumn comes, the wheat and flour will be taken to the town. Do you think that in other countries they don't gather wheat and make flour? There are thousands of towns in the world, each of them has churches and each church has its ringing bells, and everywhere pupils go to school. Does only your Van have its spring, summer and autumn?"

"Let me finish and then criticize me, brother," Kevork said angrily, not only because Ohannes had crushed his romanticism so severely making it worthless, but also because the empty bottle of raki seemed to be looking at him sarcastically. He regretted having put the last drops into his brother's glass. His brother's full glass irritated him!

"Do you want me to continue your speech for you?" continued Ohannes, surprised at his own ability to parody Kevork. "Van must see each winter, when the orchards and Mt Varag are covered with snow; when smoke rises into the sky from the chimneys and smoke-holes; and when young and old are sitting round the hot tonir, singing 'Is this your Van?' and eating nuts and raisins."

"No, that won't do," protested Kevork. He was deeply offended, but was trying at the same time to exchange his empty glass for his brother's full one. "It can't be so. Play and dance on your own."

"And would you like me to dance to your music?" Ohannes laughed complacently. He raised the glass of raki, which had somehow moved away from him by some unknown force, and swallowed it in one gulp. His head went up with the full glass and came down with the empty one. With an understandable reflex action, Kevork's head went up and down as well. Ohannes followed the raki with a piece of ghavurma, while Kevork picked up the empty bottle and called out in alarm for Satenik.

"Satenik is in the room downstairs. What do you want of her?" Ohannes said, knowing full well what his brother wanted. He cast a sidelong glance at his brother, got up by pushing against the cushions with his hands, put on his grey slippers and took up the empty bottle.

"The main essence of Van is something else. Think it over, while I go to the larder," he said and shuffled downstairs.

Once alone, Kevork reflected:

– If this man were told things he doesn't quite understand, he would appreciate your words. If you tell him that two and two make four, he will reply that he's well aware of that. But if you say two and two make fourteen, he won't be surprised and will think that perhaps wartime prices have risen and that two and two has really increased to fourteen. This is someone who, should he be told that two and two are Jerusalem, would think you're clever. I must begin with the Old Testament. –

Ohannes came out of the larder squeezing the neck of the bottle, as if to suppress its scream so that Satenik should not hear it. There is an unwritten rule that women do not want their husbands to drink without some good reason, like a wedding or a funeral.

Ohannes left his slippers on the edge of the old carpet, went to his place, sat down cross-legged and put the bottle on the low table. Kevork, having been temporarily crushed, now felt that he had to restore his intellectual advantage. He remembered the Old Testament. He had always got the highest mark in Religion as a schoolboy. Religion could at last be useful to him for once.

"Let's start from ancient times. Abraham begat Isaac; and Isaac begat Jacob; and Jacob begat Judas; and Judas begat Phares; and Phares begat Esrom; and Esrom begat A-Ram."

"Aram?" Ohannes was surprised.

"What is there to be surprised at? There are thousands of Arams both in history and out of it."

"Well, in history, yes, but what does 'out of history' mean?"

"I'll explain. For example, there's Aram Pasha, and there's also Aram Sabounjian. Is that right?"

"Right."

"Well, Aram Pasha is in history, while Aram Sabounjian, who is also an Aram, is out of history. Do you understand?"

"Yes, And what about you and I – are we in history or out of it?"

"Well, it depends. It depends on who writes that history. After the exile to Babylon, Jeconiah begat Salathiel; and Salathiel begat Zorobabel; and Zorobabel – as far as I know- begat Eleazar; and Eleazar begat Matthan; and Matthan begat Jacob; and Jacob begat Joseph, the husband of Mary, of whom was born Jesus, who is called Christ. At that time, there was no Arshak Dzetotian to take Jesus' photograph, so Abgar, Armenian king, sent a messenger with a piece of linen cloth to Jesus. Jesus wiped his face with that cloth and his image was transferred onto the cloth. This is how King Abgar obtained the picture of Jesus. He adopted Christianity and propagated it among the idolatrous Armenians."

"Did the town of Van exist at that time?"

"Van was two thousand years old when Christ was born."

"You see? And the Turks?"

"What Turk? At that time, there was no Turk, no Russian – no France and no England"

"And America?"

"Only wild cannibals lived there."

"Who else was alive at that time apart from the people of Van?"

"Romans, Byzantines – people of Egypt, Assyria, Babylon, Persia, Gaul, and other unenlightened nations. Armenia was among the enlightened nations, and later –"

"And later?"

"Later came the Tatars, Seljuks, and the Mongols under Tamerlane. The Armenian kings concluded alliances with Byzantium, and the Persians didn't like it. On the other hand, when they tried to come to terms with Persia, this time the Byzantines attacked Armenia. Unbearable conditions and desperate situations."

"Well, why did they conclude any alliances at all, why didn't they act diplomatically, why didn't they follow a neutral policy, get involved with arts and crafts and develop their economy?" Ohannes said with irritation.

"There were disagreements among the Armenian princes and feudal lords."

"Were there any political parties at that time?"

"There is no nation without parties."

"How dreadful!"

"Anyway, this was how Armenia, tired in every way of continually swinging back and forth between East and West on the one hand, and or by internal wars on the other hand, became powerless and dwindled from thirty-five million to thirty, twenty, ten, five, down to – I don't know what. There's a saying that red Easter eggs shouldn't be counted on the first day of Easter."

"What a terrible story. If you know so much, how can you sleep easily at night?"

"I'm surprised as well. On the other hand, you can't fall asleep either if you know nothing. When a man knows everything, he can sleep easier. It depends – it depends on the circumstances and the situation."

Kevork himself was also surprised at his knowledge and eloquence. He was so surprised that he felt uncomfortable taking the bottle and pouring out the raki for himself and his brother. He felt that his brother should fill the glasses, so at last accepting Kevork's superiority. As for Ohannes, his thoughts were all over the place. He was thinking about the historical past of the Armenian people, and of their fate, their present – boum-boum, trak-trak, vsh-vsh-vsh – and their unknown future.

"Shall we drink?" Kevork said casually, as if he did not really have any great wish to drink, but thought maybe it would be a good idea.

"Let's drink," Ohannes seemed to come round. "When should we drink, if not today." He took the bottle and, for the first time in his life, filled up his brother's glass. Kevork picked it up with dignity, put it on his knee and said:

"The forces of the two warring parties are totally unequal. Djevdet with his army and weapons is several times stronger than we are. But we're in a more favourable position, because they're on the offensive. We have to defend ourselves: we can stay in our unshakeable positions while they have to move out of their lines and try to break through in order to burst into the town. And above all, they have Djevdet, who is able to remove his soldiers at any time, whereas we have to continue defending our homes to the bitter end. We must either win or die. And since it's more difficult to die, we would prefer to win. Van must win. This is must be our last word."

They drank.

Later in the conversation that evening, Ohannes was still sitting in his corner of the tantun, in the place where, in the afternoon, he had drunk two bottles of raki with his brother to the sounds of the spreading gunfire. He began summarizing the events of this first day of the war while clicking his amber worry-beads. Putting down his empty glass of raki, he said:

"Well, you talk about motherland, what is this so-called motherland? The motherland is fine if there is security, abundance, wealth, prospering trade, developing crafts, herds and flocks filling up the pastures. If life is not expensive, if people can perform *Ancient Gods* in the theatre, or if they can play tavlu. A motherland must be something like that. And what is our motherland? Robbery, rape, torture, murder, slaughter! Is this a motherland? What's the value of such a motherland? To be ill-treated and insecure and to call it motherland – that's wrong! You have to live wherever there's bread, and that's your motherland. This is logical. This is our motherland."

Ohannes waved his hand to right and left, indicating the continuing gunfire. He raised his voice and filled the glasses with hands trembling with excitement.

"Is this a motherland? We didn't ask for it, we gave everything up for the sake of the devil. Where's my shop and where's our property? We had them yesterday, we have nothing today. What a wonderful motherland!"

"But this is the only motherland we have," Kevork ponderously and authoritatively declared.

"Is that all?" Ohannes replied angrily, as if someone had put a few kurush into his hands instead of the one hundred gold pieces he was owed.

"Yes, that's it," insisted his brother.

"Let it all be yours then, a motherland of the naked and the starving."

"But this is our only motherland."

"Oh, my God! " lamented Ohannes, "why didn't I convert all my goods and lands into gold and leave this Tartarus."

"And what did the ones who did get away gain?"

"What did they lose?" asked Kevork.

"To answer that question we should remember Hampartsoum's last letter."

"Hold on! Hampartsoum isn't a good example. The man got into trouble."

"If he hadn't left Van, would he have got into such a trouble? Of course not."

"If he hadn't got into that particular trouble, he would have got into this one. Is there any difference? That trouble is better than this one.

"It's a matter of taste," Kevork objected, "I would prefer to die in the defense of Van rather than of a shameful disease in Bolis."

"Then why don't you die?" Ohannes said spitefully.

"Why are you so sure that I won't die?"

Kevork stood up with solemn dignity, leaving a half-empty glass of raki for the first time in his life. He went to the door, and bad farewell. Ohannes was taken aback by this ending and wanted to get up and bring his brother back. He wanted to grab him by the hand, make him sit down and continue – no, start a new conversation about where Queen Semiramis was buried, who King Nebuchadnezzar was, and so on.

Lia reappeared the next afternoon and Souren came back in the evening. It seemed to Ohannes that both his daughter and son had got older and had become estranged from him all in one day. With his brain fuzzy from all the raki, Ohannes could just about understand that the town was surrounded by the Turks, who were trying to find a gap to break through, and that the fighters at their posts were repelling the Turkish attacks. Various committees had been formed and the Red Cross was also present, headed by Dr Sanfani. There were several merchants also included in the committees, including to Ohannes' surprise, Avetis Terzibashian.

"Who's in command?"

"Armenak Yekarian." Souren said.

"Mashallah! A Ramgavar – and what about Aram?"

"Aram turned up with his bodyguards and went into the Command Centre." Souren corrected himself while eating ravenously: "No, he didn't go in. He just spoke to Yekarian and went away with his bodyguards."

Satenik was now interested. "What did he speak to Yekarian about?"

"It's a military secret. I know, but I won't tell you."

Ohannes was angry. "If you know anything, say so. Look at you – do you think I'll go and tell Djevdet your great military secret?"

"What Aram Pasha said was: 'Baron Armenak, carry on fighting and I'll go and have some rest. Let me know when the battle is over and I'll come and take charge.' Yekarian agreed and then said, 'And why are you taking your bodyguards with you? Let them come and fight.' But I think Aram Pasha's heart trembled, as he replied, 'They are the feudal-lords of my kingdom. If they're killed accidentally, who will lead the kingdom of Van?'"

Later, Ohannes recalled this 'military secret', and thought that Souren was a crafty and knowing boy. He wondered whom he had taken after. Himself of course! He nodded off, and saw Mkho in a dream.

… Mkho was asking for a few bundles of cloth. Ohannes knew that there was a war going on and that he had lost his shop with all its goods. There wasn't a shop any more, but he didn't refuse Mkho. "Why not, why not? Take as much as you need – take even more than you need."

Hampartsoum was also there, playing with the gold chain of his watch and naming it a Zenith. "What Van, what is Van?" he said, "A plain town with plain roofs and with an even plainer life. A man lives in Van and never sees any other woman except his wife, while in Stamboul, I have seen so many things, Ohannes, so many."

"My God! My God." murmured Ohannes.

He opened his eyes and saw his manager Set, in front of him. This was no longer a dream.

"You're quite right, Effendi, to take a little rest on such a hard day," Set said, stroking his unshaven face.

"I cannot sleep, or rest. Take a seat – what's the news?"

"Is there anything that is not new?" said Set, playing with words. "Ittihat ve Terakke."

"What does that mean?" Ohannes was surprised – he always seemed to be ready to get surprised.

"It's the political party of the Young Turks. 'Ittihat ve Terakke' translates as 'Unity and Progress'. Do you see any unity? Do you see any progress? You see how they've deceived us. A constitution – freedom, equality, fraternity. Do you see any of that?"

"I see that Ittihat begins with the turkish for dog." Ohannes sneered.

This remark was too obvious, and Set could only comment, "And there are two 'k's in 'terakke'."

"You see – so what is there to be surprised at?" Ohannes was enjoying these verbal comparisons.

"Surprised or not, the words of the Patriarch Izmirlian have come true. It was Izmirlian who said: "No one can avoid his fate. All of us have already decided to become victims."

"Is that so? There's another saying as well, isn't there?"

"Yes, someone else said that Armenians need to be slaughtered in a national rebellion once more in order to gain their complete freedom."

"Has that really been said?"

"Yes, it's not my invention."

"It's a neat saying, but it's a bit stupid. Can there be any freedom after you've been massacred?"

"Well, what they mean that one half should be slaughtered, and the other half should be left to enjoy their freedom," explained Set leaning back on the cushions more comfortably.

"Why? Half of us have survived, and if half of that half also die, would we need any freedom?"

"There's another song as well: 'An honest death is always desirable.' Have you heard it?"

"I've heard it, but I haven't sung it, and I won't sing it. There can't be a desirable death, there is only desirable life."

"But there may be a situation where death is preferable."

"Never," insisted Ohannes.

"For instance – I can hardly say it – "Set looked at his fingernails, then twisted and crunched his fingers, and continued, "– suppose Van is defeated, and the Turks break into Van and begin to slaughter the people, burn and destroy the town?"

"Don't speak evil, man."

"It was only an example. And if you survived, wouldn't you prefer to die then?"

"No." The stubborn Vanetsi did not give way.

"What would you do then?"

"I'd sit on the ruins, and cry and cry. I'd have my photograph taken. Have you seen the painting of Mother Armenia? If there's a Mother Armenia, why shouldn't there be a Father Armenia, too?"

There was a silence. Set remembered the painting of Mother Armenia: ruined fortresses; walls, churches, and towns such as Kars, Van, Tigranakert; and a young woman, with her hair down and dressed in black, sitting on a stone among the ruins. Set imagined Ohannes sitting there instead of that woman. Father Armenia! He smiled slightly.

"We've got into trouble ever since Armenia became Mother and not Father," continued Ohannes, "could a Mother survive in this country of brigands?"

"This country of brigands takes no account of Mother or Father."

There was again a silence. This silence was of course only in the narrowest sense of the word. It was only between the two of them – outside it was noisy. Boum, boum. Vzh-zh-zh.

"Have they got enough bullets to keep on shooting?" Ohannes asked.

"The Turks are doing all the shooting. Our slogan is 'spare the bullets'."

"Why? Are we short of bullets?"

"We haven't got many," Set said curtly, looking at his nails.

"They've been playing at revolution for several years. They brought in weapons – so what's up?"

" _ _ _ _ — !"

"You don't say! So the hen laid an egg and the cuckoo stole it!" Ohannes said bitterly. "O good Lord, save us from all this trouble!"

"The churches of the town are now in the hands of the Turks with the exception of St Vardan's church in Norashen, where Vahan Mamigonian's finger is kept."

"One swallow doesn't make a summer."

"I hope Varag monastery at least doesn't fall into the enemy's hands. Do you know it?"

"Of course I know it. The grave of the Artsruni king, Senekerim, is there."

"Not only that."

"Is anyone else there?" said Ohannes.

"Certainly – Queen Khushush and Catholicos Getadardz are buried there."

"You have grand thoughts, Baron Set. Here you are thinking of thousand-year old figures and forgetting the living."

"Effendi, they are our national saints."

"Dead and useless saints."

"Some of the dead are useful."

"We don't want them."

"And which living saint is useful to us?"

"Our Van!" Ohannes said. "If our Van lives, all the people you mentioned will, though dead, continue to live. But if Van dies, your Queen Khushush, Vahan Mamigonian's finger and the rest, will disappear for ever. Do you understand now?"

Now it is the dead of night. The children had gone to sleep in the room downstairs. Satenik prepared their own bed in the tantun, just in the corner where Ohannes was sitting. The low-lit oil lamp was hanging on the wall. A small winged insect was flying round the glass of the lamp. When Ohannes finished considering all the day's events, he returned to the last part of his conversation with Set once again.

"The problem of the weapons is easy," Set said, "the problem of food is much more difficult, there may be famine."

Ohannes seemed to have decided not to agree with anything Set said. "Pish! There won't be any hunger. Every house has its stores, they'll live in some way."

"What stores? Do you mean money?" Set asked.

"Both money and food."

"Only very few have provisions, perhaps five in a hundred. As for money, there isn't any trade to make any money. The Turks have occupied the Khatch Street and Arark markets, and the

Norashen market is closed down. A man would be a fool to trade in a besieged town. Money has no value from now on. A man with a pound of meat won't exchange it for any amount of gold coins. Flour or bread – that's today's gold."

Despite being an experienced merchant, Ohannes had not come to any conclusion, right or wrong, about the new situation caused by the war, whereas his manager Set had already understood the issue. On the other hand, why should he think of such matters. Let the one with a big head and big aspirations think about them. Ohannes was well provided with bread and food till the next harvest. At the most, he might be short of a bit of fresh meat. Well, so be it! Ghavurma was as good as fresh meat. If there was no tava-kebab, he would eat dried meat.

He was so absorbed in these thoughts that he was not listening to what Set was saying. He had no doubt that he was speaking, because his lips were moving and the expression on his face was pitiful, like that of a man asking for something.

"I have no provisions. I always have to buy bread at the bakery. At least a little flour, please."

Ohannes did not give any flour to Set, but did not completely refuse his modest request either. He remembered Set's wife, beautiful Khushush with her red cheeks and big, black beauty spot. Every time Ohannes went to their house for the Easter celebrations, Khushush used to take particular care to seat him on the sadr, arranging the cushions in a way that let her touch him with her tight breasts. She would breathe straight into Ohannes' face and, perhaps due to the drinks he would already have had, he got pleasantly breathless. He had the same feeling when Khushush helped him to put his coat back on. When sliding his hands into his coat's sleeves and shaking himself to settle the coat well, he felt the closeness of her body. Coming out into the street, he would try to criticize the behaviour of the beautiful Khushush from a purely moral point of view, but felt that he could hardly do so. 'That's what's meant by living in Bolis,' he thought, 'she knows well how to turn a man's head.'

Bolis, Bolis. And his brother Kevork's wife. She had never been to Bolis, had she? How could she be so flirtatious? Ohannes happened once to be passing along Chaghli Street early in the morning. It was a Sunday in Spring. He was going to Simon's house to enjoy a morning rose-tea with him. Ohannes knew well enough that it would not be only tea and that he could expect a good breakfast as well. He was walking down the street thinking about it, when he saw in the distance a plump young woman sweeping the street. She was first spraying water on the ground so that no dust would rise. As he approached, he realized that the woman with the attractive body was sweeping the street in front of his brother's house. He wondered who this beautiful devil was as he passed by with his eyes fixed on the temptation. The woman straightened up, perhaps on hearing the footsteps, and Ohannes came face to face with his brother's wife, Vergine. Ohannes had not seen Vergine for a long time. During that period she had grown plump and more beautiful, as if beauty increased both in length and width.

He was astonished. "Vergine? I was looking and wondering who this beautiful girl could be."

"Good morning, Baron Ohannes." Vergine blushed like a red tulip under her brother-in-law's expressive gaze. "You're welcome, please come in."

"No, I'm in a hurry, I've something to do," Ohannes said, wondering whether his brother was in or not, "Woman, why have you got so lush?"

There are plants that can grow and become too big in one night, they are mainly harmful weeds. When Van people say 'the flower-bed has become lush,' they mean that the bed needs to be weeded. This was the meaning of Ohannes' words and the woman understood it at once.

Vergine swung the broom a couple of times at one of the willows on the edge of the babbling stream, then took a fallen willow leaf off Ohannes' shoulder and said with childish discontent, "If one doesn't weed the bed, it will grow lush. Am I not right?"

These words were said in such a tone and such a manner that Ohannes felt something shatter inside him and disappear somewhere.

"It will pass, it will pass," said Ohannes not in his normal voice, but just to have said something.

"Indeed, it will pass," agreed Vergine, looking sadly at the broom in her hand. Then she smiled – it is not clear why – and added, "Life will pass, too."

"Why don't you come to visit us?"

"Give Satenik my greetings."

Vergine was like that. Remembering all these things, Ohannes regretted that he had put off giving flour to Set immediately. He had instead sent him home, telling him to come back in a couple of days to see what could be done for him. Ohannes also thought that he should give his brother some flour, and perhaps some butter and cheese as well.

When taking his leave, Set had said something like 'the Bible says somewhere ...' Ohannes had not heard the rest. Now he would like to know what the Bible said somewhere.

Meanwhile, Satenik was sitting on the bed, sewing the buttons on Souren's shirt.

Vsh-sh-sh. Boum.

"What are you busy with, woman?"

"The buttons on our messenger's clothes. Aman! It's a terrifying night."

"Please bring me the Bible."

"What do you want with the Bible?" Satenik said, cutting the black thread with her teeth.

"I need it."

It was dark outside and the shooting was getting more terrifying. Satenik had to go to the upstairs room to fetch the Bible. But on reaching the verandah, she wanted to turn back. The bullets were flying all over the gardens, all over the place. Making an effort, she entered the room, snatched the Bible off the table and rushed out. She heard the sound of glass breaking everywhere. The enemy was causing panic. Satenik put the large Bible on Ohannes' lap.

"Turn up the wick."

The lamp flared up. Now there were two small insects flying

round it. 'How large this Bible is,' Ohannes thought, 'where shall I find that place?'

He opened a page at random and began to read with some difficulty:

> Our skin was black like an oven because of this terrible famine. They ravished the women in Zion and the maids in the cities of Judah.

Ohannes wondered whether this was about Turks.

> Princes are hanged up by their hand: the faces of the elders were not honoured. They took the young men to grind, and the children fell under the wood.

Now he was bewildered and wondered whether this was about the Adana massacres. He turned the pages back and forth, stopped somewhere at random again, and began to read out loud:

> "How beautiful are thy feet with shoes, O prince's daughter! The joints of thy thighs are like jewels, the work of a cunning workman. Thy navel is like a round goblet, which wanteth not liquor: thy belly is like an heap of wheat set about with lilies. Thy two breasts are like two young roes that are twins."

"Allah! Allah!" Ohannes gasped and closed the Bible noisily.

"You're reading shameful things," said Satenik, who had been listening to her husband with one ear.

Ohannes justified himself: "It's written in the Bible."

"What Bible is that?" complained Satenik. "Get up – let's go to bed. It's already midnight."

The bombs thundered and the guns howled all night. Ohannes' sleep was restless. He dreamed of Vergine, then Khushush, then both of them together. They were holding his coat and trying to help him put it on. He could not find the sleeve of the coat. Khushush was laughing in her devilish way while Vergine was telling him to give her regards to Satenik. Ohannes woke up. He touched and caressed his sleeping wife according to the Bible. Satenik was not asleep, but she pretended to be.

Chapter 23

From the very first day of the fighting, the spring was unusual. God knows where it went – it was spring but not spring at the same time. It was not spring, summer, autumn or winter. It seemed to be beyond the four seasons of the year, beyond the year, but within the burning and suffocating circle of gunfire.

The sun rose above Varag as usual, but ever since the monastery had been taken by the enemy, nobody now looked towards it at sunrise. The Armenians there had not been able to hold out and had retreated from the mountain and the monasteries, as well as from Shushants. Yes, they had not been able to hold out.

The birds were singing, but nobody heard. The grass had grown, the trees had blossomed and were beginning to bear fruit, but nobody noticed. The flower beds were not dug over and sown, weeds had flourished. Vergine felt equally neglected. On Ohannes' suggestion and with Satenik's consent, she had already lived under their restless, but hospitable, roof, for the two weeks since Kevork's inexplicable, and rather futile, death.

Leaving Ohannes' house, Kevork felt that he had nowhere to go. Nobody had actually told him to go round the defensive positions and encourage the soldiers. And nobody would; the posts were not cafés, his speeches were not suitable. Of course, if the posts had been cafés and restaurants, he would have carried out his mission brilliantly and successfully. However, he felt that a man like him should not stand aside like Mihran Manasserian. He decided to do some modest and useful work. The profit received from the Aghtamar affair – Kevork did not even want to think about that – had quickly melted away. That event had destroyed something important in him. He felt that he had lost his position in life, one he had never had. He felt fairly secure when he was drunk, but when things fell apart, he became frightened of himself, of others, of daylight and of the dark night. He was especially worried on rainy nights; he would toss and turn in his bed, and moan in

Vergine's ear; was not clear whether he was dreaming or awake. Vergine had got used to this, in the way a lame man accepts his limp, or a mother her disabled son.

On one occasion, he came in and put a parcel, wrapped in paper, on his wife's lap. "This is for you, for a new dress," he said.

The expensive cloth frightened Vergine. "Did Ohannes give it you?" she asked.

"Yes, of course. Ohannes already thinks about you every day."

"Ohannes likes me," said Vergine, stroking the expensive cloth up and down. She recalled the day she was sweeping the street, when her brother-in-law had appeared and gazed at her with the sort of look that only a woman understands.

"Yes, that's it, he can't get to sleep at night because of you."

With this, the conversation was over. Vergine did not want to find out where else he had taken the piece of cloth. She was pleased to think that Ohannes had wanted to see her in a fine new, green dress.

Later, there came a time when her husband would return home drunk but always with some purchases. Meanwhile, she heard some dark rumours about the Aghtamar affair. Kerovabeh Ararktsian was particularly interested in it. Once when they were talking, she expressed her surprise at the fact that Vergine did not know anything about that business, and that her husband had not given her any details. Vergine was taken unawares: how could her husband have known about what had happened? Kerovabeh was vague: "How should I know? They say he was also on the island at the time."

Whether it was on the island or under the ground was not so important. What was important was that Vergine remembered that some time ago her husband had not come home for a few days. He had knocked at the door at midnight and had come in barely able to stand. When she asked him where he had been, he could just about reply that he had gone to some wedding party in Shabagh. There was nothing she could say to that, it must certainly have been a very merry wedding party.

Then things got better. Her husband began to dress well, grew a beard, took a cane in his hand, and began to boast.

"Our Aram's eyes are hurting," he would say, "Let me go and see what can be done."

"Aram Mardigian's?" Vergin would ask casually.

"What Mardigian? Aram Pasha, of course."

Or he would say, "Ishkhan has sent a message and asked to see me. Let me go and see what he wants." And at other times he would say, "Vramian wanted to test my discretion, but I answered him in such a way that he held his tongue."

Vergine knew her husband through and through, so she was not surprised by his transformation, nor angry when eventually he lost his enthusiasm and returned to his old ways. It was clear that he had then deteriorated, physically and spiritually. He became particularly unbearable when he could not find any raki to drink, becoming mean-spirited, suspicious and angry. Once or twice he even tried to raise a hand against his wife, but when Vergine then reacted like a healthy cat with a sick mouse, he would bite his hand helplessly and weep silently without tears.

Vergine pretended not to notice when a gold ring appeared on his finger, or when that ring disappeared. He once gave her ten gold pieces when he returned home after a few days absence, but on the following morning he asked if she had enough money for bread and gave her two kurush. 'He's gone mad,' Vergine thought, 'he's lost it.' The day came, when Vergine realized that the cloth for the dress had disappeared from the trunk. A wave of anger passed over her, but she kept quiet. She felt instinctively that her difficult marriage was coming to an end.

Leaving his brother's house, Kevork walked through the streets in the best-known parts of the town, which were both dangerous and safe. No part of the town was as it used to be. All the cafés and restaurants were closed, as were all the shops. Alarm and concern could be seen on the faces of the few passers-by.

'Shall I go home?' he wondered, 'Home or the cemetery? I'd better go to the cemetery.'

"Better the cemetery," he said aloud and looked around. Had anyone heard?

He met Hagop Kandoyan, and pretended not to notice him, but Hagop tapped his cane on the ground and stopped. "Good afternoon, Baron Kevork."

"Good afternoon."

"Where are you going?"

"To the defense posts."

"And where's your revolver?"

"Some fight with revolvers, some organize and set up programmes, others inspire people."

"An unnecessary task."

"We think differently." Kevork tried to hold on to his questionable point of view. "You stick to your opinion, and I'll stick to mine."

Hagop went up close to Kevork, and stared at him with his blue eyes: "There's only one opinion and aspiration now – to fight and to die!"

"And why die at all?"

"What else can you do? Do you think they hand out raisins and nuts in the posts?"

"I see," Kevork said in a business-like way. "But the fighters shouldn't be encouraged in that way. They should be told to fight and win. But this is all pointless – why don't you fight and die yourself?"

"Aren't you aware of the situation? There are no guns to fight with?" Hagop said quietly as he looked around.

"Do you really mean that?"

Hagop took a deep breath. "Yes, you're so busy drinking raki that you don't know what's going on. I was at the Talamazians and heard Panos complaining: 'Brother, the Turkish government accused us of getting arms from Russia in order to raise a revolt. And now, when we've gathered together all our weapons, it's clear that we've got more fighters than guns.' Panos was asking what the Dashnak leaders had been doing all this time."

Kevork rubbed his brow, trying to recall something important. He succeeded and quoted the song,

> Though we have no sabre, no sword, no lance,
> We will kill them with our spades, with our spades.

"What do you mean?" Hagop sneered, "Should I take a spade and go to the posts? Let the one who made up that song go and stand with his spade in front of the forces of the state."

Kevork cheered up. "So, if I went now and asked for a gun to fight with – to win or die – wouldn't they give me one?"

"Of course not. There are no guns. Don't you understand Armenian?"

"How disgraceful, I'll go straightaway and dare them not to give me a gun. I'll show them!"

He strode off, leaving Hagop stunned and astonished. I fooled him – Kevork thought – well, let him be. He entered Khanke Street from the east and walked westwards. A new, high barrier had been built at the end of the street. The gunfire was now right in his ear. He had reached the Arark post, a square building with thick walls where soap and candles had been manufactured only a few days ago. Kevork gathered himself together and entered the yard.

The first thing he sensed was the sharp, unpleasant smell of gunpowder. It was quite dark in the former factory. The large windows were filled in with bricks leaving just a square hole in each window. These holes and the door into the yard let some light into the former workshop, now a defense post. The windows looked out at the police station in the Arark square, from where the Turks kept up continuous fire. This only occasionally produced a response from the Armenian fighters standing by each hole. If this situation could be described in terms of a conversation, it would seem that the Turks spoke all the time, shouting and yelling with a lot of noise, while the Armenians preferred to keep quiet, only breaking the long silences with a curt 'yes' or 'no'.

The first to recognize Kevork was Lorto Hampo, a well-known participant in the events of 1896, who was most probably the leader of the group defending this post. He was in his late forties – broad shouldered, with a large head, thick, drooping moustache, a deep voice, and sad, intelligent eyes. He was sitting on one of the factory machines, eating bread and cheese with great gusto. He seemed to be eating not just with his teeth but with his whole face; his moustache was moving up and down, his jaws were tensing and his brow was creasing. He swallowed the last bite and began rolling a thick cigarette in his fat fingers.

"Teacher, did you come to give us a lesson?"

"No, I came to have a lesson," said Kevork.

The defenders laughed. "Good for you," said Hampo, "shall we start with the A,B,C or do you know that already?" It was hard to tell whether the skilled fighter was serious or joking.

"If the alphabet is to load the gun, then I already know it."

"And to take aim?"

"I haven't tried."

"Well, it's said that you used a knife at Aghtamar some time ago. Is that true?" The smoke of Hampo's cigarette merged with that of the guns.

"What Aghtamar? What knife? When –"

"There's someone crawling in the square!" The talk – which was getting difficult for Kevork – was interrupted by a tall defender, Hmayak Sossoyan, standing at one of the window holes. He had been able to avoid conscription in the Turkish army. It was well-known that the government did not trust Armenian soldiers with guns, so they were drafted into so-called labour battalions to mend roads – and to be beaten and tortured. Hmayak had saved himself from all that.

"Is he an Armenian or a Turk?" Hmayak asked hesitantly.

"What's an Armenian doing in Arark square? He isn't going to church is he?" Hampo asked sarcastically.

He went up to the hole, looked out, took Hmayak's pistol, aimed, fired, looked out again and returned the weapon. The body in the square was motionless. The desolate Arark square, surrounded by closed and abandoned stalls, was now an even more terrible sight.

"Hey, teacher! You'll know, how long would it take to get to the Mohammedan paradise from this moment?" Hampo asked aloud.

"I don't know," said Kevork, regretting that he had not taken the opportunity to vanish, just as he used to when he had no money to pay the bill at a café. "I don't know. I've not been in that kind of place."

This amused the men, who were sitting together on the floor and were busy cleaning and loading their weapons. A bullet flew in through the door overlooking the yard – to be more precise, it was Souren who flew in like a bullet. It was clear that he had been running. He blinked a few times to get used to the dark, then went up to the leader of the group and handed him a piece of paper from his pocket.

"Baron Yekarian gave me this."

Hampo took the paper and strode away to read it in the light, while Souren approached his uncle with a smile.

"Souren, are you a messenger? Delivering messages is a job for girls. Why don't you come to the defense posts with your bombs?"

"Baron Yekarian has promised me a gun in a couple of days."

"Well done, my boy!" Kevork tapped Souren's shoulder, but Souren felt that his uncle was distraught.

"Seven of you must go to the Shahbenderian post." Hampo came back waving the order of the Defense Command. "Sahag, Haig, Aghavard, Haroud, Christos, Haped, and you with the black eyes. Fly!"

And they really did – accompanied by Kevork who seized his chance to avoid any more of Hampo's disturbing questions. And Souren followed them.

By the third day of fighting, Kevork was hungry, and feeling useless. He set out to go to his brother's house. The day had come when it was more frightening to look into Vergine's eyes, than go to his brother's house and look at Satenik's reproachful eyes. The homes and hearts of everyone, whether he knew them or not, seemed to have become gloomy, inaccessible and impenetrable, castles. He tried to analyse the situation.

– War... a siege ... a grave situation, life and death ... fight. There are two possible results. First, that the Turks may win, in which case they'll slaughter everyone irrespective of sex and age. This would probably be the best outcome. But if the Turks are defeated and the people of Van win, the most terrible things may happen. There would certainly be some reassessment of recent events and some revenge inflicted on some people. And in that case, I'm done for, since a Vanetsi will never spare another Vanetsi. –

He spent the nights in the barn of the Hatzhamroghian house, which was abandoned and served as a defense post. He smoked one cigarette after another to suppress his hunger. The gunfire thundered nearby. He tried to occupy his mind by thinking of peaceful things. For instance, he wondered where the surname Hatz-hamroghian – the 'bread-counters' – had come from. After lengthy and detailed consideration he came to the conclusion that their ancestors had been miserly, and had perhaps counted the loaves of bread when baking, or when lending or borrowing them. This was held to be offensive according to the unwritten rule of hospitality that counting bread was a sin.

And now, in these hard times, all Van had become Hatzhamroghians. The bakeries only made bread for the fighting soldiers, for the wounded and for the refugees who had escaped form the villages of Vaspourakan. He thought of working in a bakery. But who would take him? And even if he was taken on, would that not be shameful, what would people think? No, he should go to Ohannes. Good or bad, he was after all the man's brother.

On his way, he thought how he might go in and say with brotherly warmth, 'Ohannes, I've come to drink the remaining raki. No, I mean to empty the bottle. Ohannes, I'm hungry. Tell Satenik to bring me something to eat.'

– But wouldn't it be better if I was serious and downcast, and spoke a little about Armenian history, from the kingdom of the Artsrounis to the present day. I could criticize the Hunchaks who've been imprisoned one by one. I could pour fire and ashes on the Dashnaks for having organized the defense so badly that there are no guns for me to join in the fight. –

The garden door was locked; he slapped it with his palm. Satenik opened the door. She had folded her sleeves up to her elbows and her hands were wet – she was clearly doing the washing. She told him that Ohannes had gone and added that she was in the middle of washing, in a tone that meant she had no time to attend to him.

Kevork was disconcerted, but managed to say, "Never mind. I'll come tomorrow if I have time. By the way, I saw Souren, he came to the Arark post with orders from Yekarian. He's a messenger."

"He's been fighting with Arabo's group since yesterday," said Satenik, worried but proud, and closed the door quietly.

Standing in front of the closed door, Kevork felt that his forces were deserting him. Where should he go? Just at that moment, Satenik opened the door again, sensing perhaps that her brother-in-law had not gone.

"Have you got anything more to say?"

"Well, no," said Kevork with assumed indifference and more loudly than was necessary. "I'm wondering whether to go to the Terzibashians or to the Chanikian defense post."

"Go to the Terzibashians," Satenik advised gravely, and again shut the door on him.

It was the third evening of fighting in the terrified town. Kevork left the deserted orchards in a bitter mood and walked along the even more deserted Aghvesi Dzor until, without knowing how, he arrived at the Arark post. Hampo saw the distressed face of the interesting visitor by the light of two lamps hanging on the wall.

"So, you've come back. Don't you know that no one can hang around a defense post doing nothing. A post isn't a café but a place to fight from."

The words were stern, but they were spoken softly as if Hampo was speaking to a child. Kevork became more buoyant.

"Give me a gun, and I'll fight as well."

"Don't stand there like a target. Move over here, or they'll blame me if something happens to you. Look."

He pointed at the opposite wall. Kevork saw the wall had been hit by bullets that had passed through the holes in the windows.

"Do you want a weapon now?"

"Yes. I do," said the grown-up child

"Aless didn't have any guns either two days ago, but he has now." Two bullets went whistling towards the opposite wall one after another – shtp-shtp. "Aless, give me your gun. It's called a kuchuk-jubuk, it's an old-fashioned Turkish pistol. Do you remember the Turk I killed a few days ago? It was his. Aless crawled out at night, braving the shooting and brought it back. Could you have done that?"

Kevork was taken aback.

"There's been a decision to raise the morale of the soldiers, could you do that?"

"Why not – if I'm drunk!"

Hampo laughed and twisted the ends of his moustache to look like the horns of a ram.

"Varazdat, give the teacher a glass of raki."

Kevork quivered slightly when he held the cold, full glass. Was that because it was cold? He sniffed the shaking glass, and put on a ridiculous air. He stepped back as if putting a suitable distance between him and his audience, and began to feel completely in his element.

"Compatriots, soldiers! Our glorious Van, the wonderful capital of Vaspourakan, must not only be proud of its fourteen-hundred-years-old past. Van was born again, just three days ago. It was born like the almighty and unconquerable Vahagn, that mythical being with flaming hair and beard. Men, that evil barbarian Djevdet ... Aiee!"

Kevork was not fated to finish his speech made under such historical conditions, nor – alas – to drink up his glass. The more well-known the date of a man's birth, the more uncertain and unknown is the time and place of his death. Who would have thought that the great Frenchman would fall into eternal sleep on the island of St Helena? And Hampartsoum in Bolis? Who could have known that the unfortunate Ishkhan would be slaughtered at his friend's festive table in Herj. And, finally, who could have guessed that Vramian would be put – still wearing a tie and with his spectacles – into a sack with a heavy stone and thrown into the lake. A stray bullet, or rather one perhaps aimed especially at him, snapped the thin thread of Kevork's life in an instant.

"Teacher!" Hampo yelled, taken by surprise as he had been absorbed in the brilliant opening speech. "Teacher!" he repeated more loudly. The others ran up. There was no teacher. There was only a breathless corpse, some raki and blood.

The Vanetsi is indomitable: when he says 'yes' it means 'yes', and when he says 'no' it means 'no'. He is stubborn and enduring like the walls of the Citadel, he is as patient as the Lake, he can see further than Ishkhan's telescope, and he is clever and quick-witted.

The children – of Murad's age and older – gathered the lead bullets shot by the Turks and the empty cartridges and took them to the armoury. Someone had found out how to make a sort of gunpowder and Grigor Bulgaretsi had invented the first Armenian cannon, which though it was not all that accurate did make as much noise as a real one. Thunder was now the most important thing. Grigor, as a clever armaments specialist, was keeping up the characteristic style of the sacred cause, which is thunder, and always was. Thunder is the most important thing.

In spite of his ability to foresee events, however, no Vanetsi expected the disaster being prepared for him by Djevdet. The governor had not been able to cut the chain of defense posts encircling the town, since there was no weak link. Each defender was fighting against ten. Once peaceful citizens, they were now fighting regular government forces; they incurred very few losses and inflicted many. The cannons destroyed the Armenian positions during the night, but in the morning, the Turks were surprised and confused to see the newly restored barricades and trenches. Armenian fanfares echoed all round the posts, where it seemed that there was a feast or a wedding party being held, rather than a war.

A diabolical business. But it had now happened that there were no Dasnaks, no Hunchaks, no Ramgavars. There was only the fighting and struggling people of Van, and one Armenak (though no longer an Armenak but a Ramgavar) Yekarian.

And the days were passing by. The people of Van, including Ohannes, did not hear the sound of spring. It was deafened in the noise of the terrible gunfire. Djevdet Bey cursed the day of his appointment as Governor, as he did a thousand times every day. He lit a cigarette and ordered his chete troops – dangerous criminals released from prison – to cease killing the peaceful men of Vaspourakan causing the women and children to tremble for their lives, but instead to bring them all carefully to Van. Why had he not thought of that earlier? Let these hungry and frenzied locusts get into Aikesdan and eat up all the stocks of food. This was the only way the people of Van could be forced to their knees.

The men listened to Djevdet's order with dismay. They had been raping and kidnapping people in the villages with professional cruelty. One of them, one-eyed corporal Ahmed, who was now standing before Djevded, had three days earlier slaughtered everyone in Ermants but for a few Assyrians. Cruel, half-blind Ahmed and three others had gone to Mkho's house. There, they tortured Sira and Mariam in the dark barn, and then killed them. They tied Mkho to a post and raped the beautiful Iskouhi before his eyes. They then set her astride a pole and pressed down on her to make her, they said, more comfortable. Then they set the house on fire.

At first, the chete men were not pleased with Djevdet's order, but when the gentle governor explained his monstrous plan they were delighted at the prospect of enjoying the wealth of the town as well as the services of the Armenian women. They mounted their horses and rode out to the villages with wild shouts. Following their orders they did not harm the remaining Armenians, but set them on the road to Van.

Towards Van – towards Van!

All the roads leading to Van were full of hungry and exhausted groups of displaced villagers. They walked slowly with their eyes fixed on the distance, but they seemed to be seeing nothing. They were groaning, and the children were crying and nobody heeded them.

At first, the people of Van were pleased to see the first groups of old people, women and children fleeing from the burning and massacre. But when they saw that the stream was endless, when the people packed the gardens and came into the yards to nibble anything that was softer than stone, to demand a piece of bread, a handful of barley, to beg and to demand – then, Vanetsi joy turned into horror. The Defense Command realized the fatal significance and likely consequence of the trap Djevdet had planned. Van shivered. It became clear that this unarmed, helpless mass of Armenian villagers demanding bread and water were more of a danger than the fully-armed Turkish army.

CHAPTER 23

When Ohannes heard in detail about the death of his brother Kevork, no muscle of his face moved – only the nargileh gurgled more heavily as the water bubbled a bit more. The news was brought by Hagop Kandoyan, who was now sitting opposite and fiddling with Ohannes' worry beads.

There was another unusual thing: when Satenik came into the room to ask what she should cook for dinner, Ohannes left her question unanswered. He was recalling the previous occasion, when Kevork had boasted that he believed it would be better to die in the posts than die like Hampartsoum. Then he remembered his spiteful question, 'Why don't you die in that case?' He also recalled Kevork's answer which had been a question, 'Are you sure I won't die?' It now all seemed very obscure. He remembered how his brother had stood up leaving the bottle of raki half-full – what a miracle! – had made the sign of the cross, said goodbye and gone away. He went and did not come back. Ohannes reflected that his brother must have been very upset by his thoughts and gone to face the fire. And the nargileh gurgled even more hoarsely.

Not getting an answer to her question and learning about her brother-in-law's death, Satenik could not conceal the fact that he had come round in the evening.

"I invited him in, but he said he had to go. He didn't know whether to go to the Terzibashians or to the defense posts. I advised him to go to the Terzibashians. But it seems he went to the posts instead."

"Why should he have gone to the Terzibashians?" Hagop said. "The blessed soul liked to boast a lot. It's good he didn't go to the Kapamadjians. I saw him later myself. He was worried that there weren't enough weapons. He seemed upset."

Feeling inwardly very dejected, Ohannes suddenly remembered Vergine, he saw her image directly in front of him. He seemed to hear her voice: 'You're welcome, Baron Ohannes, come in.' He remembered her bending down to sweep the street and he felt his heart beginning to beat faster. His thoughts took another turn. Vergine had been left on her own – that fool of a husband had not understood her value. He should have kept a woman like Vergine dressed in silk, he should have burnt incense and prayed for her, washed her feet and then drank the water. Ohannes liked the last scene most of all. Could he now wash Vergine's feet and – he visibly got very excited – yes, yes! And how had his brother behaved? He hadn't had children, he hadn't carried the burden of a big family on his shoulders, he hadn't been able to keep even one woman happy. Was he a man? He was a shameful stain on the brow of the Muradkhanians!

In order to discredit his brother completely in his mind, to neutralize the pain caused by his death and to make the necessary arrangements to look after Vergine, he recalled the Aghtamar event and the vague things said about it.

– No, Kevork was not a man, he was a fool, a weak character. He went off to fight and became a needless victim, he left his wife hungry and naked and a burden round my neck. –

His own neck moved automatically, as he turned his head left and right and imagined a naked Vergine on his neck. He recalled lawyer Hrant Kaligian's words, some years ago: 'You walk in the street and the women hang themselves round your neck.'

"Satenik," he called out, as if to get rid of his thoughts, without taking into account – no, taking into account – Hagop's presence. "Satenik!"

Satenik appeared in the doorway of the pantry. "What's up?" she asked.

"Alas! My lovely wife, cover your head with a scarf, go through the gardens and bring that orphan girl here."

"What orphan girl?" Satenik was genuinely surprised. How could she know where her husband had got to in his thoughts, and how he proposed to resolve his difficult problems so easily.

"How many orphans do we have?" Ohannes replied. "Our Vergine – go and bring her, if she's still alive, the poor widow. Let her come and live with us. Let's see what God will say."

"What you're doing is pleasing to God," said Hagop, rustling Ohannes' beads, "one way or another."

Among all her relatives and acquaintances there were only two women whom Satenik inexplicably, but instinctively, did not like. One of them was the wife of Ohannes' shop manager Set, the liberally-minded Kushush, who was always ready to dance for Ohannes at parties. The other was her brother-in-law's wife Vergine. It was true that she had no reason to suspect or blame Vergine, but she had not cared for the way the ravenous eyes of that hungry woman looked at Ohannes. What eyes! This was the meaning of the words 'to eat with your eyes'. That was the situation, but when Set had come in a carriage the day before to take a sack of flour to that miserable woman, Satenik had not said a word to betray her unease. Ohannes' word was law. From this point of view, only Sultan Abdul Hamid could compete with him.

"I'm afraid and I won't go alone," she said faintly, knowing that Ohannes had to be obeyed.

"What a timid rabbit!" said Ohannes, thinking, however, that his wife was right. "And why wasn't the revolutionary Zarouhi Teroyan afraid?"

"I'm not Zarouhi Teroyan."

Hagop came to her aid. "She's right. Alone in the gardens, under the hail of bullets? Do you want me to go and bring Vergine myself?"

This was how Hagop 'helped' Satenik – he was in fact just making sure of his dinner.

"Well, no need to hurry," said Ohannes. He was grateful to Hagop whose presence resolved the rather difficult situation. Meanwhile, Satenik's previous question had remained unanswered. "Make pilaf with ghavurma," he said, "we haven't had it for a long time."

Satenik went, with a heavy heart, to the pantry to carry out her husband's order. Ohannes, who did not like to put off today's business to tomorrow, turned casually to Hagop. "There's no need to hurry. Would she come here today in any case? But if you want to, go and bring her now. Strike while the iron is hot."

"No, it should not be left until tomorrow," said Hagop, who rose and neatly placed Ohannes' beads round the neck of the nargileh.

Satenik appeared in the doorway. She had been following the conversation. "Well, what will she do with her own house? How can she leave the house and land?"

"The house and land?" Ohannes was scornful. "Nobody needs

that house and that land. Let her bring only clothes and underwear with her. Just close the door, that's all. Only clothes and underwear."

The mention of clothes and underwear left Ohannes feeling something shrivel and melt pleasantly in his heart. Vergine seemed to be very close and dear to him, like Lia – no, like Satenik. Was the raki he drank at breakfast affecting him? Ohannes now felt totally kind, devoted, and generous.

"She doesn't need to bring anything – not even underwear. She can wear Satenik's clothes." He was surprised to hear what he had said and reproached himself with a sigh, 'mashallah – mashallah!'

"My clothes won't fit her," complained Satenik, avoiding the word 'underwear'.

"Well, it's not the end of the world. Let her bring her own clothes." Ohannes straightened the crooked back of the already crooked affair and sighed deeply again.

Hagop departed. Satenik stoked up the tonir for the pilaf. Ohannes felt electricity in the air – faint flashes of lightning could be seen in the distance and the thunder of clouds could be heard, but there was no rain. The air was stifling, Ohannes closed his eyes. He pretended to be asleep, on the one hand to kill time, and on the other to avoid needless conversation with Satenik. But he did want to know what she was thinking about. It was not enough to guess, he wanted to know her thoughts fully, and then act accordingly.

The guns and cannons were firing away outside but Ohannes did not hear them. It was a matter of habit. Once, two years ago, Ohannes had entered Darbinian's weaving-shed. The deafening noise of the machines, with their shuttles and wheels, seemed to slice his feet off the ground. The people seemed impervious to the noise and were working calmly. He asked how people could work in that noise from morning till night. Darbinian shouted in his ear: "It's a matter of habit."

Yes, it really was a matter of habit. He suddenly opened his eyes, feeling as if he was standing naked in cold water. "Well, you've worked enough, come and sit down beside me," he called out to his wife.

Satenik wiped her hands on her flowery apron, left her slippers by the carpet and sat down beside her husband. Her face was calm. "Souren said there was going to be an armaments workshop. He and Arabo are going to work under Grigor Bulgaretsi."

On hearing his wife's words, Ohannes felt like a man who having dived into cold water, now felt that the water was pleasantly warm.

"Well, that's good," said Ohannes, caressing her neck, "is there any job better than that?"

There was a silence.

"I haven't sat down since morning," said Satenik, "there's a lot to do. Lia is not here either. I have a heap of clothes to be washed. Vergine will come and be able to help me."

Ohannes' spirits revived, "Of course. I know how difficult it is for you. I was only thinking of you –"

He was unable to continue. Satenik was looking at him in her slightly mocking, disbelieving but forgiving, way.

"Nevertheless," said Satenik, as she leant on her husband's knee and stood up. "Shall I make fish as well?"

"Yes, do that," said Ohannes, "and also bring something to drink."

"In short, we're having a wedding party at our home today?" It was not clear whether she was joking or was really displeased.

Ohannes wanted to reproach her by telling her that if she had anything on the tip of her tongue, she should say it. But he thought it wiser to keep quiet, and he closed his eyes again.

Not knowing how long he had drowsed, he was woken up by Hagop's voice. "We've arrived. Take away the rug – roll out the carpet."

Ohannes saw Vergine's seductive figure in the doorway. She had a black coat wrapped round her plump body, and a black lock of hair hung from under her white head-scarf over sad but watchful eyes. Satenik was not there. She had probably managed to get to the pantry in time to follow important events from there.

Nothing special happened. Vergine got rid of the package in her hand and came into the room quickly. She went up to Ohannes, knelt before him, and kissed his hand, wetting it with her tears.

"I'm your servant, master," she whispered, "thank you very much for taking care of me."

Ohannes mellowed, he was moved by her close presence. He could only release his hand with difficulty, and caress her head. "What are you saying? You're my pretty girl." Seeing Satenik coming out of the pantry, he added, "Don't cry, please don't cry. What's done can't be undone."

Vergine rescued his knees from the weight of her breasts and stood up. She went and embraced Satenik, pouring out the last drops of her tears. Satenik also wept – it was not clear whether for Vergine, for her dead brother-in-law or for something else. Who can imagine what goes on in a women's mind? A woman's soul?

They sat down to dinner.

Chapter 24

Van was stirred up with muddy and heavy waves. Hard fighting, against the odds and lasting for weeks, had upset its harmony and deprived it of its usual appearance. Van had already become unrecognizable, but it lost its features completely when the starving masses from the countryside moved in and filled it. The besieged town faced up to the threat of starvation or surrender. The soldiers were fighting with clenched teeth. It was raining.

A few Assyrians who had escaped from Ermants entered the town with the rest of the starving country-folk. They knocked at Ohannes' door; Satenik opened it. Without a word, without even a greeting, they fell down in their rags at the shed in the outer yard. Satenik recognized one of their household servants, Assyrian Hormuz, among the seven exhausted faces.

"Hormuz?" said Satenik, not believing her eyes.

"Yes, it's me, Hormuz, little Hatun." He was only just able to answer.

Ohannes entered the outer yard anxiously.

"Hormuz?"

"Yes, it's me, Hormuz, Master."

It was indeed Hormuz, he could just be recognized by his drooping, grey moustaches and big eyes, but nothing else was left of the former Hormuz.

"Mkho?" Ohannes asked without expecting to hear any good news.

"There's no Mkho, Master. There's no Ermants. Everybody was slaughtered." He passed a finger across his throat.

Something inside Ohannes flared red-hot, burnt, died away and then seemed to flare up again. Only then did he realise that Hormuz was not alone. Lying side by side were two women of indeterminate age, two men, a teenager with a bandaged eye, and a young man, who seemed to be smiling, yet after looking more carefully one could see that it was not a smile but a grimace of pain. Ohannes returned to his corner. He seemed to be not walking, but floating in the air. He could not feel the ground under his feet. And when he was seated, he seemed to be going down a hole, a trap, a well.

There was no Ermants, there was no Mkho. There was a war and during it there could be no raisins and nuts. Simon had lost his head together with everything. Panos was also in the same state, why had he not come to visit. Thank God, he had not suffered hunger yet. And he would not.

"Satenik!" he called and she came in. "Satenik, give some food to the Assyrians. Vergine, make coffee for me."

"What should I feed them with?"

"Haricot beans, lentil soup – do I need to decide that? Let them go to the stable, it's more comfortable there. O my God, O my God. Vergine!"

"What do you want of Vergine?"

"I'll say what I want of her. Tell her to make coffee."

"The world's getting ruined and you still can't forget your coffee," murmured Satenik, and put the coffee-pot on the fire.

Vergine appeared, aglow and stepping lightly despite her heavy body. "Vergine," said Satenik, "heat the cauldron, wash the lentils."

'She's forcing me to lose my way,' thought Ohannes, noticing that Satenik had just reversed the tasks he had demanded. But Satenik did not have to force Ohannes away from the path of virtue. Ohannes was only justifying himself.

Two weeks had already passed since Vergine had moved into Ohannes' house and it could not be said that things had gone smoothly without deflection or distraction. Vergine had always been the initiator; if anyone was to blame for leading Ohannes astray, it could only be Vergine. And she had a reason to behave like that: Ohannes was a rich, fertile field for her spiteful seeds. Vergine had envied Satenik ever since the first day of her own unfortunate marriage. She had envied her for having a strong and godlike husband, who had ensured a happy life for her, while she ...

Vergine had always complained to Kevork, saying, 'What shall I do – shall I go and become a maid for Satenik?' And now he was dead! And she had been commanded to live in Ohannes' house, where she worked like a maid without complaint. She felt she wanted ... what did she want? Did she want to take Ohannes away from Satenik? No. that was impossible, it would not do! She simply wanted to share Satenik's happiness, to join in and take her share in such a way that only she, Ohannes and God, if there is one, would know.

Vergine was also driven by these guilty thoughts because of the uncertain situation created by the war, the daily troubles, and the uninterrupted bombardment. She slept in the same room as the married couple, just in the opposite corner. When the lights were put out, late at night and the room was plunged into impenetrable darkness, the shooting could be heard more loudly and clearly. Vergine's only thought was that it was the end of the world. The end of the world? Who knew whether the dawn would arise or not? She thought of taking whatever she could from life that night. And what could she take, what was there for her to take?

She used to get up and hold her hand in front of her eyes to check the darkness; she would move her fingers but could see nothing. She would go to Ohannes' bed, lie down on the carpet, carefully raise the blanket and stay motionless beside him for a moment. Ohannes would wake up breathing deeply, and touch and caress her – perhaps according to the Bible, although Vergine had not read the Bible. The night would slip away. Eventually she would get up and go back tired and happy to her own bed to sleep soundly. The day would break full of all the usual troubles and concerns. Vergine would put the smoking narghileh before Ohannes and it would seem as if nothing had happened, the night seemed to be so far away, so impossible – she had simply had a dream.

Ohannes fell asleep. He woke up that night recalling Hormuz saying there was no Ermants and no Mkho anymore. He remembered the new inhabitants in the stable, as well as Hampartsoum, his mother, Kevork and Mkho. They had all gone to the same place by different roads and perhaps now they were telling each other what had happened to them. Were they not all happier? Only he remained to reign over the ruins like a blind owl. What did he have in this life? Ohannes blinked in the dark and smiled to himself, thinking that when God closed one door, he often opened another; as that blessed soul Kevork used to say, every cloud has a silver lining. Perhaps, God had sent all this trouble to Van for Vergine to fly into his house and live there like a lost pigeon. Now he wanted Vergine to come to him with her warmth and overbearing charm, without fear or remorse. If it was not for all this fighting, he would not be seeing Vergine.

'She won't come tonight,' he thought, 'she'll think I'm in mourning for Ermants and Mkho. Of course, I'm in mourning. But might she not think,' he philosophised, 'that while a man is alive, he has to live.'

Ohannes felt, rather than heard, Satenik's quiet breathing. He knew that if Satenik was asleep she would not wake up even if a drum was pounding in her ears. He raised the blanket, even its whiteness was invisible. And what if Satenik woke up and touched his bedclothes and him. She often used to do so to check whether he was lying outside the sheets. If he was, she used to cover him carefully. In that case ...

He did not want to think about that, but the thought would

not give him a moment's peace. What if he was exposed? Well, was it such a great sin? Why could he not behave like a Kurd? It was well-known that according to Kurdish custom, when a man died – God forbid! – his wife became the property of his brother. A good custom. Who else could comfort the widow if not the dear brother-in-law? It was natural and logical at the same time. Ohannes encouraged himself in this way. However, he understood very well that what was allowed by Kurds, was unacceptable to Armenians – and he was not a Kurd. Even the thought of being caught red-handed terrified him and left his brow in a cold sweat.

Ohannes decided to think of more serious things.

– Man, here we are in a fatal life-or-death situation, Van is in danger and batters itself against the walls like a slaughtered cockerel, and all you can think about is your brother's widow. What a disgrace! They say the Defense Command does not sleep day or night. Do the soldiers sleep at their posts for the Command to sleep? Do the Turks sleep, for the soldiers at their posts to sleep? Vramian and Ishkhan have perished. –

Ohannes remembered the year that now seemed to be so remote. He remembered the day when he had gone to see them both. He had always thought that Ishkhan had long hair and beard, but when he saw him, Ishkhan had short hair and an even shorter beard. He seemed to have been a good family man; after he married he had changed his appearance so as not to frighten his wife and child. Vramian had liked flowers a lot. And he ended under the sea where there were no flowers at all. That villain Djevdet! Aram had been upset and passed from post to post. He too would perish one day.

It was reported that Shirin Hagopian of Kharagonis and others had gone to the Command Centre and asked Yekarian to allow them and other fighters to leave the town and cross the border, leaving the people to Djevdet's mercy. 'What shameless scoundrels!' Ohannes thought, 'Yekarian had disarmed them and put them under arrest and Aram had congratulated him.'

Meanwhile, Mihran Manasserian was taking no part in any of the fighting. He had grown a beard and sat at home pretending to have stomachache. What nonsense! He was simply afraid. He would have paid a thousand gold pieces for a bolt-hole. And now he was running after Karmileh, but she would not take any notice of him. Karmileh had quoted the lines, "Shame on you, shame, where's your weapon?" Mihran had answered, "I'm not made of stone. I'm crazy for your love." He had moved towards the girl. Karmileh had screamed and the Grand Hatun had run to her aid. She had then said to Mihran, "I wish you hadn't been born and that the milk I gave you had been poison. The whole of Van is fighting and you look for peace cold-bloodedly and without conviction."

At the same time, Hrant Bagratouni, that representative of the new generation, had gone to the Command Centre instead of going to the lines and fighting.

"I want to fight," he told Yekarian.

"Take a weapon and go to the Chantigian post."

"But I don't want to fight with arms."

"And so what do you want to fight with?"

"With a pen."

"We're not writing love letters to Djevdet, so we don't need your pen. Panos Terlemezian is a painter, but he's put his paint-brush aside and taken arms and is fighting heroically. Just go and fight."

Hrant Bagratouni had gone home instead of going to the posts and had learnt by heart the role of Aslan from the *Valley of Tears*, so that when the fighting was over, he could play Aslan on the stage.

Ohannes banged his fists together and swore heavily:

– This is for you! May you die! Even Aram Damazian, a teacher at the Yeramian school, fought and encouraged his friends to do so as well. For according to him, every Vanetsi had a legendary patriarch Haik inside him, ready to to defeat the evil Bel. Good for you, Baron Aram. –

– Ohannes was dreaming that he was sitting in the ruins, solemnly resting his head on the palm of his left hand like a real mournful Father Armenia. All around him was desolation – ruined towns and palaces, centuries-old walls and monasteries. He was thinking that it was hard to be a Father Armenia, when you were not allowed to move and it was even awkward to think about scratching your ear. Ohannes had forgotten about hunger, but he was suffering from thirst.

There's Mother Arax flowing in the distance. And what if I get up and go beside its bank and drink some water while pretending to be looking for relics of our ancestors? No, I can't do that, I can't. If only Arshak Dzetotian would come with his camera and take my photo. I would then feel free to move. But who could find him among all these ruins?

Ohannes heard footsteps but was not allowed to look back to see who had come. Someone bent down over him from behind and put the smoking narghileh before him. It was Vergine. Ohannes was concerned to know whether Father Armenia had permission to smoke narghileh or play with Vergine.

"Oh, so you've come, courtier" he said tenderly.

"Yes, I have. Get up and roar like a lion."

"Why?"

"Because it's time for Armenia to roar," explained Vergine.

"Shall I smoke the narghileh and then roar, or first roar and then smoke quietly?"

Vergine laughed in the sophisticated manner of Kushush, his shop manager's wife. She knelt before Ohannes and embraced his knees.

"I'm your maid, Master."

Just as Ohannes was stroking Vergine's body, familiar faces appeared from behind the ruins. They looked at Ohannes and laughed. Here were the dead and buried Nakhshounian, Dyurzian, Vramian, Ishkhan, Simon, Hampartsoum, Mkho all laughing heartily. Ohannes called out to them but without disengaging from Vergine: "What is there to laugh at? Am I any worse than a Kurd?"

Ohannes woke up. He blinked quickly in the dark. How stupid his dream had been! But the thought that Vergine was only a few steps away left him full of desire. Now he wanted to check whether Vergine was there or if it was only a dream. In order to overcome temptation and frustrate evil, he tried to recall something from the Bible, and he remembered: 'Abraham begat Isaac; and Isaac begat

Jacob; and Jacob begat …'

Meanwhile, Van was living in alarming times. The food in the besieged town was dwindling very rapidly. Of course, there were no cases of actual starvation, it was scarcely possible to starve in Van after all. But two of the seven Assyrians sheltering in Ohannes' stable died. One of them was the smiling young man, and the other was the teenager with a bandaged eye. It was of course not only Assyrians who died: Armenians died as well, under the sheds, in the open yards and parks, below the walls of the Norashen church, as well as inside the American and German compounds. "Death will cut with a sharp sickle," Dr Ussher had said.

Sitting with his narghileh in the half-dark corner of the tantun, Ohannes felt as if he was a spider. The difference was that a spider emitted thread from its mouth to weave its cobweb, while in his case the threads stretched towards Ohannes from the posts, the houses, and from the people of Van, whether familiar or not. Ohannes did not go out of the house, but he was aware of everything going on.

The day came, when on the orders of the Defense Command, a group from the Supply Agency armed with a commission went from door to door to collect food – flour and domestic animals to feed the refugees and the soldiers. The last cows were being butchered and the last cauldrons of meat and wheat grits were boiling in Kevork Soukjian's yard; Mgrditch Atchemian was counting the last supplies and distributing them to authorized people.

Panos appeared in the doorway. Ohannes called out from his corner: "You're welcome, Baron Panos, come in, come in."

"If I didn't come, you wouldn't think about your brother at all, whether he's alive or not," said Panos as he entered clumsily, while getting used to the half-darkness. Yes, the expression he had used – 'your brother' – was not accidental. Panos had heard of both Kevork's and Mkho's death and he indirectly offered the first words of condolence to his old business and political friend. Alas, the business had gone and only the politics remained.

"Yes," agreed Ohannes in a sad voice, but recovering himself quickly. "You are now my only brother. Have a seat, have a seat.

What a life! Vergine, make coffee."

Vergine came out of the pantry and began making coffee at the stove.

"Well," said Panos rubbing his dulled eyes with a handkerchief and making himself comfortable, "we're both bored of sitting or of standing."

"And what about lying?" Ohannes smiled ambiguously.

'This man is stony-hearted,' thought Panos. 'He has lost his two – no, three – brothers, his shop and all his property, and he isn't concerned at all. This man will never die.'

"I wish I could lie down and not wake up," murmured Panos.

"It won't do, Baron Panos, it won't. A man is created to face up to and bear all his troubles. Why do you think they sing 'I haven't lost my hope, amidst the foamy waves'?"

"I wish I were as calm as you," said Panos, genuinely surprised at Ohannes' cheerful mood. He thought that perhaps Ohannes had gone mad due to his grief.

"Baron Panos," Ohannes continued, "even supposing that life is hard, terribly unbearably hard, nevertheless a man should never become desperate. Why do you think they sing 'It's a sin to lose hope, my friend, cheer up and be inspired'? Baron Panos, every man should have some glimmer of light in his heart, his house and his life, in order not to shrivel up his soul and body. If you don't have that ray of hope or light, I'd say in short – and you can elaborate if you want – you'll be lost from head to foot. What is death? We'll all die sooner or later. Didn't Napoleon die? Didn't Khrimian Hairig die? What is wealth? I'm sick of wealth, a man only needs a day's food. Who has consumed the world? Why should we eat it? Many people like Kevork and Mkho have come and gone, and many like ourselves will come and go. Yes, everyone will come and go, and we, too, Baron Panos. One day we came into the world and one day we'll go away. Hasn't Baron Simon gone? What did he take with him? Vanity of vanities, I want to say ..."

Vergine approached with the coffee. Panos had not noticed when Ohannes had ordered Vergine to bring it. Sitting with his back towards the stove, he had not noticed who was making the coffee. He knew only that coffee would soon be brought by

Satenik, who else? Now, when Vergine bent over him with two cups of coffee on the tray in her hand, and when his lifeless eyes met her shining ones, he understood very clearly that Ohannes' eloquence and philosophical outpourings had not been addressed to him! In fact, Panos was indeed surprised, but hid his feelings. He only indulged his curiosity by asking where Satenik was.

"She's downstairs sewing clothes on the Singer for Souren," said Ohannes, swallowing the froth of his coffee. "A man comes only once into this world. Everything depends on himself. What I am trying to say is that Armenians – people of Van – have seen so many troubles since the day of their birth that even if they were to live a hundred years and cry those hundred years, that fountain of tears will not dry up and nobody will tell him not to cry. Now, judge for yourself, should a man, who has come into this big and beautiful world created by God, just sit and cry all the time; cry because the Turks are bad; cry because the Dashnaks have power but no brains; cry because the Ramgavars have brains but no power; because the Hunchaks … Well, sit and cry then. I'm fed up with the Turks, Dashnaks, Ramgavars and so on. If I could have more than one life, I might devote one of them to those problems, but I have only one life, Baron Panos, one life. Am I an ass to give up my life for the sake of a thousand stones? Right, I've told you my thoughts – now tell me yours."

There was a studious silence. They drank their coffee silently, as if by mutual consent. Vergine came in with an empty tray, on which they put their cups; she went back to the larder. Ohannes could not help noticing that his political friend followed Vergine with a glance, and he scoffed at him in his mind.

Panos broke the silence, wiping his eyes with his handkerchief: "As far as I can see, either I've gone mad hearing views that you've never raised before, or you've gone mad, because you're saying things I've never heard before. Baron Ohannes, Van is on fire, it's burning. The lives of all Armenians are in danger. Our beautiful Van has taken on a devilish face. Yet what is your mind preoccupied with? Whatever a man does or thinks, he should first consider the national interest. You say there ought to be a glimmer of light in every man's heart and home. Would it be shameful for me to ask what glimmer of light that is? What do Armenians gain from a glimmer of light?" He glanced towards the larder. "They call it a revolution, while I call it a national movement. They call it a heroic struggle, while I call it self-defence. All our forces –"

"Very well, I get it," Ohannes interrupted him. "But now answer this question: does the national movement or national revolution exist for the good of men, or do men exist for the national movement?"

"An idle question."

"It's not an idle question." Ohannes wanted to add that it was Panos' head that was idle but did not wish to be impolite. "It's not idle; just answer it and you will see that it isn't an idle question."

"What shall I answer?" Panos was clearly beginning to get annoyed.

"Is revolution for men, or are men for revolution?"

"Not men – say an Armenian, a Vanetsi."

"Isn't a Vanetsi a man?"

"No, a Vanetsi is a Vanetsi. What is 'a man' compared with a Vanetsi?"

"No, no, Baron Panos, it won't do, you're mixing up the issues."

"Let it be my function to mix up everything."

"Very well, if you don't want to, I'll answer for you. Revolutions, or national movements, or call them what you like, are for people to live in security, to live and enjoy a dignified life. Do you understand?"

"Certainly I understand. You're singing another song, one that doesn't suit Armenians or people of Van. Your song works fine only for the great – united, wealthy and secure – nations, for the free sons of those nations. Do you understand?"

Ohannes was confused. He felt that his position was shaky. He could so easily adopt Panos' position – yes, even pleasurably – and could pour scorn on his own argument. He wondered whether it was indeed the time to speak of living and enjoying life. After all, could he not hear the sound of the guns and see the plight of the starving people, did he not feel how Van was poised on the brink of a precipice? What was this glimmer of light he was talking about?

In order to ease the heavy atmosphere of such an obvious defeat, Ohannes wanted to treat Panos to some raki. It was surprising, however, that he felt some awkwardness in calling Vergine to bring it. Why? Was he afraid of Panos? Who? He, Ohannes? Of Panos? No, why should he be? He was not afraid of Ishkhan or Aram, so now why should he be afraid of Panos? No, of course, he was not afraid. But perhaps he was ashamed or shy. But to tell the truth, why should Ohannes be ashamed before Panos? Did he depend on him, or did he live at his expense? He neither relied on him, nor needed his bread and water.

Ohannes gathered all his courage, but nobody ever knew whether he would have called Vergine again or Satenik, because at that moment Satenik herself came in.

"Satenik – let me die for you – bring raki and something to eat."

With no shooting going on, life seemed not to have changed at all. The old friends were sitting and drinking raki, chewing pasterma and soudjuk. Kevork would appear in the doorway a little later, and Mkho's tired and kindly face would turn up in the yard. Simon would enter and exclaim 'mashallah!' Mkho would say that business was going well, and Ohannes would go to the market in the morning.

But nothing was left, neither the village, nor Mkho, nor the shop, nor Baron Simon. Only the starving and struggling Van remained, with a jug buried under the pear tree and nothing else. Was there really nothing else left? Vergine came out of the larder. Ohannes could feel happy in his mind, but could he smile in his mind? Yes, Ohannes did smile in his mind: only this one sin of his last year was left. But then he became sad again as he could tell no one about either the jug in a hole, or Vergine dragged out of a hole. Yes, dragged out of a hole into the sun, where she had flourished day after day and blossomed like a rose garden. It could not now be said that she had gone to seed. No, Vergine now looked like a garden which had been weeded, cultivated, and taken care of. Ohannes realised all this but could not tell Panos about it even if he drank seven bottles of raki and wine. He could not. And it was but a thief's pleasure when he could not shout about it all over the world.

"Let's drink, Baron Ohannes, to our miserable Van and its honourable –"

The speech was interrupted. Instead of Kevork, Mkho, or Simon, several live and active men of Van appeared. They were collecting for the Supply Agency. They had come to ask for flour and meat.

"I have no meat," said Ohannes. "My animals remained in the village. My servant Usep and my white donkey have already been taken over by Simon Hovivian. Flour? How many sacks?"

"At least forty."

"I haven't so much. Twenty?"

"Thirty-five."

"Twenty-five."

They settled on thirty. Two carts arrived, the small door of the large granary was opened, thirty sacks were filled with flour and placed on the carts which then moved off.

The collecting group went on to the Houssians.

"Do you see now where we've got to?" Panos said, when Ohannes returned to his seat wiping his brow with his red handkerchief.

"I saw that long ago," murmured Ohannes.

"Nevertheless, you have just prolonged Van's life for a few more hours."

"For a few hours?"

"Well what do you expect? We've thousands of refugees, fighters, and wounded men. Take up your glass, let's drink and see what will come of it."

Panos had not moved from his place when the collecting group arrived; moreover, he had downed one or two glasses of raki in Ohannes' absence. He felt safe from the demands of the collecting group, for he knew that they were only gathering food, and that he – as the Holy Sign of Varag was his witness – had provision for only one or two months. He did have a few carpets in his house but why would they take them? To spread them under the feet of Yekarian and his soldiers to help them fight well? They could also have some ringing gold pieces, but who would give anything for gold in this besieged situation? If you put a sack of barley on one side of a refugee and a sack of gold on the other, he would take the barley and ignore the gold.

"Very well, let's drink. But the situation is grave, Baron Panos."

Panos (who, as we now know) was already in a cheerful mood began to sing in a loud and hoarse voice:

"Oh, you friend of scorched hearts,
Sing, nightingale, sing from the hill..."

'This man is stony-hearted,' thought Ohannes, 'this man will never die.'

Panos continued his song, awakening a kind of envy in Ohannes. At last, the song came to an end and the two honourable men of Van drained their glasses.

"And what will be the end of it all?" Ohannes was absorbed in his thoughts.

"Neither I nor even Yekarian know what the end will be. Only God knows what will happen at the end. If Uncle doesn't come, we won't be able to hold out."

"Yes, but is Uncle much concerned about us?"

"Not about us, but Uncle has its interests here," said Panos. "Who are the Turks to go against the Russians? O God, give strength and power to our fighters until Uncle can come!"

"Amen. May I be the only one who doesn't want that. They say Armenian groups are coming as well."

"Of course. Can there be a war without Armenians? Armenians have enrolled as volunteers."

At that moment, something surprising happened.

This is not a work of psychological research and analysis; we do not swim well enough to dive into the deep and bottomless sea, the clear and at the same time muddy sea called Ohannes Muradkhanian. We will confine ourselves only to registering this shocking — yes, shocking – fact. The fact was that while Panos was busy singing the tender song 'Kind, nice, and honest friend of man', and Ohannes was swaying to the rhythm of the song and in the mist of his own raki, Satenik and Vergine came out of the pantry together and quietly left the tantun. Ohannes looked after them with eyes agog. It was the first time he had seen them together, separate from everyone else and so close to each other. Something welled up in his throat. He wanted to say something but he could not; he wanted to take a deep breath, but could not do that either. Suddenly, he burst into tears. Panos, taken unawares, saw his tears flow down his cheeks and wet his moustache.

"Ohannes – oh, my soul – what's up?" exclaimed Panos, embracing his old friend. "Have you had a dream, or have you gone mad?"

"There's nothing special, nothing," said Ohannes, wiping his eyes and moustache with the red handkerchief and sniffling like a child. "I didn't understand either. My mother, Hampartsoum, Kevork, Mkho ..."

"It won't do, Baron Ohannes, it won't do. A man is created to face up to and bear all his troubles. Why do you think they sing, 'I haven't lost my hope, Amidst the foamy waves'?"

Later, on a day just like this one, when Panos had again come to his old friend, when the bottle of raki had already been half-emptied; when all the issues relating to the difficult situation had been examined; when, as usual, Vergine had cast passionate glances from the doorway of the larder across Panos' back towards Ohannes, to his considerable pleasure; when Panos had asked Ohannes for two sacks of flour to check on his love and friendship and had received an indefinite reply; when Ohannes had opened the Bible to reveal some surprising things, such as 'live today for tomorrow we die ... a man should not die ignorant'; Panos suddenly asked:

"Don't you notice anything, Baron Ohannes?"

"No. What is there to notice?"

"The bombardment has stopped."

Ohannes, who had not noticed that important thing because of his inner turmoil, cocked his ears.

"Shooting has been spasmodic since morning, and now there's none at all," said Panos and added, "It's a bad sign."

"It is. What's going to happen?"

"An overall offensive by the Turks. They're getting ready."

"It may not happen."

"Why may it not happen? They aren't going to fight for a thousand years, are they?"

"And what has it been so far if not an overall attack," Ohannes said.

"It has been a fight only, a partial fight."

"I don't understand."

At that moment, Set appeared in the doorway. He came forward with an inexplicable smile on his face and asked, "Haven't you heard the news?"

"An overall offensive?" Panos jumped up from his place like a spring.

"What offensive? The Turks have fled."

Ohannes did not move. The first thought that flashed across his mind was that Vergine would have to return home. She had alighted on Ohannes' shoulder like a pigeon, like a bird from a fairy tale, and given him the bitter-sweet taste of forbidden fruit. And now?

"Are you trying to say that the Armenians have won?" Ohannes slowly stood up.

"They held out," Set replied, "the Russian army and the Armenian volunteer forces are approaching. Lake Van is no longer blue, it has become white. We could hold out till –"

"Why has the sea become white?" Panos was frightened.

"Because of the offensive, perhaps" said Ohannes, though he himself also wondered why the sea should get white.

"Because of the sails of their boats. The Turks are sailing away towards Bitlis."

"Turks to Bitlis, Armenians to Tiflis," said Ohannes.

"What have the Armenians got to do in Tiflis?" Panos was worried.

"I said it to rhyme," said Ohannes. He called out for Satenik, and then turned to Panos: "How many sacks of flour did you want?"

Panos did not reply, and Satenik came in.

"Satenik, bring me my best suit. Now Baron Panos, tell me how many sacks do you want?"

"For God's sake, is this a good time to discuss flour?" Panos tried to avoid the question. Satenik stood amazed. She looked at the guests' faces trying to understand her husband's extraordinary request. Everyone was smiling.

"Tell me what's going on," she said.

"Bring me my best suit – I'm yours forever. The Turks have fled."

Chapter 25

Van was free at last. It was bellowing like a horse that has been locked up in a sunless stable and become accustomed to the dark, but which is now free and standing on its hind legs with its eyes blinking in the sun and its nostrils filled with fresh, exhilarating air. Like a head wounded and bleeding in some supernatural massacre, the sun was searching for a place to rest. The white sails of the Turkish ships were sailing away to the west to be blessed with the last bleeding rays of the sun. To the west, to the west.

The guns and cannons were silent. On this sixteenth day of May in 1915, there were no more bullets flying through the air. It was, instead, full of spontaneous cries, songs, congratulations and condolences, as people streamed to the Command Centre to learn what they already knew, to be assured of what had already been confirmed, to grasp the miracle.

Something new rippled through the excited gardens. The fortress overlooking the town from Toprak-Kale, which only the previous day had spread terror from the muzzles of its cannons and smaller guns, was suddenly ablaze. There was no smoke, or perhaps it was invisible, only a huge flame burning like a chandelier or a torch. It was a fiery symbol of freedom, achieved at the cost of many lives.

Van was shouting in one voice: "The fort is burning."

Yekarian came out of the headquarters, he was animated and smiling. Seeing the gathered crowd, he narrowed his eyes in the way people do when looking into the sun. Perhaps the people knew what he was trying to say above all the noise. "Long live free Van," they shouted. "Long live our free Van," screamed the women and the children.

Here were the fighters: they were no longer carrying their weapons to fight with but just to impress. Here, led by Dr Sanfani, were the Red Cross nurses and the children with curly hair who had acted as messengers – they all looked significantly thin. Here were the heroic sappers who had maintained the barricades and defense posts; the ramparts they had built could have enclosed the town several times. They were led by Shavarsh Hovivian, and among them was Ohannes' servant, Usep, and his exhausted, white, horse-like donkey – or perhaps it was a donkey-like horse. The band began playing the song of the Italian girl, *To the centre of the town*.

The men who had fought in the two parts of Van met up on the wide avenue connecting the city centre and Aikesdan. These unshaven men who had been as strong and steadfast as a rock the previous day, now kissed each other, cried like children, and roared with deafening laughter. Mihrtad Mirzakhanian was there, with Haig Gossoyan and Haroutioun Nergarian, as well as Mardiros Maroutian, who was cheerfully waving his long arms as he recounted an episode of the struggle.

"Four of us were sitting at our post at midnight, drinking brandy. We drank glass after glass. We were raising and clinking glasses when, suddenly, a shell hit our post, the earth from the roof fell down on us and, moreover, into the glasses. But we didn't take any notice and drank up. We then picked up our rifles and shot two snipers who were firing from the fort."

"It was teacher Yesnig," Mihrtad gently corrected him.

"Does that make any difference." The whole group burst out laughing, and Mardiros laughed loudest.

A large crowd was gathered at the fort on Toprak-Kale. The mythical giant, Mher, peered down from his stony perch and seemed not to be believing his eyes. Sahag Djankoyan climbed up the fort with his long, ostrich-like legs and placed the Armenian flag on its highest point. There was a loud and exultant cry: "Long live free Vaspourakan!"

Panos Terlemezian, the painter, climbed onto a rock; he was himself like a piece of rock as he spoke. He noted the grandeur of this historical moment. He recalled Haik Nahabed, Vartan Mamigonian, and Khrimian Hairig. He said the defenders of Van were tigers, eagles, hawks, as well as other animals and birds famous for their courage and steadfastness, ending with the ant. "Over the centuries, a Vanetsi has like a diligent and hard-working ant . . . " His speech received thunderous applause and more cries of 'Long live free Vaspourakan!'.

Then a short priest stood up – who else but teacher Yesnig? He called the enemy bloody beasts, hyenas, wild vultures, which had over the centuries, and so on. "But today, the eagle of freedom is flying over Van and Vaspourakan. Van will endure, and it can't help enduring, because the blood of Chaldeans and Urartians flows in its veins."

Thereupon a Chaldean and Urartian rejoicing sprang up, the crowd was excited and Van celebrated its victory late into the night. The reserved stocks of wine were opened; the rich got drunk with wine and raki, while the poor, joined by the refugees, moved into the abandoned Turkish districts.

Roses were blooming in the gardens of Van. There was a time when red, pink, white, and yellow roses always flowered in season, and when the scent of marjoram spread like incense in a church. There was such a time. But now the roses were blooming again. Could there be a spring without roses? But nobody looked at them and they were angry. The roses did not care for this indifference and inattention: they were angry, and perhaps it was this that made them seem even more red.

What has happened to you, my beautiful, but mourning Van? Believe it or not, there are no Turks left, no Djevdet, no Agyah. The homes of the Turks, rich and poor, are empty today, as are the government buildings and the barracks that were spreading terror yesterday. The six Armenian vilayets are being trampled on. People are being massacred without remorse – women and children, masters and servants. Hundreds of thousands are being killed, hundreds of thousands are being robbed and deported, to be slaughtered in the valleys, ravines and gorges ... lest the towns be contaminated, lest the plague devouring the bleeding hordes spreads death and destruction.

But you are free! Long live freedom, now, always and forever! A plague upon you!

And, what is even more surprising, God himself sees how the churches in the towns and villages, as well as the monasteries and sanctuaries, have suffered so much criminal barbarity, yet he does not intervene. No, his ears do not hear the cries of the millions of dying victims, and his nose does not smell the blood. Nor does the smoke of the burning towns and villages reach his long, white beard.

Having slipped out of sight, Mihran Manasserian slapped his knee-high boot with his cane and entered the home of a Turk. It was a one-and-a-half-storeyed house. The rooms were full of empty trunks, pieces of wool and cotton, battered furniture, broken crockery, rusted garden tools, and some old slippers lay about here and there. There was a worn-out saddle in the corner of the yard and a twisted bucket by the well – the rope had been probably taken away.

Mihran came out into the street. He went from house to house always hoping to find a better one. He did not notice how he had reached the former Turkish barracks. There was a notice stuck – perhaps with dough – on one of the doors. He went up to read it. 'Honoured compatriots, this house belongs to Hagop Kandoyan. Do not burn it.' He smiled and carried on. But Mihran was tired of wandering from one house to another. He realised that he was not going round the houses, climbing up stairs and seeing what household goods were left in the rooms, just because he wanted to find a house for himself.

He stood for a long time in a corner in one house. There was something shining on the floor; he bent down and picked it up. It was a button, perhaps a beautiful woman's button. Perhaps Nana had lived in this very house with her husband Kamal, the district governor of Hayots Dzor. What evidence was there? Could a single button serve as evidence for such a conclusion? Of course, not! He felt something soft touch his feet, even through his knee-high boots. He trembled, well, almost trembled. It was a white house-cat, a shaggy cat with one eye yellow and the other blue. It was a Van cat, but it had belonged to a Turk He picked it up, it was heavy but well-groomed. He looked at its eyes, and he saw Nana! Mihran pocketed the shiny button, left the abandoned house with the cat in his arms, and went home.

On the following day, and on the days after that, Nana followed Mihran like a dog. Mihran had not been involved in the fighting in any way, except for the fact that the carts that came by regularly to collect the dead, stopped twice at his house and left loaded up. He had been terrified of the idea of being in one of the defense posts. Of course, if Aram had been in charge of the fighting, he would have gone to him for some suitable work as a clerk, store-keeper or something like that. He did not know Gaidsag Arakel or Grigor Bulgaretsi personally at all. If he had gone to Yekarian with such a request he would have been mocked and dishonoured. While there had been a united front rather than separate parties, the fact was that there was nothing Mihran could have done. There would have been those who would have killed him right there in the post during the fighting and nobody would have been able to establish whether he had been killed by another Armenian rather than the enemy.

No, there was nothing Mihran could do. He had sentenced himself to house arrest. In short, he had deserted. This man, a sworn Dashnak, Aram Pasha's trusted henchman, the head of the Hayots Dzor committee, the owner of the Khek monastery and its land as well as other properties, had deserted! Mihran, who had never baulked at anything for the cause, and who had widowed his sister and orphaned her children, could see no way forward for himself. During the days of gunfire, the bullets pierced his heart. This feeling was especially acute during the first days of the fighting. Then he gradually got used to the serious situation. He recalled his life in detail, examined it and arrived at a dreadful conclusion.

His Ramgavar tenants, Hmayak and Armenak Sossoyan, were rarely at home, they were serving at different defense posts. Karmileh worked in the sewing workshop; she went out in the morning and returned home in the evening. Mihran locked himself in his room; he would go down to eat something and then return to his den. His bed was unmade. Karmileh was busy and so was his mother – or the Grand Mother, as she was called by everyone and especially by her orphaned grandchildren. She was sitting in a corner of the tantun, knitting one of her endless socks. Burdened with sad thoughts, she would from time to time look up at the logs burning in the hearth and murmur, "May the good Lord grant us peace!"

The trouble began the very day the Dashnak leaders – Ishkhan, Aram, Goms – came to Van. If they had not, Mihran would not have lost himself and misfortune would not have come to his house. There is nothing more to be said: tyranny is tyranny and it was decided that Armenians be eaten up. But with so many innocent victims, who was there left to live and fight?

The Grand Mother thought of her son-in-law; then she heard Mihran's dry cough from the room upstairs and she became confused. All Van, young and old, had stood to a man against the Turks, and yet her Mihran was afraid to leave the house. She understood very well why Mihran had chosen this shameful course, but the question was how had it happened. "May the day never dawn," she murmured, and her needles began to move more rapidly.

– If only he got married. If he were married, he'd be shamed by his wife and he'd go to the posts. He'd be better dead than a coward. Ishkhan is dead, and who now thinks about what happened at Aghtamar? Those who had perished there had been forgiven, they'd become saints. –

Karmileh, too, had changed. The first cool wind blew in when she learned that they had asked for Muradkhanian's daughter and had been refused. And when she learned on the third day of the fighting that Mihran had locked himself up in his room instead of going to the posts, her hair stood on end. There were rumours in the town that Mihran yearned for her, but the truth was that

Mihran did not want to see Karmileh at all. He had gone mad because of his desperate and difficult situation.

Yes, that was the truth. And it was also true that the Grand Mother, knowing her son's greediness, was frightened when she heard that some weak-willed men had become thieves since the departure of the Turks. She decided that no wickedly stolen goods should enter the house, and prepared herself for persistent argument with her own son. She relaxed when Mihran came home in the evening with a pretty cat in his arms.

The arrival of the Russian army and its Armenian volunteer brigades was splendid and astonishing. Even the stone statues of the bride and bridegroom at the Ak-Küpri rock seemed more solemn. There were no sculptors in the province, the only sculptor was nature. The people had gathered there, on the wide road to Shabagh, in the field where in more peaceful days horse races used to be held several times a year.

The people had come here again. The traditional drums and flutes were playing loudly, and the military band of the college was standing by. The whole staff of the arms-manufacturing workshop, led by Grigor Bulgaretsi, was here. Grigor himself was standing like a guard of honour beside the first – and the last – cannon that he had designed in Van. It was known to have had little effect on the fighting, and seemed rather to have been made for peacetime celebrations. It never did more than make a thunderous noise.

Dust rose in the distance on the wide road below Shabagh. What did that mean? The sea of people stirred. At last, the cavalry came into sight, and then the clatter of hooves was heard. There were four riders in the first row – Ozali, the Russian colonel, with Khecho, an armed priest, and a fifteen-year-old volunteer – and the cavalry squadron followed behind.

Aram, Yekarian, Arakel and Bulgaretsi, stepped forward. Oza,li, Khecho and the priest dismounted and greeted them. Just as they were doing so, the band roared, the cannon thundered, and the crowd shouted in unison. There was such a hubbub that the Ak-Küpri rock shook and the bride and bridegroom embraced each other even more tightly. Ozali and Khecho shook hands with Aram, congratulating him on the victorious liberation of Van. "A Vanetsi and the men of Van rescued the town," said Aram. "There are the men of Van," he pointed to the crowd, "and here is the Vanetsi – Armenak Yekarian, our military leader."

The Armenian priest then raised his hand and blessed the people. The cavalry set off and the people followed them, together with the cannon which had accomplished its honourable duty. They came to Aikesdan, where they were greeted with great excitement and joy by the men and women standing on both sides of the wide avenue and by the children who had climbed up trees.

That is how things were. Hagop Kandoyan could not control his tears; he grabbed Ohannes' arm and through his tears said: "What a time this is." Ohannes thought that Hagop wanted to know what time it was and began to pull his watch out of his pocket. His hand was already on the chain, when Hagop clarified the matter: "This is an unforgettable moment in Armenian history!" And he wiped his eyes with his handkerchief.

The Van Government. The college of the French Dominicans was honoured to be the seat of government in Van. According to the evidence of later historians – evidence which is consistent with the truth – this two-storey building, with its long balcony, was to the east of the Hamud Agha barracks, which had been blown up by the Armenians. To locate the building more precisely, it should be added that it was on the eastern corner of Santi Street and Khatch Street, opposite the Yeramian school and the house of its owner, Hampartsoum Yeramian. This historical building was not far from the deceased Vramian's house and just opposite it was the Gir bookstore, whose front – the reader might recall – was decorated with a huge pen. Nobody knew where that pen was now, but it was being said that Grigor Bulgaretsi had thrown it into a large cauldron and had melted it down when making his famous cannon.

To be brief. Later historians would describe each detail of the former Dominican college, now the seat of the government. They would even count the stairs leading to the second floor of the building not forgetting to mention that the fifteenth stair was a little askew – though not visibly so to the naked eye.

Nikolayev, the major-general of the Imperial Russian army, confirmed the appointment of the Russian-Armenian Aram as a provisional governor of the region round Van. When the people read the order pinned up on the walls of the schools and churches of the town, they eventually considered this to be both natural and reasonable.

"Wasn't there anyone else? Let a Vanetsi be the governor of Van."

"Yes, Aram is a revolutionary. We need an experienced national politician here. Not Yekarian – he's a military man. Someone like Avetis Terzibashian should be the governor."

"But it's clearly mentioned in the order. Russian-Armenian Aram. The governor of the country occupied by the Russian army, should be either a Russian or a Russian-Armenian. It's natural and reasonable."

The argument was convincing. Aram's appointment gradually came to be seen as natural, reasonable and, above all, inevitable.

The following newly-formed departments were to be found in this seat of government, which was in fact nothing other than a regional administrative centre: Police (to arrest and set criminals free); Legal (to judge Armenians); Agriculture (to find out how many male peasants had survived); Refugees (its function is clear); Urban (to rebuild the burnt houses). Even a jail was created in one of the cellars of the building, though here were some difficulties in appointing a warden, nobody wanted to be a prison guard.

Autonomy for Van. A government for Van.

Day and night, the yard was full of locals and peasants from the villages The provincial government and all its departments were working at full stretch. As provincial governor, Aram felt that a narrow political approach to the appointment of officials could have destructive consequences, so he appointed people irrespective of their party affiliations. The Ramgavars said sarcastically that he had at last recovered his wits. The Dashnaks murmured that he had lost his appetite for revolution.

Aram had already heard the first vague rumours of a Russian retreat, when as he was sitting in his study one day reading some reports about the properties left by the Turks, Mihran entered and stood at the door.

"What's up, Mihran?" The governor looked up casually as if they had met the day before.

Mihran felt encouraged. "Baron Aram, what orders do you have for me? Should I look into the matter of the monastery?"

Aram carefully looked at Mihran's gaunt face. 'What naiveté,' he thought, 'let's make the man happy for at least one or two more days.'

"What a question!" he said aloud. "The monastery is yours, and it will remain yours. Just do whatever's necessary."

Mihran thanked him and rushed out, somewhat surprised. He hurried home. He had shut Nana up in his room to stop her following him She met him joyfully. An inspired Mihran spoke enthusiastically to his mother about his conversation with Aram. The Grand Mother listened to him, and rejoiced in her son's happiness, but when she was alone, she shook her head incredulously. She felt there was something evil going on, and, in order to get rid of her grave thoughts, she called out, "Nana, you black-hearted cat, come and eat." Nana approached her like a modest bride.

Chapter 26

Ohannes was sitting on the rich carpet in the high kiosk looking over Aikesdan, leaning back on the soft cushions and smoking his usual narghileh. The summer sun was shining over the gardens. The sun's rays had fallen on the triangular crystal pendants round the large lamp hanging from the ceiling and their reflections had fallen on the opposite wall in the seven colours of the rainbow. If you touched the hanging lamp with a finger, it would swing and the rainbow on the wall would move as well.

Little by little, day by day, Ohannes' life, together with that of Van as a whole, had returned to its old routine. The refugees had returned to their villages. The Assyrians had departed from Ohannes' stable, having lost two of their members. Vergine and Satenik dug and sowed the flowerbeds and set out the chairs in the rose-garden. Usep and the white donkey began working again. A cart in the outer yard, that had come from the village long before, was still there. Mkho had brought it several years before. He had left the old cart there, purchased a new one and gone back to the village. Ohannes could not now look at that cart without bringing back to mind the unlucky Mkho, his family, Ermants, and even his mother.

"Take away that cart, I don't want to see it," he ordered Usep.

"What shall I do with it?"

"Burn it, take it away. I don't want to see it any more."

Usep, being a peasant and knowing well the value of the cart, dragged it under the shed, covered it with grass and thus Ohannes did not see it any more.

Lia and Souren arranged the flower garden of the big yard. Bullets had made several holes in the wooden walls of the kiosk. Souren suggested closing those holes in some way, but Ohannes did not agree, saying that they would be better left, to let in fresh air.

The most difficult of all the problems was the matter of Vergine. On the third or fourth day after the war was over, Vergine knelt before Ohannes when giving him his coffee, embraced his knees and said with tears in her eyes:

"Master, shall I go away?"

"Where to?" asked Ohannes, knowing very well where.

"To our house."

"Do you really want to go?" said Ohannes, touching Vergine's hair with his moustache.

"No, I don't."

"What can I say, my girl? Try to get Satenik's support, you've already got mine." Ohannes was surprised at what he said, wondering what Satenik might say if she had heard him.

Vergine went away without another word. Ohannes did not really need to tell her what to do. She had behaved like this from the very first day. She called Satenik 'Hanum', she had undertaken all the hard work and did her best to satisfy Satenik. And it was obvious, as Ohannes once realised, that this was like the saying that people kiss the child to please the mother – and he was the mother in this case.

The same evening, when the couple were alone, Satenik asked him whether Vergine had said anything.

"No, what's up?" Ohannes tried to sound casual.

"She said she had spoken to you and you had agreed."

"To what?" Ohannes became a bit anxious.

"She wants to go home."

Ohannes breathed a sigh of relief. "Yes, she did mention that, but my mind was busy. But to tell the truth, the girl is right. The war is over so everybody can go back to their own home."

"Home, what home? Her house is worthless. Let her stay at our house, she doesn't lack anything here. Take pity on me, I'm so busy with all the household chores."

"I don't know," said Ohannes wiping his brow with his handkerchief. "You two decide. I won't interfere with women's affairs."

"Is that all you can say? You're the head of the house, tell her in a few words to stay. To tell the truth, although she isn't very likeable, she is very good at housework."

So the problem which had been so tricky for Ohannes was resolved in a flash. And now, he was smoking his usual narghileh with his eyes on the rainbow on the wall. He was thinking that if anyone had told him two months before that in two months he would have neither Mkho, nor Kevork, nor the shop, nor Ermants, and that the Turks would kill Simon on the road to the town centre, while he would be sitting in his kiosk and smoking his narghile, he would have said to that man: "Go away, you dog, do you think I'm a beast or a man without any feelings to be able to sit down after all that and smoke my narghileh. If such things really happened, I'd throw myself into the sea and become food for the fish." Ohannes would have answered like that, but now, after all, he was indeed sitting and smoking his narghileh. People were right when they said that even a dog would not be able to endure what a man can endure.

He had no plan for the day. He did not go to the town to have a look at the burnt-out market. It never crossed his mind even to think of restoring his shop. Let Panos do that if he wanted to. Maybe he would go to Ermants, to see what had been sown in the autumn and whether it was worth continuing that work. Ohannes had an entirely different, exceptional plan. After the Russians came, the town was filled with Russian sugar, soap and various kinds of cigarettes. Russian money – banknotes and silver coins – appeared, and even Russian gold. According to Set, Turkish gold was more valuable than Russian. Ohannes often went into the garden for a stroll, and he would pass by that pear tree, look there, and feel better and safer.

There were also some new kind of caps received from Russia that were called 'kepi'or something like that. Everybody threw away their fezzes and put the new caps on. Ohannes could understand almost everything, but not this. Could there be a Vanetsi without a fez? No, Ohannes could throw away his head, but not his fez.

The war was a cursed thing; what good fortune that it was over and that Van could breathe again. Ohannes and Satenik could also breathe again. Now they were again sleeping in the upper room. But what a combination of joy and sadness he felt, recalling the terrible and dark nights spent in the scanty tantun. War and peace were different things, but there was a difference in the difference, thought Ohannes, and his narghileh gurgled more deeply.

The song, *A rose has blossomed*, was heard from the yard. Lia, usually so sad, was singing.

> "O pretty one with your thorns, whose are you,
> The world knows, everyone knows, you are mine."

Ohannes reflected:

– That's not true. The truth is that not everyone knows that you are mine. You need to know how to fit the right words, like the poets Bedros Tourian or Ghevond Alishan. 'Let my soul burn in pain at least you'll know I'm still alive.' Well done, Tourian, well done! –

Nobody knew where Ohannes might have reached with his literary explorations, if Hagop Kandoyan's voice had not been heard from the yard asking for him. His footsteps were heard coming up. and he appeared in the doorway. "Mashallah! A pigeon was asked where the best place in the world was and it answered that it's nest was. You have done it up well."

It should be made clear that Hagop was also gifted with the ability to fit the words to the occasion. Instead of saying it was the dog that was asked, he had said it was the pigeon. It is not known whether Ohannes knew the original version of this fable or not, but even if he knew it, he must have been impressed since not everyone would have had such a quick wit to change the old-established folk proverb. On the other hand, perhaps Ohannes did not think so, because he made a sour face and said:

"That may be a proverb that fits its teller more than its listener."

"I wish it were so, I wish it were. You know very well, Baron Ohannes, that I am a man without a house and home. Even a dog wouldn't live in the hovel where I live. I had just taken over a Turk's house, but now the municipality wants to take it back from me. Is this humane?"

"Have a seat, Baron Hagop, have a seat," Ohannes said gently. He stood up, leant out of the window and called, "Vergine, Satenik, Lia," and sat down again. Hagop sat down opposite him and pulled his beads out of his pocket.

Vergine entered like a rose that had just blossomed that morning.

"Vergine, my girl, coffee!"

After Vergine had gone out followed by his glance, Hagop said, almost indifferently, "So, she's been staying here?"

"Satenik wouldn't let her leave," said Ohannes with nearly the same pretence of indifference, and he yawned to make his unconcern more convincing.

"I would tell you that we live in a period of real turmoil. You know that man, Mihrtad Ptotian? He and his family used to spend their day eating only bread and cheese. But now, he's one of the seven richest men in Van, with antique carpets, rolls of silk, gold plates, golden bracelets, ear-rings, and rings from houses abandoned by the Turks –"

Ohannes interrupted: "The last can't be true."

"Why?"

"Because you're not a child. How foolish it would be for a Turk to leave golden bracelets, ear-rings and rings in the house for Ptotian to come and take them for himself. The lady of the house would have put the bracelets on her arms, the ear-rings on her ears and the rings on her fingers, and only then would the family have left the house and escaped."

Hagop had not thought about it that way, but he did not back down.

"Ohannes, you are a surprising man. Was the Turkish woman going to the theatre to see *Ancient Gods*, to be putting bracelets on her arms, ear-rings on her ears and rings on her fingers. No it seems they've left everything in that turmoil and fled."

"All right, I admit it. Go on," said Ohannes, giving way.

"What I want to say is that many poor people got hold of some property, a house perhaps or some gardens. Why not? The more a Vanetsi has, the better for Van and our own honour. Now you might say that it's none of my business."

"No, I wouldn't say that."

"Good for you! We have seen many problems arise due to indifference. If everyone was to say that it was none of their business and looked the other way, Van would become like Sodom and Gomorrah."

"You're quite right."

"Now, I also want to ask another question. Do I have the right to a house?"

Vergine entered with the steaming coffee cups. Hagop took his coffee and, trying to catch Vergine's eye, said more loudly:

"Don't I have the right to end my loneliness and have a house. The years are passing by and what does our municipality do about it."

"What does our municipality do about what?" Ohannes answered with a question of his own and wondered what was going on.

Hagop Kandoyan had had no noticeable achievements in his life. He had been lonely, and if his home, referred to by him as a hovel, had been set on fire and burnt down, there would be no smell of burning. However, like any other Vanetsi he was not devoid of cunning, practical sense. Oh no, Hagop was not one to build his house on sand. If he had decided to visit Ohannes and deliberately start a conversation about all his personal concerns and his wish to get married in such a way that Vergine could hear him, you can be sure that he had very clear reasons for pressing on with the matter in the hope of a successful conclusion.

However, the confused reader might well ask what reason could Hagop possibly have had for thinking that he might be successful with Vergine. Well, the fact is that Hagop was aware of many matters that the reader does not know about. For instance, the reader is not aware of what happened between them the day he was sent by Ohannes to bring the newly-widowed Vergine back to Ohannes' house.

On that remarkable day, when Hagop went to accomplish that mission, he expected to see Vergine bent over in grief, and so he had prepared a speech in his mind to console the unfortunate widow. To be on the safe side, he chose the path that led through the gardens and entered Vergine's small room without any warning. As expected, he did indeed find Vergine bent over, but not in any way due to grief. She was bent down over an old trunk which was open and was picking out some things. She was barefooted. She straightened up, turned and looked at the guest calmly. Hagop saw a woman before him capable of arousing great temptation and disturbing thoughts, rather than one exhausted by sadness. His consoling speech flew out of his mind; instead he loudly said he had come to take her.

"Where?" Vergine asked with a mischievous smile.

"To our house." The words came not from his mouth but from his heart.

"I wish you had a house and could indeed take me there, Baron Hagop." said Vergine sadly thinking to herself that here was but a featherless rooster.

Something broke inside him and crumbled, but he controlled himself and told her of Ohannes' wishes and the purpose of his arrival. Vergine's eyes burnt with joy while Hagop became a bit sad. Then Vergine, quite deliberately ignoring Hagop's presence, began to take some things out of the trunk, while Hagop looked on thinking to himself that she was deliberately ignoring him in order to stimulate his attention. She tried some things on and packed some clothes. Then she shut the door and they both set off through the gardens. Vergine heartily breathed in the fresh air of spring in Aikesdan and smiled to herself, thinking that it was all coming out like a dream that Baron Ohannes had sent for her. Then she remembered Satenik, and a cloud passed over her, but she decided that she would need to be very sweet and tender with Satenik.

The gardens blossomed as they did every year and flourished while ignoring both the war and all the human troubles. Old men and women were digging up the earth here and there, sowing seeds and planting vegetables and various kinds of flowers. The earth smelled sweet and warm like a baby that has been washed and wrapped in clean, white linen. Hagop's heart was full of a vague desire which after all was perfectly explicable. Of course, such a thing could happen only once in a thousand years. Hagop was walking through the gardens of Van with a beautiful and widowed woman by his side. Everything was just right for him to open his heart to Vergine who was perfumed like this garden. He was ready to tell her surprising and incredible words in such a way that she would sit down on the flower-bed in excitement, and Hagop would throw his stick away on the grass and kneel before her, caressing her knees with his grey moustache.

But this dream was entirely spoilt by all the gunfire. If there had been no shots and a decent, solemn silence had reigned, allowing the birds' singing and the nightingale's warble to be heard, Hagop could have worked wonders. But no one would want to listen to his yearning words in all this thunder.

Hagop occasionally walked behind Vergine in order to admire her figure. When they had already gone half of the way, he was able to say. "So, let's be logical. If I did have a house, would you come to live with me?"

Vergine's thoughts were far away. She was drawing up a plan for her future life. Thinking that her silence was due to her shyness and to help her to reply, Hagop said, "Well, wouldn't it be good?"

"Why not," said Vergine, probably answering her own thoughts rather than Hagop's. "Why not?" she repeated and quickened her steps so that Hagop could hardly keep up with her.

Hagop was certainly not a man to start on anything awkward or to build a house on sand. He would not, without encouragement, have raised the issue in such a way that Vergine could overhear.

Hagop took up his coffee and continued, "The municipality has decided to take over all the empty houses. Any further looting is strictly forbidden, so why should they be concerned about my home."

"So you can't have anything?"

"Why should I lose everything, Baron Ohannes. I'm currently homeless, but I'm not entirely neglected. Lawyer Hrant Kaligian told me that the municipality know that I have decided to end my celibate state and that I will therefore want to have a house and a family, and so my circumstances will be taken into account."

"What else do you need?" said Ohannes, " I'll pay all the expenses of your wedding party."

Hagop went straight to seventh heaven. Meanwhile, Vergine gathered the empty glasses and went downstairs.

To avoid any further misunderstanding, it should be quickly added that it had not even occured to Ohannes that Hagop had already chosen not only his future house, but also who was to be the lady of that house, nobody else but … As for Hagop himself, he had the impression that Vergine must have whispered in Satenik's ear, and Satenik in Ohannes' ear, about Hagop's serious intentions regarding Vergine. Yet Vergine had never considered Hagop as a mate; she would have preferred the Ak-Küpri statue to be her bridegroom rather than Kandoyan. She did not even remember the words she had said in her house or when walking back through the gardens – words which had deprived Hagop of sleep. But now he would sleep without any more worries, because Ohannes had even promised to bear the expenses of his wedding party.

After all this, could there be any more doubt that Hagop was not a man to lie in a damp bed or build his house on sand, or that he was imagining a situation which did not in fact exist?

The conversation continued with references to the affairs of the Armenian government and the everyday life of the town.

"Aram's guards have long faces," said Hagop, "and to tell the truth they have a right to."

"Why?"

"Why? All the other soldiers have been paid and become rich while, because they were guarding him day and night, they were unable even to pick up one or two carpets."

"And what does Aram say?"

"What can he say? Aram tells them that as they had only gone round with him during the fighting, they had had no problems and so had survived."

"And what do the guards say to that?" said Ohannes scarcely listening to Hagop's answer.

Ohannes' thoughts were far away. He hardly heard all Hagop's gossip: that the young widows of the perished Hunchaks had vowed not to marry again; that Paramaz appeared to have been hanged in Stamboul; that Aram Pasha had appointed the husband of his fiery landlady as a storekeeper in the town hall; that a violinist from Bolis, Aram Atchemian, would soon be playing at a concert in the Central Hall to be given on behalf of the starving refugees; that Hampartsoum Yeramian had sent a letter from Cairo, in which he had expressed his regret that because of some unhappy circumstances (a lie!) he was unable to contribute his efforts to the heroic battle of his adorable Van, but that he was proud of the city from afar – the Grand Mother had commented that she too could have been proud from afar, but that if he had been a man he would not have left his 'adorable Van' and shed crocodile tears sitting on the banks of the Nile; that Mihran

Manasserian had taken the cat from the house of the district governor of Hayots Dzor and had brought it to his own house – it was not like a cat but more like a faithful dog, which followed him wherever he went; and that Dr Ussher had written to America to ask for more money and medical instruments so as to be able to carry out complicated operations.

"I don't understand, Baron Ohannes. The war is over, the wounded have either died or recovered, what complicated operations does he mean? This is the Dr Ussher who said that he would build something in the American compound which allows light to pass through wires to houses. Just tell me, how can light pass through wires? They'd burn up in a moment?"

"Yes, there is such light." Ohannes began concentrating: "Baron Simon – may he rest in peace – told me. It's called … yes, electricity. Baron Simon had seen it in Stamboul."

"What is wire and what can its light be, Baron Ohannes? Oh my God! And do you believe all these lies?" Hagop was quite angry.

"Man, science is not lies, science is – in a word – science. One of these days I'll go to Stamboul myself and see everything with my own eyes, and then I'll come and tell you."

"Oh, are you going to Stamboul?"

"I have such an intention, either to Stamboul, or to Tiflis."

There was a silence, which was broken by Hagop. "You can't go to Stamboul. There's no way – there are massacres everywhere. Tiflis? Yes, you can go to Tiflis, the way there is open. But Stamboul? Do you want to come out of the river to fall into a flood? Tiflis? On what business, or is it just a trip?"

"To tell the truth I want to go on business," said Ohannes, "as far as I know, Tiflis is a big commercial town. I'll go and see what I can find there."

These were Ohannes' thoughts. He was not the kind of man to march on the spot. He wanted to go to Tiflis, to see the commercial life and the situation in these big cities, to establish relations with some great merchants, to buy and sell goods that Van had never seen or dreamed of. He had money, the leafy pear tree was witness to that. He would find a few faithful Assyrians to carry on the farm in Ermants, and he would appoint a new manager. He would build a new summer-house in Artemid. He would not sell his donkey, it might turn out to be useful, but he would need his own carriage when going to Artemid on hot summer days. Furthermore, he had to marry Lia off, and send Souren to Tiflis to be educated. Only Vostanig, whose real name was Murad, would stay at home. Vostanig would soon become Murad Muradkhanian.

"The Shirak cafe has re-opened." Hagop continued giving information. "The Russian Cossacks come and sit and ask for raki. Shirak always keeps raki for them."

"And do they pay?"

"They give whatever you ask, they don't haggle at all."

"That's good."

"Yes the Russians are generous people."

"That's good, it's good. People should be generous so that trade can pick up again."

"Of course – what trade can there be if the customer is too greedy?"

"Well, the world has changed," said Ohannes shutting one eye as if to see the changes taking place better. "We can't go to Stamboul, so now we must deal with Tiflis, Moscow, St Petersburg."

"You know the Russian cities well?"

"Why shouldn't I know that much?" said Ohannes, remembering that he had heard those names from the late Kevork and from Set. People hear many things, some of which go in at one ear and out at the other. One should hear like Ohannes, hear and keep it in one's mind.

When Ohannes had heard that the Turks had fled, he had rhymed, 'Turks to Bitlis, Armenians to Tiflis.' Now he thought that this rhyme should be changed to 'Djevded Bey to Bitlis, Ohannes Oglu to Tiflis.' Well, a man does not know what can befall him.

"What is the name of the light in the wire?" said Hagop mischievously.

"Electricity."

"And do you know what an otomobil is?"

"No, what is it?"

"You see, I saw it with my own eyes. It passed from Santi Street into the Houssians street. This was me, and that was the otomobil." Hagop pointed to the high table in the corner, on which was a four-branch candlestick. "The driver was sitting in the front and there were two military officers in the back. I think they were Russian high-ranking officers."

"What was it? A carriage?"

"It serves as a carriage but with rubber wheels. It moves without a horse or anything else pulling it."

"I've heard of it The dear, departed Baron Simon told me. He'd got into one in Stamboul."

"I wouldn't get in one, even if I die."

"Why?"

"It poured out smoke when it passed. Moreover, it also gave out an unbearable smell."

Ohannes, a progressive man from top to toe, could not help coming to the defense of this scientific achievement. "Well, when you go in a carriage, doesn't the horse give off a smell? An otomobil? Look how developed science is in Russia!"

"Yes, you're right."

"So, it's good, it's good."

Who knows what other problems they would have talked about, if Hagop had not jumped up like a man who had suddenly remembered something very important.

"I'll have to go, Baron Ohannes, I'd forgotten –"

"Where? What have you forgotten?"

"I've got to go and see a house."

"Is it a good one?"

"A king's palace, Baron Ohannes."

"Only the queen is missing!"

"Yes, the queen. You know it well, Baron Ohannes, your word is law."

"Go, go!" Ohannes stood up and patted Hagop's back. "We'll arrange such a wedding party, that the Ak-Küpri Bride and Bridegroom will tremble with horror."

Hagop didn't care for the word 'horror'. Why should the Bride and Bridegroom tremble?

"Why should they be horrified? Let them also rejoice."

"Let them envy and rejoice." Ohannes closed the subject.

Hagop went out into the street encouraged and full of joy. And he had some reason – he had misunderstood the whole situation.

An hour later, Set came in just when Ohannes was about to go down for dinner having carefully read some more of the Bible.

"I congratulate you. I do congratulate you – you have decided well, a very good decision."

Ohannes had talked to Panos about his proposed journey to Tiflis, and he thought that perhaps Set had heard about this from him.

"Yes, I do have such an intention. I considered all the pros and cons, and came to that conclusion. Of course, I'll spend a lot, but I'll make a big profit out of it."

Set wondered what profit could be made by marrying Vergine off to Kando and paying all the expenses? He had not believed it when Hagop Kandoyan had told him about this a few minutes before, but now it seemed to be true. What possible profit could there be in it?

"I can't say anything about any benefits and losses, but you have decided very well, Baron Ohannes," said Set.

"I think so too. Before starting any business, a man should examine the new place, establish local relationships and study the situation."

The expression on Set's face changed so much that Ohannes could not help noticing it, and continued.

"Why do you suddenly look so confused? Am I mad to commit myself to anything without considering and examining all the circumstances. Baron Simon – the blessed soul – always used to say that what we did in Van is old-fashioned, unprofitable and senseless compared with Bolis. And you – Allah be praised – are a man who has been to Bolis. Put your hand on your heart and tell me truly whether the business we do here is really much good."

"What business? Which business, Baron Ohannes?" Set who was always so quiet and respectful, lost his patience.

Ohannes looked closely at the perplexed face of his former shop manager.

"Are you drunk?"

"You've known me for so many years, Baron Ohannes, have you ever seen me drunk?"

"If you're sober, tell me, what business are we talking about. We're speaking about my journey to Tiflis to study the commercial life there and start a new business, aren't we?"

"No, Baron Ohannes, not that."

"So, what are we talking about?" shouted Ohannes at the top of his voice.

"I came to congratulate you on your decision to marry Vergine off to Hagop Kandoyan, and on your promise to bear all the expenses of the wedding party."

Ohannes stopped breathing. He wondered whether Vergine had promised anything to that stupid man.

Chapter 27

> The lake was the partner of the gunman …
> (Shahan Shahnour)

July. The ancient town lies not far from the lake like a beautiful green-haired goddess in a fairy-tale. The gardens, orchards and vineyards, the lake now again coloured a spectacular, incredible and impossible, blue, and the watered and swept streets, feeling cool and fresh again, have now all become the site of an inexpensive bazaar. Outside almost all the houses and at street corners, there are tables laden with light refreshments, cold milk or yoghourt, tobacco and cigarette paper. The vendors are short-haired, young boys mainly dressed like girls in gowns – the ones in trousers are more than ten-years-old. The customers are Russian Cossacks, they pass by on horse and on foot, stop at a table, point to what they want and ask how much it cost – "Pachyom?" Nothing on the table costs more than ten kopecks, and the young traders have learned to count in Russian from one to ten. They have also learned to say 'pazhalsta' (please) and 'kharasho' (good).

It is possible to live. The Russians are generous. As one of our heroes has well observed, if you ask one for five kopecks, he will give you five, and if for ten – ten. And he will not be surprised if you charge one kopeck for something costing ten. Nor will he be angry if you charge ten kopecks for something costing one; he will not get angry, he will take it and even thank you: "Spasibo."

These Cossacks have blue eyes and fair, wispy moustaches. The Van girls are scared of them, but very much like to look at their horses until the rider turns round the corner of the street and disappears. The braver ones open a window overlooking the street, shout "Rus-si-an" in piercing tones and quickly close the shutters.

Yes, life is really promising. But it should also be said that the gardens are damaged. There was a poplar in the Darbinians' orchard keeping watch on Aikesdan like Aram, or like Ohannes' kiosk. One morning, a hostile cannon-ball sliced off its top, causing it to fall to the ground together with a stork's nest. And now some people cry and some laugh when they see it; then, of course the roles change, for there is now nothing to worry about. But trading opportunities were being reviewed: in many gardens, the annual spring flowers were being replaced by potatoes, carrots, cabbages, and beans.

On the day after seeing Aram, Mihran decided to waste no more time and to review his own trading opportunities. He saddled his horse; the Grand Mother was as usual sceptical, but she filled his saddle-bag with bread, boiled eggs, cheese, and a bottle of raki. She asked him whether he had taken the key of his room at the monastery; he scornfully assured her that he had. Nana was walking round the horse trying to catch his attention. She even tried, unsuccessfully, to jump onto the saddle. Mihran went back inside and Nana followed him. He put on his hat, closed the door on Nana and went out. Everything seemed in order; he said goodbye to his mother, and led his horse out.

CHAPTER 27

He mounted his horse at the eastern gate at Nakhri Street, and rode along the familiar road. It was a sunny Friday morning and, as the song has it, tomorrow would be a Saturday. He reached Gurubash. No sound could be heard in the village, the doors of the houses were open, many of them broken. The millstones of the water-mill were turning, stone was grinding against stone, but there was no grain between them. Otherwise silence: no, his horse was stamping on the wide road dividing the village into two, and there was a loud mewing of cats, at first far off but now getting closer. Mihran noticed a small, limping dog running out of a path followed by a group of angry, dishevelled cats. They chased the dog towards the water-mill; Mihran thought that it would get eaten.

He stopped in front of a hut, where a barely human old man was sitting with a piece of wood in his mouth, pretending to be smoking. His rags did not cover his lean and sunburnt body, he was half-naked and seemed to be only just alive. Mihran greeted him. The lines of his hairy face rippled, he opened his toothless mouth and mumbled something in a thick, petulant tone. Mihran understood the old man to say that the wedding party had gone to Varag, he was sitting there, waiting for them to return. Mihran rode away from the lifeless village; he wanted to leave it behind him, but could not, it was running after him, catching up with him, overtaking him.

He reached Gyaduk without taking a break. As usual, he dismounted, but did not sit down for a rest, he had lost all his appetite. He looked down on Hayots Dzor spread out from east to west. In the distance, the monastery buildings seemed smaller and bunched up. There were the villages – Noraber, Astvadzashen, Khek, Aradents. There was no smoke rising from any of the villages, no dust from any road. The winter crops had sprouted, but the green shoots did not please his eye, they reminded him of the green moss of a graveyard.

– Why did I come here? What am I here for? Oh, yes, I need to think about restoring the monastery. But how? The most important thing is that there's nobody left. –

Mihran recalled Hagop Mudoyan, who had lived in the valley, but had managed to escape to Van and had been able to arrange for two hundred others to escape as well, including women, old people, and children. This heroic deed had, of course, coincided with Djevdet Bey ordering his men to stop the slaughter and drive the survivors into Van to force the town to starve and so surrender. This Hagop had come to Mihran. He said he had been to the Eremer monastery and had seen Manuel's dead body. Manuel had been busy drawing a map of Armenia at the time of Tigran the Great, when the murderers had rushed in. They had trampled over the map, and had killed Manuel with an axe. Hagop had seen his body lying on the map with the red blood seeping into the bright colours of the map of Armenia. Mihran wondered whether Avdo and the herdsmen had stayed in the monastery. He decide that since he had already come so far, he might as well carry on to the end. He began walking slowly down, leading the horse behind him.

Astvadzashen was as deserted as Gurubash. There were dead bodies everywhere. Mihran was deeply moved when he saw the first one, but then got used to them. He did not see any cats, but instead there were dogs who – tired of feeding on corpses and detecting live flesh – ran towards him, barking hoarsely. He took out his revolver and fired a number of times. The gunshots echoed round the deserted village and the dogs ran away.

It was the same in Aradents. A man looking like the headman Naho was standing under a willow, not far from the water-mill. Mihran approached: it was indeed Naho, not standing but tied to the tree, having been tortured and killed. Outside the village, in the rose-hip bushes, there were bodies of half-naked girls and women. He recognized some of them. He left Aradents with a heavy heart, and eventually could no longer smell the decaying corpses and villages. Mihran took a deep breath – it was a sigh.

He rode the horse across the Khoshab river. The water splashing under the horse's feet reminded him of peaceful days in the flourishing and populated Hayots Dzor and of the wealthy and productive monastery. The road wound round into the familiar and friendly atmosphere of the monastery meadows. The horse neighed as usual to announce its arrival. Avdo should now be slowly coming down from the monastery. But there was no one. Mihran dismounted and left the horse free to graze in the meadow.

He walked cautiously up the steps to the monastery. What if there were Turks hiding there? Or in the villages? Should he be entering this world of death alone, relying only on his revolver? The door of the monastery was open as usual. He entered – to total silence.

"Avdo!" he nervously called out and did not recognize his own voice.

The first human figure he saw was Avdo's. It is true that it was not at all like him, but it was Avdo. He was lying on the threshold of the stable with his feet sticking out into the yard. There was dry straw in his moustache and his face lying in the sun was swarming with flies. Mihran remembered Avdo when he was alive – kind and friendly, though always swearing. He remembered the expression on his face when he found out that the boy in trousers he had embraced was not the governor's son but his wife. Avdo had been tortured and was lying in eternal sleep. He could no longer swear, or be surprised by anything.

Mihran entered the main room; enclosed by its blackened walls and ceiling, the herdsmen would every day bake bread, boil milk in huge cauldrons on the stove and make cheese and butter. Many kinds of meals would be prepared in this room but it was the familiar smell of bread that Mihran particularly recalled and his heart filled with tears. Indeed, thousands of years could pass over the Armenian monasteries, but the smell of bread would never vanish from their ruined and desolate kitchens. He felt hungry, but also knew that he could not eat.

It seemed to Mihran that the ashes in the big stove were still hot. His attention was caught by some unusual, white ash. He picked up a wooden-handled, iron hook leaning against the wall not far from the stove, and began to stir the ashes to reveal some bones, which were as light as a sponge. When he began to stir the ashes more vigorously, he was taken aback to see the skull of a small child. He realized that they had burnt a child in the stove. His brow was sweating He threw away the hook and bent down over the hearth to see the same white ashes.

He went out through the deserted yard to the church. When he opened the door, the first thing he could sense was the heavy and humid air. The bodies of the hard-working, quarrrelsome housemaids were lying on the damp floor. It was not hard to guess what torture they had suffered before dying. A huge rat ran past Mihran and disappeared behind the altar. He left with a heavy heart.

He did not need a key to get into his room. The furniture was broken, as were the window panes and the lamp hanging from the ceiling. Traces of kerosene could be seen on the floorboards. Torn pieces of bed linen were scattered here and there. Tired and broken-hearted, he sat down on the undamaged sadr and murmured aloud, "A cross against the monastery!"

Yes, a cross should be put on the monastery. The fields were of no value without labourers to work them, nor was the building itself. Aram could give him the whole of Hayots Dzor, let alone the monastery, and he would give it all back to Aram. 'Take it,' he would say, 'it's yours, enjoy it'.

He rolled a cigarette with trembling fingers and lit it with a wax match. He heard the troubled whinny of the horse through the open window, it seemed to be asking for help. He threw the still burning match on the floor and jumped up. He could have put the resulting flame out with his foot but he did not. Mihran wanted to forget the monastery.

He ran out and went down the hill without thinking. Now he could hear some dogs barking. He entered the meadow and found the horse trying heroically to protect itself from five dogs. One of the dogs had managed to jump onto the horse's saddle. The smell of food had brought them there. Mihran fired a few times and the dogs ran off towards Khek. The horse was sweating from the unequal struggle. Mihran stroked it, and it neighed and calmed down.

Why did he come here? What for? He came to be able to escape without looking back, to escape from this deserted and dead monastery, from Hayots Dzor, from this deadly emptiness. Something glistened in the grass; he bent down and picked it up, it was a spent bullet. He remembered Ishkhan firing a shotgun while riding his horse. Here was the stove with blackened stones – Kotot Boghos, Mushegh Baldoshian and the others used to grill meat out here. He wanted to escape from this land of death, from this monastery and meadow quivering with ghosts and memories.

Mihran put the reins on the horse, arranged the saddle-bag,

mounted and rode off slowly along the meadow without looking back. He smelled the oleander once again and as soon as he had left the meadow he galloped quickly away. It was only the heavy atmosphere that made him realise that he had passed Aradents and Astvadzashen, he carried straight on up the slope to Gyaduk. He stopped on the top of the hill. This time he could not help turning his horse round and looking back towards the monastery.

The Khek monastery was on fire. It was enveloped in smoke, which was spreading over the meadow, fanned perhaps by the cool wind blowing down from Mt St Abraham.

He rode on to Gurubash. He breathed more easily when the village came in sight, and he slowed the horse down. The toothless and half-human creature sitting by the wall of the hut was still there. Mihran again asked the man what he was doing. The answer was the same: the wedding party had gone to Varag and he was sitting and waiting for them to return. He had married off his granddaughter; did Mihran know the groom, Sakho, with the long neck and black hat? He invited Mihran to dismount and drink a jug of wine.

Back in Van, it seemed strange that people were coming and going, that the children were playing in the street screaming happily and spraying water over each other. Karmileh opened the door. Mihran wanted to tap her on the chin with his finger and say 'hey', but the girl evaded him and quickly went upstairs. The Grand Mother was knitting socks, seated on a divan in the garden. She was not surprised at the expression on Mihran's face. She had already imagined it.

"Did you see the monastery?"

"Yes, I did. A sullen, empty monastery without a single soul."

"Hand it over to Aram and let him enjoy it."

Nana ran up rubbed against his feet. He did not smile.

To begin with, there were rumours. Perhaps everything begins with rumours. Migration? Retreat?

First, what is a migration? Not much can be said: it was a flight when the surviving Armenian peasants left the villages of various provinces of Vaspourakan and came to Van. Where could a Vanetsi migrate to now? To Russia? Can Van live without a Vanetsi? No, no – the question is whether a Vanetsi can live without Van. Well it might be agreed that a Vanetsi is a practical man and can busy himself with trade or craft and support his family, but what about Van? If a Vanetsi leaves Van, will anything else remain?

What if Hampartsoum Yeramian went to Egypt on some supposedly important business, and Tatchat Talamazian killed Davo and escaped to America, and Mushegh Baldoshian was compelled through unlucky circumstances to go to Persia? That does not mean that Van would be emptied, does it? Would it be natural if everybody in Van became migrants and moved away? What would become of Van?

Then there's 'retreat'. The issue needs to be examined dispassionately. What is a retreat? Who invented the idea? They wrote saying that the Turks had retreated across the lake to Tatvan. That was natural, but where could the people of Van retreat to? It was now a matter of tens of thousands of them. To Russia? Russia and Van do not mix very well. It is well known that the Russian army has reached Erzinjan and no sword of Damocles is hanging over the head of Van, so what retreat are people talking about? What retreat are people in cafés, on street-corners, and in the churchyards, whispering about? Only the Governor and the Government are silent. Why are they silent? Why?

Ohannes woke up from the midnight cock-crow from the gardens. When going to bed in the evening, he had been afraid of oversleeping and not waking up until the morning. Heaven be praised! He could get up in time. He did so and as on that remarkable earlier day, he dressed and put on his outdoor shoes, went down to the barn, took a spade, quietly opened the garden door and walked along the path dividing the garden into two parts. There stood the Hadji-Nana pear tree.

The night was cool and pleasant, there was no moon, but the sky was fill of stars. A cool wind was blowing from Mt Varag and the gardens were full of whispers and rustling. The magical night filled his heart and soul. He could have admired the nameless charms of this surprising night for hours if he had not felt the spade in his hand to remind him why he had come here. Despite the darkness, he could tell the spot precisely and he began to dig – khrt, khrt, khrt. Ohannes was digging and recalling all the important events of the past weeks. And Ohannes – glory be to God – was not a man whose life was in any way deprived from the point of view of the proverb, 'Man is born to live and to experience life to the full'.

On that evening, when Ohannes was resting in the kiosk and had the conversation – already known to the reader – with Set, Vergine had entered with a cup of coffee.

"What's Satenik doing?" asked Ohannes, taking the coffee.

Vergine looked out of the window into the garden. "She's picking some roses."

"Are you Kando's wife?" said Ohannes, and corrected himself, "bride?"

"So I've heard," Vergine replied calmly and quietly.

"Who said so?"

"Siroun Terdzakian, Aghavni Darbinian, and –"

"Yes, yes. Where've they heard it from?"

"Perhaps Kando told someone and then it got passed on from mouth to mouth," Vergine explained with a smile.

"Well, you seem to be pleased. Have you made any promise?"

"According to Kando, yes."

"And in reality?"

"Well, let them talk, Master. The more they talk the better. Pass it on yourself as well and I will also." Vergine spoke softly and for some reason her tone left Ohannes tingling with goose-pimples inside.

Ohannes was puzzled. "What for?" he asked, also speaking quietly.

And it was here that Vergine astonished Ohannes by her wisdom and far-sightedness. She said that the more that false news was spread, the better, because nobody would then suspect them, and, moreover, Satenik would be more at ease. The lie would swallow the truth and at the same time it would remain a lie. Anyone would be astonished by such cunning.

Khrt, khrt, khrt. Ohannes was digging and smiling. He thought that Eve who was deceived by the snake was naive. If it had been Vergine instead of Eve, the snake would not have been able to deceive her, and she and the rest of mankind would not have been deprived of paradise. Ohannes thought Vergine must have been born three days before Satan. The reader will more or less know Vergine well by now. It cannot, of course, be said that she is naive, but it can be said that she was a devil. But to say that she was born three days before Satan is quite an exaggeration. But Ohannes is also well-known. Could he make improper observations without weighing and considering everything? No, twice no! Ohannes would not say anything without checking. Why would Ohannes want to determine Vergine's date of birth so precisely?

Khrt, khrt, khrt. Ohannes was digging – and also deep into his mind.

– It's pointless going to Ermants, it's an unnecessary waste of time. To Russia? Yes, there's some sense in that. First, he could see the world, and secondly, he could start a new business, a new business like Russian merchants. Or, maybe, he would sell his house and garden and take his family to Russia? It's clear, that in that case Vergine … No, no! What is a Vanetsi without Van? A nothing, a round zero. –

Now, the hole had got so deep that it was impossible to take the earth out just with the spade. He knelt down and cautiously scooped the earth out with his hands. He thought that he should be careful lest the spade break the jug, for it would then it would be difficult to separate the gold from the earth in the dark. "Slow and steady wins the race," he muttered aloud, and continued to dig. Khrt, khrt, khrt.

– As for the expenses of Kando's wedding party, I'll keep my word. Let him marry Vergine if he can. Hm, look at that stupid idiot, he wants to marry Vergine! Honey's not for a donkey's mouth. Or is it? Well, even supposing it is for him, who'll give honey to the donkey? Anyone giving honey to this particular donkey would be at least an ass himself. –

Ohannes felt the spade touch the jug. He knelt down again and began to release the jug carefully from the earth with the spade. He moved the heavy jug; it shifted and he pulled it out. He put it to one side and began re-filling the hole. That was almost done when he became aware again of the warm, starry night, its beauty was intoxicating. He took a deep breath – "Akh, Akh, Akh!"

"All right, I've nothing more to say. Migration or retreat – it's all the same. But I want to understand. What for? Are the Turks approaching?"

"No."

"Is the sword of Damocles hanging over our heads?"

"No."

"Against what force do we have to retreat. Why should we run away? Is there any sense or logic in that?"

"There is sense, but no logic."

"So, what is there?"

"An instruction, an order."

This significant – and, as it turned out later, historic – conversation took place in the kiosk of Baron Ohannes Muradkhanian between him and his former shop manager, Baron Set, on the 30th of July in the year 1915.

Before that conversation, when the sun was still setting, someone had knocked at the door and had tramped heavily up the stairs. Ohannes was reminded of the day when Panos had come and told him about the murder of Simon. And when Panos' confused and anxious face appeared in the doorway, he braced himself to face a heavy blow, which turned out to be even heavier than he had anticipated.

"Is it true or just a rumour?" he asked like a drowning man, seeking to clutch at least one straw. There was not even one.

"There is Nikolayev's order: no one must be left in Van by tomorrow evening."

"And this house, and all the property?" Ohannes did not want to give in.

Panos smiled bitterly.

"What's happened already to your property at Ermants and your shop?"

"Yes, yes." Ohannes understood.

"If you've got gold, rings and bracelets, fine; but the rest can't be saved."

Ohannes reflected and muttered, "How could I have been so stupid?"

There was a heavy, a really heavy, silence.

"And you?" Ohannes said briefly.

"Like you," said Panos and he added, "Do you think I'm any less stupid than you?"

They looked at each other and smiled. There came a moment when Ohannes wanted to stand up, go to the window and call out, like he used to in the past, 'Satenig, Vergine, Lia, bring raki and something to eat' – but he realised times had changed. Instead he said:

"Alas! Glory be to the dead. The destruction of Van –"

"Van will not be destroyed, Baron Ohannes For God's sake, why should Van be ruined? The people of Van, yes, they will be destroyed –"

"That's nonsense, idle thinking, Baron Panos. If the people are ruined, then Van will certainly be ruined."

For a moment it seemed that both of them were right, but that could not be so. The issue had to be examined radically.

"Baron Ohannes, answer my question: Which came first, Van or its people?"

"Nonsense. If there was no Van to start with, where would the people have come from?"

"Well, suppose you're right. Who built that Van?"

"Who built Van? A Vanetsi"

"So, first there had to be a Vanetsi to build Van."

"No, Van came first and then a Vanetsi was born."

Panos was losing patience. "In that case, I say again, who built that Van?"

"A Vanetsi," insisted Ohannes, but he was beginning to feel that the problem was not as simple and clear as he had thought. Which was first? It had to be Van for a Vanetsi to be born there. But who built Van? Could a Vanetsi be born in a Van built by a stranger? Of course not, Van was built by a Vanetsi!

"You are very good at muddling things," said Ohannes in a

conciliatory manner. He even smiled, though the smile came and went at lightning speed. "Well, Baron Panos, what shall we take with us?" he almost whispered.

"What can we take? Bread, cheese."

"What else?"

"What else? It's only a few days' away. What could you take? Have you a cart?

"And what if I had?"

"A cart would be a blessing. You could take one or two carpets, beds, clothes and some food, and go."

"I had a cart, but I told Usep to demolish it," Ohannes was annoyed, but soon recovered. "The cart would have had to have an ox. The donkey's no use."

"Baron Ohannes, you're thinking in the way you would if you were going to a Varag church festival. This is a flight – whether it's pleasant or not shouldn't be taken into account. You'll put what's necessary into the cart and pull it. And go pushing and shoving. A cart's a fine thing."

Panos prepared to say goodbye, but he paused and said, almost as if to himself, "I too don't understand. There's no danger from the Turks, there isn't a sword of Damocles hanging over our heads. Why do they remove the people from Van? I don't understand. Well, I must go. Let's say our goodbyes."

Ohannes got excited, really excited. He took his friend's hand, shook it a few times and was able to ask in a trembling voice, "When shall we meet again?"

"And you could ask where? When and where are unknown. Probably one of these days with Baron Simon. Our Van is ruined."

The two worthy men of Van embraced each other and cried like children who had been beaten and unfairly punished.

"Oh that we should have seen such a day," said Panos, "My heart aches. Don't cry, Ohannes. Alas, alas! Getdi gyul, getdi byulbyul – fly away, fly away nightingale."

After Panos had left, Ohannes wiped his tears and moustache, coughed several times to settle his throat and steady his voice, and walked up and down the room. 'It's pointless crying or laughing, crying is bad for the health,' he thought. 'Everything will have to be arranged in a night. How clever to have taken the jug out of the earth a few days ago.'

There was something else important. That morning Satenik had said that Vergine was ill, that she felt sick in the mornings. She had thought Kando might have had a hand in that. He had laughed, but after she had gone out he'd been worried. What news!

Ohannes could not help noticing that after the fighting was over, Vergine had become somehow estranged. It was clear why: he slept now with Satenik in the room upstairs and Vergine was with the children downstairs. They did not meet, and probably would not be able to. But Vergine had once let him know that it had been his brother Kevork's fault that she had not had children, that she was now disgusted at the thought of marrying again, and that she had but one wish – to have a child and bring it up.

And now there was Satenik's news. What a surprise! It was clear that Kando had nothing to do with it. But neither had Ohannes, he knew his capacity and virility well enough. Oh, naughty Vergine! How had she managed to carry the thing out to the end? He also thought that she was not so foolish as to have a child without a father under present conditions. She would become a subject of gossip and disgrace in the town. Vergine was a devil; clearly she had someone, but who was that mysterious and invisible bridegroom? Ohannes even tried to smile and he managed to do so. Yes, yes, he smiled – gloomily.

Just when he decided to go down, Satenik came in. She was excited. "What bad news is there in the town?"

Ohannes, now controlled, stuck firmly to his original decision.

"I have to tell you my dear Satenik, that we're going on a trip to Russia. Now listen to me. There has to be no one left in Van by tomorrow evening. Early in the morning, we'll take an emigrant's walking staff and –"

"Where should we find such a staff?" Satenik was annoyed.

"They write about that in books and newspapers. We can flee without a staff. Bake some bread and pies for a few days, make some rolls of pokhind, eggs, cheese, and so on. In a word – as if we're going to a Varag festival. Get everything ready like that."

"And what about our house and possessions?"

"No house and no possessions, woman. It's flight we're engaged in. Go, go! Let Vergine and Lia help you. Get everything ready, we're leaving in the morning."

And as a sign of inner calm, he began to sing.

"In the morning when it was cool
Our Hrep fell down into the sea."

"Get serious, man." Satenik could not help smiling, but when Ohannes did get serious, her smile faded and she went out shedding tears.

Ohannes cleared his throat once more and, without knowing how, appeared in the outer yard. Usep was sitting on the threshold of the stable, repairing his rope shoes.

"Usep, have you given water to the donkey," said Ohannes and added, "We once had a cart – where is it?" He asked the question knowing full well what Usep's reply would be. And it was as he thought.

"You told me to lose it, and I –"

"I did say so but what did you imagine? Now, take off your rope shoes, put on my strong ones and go and look for a cart in the town. Today we couldn't buy draught cattle even for a thousand gold pieces.

"No one's selling a cart, Master."

"You'll see. Promise three, five or ten singing gold pieces. We'll be lost without a cart. Find one, take a yoke and pull the cart here yourself. Bring the owner of the cart as well, to collect his money."

Usep finished his work and stood up decisively. He gave Ohannes an inexplicable smile. "You said ten gold pieces, Master?"

"Ten – even twelve."

"Give me one gold piece and I'll bring you a good cart."

Ohannes pulled his red purse out of his pocket and opened it in a hurry lest Usep took back his promise. He shook out one gold coin and handed it to Usep. "Here you are."

Usep took the coin, held it in his teeth while he ruffled the shawl on his back and pulled out a dirty piece of cloth He wrapped the coin up in it, tied the ends, tossed it up and caught it. He picked up his rope shoes and went into the stable, where he probably hid his treasure. At last he came out and without looking at Ohannes went briskly to the haystack under the shed in the corner of the yard. He picked up a hayfork and began ... and the cart appeared from under the hay.

"You dog," Ohannes shouted with mixed feelings of anger and joy, "you're selling me my own property?"

Usep, caught red-handed, smiled with his bright, white teeth. He wanted now to go back to the stable, and return with the coin to hand it back to its rightful owner.

"Good for you, Usep. May you be blessed. Pull the cart out and clean it."

Ohannes was so delighted that for a moment he forgot the serious situation which had made the cart, which had been worthless the day before, a real treasure today. Those who are well aware of the changing, enduring, inexplicable – and, at the same time, simple – nature of Ohannes' soul, would not be surprised.

By the time he had returned to the house, his delight had already passed away. His brow was clouded with new worries. The most important, of course, was the problem of the gold coins. Where should he hide them? How to keep them till the end of the journey? He recalled that Usep had wrapped the coin in a piece of cloth, which he had then tied up. That was all he had to do, the lucky man.

– We'll put Vostanig and the food on the donkey and on the cart, the important clothes, one or two carpets, and some silver and gold items in a box. Should he divide the gold and sew some in a few belts, for each of them to wear as they set out? No, that was not a good idea. Some may be lost on the way, or may fall behind and never catch up. –

Work was in full swing in the main room. Vergine was bent over the big pan, and Satenik over the small one, mixing dough for the bread and pies. Lia was helping both of them with a worried face. Souren was walking aimlessly in the garden, looking at the ripening fruit and thinking that it would now be eaten by Turks. And Vostanig had climbed up onto the roof and, being unaware of the current situation, was trying to protect the fruit, lying there ready to be dried, from the birds. Ksh, ksh, ksh.

"Is there any flour left?" asked Ohannes tapping the jar with the knuckle of his index finger. "Will there be enough until a new lot comes from Ermants?"

"Yes," said Satenik, "let those dogs come and eat it."

The air of the room seemed stifling to Ohannes. He went up to the verandah. His mind suddenly cleared. Satenik could sew the coins into a belt of tough cloth and he would tie it on his back. While the rest of the coins would be tied up one by one in pieces of cloth, like Usep had done, and tucked into the wool of the blanket. "That's it," he said aloud, "that's it."

He went up to the kiosk with a light heart, sat down in his place in front of the cold nargileh and began to finger his beads – Kher, Shar, Astvadz...

It was just then that Set came in and the conversation already referred to took place between them.

Ohannes grumbled: "Of course, the one who's given that order must know something to give such an order. But why don't they tell the people the real reason? Why do they assume people are donkeys?"

Set did not know why people were assumed to be donkeys; he really did not know, so he thought it better to keep quiet.

"What should we take with us, Baron Set?"

"Our heads," the manager replied with his former eagerness, "and bread if there is some."

'This man hasn't any bread,' Ohannes thought. In some unknown corner of his mind the image of a smiling Khushush deceptively appeared, but quickly vanished. 'It's just the same,' he continued reasoning, 'instead of leaving it to the dogs, let Kushush eat it.'

"Well, have you got any bread yourself? If not, don't be embarrased to say if you haven't. On such a day –"

"I haven't any, Baron Ohannes. The lady of the house sends you her regards and said –"

"Usep," Ohannes called out from the high window of the kiosk. "Don't come up. Listen, take some sacks for Baron Set." He asked how many sacks Set wanted and was told three if he did not mind. He called out again to Usep: "Four sacks of flour for Baron Set. Do you understand?"

He went up to his former manager and said in a broken voice, "Go, my son, go. May the house of he who ruined ours be ruined."

As if in a dream, Ohannes felt Set kiss his hand. Taken by surprise, he withdrew it and realised that it was wet. Then he heard his own desperate cry: "Where have we got to?. What are they doing to us?"

The final night loomed over Van. Why final? Was there not going to be another dark night? Of course, there was. And now, after so many years is there not still going to be another dark night – even with the same moon, and with the same sun about to rise. And, as a writer born in Bitlis and now living in America has said, Mt Varag, the Citadel, the Lake, and Aghtamar, are all still there. Indeed, the lake – the 'little sea' – is still calling out, but nobody now understands its language. Did the writer born in Bitlis understand it? Did that cry pierce his heart or not? As far as one can tell, it did; for as the wise men of Van would say, blood is thicker than water. It is true that some people came and proved that water can be very easily turned into blood. However, this purely chemical conversion has not affected the invulnerable and immortal saying of the Van sages. It was, of course, the final night for Ohannes, and for the people of Van in general. Perhaps this should have been stated from the start.

Ohannes ordered that anything valuable be taken into the kiosk. Usep was also engaged in this activity. Nobody realized the meaning of the order and nobody asked. The expensive belt was already tied on Ohannes' back. Two blankets were fitted up in the way Ohannes had envisaged. It would not be possible to find a third blanket as heavy and as valuable in the whole world. Of course, here the wide world excludes Van, for that night it was perfectly possible to find – if not blankets – mattresses, pillows, and even winter coats, that were more or less the same.

Ohannes chose an ordinary box, smaller than an ordinary trunk and larger than a suitcase, for the silver and gold household items, which were usually kept in his famous cupboard and only taken out for special occasions. He covered them with the portraits of his ancestor, Vartan Muradkhan. He closed the lid and locked the box with a small key. He ordered the trunk and the blankets, two pillows, one carpet, and some essential clothes – as had been previously decided – to be put on the cart. There were things Satenik wanted to save, but Ohannes considered them unimportant and threw them away.

Though it was midnight, the smell of fresh bread being baked spread over Aikesdan. It was as if the people of Van were getting ready to go in the morning to a festival at the Varag monastery. Though it was midnight, the lamps were lit in all the houses. That was a surprising thing: why was Van not sleeping? And Ohannes? What about Ohannes? There had been so many times when all Van had fallen quietly and peacefully into the arms of Morpheus, while he had not slept and had guarded the town's slumber like an unpaid watchman. And now, when even the children were not asleep in their cradles because of all the unusual noise and fuss, and when the town was buzzing in the night like a beehive or a disturbed anthill, how could Ohannes fall asleep?

Ohannes put his jacket on over his night-gown, donned his fez and went downstairs to the outer yard. He walked round the cart and felt pleased. He wanted to enter the stable to check the well-being of his animals, but decided not to disturb Usep's rest. He went to the inner yard, and, without announcing his presence, kept an eye on the hectic work going on in the tantun. He went into the garden: perhaps he had decided to take his leave of the trees and bushes, the vegetables and flowers, but he tried not to think about it to avoid getting upset. Ohannes knew very well that such disturbances were very bad for his health. He slowly carried on along the wide path through the garden. 'Farewell to my homeland, the cradle of my childhood.' Where had he read or heard those lines? Why should he remember them at just this time and in just this place? It appeared that the life of an Armenian had always been a 'farewell', with no one wishing him 'good luck'. Ohannes carried on walking.

The gardens were cradled in the arms of the mild, grey night. A slight wind passed from garden to garden, from tree to tree, from branch to branch, from leaf to leaf. Ohannes had heard these sounds from early childhood, had heard them when he grew into an adolescent, and then a young man. He had heard these sounds in different periods of his life, with different awarenesses. They had said different things to him, but had always been inexplicable and incomprehensible. Yet today, the trees whispered and murmured something new, something that had not been said before. It seemed to Ohannes that the trees were plainly bidding him farewell. Fa-re-we-ell.

He wondered who it was who had bidden him farewell and wished him a safe journey. Was it Simon, or Panos, or he himself, who had said he would go to Russia and get richer, and had hoped his business would run as smoothly as a Singer sewing machine. 'And what homeland?' he asked himself, 'Homeland is only where there is bread.'

It seemed to Ohannes that there was a body lying on the grass near the rose garden with something white beside it. Jesus Christ! Was this a mirage?

"It's me, Master," Usep called out from the dark.

"Usep? What are you doing here?"

"I don't myself know what I'm doing," Usep replied as he sat up. "I'm speaking with God."

"Is that the cat?"

"It's our cat, Master. It's also upset like me. It came and huddled down beside me."

"How are we going to end up, Usep?" He noticed that Usep was well dressed with a white hat and grey scarf, as though he were going to the Varag festival.

Usep, who was usually an amiable man, had been a child at the time of the great events, when Turks had massacred the population of Marmet; he had been left an orphan and had come to Van. One spring day, as Ohannes returned home from his shop, he had seen a peasant boy sitting on an old saddle in the outer yard and eating bread and cheese with great appetite. His blessed mother had said, "He's an orphan, I took him in to dig the garden. Let him live with us, he's a good-natured boy. He'll be a help."

And he stayed. Nobody heard him say a word except a 'yes' or a 'no'. He was scrupulous, strong and diligent. He put some clean boards in a corner of the stable, spread a carpet over them – his bed was always clean. He had done his own washing, sewing and mending over the years. Ohannes had several times suggested, half-seriously and half-jokingly, that it was time he got married. Usep had blushed and said it was not a good time for that. The years passed by.

"How old are you, Usep?" Ohannes now asked.

"About forty," Usep said, stroking the cat's back.

"It's time to get married."

"Well, Master, I took something on. A secret kept from God or anyone else. And the world stirred up like this. We'll see, may it turn out well. Who knows? Perhaps it's good for all of us."

Ohannes wondered what the man was talking about. But he did not want to know, or could not find, the real meaning of the issues raised by Usep. He thought it better to repeat his unanswered question.

"How are we going to end up, Usep?"

"Don't say 'we', Master. Each man has his own end. We'll go to Russia. Are there any Armenians in Russia?"

"There's nowhere in the world without Armenians."

"So, we shouldn't be worried. The only thing is that we won't be able to find anywhere in the world as beautiful as our Van. How sad for our Van."

To hide his turmoil, Ohannes walked along the wide garden path. His thoughts were stirred up and he could not concentrate. He stopped under the Hadji-Nana pear tree. 'Farewell to my homeland, the cradle of my childhood.'

Some sounds were heard from the Dankovians' garden. He went up to the wall, raised his head and looked across. There were lights burning some twenty paces away in the depth of the garden, where he could see a deep pit. The Dankovian brothers were probably hiding valuable items from the house.

He heard Sirak's voice: "There's no need, it would only decay."

"It won't decay, bury it," said Varazdat.

Ohannes stepped back. He realised that they had made a chest. Varazdat was right, the chest would decay underground, but the gold would not. Ohannes had thought about his house and its contents. Nobody would come to his house and nobody would use the fine furniture and household goods. He looked at the trees laden with fruit. Should he and Usep take two axes and cut down all the trees until daybreak and so destroy the whole garden? Ohannes shivered at the thought. Had he gone mad? To raise a hand to the garden and the earth, would be the same as raising a hand to a pregnant woman. It would be a sin, a sin.

He went back along the wide path; he did not want to approach Usep. 'Let him lie,' he thought, 'and say a few words to God.'

As he was coming up to the garden door, he met Vergine. "What's up, Vergine?" he whispered.

"I've a headache, Master. I want to breathe some fresh air," Vergine replied and quickly vanished into the garden shadows.

He recalled Usep's words: 'A secret kept from God or anyone else'. No, he had no time – and did not wish – to reason it out in cold-blood. He could not be bothered with unimportant things. 'Farewell, my homeland ...'

The smell of the pies and the bread was in the air. Ohannes passed by the tantun without being noticed. He heard Satenik say, "Who knows who will die and who will survive?" He wondered how she found the time for philosophising. She then said, "Vergine knows her business well enough." Satenik added something else, which he did not hear.

Overcome with fatigue and strain, he went upstairs. The air was stifling, or so it seemed to him. His soul felt drained, without a scrap of light. The heavy belt was weighing him down; he untied it and threw it over the chair. Then he fell on the soft bed, that had nevertheless been made up that evening, and sobbed bitterly without tears, but with all his heart and soul, like a child thrown out of its house.

The sun must have risen in the morning, but neither sun nor morning were visible. They were not seen because dust stood between the morning and the sun, between light and justice. Dust. People were swimming in the dust – women, children, carts and cattle.

Van began to empty early in the morning. First went the common people. What an unecessary word! Who were common, who were special? Everyone lived well in Van. Nevertheless, the common people were the first to set off.

The barefooted children with pieces of bread in their hands, and the newborn children in the arms of women with dirty packages on their backs, all turned their faces to the east, towards Mt Varag and called on the burnt monastery's Holy Sign to help them. Then they turned their anxious faces to the west, then to the north, and carried on, forward and forward and forward. Cursing – crying – dust – migration.

A little later, the middle class also started to move off. Barrows, loaded cows tied to each other by their horns, bemused goats calling for help, stubborn oxen, donkeys bent down under their loads, and people – women, children, the aged. Where had all the animals been during the fighting? It must certainly be true that should the Russians have arrived later, Van could have endured another month if all these animals had been put at the disposal of Kevork Sudjian and Mgirditch Atchemian. But it is probable there would have been no such intention.

Here was Effendi Khanjian's family lost in the dust and crowd. His son Aghasi was ill and they had tied him on the back of a skinny cow. The cow did not refuse to carry out its unusual role; perhaps it was far-seeing, like Hampartsoum Yeramian sitting on the bank of the Nile, and it knew who was tied on its back. It was walking along obediently.

And now, the whole town – its districts and streets, its small and large houses,, irrespective of class, sex and age – was humming and stirring. Van was emptying.

When early in the morning the preparations for the flight and retreat were coming to an end at Mihran Manasserian's house, his widowed sister came in through the garden door, followed by her four orphans, each of them holding a small package. Only the eldest daughter did not have anything in her hand, because she had thrown away her light package on the way. She had cried and sung without words – yes, without words – for she had lost her speech and her wits since her father's death. She had, however, retained if not the ability to feel, at least the instinct to do so. And due to that instinct, when she saw her uncle, she let out a cry like a frightened bird and showed him her palms with ten fingers spread out as a curse.

Mihran frowned and pretended not to notice, but made everybody understand that this was a migration which was a flight, and that everyone would have to rely only on themselves, that young and old, should all try to keep their head. "It's a matter of life and death," he said. Once all of them were in the street, so was Nana, who was always inseparable from Mihran. Deeply enraged, and maddened in his soul, Mihran cast a malicious glance at his sister's sorrowful orphans, then at Nana and went into the garden with an ominous look. Nana followed him. Mihran went towards the rose-garden. Nana was very delighted with, and besotted by, the sharp scent of marjoram. She turned a somersault at Mihran's feet and stood up on her two hind legs like a trained dog. Mihran took a revolver out of his pocket and shot Nana, without blinking an eye. She fell to one side, coating her snow-white fur and the green marjoram with her crimson blood. Nana's charming looks and her tragic demise will never be forgotten in the history of Van cats.

Souren and Usep pulled the cart out into the street and the others followed. Satenik arranged the hair on Lia's brow. Margar, known in the town as 'Margar Nevertheless', was coming straight towards them with red eyes. Margar, a lonely man with his own vineyard, was fond of drinking and crying. Before crying, he used to say 'nevertheless' and would then burst into tears. Seeing Ohannes, he put his saddle-bag over his shoulder, came up and kissed Ohannes on his moustache with his wine-smelling lips. To make himsefl heard in the reigning noise, he shouted in Ohannes' ear.

"Are we going to Russia?"
Ohannes nodded. "What's in your saddle-bag?"
"Bread and wine. What a tragedy about our Van!"
"Yes, it's terrible."
"Nevertheless," Margar said and burst into tears. He moved away quickly, swallowing his tears.

Something else happened as well: Usep knelt before Vergine

and quickly tied her brown shoe-laces with his skilful fingers. Vergine blushed like an Adonis. Satenik jabbed Ohannes in his side. He pretended not to see anything. Vostanig jumped onto the cart with the cat in his arms. The donkey with its heavy load shook its head and its bells tinkled.

When everything was ready, when all the shoe-laces were checked and tied, when all of them were waiting for Ohannes to give the order to start, he went back into the house with heavy steps. He entered the tantun almost running, took the half-filled kerosene-can and went up into the kiosk like a thief. He poured out the entire contents of the can and then threw it away. He took a deep breath. Should he close the door from inside and throw the key out of the window, so that he could not do anything about it if he repented? And then set the kiosk on fire and get burnt alive, together with his grandfathers' house, as a sacrifice for beautiful Van?

But the unshakeable man of Van reasoned to himself: 'Why? Am I mad? Am I out of my mind? Suppose Van is alone in the world. And Ohannes? Are there two of us? Van will need me one day.'

And he lit the match.

The rest happened very quickly. In the street he heard himself saying in a strange voice, "Get a move on. Why are you standing about?" The procession started up. Ohannes sensed – as if not with his eyes – that Kando was also walking with them, and sorrowfully looking at Vergine. Ohannes loosened his belt and felt that there could be no comparison between him and Kando.

Ancient Van was being emptied of its people. But Van remained behind covered with dust. Lamentation – execration – exclamation. The people were leaving with tears, curses, and cries, while Van itself was motionless. Thus, the great issue – which came first, Van or the Vanetsi? – was resolved. It was clear that Van had come first, for anyone could see for themselves that the last Vanetsi had left Van, while Van stood fixed and unshakeable, looking with one of its green eyes back to the past and the other towards the coming centuries.

Ne-ver-the—less.

When they reached the end of the street, Ohannes looked back. Black smoke was rising from his kiosk in thick clouds and coming down over the gardens mixed with dust. It seemed that a thousand-and-one, invisible and magic, hands had simultaneously set the whole place on fire. Now there was no fire or flame to be seen. The devastated gardens, bound up with inner distress and choking in their own smoke, were burning without fire or flame.

Epilogue

Like everything else in the world, books also have their beginning and their end. This book would have finished with the previous chapter, if its author had not loved fairy-tales since his early childhood and if he had not considered life as a carefully built fairy-tale embellished with all the charming colours of the rainbow. The life and everyday activities of the town, to which every chapter has been dedicated, were all embroidered with the colours of the rainbow. Furthermore, this life and these everyday activities had one remarkable, dominating colour that all the rainbows in the world lack. That colour was black. And as has been seen, the black rainbow had appeared many times in the dome of the sky over the town.

    And the fairy-tale starts here.

According to this astonishing and terrifying tale, there is a night once a year – or maybe every two, five, or ten (though in my opinion every fifty) years – when the now dead town of Van comes to life at a certain hour. The tale relates that the once silent ghost town is filled with noise, with shouts, with the joyful clamour of feasts and wedding parties, with inspired speeches, tenacious debates, toasts, complaints, grumbles, and with weeping and lamentation. The tale states the unbelievable; it tells how we can meet the now familiar people of Van in the same clothes and at the same age as before. They carried the town in their time on their shoulders and now, it is said, they have a second life. An incredible thing! There is no moon, no light, no lamp, but their eyes are burning with the light of a magic lamp and illuminating each other. They are tearing up the night and continually ploughing it into zigzag patterns.

In these terrible few hours, the dead town becomes an open colony of madmen, where people can see each other with their dreadful eyes, but can not hear anything, because this second life is too short, hardly two or three hours, a period of time which is too short to say what they have to say, let alone listen to anyone. Among these people with burning eyes, there is only one man with unseeing, cold eyes. He is blind, and an indefatigable educator. He moves forward feeling his way with his stick and assures everyone to his right and left that he has been wrongly held to have abjured and betrayed Van, and that, while sitting on the banks of the Nile, he has built a monument for Vaspourakan, which will survive undamaged like the Egyptian pyramids.

And who is this other man bearing his cane on his shoulder in a military pose? It is perhaps the former teacher who had heroically fallen victim at the Araruts defense post. He assures everyone, that it was not a random bullet that cut the thread of his life and that he had died an intended death.

A pale-faced man passes by. He has thick glasses and a hat on his head instead of a fez, and is carrying an official brief-case instead of a revolver. He cries out, "Woe on me! I didn't want to die on the road to freedom, but I perished in the labyrinthine corridors of the office of internal affairs of the tiny Ararat republic. I died of typhus, not in Tiflis but in the capital village of Yerevan – a shameful death for a revolutionary, much like the death of an aeroplane pilot crushed under a cart."

A sparsely bearded man is standing on the trunk of a cut-down tree and is making a speech. The main essence of his speech is that the crimes he did or did not commit are remembered in vain, for he has already washed away his guilt by being killed at the bloody hands of the enemy.

Ohannes is persuading Simon that he lost everything on the journey, and that the remarkable blankets were lost because of Vergine. Usep and Vergine have gone to Buenos Aires under those blankets and now they are bringing up their twins. And here is Makrouhi's husband, Setrak, who is shouting at the top of his voice, "By all means greet the revolution with open arms, but don't let the revolutionary enter your house."

There are many other known and unknown people here, each of them with their own heartaches and their own story. Who should you listen to? Which account should you write down?

Paramaz comes by with tumbled hair and a long rope round his neck instead of a tie. "Though I was hanged in Bolis," he says, "I was hanged for Van, my beloved nation. Give me a corner in the pantheon of Van."

Set asks the passers-by whether they have seen Khushush. She had not come home yet, she was enjoying herself eating chocolate with the Armenian officers in the Ortochala square in Tiflis.

Here is Vramian. He raises his hand like Jesus: "Diplomacy – that's what we lack. With my watery death I proved the dry necessity of diplomacy."

Mkho appears, the only man who is not speaking, but is instead emitting screams through tight lips like a frightened beast.

Dr Ussher is preaching, hurling sparks from his blue eyes and proving that if the Turks had only read the Bible, they would not have had time to massacre Armenians.

Armenak Yekarian is thundering: "What a world this is! I sow while others reap the laurels."

Dikran of Khorkom is preaching morality, adding that he is as innocent as the Holy Lamb and Mihran Manasserian, and that the guilt for what had happened on the way to Khorkom belongs to the district governor's short-haired wife in trousers.

The widows of Abraham Broutian and Artashes Solakian are hiding behind the bushes. They are ashamed to meet their husbands because they have broken their vows and married again – and, moreover, not to Hunchaks.

Panos passes Ohannes; one of them is facing Arark and the other Varag and they do not greet each other. What has happened? Both of them have opened fruit-stores on Astafian Street in Yerevan and are now rivals.

Lia is following Ishkhan and directing the spotlight of her eyes at him. Her face is blue, her hair tumbled and her dress soaking. In Bergri, where the people of Van on their journey into exile had faced Turkish attacks, she had thrown herself into the Bendi-Mahu river.

The Grand Mother of the monastery, disabled by torture, is sitting on the grass having a pleasant conversation with Takouhi Sossoyan. "You're lucky, you were buried decently, while I was eaten by wolves during the deportation."

Kotcho passes by on a horse, trying not to meet Aram.

Manvel from the Eremer monastery is running around with the blood-stained map on his shoulders, while the old man from Gurubash village asks everyone whether they have seen his son-in-law, long-necked Sakho in a dark hat.

In this world of ghosts, one can also meet the people of Van who are still alive. When the first light-blue lacing of the chapel rises from Mt Varag, silence falls, the ghosts disappear and each still living Vanetsi goes his own way. They leave bright pebbles behind them, so as not to forget their way back when the time comes for the ghosts to return.

Now there is silence in the dead town, and only the last sound of Hagop Kandoyan's heartbreaking melody still lingers in the air – Vaspoura-a-a... No one knows, dear reader, when Hagop will be able to add his final 'kan'. No one knows.

That is the fairy-tale.

And if, as is the custom, three apples fall down at the end of all Armenian tales, then let these here be apples from Artemid. Let the apples of the fairy-tale fall.

Let the first apple be for every Vanetsi living in every corner of the world and missing Van, and for their children and grandchildren.

Let the second apple be for the people of the homeland, who love Van with the love of a Vanetsi.

And the third? Well, I was recently in Moscow and there I saw the best apples in the world. Only the third apple of our fairy-tale was missing.

Ne-ver-the-less...

Map of Aikesdan

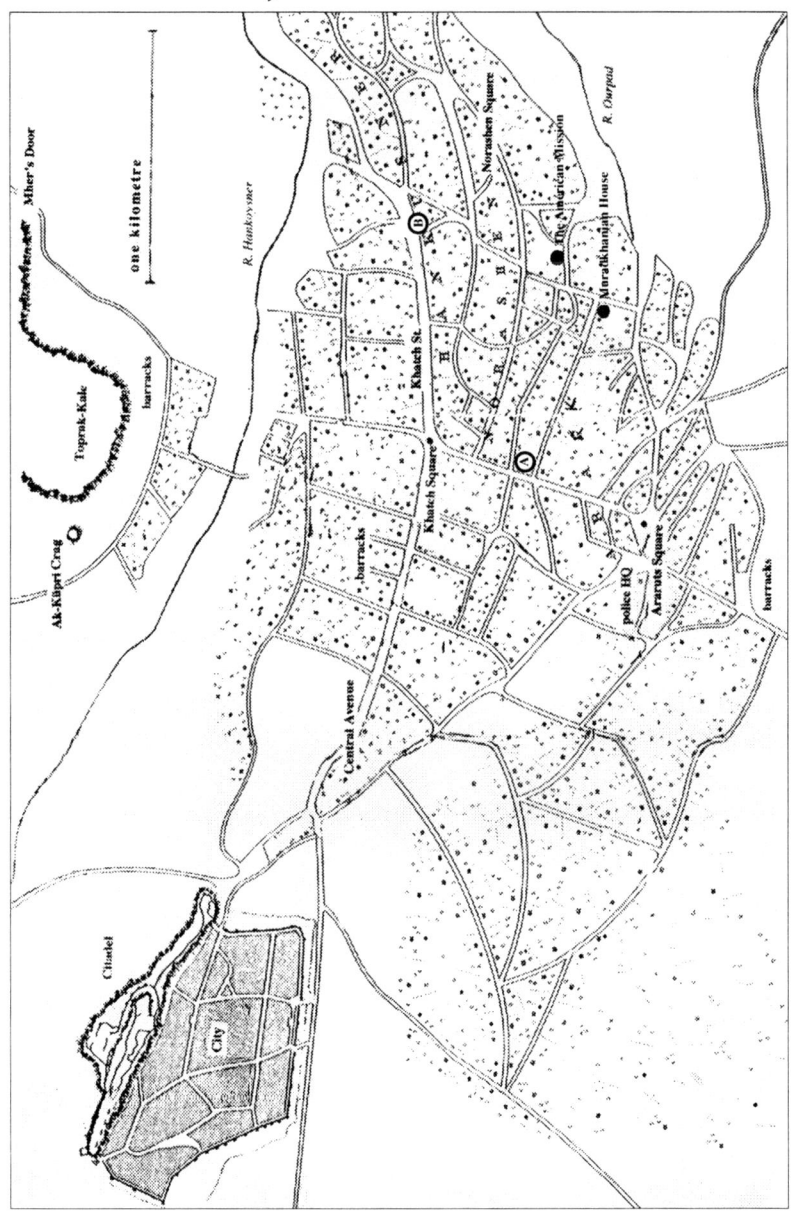

The map names the districts in the mainly Armenian eastern part of the suburb that were being defended during the siege of Van in 1915.
A is the Freedom and Light library, the French consulate and Kiligian house
B is the Dominican College and Yeramian school on Khatch Street

Glossary

Abovian, Khatchadour: (1805-1848) teacher and author of the first novel in spoken Armenian rather than the classical language, influenced the nineteenth century literary revival.

Aghtamar: island on Lake Van with famous 10th century church and formerly a monastery.

Aghbiur, Serop: 1864-1899) famous fedayeen leader, recruited the young Antranik.

Aikesdan: the 'garden city' suburb of Van, now site of the present town.

Aklatiz: the doll of an old man with one leg, hung during Lent with an onion stuck with seven feathers withdrawn one at a time at each of the seven weeks.

Alishan, Ghevond: (1820-1901) armenian catholic priest in Venice, teacher and poet.

Antranik (Ozanian): (1865-1927) led an Armenian legion fighting with Russians when they arrived in Van, later dissuaded by British from occupying Karabagh.

Arakel, Gaidsag: Dashnak military commander during defense of Van.

Aram (Manoukian): pseudonym of Sergei Hovhannessian (1879-1919), usually known by his first name, Dashnak leader during defense of Van, one of founders of first Armenian Republic.

Armenak: member of the first Armenian political party, founded by Portugalian; the party planned for some Armenian independence, but this was a long-term goal.

Armenian flag: a yellow-red-green tricolour orginally designed for the Hunchak party, and used in Van in 1915, the current republic uses the red-blue-yellow tricolour of the 1918 republic.

Artsrouni: royal dynasty, kings include Gagik (C10) and Senekerim (C11).

Ashkhadank: name (Labour) of a Dashnak weekly published in Van.

Astghik: Armenian pagan goddess of love, her shrine was on a mountain to the west of Lake Van.

Avetisian: pseudonym of Mgirditch Terlemezian (1864-1896), Armenak leader in the Van uprising of 1896.

Biainili-Bznuni-Van: composite name of Lake Van, the first is the name of the kingdom called Urartu by the Assyrians, the second is that of an ancient principality on the western shore.

Boghossian: a reactionary subgroup of the Hunchak party, opposed by people who then called themselves A-Boghossians.

Bolis: version of Greek Polis (the city) referring to Constantinople, Istanbul, Stamboul – note a person from Bolis is a Bolsetsi.

Boyadjian, Zhirair: Hunchak pioneer, hanged in 1893.

Bulgaratsi, Grigor: (i.e. of Bulgaria), Dashnak colleague of Aram Manoukian during defense of Van, designed successful cannon.

Dashnak: member of the principal Armenian revolutionary and nationalist party, led initially by Russian Armenians; the party was dominant in Van in 1915 and in the first republic, it tended to socialism, but was later anti-soviet.

Davo: Dashnak who in 1907 informed the police about large stocks of arms in Van – there are various explanations of this shocking event, Mahari took the view that he had angrily broken with the party after his fiancée had left him for Aram, the Dashnaks claimed he had been expelled for getting some girl pregnant.

David of Sassoun: hero of national epic, son of giant Mher, half-brother of Melik of Misra (Assyria) who he quarrels with and eventually kills.

Djevdet Bey: notoriously cruel Turkish Governor of Van, his father Tahir Bey had also been a governor of Van but a relatively benign one.

Djilbur: tarragon omelette.

Djitechian, Kevork: chairman of national council in Van, a childhood friend of Djevdet who – unusually – spared him, his family and his house in the Turkish quarter of Aikesdan.

Droshak: (the Banner) a Dashnak monthly newsletter.

Ebbers, George: (1837-98) German Egyptologist and novelist, discovered important papyrus, novels include 'Homo Sum' and 'Der Kaiser'.

Freedom and Light: political or religious slogan (originally from St Augustine), name of the Dashnak library and centre in Van.

Getardardz, Petros: (1019-58) Catholicos who helped persuade king Gagik of Ani to cede the town to Byzantium.

Ghavurma: fried meat with a lot of melted butter.

Giumretsi, Peto: pseudonym of Alexander Petrosian, Dashnak colleague of Aghbiur.

Goms: pseudonym of Vahan Papazian (1876-1973), leading Dashnak activist.

Grigor, Saint: (257?-337?), Gregory the Illuminator, the founder of the Armenian church.

Hadji: one who has made the pilgrimage to Mecca, generally a learned man.

Hamid: Sultan Abdul Hamid (1842-1918), initiated the 1895 massacres of Armenians; he was deposed by the Young Turks in 1908.

Hayots Dzor: (the valley of the Armenians) lies south of Van down to the river Khoshab, it was a sub-districts (kaza) of the district (sanjak) of Van.

Hunchak: member of an Armenian revolutionary 'social democrat' party, led initially by European-based marxist Armenians; the party later split with some members joining Ramgavars.

Ignatios: C14 painter in Cilicia.

Ishkhan: pseudonym of Nicoghagos Boghossian (1879-1915), Dashnak leader murdered in 1915 on mission organised by Djevdet supposedly to investigate deaths in an outlying village of Van.

Izmirlian, Mateos: (1848-1911) patriarch of Constantinople, and later Catholicos, who supported revolutionary movements.

Jajik: yogurt, cucumber and garlic.

Khatch: (cross) when naming a church it refers to the Cross, supposed fragments of which being owned by the church, here also the name of a main street in Aikesdan.

Khatchkar: memorial stones with complex interweaving patterns rather like Celtic designs.

Khanasor: a valley on the Persian border where in 1897 Armenians successfully defeated a Kurdish tribe which had massacred Armenian villagers in the area, the victory is often referred to as the first organised resistance by the revolutionary parties.

Kher, Sher, Astvadz: multilingual words for good and evil invoked when clicking worry-beads.

Khizanetsi, Mesrob: C16 writer.

Khrimian (Hairig): (1820-1907) famous patriot priest, attended Berlin Congress, printed journals in Constantinople and also at monastery of Varag, became much-admired Catholicos.

Khushush: wife of king Senekerim, daughter of the Bagratuni king, Gagik of Ani.

Kurush: silver or gold coins, sometimes called piastres.

Lavash: A soft, thin flatbread.

Mardig: Hunchak leader, killed in Van in 1896.

Masis: the Armenian name for the mountain others call Ararat.

Mher's Door: in the Armenian epic of Sassoun, the entrance to sealed cave on Toprak-Kale which the giant Little Mher will open at the end of time.

Mushkil Gusha: in persian folk-tales, the 'remover of difficulties'.

Naregatsi, Grigor: (950-1000) poet and priest, his much prized 'Book of Lamentations' was often just known as Nareg, which was also the name of the monastery where he spent most of his life.

Ottoman Bank: reference to raid by young Dashnaks on the Ottoman bank in Istanbul in 1896, holding staff as hostages – the situation was soon resolved, the Dashnaks were allowed to leave, but there was then an outbreak of violence against Armenians in the city.

Paramaz: pen-name of Matteos Sarkissian (1863-1915), a Hunchak leader (not known in fact to have been in Van after 1896), hanged in Istanbul in 1915.

Para: a copper coin, a small fraction of a penny.

Pasterma: Armenian specialty – beef marinated in spices.

Portugalian, Mgirditch: (1845-1921) teacher in Van, went to France in 1885, founder of Armenak party.

Raffi: pen-name of Hakob Melik-Hakobia (1835-1888), author of famous novel, 'The Fool'.

Raki: aniseed-flavoured alcoholic drink.

Ramgavar: member of Armenian 'liberal' party, which also attracted some disaffected Hunchaks.

Sabounjian, Aram: leader of post in Arark region, during siege of Van.

Salavat: persian islamic greeting: 'blessed be the prophet and his household'.

Sanfani: professional name of Khosrov Chitjian, a Red Cross doctor in Van.

Senekerim: last king of Artsruni dynasty, ceded his kingdom of Vaspourakan to the Byzantines in 1021, this lead to his memorial at Varag being stripped of its ornaments by Khrimian.

Servantsdian, Karekin: (1840-1892) bishop and writer, follower of Khrimian.

Shanour, Shahan: pen-name of Shanour Kevrestedjian (1903-1947), novelist who settled in France and had warm correspondence with Mahari who dedicated his novel to him.

Shant, Levon: (1869-1951) Armenian poet, novelist, author of a well-known play, 'Ancient Gods', and the story about Seda, a princess.

Siamanto: pen-name of Atom Yardjanian (1878-1915), poet, one of the first murdered deportees.

Soudjuk: Armenian highly spiced sausage of beef, tomato and garlic.

Tahsin Bey: governor of Van replaced by Djevdet Bey in 1914.

Tantun: main ground-floor room of houses in Aikesdan.

Tavlu: turkish name for the popular game, known in English as backgammon.

Terlemezian, Panos: (1865-1941) artist, veteran Armenak in Van, travelled widely before settling in Armenia where he was an honoured painter.

Terian, Vahan: (1885-1920) poet, wrote epic 'Land of Nairi', probably the great poet mentioned at start of the interlude between chapters 17,18.

Terzibashian, Avetis: Dashnak colleague of Vramian, survived siege and settled in France.

Tigran: (c140-55 BCE), king of a large Armenian empire, a vassal of Rome.

Tigranakert: capital city of Tigran, near present-day Diyarbekir.

Tonir: an oven dug into the floor or raised as a stone hearth.

Tossoun: endearing nick-name for a young boy, from Turkish for bullock.

Tourian, Bedros: (1851-1872) poet who wrote about Lake Van.

Ussher, Clarence: American missionary doctor in Van.

Vahagn: Armenian pagan god of victory, his shrine with that of Ashtig (see above).

Vahan (Mamigonian): nephew of Vartan, ruled under Persian occupation.

Vanetsi: someone from Van, also as a surname, eg C15 writer, Grigor Vanetsi.

Van-Tosp: another name for Van that includes the orginal armenian name of the district below the Rock – but here the name of a Ramgavar weekly published in Van.

Varag: mountain, nine kilometres east of Van, with monastery (Varagavank).

Vartan (Mamigonian): heroic leader who died at the battle of Avarayr (451) against the Persians.

Vardan: pseudonym of Sarkis Mehropian (? - 1943), Dasnak leader at Khanasor, and with the Armenian volunteers who came to Van with the Russians.

Varujan, Daniel: (1884-1915) poet and teacher, deported and brutally tortured to death.

Vramian: pseudonym of Onnig Tertzagian (1871-1926), highly respected Dashnak deputy for Van in second Ottoman parliament, imprisoned by Djevdet and then murdered.

Yekarian, Armenak: (1869-1926), Ramgavar military commander during defense of Van.

Yilditz Kiosk: palace of Sultan Abdul Hamid.

Zen Hokevor: title of work (' Suffering and sacrifice', 1859) by Hagop Badriark.

Zum Zum Maghara: Turkish name for Mher's Door (see above)